THE CASSAN

by

J.D. GREENFIELD

Cassandra was a princess of ancient Troy, cursed by Apollo to see the future but never to be believed.

"Cassandra, you will pay for your treachery. I will leave you the gift of sight, but no one will ever believe your truth and you will never change your fate."

Warmest Wishes,

JD Greenfield

Acknowledgements

This book would not have been possible without the love and support of some very special and amazing people. Thank you to James for your constant love and support. You are my touchstone. Thank you to my son C for challenging me and inspiring me. You are my miracle. Thank you to my dad for giving me a strong sense of self and home and what family really means. You are my roots. Thank you to my mama for never giving up on me or my dreams. You are my wings.

Cover design by: Denise Henkle Owen
Cover photo by: Mike Morehead
Edited by: Tedde Lou Holcomb

Note: The clipart image of the phoenix above is free of copyright and is in the Public Domain. http://insertmedia.office.microsoft.com

ISBN-13: 978-1537777825

ISBN-10: 1537777823

PROLOGUE:

Dearest,

   I don't even know your name. You and I have never met, and I only have a glimpse of what this will be. I saw your face in a vision and I felt drawn toward you in a way I don't fully understand and have never known. It terrified me because I can't change my fate. The visions have always come to pass just as I've seen them and in the last one you were hurt. I don't know if you live or die. The not knowing scares me the most.

   I have nowhere to send this letter. I write it as my vow to find a way to save you; to somehow change my fate and yours. My eyes have not seen you but I know you are real and I will love you. My first real love is still only a face in my mind and an ache in my heart.

Your Olivia xo

CHAPTER ONE

November, 2010

Violence is nothing like what you see in the movies. When someone hits you and your body and soul give way to the pain of bruising and sometimes broken parts, it isn't funny. It isn't curious or interesting or even entertaining at all. It's terrifying and shameful and you carry it with you like invisible bricks you can't put down.

For that reason, Olivia Curtis-Montgomery could not believe she'd let it go on for so long. Much to her dismay, there was no way to explain it or reconcile it at all.

Her husband had beaten her down in every way possible and ironically, it wasn't even the worst thing she'd ever endured.

This is how it was all the time lately; with thoughts of Jackson, her now dead husband haunting her mind whether dreaming or awake. It didn't matter he was dead. She thought about his death with nary a flinch and when forced to speak of it, she had perfected the act of a grieving widow. It *was* only an act. She grieved but never a moment for Jackson Montgomery. He never earned her sorrow. She couldn't even force herself to miss him or remember one good thing about him. That was what her marriage had been. It was an endless trail of egg shells to walk on. Now all of it was gone.

It was strange, this new reality. She was left with only a huge knot in her stomach, her son's name always on the tip of her tongue and her dog.

Her dog Harper was small, white and fluffy. She looked as though someone had left a pile of cotton on the floor. Olivia was pretty sure Harper had a mix of several breeds in her small frame but she was a pound puppy so there was no way to tell. Harper was the one living reminder of a life Olivia could never have back.
The life she had with her son was now only a memory.

It wasn't healthy to dwell on that. Every doctor she'd ever seen told her some version of the same thing, hadn't they? Isn't that what Doctor Cline had said countless times? She must grieve and finally come back to a place of peace. If she'd been one hundred percent honest with Dr. C she would have told him her life had never been peaceful. Hers was a life of torment.

But, the torment hadn't begun with her painful marriage to Jackson. It began the day she was raped.

She was only 15 years old when her innocence was stolen and in its place a curse took hold. It felt terminal, inescapable. She feared it had no end. She could see the future, the dark and scariest parts that affected her life. Only no one ever believed her when she dared speak of them. No one even heard her as she told of the awful things she saw. And when people did listen she was labeled 'crazy'. Just like the invisible bricks she carried, the curse was invisible too.

Life with Jackson had not been easy, but she barely remembered a time when life in general was easy. Her life was filled with anxiety and fear. It was anything but easy. Olivia wasn't stupid. She knew about abuse. The emotional abuse sucked the life out of her more than any physical beating she'd ever endured. Or maybe that wasn't true but it felt true.

"Ugh" she thought. "Why can't I just shut off my brain?" Olivia sighed heavily and reached for Harper. Cuddling her dog was her only comfort when she was stuck in the dark places inside her own head. It didn't matter. It would be time to get up soon.

Soon, Mr. Jameson would be getting ready for his day. Her new neighbor was always an early riser and the walls were thin. She was pretty sure she could hear his alarm clock most mornings. She glanced at the time.

"Five a.m. is not a decent hour. " She yawned. "I should probably just get up." She said aloud as Harper copied her yawn.

Sleep was a friend she saw too rarely and when it arrived always seemed to show up with nightmares in tow. She was new in town, new to this independent life she was living and today was an important day. She could feel it and had felt it coming for some time now. "I think I meet him today. I'm so scared girl. Maybe I should call in sick. What if I really do fall in love with him? Do you think it's possible? Of course it is. It always happens like I see it, and I saw myself in love with him. Love, Oh, God." She rambled on to her dog that seemed less than interested.

Harper was such a good little dog. She had a sweet nature and never barked unnecessarily. Olivia remembered how Harper crawled on her lap as she cried; the day she got the news about her family. Even though she shouldn't think about it again, the memory came rushing back. It always did. It was strong, like a smell that won't leave a room.

Olivia was alone in the house. She was excited for her son's return home from his annual sailing trip with Jackson.

She had worried over it so much. This time in particular. She even told her son as much, though he passed it off saying, "Mom, you worry too much. Nothing's going to happen to me." Then the doorbell rang.

"No", she thought. It felt too familiar. Her vision had not been clear but she knew her son was in danger. "Why did I let him go?" she whispered. Her hand was unable to open the door. Maybe she could stop the pain for just a second longer. She just needed a second. The doorbell rang again.

Torturous thoughts raced through her head. Why did I enjoy even a moment of life without him? She kicked herself for all the things she should have done differently. It was easier to breathe with Jackson gone. There was no one to tell her how to do anything. There was no one to give her looks of disapproval. No one yelled. No one told her she'd had enough wine or she shouldn't watch a certain TV show. No one called her names. Shame grew inside and became more of the invisible bricks she would carry through life. She forced herself to open the door.

It was a police officer. Before he spoke, it was as if time stopped for everything and everyone. She saw the name on the officer's badge: Hyatt, like the hotels. It didn't matter his name or what he looked like at all. On a cellular level, somewhere in the pit of her stomach, the fear grew and spread and she knew. She had known this was coming but she couldn't stop it. No one ever believed her; and now again, it was too late.

She knew her life would never be the same. Her husband, her son; they were dead. A car wreck, the officer said. Olivia heard but it didn't matter how. It only mattered her angel was gone. That's it.

She wasn't sure who screamed her son's name, as loud and piercing as to break windows and hearts. It didn't sound like her. She had never sounded so broken. She'd never sounded like an animal, primal and scared. It couldn't be her. "NO, NO, NO" she screamed at the officer!

She crumpled to the floor. She sobbed and sobbed. She cried for her beautiful boy like a flood had come. She spoke his name one last time at the funeral and then vowed to never speak it again. Like a prayer his name would go through her mind a thousand times a day but no one deserved to hear it. No one earned the right to speak it, not anymore. He was hers and she would keep what was left of him all to herself.

She named her son without Jackson, before him in fact. Just one more thing she silently paid for throughout their years together. Jackson never liked her son's name and even told her to change it to Jackson Frederic Montgomery III. She refused.

Her son's death was the one moment she would have given anything to not see coming and the one thing she wished she could change. She would give her own life to keep him safe but that was simply not the way life worked.

Olivia dragged herself back from the horrible memories, "Thank God for coffee" she said aloud, shaking her head and wiping away a stray tear.

She put on her polyester uniform. No matter how much she washed it, it was still polyester. It was nothing close to the cashmere and silk she once wore but it was honest work at the diner. It kept her out of her own head and there were still some financial obligations back in Oregon. She wasn't sure exactly. She just knew that working hard and staying busy were like interminably rolling a heavy stone up a mountain. Like Sisyphus, she needed to pay, if only for how she couldn't save her son.

In her old life money had been the focus of everything. Now she barely thought about it. Jackson always made sure they were showing off their wealth or rather *his wealth* as long as they weren't obvious about it. But he'd accrued some very large debts as well, and she couldn't honestly say how much had been paid after the auction. She remembered how strange it was to see movers taking furniture out her front door.

Now she couldn't help but wonder if she still owed money to anyone. She should probably ask her brother Miles to be certain.

After the auction, she decided to move. There was really nothing she could say about moving to Troy, Montana except it was small and far away from her memories. Olivia had seen it in one of her many premonitions. Her visions always drew her in, as a moth to a flame. And desire to meet the man she would love felt like a rope wrapped around her heart, dragging her here, even though it could cost him his life. She couldn't stop herself from following her fate here to Troy.

She'd grown up living next to a lake and frequenting the country club her family belonged to. It was so far removed from the small town life she was living now.

Olivia sipped her coffee and looked around her new place. There was nothing pretty or homey about the duplex. Everything was bland. There were beige walls, no pictures. The dark grey couch was purchased in town from a small second hand store. She didn't even sit in it before she bought it.

The kitchen table and two chairs had come with the apartment. Olivia was pretty sure they were from the sixties, possibly earlier and the place had a musty smell that wouldn't go away no matter how often she cleaned. She'd been here for almost a month and still the walls were empty. There were none of the little touches that decorated her old life.

Almost everything of value had been sold and everything sentimental was still packed in boxes. The boxes were purposely stacked high and deep in a room she never entered.

"Well Harper, I'm off to work." The fluff ball pawed at her ankles. She really needed to find another way to keep busy. She'd spent too many mornings remembering.

"I'll probably be late. Fridays get pretty busy." Olivia turned and shut the door. As she was hurrying, she almost ran into Mr. Jameson.

"Oh, uh, good morning, Olivia" He said kindly.

Olivia smiled. "Good morning Mr. Jameson. Guess I should have checked the weather report, huh?" Olivia asked as she eyed the storm clouds but it was already almost nine. The upshot of living so close to work was she hadn't been late yet and she didn't intend to start today.

"You could still grab a coat. You haven't even gotten in your car yet,"

"No, I don't want to be late. I'll just deal with it," she said.

She smiled another pretty but incomplete smile.

"Have a good day," she called.

"Thank you dear, you too."

Mitch Jameson was only 58 years old but had been on disability since the accident at the only lumber mill left open three years back. At his age, he was old enough to look upon Olivia much like a daughter but still young enough to really appreciate her beauty.

Olivia had a way of making him miss his wife. His beloved Dana had died of breast cancer six years prior but he still thought of her and missed her every day. He was devoted to her, even in death.

He watched as Olivia drove her black Ford Thunderbird down the street toward Missoula Ave. The duplex was only a block and a half from where Olivia worked at the local diner.

He remembered how beautiful she looked the day she moved in. She had long auburn hair that fell in waves down her back and green eyes that could be seen from across the yard. They were made brighter by the green sweater she wore. You could smell the money on her but here she was moving into this low rent duplex next to him. She didn't fit in here at all, but Mitch had certainly had worse neighbors.

Mitch was good at reading people. He knew Olivia Curtis had lots of secrets and he could respect that. Though the town was ablaze with curiosity about its' newest resident.

Small towns were always the same. Gossip spread like wildfire and everyone felt a sense of entitlement to everyone's life. Olivia Curtis was different. No one seemed to know much about her. She had Oregon plates on her car but when Jim Reed at the gas station asked her about them she said only, "I'm moving here from Oregon." Then she smiled at him. He retold that story later at Max's bar, embellishing it some for his benefit.

He remembered Jim saying, "A smile like that makes a man forget his own name." Mitch knew he was right about that. Olivia had a beautiful smile but he'd yet to see it truly reach her eyes. He wondered if Olivia had made any friends in town yet. He'd overheard Ella Russell, another waitress at the diner; say she was 'quiet as a church mouse'.

Mitch ended up hearing a lot of local gossip. He often went to Maggie's Diner for dinner. The food was good and reasonably priced. He thought Ella sounded a bit jealous when she spoke about Olivia. Ella was not good at being friends with other women. "It's too bad" he thought. "Everyone needs a friend.

Olivia pulled up to Maggie's Diner just two minutes before nine. "Perfect", she thought. She knew Ella would love nothing more than to see her get chastised for being late. Ella didn't like her very much and was all kinds of fake to her. It was the type of false kindness other women often showed.

Olivia jumped out of the car and dashed in through the back; tying her white eyelet apron on the run and grabbing a notepad and pen off the counter as she breezed past Tag. He was the cook; possibly the best in the county.

The diner smelled like a big family breakfast on Sunday. Bacon frying and coffee brewing was the constant aroma. Olivia couldn't help taking in a big whiff as she walked through the door.

She hadn't tired of it yet though the smell of her uniform at the end of the day was less than desirable.

Maggie's was the perfect small town diner. It had light blue gingham curtains on the front windows and a long counter with 50's style stools next to it. There were vinyl seats on the booths and a homemade sign that read 'Take Yer Spurs Off' over the kitchen pass-through.

"Hey Tag, did I miss anything?" She asked.

"Nope", he said, "well, Ella isn't going to be in today. Are you up for pulling a double with me?" He asked hopefully.

"Sure, maybe it'll be good tips tonight."

"Eh, maybe," he said, "but if you're looking to make a lot of money, you need to work at Max's. The drunks always pay better. Do you know how to tend bar?"

"Not really. Besides, I don't think I'd make a good cocktail waitress and I don't want to play therapist to a bunch of drunks," she mumbled, sounding slightly irritated.

"Oh, I'm sorry Olivia; I didn't mean to offend you."

"No, no you didn't; I'm sorry. I didn't get enough sleep I guess. I appreciate the suggestion but I'm happy here." She reached over and put her hand on Tag's arm. "Really, I'm grateful." She added.

"Ok", he said looking at her delicate hand on his arm. "I'm grateful you're here." He blushed. "What's this bracelet you always wear? I like it."

Olivia pulled her hand back quickly. "It's a phoenix." She said covering the wide leather cuff with her other hand. "I've had it a long time." She needed to change the subject.

"Tag is an unusual name. How did you end up with a name like Tag?" she asked.

"Well it's actually Rowtag but please don't tell anyone. I have a few friends that know but everyone just calls me Tag. It means fire in Algonquin."

"Fire, I won't tell anyone. I like it." She liked Tag Porter from the first day they were introduced. He was tall and lanky with beautiful dark skin and looked all of about 12 years old; though she knew he was in his thirties, as well. When she asked him how he stayed so young looking, he said it was a Kootenai Tribal secret. She considered Tag her first pseudo-friend in Troy.

"Thanks" he replied and reached to put his hand on Olivia's shoulder but she stepped back awkwardly.

Just then Dan, the manager walked in. Dan was a squat, balding, mustachioed man who seemed to smoke cigars in back of the building more than he actually worked and hardly said two words to Olivia usually.

Dan looked quizzically at Olivia. To him, she always seemed like a nervous bird but she worked hard and the customers liked her. That was all that mattered to him.

"Good morning. Olivia, did Tag tell you about Ella? She won't be in today," said Dan.

"Yes, that's fine. I can work both shifts." Olivia never wanted to seem desperate. Desperation always opened the door to questions.

"That would be great. I guess Ella has the flu. It's probably the brown bottle flu if you ask me but I could be wrong." Dan complained in his smoke filled voice. There was no smoking in the diner but Olivia knew he'd probably come from out back on another 'break'.

"We'd better get rolling. The regulars are already out front waiting," said Dan.

Olivia rushed past him, grabbing a pot of coffee and headed to the booth where four local truck drivers always sat.

"Good morning, what can I get for you?"

"Well Miss Olivia, how about the usual."

Olivia had never seen anyone eat the same breakfast day after day without fail the way these guys did. It amused her. The breakfast special was ham, eggs, hash browns and toast.

"How would you like your eggs Robert?" Olivia asked politely.

"Over easy, just like me." He grinned looking up. Olivia smiled, took the rest of the orders topped off the men's coffee and placed the orders with Tag.

The bell on the glass door jingled.

CHAPTER TWO

On instinct, Olivia's heart raced. She looked up as a man she'd never seen, walked through the door. Her heart was pounding harder in her chest. She pictured him differently but it was definitely him. The rope around her heart tightened its' grip. "He's..." she thought. She didn't have the words.

Nervously, she bit her lip. She'd met all manner of people in her old life but this man was so unexpected. For starters, he was incredibly sexy and Olivia never described *anyone* like that. More than anything, it was his imposing physicality that had her struggling for more oxygen. He was big, strong, like he worked outdoors. He had dark hair, and warm brown eyes. He wore a crisp button up shirt with the sleeves rolled up. His jeans were pressed and he wore cowboy boots.

He reminded Olivia of a businessman and a cowboy all rolled up into one delicious package. It was fascinating and unnerving. This was the man who walked out of her vision right into her life. This was the face, this was him. Now what? She must decide what to do; stay and fall in love or run from her fate? What would save him? Could she save him? And did she have the courage? Her vision told her she would not save him no matter what she did or how much courage she mustered. Why wasn't there an easier choice and why did her heart feel like it was about to pound out of her chest?

"What am I doing?" she thought frustratingly. "I have a job and a, a, a what? What do I really have? I have an apartment that sucks, no friends and only memories of a life that no longer exists." If she could stop herself from falling in love then maybe, just maybe she could stop the vision from coming true. "I don't need him" she told herself. "And I don't want him." All evidence to the contrary.

"A man is merely a complication, especially this gorgeous man in front of me." Complications were the last thing Olivia wanted. Though it would likely be in vain, she had to try. She had to save this man from her curse, though the rope around her heart tugged harder still as she thought it. She must try to stay away from him. Perhaps he could be saved if she could only keep her distance. She had to change her fate and his. This man would be the way it would change, once and for all. She intended that Jackson Montgomery be the last *complication* she ever had. Humph!

Olivia took a deep breath. It was ridiculous really. "What am I, some kind of giggly teenager?" she scolded herself. "No" she told herself sternly. "I'm a grown-ass woman who survived more than most people could possibly fathom and I will not fall in love! I will **not!**"

She straightened her shoulders and took a deep breath. "I can do this," she thought. "Who cares if he looks like a rugged male model with perfect white teeth and forearms from some Popeye cartoon?" Olivia sighed. "Damn it" she said aloud.

"Is something wrong?" asked Tag from behind her.

"Huh? Uh, no, I, well, I just um, just a new customer." She smiled pathetically at Tag, knowing she sounded ridiculous.

"Who, him? He's not new. That's my friend Jake. I guess he's finally back in town. He's been in New York for a while now, living with his sister. Guess he's had enough of Jess, the big city or maybe both." He laughed.

Olivia thought about his name. It fit him perfectly. She hadn't known his name from the vision. "He lives here in Troy?" she asked, trying to sound casual and failing.

"Yeah a whole bunch of us grew up around here and stayed I guess." Tag laughed again. "Jake and Ben and I have been friends forever. Well, Ben and Jake aren't close anymore but Jake's like family to me. We all went to school together." He smiled at the memory.

He couldn't help but notice how Olivia looked at Jake. He'd seen that look many times and had given up trying to compete, at least until Olivia started working here.

"I'd better take his order."

"Yeah, oh and order up on table four," he said turning back to his grill.

"Ok, I'll grab it in just a sec."

She walked over to Jake's table trying to seem nonchalant but feeling nervous and conspicuous. "Good morning Sir. What can I get for you?" she asked, hoping her voice didn't crack.

Jake looked up from the laptop computer he'd been working on and gave Olivia a half-cocked smile. "Good morning beautiful; I don't think we've met."

"No we haven't," she said, suddenly feeling a loss for words but trying desperately to sound aloof and uninterested.

"Well darlin' what's your name?" He smiled again.

"My name is on my tag. Now what can I get for you or are you here just to hold a table?" asked Olivia. She was getting flustered already.

"Whoa! Now I didn't mean to ruffle your pretty feathers. I'll have a ham and American cheese omelet with whole wheat toast and orange juice," he said sounding amused.

"Fine, would you like coffee or just the juice?" finding it nearly impossible to sound polite but detached.

"Coffee would be great. O-LIV-I-A," he enunciated just to tease her. "I prefer lots of cream. I can't stand black coffee."

"I'll bring extra cream to the table and be back with the rest of your order in a bit. Anything else?" Sounding clipped. Clipped was the best she could manage. She wished he'd picked any other place to eat this morning. It was nearly ten o'clock; didn't he have someplace to go, like a job perhaps?

He smiled one more cocky, lopsided smile at her. "No Ma'am, that's it."

She didn't even look at him again. She went back to the kitchen and placed the order.

Jake sat in the booth thinking about this interesting turn of events. Who was this bewitching creature? Obviously she was new in town. Had he really been gone that long? His trip to New York to help Jessica get her life in order had been pretty consuming but how did he miss Troy's newest resident? He'd been gone the better part of three months helping out his sister and doing some business for his family.

Jake was glad to be back home. He was especially happy to see a beautiful green-eyed waitress taking his order this morning. Nothing about her seemed to fit. She didn't fit here in Troy, not in that polyester uniform Dan had the girls wear and she didn't fit waiting tables. Yet, here she was glaring at him from behind the front counter, filling a small white cup with extra cream.

He liked that she appeared to *dislike* him. "I've always loved a challenge." He mused.

She promptly brought over the cream and juice, and then poured his coffee. She seemed unable to get away from him quickly enough. Jake watched her with a smile on his face.

"Order up Olivia," Tag shouted.

"Thanks Tag," she answered.

~ 14 ~

She picked up Jake's order, walked swiftly over and placed it in front of him unceremoniously.

"Uh excuse me, Olivia" He turned those warm eyes on her.

She stopped and turned back. "Why does he have to have a voice like that?" she thought. "He sounds like, like maybe his father could be Sam Elliott or James Earl Jones! This just isn't fair! Haven't I been through enough? What is it about him that makes me feel like crying or screaming and maybe a few other things I can't believe I'm thinking about?" All this went through her head in seconds as she stared at him.

"Yes Sir?" she said coldly.

"You can call me Jake."

She rolled her eyes. "Is there something else I can get for you, *Sir*?" she asked pointedly.

"Yes, I would love your phone number," he drawled. "But only when you get a minute." He smiled broadly this time.

Olivia looked around and realized there was no one in the diner except him. The truckers must have already paid their bill with Dan and left. She hadn't even noticed.

"My number isn't on the menu," she blushed. She tried not to smile at him.

"That's a shame because you just light up this room."

"Let me stop you right there," she said, holding her hand up and meeting his eyes briefly.

"Did I say something wrong?" he asked.

"No, yes, well, no, but let me assure you, *this*" she pointed at the two of them, "this is not happening. I am not interested...not in flirting or anything else you had in mind." She said, trying to sound serious.

It was difficult to keep her composure facing that glowing smile. She was proud of herself for setting a boundary before he got the wrong idea. She would not be his conquest. She *wanted* to be left alone. She *needed* him to leave her alone. The pull of the curse tugged at her again as if knowing her efforts would be futile.

"The only thing I have in mind is getting to know you. But since you aren't interested, YET; you should know I'm a very patient man and you are definitely worth the wait." Jake said seriously. He was used to getting what he wanted in all things. He would wait. She would come around, he was sure of it. He smiled to himself. He looked forward to it too, more than she could know.

~ 15 ~

"Patient or not, I'm not someone you should waste your time on." She turned and breezed back through the kitchen straight to the employee bathroom.

"Tag, I need a break. There isn't anyone out front right now except the one customer." She refused to say his name.

"Sure Olivia. No problem. Are you ok?"
She didn't answer. She shut the door to the bathroom and locked it. She sat on the floor holding her knees. She tried desperately to stop the tears from falling.

"I hate this," she thought. "One man, one moment and I get turned into a mess of nerves and emotions. You knew he'd be coming Olivia. You *knew* this was coming." She lectured herself.

She felt ashamed. "I need to toughen up," she told herself. "He won't be the last man to hit on you. Get over yourself, Slugger." She whispered quietly in her best 'Dad' voice. She stood up, straightened her uniform, splashed her face with water, pinched her cheeks and walked out.

Tag looked at her with questions in his eyes but said nothing. He turned back to the pie he'd been putting together.

Olivia was grateful for the silence, but sighed audibly. She walked back to the front but the diner was empty. She grabbed her tray and began clearing the two breakfast tables.

The truckers had left their usual mess of opened sugar packets but their plates were practically licked clean. She picked up the dishes and her usual tip then moved to the other table. She cringed. How could she let herself get so upset over a stranger? There was a twenty dollar bill next to Jake's mostly uneaten breakfast. She picked up the plate and underneath was a crisp one hundred dollar bill. She looked around. He couldn't have meant to leave so much for crappy service and an even worse attitude.

The food was good but it wasn't *that* good. She finished cleaning and took the tray back to the kitchen. She figured with no one in the diner she would help with the dishes.

"Tag, your friend left a hundred dollar bill," she said putting dishes in the sink.

"What? Are talking about Jake?"

Olivia could tell he was amused. Once upon a time she might have been amused too but not anymore. Instead she just felt off balance and nervous. "Yeah."

"I'm pretty sure none of it was intended for *me*," he said. "Did he pay the bill?"

"Yeah, he left extra. I don't care who it was intended for. I split all my other tips with you and this one is no different." She protested, holding out the bill to him.

"Olivia I don't mean any disrespect but Jake would never let me live it down and I really *want* you to have it. Maybe you could buy yourself something nice," he suggested.

"I don't feel right about keeping it, any of it really." She bit her lip.

"I insist. I want you to have it and Jake won't miss it." He smirked. "If it makes you feel better; I can call and ask him about it."

"Oh no, please don't. I'll just take it then. It's just..." she didn't know what else to say. What could she say?

"Take it Olivia and buy some new boots. You live in Montana now. You're going to need something for the snow."

"Ok, thanks" she said reluctantly, looking at the floor and now vigorously chewing her lip.

She shrugged. She knew it was no use arguing.

The rest of the day passed without incident. Olivia felt dead on her feet by the time Dan locked up at ten that night. The diner was clean and ready for Saturday morning.

"Thank goodness Ella is coming tomorrow," she thought.

Olivia felt like she could use some down time with Harper. Maybe she would go shop for some new boots like Tag suggested. Winter was just around the corner and Mr. Jameson had already warned her once about the difficult Montana winters. Maybe she should dig out that sweater she once bought on a whim for Harper. She wasn't one to dress up dogs but when it was practical, she supposed there was no harm.

"Goodnight Tag, Dan," she yawned as they were all walking out the door. "See you tomorrow."

"Yep," Dan said, puffing on his cigar already. "We'll see you at two o'clock."

"I'll be here," she answered. She walked around the building to the spot where she always parked her car.

"Why didn't I listen to Mr. Jameson?" she thought. It was more than just a little cold, it was freezing. The ground beneath her feet crunched with frost. "Shit, it's cold!" She cussed.

"Now that's an awfully dirty word coming from such a pretty girl, darlin'." Jake said with amusement.

Olivia spun around, screamed and hit him with her purse in the chest, backing up toward her car. When she realized who it was; she was nervous in a whole different way.

"Easy, I didn't mean to frighten you. I got a message from Tag. He said you were put off by the tip I left," Jake grinned.

"Well, yes and as a matter of fact, here." She pulled the hundred dollar bill out of her pocket and held it out on the tips of her fingers. She hoped he wouldn't touch her. She wasn't sure if she could stand it. He was just too beautiful for words. He was too perfect, too tall. His skin was too tan; his eyelashes too long. So why did she desire to reach out and touch them?

"Dear God," she thought. "What is wrong with you Olivia? Get a freaking grip! He is a man. Just a man and men equaled trouble." If she could have, she would have slapped herself.

Jake held up his hand but didn't take the money.

"Of course he won't take it," she thought. She wanted to scream at him but didn't. Instead, she looked up at him through her own long lashes and said sweetly, "I really can't accept it. It's much too generous and I don't feel right about it."

"Wow", Jake thought, "this girl knows how to play a man like a fiddle." He didn't mind admitting he liked this tune. The look on her face was two parts charm and eight parts bullshit. He wished she would smile at him but she was far too stubborn for that.

"Ma'am," he said, "it's your money now. Do what you want with it. Perhaps you could buy yourself a proper winter coat."

He could see she was shivering and if she pried that beautiful mouth of hers out of the scowl she was wearing, her teeth would probably start chattering.

"I'm fine," she said, "I just need to get home."

"Here," he said, "take mine. My truck is all warmed up and I wouldn't dare leave a lady out her in the cold night air without a coat."

He removed his coat and walked up to her. He was close, too close. She could smell his cologne. It was a heady, an earthy scent like leather and something Olivia couldn't name. She hadn't expected to be so drawn to him, not like this and not so quickly.

He placed the coat on her shoulders. It was warm and completely comforting.

She suppressed the urge to bury her face in it and sigh. "Thank you," she said, gulping.

"Of course, just give it to Tag tomorrow and he can bring it to our poker night for me."

"Is that why he said you wouldn't miss the money?" she asked, unable to stop her insatiable curiosity and kicking herself inwardly for it.

Jake laughed. "Yeah probably, I've had a bit of good luck lately at the card table."

"So you're a gambling man then Mr. uh, I'm sorry, I don't know your name," she puzzled.

"No and since you're wearing my coat, I guess you should. I'm Jake Weidner and you are?" Jake held out his hand.
Olivia just didn't know what to make of him.

"Olivia Curtis" she said, shaking his hand firmly. She always detested when women didn't shake hands well. It was almost as bad as a man with a weak handshake. Her mother always disagreed with her in this matter, but she felt certain that a handshake said a lot about a person, regardless of gender.

"Well Olivia now that we're properly acquainted, what do you say about joining me at Max's for a drink?" he asked hopefully.

"No, uh, thank you but as I said before, I'm not interested. I'll return your coat tomorrow to Tag. Thank you," she said quickly. Her nerves were showing.

She could feel herself losing control so she pulled out her car keys, unlocked the door and got in without glancing at him. She wasn't even sure if he said anything else. She wouldn't have heard it over the sound of her heartbeat.

She started her car and drove away as fast as was safe. She didn't want to seem jumpy but that is exactly what she was. Jake Weidner made her nervous.

Jake hopped into his truck and started it again. "Damn, it *is* cold," he thought, "and that beautiful creature just drove away with my coat." He laughed.

He thought if she would accept the coat she might accept the drink but no such luck. "Olivia Curtis has some iron clad walls built around her." He mused, deciding to head home. Suddenly a drink didn't sound so good.

CHAPTER THREE

"Hi Harper," Olivia said lovingly. "Well, I met him and he sure isn't what I expected. Do you remember how I told you I'd be meeting a handsome stranger? He's handsome alright and trouble. I have to change this part. I have to, don't I girl? You want to know something though?"

Harper looked at her expectantly. "He's wonderful. I mean he's got a great big ego but I think it's just an act. But oh, to look at him, he's better than the vision." Olivia couldn't help the romantic sigh as she chattered on about Jake. Harper wagged her little tail.

"Sorry I'm so late. We should probably take you out for a walk huh?"

She took off the borrowed coat and set it down on the couch. She went into her bedroom and changed into an oversized sweatshirt, capris sweatpants and tennis shoes. She went to the hall closet and pulled out a white Nike ball cap she'd had since her days of playing tennis on a twice weekly basis at the club. She thought of it for a moment and then looked over at the coat sitting on her couch, tempting her.

"Should I wear it?" The dog was waiting impatiently by the door. Olivia had jackets of her own in the closet but she longed to put Jake's coat back on and smell the scent of his cologne all around her. She wanted to feel the weight and the warmth of it.

"I'm going crazy. That's what it is Harper! I'm losing my mind. I told Dr. Cline this would happen but would he listen to me? No! No one ever listens to me."

Harper whined. "Sorry girl, we're going. We're going." Olivia threw on Jake's coat, grabbed Harper's leash and her keys and they walked out the door.

Harper was happy to be outside. Olivia snapped the leash to Harper's collar and they began walking. The exercise would do them both good. They headed down the street toward the park with her happy little dog taking the lead. It was quiet. The only sounds were from an owl somewhere high in the trees and the soothing sound of the rushing river.

Olivia had made a habit of walking Harper every night after work. She kept hoping it would help distract her but since the accident, very little seemed to help. However, she was nothing if not persistent.

The hair on the back of Harper's neck rose up and she began to growl at something in the darkness beyond the trees in the park. "Harper, what is it girl?" She asked, silently wishing Harper was a Great Dane instead of a cotton ball with eyes.

She tried to see through the darkness, praying it wasn't a bear or a wolf. "Oh God," she said nervously, quietly.

A figure of a man came out of the park and into the light from the street. Olivia debated on running. She was always a fast runner but with Harper, she thought it best to stand her ground. At least it wasn't an animal. It was a man, a strange man but it wasn't likely he intended her harm. She hoped.

"The park isn't really safe at night," he said, as Harper barked at him with false braveness.

"I'll remember that" she said, trying to keep her voice level.

"No, I mean it. We've had bears come right into this park before. You and your dog would be easy prey."

Harper continued to bark which didn't help Olivia's nerves one bit. "Harper! Hush!" she snapped.

"Sorry, I didn't mean to scare you. I'm Billy." He didn't seem to want to elaborate.

If this was a pick up line then he needed to work on his material. "It's ok, it's just one of those nights, I guess," she said and sighed. "I'd better be getting home anyhow." Thanks for the warning. I'm glad you weren't a bear."

"Are you new in town?" he asked hoping to continue the conversation.

"Goodnight Billy," she said pulling Harper toward home.

"Wait, you didn't tell me your name."

"No I didn't," she said over her shoulder. She moved faster, happy to leave Billy and the dark cold night behind.

"Ok, have it your way," he yelled to her. Billy leaned against a tree and pulled out another cigarette.

When she and Harper got back to the duplex Olivia was beginning to seriously question her choices. Why had she moved to this small town with wild animals and even wilder men? She sunk into a hot bubble bath with a washcloth over her eyes and Harper parked on the bathmat licking her paws.

"Where else could I go?" she thought. "Back home? That was definitely out of the question."

It was pointless to fight it. The answer was always the same. Her visions always pulled her toward her fate.

"Olivia, you are an idiot," she told herself out loud. "Did you really think you would recreate yourself here?" She didn't care she was talking to herself again. "You don't belong here! You belong in a nice padded room somewhere near a country club so your mother can visit. Wouldn't *that* be fun."

"NO! NO! NO!" she said, again out loud.

Her thoughts fired away at her. "What did Doctor Cline tell me? He said a change of scenery would do me good. And after all, this is the place in my vision. Why not here?" "Well, here I am and this scenery is definitely different," she analyzed.

No longer was she surrounded by the pretense of her old life. The people here weren't nearly so polished and full of shit. She liked it but she also feared it. No one seemed to take her at face value anymore. It felt like everyone she met wanted to know too much about her. How long before she would be seen as broken? She despised feeling this way but it was unavoidable. She started to cry from beneath the washcloth on her face. "I hate this," she cried. "I hate this so much!"

She climbed out of the tub and wrapped herself in a towel. Olivia crawled into bed, grabbing Harper on the way. Harper curled up in a blanket beside her and looked at her with canine understanding. Olivia rolled onto her side, her wet hair mixing with the tears still streaming down her face. She couldn't count all the nights she'd cried herself to sleep.

This night would be no different. The nightmares came again.

"Jackson, I'm sorry!" She cried. "I didn't know you didn't want me to say anything about the partnership."
Jackson had that same old look of disapproval mixed with anger. "Dammit Olivia, how many times have I told you to restrict your comments to shopping and tennis or something you fucking know about?! You made me look like a horse's ass. I won't have it! I WON'T HAVE IT! Do you understand me?! Why you women find it necessary to one up each other all the time is beyond me. Shit Olivia, use your fucking head, would you please? You really disappoint me!"

She knew she should keep her mouth shut now but it was never her strong suit. "But Jackson, I wasn't bragging. I was sharing good news with our friends. I don't think Justine and Blake thought I was bragging. They're our friends and they're happy for us when something good happens. I just didn't think..."

"Right", he cut her off "you *just* didn't think! You never think about anyone but yourself! You're a selfish bitch Olivia!" He yelled as he pulled the Mercedes into their garage.

She didn't see his hand coming as he slapped her hard across the face. A gasp escaped her lips before she could clamp them down.

"I'm sorry Jackson" she whispered sadly.

"Clean up your face and pull yourself together before you come inside. I don't need the babysitter telling the neighborhood our business *too*!" He yelled.

"Ok. Ok, Jackson. I'm so sorry. Please don't be angry with me. I can't take it," she pleaded.

"You should have thought of that before you opened that goddamned mouth of yours!" He slammed the door on his words.

Olivia sobbed into a napkin she'd found in the car. Why did he hate her so? He was always so angry at her and yet he said he loved her.

She wondered how love could feel like this. Here she was stuck with this angry love and a beautiful child to protect from it. She could only hope the way she loved her son made the bigger impact.

She wiped her face and quietly went inside.
Jackson was already engrossed in the financial news in the den, actively ignoring her presence.

"Megan, did Mr. Montgomery pay you?" she asked their young neighbor and longtime babysitter.

"Yes Mrs. Montgomery; he did. Everything went just fine tonight. We played games, had popcorn, after dinner of course." Megan replied smiling.

"Thank you Megan. Tell your parents hello and be sure to let your mother know brunch has been moved to Wednesday." Olivia said.

"Sure, you take care Mrs. Montgomery." Megan replied knowingly.

Olivia walked Megan to the door and watched her walk across the street to her house. Then she shut the door, slipped out of her heels and practically sprinted up the stairs to check on her sweet boy.

Suddenly Olivia's dream became foggy, heavy and darker. She wanted to go in and see her son but everything began to bog down like she was walking in quicksand. Finally, she made it to his door. Her son sat up in bed and cried out. He had cuts all over his face and he held out his hands to her. "My God," he was covered in blood.

Olivia couldn't make the scene make sense. She thought he should be a little boy but he was sixteen and badly injured.

She screamed and tried to get to him but was held back. She turned to look into the dead eyes of her husband.

Olivia screamed and screamed. There was a knock on the door. "Let me go! He needs me! Please let me go!" she screamed.

Somehow Olivia pulled herself out of the nightmare; frustrated and scared. She sat up in bed and realized the knocking wasn't in her dream but at her door in Troy, Montana. She was soaking wet from the sweat and tears. She found the towel from her earlier bath and wiped her face.

"I'm coming, just a minute." She croaked. Olivia grabbed her bathrobe and pulled it tight around her. She felt like she had been run over by a train. She looked through the peep hole in the door and then opened it.

"Hello Mr. Jameson."

"Olivia, are you alright? I heard yelling." he looked past her into the house.

"Yes. I'm so sorry I disturbed you. I had a nightmare and I guess I was yelling. My apologies," she blushed.

"That's alright my dear. I was just worried about you," he said kindly. "I'll let you get back to sleep now, if you're sure you're alright."

"I'm, yes, thank you for checking on me." Olivia gently shut the door and walked back to her bedroom.

The clock read just after two a.m.

CHAPTER FOUR

Olivia's eyes blinked open again around seven the next morning. Harper had jumped off the bed and was licking Olivia's hand dangling toward the floor.

"Hungry girl?" she asked. She rolled out of bed and yawned her way to the bathroom. Harper sat in her usual spot by the door.

After she got ready for her day and made sure Harper had some outside time, Olivia decided she would go get some much needed winter clothing. The shopping was beyond depressing in Troy as far as she could tell so she decided she would drive to Spokane. At least she knew the selection would be better in the city.

By the time she pulled up to her duplex there was only thirty minutes until she was due at work. She quickly dropped off her purchases, let Harper outside and changed her clothes. She wished she would have made time to wash her uniform but it was too late now. She put on her new down coat and grabbed Jake's loaner coat. She secretly wanted to keep his coat for a day or two longer but that was only asking for trouble.

The drive to Spokane had rejuvenated her. Beautiful country, good shopping and one perfect peppermint mocha were just what the doctor ordered. She was determined to put the tribulations of last night behind her starting with a coat that belonged to Jake Weidner.

"Bye Harper, don't worry, I shouldn't be too late tonight."

Snow began to fall lightly as she was driving to work. She wondered if it would stick or if the ground was still too warm. She pulled into the parking lot and around to the back where she usually parked. In her 'spot' was a big black pickup truck with a man inside. Her temper flared. She pulled in fast behind the truck and blocked him in. Jumping out of her car, she knocked on the driver's side window of the truck.

"What the hell do you think you are doing?" She yelled. The man inside held his hand up to the window as if to say, 'hold on'. Olivia wasn't in the mood to wait for some jackass to get out of her way. She could have parked somewhere else but today she was late and frustrated. The man in the truck was looking at a computer on his center console. Olivia was standing in the light snow with her car door wide open. She was about to pound on the window again when Jake Weidner turned his face to her.

Jake thought she looked like an angel that had fallen from the sky. She was wearing her obviously new coat. It was dark grey and she wore a hunter green scarf, setting her eyes afire. She had a pout on her lips turning her face into that of a child. For a moment Jake was lost in thoughts of Olivia Curtis.

He couldn't remember ever feeling this way about anyone. The feeling jolted him to the core. He decided to push her buttons a little more, so he rolled down his window.

"Yes?" he drawled, "can I help you with something Miss Olivia?"

"Can you help me?" she almost yelled. "Yes, as a matter of fact, you can get out of my way. This is where I park and now you've made me late."

"Now Darlin', I think *you* have made you late by standing out here in the snow when you should have gone in and gotten to work," he prodded. "Don't you think?"

"You, you, you...ugh," she wanted to stamp her foot like a child but decided against it.

"He's had the upper hand long enough," she thought. "Fine" she said as calmly as she could. "Fine, you're right."

"Since you're already late, you can just give me my coat back now if you want to." He laughed.

She cast him one last dirty look, grabbed her purse, turned off the car, tossed his coat on the seat, and locked the doors. The sound of her car alarm beeped. Olivia walked into work just as Dan was coming out the back door.

"Olivia, do you plan on working today or just hanging out in the back lot?" he asked. Dan looked up at Jake and smiled.

"Hey Jake, what's going on?" he asked and then realized that Jake Weidner had just been trumped.

"Hey Dan, could you excuse Olivia for a moment? She needs to move her car so I can get out of here." He said, amused.

"Sorry Jake but I'm afraid she needs to get to work, though you're welcome to wait inside until her break time if you'd like." Dan laughed heartily and went inside.

Jake shrugged and walked in the back door of the diner right behind him. Dan disappeared into his office and Olivia was already out front waiting on customers. Jake stood in the kitchen at Maggie's and burst out laughing.

"Hey Jake, what's up? What's so funny?" asked Tag. He'd been frying up hamburgers.

"Olivia is funny. I thought I would give her a hard time this afternoon but instead she's giving me one," Jake chuckled.

"You come for your coat?" he asked. "I could have brought it to you tonight."

"Yeah, I was hoping to get my coat and maybe even a date but I think the coat has a new owner and the jury's still out about a date." Jake smiled. "Wait, did Olivia tell you about the coat?" he asked.

"Yeah, she said something about me bringing it to you but she'd changed her mind," Tag smiled a big shit-eating grin. "I don't know what you did to piss her off but I should probably say 'thanks'."

"What are you talking about?" Jake asked starting to get irritated.

"Your loss is my gain. If she's pissed at you, that leaves the door wide open for me my man." Tag couldn't help but feel good about his chances with Olivia now.

Jake simmered a little but reminded himself that this was his friend and he had no claim on Olivia Curtis.

"Listen Porter," Jake always called him Porter when they were competing for something. "I'll bet all my winnings from tonight's poker game that you don't have a chance in hell with the lovely Miss Olivia Curtis," Jake wagered.

"Is that so?" he replied. "You want to bet money you haven't even won yet? That just doesn't seem right at all."

"Hey", Jake said, "I was just trying to save you from having to pay me twice but if that doesn't sit right with you, then *you* name the terms."

"Ok," said Tag, "let's keep the game out of it. A hundred bucks if I can't get a date with Olivia."

Just then she walked back into the kitchen. "Are you guys talking about me?" she asked with a look that could break ice.

"No" they both lied.

"What are you even doing back here?" she asked Jake. "Don't you have someplace to go?" Olivia smirked.

"Yes, as a matter of fact I do have some things I need to get done. I'm just here to borrow Tag's truck."
Jake gave him a meaningful look.

"Sure man, here's the keys. Don't run the truck out of gas...like last time." He laughed.

Jake could see Tag was ready to play hardball.

He grabbed the keys, shut the door firmly behind him and strode out.

Jacob Knox Weidner was considered steady, reliable. Everyone in town knew him to be honest, hardworking and trustworthy, if not somewhat of a playboy. He was the one people called when they needed business advice or help moving cattle and pretty much anything in between. His parents had raised him to have a strong work ethic and never gave him the easy way out.

He grew up in the shadow of the Cabinet Mountains and spent most of his time outdoors; hunting, fishing and working the cattle ranch his family owned. That education was courtesy of his dad but he also became quickly accustomed to the finer things thanks to his mother's love of art and culture.

Jake was well traveled by the time he was a teenager but his true love was the small town of Troy and the laid back atmosphere of Montana. His parents, long since retired, now spent most of their time seeing the world together.

The majority of the business responsibilities rested on Jake's shoulders now, of which there were many. Jake's favorite was the outfitting company his dad purchased when Jake was just a boy. Before his dad retired, Jake guided hunts of all kinds for clients who traveled from many parts of the world to hunt in Montana. And even now, much of Jake's free time was spent with the crew at Weidner Outfitting Company. He loved the horses, the people, the fresh air and once upon a time, he was pretty sure he loved Samantha Duncan, his high school crush, best friend and bookkeeper for the outfitters.

Jake drove Tag's truck up the hill toward the main office for Weidner Outfitting. The snow was letting up. Jake thought an afternoon ride might be just the trick to get his mind off Olivia. He hoped it would.

"I hope I see her again soon," he thought. "Or maybe it's best to just leave the truck and let the whole Olivia thing breathe. Nah" he said aloud, chuckling to himself.

Something about that pout she had on her face earlier gave him the urge to throw her over his knee and give her a proper spanking. The thought had him smiling to himself.

He hated feeling helpless, usually all he had to do was turn on the charm a little and the women he fancied turned into putty. He got out of the truck and walked up to the office. When he opened the door Samantha was at her desk knee deep in paperwork. She looked up when she heard the door.

"Shit Jake, why don't you let all the cold air in. I'm freezing in here already. I thought someone was coming today to fix this heater?" Samantha said grumpily.

"They were supposed to. I'll call them back on my way to the ranch." Jake replied somewhat amused.

"Didn't you get my text, I needed you to stop by there and pick up last year's tax returns?" She complained.

"Huh?" Jake asked, not listening to his friend at all.

"JAKE! Hello? Kinda tryin' to help you run a business here," she said, noticing the dreamy state he was in. He was staring out the window at the corrals.

"Jacob Knox Weidner, what the hell's going on with you?" she yelled as she threw a notepad at his head.

He turned and smiled at her. "Nothing" he lied.
"Right and you may call me the Queen of England," she said. "Talk to me Jake before I call up your sister in New York and ask *her* what's going on." She threatened. "What did Jessica do now?"

"No everything with Jess is ok, I got her straightened out and I think she may stick with this job. She's working at an art gallery," he said, still only half in the conversation.

"Oh, well that's good," Sam said, "So what's with the dopey look on your face and the fact that you can't concentrate?"

Jake gave her a lop-sided grin. "I met someone."

"Of course you did. Who's the latest Mensa candidate? Is she from New York? It'd better not be a New Yorker because you know you'd hate living there permanently. Details, Man, tell me everything," she paused to take a breath.

"Well if you'd shut up for a minute, I would."

She put her hand over her mouth as if to say, 'proceed'.

"Her name's Olivia Curtis. She's a waitress down at Maggie's."

"Oh yeah, Tag mentioned something about her. She's been in town about a month he said. She must keep to herself a lot because I haven't seen her around town at all."

"Isn't she something?"

"Yeah, I was thinking of asking her out but since I'm not into girls...well, you know?" Sam teased.

Jake rolled his eyes but Sam knew her friend. He had a tendency to go for mindless, money grubbing, ditzy types; generally with very large breasts.

She always thought it was because he never really wanted to get involved, not seriously at least. The look on his face now was telling her this might be different.

Jake ignored Sam's sarcasm. "She's gorgeous. I mean really stunning. Have you seen her, up close? She has big green eyes, long auburn hair and a voice like melted butter."

"Ok lover boy, I get the point, she's a beauty, what else?" Sam pretended to gag. "Does this girl have anything between her ears other than those *big green eyes*?" She enunciated carefully for effect.

"Oh yeah, she's smart and funny and she, she *hates* me," he laughed and plopped in the office chair throwing his hands up like he just couldn't understand it.

"Well that's saying something for her." Sam giggled.

"No Sam I mean she wants to hate me, I think." He pondered that thought.

"What the hell does that mean?" she asked, slightly irritated.

"It means when I look at her, there's something about her. I don't know what it is." He replied in frustration. "It's almost like she's *trying* not to like me. Also..." he stopped.

"Also what?" she had never seen Jake like this. He was positively goofy.

"She said she wasn't someone I should waste my time on", he sighed. "I don't get it Sam. She's still new in town. She's all alone as far as I've heard and she seems to want to keep it that way. Tag told me she lives in those horrible duplexes on the end of Third. You know the ones Mr. Jameson lives in? And yet she doesn't seem to fit in there at all." Jake smiled without realizing it.

Sam burst out laughing. "Oh my God you've got it bad for this girl. I mean *really* over the top bad. I've never seen you like this. I've never heard you talk this way, **EVER**. Are you sure it's not just another challenge you're looking for?"

"No, that's not it. Sam, you aren't helping," he complained.

"Jake my friend, there's no help for you. Not this time. What do you want me to do, pass her a note in class?" She teased.

Jake got up and walked out the door leaving it wide open just to piss her off.

"See you at the poker game tonight lover boy," she yelled after him, laughing loudly.

Jake decided he didn't have time to go for a ride and didn't much feel like it anymore.

He drove Tag's truck back down the hill and turned toward the ranch road when he remembered Tag would have to drive *his* truck out for him otherwise he'd be stranded.

Jake didn't want to give any more ammunition to Tag when it came to Olivia, so he called him up.

"Hello Jake. If you're calling to tell me you wrecked my truck, man, I don't think we can be friends anymore," he joked.

"No you bastard, I'm calling because I gotta head straight out to the ranch and get some papers together for Sam, so I thought you could just drive my truck out here?"

"Sure, are the keys in it?" he asked, not really needing to. He knew Jake well enough to know the keys were always in it. Besides no one would be able to steal it with Olivia's car blocking him in.

"Yeah, they're on the floor boards." Jake replied. "I'll see you at seven? That is unless Olivia won't move her car for you either." Jake smiled thinking how poetic that would be. He liked Olivia's stubbornness. He found it charming.

"No problem, man," Tag said, "Olivia actually *likes me*."

Tag was still laughing when Jake hung up in his ear. He put his cell phone in his pocket and turned around to see Olivia placing an order in the window. "Hey Olivia, come here a second would you?"

"Sure, what's up?" she came around the end of the counter into the kitchen.

Tag smiled at her. "Would you mind moving your car for me? I've got to take Jake's truck out to the ranch for poker night,"

"Oh I'm sorry, I should have realized. I thought he would bring your truck back to you. What a jerk!"

"Aw, its ok, Jake called me. I was heading that way tonight for the card game. Hey, how would you like to come with me? I could probably get Dan to give you the rest of the night off," he asked hopefully. "It'll be fun."

"No; thank you for offering though. I'm sure it would be fun but I'm kind of looking forward to some quiet time at home," trying not to hurt his feelings. "You understand, don't you?"

"Sure, sure I understand. Maybe we could go out sometime though? How does dinner and a movie sound?" he prayed she would say yes.

"Tag, since we work together, I really think it best to avoid that sort of personal relationship. I want to be your friend but nothing more. Please don't be upset."

She really enjoyed working with him and the friendship they had begun to develop. She hoped she hadn't just ruined it for both of them.

"No, I understand. You're probably right," he said. "I shouldn't have made that bet I guess," he mumbled turning back to the grill.

"What?" she asked, not sure she heard him correctly. "What did you say?"

"Oh nothing," he replied, "I just wish I wouldn't have made that bet with Jake."

"You made a bet with him, about me? What kind of bet?" She asked, beginning to boil.

"He bet me a hundred dollars you wouldn't go on a date with me," he said guiltily, unable to look her in the eyes.

"Is that so?" she paused. "I should be really mad at you, but I'm not. It's kind of sweet, kind of. Listen, just tell him I said 'yes'."

"No, I couldn't lie to him. I told you, Jake's like family."

"This really is a small town isn't it?" Olivia noted.

"Yeah, but I love it."

"I'm really sorry about the money." Olivia said.

"Don't be sorry. Who knows, maybe I'll win at poker tonight and break even." He smiled meekly at her.

"I'll go move my car so you can get going," she said turning toward the back door.

"Thank you. I'm sorry about all this," he replied sincerely.

"A compliment is a compliment."

Jake was still getting paperwork together for Sam when Carmella, his housekeeper, quietly knocked on the open door to his home office.

"Jacob, your guests are beginning to arrive and Tag says to tell you to 'get your lazy ass out there so he can win some money'." Carmella giggled, as she headed down the hallway.

"Yeah, yeah," Jake said aloud, though Carmella was already too far away to hear. Jake grabbed the envelope for Sam and walked through the house to the parlor. He was fond of calling it his 'man cave' but it had been designed by his mother who was obsessed with all things plantation style, so technically it was the parlor.

Tag and Sam were already seated at the round oak table they used for poker and Cameron, Jake's cousin was just arriving.

"Hey lover boy," said Sam.

"Who are you talking about?" asked Tag.

Cameron's eyes lit up. It was always good fun teasing Jake about his 'flavor of the month'.

"Didn't Jake tell you about...?" She was cut off.

"Nobody. Sam just wanted to see if she could throw me off my game tonight," Jake interrupted her.

Tag said sadly, "it's OK. If you're talking about Olivia, I crashed and burned. You don't have to spare my feelings; besides it's obvious you like her, Jake."

"Wait, Tag? You're into this chick, too?" Sam asked starting to bristle.

Cameron interjected, "Why haven't I met her? Who are we even talking about?"

"What is it with her anyhow? I've seen her, sort of. Does she have a solid gold ass or what? I don't get it." Sam said sounding more jealous than she intended.

"Who are we talking about?" Cameron asked again, getting frustrated.

"Her name's Olivia Curtis. She's new in town and she works at the diner with Tag. And apparently she has every man in town drooling; from the sounds of it." Sam explained to Cameron.

"Perhaps I need to introduce this girl to the best Troy has to offer." Cameron bragged.

"I've already met her Cam so it won't be necessary." Jake replied proudly, letting Cameron simmer.

"Ha! That poor girl probably thinks Troy is filled with dumbass cowboys with no manners then. It's official; she needs to meet me, if only to save this town's reputation." Cameron poked back.

Sam stood up from the poker table and walked over to the bar and fixed herself a drink. "Why do men have to be so dumb?" she said aloud. Samantha had loved Tag Porter for as long as she could remember and now this new girl comes into town and turns all 'her boys' heads. She thought of them as 'hers' because none of them ever really got serious about anyone and she was like one of the guys to them. They were important to her, especially Jake and Tag. Jake and Cameron were more like pesky brothers but she held a special place in her heart for Tag. She refused to share him, no matter who this Olivia girl thought she was.

Jake walked up behind her. "It's ok Sam," he whispered, "You know Tag loves you, right?"

"Yeah right, that's why he's asking out the new waitress at the diner." She shook her blond curls at him "Listen Jake, I'm suddenly not feeling up to playing cards tonight."

"Oh no you don't; go sit down. We're playing poker and maybe even getting drunk tonight. You can sleep here," Jake smiled.

"Fine but I intend on taking all your money, lover boy," she replied, trying to snap out of her melancholy mood.

"You can *intend* all you want," he took her hand and led her back to the table. "Let's get this game started, shall we?" he said to his friends.

Two other guys they'd all known for many years arrived and sat down to join them. After a while, Tag leaned over to Jake and pressed a hundred dollar bill into his hand. "You won Jake. She turned me down flat," he whispered.

"Keep it. I don't feel right about it."

"No, a bet is a bet." Tag replied, looking at his hand of cards. He figured he still might have a chance of winning it back from Jake.

The poker game lasted well after midnight. Jake had faired pretty well considering all the drinks he had. He made sure Sam was situated in one of the guest bedrooms then stumbled up the stairs to his own room. In only his jeans, he lay on his bed staring at the ceiling bathed in moonlight.

Sleep finally took him. He dreamt of a bird with green eyes and long red and gold feathers. She called to him in a cry of music and he could feel it deep in his heart. The music told of a woman who was born of fire. Then the fire rose up and consumed the calling bird. He raced toward her but she flew away, alight with flames. Suddenly, on the ground at his feet was left a pile of ash. He reached down and felt it soft and powdered in his fingers. Again, he looked toward the sky but it was blindingly bright.

It was a vivid dream, the kind so real and intense you feel like you can't escape it. There was no line between reality and the dream. Jake would forever remember the face of the bird and the sound that echoed in his heart. He belonged to her and she belonged to the fire, but why?

CHAPTER FIVE

Olivia leaned back lazily on her bed pillows. She found it comforting to have a lot of pillows. Jackson hated that. She remembered once he threw every pillow on the bedroom floor. He was angry about something and took it out on her and the pillows. She laid quietly pillow-less until Jackson fell asleep. Only then did she grab a couple from the floor to comfort her fitful sleep.

The following morning, he was ominously quiet. Suddenly, he ordered her to stand by the bed. She waited barely breathing when he left the room and returned with a kitchen knife in his hand. She began to shake uncontrollably. "What are you going to do?" she whispered.

He took the knife and slashed it into the pillows until every one of them was destroyed. The room filled with fluff and fabric as Olivia watched Jackson in horror. He was out of breath as he took the knife and jabbed the point of it under her chin. She gasped.

"If you ever disobey me again, I'll kill you!" He panted. He walked out of the room as though nothing had happened.

Olivia, choking on tears and dropping to her knees began gathering up the fluff into a large pile. Her son came in and knelt beside her. "Mom, are you ok?"

"Yeah, thanks Bud." They cleaned the room in silence.

Olivia slept without a pillow the better part of a month. Eventually, Jackson bought two new pillows, one for her and one for him. She wasn't allowed to have more than that. He called it 'excessive bullshit'.

It was still so hard to believe he was dead. Olivia was a widow, so strange. She always thought of widows as little old ladies in church but here she was with a dead husband. She didn't have *anyone*, not really. Her brother Miles, her parents but it wasn't the same; not the same as having a husband, even though her husband had been horrible.

She reached over and opened the drawer on her bedside table. She pulled out a wooden cigar box and sat it on her bed. She turned on the lamp and opened the box. She'd had it since she was a child from her grandfather's estate.

Over her lifetime, she put many different things in that box. Most recently she put the letter she'd written to Jake. She hadn't known his name when she wrote it.

It seemed silly to add it now. She set it aside. The box held many other things; notes and pictures from school friends, her son's birth certificate and now it held two death certificates, a check she hadn't deposited and her wedding ring. The ring was a gaudy thing, oozing with excess and lies. The biggest lie of all; that she ever loved Jackson Montgomery.

There had been a message on her cell phone a couple days ago from the insurance company reminding her of the expiration date on the check and that it should be cashed or it would be voided. She picked up the check and turned it over in her hand to read the name on it.
Olivia K. Curtis-Montgomery

Olivia wished she knew what to do with this money. She felt like working hard and paying old debts was part of her penance, her payment for all the ways she had failed. She had let her son down most of all. She couldn't save him and for that, she would never forgive herself. Though she knew it wasn't right letting all that money slip away. Maybe the thing to do was to cash the check, pay the debts but still continue on her path here in Troy. And that would mean facing her fate. She took a deep breath.

"Yes", she said out loud, "that feels right. Dr. Cline would be proud of me." She decided to send her brother a text...

I made a decision about the life insurance but time is ticking. Call me tomorrow. I need your help. What needs to be paid first? What debt is left? Let me know. Love, Liv

Olivia picked up the ring and slipped it on her finger. It was looser than before but she knew she'd lost weight. Eating had been a pretty low priority since the funeral and her stay in the hospital. She took off the ring as quickly as she had put it on. It was the sign of her imprisonment and she refused to ever feel that way again. She would never again be a prisoner, the warden known as Jackson Montgomery was dead.

Olivia put the box away and went into the kitchen for a glass of wine, hoping to finally get some sleep. She poured herself a glass of white Zinfandel. The taste was perfect, soothing and cool on her lips and down her throat. She walked back to bed, turned off her lamp and sat sipping wine in the moonlight.

Jake lifted Olivia's hand to his lips and kissed her palm, then her forearm. Olivia felt breathless and flushed. She couldn't believe how he made her feel. He kissed his way up her arm toward her neck, covering every inch with gentle kisses. She sighed and felt so peaceful. Jake began kissing her lower lip, sucking it into his mouth. She moaned and moved in closer to deepen the kiss. He smiled and then kissed her some more, deeply and passionately. He put his hands on her shoulders and pushed her back just enough to clearly look at her face.

"Jake please, don't stop" she said in a desperate whisper. Suddenly Jake's face changed into Jackson. Jackson hovered over her, angry and threatening.

"Damn it Olivia, use your fucking head!" He yelled at her.

Olivia jerked awake and sat bolt upright in her bed filled with pillows.

"Ugh!" Olivia yelled, "Why do we have to have dreams at all? Dreams suck!"

Harper looked up at her and cowered near the foot of the bed. "Sorry girl, you aren't in trouble. I'm just, venting I guess." She reached over and petted her dog softly. Olivia looked at the clock.

"Ten o'clock?" she said. "I must have been really tired."

Jake was waking up that same Sunday morning to sunlight streaming in the window. He hadn't closed the drapes before he fell asleep and he was very hung over. He rolled over and pushed the intercom button:

"Carmella dear, I could desperately use some coffee and some ibuprofen, please." He croaked.

Carmella had been in charge of the Weidner household since Jake was a young boy. She was practically part of the family and with his parents' retirement, she made the perfect surrogate mom.

Carmella's Italian accented voice answered back, "Jacob, you get up and come downstairs. You still have guests in this house you know?"

Jake pushed the button again: "Carmella, my guests are all grown up and can figure out what to do without me for a little while and my head is pounding," he yelled, and then thought better of it as it made his headache ten times worse.

Carmella yelled back, "Don't you get loud with me Jacob Knox Weidner" and then scolded him in a string of Italian cusswords.

He knew this wasn't a battle he was going to win so he took a hot shower.

Twenty minutes later he came downstairs dressed in fresh clothes and feeling much better though still a little burned about not getting any coffee.

"Good morning Carmella dear. I'm very sorry." Jake purred. "Would there happen to be any coffee left?"

"Yes of course there is, not that it's hardly morning anymore." She said grumpily.

Carmella was in the middle of putting together lasagna for their dinner. Sunday dinner at the Weidner Ranch had been a tradition since he was a kid. After Jake's sister moved out it was often Carmella and Jake by themselves; though Jake could usually rope Sam or Tag or some of the many ranch hands into joining them for dinner. It wasn't difficult since Carmella was an excellent cook.

Carmella stopped the preparations long enough to pour Jake a cup of coffee with lots of creamer, just how he liked it; then she leaned on the counter and looked seriously at him.

"Jacob, it's time you got married," she said in earnest.

"Are you asking me to marry you Carmella?" he teased.

"Certainly not; you know better," she replied. "But it is time you think about settling down with a nice girl. Did you hear me, a nice girl, and not some girl with only air in her head?"

"Awe Carmella, those girls aren't so bad. You shouldn't be so hard on them," he teased. "Listen, I love you but it's kind of hard to get married when I haven't even met anyone I really like," he smirked.

"I hear differently. Samantha says you found a girl you do like." She smiled.

"Where is Sam anyway?" he asked.

"Don't change the subject. Samantha is swimming. I'm sure she got tired of waiting for you to wake up," she pointed at him.

"Sam doesn't have a swimsuit here, does she?" he said knowing perfectly well that she didn't and smiling mischievously.

"No, and that is exactly why you will stay right here and leave her alone," she told him.

"Yes Ma'am," he said, though he was tempted to go take a peek. Sam might be his best friend but she had a gorgeous body.

"I think I'll go to my office for a bit."

"Sit down Jacob; you don't fool me." Carmella pointed to the stool at the island.

"I'll get you that ibuprofen now *and* you need to eat something.

You **don't** need to go invade that girl's privacy like some sort of horny teenager."

"Horny teenager?" Jake laughed. "I haven't been one of those in quite a while."

"Then prove it. Sit down and eat," she ordered again.

"Ok, ok" he sat down at the island to enjoy his very belated breakfast of homemade cinnamon rolls.

"Your parents and I tried to raise a gentleman but sometimes I wonder," she smiled.

In between bites, Jake said, "You did Ma'am, you did."

Sam walked in just then looking like a sunflower on a sunny day. "Good morning lover boy," she patted Jake on the head like a puppy. "I was going to take off early this morning but Carmella and I got to talking and well, I don't have a pool at my house."

"You looked good in there. Good form." He teased.

"What? You were watching me? She asked, suddenly feeling uncomfortable.

"No but next time you decide to skinny dip in my pool; the least you could do is invite me." He laughed.

"Ha! I'm not the one you want to jump in the pool with, am I?"

Carmella started shaking her head at them. "Jacob, I told you not to change the subject. I want you to tell me about this woman that has your head on backwards." Carmella looked to Sam to see if she had gotten the expression right.

"It's actually 'whipped your hair back' but Jake knows what you mean," Sam smiled at her. "Don't you Jake?"

"There's nothing to say. I don't even really know her. She doesn't want anything to do with me. I loaned her a coat and that's it." He smiled thinking of her in only his coat and nothing else.

"See?! See Carmella? See that dopey look on his face? Our Jakey boy is a fish on a hook and he won't even admit it." Sam teased.

"Jacob, I think you should invite her out here for dinner tonight. She will love my lasagna and I'll chaperone." She said, thinking herself brilliant.

"I don't need a chaperone. Besides, she won't come." He said, sounding irritated.

"How do you know unless you ask her?" Carmella said.

"I did ask her. I asked her out the other night and she said 'No'." In fact not just 'No' but 'Hell No'!" he frowned.

"That can't be. You're a good man. You asked her here and she said, 'No'? Did you tell her I make the best lasagna she'll ever taste?" Carmella asked. She prided herself on her cooking.

"Well no. I asked her for a drink at Max's," he said staring down into his now empty coffee cup.

"Jake you are a dumbass! You, Tag, Cameron and pretty much every other man in this county have me convinced that men in general are not bright." Sam said pointedly. "You can't just ask her out to a bar. If you really like her then you need to *court* her," Sam scolded him.

"Ci, I agree Jacob" Carmella added. "Samantha is right. Go to her house with flowers in hand and invite her for dinner, here to your home. It's much nicer than a *bar*."

Jake knew Carmella just wanted to get a look at her. He also knew if Sam could think of a reason to join them for dinner that she would, too. Jake sighed.

"Fine, I'll invite Olivia for dinner but if she turns me down again I'm coming after the two of you" he teased.

"Don't worry Jake, "Sam smiled knowingly, "she won't turn you down. You're too irresistible." She patted his face gently.

"Yeah right, says the girl who turned me down flat in high school," he gave her a pitiful look.

"That's just because we were meant to be friends," she replied honestly.

"You're probably right though my ego is still bruised from it."

"Your ego barely fits through the door, lover boy."

"So how do I look?" Jake asked two of his favorite ladies.

"You need to brush your teeth again." Sam evaluated.

"...and don't wear that shirt. It's not a great color on you. Wear the blue one I pressed for you earlier." Carmella added.

"Have you two been scheming all morning about this?" he asked. "What about flowers, it's Sunday?"

"Don't worry. I called Martha at the flower shop and she'll have something all ready for you," Sam said innocently.

"You **have** been scheming! What if neither of you even likes her? Then you'll have put me through all of this for nothing?"

"Don't be such a pussy, Jake. What's the worst that could happen?" Sam asked.

Carmella gave Sam a look about the language but agreed nonetheless.

"Well let's see? She could slap me, slam the door in my face, call the sheriff because she thinks I'm stalking her, sic her dog on me, you name it."

"Wow, maybe I did kill your ego. Since when did you lose all your confidence?" Sam asked.

"Since I met Olivia Curtis, I guess." He smiled half-heartedly.

"Don't worry, Jake. I have a good feeling about this. Besides, if Carmella and I decide we don't like her then we'll kill her and bury her body out in your pasture somewhere. Problem solved." Sam teased.

Carmella nodded happily. "Jacob, you need to get a move on, it's nearly noon and she will want time to get ready." Carmella pushed.

Jake wanted to complain but there was no point. In spite of everything, he was looking forward to seeing Olivia again; even if she did decide to slam the door in his face.

CHAPTER SIX

Olivia sat in the middle of her small living room floor, cross legged on her yoga mat. Meditation had become a very important part of her new routine. The yoga made her feel a little better. She closed her eyes and listened to the soothing voice on the DVD. Her mind was peaceful thinking of her quiet space. In her head she pictured clouds rolling by and birds flying, a sandy beach and a cold drink with water condensing on the glass beside her. There was a pretty hut on stilts over blue water. It was a place she'd never been and yet been many times in her meditations.

There was a knock at the door. Olivia sighed. "Just a minute" she said, frustrated by the interruption. Harper started barking in excitement. Olivia figured it was probably Mr. Jameson again about snow tires or something. She would smile and agree and tell him she would take care of it. She wasn't too worried about it really. She knew she could always walk to and from work. It was part of the reason she had picked this apartment. She didn't even look through the peep hole, she just opened the door.

"Miles!! Oh my God. What are you doing here? In Montana?" she asked, utterly shocked. "I told you to call me."

"Liv is that any way to talk to your handsome older brother who took a very early, **very early**, flight into Spokane on a Sunday and then drove a rental car all the way here to see you?" Miles asked happily.

"No. No. Gosh. Sorry.'" she hugged him tightly. She suddenly felt like crying. She hadn't seen Miles since the auction in her hometown of Lake Oswego. It was a place she couldn't even think about returning to.

She couldn't help it; tears began rolling down her face. Miles just kept hugging her. He figured she was long overdue for some family connection and some hug therapy from her big brother. Harper finally quieted down after sniffing around Miles ankles. Olivia and Miles stood in the doorway while she cried her heart out into his overpriced white dress shirt.

"Liv, we're letting all the cold air into your shithole," he teased.

She laughed and smacked his shoulder. "You jerk, it's not that bad."

"Um honey, it's a dump, but if you dig it, then that's cool." Miles eyed the place and then bent down to pet Harper.

"Hiya Harper, are you taking good care of my Sis?" Miles asked.

"She is," Olivia answered. "Come in and have a seat. We have a lot to catch up on and I need your help with this insurance check."

"Riiiight! It's hard to know what to do with a million dollar life insurance check. Holy shit Liv, save it or invest it, but do *something* with it. Don't just let it sit in that stupid box of yours." Miles said seriously.

Olivia smiled that Miles remembered her cigar box. "Miles, you're the accountant. You know I can't just stick it in the bank and forget about it."

"Olivia," Miles used her whole name to prove he was serious. "You should know most of the debt you and Jackson had during your marriage was covered by the auction. You don't have the kind of debt you think you have. I told you to wait until after the insurance paid to have that damn auction. You could have kept a lot of your things."

"I didn't want to Miles. I couldn't look at all of that stuff every day or live in that house with so many memories."

"I understand that but you didn't have to leave town. Mom and Dad are worried sick over you. Mom is convinced you'll be murdered or eaten by a bear." Miles joked.

"Tell Mother I'm fine, really."

"*I* know you are, but how long are you going to stay here in *this town*? It's barely a blip on the radar."

"When did you turn into such a snob?"

"I'm not a snob. I'm just being real. This isn't even close to what you're used to. I think you chose this place to punish yourself. For what, I don't know but it's sick Olivia. You need to get your well-manicured hands around a tennis racket or a cabernet," Miles emphasized, lifting up her delicate hands.

"Don't be a dick," she said. "And I hate cabernet. This blip on the radar is starting to grow on me. This is where I'm supposed to be. It's not a delusion either. I belong here. The people are real and kind and not full of crap like all my so-called friends from the country club."

"I'm sorry Liv, really. I just figured you needed an excuse to get out of here. How about I stay a couple days, get this money stuff all straightened out and you can show me what 'real' life looks like?" he smiled.

"That sounds good, though you may like it so much you won't want to leave."

Just then there was another knock on the door. "Miles would you get that it's probably my neighbor Mr. Jameson. He's been worried sick about my lack of snow tires. Apparently he thinks winter is going to happen tomorrow. I'm going to make us some coffee."

"Sure Liv," Miles said. He opened the door to a strange man with flowers in his hand. Leaning back toward the kitchen, Miles said "Uh, Liv this town *is* nice; Mr. Jameson just brought me flowers."

"What?" Olivia asked, still making coffee.

"Oh no, I'm not Mr. Jameson. My name is Jake Weidner. I, um, I..." he looked down at the daisies in his hand. "I was coming to extend an invitation." Jake knew he needed to switch gears especially with Olivia's boyfriend standing in the doorway.

"How could I not realize she would have a boyfriend? Of course she would have a boyfriend." He thought, kicking himself.

"Oh" Miles said, "How nice; invite to what?"

Olivia leaned around her brother's shoulder to see who was at her door. She opened her mouth to speak but didn't have the slightest idea what to say. Miles decided he would take over this obviously awkward situation. He stuck his hand out. "Hi Jake, I'm Miles Curtis. I'm Olivia's brother." He said kindly. Jake shook hands with Miles. "I decided to surprise my little sister with a long overdue visit."

"Yes Jake, this is my brother," she said awkwardly. She had no idea why she felt the need to repeat that information.

Jake smiled broadly. "What a nice surprise. Well you are both welcome to come. I'm having a little dinner party at my house at six and would love for you both to join me as my guests," he said formally.

"No thank you, Jake." Olivia quickly responded.

"Hold on a minute, Jake." Miles shut the door on him.

"Miles what are you doing?" Olivia asked.

"Liv, if you are going to introduce me to all the fine things in your *new* life then you actually have to **have** a life..." Miles waited patiently for Olivia to cave in.

"Fine but if it ends up an unmitigated disaster I'm never speaking to you again." Olivia threatened.

The two of them either didn't realize or didn't care that the walls and door were paper thin. Jake could hear every word. He decided right then and there, he liked Olivia's brother very much.

He knew he'd better call Carmella as soon as he could to inform her of the extra guests and that he had turned his intimate dinner for two into an intimate dinner party. It looked like Sam would get to join him after all.

The door opened and Miles shoved Olivia out in front of him. "Jake we would be delighted to join you tonight. Where do we need to go? I'm afraid I have no idea where you live." Olivia confessed.

"Oh no problem; it's very easy to find. Just cross the bridge on Roosevelt Parkway and then head south on Kootenai River Road until you see the sign. It's on the left. I'll see you at six then? Oh and here, these *are* for you," Jake said and held out the bouquet of daisies to Olivia.

She took them and smiled. Jake's breath caught in his throat as he turned to walk toward his truck.

"Thank you, they're beautiful. Jake, Jake wait," she followed after him. He stopped and turned back toward her.

"You said 'the sign', what sign?" She asked, confused.

"There is a sign at our lane. Don't worry, you'll see it. It's hard to miss, but if you prefer I can come pick you up?" he offered.

"No. That won't be necessary. We can manage," she replied.

"Somehow I knew you would say that," Jake smiled. "See you tonight."

Olivia shut the door behind her and stared at the daisies in her hand.

Miles sat on the couch looking smug. "Oh Liv he seems nice enough and it'll be fun because I'll be there." Miles laughed.

"Sure, fun," she sneered. "Miles you don't know Jake, he's...he's an ass. I'm quite certain he...he..."

"He what? Stole your bike?"

"Well no but he did steal my parking spot at work; on purpose." She said trying to sound convincing.

"Then shit Liv, why didn't you have him arrested? They shouldn't let hardened criminals like Jake Weidner walk the streets." He laughed out loud.

"You think you're pretty funny don't you big brother?"

"I know I'm funny; now go and get in the shower. I'm going to bring my suitcase in and find a fresh shirt to wear'"

"Yeah, sorry I messed up your shirt Miles," she apologized.

"No biggy. Do you have an iron I could use though? I have a feeling I'll need it."

"Sure, it's in the hall closet with the ironing board."

Two hours later Olivia emerged from her bedroom. Miles was flipping through her meager channels on the television.

"Damn, took you long enough. It's already almost five and we have to be there by six. Do you think it's far?" Miles asked.

He hadn't really looked up to see Olivia but when she was quiet, he did. "Liv, what are you wearing?" he wrinkled his nose.

"Jeans and a blouse, why?"

"Because you look like you've been dumpster diving for your wardrobe. Do those jeans have an elastic waist?" Miles scoffed.

"No they don't, thank you very much. You're wearing jeans too."

"Yes, but these are Ralph Lauren jeans, not thrift store specials. I mean, I get you wanting to fit in with the locals but those are just ugly."

"This is the country and besides I don't have anything else to wear." Olivia bit her lip.

"You're lying. I know you too well. You had two closets full of designer clothes. What gives?"

"If you must know, all my other clothes are still in boxes in the spare bedroom and well, um, I just, I don't go in there," she sighed.

"Ok well that outfit just won't do so tell me what box to dig through because we can't have you going to dinner looking like a hobo," Miles teased.

"Nobody says 'hobo' anymore," she smiled at him.

"No but they should, it's funny. Now, what box?" he asked again.

"Dresses; the box marked dresses, I guess," she answered reluctantly.

The spare bedroom was piled high and deep with boxes all neatly labeled and stacked of course. Olivia was nothing if not tidy. Miles started to wish he wouldn't have put down her outfit. He saw several boxes marked with his nephew's name. A sick feeling rose from the pit of his stomach. He loved that boy so much. He was bright and charming like his mom and he had her eyes too, big and green. Miles sighed. "I miss you buddy," he said aloud softly. A knot that ached lodged itself in his throat. Miles shook his head.

Dresses, there it was. He grabbed the box and started digging. He pulled out an emerald green sweater dress and even found light grey suede boots in the box marked shoes. He hoped she would hurry. Miles detested being late. He came out, shut the door but Olivia wasn't in the living room.

"Liv" Miles called.

"Yeah, in the bathroom, just bring me the dress and I'll change."

"Here" Miles held out the dress and boots at the bathroom door.

"Oh Miles this dress is perfect. I haven't worn it in so long. Will you go start the car? I'll change and then we'll go."

Miles grabbed her keys and ran out to her T-Bird. It had been snowing. Perhaps Olivia's neighbor had been right about winter. He hopped in the car and started it up turning on the defrost hoping it would warm up quickly. The car smelled of Olivia's perfume and was full of memories.

"Wow" he said when he saw her. "You look incredible." She had pulled her hair back into a smooth chignon and had done her makeup. It was a huge improvement from the scrubbed up denim look she'd been rocking earlier.

"Thanks. I decided if I'm going to do this then I should do it right."

"Are you ready to go? You'd better grab a coat and scarf, it's been snowing."

"It has?" she asked. "Do you think we'll have trouble with the drive?"

"No we should be alright. It will probably lighten up soon."

She threw on her scarf and new coat and they headed on their way. Mr. Jameson waved from his window as they backed out of the shared driveway.

"That's Mr. Jameson," Olivia told Miles.

"Oh, well he's no Jake Weidner is he Liv?" Miles teased.

"No he certainly isn't," she admitted.

CHAPTER SEVEN

Sam walked into the dining room in a topaz blue sweater, ivory slacks and five inch stiletto boots. "You look beautiful Sam." Jake mentioned casually. "I hope you and Olivia get along alright. I don't need any cat fights in my dining room."

"Jake I've never known you to worry so much. You shouldn't start now. Hey what time is it anyhow?"

"Ten till" Jake replied, "I probably should have insisted on picking them up. I didn't plan on this much snow tonight."

"Yes, you should have Jacob. If this woman and her brother aren't here at six I want you to get in your truck and go get them." Carmella ordered as she set places at the dining table.

"Yes Ma'am," He had been thinking the same thing.

Twelve minutes later Jake had a coat on and was heading to his pickup when car lights pulled up the drive and Olivia's car stopped out front. Miles got out and started to come around to open the door for Olivia but Jake beat him to it. Jake smiled brightly at her.

"Olivia, Miles, I'm so glad you made it." Jake beamed.

He held out a hand to assist Olivia from the car. She looked up at Jake's house. It was a classic plantation style with a graceful sweeping porch. It reminded Olivia of Gone with the Wind.

"*This* is your house?" she marveled. "It's gorgeous." She knew she was gushing but she couldn't help herself.

"Thank you. Welcome to Weidner Ranch," Jake replied.

"I understand now what you meant about the sign. It's the only sign and the ranch bears your name. You could have just told us," she smiled.

"I didn't want you to think I was bragging. Come on in before we all freeze out here." Jake motioned toward the wide front stairs.

Olivia and Miles followed Jake in through the grand double entry doors. The foyer was lit softly by a glowing chandelier that looked antique, it reinforced the plantation style. Somehow the house had been decorated to perfectly marry modern conveniences with a turn of the century style.

"May I take your coat Olivia?" Jake asked.

"Yes of course, thank you."

Just then Carmella walked down the hall.

"Here I'll take the coats and you show our guests to the dining room Jacob. Dinner is about ready," Carmella said brightly. "I'm Carmella, the housekeeper here."

"Oh hello, it's a pleasure to meet you." Miles shook hands with Carmella but she pulled him in and kissed his cheeks then she did the same with Olivia. She took their coats, made quick work of hanging them into a nearby closet and disappeared down the hall just as quickly as she'd arrived.

"Carmella is more than just the housekeeper; she is also my friend. She's like another mom to me." Jake added.

Olivia smiled at him. She could hear the love and adoration in his voice. Perhaps he wasn't the jackass she had thought.

They followed Jake to the dining room and were seated at one end of a very large table. Low lights and candles on the sideboard warmed the room and gave it a romantic feel.

"Are we your only guests this evening, I thought this was a dinner party?" Olivia puzzled.

"No Darlin', as a matter of fact..." Jake looked behind him.

"I'm coming. I had to pee." Sam laughed entering the room with a splash. "Carmella damn near bit my head off but when you gotta go, you gotta go."

Jake laughed, but sounded more nervous than anything. "Ah there you are. Olivia and Miles Curtis let me introduce you to my friend Samantha Duncan." Jake said.

"Hello, it's a pleasure to meet you Samantha," Olivia said.

"Just call me Sam. I'm so happy we could all get together like this. I've been dying to meet you Olivia. Between Jake and Tag I've heard nothing but good things."

Olivia wasn't sure if she meant it but just smiled. Miles was instantly taken with Samantha; Olivia could read her brother so well.

Miles shook her hand and lingered for a moment longer than necessary. Samantha was an effervescent blond with naturally curly hair. She was petite but perfectly proportioned and completely self-assured. Olivia suppressed the urge to roll her eyes at Miles's reaction.

"Let's sit down shall we. I'll get the wine," Jake offered.

As Jake poured wine, he took the opportunity to really look at Olivia. She wore an emerald green sweater dress that hugged every curve. It looked to be cashmere and he hoped to find out for sure.

Her eyes sparkled in the candlelight. Jake was suddenly and powerfully aroused. He listened and watched as Sam told amusing stories of their childhood together.

After a while, Sam said, "Sorry, I've been completely monopolizing the conversation. Let's talk about the two of you."

"I'm afraid there isn't much to tell," Olivia answered quickly beginning to wonder why she agreed to this dinner.

"Well let's see, I know you're from Oregon, you work at Maggie's and you have a gorgeous brother. What else?" Sam looked directly at Miles. Playing hard to get was not her strong suit.

He *was* good looking, too. Sam couldn't help but notice that Miles cut a striking figure. Where Olivia was this odd combination of dark red hair, fair skin, and light green eyes; Miles had darker skin and ash blond hair. His eyes were blue and he was tall and athletic looking. He wasn't at all similar to Jake but had something completely unique.

"Well, thank you Sam. I was just thinking there is an influx of beautiful people here in Montana. I guess I know what I've been missing." Miles replied staring into Sam's eyes.

Olivia suddenly felt like a twelve year old and wished she could make puking sounds.

"How is it that you aren't married Sam?" Miles asked.

"Oh my God Miles stop it. You're embarrassing her." Olivia had had enough. Jake chuckled softly.

"It's ok, Olivia, It takes a lot more than that to embarrass me. And, to answer your question it's because I keep waiting for the right guy to come along."

Jake realized maybe he wasn't the only person at the table with a dopey look on his face. The thought amused him.

Carmella had been serving them lovingly all evening, urging them in her very Italian way to eat more. Jake tried to get her to join them several times but she refused; though she kept checking on them. Jake figured it was her way of chaperoning them.

Olivia liked Carmella very much. She held her firmly by the shoulders and kissed both her cheeks but not the way her old friends did kissing the air, but real honest to goodness kisses on her cheeks. She called Olivia, "bella ragazza" and Olivia knew just enough Italian to know Carmella had called her a *beautiful girl.*

"Grazie", Olivia replied. Jake's eyes lit up when he heard Olivia speak Italian.

He pictured telling her many things in Italian. Sweet nothings whispered in her ear.

"Jake" Sam said sharply, "Jake! Quit daydreaming and make Olivia tell me something about herself."

"Sam I promise you I've got nothing so interesting as your life here in Troy," said Olivia.

Sam pouted a bit and Miles snorted. His sister had once been vibrant and full of life and stories. It was so long ago but he remembered a girl who entertained people. Olivia gave him a stern look.

"Miles, tell us about you then and we'll get back to Olivia." Sam said.

"Well that's easy enough. I'm single." He looked right at Sam who blushed uncharacteristically. "I live just outside of Portland and I've got the world's most fascinating career, I'm an accountant." Miles said and Sam laughed at his little joke.

"Actually I enjoy it. I'm good with numbers, I always have been. Anyway our dad is a retired investment banker and our mom is a cellist. She has been touring with a symphony recently but also does solo performances. You should hear her play Bach's Cello Suite Number One in G Major. She plays the prelude and I get goose bumps, no joke. Liv can play the cello too but she was a rebel and focused mainly on the piano instead. Didn't you Liv?" Miles looked at her with brotherly pride.

Olivia nodded but said nothing.

"Do you play an instrument as well Miles?" Jake asked. Sam looked deflated when Jake beat her to the question.

The wine was beginning to go to Olivia's head. She touched her fingertips to her forehead. The gesture didn't go unnoticed by Jake.

"No, I never had the musical talent the Curtis women have." Miles laughed. "I'm blaming my lack of talent on my lack of ovaries. It makes me feel better about my shortcomings." Everyone laughed. Olivia only smiled and then stood up. Jake and Miles both stood as well.

"Excuse me, where is the restroom?" Olivia asked feeling tipsy and flushed.

"Here, right this way. I'll show you." Jake offered. Jake took Olivia's arm and led her down a hall to the bathroom.

"Are you feeling alright?" Jake asked.

"Yes I'm fine. I think the wine is getting to me a little." Olivia blushed. Jake looked at her skeptically.

"I'm fine really." Olivia walked in, shut the door behind her and looked at herself in the mirror. "Get it together Olivia. You don't even know these people. They do not need to see you make a fool of yourself." she told herself quietly. There was a knock on the door.

"Just a minute please," she replied.

"Liv, its Miles, are you alright?" He asked.

"Yes, please go back and enjoy the evening. I'll be along in a moment," she begged.

"We're going to have coffee in the sitting room. I'll wait for you," Miles insisted.

"Miles I am perfectly capable of finding the sitting room. I'll simply follow the sound of your loud, annoying voice," she said forcefully.

"Ok, ok, sheesh."

Olivia sat on a dainty looking Victorian chair facing the sink. "Breathe Olivia. Breathe," she sighed.

After a moment or two, she wasn't sure how long; she walked out of the bathroom to find Jake sitting on the floor in the hallway with his arms resting on his knees.

"Uh hi" she almost giggled. "Damn wine," she thought.

Jake looked up at her smiling then easily got to his feet. "It's a big house and I didn't want you to get lost."

"I'm sure I could have managed but thank you just the same." Olivia replied. "Where are Miles and Sam? Miles said you'd be having coffee in the sitting room. Should we join them? We probably should don't you think?" Olivia rambled.

"Well, Darlin' I think they would like a little alone time. How about I take you on a tour of the house?" he offered.

"Oh, well, um, uh, ok," she stammered.

"Why do I get the feeling I make you nervous?" he asked.

"Because you do" she said candidly and then clapped her hand over her mouth.

Jake laughed and then she laughed too. He thought she had the best laugh he'd ever heard. Olivia couldn't seem to stop laughing. She couldn't remember the last time she felt so light and so free. She finally got it under control and sighed like a satisfied child.

"So how about that coffee?"

"Or we could just have some more wine. I'm happy to open another bottle, your choice," he suggested.

"No I really shouldn't."

"Olivia, it's ok to break the rules once in a while." He smiled at her.

"I guess it wouldn't hurt. Let's open another bottle, then."

"Well first we have to pick one." He said lightly as he grabbed her hand and led her down the hallway to a large wooden door. He opened it and they went down a dimly lit staircase that opened up into a beautiful and cool wine cellar.

"My mom designed this house around the plantation houses in the South. She's a sucker for Gone with the Wind." Jake announced.

Olivia smiled. "I can relate to that. There's something so timeless and romantic about it. The way people spoke to each other, the clothing, the architecture; it's all so wonderfully charming."

Jake could tell she was a romantic like his mom. It was sweet and he couldn't help but smile as she spoke.

"Do you still play music?" Jake asked.

"No, not for a while now," she said darkly.

"I'm sorry, is that a touchy subject? I didn't mean to pry." He could tell it was an open wound he had stumbled upon.

"You didn't pry. It's fine." Olivia lied.

Jake wanted to kick himself. He felt like he'd ruined the mood with one question.

"Here" Olivia said, "how about this one?" She held up a bottle of wine.

"You want to open a bottle of Chateau Lafite?" he asked, sounding surprised at her choice.

"Sure. I mean, if you don't mind," she smiled.

The cashmere dress, the investment banker father, her taste in wine; the whole thing didn't add up. Olivia carried herself like she had been born to privilege and yet she worked in a diner and rented a less than glamorous duplex in a town where she had no connections.

"I don't mind. It's an excellent choice." He answered. "Let's take it into the library. I'll start a fire."

"Perfect." She whispered, turning toward the stairs.

"Perfect." He thought.

They made their way into the library, hearing sounds of laughter from Miles and Sam as they passed by the sitting room. Jake carried the bottle of wine and two glasses.

The library was a huge elegant room with a fireplace big enough to stand in and cozy, overstuffed couches in the center facing it, but the shelves of books were the most impressive feature of the high-ceilinged room.

The bookcases lined the walls reaching to the ceiling on one side of the room. The opposite side of the room had a large picture window framed with dark heavy drapes. Toward one side was a spiral staircase leading to the upper floor filled with more books.

Jake started a fire while Olivia marveled at the grandeur of the place. Above the fireplace was a painting that felt familiar to her. "I feel like I've seen this painting somewhere before." She said, staring up.

"You probably have if you've been to The Metropolitan Museum of Art in New York. It's the Portrait of Madame X by John Singer Sargent. This one is a reproduction of course, though a good one. My dad saw it once when he and my mom were traveling and decided he needed to own this one. He said she reminded him of a picture he has of his grandmother. In truth Olivia, now that I look at her again, she rather reminds me of you."

"Thank you, that's kind of you. It's probably just the red hair." Olivia smiled.

"I think it's something else." Jake replied mysteriously, turning back to his fire building.

Olivia admired the view of Jake, too. Goosebumps rose on her arms but it wasn't because she was cold. She suppressed the urge to sigh like something out of a corny teenage movie.

Jake stood up and looked questioningly at her. He uncorked the wine and then sat next to her. "What are you thinking about?"

"I'm admiring this room. It's amazing. You didn't take me on a tour of your house you know?" she said, trying to find a safe subject.

"Did you still want one?" he asked.

"No I'm pretty comfortable here; maybe another time." She smiled.

Jake poured the wine and handed a glass to Olivia. She took a sip. "It's lovely."

"Yes, it is good. You chose a great bottle of wine."

They both stared at the fire for a while sipping their wine.

Jake broke the silence first. "Olivia, I..."

"It was really nice of you to invite us to dinner," she said interrupting him.

She wasn't sure she wanted him to finish his sentence. Her insides felt like jelly. The feeling had been there since he opened her car door. If she were honest, she'd felt this way since the day he walked into Maggie's Diner. What was it? Three days ago? It felt like she'd known Jake for much longer. That was the trouble with knowing who would walk into your life but not knowing how it would feel when they did.

"I'm glad you came. I really want to get to know you better." He said. "Isn't there anything you'll tell me about yourself?"

Olivia could feel the wine had really gotten to her now. Out of nowhere a flood of emotion overwhelmed her.

"I can't Jake. I can't...get to know you. I'm broken. You don't want me in your life. I'm trouble." Her lower lip began to quiver and a tear slid down her cheek. Jake felt like his heart was being torn from his chest as she cried. He tried to move closer.

She stood up, suddenly feeling claustrophobic even though the room was so large. She felt like she needed to be outside. "I'm sorry Jake but I should go. I can't be here right now. I'm so sorry." Then the tears came down in heavy streams.

Jake reached out and pulled her to him. "Tell me what's going on," he said soothingly.

"I...I can't. I'm sorry, this isn't your problem. This really isn't your problem," she whispered.

Jake hugged her tightly. "Shhh, you have nothing to be sorry for," he said softly. He sat back down on the sofa and pulled her onto his lap. She couldn't even resist, so she buried her face in his neck gaining comfort from the warmth of him, the smell of him, and the closeness of him. She began to calm down and then was instantly embarrassed.

"Oh Jake this is inexcusable. I can't believe I did this. I don't even know you. I'm so, so sorry." She leaned back just enough to realize she was still sitting on his lap. Olivia blushed anew.

"Darlin' if it means I get to have you on my lap then by all means." He teased gently.

Olivia sighed. "I'm a widow. I don't think I have ever said it out loud to anyone. I still can't believe it myself. I have so much going on."

"I'm sorry Darlin'." Jake said. "I can't imagine what you're going through."

"I'm trying to get my life back, that's what I'm going through. I should have known but I didn't want to believe I would feel this way about you," she said, unable to meet his eyes.

Jake thought it was strange she put it that way. It sounded almost as if she knew they would meet. It was yet another mystery about Olivia Curtis. "If it helps, you should know I already feel strongly for you, as well." He said slowly, as if it only just occurred to him. "I know something that'll take your mind off this. Do you want to go swimming?"

"Swimming? Jake I didn't bring a swimsuit," she said, smiling in spite of herself.

"I don't mind if you go without." He smiled mischievously.

Olivia laughed. Jake pulled her in closer and kissed her on the mouth ever so gently until her lips parted. And like a thirst finally quenched, she moved in for more. It was better than the dream. He kissed her again. He held her head and moved her body closer to him. Jake found he loved kissing Olivia. Hers was not the only thirst being quenched. Her kisses were warm, soft and she still tasted of the wine.

Olivia relaxed against him and let her hands explore his strong arms and shoulders, neck and hair. She moaned slightly as he kissed her. The sound set something loose in Jake and he deepened the kiss, feeling more urgent and needy. He wanted her so badly. His mind leaped ahead to making love with her; the thought was intoxicating.

Breathless and dizzy, Olivia pulled back. "Jake I can't. You don't know me at all really and..." Olivia whispered, breathing heavily.

"I know. You're right. Just promise me you'll see me again. We'll take it slowly. We'll take it as slowly as you want. Just, just promise me." Jake said seriously.

"I promise." Olivia said. "I *would* like to see you again." She eased off his lap and smoothed out her dress. She touched her hair like she was trying to put herself back together. The gesture was utterly feminine.

Jake smiled and stood up next to her taking her hand. He looked into her eyes and had to resist the strong desire to kiss her again. If he did, he wasn't sure he'd be able to stop. He found her irresistible, but he knew her pain was real and he hadn't even scratched the surface of it. He didn't care if she was broken, he wanted her anyway. He wanted to take the pain away for her. He wanted to protect her like the bird from his dream.

She sat down again.

"Olivia, are you ok?"

"Not really. I think I'm a little drunk and my head is spinning. Could you find Miles and tell him I need to go home?"

"Yes of course, I'll go get him. You just wait here and relax ok?"

"Ok, that's a good idea. This is your fault you know?" She smiled up at him.

"Oh it is, is it?"

"Yes, you had to give me more wine, didn't you?"

"Sure Darlin' I'll take the blame for this one. Next time we'll have coffee and polite conversation instead of wine and kissing." Jake touched her cheek gently as he said it. "I'll be right back, just rest."

"Thank you," Olivia murmured as her eyes became heavy. When he had gone she laid her head on the decorative pillow, kicked her boots off and curled her legs up underneath her. She felt heavy, tired and cozy here on the sofa bathed in firelight. Olivia slept.

Jake went into the kitchen where Carmella could usually be found. "Carmella dinner was incredible. Thank you so much for everything." He said sincerely.

"You're welcome Jacob." Carmella patted his cheek. "I'm about to turn in unless there is something else you need?"

"I don't suppose you've seen Sam or Miles? They aren't in the sitting room any longer and I really don't feel like hunting them down."

"Yes" Carmella giggled. "I saw them. Those two are worse than a couple of teenagers."

Jake rubbed his eyes. "Where Carmella, please?"

"I think they were headed out to the stables. Samantha wanted to show Miles the horses or maybe something else." Carmella smiled.

"Ugh. I really don't want to go out there, but Olivia is ready to go home." Jake said feeling frustrated in a number of ways.

"Well Jacob you could use the intercom. That is why you bought it you know. I don't think Miss Olivia's car will make it home tonight with all this snow." She added.

"What? Has it been snowing that much?"

"Yes, didn't you notice?" Carmella asked sarcastically.

"No not really," Jake smirked.

Carmella threw her hands in the air. "Teenagers!

Jacob act your age and take care of your guests. These people aren't from Montana like you, they probably don't have a clue how to drive on country roads in the snow."

"Yes, you're right. I will take care of everything. Don't fret. Goodnight Carmella. Thank you again for a lovely dinner." He replied lightly kissing the top of her head.

"You're welcome Jacob. There are clean linens in all the guest rooms. Make them feel welcome, ok? Goodnight 'cara'." She walked past him and up to her room.

"Goodnight Carmella." He said sounding distracted.

Jake walked to the wall and pressed the button on the intercom. "Sam? Are you out there?" Jake asked.

Muffled sounds and voices came through. "Jake, um, Miles and I are otherwise occupied. Could you maybe call back later?" Sam laughed.

"Olivia would like to go home now but the snow has gotten worse and I don't think it's safe with that little car of hers." Jake replied, sounding irritated.

Miles voice came on the intercom. "Jake I'm sorry about this. We shouldn't have stayed so late. Sam and I will be right back up to the house,"

Jake could hear Sam complain before the intercom clicked off. Jake definitely liked Miles Curtis.

Jake walked back into the library. The room was a bit darker than before as the fire had died down. He walked over and sat on the edge of the sofa. Olivia slept quietly. She had taken her boots off and was curled up on her side, her face lit softly in the fire's glow. Jake didn't touch her. He sat there for a moment, thinking about her. He wondered what had happened to hurt this lovely creature. Though she was a widow, he felt there was much more to her story, more pain behind those green eyes. He worried about feeling so strongly for her, so quickly. How broken was she? And what or who had made her feel this way? And, why did he have the urge to punch someone for her sake when he really didn't have the answers? Maybe there was no one to punch. He would feel better if she would open up to him. Maybe she would come around. Maybe she needed his story, and time. She needed time to trust him.

He was more relaxed thinking of it that way. His dad had always told him, "...pressures in matters of business are good, they keep a man on his toes, but pressures in matters of the heart are never good...they can ruin a person." The last thing he wanted to do was pressure Olivia. He worried with too much pressure, she would run away. He had a hunch that's how she wound up here in Troy. He heard voices coming from the foyer so he stood up and went to talk to Miles.

"Hey guys sorry to interrupt." Jake smiled at the two of them. They seemed more than a little cozy.

"No problem," Miles said, "Is Liv ok? Where is she?"

"She's sleeping soundly in the library. I didn't think we drank *that* much wine but maybe we did." Jake wondered.

"That's ok. Is she feeling sick?" Miles worried.

"No not sick just tired, I think. She passed out on the sofa."

Sam piped in, "Miles was telling me Olivia has a dog we should look in on. How about Olivia stays here tonight and Miles and I can take my truck to go check on her dog."

"Yeah, that would be fine but you're in no condition to drive." Jake replied.

Miles offered a solution. "I'll drive. I only had one glass of wine with dinner. I'll drive Sam's truck and we'll go check on Harper and just stay there tonight. Or we can take Olivia with us too, Jake."

"No. She can stay here. I think that would be better." Jake replied, not realizing how it sounded.

"As long as you're comfortable with it Jake, that would be great. It was never our intention to be such a bother."

"Honestly Miles, you aren't a bother. I have plenty of rooms and if it weren't for the dog, I'd suggest you all stay. Did you want to see Olivia before you go? She's in the library."

"Yeah, not that she'll even notice, but I'd better." Miles chuckled and walked away toward the library.

Jake whispered, "Sam; are you ok with this?"

"It was my idea. I really doubt Olivia would like to find out her dog spent the night alone in her apartment. Besides that, Miles is really great Jake and he's such a gentleman. Neither of us is ready for the night to be over. If you tease me about this I will kill you in your sleep but I'm kinda smitten." Sam smiled coyly at him.

"Ok well tear it up then, cowgirl. Just be careful with him; he is a city boy." Jake teased.

"Who's a *city boy*?" Miles asked, chuckling.

"Nobody." Sam smiled. "Are you ready Miles?"

"Yeah. Jake, are you sure you don't want me to take the drunkard off your hands? I feel badly dumping her on you like this."

"She's already sleeping, may as well let her. Did she wake up at all?"

"Not really, she was talking a little but it was hard to understand. She didn't realize I was there."

"Ok, well before the weather gets any worse, you should get going. Sam has my number. Text me when you get there so I know you made it safely."

"Sure Jake and thanks again. This was great. Be sure to thank Carmella again for me, too."

"See you tomorrow Jake." Sam kissed his cheek and took Miles hand as they moved through the foyer.

"Ok, good night you two."

Jake shut the door and turned off the foyer light then walked upstairs to one of the guest bedrooms. He turned on a bedside lamp and turned down the covers. He grabbed a fluffy white robe from the adjoining bathroom and placed it on the bench at the end of the bed. Then he filled a small glass with water and set it next to the bed along with a bottle of ibuprofen. He had a feeling Olivia might be in need of it when she awoke in the morning.

He returned to the library and scooped her up in his arms. She cuddled around him and rested her head on his shoulder.

"God you feel good," Jake whispered to her. He noticed the curves of her body, the smoothness of her skin, the silkiness of her hair. He noticed everything, even her unusual resemblance to Madame X. He didn't want to admit he'd had a crush on that painting since he was a young boy. Olivia didn't have the sharp nose of Madame X, but she had the same mysterious appeal.

Jake easily carried her upstairs and gently laid her on the bed. She made an indistinct sound but didn't wake. He smiled, though it was lost on her sleeping face. He felt like he should say something before he undressed her.

"Olivia, I'm going to help you get out of your dress." He said quietly, but felt like an idiot. She didn't know and definitely didn't care; not in the state she was in.

Jake wanted to be the gentleman his parents and Carmella had raised him to be. He slid the dress up her thighs and up around her waist. He thought it might be akin to undressing a ragdoll.

He knew he shouldn't look but he couldn't help himself. She wasn't the first woman he'd ever undressed though the others were generally awake for it. Olivia was wearing black silk and lace panties. Jake sighed. He sat her up and pulled the dress over her head and set it aside. He tried not to dwell on the matching bra or the feel of her smooth ivory skin. "Ok Jake, be a gentleman. Be a gentleman." He told himself repeatedly.

Sometimes he wished he *wasn't* such a gentleman. He lay her back down softly. Her hand rested of its own accord on his thigh. She wore a thick bracelet and as he turned her hand over he saw the bird from his dream, inlaid into the leather. This was disconcerting. He'd never experienced this sort of déjà vu before. He slowly moved aside the bracelet and saw a wicked scar on her wrist. His breath caught in his throat. He needed to understand this, but for tonight, it would have to wait. He rolled the wide cuff back covering the scar. Gently he pulled the covers up over her. He touched her cheek softly with his hand.

He suspected regardless of how he conducted himself; she was going to be angry and embarrassed tomorrow. "It's too late now," he thought, so he kissed her gently on the lips. "Goodnight, Olivia." He said, turning off the lamp.

The image of her sleeping peacefully in that big white bed, in his house would stay with him always. Jake felt strange. He never reacted this way with a woman and his dreams had never come to life before. She wasn't just a woman, she was much more. There was something special about her he couldn't give a name to. "Sam was right" he thought. "I do have it bad for this girl."

That night Jake dreamt again of the phoenix and the song that called him to her. This time the song changed to words he could understand. The bird's song said, "Leave me. Fight against the desire to stay. I can't save you and you can't save me." Again he looked toward the sky to tell his phoenix she was wrong and found nothing but bright and blinding flame. The song ended and she was gone leaving a terrible ache in his heart.

CHAPTER EIGHT

Monday morning Olivia woke feeling unsure of herself and disoriented. She had slept without any nightmares and that was a surprise. She was also surprised to be in a big white bed in a big white room. The comforter on the bed was an overstuffed box-stitched down thing and the sheets had eyelet trim and touches of yellow in the stitching. The fabric on the window coverings was white eyelet, as well. It was like sleeping in a cloud. It was "charming", she thought. There was no other word for it.

Everything about Jake and his life was charming. She sat up and stretched and continued to look around. The antique white bedside table had water and ibuprofen. Olivia smiled. Thinking of Jake made her nervous and excited. She didn't want to like him as much as she did. She was trying desperately hard not to like him.

Then suddenly it occurred to her she was only wearing a bra and panties. Olivia sighed heavily. She put her hands to her face. That ibuprofen was now a necessity. She took four and held her glass of water sipping slowly and thinking. She wondered if it was going to be possible to slip out of the house unnoticed. She doubted it. First, she would have to find her clothes.

"Damn," she cursed. She was irritated with Jake but more with herself. "I drank too much, and cried, and then practically threw myself at him. I'm going to Hell. I'm in Hell." She thought. "Men are trouble. What am I doing?" She slammed her fist into the soft bedding. It only rustled as if to say, 'your little tantrum doesn't impress me'.

At the end of the bed lay a plushy robe. "At least he left me *something* to wear." She said quietly. She put her feet on the floor and was relieved to know she wasn't feeling shaky. She reached for the robe and tied it tightly around herself. It was a heavenly, oversized robe that felt cozy and comforting. She went into the bathroom and tried to be as quiet as possible; hoping no one would hear the water running.

She had no idea what time it was but she prayed it was early enough that Jake might still be sleeping. She was sure she could handle seeing Carmella this morning but less sure about seeing Jake.

"Dear Lord, let Jake be sleeping somewhere on the opposite end of this house," she whispered.

Olivia turned the doorknob slowly; as quietly as humanly possible and opened the door. It barely made a sound. She peeked into the hallway and there, propped up on a very uncomfortable looking bench was Jake; asleep. Olivia detested when only half her prayers were answered. She suppressed the urge to groan.

She tiptoed out into the hallway, hoping the floor didn't squeak. For the first time, she was able to really look at Jake without the necessity of looking away. He was so very handsome but he was more than that, he was rugged looking. He was dashing with his dark hair slightly long and curling around his ears. She stood frozen like a statue and noticed his jeans, different from the ones he had on last night. These jeans were worn, like work jeans. His hands were a working man's hands, big and strong looking.

Jake was a big guy, not heavy; just tall and strong and sturdy like he could move a mountain if he wanted. The thought made Olivia smile a little to herself. He had long, dark eyelashes similar to her own but so different on his masculine face. He hadn't shaved today and Olivia yearned to reach out and feel the rough stubble under her fingertips. Jake looked like a cowboy; at least what she had always imagined a real cowboy should look like. There was a scar in his left eyebrow that made him look boyish and charming and somewhat mischievous.

Olivia hoped Jake was a heavy sleeper. She started to move past him further down the hallway. He was obviously exhausted and she was more than a little embarrassed about her behavior.

Jake wasn't really asleep. He had come to check on Olivia and decided to rest his eyes and wait for her to wake up. He wondered how long before she would say something to him. So he waited patiently with his eyes closed. "Stubborn," he thought.

Olivia definitely had a stubborn streak he could not only relate to, but he found endearing. He opened his eyes a little and looked over. She looked like a cat burglar from one of those old silent movies. The oversized robe swished around her as she moved slowly toward the staircase. Jake grinned.

"Well good morning, Darlin'."

Olivia stopped in her tracks. "Shit."

"Ooh you got a mouth on you." Jake laughed.

"You scared me. I don't usually cuss. I didn't see you there. I was just, I was trying to, I..." Olivia lied and stuttered.

"Darlin' you're a terrible liar." He replied sitting up on the bench.

"I *am* not," Olivia protested, "I mean I'm not lying." She corrected herself. "I have nothing to lie to you about."

"Yeah that's true." Jake stood up and moved in for a hug. His arms ached to touch her again; to wrap around her and feel her warmth. Olivia stepped back, fear lighting her eyes. She stiffened and suddenly retreated to formality.

"I'm sorry Jake. What I should have said was 'good morning'. Now where are my clothes so that I may go home?" she bit her lip nervously.

Jake ignored the wall she tried to throw up and reached around her anyway. He held her against him with his arms easily wrapped around her waist. Olivia trembled a little and looked up at him still biting her lower lip. Jake thought she looked like a nervous little bird and it worried him. Were his dreams really trying to tell him something?

"What do you want from me?" she asked feeling overwhelmed and overstimulated being so close to him.

"Now that's a loaded question, but let's start with; I want you to relax and have some," he looked at his watch, "brunch with me." He smiled brightly.

She began to protest. Jake held up his hand "and, I hear you don't work on Monday so there is no reason to rush off anywhere. Your brother is looking after your dog and as far as I can tell, unless you have a spare key, you're kind of stuck here with me until Miles comes back."

Olivia felt herself give just a little. "Ok" She said and leaned her head on his chest.

"Ok? Ok? Did I hear you correctly? I'm not sure I did." Jake teased lightly.

"Yes. I give up Jake. I'm hung over, I'm hungry, and arguing with you seems futile." She looked up at him and smiled.

"Mmm, good" He rubbed her back softly. He had prepared himself for a whole lot more debate on the subject.

"Let's get something to eat." Jake said happily.

"Uh Jake, my clothes?" she stopped him.

"We'll get to that and anyhow that robe covers up more than the dress you wore last night." Jake replied, smiling.

"Speaking of which", she said, "did you...uh, did you undress me?"

"Yes I did Darlin' but before you freak out about it; you should know I hardly looked." Jake grinned.

Olivia threw her hands in the air and the overly long sleeves flapped around. "Ugh, I can't believe this, it's so embarrassing. You, you saw me naked practically." She yelled.

He reached for her hand and held it softly. "Try not to overreact, Darlin'. You'll ruin your appetite," Jake laughed.

Olivia took a deep breath and tried to calm herself. "Fine, what's done is done, right?" she looked at Jake. He looked amused but she tried to ignore it.

They went down to the kitchen and Carmella was sipping coffee and looking at the screen of a laptop computer.

"Good morning Carmella," Jake said politely. Suddenly Olivia felt more embarrassed than ever. Here she was an overnight guest. Who knew what Carmella imagined had happened. Olivia blushed anew.

"Oh, good morning; bella ragazza, how did you sleep?" Carmella asked.

"Good morning. I slept very well thank you. But, I feel as though I have overstayed my welcome," Olivia replied.

"Nonsense; you are most welcome. I prefer people don't drive when the roads are bad. There is a breakfast casserole in the oven just waiting to be eaten so, manga, eat, please," Carmella insisted.

Jake was already getting plates and silverware out and set them at the island. He pulled Olivia by the elbow and set her on a bar stool rather unceremoniously. Then he put on an oven mitt, took the casserole out of the oven and dished them both up. "Carmella, would you like some, too?" Jake asked.

"No Jacob dear, I've already eaten." She replied sounding somewhat distracted.

"Carmella, may I ask what you're working on?" Olivia said. "Facebook" Carmella giggled. "Are you on here Olivia? If you are I'll friend you?"

"No I'm not. I don't even have a computer anymore." Olivia sighed. "I used to but there are some people I don't wish to hear from anymore."

"Oh well that's understandable. Sometimes I have to 'unfriend' people but I still like it. It's how I keep up with family and friends, especially in Italy."

Olivia just smiled. She didn't think she should elaborate, so she let Carmella go on about her Facebook life. Carmella was full of great stories.

Jake ate, quietly listening to the female banter. They spoke of cooking, shopping, Italy and various other things. He could feel Olivia's walls crumbling. When there was a lull in their conversation Jake asked, "How would you like that tour of the house now Olivia?"

Olivia looked at Carmella with concern. "Oh go on, Jake tells the history of this house very well. It will be fun for you."

"Shouldn't I get dressed first Jake?" she asked seriously.
"If you must," Jake teased. "Carmella will bring your clothes up to the White Room."

"The White Room?" Olivia asked, confused.

"Yes, the guest bedroom where you slept; we call it the White Room. Sorry, Jake should have mentioned that." Carmella offered.

"Oh, ok thank you." Olivia replied.

"When you are ready I'll be in my office. It's the third door to the right of the stairs, or just press three on the intercom system and I'll come up." Jake offered.

Jake left the kitchen and Olivia went upstairs to the 'White Room'. Looking at the room again with eyes that were now more awake; it was easy to see why they called it that. Everything *was* white; the carpeting, the drapes, the linens, and even the furniture. There were little touches of butter yellow that created a cottagey feeling. It seemed almost magical. Someone had an eye for decorating and she guessed that *someone* was not Jake.

Carmella knocked on the door. "Yes come in." Olivia replied.

"Here dear, I brought your boots and purse up from the library and your dress is hanging in the closet. We women feel better with our personal items at hand, don't you think?"

"Yes, thank you Carmella." she said. You didn't have to go to so much trouble."

"It's no trouble. Jacob is the only one who lets me fuss over him anymore and he really doesn't need much from me these days. Now, if there is nothing more you need?"

"No, no Ma'am, I'm fine, thank you." Olivia replied sincerely.

Olivia decided to take a shower. She knew it would make her feel better and since Miles was taking care of Harper and there seemed to be no rushing here at the Weidner Ranch, she thought, "why not?"

After the shower she searched the cabinet for some essentials, like a hairbrush. Gratefully, she found everything she needed and was beginning to feel human again. She cleaned up after herself in the bathroom and walked back into the bedroom. Carmella had already made the bed so Olivia went to find Jake's office.

The double doors were open. "I'm ready," Olivia said stepping inside.

Jake was looking over paperwork at his large polished wooden desk. An Irish setter thumped his tail on the floor at the sound of Olivia's voice. Jake looked up and smiled.

"You look beautiful Darlin'."

"You have a dog," Olivia commented. "I mean, thank you."

"Yeah, we have lots of dogs around the ranch but Whitman here is more of a companion and less of a working dog. He's kind of a couch potato and spends a lot of time by the fire."

Whitman came over to greet Olivia. "Whitman, huh?" she asked.

"Yeah, I wanted to name him Walt but Carmella said it sounded like an old man. She was probably right. He was just a pup when I brought him home."

"That's funny; my dog is named after an author too, Harper Lee."

"That *is* funny," he said. "Let me just finish this up and then I'm all yours."

"Ok, any word from my brother or Sam? I tried texting Miles but he isn't responding."

"Nope, just last night, Miles sent a text that they made it safely to your house."

"Olivia, you aren't a prisoner here you know? If you need to get home or just *want* to leave I'd be happy to drive you. I can get your car back to you later." Jake hoped he sounded sincere. He also hoped she wasn't in a hurry to leave.

Olivia patted Whitman on the head thoughtfully. "No, I'm fine. I don't mind waiting for Miles unless of course I'm in your way here. You probably have work to do."

"Darlin' you aren't in my way in the slightest." He said, relieved. "In fact I'd be happy if you never left." Jake knew instantly he'd gone too far. He couldn't believe those words popped out of his mouth.

Olivia froze and stared at him. She had that deer in the headlights look about her again. Jake silently cursed himself.

"I just meant you are welcome here and you aren't in my way."

"Oh ok, well good." She replied, trying to sound calm.

He stood to escort her on a tour of the house as promised. Olivia found herself getting lost in the stories of his family, his childhood here in Montana and his travels with his mom and sister.

"Didn't your dad ever go with you?" she asked after one such story.

"Sure sometimes he did," Jake replied. "But my dad has always loved Montana so much. He would rather be on the ranch or hunting or just go on a trail ride more than anything else. Now that he's retired though, he travels a lot with my mom and seems to enjoy that, too. He still sneaks in a little business here and there."

"Mom believes it's important for children to see the world. My dad likes to tease her that it's just the New Yorker in her." Jake laughed.

"Your mom is from New York?" Olivia asked.

"Well sort of, she lived there before she married dad. They actually met there. Dad was there on business and my mom was working in a real estate office at the time. He says he walked in; saw her and his heart stayed behind. He went back a couple days later and asked her out on a date."

"That's really sweet. Where are they now?"

"I'm not exactly sure. My mother keeps me updated with emails and pictures of their adventures but I haven't been checking them lately. The last one I did check, they were in Canada somewhere. I don't know. They're having fun; that's all that matters, I guess. They have a house in town not too far from your duplex. When Dad retired they decided to move into town and it made more sense for me to live here on the ranch."

Jake explained further, "My office is here and it's closer to Weidner Outfitting, another of our family businesses. When my parents aren't traveling they either stay here or in town. The house in town was my great grandfather's home. Great Grandpa Henry built the house in 1920. It's been in our family ever since."

"Wow. I can't even imagine what that would be like. My family tree doesn't have such deep roots. My parents still live in the house I grew up in but it hasn't been in our family for longer than that. I think I was three when they bought it. It's on the lake, not far from the country club in a prestigious neighborhood. That is all the more attached they are to it."

"What about you? Don't you miss it? Everyone gets nostalgic about their childhood home; except me I guess but then I still live here. I bet it's beautiful on the lake."

"It is beautiful. And no, I don't." she said simply and didn't elaborate. Jake felt the temperature in the room shift. Olivia's mood darkened.

Jake led Olivia through large double doors into an enormous ballroom. There were Italian marble floors that softly glowed in the daylight from the tall window wall looking out to a lovely courtyard and garden. Three exquisite chandeliers hung from the tall ceiling, grander than the one hanging in the foyer. Near the entry of this huge room stood a beautiful dark baby grand piano. Olivia suddenly got nervous. She wished her stupid brother had kept his mouth shut about her 'musical talent'. People always expected if you knew how to play piano you would play at every opportunity.

Jake could still feel the tension coming off of Olivia in waves. He knew not to say anything more about her childhood home. He would like to hear her play piano but he was beginning to wonder if the painful story of her life was somehow attached to her music.

"Is your mom well known for her music?" he asked, hoping it was a benign enough question.

"Yes in certain circles she is." Olivia relaxed a little. "My mother is very passionate about music. Miles was right about the way it feels to hear her play but her passion is only for music. It doesn't translate to the rest of her life." Olivia said, surprised at her own candor.

"Is that why your big brother is here checking up on you instead of your parents?" Jake asked, trying to put the puzzle together.

Olivia's fingers longed to play. She hadn't expected to feel this way. It was a beautiful instrument; a Steinway. It was simple in design but elegant just like the rest of this home.

"I suppose that's why Miles is here. I asked my family not to come. I've needed to be on my own."

"And yet your brother's here." Jake noted.

"I asked him for some advice and he decided to visit instead of calling. Miles never does what I tell him."

"Brothers usually don't. I don't when it comes to my sister, Jessica. She had her heart broken by some loser and ended up quitting another job because of it. I went to New York to help her out.

She may have asked me not to come, but I didn't listen. I was there for about three months."

"I know what it's like when people don't listen. So, you ignored her request and went to rescue her?" Olivia asked, trying to sound lighthearted.

"Yes I did. She needed my help and that piece of trash she called a boyfriend needed his ass handed to him. I worked while I was there, too though."

Olivia understood feeling protective of someone. She thought about her son and couldn't help thinking of Jake, as well. She had been so protective of her son and that feeling was hard to let go. Now she was faced with how to protect Jake, without leaving him.

Olivia continued to look at the piano. Jake had unknowingly hit a nerve. Without really understanding or analyzing it, she sat down at the piano and began to play Beethoven's Moonlight Sonata. It was always her son's favorite. It was his lullaby. Jake stepped back and watched as she played. The moment was heartbreaking; the only word for it.

Tears began to fill Olivia's eyes and threatened to spill over. She hadn't played since the funeral. Jake watched as a single tear dropped onto the keys. Somehow he knew she didn't play for him and she didn't play for a lost husband. This was something else, something deeper and more painful. *This* was for someone else.

Olivia finished and patted her face. She turned around to look at Jake as if facing the firing squad. There weren't any words. What could she say without saying everything? He came closer and put a hand on her shoulder.

He pulled a handkerchief out of his pocket and dabbed her cheek. He sat next to her on the piano bench.

"Thank you."

"No, thank you."

Carmella entered the ballroom. "Jacob, Samantha and Mr. Curtis are here," she announced.

Jake didn't take his eyes off Olivia. "Ok, thank you Carmella."

Olivia felt like she was falling into Jake's warm brown eyes. He leaned into kiss her and her lips parted in response. He kissed the salty tears from her lips and yearned for more. She kissed him back, licking his lips and tongue with her own. She sucked on his bottom lip and lost herself in his kisses. To her, they were the only two people in the world.

His hands lay gently near her throat and he could feel her pulse racing to match his own. She couldn't know the effect she had on him. He couldn't know how close she was to losing all control. Jake was supposed to be the part of her fate she would change.

Jake felt the slight shift in her and leaned back. "We should get you home I suppose," he said reluctantly.

"Yes, you probably have work I'm keeping you from," she said looking down to her hands folded in her lap. Together they stood up and walked into the foyer.

"It'll keep." Jake held her hand softly. She didn't resist as they walked together down the long hallway.

Sam and Miles were full-on making out in the foyer. Olivia blushed and Jake purposely and loudly cleared his throat.

"Oh sorry, we didn't realize you were here" Sam laughed.

"You ready to go Liv?" Miles asked, smiling like the cat that swallowed the canary.

"Yes." She replied and then turned to Jake. "Thank you for dinner and for everything." She smiled at him and his heart melted. He kissed her cheek.

"It was my pleasure, Darlin'." Reluctantly he walked her to her car.

Before Miles got in Jake said, "Miles how long are you in town for?"

"I fly out of Spokane on Wednesday."

"Well it was nice meeting you. Enjoy the rest of your visit."

"Thanks Jake."

Sam and Jake watched them drive away. Sam punched Jake in the arm.

"Ouch, what was that for?"

"Thanks for dinner and for 'everything'. What happened with you last night, lover boy? You didn't sleep with her, did you?" she asked bluntly.

"Oh you're one to talk" Jake teased her.

Sam smiled. "I was good" she paused. "I was very, very good." She said, pretending to dust her shoulder off.

Jake couldn't help but laugh. "I'm sure you were but unlike you, I don't want all the dirty details."

"Listen Jake," suddenly sounding serious, "we should talk."

"What do you want to talk about?"

"Let's go inside, have some coffee and a little heart to heart."

"Will it keep? I really do need to get some work done. Besides, I thought you were knee deep in paperwork at the office and don't we have some new clients coming in this afternoon?"

"Yeah. Ok, but call me tonight. Seriously! We need to talk."

"Sure." Jake replied and walked Sam to her truck.

She needed him to mean it. "Jake!" she emphasized.

"Yes Samantha, I will call you tonight."

CHAPTER NINE

"You're awfully quiet Miles." Olivia said on the drive back to her apartment.

"Yeah, I guess I just have a lot on my mind," Miles replied without looking over.

"Hey, thanks for leaving me stranded at a perfect stranger's house," she teased.

"Well, was he a *perfect* stranger or just a perfect *stranger*? Besides, it seemed like the best option considering this car you drive and the fact you were passed out drunk in the library," he said teasingly.

"Miles it wasn't just the wine and this is a *great* car, she said without thinking.

"What do you mean?" Miles asked seriously.

"I mean this is the car Dad bought me on my 25th birthday, don't you remember he left the note inside. It said, "A bird sitting on a tree is never afraid of the branch breaking because her trust is not on the branch but on her own wings"...?"

"I remember." he interrupted. "I mean, about the wine?"

"Oh. Well I took a little something to calm my nerves before. That's all it was. It was just an herbal thing."

"That was stupid; and *herbal* my ass, Olivia."

"It's not like I knew it was going to affect me that way; and it *was* herbal."

They pulled up to the apartment and Miles came around the car to open Olivia's door but instead of stepping aside he leaned down in front of her. "You ever pull that kind of shit again I will pack up your stuff and haul you back to Oregon where you can get some *real* help." Miles said angrily.

"Miles, you'll do no such thing! I'm not a child! You don't get to tell me what to do!" Olivia yelled back. "Besides, it wasn't like I did it on purpose. I wasn't trying to hurt myself!"

"No, not yet! Not this time, but what about when you do and there's no one around to help you? What if I'm not here? You don't have *anyone* here!" he growled at her.

"I don't want anyone here! I shouldn't have told you! I knew you'd act this way! I knew you'd overreact!"

"I don't think I *am* overreacting. I'm genuinely worried about you Olivia. Do you have any idea what this is like for me, for Mom and Dad? This is just the tip of the iceberg with you and your grief over..." Miles began.

"DON'T SAY HIS NAME! DON'T EVER SAY IT!" Olivia threatened, pointing her finger in Miles's chest.

Miles grabbed her left wrist and pulled aside her wide bracelet and revealed her gnarly scar. Miles cringed at the sight of it. He hated that he couldn't fix this for her. Angry and scared, he showed her the scar.

"Look at it! **LOOK** Olivia!" He yelled at her standing in her driveway in the cold. "Look what you almost did!" His eyes turned glossy and wet.

Olivia stared at him, tears suddenly streaming down her face. Miles held her wrist up between them angrily.

"Olivia! Is everything alright?" Mr. Jameson asked walking toward them. Miles dropped her wrist. Olivia wiped her face quickly.

"My brother and I were having a disagreement. I'm fine."

"Ok, just checking." Mitch said, still sounding suspicious. It had looked like more than a disagreement to him.

Miles walked up to the apartment door and then turned back to his sister. "Come on Liv, let's go inside," he coaxed.

Olivia followed slowly looking stunned and shaken. "Sorry, Mr. Jameson. I'm really ok."

Miles was sitting at the kitchen table expectantly when Olivia walked in and closed the door. "You should just go home Miles." She said quietly. She sat down at the table across from him and stared out the window.

"I'm not leaving, not yet."

"I don't have anything else to say to you."

"Fine Olivia, that's fine, but I still have plenty to say to you."

"Don't. Please," Olivia begged rubbing her temple. She couldn't handle any more of this; she didn't want to talk about it anymore.

"Olivia I'm your brother and I love you. I don't want to hurt you. I want to help you."

"If you really want to help me; then leave me here. Leave me alone. Or, just take care of the financial stuff and then go. I don't care, I just don't want to talk about this."

"Fine but can I just ask one question?"

"No Miles. NO! I'm done talking about this! Don't you see...I'm fine? I'm..."

"Tell me when you saw Dr. Cline last?" deciding to push her further.

"**That** is none of your business," she replied angrily.

"Should I call him?" he continued. "I thought you were supposed to be seeing someone on a regular basis?" He ignored the look of desperation on her face.

Olivia laid her forehead on the table. "Yes Miles, I am but it didn't do me any good. There isn't a doctor who can make this right. No one can change my fate. Seeing Dr. Cline didn't make me feel any better," she said sadly against the polished wood of her table. "I couldn't tell him...I just...I couldn't say the things that...I couldn't."

His heart broke for his sister. She was so different than the girl he once knew. The easy laughter and sassy attitude were gone. He reached over and grabbed her hand.

"I'm sorry Livi. I get overprotective; just like I always have I guess." He smiled. "Do you remember the time I chased that Michael kid down the street and pummeled him because I heard he was spreading rumors about you?

Olivia lifted her head slightly and giggled, "Yeah, and then we found out he wasn't even the one who started the rumors. Dad was pissed."

She lifted her head and gave him a half-smile. "I'm sorry."

"Would you please give Dr. Cline a call? Just check in. See what he says? Or if you don't like him then we'll find someone else." Miles offered.

Olivia squeezed her brother's hand. "Ok Miles. Ok, I will."

"Now go grab that check and anything else you want me to deal with so I can crunch some numbers for you and get this taken care of today." He said brightly.

Olivia gave him another half-smile and rose from the table. "While you're doing that; I'm taking Harper for a walk," she said, rounding her shoulders as she left the room.

"Liv, about that; um, maybe don't go to the park. I wasn't sure if I should tell you but some guy named Billy was here in the middle of the night. I doubt he'll be back after seeing me here but he said he met you over in the park. Was it you?"

~ 75 ~

"Yeah, but I didn't tell him my name. I barely spoke to him. What did he want?"

"You, I imagine. He didn't say exactly, I'm pretty sure he was wasted. I think you should carry some mace or something, just in case." Miles suggested.

"I don't have any. I didn't think I would need it in this town. It's so quiet here, peaceful."

"It's always the quiet ones. I'll pick you up some pepper spray at the store while I'm out but in the meantime, just stick to the main streets?" He said it like a question, but it was a demand. She detested when he acted like this, it reminded her of Jackson.

"Well there is only one *main street* but I know what you mean." She replied and went to change. After a few minutes she came back out to the kitchen, check in hand ready to take a walk.

"Here, I'll be back in about an hour. There's a bank branch just right down the street."

"Ok, take your cell with you."

"I have it" is all she said grabbing Harper's leash.

It burned her so much that Miles thought he could act this way. She knew he loved her and she had even asked for his help but sometimes it was more than she bargained for. Part of the reason for leaving her hometown was to be truly independent. She didn't want people telling her where to go and when to go there; who she should talk to and who she shouldn't. Miles had inherited some of their mothers' bossiness. Her mother liked to be in control and her favorite thing to control was Olivia.

The day was gray and biting. The snow had melted off the roads and sidewalks but the sky threatened to dump on them again. Harper was happy to be out with Olivia. True to her word, Olivia walked briskly along the main streets and avoided the park. She tried only to think of the pace and about getting exercise but her head had other plans.

Olivia wanted to forget what Miles had said but his words kept running through her mind as if the whole conversation were on 'repeat' in her brain. She was still shocked and hurt that he would bring up her scars. Olivia was flooded with guilt. She wondered if Jake had seen them, too.

"Maybe he hadn't noticed." She hoped but figured she wasn't that lucky. She was relieved he hadn't asked her about it. It was definitely not the kind of conversation for a first date, or whatever that was. Olivia turned and headed toward home. She had done enough walking and thinking and it wasn't getting her anywhere.

Miles was gone when Olivia got back to her duplex. She guessed he was probably at the bank and she was glad for a little peace and the time to catch up on housekeeping. Though, there was never very much to do in such a small, undecorated place. She wet a washcloth and starting wiping down cabinets vigorously.

The duplex was vastly different from her house on the lake with Jackson and her son. Sometimes she missed its' beauty, and elegance but mostly she missed the moments shared with her son in that house. She would give everything to have one more moment with him; one smile, one laugh, one hug. One.

"I'm afraid something is going to happen to you."
"Mom, you worry too much. Dad and I take this trip every year. I'll be fine."

Olivia finished her housework and decided to call Dr. Cline. She knew Miles wouldn't get off her back until she did.

"Yes hello, this is Olivia Curtis calling for Dr. Cline." A receptionist answered politely.

"Yes I'll hold." She told the voice on the phone. After a brief moment, she heard Dr. Cline's familiar voice.

"Olivia I've been concerned. I've tried to contact you several times. How are you doing?" Dr. Cline asked kindly. It was Olivia's least favorite question.

"I'm as well as can be expected, I guess. I'm sorry I haven't been in. Spokane isn't exactly a short drive."

"Yes, well about that, I've been thinking the best thing would be to refer you to someone local and believe it or not, I have found someone in Troy for you to see. The doctor's name is Ben Thompson."

Olivia was quiet, so Dr. Cline continued, "From what I understand and have been able to learn about him, he is well-qualified and much respected in the medical and psychiatric community. Can I forward him your file Olivia? Mixed delusional disorder isn't something that just goes away on its' own. Continued therapy is vital." he said.

It seemed to Olivia, it was another question that wasn't really a question. "Yes I suppose that would be fine." Olivia said, resigned.

"Please understand, if you are not comfortable with Dr. Thompson then we'll find a better alternative but I want you to give it a try Olivia. If he ends up the wrong fit, then leave word with my office and I will figure something else out. Though I will say I think you lucked out considering the small size of Troy. It seems Dr. Thompson is from there and decided to open a practice in his home town." Dr. Cline said enthusiastically. "He comes highly recommended."

"Alright Dr. C, whatever you think is best."

"Good, I'll text you the number."

"Thank you Doc, good day."

"You're welcome Olivia. Try to really open up to Dr. Thompson, would you?"

"I'll try", Olivia said and hung up the phone.

Shortly after, Miles walked in the door. "Hey Liv, I have good news. I've got everything squared away. All you have to do is sign some papers at the bank and then you are all taken care of. It's like a fresh start but better because not only are you debt- free but you have a substantial savings."

Miles looked like a kid in a candy store. Ever since they were children, Miles had special ability when it came to numbers, money and math. Olivia couldn't help but smile. He showed her what he'd done and she pretended to be interested.

"So what do I owe you for taking care of all this for me?"

"Oh, I took my usual fee. I don't come cheap you know?" he teased.

"I guess that means I'm not broke, huh?" she asked lightly.

"Better than that, it means you can retire from waitressing." He said hopefully.

"Miles I like my job. It's good, honest work and the people are nice."

"Oh there's more. I nearly forgot. I bought you a new car." He smiled broadly.

"What did you do that for?" she asked angrily. She went to the window to look but her own car was still there.

"You're joking."

"No I'm not. The dealership in Libby will be delivering your new car tomorrow and I'll be putting your old one in storage over there for you." he said happily.

"Miles!" she complained. "Explain yourself and fast before I kick you out of my apartment *and* out of this town."

"I'd like to see you try." He grinned. "Ok, ok, so everyone I talked to at the bank and the store was asking about you. They wanted to know what you drove, did you have snow tires, etc. etc. So I thought you should probably have something with four-wheel drive. I can't wait for you to see it."

Olivia shrugged in acceptance. "Thank you, Miles. I'm just glad you didn't trade in my T-Bird. Even though Jackson hated it, I always loved it. I still have that note I was telling you about. It's in the glove box," she reflected.

"I think Dad wanted you to realize how strong you are Liv. So do I."

Olivia looked down. "Thanks", quietly. "Do I get to know what I'm getting?" she asked, changing the subject.

"It's a surprise but since I knew you might find all of this overwhelming, I stopped and got us movies and a pizza. I hope you don't mind."

Olivia hugged him tightly. "I lucked out in the brother department, you know that?"

"Yes, yes you did. Anymore run-ins with that Billy character?" he asked.

"No I'm sure it was just a fluke. I doubt he means me any harm."

Miles's phone buzzed. "Let's hope you're right. Hey, I got a text from Jake. He'd like to take me horseback riding tomorrow." Miles said looking cautiously at Olivia.

"Why would he do that?"

"It's because I'm awesome and he wants to spend more time with me. What do you mean, why would he do that?"

"Well just don't break your neck." Olivia skeptically gave him a raised eyebrow.

CHAPTER TEN

On the third ring, Sam picked up the phone. "Hello Jake. It's about time you called me. It's almost nine thirty and..."

"...and what? You turn into a pumpkin at midnight?" Jake ribbed.

"I just wanted to tell you when Miles and I were together at Olivia's apartment we..." Sam paused.

"What? Please don't give me details Sam. I don't want to know. I told you that."

"Jake, you ass, I wasn't going to. It's just well, Billy Frazier showed up at her apartment drunk out of his mind, banged on the door so hard I thought he was going to break it down, and demanded to talk to Olivia."

"Damn it Sam, why didn't you tell me?"

"I tried but you had work to do, remember?"

"Did you call the police?"

"No, I didn't want Miles to flip out even more than he already was. So, I explained that Billy is the town drunk and not to worry about it. Miles sent him away but you know Billy isn't exactly stable."

"No he's not. You should have called the police."

"I know, but that's why I'm telling you. I thought maybe you would give Brad a call, at least so he's aware of a problem with Billy."

"Just because Brad is a cop doesn't mean he wants to be in charge of his idiot brother."

"What if he isn't *just* an idiot, Jake? What if Billy really causes trouble?"

"Then we'll deal with it." Jake sighed. "I'll call Brad but I think Olivia is better off not knowing all the details."

"Oh, and about that; there is a whole lot of details you don't know about her Jake. I'm worried about you, too."

"Why? What did Miles tell you? Do you know something I don't?"

"I know a shit-ton you don't. She's on the edge; hanging by a very thin thread and although I feel sorry for her I don't think you want to get tangled up in everything she's dealing with. I don't. I think you're going to get your heart broken, for real this time."

"Who's the worrywart now?" Jake teased.

"Jake I'm serious. She came here to make a fresh start but that doesn't have to include you."

"I think it might be too late for that." Jake said honestly.

"If that's true then I hope you know what you're doing."

"What is going on with her?"

"Just tread lightly my friend. Miles is really worried about her. He said she's supposed to be in regular therapy sessions because of some disorder she has and something else he wouldn't talk about. Anyway, he doesn't think she's been going to therapy at all. Plus, he said she left home without so much as a word about where she was going or even if she'd be back. She just took off and they have only known where she was for a little while now."

Sam continued, "Miles got a text that said she was safe and they should leave her alone. He said he was afraid to come see her because he didn't want her to run again but then he got another text in the middle of the night last week and she asked for his help. He figured it might be his only chance to see her. That's when he showed up. He said he was surprised at how good she seems here but he doesn't trust it. I guess I can't blame him." Sam explained.

"Did he say why she left? Do you know what happened to her? What kind of disorder?" Jake asked seriously.

"I don't know; he was reluctant to talk about it. He just said she lost her family and it was complicated."

"Miles said, 'family' or did he say 'husband'?"

"No, he said 'family'. I guess they had kids, too. I don't know for sure, he didn't elaborate."

"Listen I'm going to go. I'll talk to you tomorrow." Jake replied taking it all in. He hung up the phone staring at it. Maybe Miles would tell him more tomorrow. Somehow Jake knew if he was ever to have any chance with Olivia he needed to know what had happened to her. There was pain in those beautiful green eyes and she had definitely been fighting some sort of demon; her scars were the obvious evidence. He had to know more.

Miles drove Olivia to work the next morning and then waited back at her apartment for her new Jeep to arrive and for Jake to come pick him up. He was looking forward to both. He couldn't wait for Olivia to see her new car but also he was looking forward to the horseback ride. He hadn't really done much of it; that had always been Olivia's thing. She loved equestrian classes as a child but was forced to stop when her talent on the piano had been discovered by their mother.

Jake pulled up a few minutes after the Jeep had been delivered. "Hey Miles, what's going on?" Jake asked.

"This is Olivia's new car. I'll feel better if she has something with four wheel drive." Miles explained.

"Did she pick it out?" Jake asked cocking his head toward Miles.

"No I did."

"I'm surprised you didn't get her a tank to drive." Jake teased.

"I thought about a "Hummer" but this is as extravagant as I could go without her freaking out on me." Miles joked.

"Are we still going for that ride or do you need to be here?" Jake asked.

"I did all the paperwork yesterday so I just have to run her T-Bird to the storage unit then I'm ready. I will have to be back in time to pick up Liv from work."

"Great."

Jake followed Miles to the storage unit to drop off the T-Bird and then they made their way back out to Weidner Outfitting Company. It was a nice day and an easy drive. Miles thought about driving Olivia's new Jeep but Jake suggested they take his truck.

Jake and Miles found they had a lot in common and a similar sense of humor. They talked about family, business and their shared love of the outdoors. Miles stepped into the office to visit with Sam for a minute before they saddled up.

On the ride Miles said, "This is amazing Jake. I can see why you love it here."

"Yeah, there's something special about these mountains and seeing them from the back of a horse is the only way to go."

"Liv would love this. She took riding lessons as a kid but my mom put a stop to it. She was afraid Liv would break her fingers or something."

"She played the piano at my house, it was amazing." Jake added.

Miles stared at Jake. "She did? That surprises me. She hasn't played since...well; it's been a long time. She is pretty incredible isn't she? You know she played at Carnegie Hall once?"

"I can believe it. She plays with a lot of passion." Jake smiled, thinking of it. "Listen Miles, I really care for your sister. I want you to know that. I realize we haven't known each other long at all but I do care for her."

"Honestly it doesn't surprise me to hear you say that. People have always been drawn to Liv. Men are drawn to her.

Once upon a time she was so trusting and open but now; well, now she doesn't trust anyone, not even me really."

"What happened to her?" Jake asked figuring the direct approach was best.

"More than should ever happen to anyone." Miles said darkly. "Jake, you seem like a good guy, you do; but it isn't my story to tell. It's her story and maybe she'll talk about it. Maybe she won't. If you really care for her like you say, then stick around and prove she can trust you. I don't know if she'll ever talk about it with anyone. I just don't know." Miles said sadly.

After their ride Jake asked if he could be there when Miles picked up Olivia in her new Jeep so they waited together at her apartment until it was time.

"Do you want some left over pizza Jake? I forget Livi eats like a bird."

"Sure" Jake replied. "So how come you're here and not your parents, if you don't mind my asking?"

"Mom has told everyone at the club that Olivia is touring in France with an orchestra. She's not exactly facing this and Dad has left it up to me to take care of things where Liv is concerned for as long as I can remember. That and she didn't want them here. I wasn't sure she'd want *me* here but I came anyway. I had to see for myself she hasn't turned into a pile of ash." Miles said sincerely.

"I can relate to that. I have a younger sister too but Jessica is tougher I think. No offense but Olivia seems..." Jake searched for the word, "fragile."

"She didn't used to be. If you would have known her before, fragile would be the last word you'd use to describe her. As a kid she was so self-assured. She didn't let anyone push her around. Not even Mom. That's why she didn't play the cello."

Miles set the plate of pizza and two sodas on the table and continued, "When she got pregnant my parents were convinced she would never make anything of herself; she would never go to college. Mom cried and screamed and threatened Olivia with everything she could think of. She tried to convince Liv to get an abortion but she refused. And Dad, he couldn't handle it so he pretended it wasn't happening."

"But, you know, Olivia had that baby, finished high school and even went to college. She went to the University of Oregon School of Music and Dance.

To this day I don't know how she managed to graduate from college with a baby on her hip. It couldn't have been easy, I'm sure. My parents weren't exactly helpful. I did what I could but I was still getting established so she was mostly on her own."

Suddenly Miles realized how much he had said. "Damn it. Jake I hope you won't say anything. Liv will be so pissed at me if she finds out I told you all of that."

"I won't say anything Miles. Don't worry. It does make things more clear. So Olivia has a child?" Jake asked wondering if he'd gone too far.

"No, my nephew died in a car wreck along with Jackson, Olivia's husband. There is no making sense of it when kids die. He was only sixteen. Olivia couldn't deal with it. She can't deal with it, even now. I can't say I blame her."

"I'm sorry Miles; truly." Jake said staring at his plate.

"Thanks Jake. Hey, we'd better roll. I don't want Liv to wait; she'll just start walking home if we aren't there."

Jake and Miles pulled up to the rear entrance of Maggie's just as Olivia was walking out the door. Once again, Jake's breath caught in his throat. She never seemed to look real to him at first glance. She appeared more like a mirage of water and he was thirsty.

Miles pulled to a stop and hopped out, excited. Jake got out and waited, letting Miles have his moment.

"This is what you picked out for me?" Olivia giggled. "Miles, it's a lifted four door Jeep Wrangler."

"I know, it's hot, huh?" he grinned.

"I love it and you picked a great color, too. Black matches my T-Bird." She exclaimed and hugged him fiercely.

Miles kissed the top of her head. "Your chariot awaits," he joked. "Come on Jake, hop in."

Olivia drove the three of them down the block to her apartment. She had to smile at the obvious camaraderie developing between her brother and Jake. Miles was never close with Jackson. No one got very close to Jackson, not even his own family. He was always like a closed book so when his temper exploded it was always a shock.

As she pulled her new car into the driveway, Miles said, "Jake, why don't you come in and have a beer with me?"

"No thanks, I don't want to intrude. Isn't this your last night in town?" Jake asked.

"Yeah, but we don't mind the company. Do we Liv?" Miles looked expectantly at Olivia.

"Jake you are welcome to stay. I'm going to take a hot bath and go to bed. I'll visit with Miles in the morning before he leaves for Spokane," she explained through a yawn.

"I'd be happy to stay then but I'll pass on the beer. I have to drive home."

The rest of the night was pleasant. Olivia took a nice long bath and listened as Jake and Miles argued over the best team in the NFL and who had a shot at the Super Bowl. Olivia walked out in a bathrobe and a towel wrapped on her head.

"I'm going to bed. Good night, gentlemen."

Jake and Miles both looked up from the couch.

"Good night Liv, sweet dreams." Miles said.

"Good night Olivia. I should probably go." Jake said.

"Jake you don't have to leave. Stay if you'd like. I'm sure Miles would appreciate the company. He's the night owl in our family." Olivia smiled.

She kissed her brother on the cheek and Jake reached out to squeeze her hand briefly. She blushed suddenly and retreated with Harper to the privacy of her room. Olivia sat on her bed in the lamplight thinking about Jake. She continued to be surprised at the strong reaction she had to him. In her room, she could still hear his voice, so deep and sexy. It perfectly matched the rest of him. She wished now she had been awake when he carried her to the pretty 'White Room' on Sunday night. It would be nice to know what those arms felt like lifting her.

"Ugh" she thought. "Olivia, what is wrong with you? He is just a man. You **don't** need him. You need to figure out how to move on...*alone* and you have to change your fate."

She had to admit when Jake was around she felt better, more normal. She felt alive and not like just a walking corpse. Already she was beginning to crave the feelings. It would be much more difficult than she anticipated but somehow she had to cut him out of her life. It might be the only way to change what was coming.

Olivia woke around seven on Wednesday morning. She was no longer able to stave off the nightmares constantly plaguing her nights. She threw on her oversized t-shirt and walked into the living room to let Harper out. There sleeping like a baby on the couch was her brother. On the floor also sleeping like a baby was Jake Weidner.

Before Olivia could get back into her room, Harper licked Jake's hand and woke him up. He looked up at Olivia and smiled. "Well good morning Darlin'. I hope you don't mind I crashed on your floor. I had a couple beers with Miles and so..."

"No it's fine." She wrapped her arms around herself. "Would you mind letting Harper out for me?" she asked.

Jake got up nimbly. "No problem. Come on Harper." He put his boots on and grabbed his coat. Then, grabbing the leash near the door, he walked outside with her dog.

Olivia darted into her room and quickly put on a bra, t-shirt and jeans.

"Liv?" Miles yawned. "What's up?"

"I didn't realize we still had company and I just came out here in an old ratty shirt and no bra,." she complained.

"Then you probably made Jake's day." Miles replied happily.

"Men! I'm going to make some coffee for my permanent house guest."

"Bullshit Liv. I know you like him. It's so obvious. You wouldn't be acting like this otherwise. You can pretend all you want but..."

Jake interrupted. "Olivia, I think Harper is hungry. Where do you keep her food and I'll feed her for you?" Harper did her usual happy dance around her food bowl.

"Just there under the cabinet, thank you." Olivia replied embarrassed hoping he had not heard her complaining.

Jake bent down and Olivia glared at Miles over the top of him. Jake fed Harper and reached to shake Miles' hand. "Miles, it's been a pleasure. Don't be a stranger around here." He turned to Olivia, "Thank you for putting up with me. If you ever need anything, you can call me anytime. Here's my card. It has all my numbers and I wrote Carmella's number on there for you, too." Jake said smiling. He set the card on the table, reached for Olivia's hand and pulled her in closer. She could have been in a trance for all the resistance she gave. He leaned down and kissed her cheek; lingering for longer than necessary.

She bit down on a sigh that waited for a chance to escape her lips. "You're welcome Jake. I, I'll see you soon maybe."

"I hope so." He turned to Miles, "Have a safe trip home Miles."

When Jake left, Olivia sat at the kitchen table with Miles drinking coffee, her mind still reeling with thoughts of Jake. Harper perched herself on Olivia's bare feet. Her favorite spot whenever Olivia sat down.

"When do you have to be in Spokane?" she asked absently.

"My flight leaves at two. I'm going to leave here about nine."

"Miles you don't need to check into your flight *that* far in advance. Three hours is overkill, don't you think?"

"I have a stop to make in Spokane before my flight." Miles said vaguely.

"Is this about Dr. Cline? I can save you the trouble. I called him." Olivia said, again feeling frustration with her brother.

"You did? What did he say?"

"He said there is no hope for me. I'm a lost cause and therefore, I should join the circus." She replied trying to sound funny but failing.

"Liv really, what did he say?" Miles probed.

"He gave me a referral to a local doctor. Supposedly, this guy is pretty great and his office is here in Troy of all things. I have an appointment with Dr. Ben Thompson tomorrow." Olivia replied.

"Good. That's really good Liv." Miles was pleased.

"Do I get a special treat? Have I earned an ice cream sundae?" Olivia asked sarcastically. She couldn't quite get over the condescension in Miles' voice.

A short time later, she watched her brother drive away in his rental car. She was a tangle of emotions. She needed his visit and found she had missed him more than she realized; but also she was relieved to be alone again.

On her counter sat Jake's business card. She held it in her hand and turned it over slowly, looking at the handwriting. She sighed in spite of herself.

Jacob K. Weidner
Weidner Corporation, LLC.
Phone: (406) 555-9210
Fax: (406) 555-7376

Olivia looked at the card. It was a funny coincidence she and Jake shared the same middle initial. She wondered what it stood for; Kevin maybe, Kyle perhaps? She couldn't guess.

She was struck with the urge to call him though she couldn't think of a good reason for it and then realized thinking of Jake at all was such a bad idea. She tried to squelch all thoughts of Jake Weidner and left for work. Though she secretly hoped he might come into the diner. He never did.

The next day Olivia didn't have to be at work until two and her appointment with Dr. Thompson was at nine a.m. She had questioned the receptionist about it because she'd been scheduled for a four hour appointment. Olivia thought it was more than a little strange but the receptionist told her it was what Dr. Thompson and Dr. Cline agreed upon. Olivia went, though she wasn't pleased. Again she felt railroaded by men and their expectations of her.

"Olivia, it's important for you to separate your delusions from reality. You have not been cursed with precognition. You cannot see the future. You have suffered many traumas and this is your mind's way of coping."

Olivia remembered vividly the conversation with a doctor though she couldn't seem to remember this doctor's face at all. It was during one of the many individual sessions at Oregon State Hospital where she was committed involuntarily. It was the day she stopped telling anyone about the future. It was also the day she knew the remainder of her fate waited for her in Montana.

She had been sitting on a very hard chair in the activity room of the hospital. The meds she was on had her in a constant state of drowsiness, though she still slept terribly. It was always loud in the activity room or maybe it just felt that way. *Suddenly, a flash of a man's face, her lover's face filled her sight. For a blink of time she felt how much she loved him. Their love filled up her heart so fully she lost all touch with where she was. There was only him. She saw herself kiss him hard. Then, as the curse toyed with her, she saw the name of the town and it glowed with fire. She heard a noise. It was something unnatural and terrifying. It rained blood and darkness on the blissful glimpse of love. She looked at her fingers. They were covered in blood, his blood. There was so much of it. He fell and then he fell from her sight. It was so similar to the vision of her son before his death there was no other conclusion to be drawn. Another sound filled her ears. This one she recognized. It was the sound of her heart breaking again. For the curse would reveal no more. Her eyes opened to the activity room; tears falling down her face.*

At the time of the vision she didn't know Jake's name. She only knew she had to stop him from being hurt. Somehow she had to save him the way she couldn't save her son.

She convinced herself she would keep him safe by staying away but the pull toward her fate was as strong as it had ever been. The day she left her hometown it wasn't exactly her plan to drive to Troy. It had been her fate. She arrived, barely remembering the drive. She never looked at a map. She traveled the way a bird knows its migratory route.

THERAPY SESSION I
Ben Thompson, M.D.

"Sit down Olivia, make yourself comfortable. I'm Dr. Thompson," he said formally. "You may call me Ben."

Olivia was surprised at Dr. Ben Thompson's youth. He looked much younger than she had expected. He was probably close to her age, mid-thirties she guessed. He was handsome. He had good skin, dark blonde hair and blue eyes. His features reminded her somewhat of Miles. "Well put together," she thought.

"How do you do, I'm Olivia Curtis." She introduced herself.

"I'm well. May I get you anything? Would you like a water, juice or a cup of coffee?" he asked politely, gesturing toward a comfortable-looking sofa.

"No thank you." Olivia sat down. The couch was cozy and meant to be. Therapy was no place for uncomfortable furniture. There were simple prints on the walls, mountain landscapes mostly and a dark mahogany desk off to one side of the room. There were papers neatly stacked and a classic green shaded desk lamp on one side. It reminded her of Jackson's office, proper.

"Well Olivia, I'd prefer to begin with any questions you might have of me. Then, we'll go over a little background information and proceed from there. Are you comfortable with that?" He asked politely, clinically.

"Yes that's fine. I do have one question; why was I scheduled for a *four hour session*?"

"That's pretty standard with new patients so we can hit the ground running. I was informed you haven't seen Dr. Cline in some time. I thought it best to give ourselves plenty of time. However, if you aren't comfortable with it, we can stop whenever you like. You have the control here, Olivia."

"Liar" she thought. "Yes fine. Do you have my file, then?"

"Yes I do but it's not the same as hearing what you have to say," he admitted.

Olivia stared at him. The room was perfectly quiet.

Olivia was skilled at staring down psychiatrists but most of them were skilled at dealing with it. She decided she had better things to do so she broke the silence first.

"Where shall I start because I didn't come here to nap on your couch?" she said, frustrated.

"Well, let's start there. Why did you come? Your report says you spent some time recently in Oregon State Hospital." He said flatly.

"That's one way of putting it. I was committed, involuntarily by my overbearing mother. Of course she would never admit to having any part of it." Olivia said angrily.

"Do you realize she didn't have you committed all by herself? There was a hearing and doctors' recommendations. A judge signed off on it. Do you understand that?"

"Yes, of course. I'm not saying she did it alone. I'm saying she pushed extremely hard for it to happen. She was there in court, I'm sure of it."

"So you blame your mother?"

"Not for slicing my wrist with a razor blade, no. But, do I blame her for the 'hospital stay'? Yeah, I do."

Ben ignored the anger and moved forward. "Who found you, Olivia?"

"My mother found me that time; the fabulous and renowned Antoinette Curtis. Doesn't it say that in my file?" She said sarcastically.

"Yes it does but as I said, I would like to hear from you." He responded kindly. "So you think she overreacted?"

"Yes, I do. I was committed to the state hospital like some kind of drooling psychotic. Do you realize doctor, that I was committed to the very place they filmed "One Flew over the Cuckoo's Nest"?" She asked angrily. "It's not exactly a comforting thought."

"No I was unaware of where that movie was filmed. Does that insult you?"

"**Insult me? Insult me? It pisses me off!**" She yelled.

"Were you treated poorly?"

"No" she replied flatly.

Olivia attempted to rein in her temper and leaned back on the sofa. She hadn't realized her posture. Ben sat in his leather chair looking unruffled and unaffected by her reaction. They were both quiet for a moment.

"What do you think would have been an appropriate response from your mother? What should she have done, Olivia?" He asked, and then continued. "Should she have put you in a luxury hotel for a few weeks so you could bleed out in *their* bathtub?"

Olivia's head snapped up. She was angry and shocked to hear a doctor speak to her that way. She had been here twenty minutes at the most and already he was painting agonizing pictures of her blood-soaked body in a tub. She felt the desire to punch him. "You're an asshole," she said simply.

"That may be, but *you* are a woman who endured a horrible tragedy and possess zero skills for dealing with your grief. Yelling at me and blaming your mother is not going to help you. I'm wondering why you think your mother overreacted in the face of possibly losing her daughter. My goal is to help you *find* your strength; to help you deal with the grief so you may move forward with your life." He explained.

She knew he meant well but the whole thing sounded like a challenge to her. "You said I have zero skills. I have skills" she said defensively. "I don't want to talk about my commitment anymore."

"It wasn't just the suicide attempt, was it?"

"I don't want to talk about it."

"You were diagnosed with mixed delusional disorder, were you not?"

"Yes I was but that's over."

"So you don't think you can see the future anymore?" he asked bluntly.

"No, of course I can't see the future. That's crazy, right?"

"You tell me. Because, what I'm hearing so far is you would like to take your anger out on someone and you're trying to convince me of something you don't even believe yourself."

"I'm not delusional." She protested again.

"Can you see the future?"

"No" she said quietly, looking down at her hands.

"Did you ever?"

"No" she replied.

"Olivia, we aren't going to get very far if you don't talk to me."

"I won't be committed again."

"Is that why you won't be honest with me?"

She let out a deep breath. "I know how it seems to everyone else. I know how crazy it all seems. I know it's easier for everyone to call it delusions and grief, but for me..."

"For you it felt real."

She hadn't planned on this. There were reasons she avoided therapy for so long and having someone take a microscope to her emotions was the main one. What could she say that would be honest but wouldn't make her the subject of a new witch hunt? "Yes, it did, but now I'm less sure." she answered.

"That's ok; to question yourself and your decisions is normal. I would be more concerned if you were completely sure of yourself especially after everything you've been through."

"Would you have had me committed?" she asked suddenly, though she wasn't sure why the answer mattered to her.

"I don't know. Truly I can't answer that. I only know your family and your doctors thought it was appropriate at the time," he replied diplomatically.

"Ok, I guess that's fair," she said quietly conceding.

"How about we go back further and talk about your son?" he suggested.

"No." Olivia stood up. "I **won't** talk about him."

"I understand you refuse to say his name or let anyone around you say it either." He added.

"I said, 'no'. I will walk out of this office." She threatened, starting for the door.

"Fine, eventually though, we will have to talk about him." He said gesturing for her to sit back down.

"Fine" she said, devoid of emotion.

"So what shall we talk about?"

Ben Thompson was not new to this. He knew he needed to take a different approach with Olivia Curtis or he would get nowhere.

"Why don't you tell me about your life now? What's it like for you here in Troy?"

Breathing again, Olivia said, "Troy is nice. It's real and I like how different it is from *everything*. I work. I walk my dog. I watch TV. I eat, drink, exercise, and meditate. It's quiet here. It's small. I have a life. I have a *new* life." She explained, not sure who she was trying to convince more.

"Are you happy?" he asked simply.

"No." She responded honestly.

"Have you made any friends here?"

"Do you mean other than you?" she replied, smirking.

"Yes, other than me." He smiled.

"I don't know. I guess so." She said turning up the corners of her mouth.

"What?" He inquired looking at her.

"Nothing."

"It's not 'nothing'. I ask if you've made any friends and you smiled." He pushed. "What is it or rather who is it?"

"Well my brother came for a visit and we went to a dinner party. It was *nice*." She finished.

"Oh, how did that come about? Who was your host or hostess?"

"Just by chance, I guess. I met this guy where I work and he invited me, um, us. His name is Jake Weidner." She announced, smiling, unable to help it.

Ben's eyebrows raised and he pursed his lips but said nothing. He knew Jake Weidner. Everyone in Troy knew Jake Weidner but Ben thought it best not to go down that road with Olivia Curtis.

"Did you enjoy yourself?" he asked. "Would you consider Jake Weidner a friend?"

Olivia looked around the office for a minute trying to compose her thoughts. "Yes, I think he is my friend" she replied.

"I want you to be cautious about the connections you make. Having friends is great and can be very helpful through difficult times but what happens when friendship is not what Jake Weidner is looking for? What if all he really wants is a physical relationship, a romantic relationship? Are you ready for something like that and what if you aren't?" Ben said seriously, almost sorry he'd opened this can of worms.

"Why am I not ready? I don't think I'll ever be happy again, not really. I don't believe I'll ever feel any better. So should I never have sex again? Should I never have someone in my life because I'm sad *all the time?"*

She couldn't help but think about Jake and the way her body responded to him. She forgot about her sadness, her loss, if only for a moment when he kissed her. It would be so easy to let herself be lost in those feelings, to pour out her sadness into his kisses and sweaty, mindless sex with Jake Weidner. The thought tempted her. It was like telling an addict there were drugs just beyond the door. She wished for simple. She wished for easy. Though she knew it wasn't fair to Jake and she knew the time hadn't come for that.

Ben watched her for a moment and then replied. "No that's not what I'm saying. I'm saying whether you believe it or not, you *won't* always feel this sad. It's best to wait. I'm saying you should hold off on a physical relationship until you are emotionally ready." He explained carefully.

"Doc you make me sound like some teenage kid who has never done it before," she said, exasperated.

"On the contrary; I want you to have a healthy sex life with an appropriate partner. I just hope you'll wait until you are more in control of your emotions." He stated, pleased that she had relaxed enough to call him 'Doc'.

"You're probably right," she admitted. "I should be honest with you then, and tell you I already kissed him."

"Did you kiss him or did he kiss you?" Ben asked, sounding rather petulant.

"I don't know. Does it matter?"

~ 95 ~

"Were you under the influence of anything at the time? Was alcohol involved?"

"Did you speak to my brother?" she glared angrily.

"Olivia you have a family who loves you. They're concerned for your safety and well-being. I think you should focus on the goal of getting well and not let anything or anyone get in the way of that goal."

"When did you speak to Miles?" she asked again.

"I didn't. I simply want to know if you kissed this man with a clear head and it's obvious to me you didn't."

"Fine, you want to know, fine. I took an antianxiety drug and I drank some wine. The combination was more potent than I realized. Are you satisfied?"

"No I'm not, and you shouldn't be either. You were out of control and acting impulsively and the fact you don't recognize it indicates just how much of a danger you still are to yourself. Do you think you would have kissed him if you hadn't been drinking or taking drugs?" He asked calmly looking at the papers in his lap.

"Ha! Drugs and alcohol are the only reason I'm..." she didn't know how to finish that sentence.

"That you're what? Not crazy? That you're coherent?" he asked calmly.

"I don't know. I really don't know." Her eyes burned with unshed tears.

Ben handed her a tissue. "Listen Olivia you and I both know you aren't ready. You cannot mask your obvious pain. Sex isn't going to help you. Drugs aren't going to help you. Your grief will remain until you deal with it. If I am doing my job at all, then I will help you to discover a healthy way to get through this." He said earnestly.

"I'd rather have a pill." She grunted and tried to smile.

"Wouldn't we all?" he said, "but there's no easy way out."

Olivia sighed, wishing she was somewhere else-anywhere else.

He straightened his shoulders and leaned forward. "I'd like you to tell me about Jackson." He began again.

She hesitated and then replied slowly. "I don't know what to say. He was my husband and now he's dead."

He was surprised at the way she said 'he's dead'. She didn't sound the way one sounds when discussing their dead spouse, someone she had married. "Are you sad? Do you think about him a lot?"

"Well the other night I had a dream about him. It was something that really happened, but in the end Jackson was there, only he was...he was..." Olivia stopped.

"Different?"

"No...Dead; he was dead and grabbing me. He was trying to keep me away from D... from my son." She said, unwilling to speak her son's name. She had almost said it. She felt like screaming but it didn't help, it had never helped.

"Did Jackson scare you? In life, did he scare you? Obviously, you had a terrible nightmare; but in your marriage, were you afraid of Jackson?"

"I wish I could say, no".

"What do you mean?"

"I mean, I never wanted to be that kind of girl. Nobody ever intimidated me. I am Antoinette Curtis' daughter for hell's sake. I have the ultimate dragon-lady for a mother. I don't intimidate easily or I didn't want to. I didn't used to. I regret I let Jackson bully me," she admitted.

"Did he bully you or did he abuse you?" Dr. Thompson asked bluntly.

Olivia sighed. "Both."

"How old were you when you met Jackson?"

"I was ten years old the first time I met him. There was a benefit concert Mother had organized. Jackson attended the party afterward. It was at their house."

"Whose house?" he asked, confused.

"My parent's"

It seemed to Ben that Olivia had detached herself from any bond to her childhood home. "Do you remember what happened?"

"Then, I didn't see him again for a long time. I was eighteen and going to college. I was very busy and overwhelmed with school. I was a single mom. I realized Jackson had become chummy with my mother and ran in the same circles as my parents. My son and I went to my parents for a holiday break and Jackson was there. Mother spent the whole visit shoving Jackson down my throat or perhaps it was the other way around. She had found my husband and she wanted to make sure I knew it. She adored Jackson because he was older, he was established in his career and he had money. She didn't care what kind of a person he was. Her only concern was how to make her only daughter respectable again in the eyes of her peers. It wasn't enough I was going to college or that I would graduate with honors. It wasn't enough that I took care of my son's every need all by myself. I have never been good enough for her."

Ben sat back thoughtfully. He found himself distracted by her beauty. He suddenly wished he didn't have to see her professionally. "Occupational hazard" he mused. She was beautiful, though. It was undeniable but also Ben had to admit to himself she *was* sad and he was a sucker for girls who needed fixing. It was probably why he chose psychiatry as a career.

"Did you graduate from college and then get married?"

"Yes, all in the same month, and then I became a housewife."

"Were you happily married?"

"I don't think there is such a thing." She replied bluntly. "I thought maybe we would be happy. At first I thought we might be. I learned quickly it would not be the fairy tale."

"So you don't think any married couple finds happiness?"

"No, I don't. It's life. There are good moments and there are bad moments but happily married is crap."

"Do you regret marrying Jackson?"

"Yes, every day."

"Why did you marry him then? What made you say yes to a man you didn't really care for? Why the regret?" he asked pushing harder now.

~ 98 ~

"I regret him because if I'd never married Jackson, then my son would not have been in that car. There wouldn't have been a sailing trip. My son would be here with me. He would be safe. Don't you get it? Don't you see?"

"I married Jackson because I was tired of working so hard. I was tired of fighting for my mother's approval. I was tired of living paycheck to paycheck and Jackson looked like the only way to get what I wanted. I couldn't change what happened. He was the man who would win my mother's love. He would be the father my son never had. He would swoop in and rescue me. Only the joke was on me. The joke was always on me. My mother will never be proud of me. My son never loved Jackson as his father, and every beautiful thing I was given came at a very high price. Now I pay. I pay for my greed and my sins. I pay for my laziness."

"I lost the one person I loved the most. I lost the most magical part of my life; the only magical part of my life. Every part of me hurts from it. I feel like someone ripped out my heart and yet it still beats. It doesn't make sense to me; my heart...still...beats! It's wrong. It's so wrong when I breathe. It's wrong when I smile. It's wrong that I'm here and he's not. I want him back! I want him back! You say I won't always feel like this. I say, you're wrong." She sobbed.

Ben handed her the tissue box. He watched her carefully for a moment. He waited for the flood of emotion to recede a bit. "That's an awfully heavy burden you're carrying around." Ben said at last. "Olivia, what if I told you that regardless of your choices, the outcome would be the same? Your husband and your son would still be deceased and you would still be left to pick up the pieces of your life?"

Olivia sniffed, holding her tissue up to her nose with both hands. "I would say I already knew that Ben."

He noticed it was the first time she had said his name. "What if I knew without any question that what happened was going to happen regardless of what you did?" he asked. "It would set you free from unnecessary guilt, would it not?"

"You would think so, but it doesn't," she said knowingly.

"I thought you said the delusions were gone?"

"They *are* gone. I just meant you'd be surprised how easy it is to feel guilty. It is so easy to wish you could go back and do something differently so you can change that one moment."

"Do you believe in God?" he asked.

"I went to church as a child, when it was convenient for Mother."

"No that's not what I asked. Are you a believer?"

"I didn't know you were a pastor *and* a therapist?" she said sarcastically, deflecting.

He ignored the sarcasm. "People of faith often have better coping skills when dealing with grief." he explained.

"Why is that?"

"I think it's because they know they don't choose who lives and who dies. They are able to let go of guilt and face the other aspects of grief unburdened. You didn't run that car off the road. You didn't have your hands on the wheel and therefore those deaths are not your fault." He paused.

She was processing what he said and he wanted to make sure she understood before moving on. "Who was driving the car?" He asked.

"Jackson."

"Are you angry at him?"

"No" she lied.

"Why not? You said yourself he intimidated you. He was driving the car that killed your son. He wasn't a very nice person from the sounds of it. Isn't that reason enough to be angry at him?"

"You're saying I *should* be angry at Jackson? I wish I wouldn't have married him, but I don't see the point in being angry at him, he's dead." She replied, sounding more frustrated than before.

"I'm saying being angry at Jackson is a normal response. Blame and guilt have an intimate relationship. The only difference is, one lives inside you and the other you cast onto someone else but neither will help you deal with the sadness or loss."

"Right, I get it. Guilt is bad. Blame is bad."

"Yes but unfortunately it isn't that simple. I can't magically make you stop feeling guilty."

"I wish you could." She smiled meekly.

"I wish I could too." He replied honestly. The pain oozing from her was palpable. He could see it fill up all the spaces in the room.

"What was Jackson like?" he asked.

"Didn't we already go over that?"

"No we didn't. Not really. I mean describe his character."

"He was very self-assured. He always knew exactly what he wanted and he was brilliant, crafty; so he usually got it. He had become a successful lawyer at a very early age. He liked control, he had to be in control and he was a very serious person. I don't remember that he ever laughed, or made a joke. He was very concerned with appearance. He and his brother would often compete with each other, in everything. They didn't know how to be happy for the success of the other. Jackson made sure I went to the right parties, wore the right clothes, and spoke the right way. He was the male version of my mother and like her, he was very good at manipulation."

"Did he love you?"

"Yes. No. I don't know. He loved me like one loves a fancy sports car or a nice watch." She said bitterly.

"So is it safe to say he treated you like his possession?"

"Oh make no mistake; I was Jackson Montgomery's possession."

"Hmm" Ben replied. "If you could say anything at all to Jackson now, what would you say?"

"I don't want to play this game."

"It's not a game, I assure you. Imagine I'm Jackson. What do you have to say to me Olivia?" he asked sharply, trying to get her to bite.

"Nothing; I don't know." She looked down answering with obvious frustration.

"Yes you do. I think there is unfinished business.

Did I yell at you? Did I beat you? Did I make you feel like trash? Tell me I was pushy! Tell me I was overbearing! Tell me how it made you feel to be treated like a piece of my property! Tell me you're angry I was driving the car that killed **your son**!" He yelled.

Olivia cried but took the bait. "I hate you Jackson! I hate you! I hated every day with you! I hate that I gave so much of myself to you and you took my son away from me! My son! He was mine, you son of a bitch! You took the only person who ever loved me! I will never forgive you; NEVER!" She screamed.

Olivia felt the room tilt and spin. She couldn't breathe. Her head had lifted off her neck and floated around the room.

Ben knelt in front of her and held her hand. "Just breathe. It was only an exercise. Just breathe. Jackson is gone." He soothed calmly.

"But..." she began when the room stopped spinning.

"But what?" he asked, moving back to his chair.

"I'm angrier at myself." She broke into sobs. "Jackson was being Jackson. He took care of us, at least financially. He did what he always did. It wasn't like he changed. He was always the same jerk, the jerk I married. I chose and I knew what I was getting. Believe me I knew. But I changed; only it didn't change what happened. I lost myself when I married him. I let myself be lost. I lost my voice. Or, I guess it had been lost before Jackson but I let him control me. I let him beat me. I let him treat me like shit and all I have to show for it is shame," she explained puffing breaths out with nearly each word.

"So maybe if you can remember who you were and find *that* voice, you'll be able to deal with this loss." He explained. "Just maybe if you find your true voice, you'll be set free from the shame."

"Maybe", she agreed. Olivia tried to calm her breathing. She hated feeling so helpless and out of control.

"I think perhaps we should stop there for today." Ben said, "One more question, though. Call it something to think about for next week. Do you think Jackson trusted you?"

Olivia hadn't expected that. She didn't need a week to think about it though. "No, he didn't trust me but I wasn't always trustworthy." She answered honestly.

"Let me let you in on a little secret; no one is. No one is trustworthy one hundred percent of the time. We're human. We make mistakes." He smiled. "Just make an appointment with LeAnn out front for next week. Ok?"

CHAPTER ELEVEN

Olivia was relieved to be done with therapy for the day. She felt exhausted. Work wasn't a much better alternative to therapy but then the only other option was her bleak apartment. She hoped work would keep her mind occupied. She checked her watch. It hadn't been a four hour session like she expected so Olivia had plenty of time to change and eat some lunch. Food didn't sound appealing so she drove herself to the park and sat in the quiet of her new Jeep by the river. She loved the new car. Miles had done a really nice thing. It wasn't something she would have ever done for herself. The Jeep was sporty, rugged and fun and a much better fit for winter in Montana.

She hadn't felt like a 'fun' person in a very long time. She hadn't felt like a whole person at all; just bits and pieces scattered around like her son's toys from when he was little.

Olivia was staring at the fresh skiff of snow on the ground. She ached for her child. "I can't believe you're gone?" she cried aloud. Tears began sliding down her face blurring her vision. The park became awash in salty streams of pain. She laid her head on the steering wheel and let the tears flow. Suddenly, there was a knock on her window and she jerked her head up, nearly jumping out of her seat.

"Olivia?" Jake asked through the glass. "Are you alright?"

Jake had been driving up to the Outfitters to work with Sam in the office when he saw her new Jeep in the lot of the river parkway. Olivia looked at him with huge crocodile tears streaming down her face. She didn't roll down the window. Instead she opened the car door; put her arms around his waist pulling herself out of the car. Jake held her quietly, gently as she sobbed into his shirt. He wondered what had happened but waited patiently for her to speak.

Finally, she took a deep breath and looked up at him, her arms still wound around his waist. "I don't know what to say. I'm so sorry."

"It seems to me Darlin', you don't need to say anything." He replied, just happy to be holding her again.

"I just came from therapy and I'm a little rocky; emotional, I guess," she said, trying to step away from him. "Jake I should go. I'm sorry you had to see this. I, I should go. I have to go to work." She said sounding unsure and turning toward the steering wheel.

"How about I stop by during your dinner break? Dan does give you breaks doesn't he?"

"Yeah, he does. I usually take mine around eight."

"Well then if you're interested, I'll be there at eight so we can have some dinner together. How does that sound?"

"It sounds nice. I promise not to cry." She smiled pathetically.

"Darlin' don't make promises you can't keep." He teased.

She laughed, her face still wet from tears. She couldn't get over the way he changed things for her. She went from some of her darkest moments to the world suddenly looking brighter.

"Dr. Thompson was wrong." She thought. "Not everything was a mask for her pain. Jake really made her feel better; if only for a few moments at a time."

"I'll see you at eight then and I'll have Tag make us something."

"Perfect." Jake kissed her on the mouth as if it was the most natural thing in the world. He lifted her off the ground as they kissed. Olivia blinked her surprise but then couldn't help relaxing into it. It did feel natural kissing him. His lips had her warming up from head to toe; it could have been a sunny day in July. He slowly set her back on her feet.

"See you tonight." He said as he turned back to his truck.

"Ooh, I like watching that man walk away." She stood there for a moment in a daze left with a dopey smile on her face.

This was the moment she realized it was futile to fight her feelings for Jake. She didn't want to fight anymore. As with everything, she couldn't change what was coming. Perhaps she should quit trying to change this part. She had so many difficulties in her life and then there was Jake. Everything about him was easy. There was no pretense. He didn't hide anything or seem to have anything *to* hide. To her, he was like the only port in the storm. How could stupid Dr. Ben Thompson not want her to have this? She would have to ask him about that next week. "Eight p.m. won't come soon enough" she thought.

When Jake walked into the diner later that night, Olivia was sitting at a booth with two plates in front of her. She had her back to the door but turned around and smiled at the sound of the bell. She knew it was him. She had felt him coming. He walked over to her, leaned down and kissed her warmly on the cheek.

"Hello Darlin'. How's work going?" he asked as he took a seat across from her.

"Same as always I guess. I asked Tag to make us the special, meat loaf and mashed potatoes. I hope that's ok?"

"That's great." He smiled again.

"How was your day?" she asked in return. She didn't know how to make idle conversation with him. He made her nervous so everything seemed silly when she said it.

"I had a busy day; very productive. I worked at the Outfitter's with Sam and we caught up on some long overdue paperwork. It was boring stuff but a necessary evil. I thought about you a lot." He grinned.

She wasn't sure she even heard him correctly but blush colored her cheeks and she looked at him from behind her heavy, dark eyelashes. "Really?" she questioned.

"Yes, really; I can't stop thinking about you Olivia. You're becoming all consuming. I wouldn't stop it even if I could." He answered, and reached over the table to hold her hand.

"Jake, I..." she began.

"It's ok; you don't have to say anything. I'm not trying to pressure you. I just need you to know what I'm feeling."

"I do need to say something." She said seriously.

"Sure, Darlin'. Shoot."

"Jake, there should be a warning label on me."

He laughed. "Is that so?"

"Yes. I feel like you need to hear this. I'm a big, big mess and I care enough to try and warn you about it. I don't *want* you to go anywhere but I feel like if I don't say this then I'll never be satisfied that I tried to keep you out of harm's way. If you decide I am not the girl for you, I would say that was a prudent and wise decision. I would understand. I've been told I'm nowhere near ready for a relationship and honestly; he's probably right. I just think you should know what you're getting into." She said, feeling breathless.

Hadn't she told herself she was just going to let this feeling with Jake take her away? Hadn't she decided to stop fighting these feelings she was having? She wished she could be more decisive. Had she ever just gone along with the visions in her head? She couldn't remember a time when she didn't fight them somehow. It wasn't just meeting him and falling for him. It was the part that came next she had to stop. But how?

"It's too late." Jake replied earnestly.

"Are you sure?" Her face was a mixture of relief and fear.

"Darlin', you need to stop telling me why you *think* we shouldn't be together because I know you're wrong. When I hold you in my arms nothing ever felt so right. Nothing" he said and then took a bite of his dinner as if he was placing a large exclamation point on his declaration.

He watched her. He waited for her reaction but she just smiled.

"Ok, just don't say I didn't warn you."

Jake decided to change the subject before she could change her mind. "How would you like to go for a ride with me tomorrow?"

"A ride? Like on a horse?" she asked cautiously.

"Yes Darlin' on a horse." He chuckled.

"Oh I don't know. I haven't been on a horse in a long time. It's been since I was a kid."

"It's like riding a bike. It'll be great. I promise you'll have fun."

"What time are we talking about? I have to work in the afternoon."

"I thought we would go early, say seven?"

Olivia sighed but was completely tempted. "Alright" she said at last.

"Great, I'll pick you up tomorrow about six thirty. Make sure you dress warmly."

"Jake I don't have proper riding clothes," she said, beginning to rethink it.

"That's ok, just wear jeans. I'll take care of the rest. What size shoes do you wear?"

"Um, a size eight, why?"

"Just let me handle this. You wear some jeans, a sweatshirt, and a coat. *My* coat might actually work best for this unless you burned it or something." Jake laughed.

Olivia laughed too. "No I didn't burn it. I still have it." Suddenly she felt like a high school girl who borrowed her boyfriend's letterman jacket. "I can't let you buy me boots." She said firmly.

"Of course you can. If it bothers you that much then you're welcome to donate them later."

"No I couldn't. I can buy my own boots."

"I'm sure you can but *I* can get you some tonight."

Olivia just smiled. It was easy to tell Jake was used to having things his own way. "I should get back to work before Dan starts glaring at me."

"Ok, tell Tag he makes a mean meatloaf and thank you." Jake smiled, stood up and placed cash on the table then leaned down to kiss Olivia, again on the cheek. It was nice but not what she was hoping for, she pursed her lips.

"I'll see you tomorrow morning Darlin'."

"Jake, you should probably have my phone number," she offered. She took the notepad out of her pocket and wrote her number. "Just in case."

"Have a good night." He wished he could just take her home with him.

"Thank you." She wished he didn't have to leave. She put her arms around his neck, stretched up and kissed him on the mouth. It's what she had wanted and what she'd been thinking about since he arrived.

He was pleased. This was the first time she had taken the initiative. There was an undeniable attraction between them. It was like lightning struck when they touched.

When he got out to his truck Jake thought more about Olivia. She hadn't eaten very much. Like a bird, she had picked at her food. It worried him some. He'd seen eating disorders first hand and knew how difficult they could be to overcome. He hoped he was wrong. Jake considered calling Miles but thought better of it. From the little he knew of the Curtis family, it might just make things harder for her. That, he wouldn't do.

He picked up his cell phone and dialed up Sam.

"Jake didn't you and I spend the better part of the day together? I know you love the pleasure of my company but this is a bit much." she answered teasingly.

"I have a little problem I need your help with." He said, accustomed to her teasing.

"Yeah? What do you need?"

"Is there any way you could get some boots for Olivia to wear riding tomorrow? She wears a size eight." He said hopefully.

"Jake you know perfectly well what you need to do. You own The Boot Barn. Just call up Pamela and tell her you need to do a little 'after hours' shopping." She directed, slightly irritated.

"Yeah I know." Jake grumbled. "It's just that you're a woman and I thought maybe you would come with me."

"Jake, I told you not to get involved with Pamela but did you listen? No! Of course you didn't listen.

Now you have an awkward relationship with one of your employees. What a surprise!" Sam scolded.

"I know, you told me. I should have listened. Pamela and I were a disaster waiting to happen. I'm sorry. Just please come be a buffer for me?"

"I was just going to take a bath and maybe call Miles..." she sighed. "Oh never mind. I'll meet you there, but you are going to call Pamela yourself because I'm not doing it."

"Fine, I'll call her and meet you there in twenty." He said, frustrated at his own stupidity.

Pamela George had truly been a mistake of gigantic proportions. She was a great employee. She managed The Boot Barn with ease and had never given Jake a moment of trouble, until he asked her out. That was all it took. She jumped at the offer like she had just won the lottery. When he tried to explain he wasn't looking for anything serious, well, it got ugly. He was surprised she didn't quit, or sue him or worse. She did not take the rejection well at all.

Jake just hoped Sam would keep her mouth shut. He loved Sam. She really was the best friend a guy could have but she had no filter, none. She blurted out everything that came to her mind. Sometimes it was more irritating than funny but he was used to it.

Jake was still parked at the diner and he could see Olivia through the window. She was beautiful. He pictured her wearing a silk dress, smelling like Christmas cookies and dancing with him in the candlelit ballroom. "Nope, the uniform just doesn't fit her." He mused.

He figured the least he could do for Olivia's sake was to have the balls to deal with Pam. He dialed her number.

She answered on the third ring. "Boot Barn, this is Pamela."

"Hi Pam, its Jake."

"Yes?" she said, sounding short.

"I wasn't sure you'd still be there. Um, I need to do a little shopping tonight and my store keys are at home."

"That's fine." she replied in a clipped tone.

"Great, I'll be there in just a few minutes. Thank you." He silently cursed her work ethic. He had no desire to confront her in person or answer any questions about why he was buying women's boots.

"Just come to the back door." She hung up.

He drove to the store and waved Sam around to the back of the building.

She pulled her truck around and hopped out. "Glad to see you found your balls, Jake. Were they deep in Pamela's handbag?" Sam teased.

"Very funny."

"How about, thank you Sam. You are the best friend any gutless turd could ever have, Sam. How did I get so lucky?" She loved teasing Jake about his love life. It had become one of her favorite pastimes over the years. For whatever reason, he tolerated it.

"Thank you, Sam. Listen, Pam is still here, so I'd appreciate it if you wouldn't mention who I'm buying boots for," Jake replied, ignoring her teasing.

"You know she'll ask us what we're up to. Have you spoken to her since you broke her heart?" Sam asked, genuinely curious.

"I didn't break her heart and yes, we've talked about work...when it's necessary. If she asks you anything, just deflect, change the subject, something. Just don't tell her about Olivia. Please?" He pleaded.

"I'll do my best," she replied, and smiled mischievously.

Jake knocked at the back door. Pamela opened it and glared at Jake, but let them in.

"Hi Pamela," Sam smiled, amused by the obvious distaste Pam had for her.

"Samantha," she said, lifting her eyebrows slightly.

"Thank you Pam for helping me out. I appreciate it." Jake said, trying to break the tension.

"It's fine. It *is* your store after all. Like I said, I was here anyway. So, who needs boots at ten o'clock at night?" she asked suspiciously.

Jake walked past her into the store, not answering. Sam smiled and followed him. "Um, they're for me." Sam lied.

Pamela's eyebrows shot up all the way this time. "Sure Samantha. You have every boot ever made I think. What's the deal?" She probed.

"There is no deal. They're actually for Jake's sister. She and I wear the same size. Jake just needed my help. You know how he is? He can't pick out gifts for women." Sam replied, hoping she would buy it.

"That's true. I think the only nice thing he ever did for me was put fuel in my car...once." she snipped.

Sam laughed nervously and went to find Jake.

He was sitting on a bench holding up two different boots. "Jake, you owe me for this. Pam is such a nosy bitch. I don't know what you ever saw in her." Sam whispered.

"What do you think?" Jake replied, ignoring the subject of Pamela George.

"Get her both and let her pick. It's not like you can't afford it." Sam said, smiling.

"I can't. She doesn't want me to get her anything. I can't show up with *two* pairs of new boots."

"Get her the blue ones. They'll match any pair of jeans she puts on and they're comfortable. I would get her some good socks too and a belt. She needs a belt." Sam said thrusting a belt at him.

"Ok but she's going to be pissed."

"No she won't. She might act pissed at first but she'll love it. Look at how she was about that new Jeep Miles bought her?"

"Yeah, but that's her brother. I'm still a guy she just met."

"Even so, it sounds like they come from money. She should be used to accepting gifts. You know why they bought her that Jeep don't you?"

"Yeah, they got it so her cute little T-Bird wouldn't get stuck in the snow." Jake replied as though the answer were obvious.

"No Jake, they were hoping she would finally come to her senses and move back to Oregon or at least quit her job at the diner."

"They did? I get the moving back thing, I guess. I'm sure they miss her but what do they have against her working?"

"Seriously, you really don't get it? These are the original rich kids. I would think you would understand better than anyone. I guess it just proves how little you think about money,"

"Do they think she's too good for waitressing?"

"Of course they do. This is Miles' little sister we're talking about. She's the daughter of an investment banker. She's an accomplished concert pianist, socialite and country clubber from a well-to-do family. Duh, Jake" She explained, exasperated.

"Yeah, I guess so. I mean I get it. I don't think the job really *fits* her either. But Miles doesn't seem snobby to me and you would think he would want her to just be happy."

"I don't think Miles and Olivia are snobby, either. Miles just wants better for her. He told me his mother is freaking out over this whole thing, like *really* freaking out. I guess she told him to do whatever it takes to bring Olivia home to the city, where she belongs."

"That can't be true."

"I think it is." Sam replied. "I get the impression it isn't over, either."

"Olivia must have won that little battle because Miles left and she's still here." Jake observed.

"Yeah, we'll see who wins the war. Let's go before 'Nazi' Pamela comes back."

"Thanks for your help." Jake hugged Sam.

"You're welcome lover boy." She laughed.

"Loverboy?" Pamela asked appearing in the doorway. "What's really going on, Jake?"

"Pam, it's personal. I'll take these. Just put them on my account." Jake answered.

"Why did Samantha call you 'lover boy'? Are you seeing someone?" Pamela probed.

"Pam, I really, really don't want to get into this with you." Jake replied.

"No, you didn't want to get into anything except my pants." Pamela said angrily.

Sam's eyes got big and she couldn't help but smirk. She knew Jake could handle this and she couldn't help but think it was high time he did.

Jake exhaled loudly, "I was completely honest with you. We were never going to have a future together. I never wanted to hurt you, though."

"You and I were so good together! How could you say we never had a future? I saw how you looked at me!" Pamela sniffed.

"If I did, it was a mistake, I *am* sorry. Pam, I like you, but I don't love you and it was certainly not my intention to hurt you. Jake replied softly.

Sam just watched with wide eyes as Pamela started to cry.

"Well you did! Just see yourselves out!" She hissed, turned on one heel and walked back to her office, slamming the door.

Sam looked at Jake, ready to say something when he stopped her. "Don't say it!"

CHAPTER TWELVE

Jake and Sam both left. Sam had patted him on the shoulder as if to say, "It had to be done". He felt badly about what happened but it seemed it only took the slightest kindness for Pamela to have renewed hope in some future she imagined between them. He had to be clear.

Sam went home to call Miles and Jake went home to wrap up the gifts for Olivia. He was so excited for the morning he could barely sleep and thoughts of her kept running through his mind.

Promptly at six thirty the next morning, Jake was knocking on Olivia's door. He held two boxes, one containing his gifts and the other held breakfast, two coffees and croissants.

She opened the door wearing jeans, a black hoodie and a baseball cap. She looked weary but still beautiful. She smiled at him.

"Good morning Jake." She just stood in the doorway staring into his eyes.

"Good morning Darlin'" he replied. "May I come in?"

"Of course, please." Harper was jumping and wagging her little tail furiously. Jake set the boxes on the kitchen table and bent to pet Harper.

"She really likes you."

"I think she likes everyone." Jake smiled up at her.

"No, she hated my husband" Olivia replied honestly.

He pointed to the boxes. "Those are for you."

She unwrapped the box, opened it and held up the boots. She smiled. "Jake these are beautiful. It is so kind of you but..."

"Don't say it. Please don't say you can't accept them because I cannot take them back, trust me. The other box is some coffee and croissants for us. I'm starving."

She wanted to argue further but didn't, she just sat to try on her new boots. As she pulled on the second one, she looked up at Jake. "Thank you so much." She stood up, "They're perfect. I love them. I've never had western boots before. I always rode English."

She wrapped her arms around his neck and kissed him. Her lips were warm and soft and fit perfectly with his. He held her tightly and deepened the kiss. She was again surprised how her body responded to him. She felt tingly and was covered in goose bumps. It was delicious. Her mind was left to wander; not stuck in painful reality but floating somewhere in blissful oblivion.

His self-control was suddenly gone. He let himself be lost too, floating alongside Olivia's mind. Both were transported somewhere by the perfectness of their kisses. Then suddenly he stopped. She was surprised.

"What? Did I do something wrong?" she asked.

"No Darlin' not at all. You are so tempting and believe me, I'm tempted but I don't think it's the right time. I think it's best if we slow down a little."

"Best for who?" she demanded. Her fingertips lifted to her still wet lips. She hadn't expected to feel so sexual and so needy and *now* he had the nerve to shut her down. It was maddening.

He saw her temper flair. She looked like she wanted to wring his neck. Oh, if only she knew how much that pouty, angry face turned him on.

"It's best for both of us." He simply reached out for her hand.

"Maybe it would be best if you leave!" she said bitterly, tugging her hand away from him.

"No. Now Olivia, I've had just about all I'm going to take. I care for you. And believe me when I tell you all I really want to do right now is make love with you. I want it more than you can imagine, but I want to be more to you than that. I want more than a one night stand or a, a booty call. I want more for both of us. If that upsets you, I'm sorry. I won't settle for less than everything. Not with you."

She was looking down at the floor and Jake couldn't tell if she was about to slap him, or kiss him, or kick him out. Finally she looked up and started laughing. He looked at her, confused. He chuckled and reached for her hand again. This time she didn't pull away.

"I'm sorry, Jake. I guess I thought I knew what you wanted. I thought I knew what I wanted.
After what Ben said, I just..." she paused.

"*Ben* Thompson? What did he say?"

"Well, he's my therapist. He just said you were going to want us to have a physical relationship before I was emotionally ready. He also said that I wasn't ready even if I thought I was. I wanted to prove him wrong."

"*Dr. Ben Thompson* doesn't know me as well as he thinks he does." Jake responded.

"I'm sorry. I shouldn't have said anything."

"You didn't say anything wrong Darlin'. I just don't want him or anyone telling *you* who I am.

I want you to decide for yourself. I've known Ben a long time so he might be less than impartial when it comes to me."

"Is that one of the many 'small town' idiosyncrasies I'm going to have to get used to?"

"Yes, it probably is. Let's get going, shall we?" he leaned down to kiss her as if he was checking to see if she was ok.

Olivia didn't mind. Whatever it took to kiss him more was alright with her. "Ok." She drank the coffee but only nibbled at the croissant. Jake noticed.

When they arrived at the Outfitter's there were only a few people there. One of the hands had already saddled up two horses and they were tied to the hitching rail waiting for them. She figured Jake must have called ahead and had someone take care of it for him.

The sun wasn't quite up yet. Jake went over some basics with Olivia and then helped her up into the saddle. The horses were beautiful. The landscape was spectacular. It stirred something inside her. She had missed being on horseback, missed seeing the world from that vantage point. It brought back memories of her childhood and her time spent in equestrian classes dressed in English riding togs and being happy. It was one of the few happy memories she held onto.

Jake led her down a trail, at a leisurely pace. The air was crisp and cold and there was a little fresh snow on the ground but the sun started to peek through the trees. The earth smelled wet and green like pine and fir trees. It was so quiet and serene in the woods. It felt like they were all alone in the world, just two people and two horses. This was beyond anything she had ever experienced. When she was little, horses were about discipline, competition and perfection. This was perfection without the competition.

Jake hummed softly. The horses were calm and surefooted as if the trail they followed was a part of them. Olivia was lost in her thoughts when Jake stopped their progress. She pulled her horse up and looked over at him, questioningly. He pointed ahead of them and there in the trees stood a huge bull elk. Olivia had never seen elk in the wild. She wondered why she hadn't thought to bring a camera. After a moment the elk turned away disappearing over a rise. They cued their mounts forward again.

"That was amazing. It was so beautiful." She gushed.

Jake smiled. He was glad Olivia was enjoying herself. He wanted to share this with her. Being here he felt as though he was exposing the deepest parts of himself.

The trail began to rise after about an hour and as the crest of the hill broke open the view, the wind picked up and it began to snow. It didn't take long before the snowfall was heavy and wet. Olivia put the hood up on Jake's coat and tried her best to stay warm but her hands were freezing. The gloves she had were not meant to be worn in a blizzard. She watched as she thought Jake was turning his horse to head back but instead he stopped next to her. She didn't understand when he hopped lightly to the ground. He opened the saddlebag and retrieved a pair of heavy winter gloves. Then, he tied her horse to his.

"What are you doing?" she asked, shivering and putting the gloves on he had held out to her.

"This weather came up fast so I'm going to lead your horse and you'll ride double behind me. You'll be warmer."

"Did you plan this?" she asked teasingly.

"Yes, I planned ahead for winds and heavy snow." He replied, as he worked.

He helped her down and stepped up on his horse. "Here, grab my hand, use the stirrup and swing up behind me."

She did as he instructed and wrapped her arms around his waist. She was instantly warmer being so close to him. She laid her head on his back and felt so safe and protected.

She relaxed and thought about the kind of man Jake was proving to be. He knew things that metrosexual, country club boys just didn't know. Her dad would describe him as a 'jack of all trades'. "There is something to be said for country boys" she mused. He was funny, charming, intelligent, and handy. He knew how to run a business and how to saddle a horse. He could probably even build her a fire in this blizzard and kill an animal and cook it for dinner. She had never known a man like him. It was like spending the day with McGyver...and *that* was so appealing. She wanted him so badly but he was right, she wasn't ready. He hadn't said that exactly but she knew it's what he meant. She was glad he wanted more than just sex from her but she also found it frustrating. Sex was easier than opening up emotionally.

How much would he want to know? She couldn't tell him everything. She couldn't tell *anyone* everything. She thought about his reaction when she mentioned Ben. It was obvious they were not exactly friends.

Olivia's thoughts began to drift. The motion of the horse and the rhythmic sound of their steps on the ground and soon, she was asleep.

Jake could tell the moment she slept. Her grip around his waist went slack and she leaned heavier against him. He wanted to laugh but was afraid to wake her. Instead he reached around her to make sure she was balanced and wouldn't fall off. He couldn't believe anyone could fall asleep in a snowstorm riding on a horse. When they arrived back at the Outfitter's, Dennis, one of the young cowboys approached them.

Jake put a finger to his lips and the young man smiled when he realized why. Whispering, he said, "Take this one into the stable and get him groomed. I'll be along shortly." Jake handed Dennis the reins and then rode into the cover of the stables.

"Darlin', we're here." Jake said gently, rubbing her leg softly.

Olivia woke up with a start and the horse shifted. She would have fallen but Jake grabbed her.

"Oh, oh no!" she said feeling so embarrassed. She looked at the back of Jake's coat and realized she had drooled on it. Silently she cursed herself.

"You're just tired is all," he said sweetly.

"I guess so." Blush colored her cheeks. "I'm so sorry. I wasn't very good company was I?" she asked, still feeling humiliated.

"On the contrary, I quite enjoyed having you sleep on me. I'm just glad you didn't fall off the horse." He laughed.

She took his arm and dismounted. He hopped down next to her and handed the reins over to another young cowboy who was waiting nearby. Jake couldn't help but smile.

"Did everyone see? Um, never mind. I don't want to know," she said and began walking toward the wrong end of the stables.

"Darlin', uh, the truck is down this way," he said, unable to stop smiling.

"Oh," she whirled around. She marched toward the direction of the truck but Jake easily caught up to her, grabbed her hand, turned her around into his arms and kissed her.

Olivia closed her eyes and sighed. She bit his bottom lip and he quivered. He was beginning to regret what he had said that morning. He pulled her in closer. Olivia could feel his need. Her mind was spinning but she tried to get her wits about her. She stayed in Jake's strong embrace but leaned back slightly.

"I should go home. I have to work this afternoon, remember?"

Jake took a deep breath. He placed his forehead lightly against the bill of her ball cap. "Ok" he sighed, and kissed her again, this time softer and less intense.

He walked hand in hand with her to the office leaving her to visit with Sam while he went out to warm up his truck.

"Nice boots, Olivia" Sam said, smiling.

"Thank you. Jake bought them for me. I guess he didn't want me riding in my tennis shoes" she said happily.

"Tennis shoes probably wouldn't have been too great especially on a shitty day like today."

"It wasn't bad. Before the snow hit, it was beautiful."

"That's good, so I don't know if Jake mentioned it or not, but I'm having a 'girls night' next Friday, if you're interested. My friend Ali gets her husband to drive us around so we can drink as much as we want. Oh, and Jake can't come. It's girls' night." She winked. "But if someone asks you to dance, it's perfectly acceptable."

"Dance? Where?" Olivia asked.

"Max's is the only place in Troy with a dance floor; that is unless Jake throws a party. Did he show you the ballroom at his house?"

"Yeah, he did. I'm supposed to work next Friday but I could ask Dan for the night off or maybe he could switch me to the early shift."

"Or you could just quit." Sam said bluntly.

"I gather you and my brother have been discussing my career choice then?" Olivia replied figuring Miles had opened his mouth again.

"I just know he really wants you to find something more *suitable*." Sam replied honestly. "I'm not saying I agree with him."

"I am perfectly aware of what my family finds suitable. I love my brother but he should keep his big, fat opinion to himself." Olivia ranted.

"It's ok Olivia, I understand. He is a good looking hunk of man your brother; but he's still *just a man*." Sam smiled and they both started laughing. They were still laughing when Jake came back inside. He put his arm around Olivia. His cowboy hat was dusted with snow.

"What's so funny?" he asked.

"Men" Sam giggled.

"Boy, did I ever come in at the wrong time?"

"That's ok. Where'd you go? I thought you were just starting the truck?" Olivia asked.

"I had a little business to tend to. We have a few big clients coming into town for hunts soon and..." Jake began.

"...and Jake likes to micromanage the crew here." Sam teased.

"Sorry Sam. I know you've got it handled. Just let me know if Mr. Kimble has any special requests."

"Don't I always? It was good to see you again Olivia. Give me a call if you're interested about Friday. Jake has my number." Sam smiled sweetly.

"Do I ever?" Jake teased.

"I'll call you either way. Thank you, Sam." Olivia replied.

Jake led Olivia outside into the cold, blowing storm but his truck was warm and cozy.

"What's going on this Friday?" Jake asked her. He drove them back down the hill toward her apartment.

"Sam asked me along for a girl's night out." Olivia smiled.

"Oh shit, yeah, I was supposed to tell you about that."

She noticed he made a face. "What's that look for?" she asked trying to figure him.

"Nothing, you should go. You'll have fun."

"Are you jealous?" Olivia teased.

"No. No, of course not" Though; he wasn't sure who he was trying to convince, himself or her. "Maybe I'll just happen to show up at Max's next Friday night."

"Sam said you can't come. No boys allowed." Olivia giggled.

"Well then, it's a good thing I'm not a boy." Jake smiled.

Olivia agreed silently. "Jake, I want to thank you for today. It was so beautiful and I'm just sorry I fell asleep. I think I might have drooled on your coat." She blushed anew.

"So, another one of my coats has become your victim?" He teased. "That's ok; I enjoy spending time with you even if you are sleeping. I hope you stayed warm enough."

"I did. Your coat is toasty warm." She smiled.

"You mean *your* coat." He said, grinning at her.

"I can't keep it Jake."

"Do you want to?"

"Yes." She smiled coyly.

"Then you should. Besides I wouldn't mind some visitation rights to it."

"You have a deal. Do you want to come in for some coffee or something? Or I could make some lunch?"

"That sounds great, but do you have time?"

"Sure; I don't have to be at work until two and it's just eleven now."

When they walked into her apartment, Harper bounded up happily.

"I'm going to take her out. Make yourself comfortable, I'll just be a minute."

Olivia took Harper outside and Jake began rummaging through her kitchen. When she came back inside, Jake was putting together two enormous sandwiches.

"Jake, I can't eat all that."

"I'll finish what you don't eat." He handed her a plate.

"Do you want to sit on the couch and eat? We could turn on the TV for a bit?" She offered.

They took their boots off and sat close together on the couch. Jake finished his sandwich in record time and Olivia took a few bites and set her plate on the side table. He was about to mention her lack of appetite when she curled her legs up under her and leaned against his strong chest. She tucked her arm under his and yawned. Being close to him was so comforting.

"Darlin' if you want to catch a quick nap before work I can go."

"No, don't go. I don't need to nap *again*." She smiled, yawning as she said it. "It's just I don't sleep very well at night."

"If you're sure?"

"I am."

"I understand how you feel. Sometimes I don't sleep well either. Last week after poker night I thought I would sleep like a baby. I'd had a few drinks and was definitely tired but I couldn't sleep. It was a full moon, though. I've never slept very well during the full moon. And..." he paused. "I kept thinking about you." He looked over at Olivia and again she was fast asleep on him.

Jake smiled. "So much for not needing another nap" he whispered.

He propped his feet up and pulled himself and her down further into the cushions of the couch. He tried to stay awake. He knew she needed to go to work in a couple hours; but he couldn't stay awake either. With Olivia snuggled up against him, he was perfectly contented and drifted off.

Olivia woke with a start at the sound of her cell phone.

Jakes arms were draped heavily around her so she could barely move.

"Oh my God! Jake! Jake! Wake up!"

"What is it? Are you alright? What's the matter?" He was disoriented.

"Shit! Shit! We fell asleep! My phone is ringing, grab my phone!"

He reached for her cell phone and answered instead of handing it to her. "Olivia Curtis' phone."

"Oh, hey Dan, no she's here. She's fine. We just overslept."

Olivia felt like screaming. She couldn't understand why he was so nonchalant having a conversation on *her* phone with *her* boss. Jake still had her trapped under his heavy arm. She shoved against him and he finally moved. She stood up next to the couch.

"No Dan. I don't think you want to do that." He said into the phone. "Yeah? We'll see about that." Jake replied, sounding angry. He hung up the phone and reached for her hand. She stepped back feeling her heart swan dive into her stomach.

"Why didn't you let me answer it?" Olivia demanded. "You had no right to answer my phone! You should have handed it to me!"

Jake sat up. He had just been so happy but now she was angry. He knew he was about to get shot by her temper with both barrels. "Olivia, I'm sorry. You're right; I should have let you answer it. I guess I was a bit out of it still."

"What did he say?" Olivia asked, as calmly as possible.

"Well, he said, uh...he says you're fired. Listen, I know it sounds bad but Dan's always been a hothead, he'll cool off."

"What? That can't be. This is your fault! If you, if we, if I, you, you, how could you?"
She made no sense but continued to ramble angrily.

"Darlin' you need to calm down. This isn't the end of the world." He said soothingly.

"No you can be calm! You didn't just lose your job! Get out! GET OUT! You make me weak! GET OUT, JACKSON!" she screamed at him.

He just stood there staring at her with his mouth open. She had called him, "Jackson." She didn't start crying like he had expected but she was definitely not ok. He watched as she paced the floor for a few seconds and then sat down heavily; pulling her knees to her chest as she rocked herself.

He couldn't leave her alone; he leaned over her and lightly stroked her hair. "Darlin' it's ok.

Dan just likes to flex his muscles sometimes. We'll make this right. You are the best waitress he has." He rubbed her back and continued to speak softly to her but still she rocked and chewed her lip.

She was staring off into the abyss. It was as if she wasn't there at all.

Finally she spoke, "Get out" she said flatly.

"I'm not leaving you." He whispered.

She felt like she couldn't breathe. She tried to slow her thoughts but all she could do was pant and then the tears came. "Panic attack" she managed to get out between breaths. Harper was pacing in a circle and whining.

Jake jumped up and ran to her bathroom. He opened the medicine cabinet, hoping to find something helpful. What he found was a 'drug store'; way overstocked with medications.

"Shit" he cursed. He looked at all the bottles and labels until he found an antianxiety medicine he recognized. He grabbed a bottle of water and the pills and took them to her. Gently, he coaxed her to take one, though she continued to rock, still breathing shallowly. After about fifteen minutes, Olivia slowed. It was a visible change and she slumped. Jake picked her up and carried her to the bed; her head lolled. She was a beautiful rag doll again. The way she reacted to things absolutely scared him. She had that scar on her wrist. She barely ate. She was in therapy. She cried a hell of a lot.

"Maybe Sam was right" he thought sadly. "Maybe this was a mistake."

He sat on the edge of her bed watching. He never expected her to be this way. She had tried to warn him. He didn't want to believe it was like this. He hadn't wanted to believe her. If only she would open up to him, to talk about it with him. If only she would tell him something, anything she was dealing with. He needed to do something. He couldn't just sit here and watch this beautiful creature unravel this way.

Harper was curled in her own little bed watching him quietly, now. He went to the kitchen and wrote a note. He locked the apartment door and left Olivia sleeping soundly on her bed.

As Jake pulled his truck into the parking lot of Dr. Thompson's office he started second guessing himself. "What are you doing Jake? Ben isn't going to tell you anything." He thought. He got out anyway and walked into the reception area and was grateful that Ben's outer office was empty of patients.

The receptionist LeAnn was the only person there. "Well hi Jake, how are you?"

"Is he in?" Jake asked pointing toward Ben's closed door.

"He isn't to be disturbed right now. Did you want to make an appointment?" she asked politely.

"Does he have a patient in there right now?"

"No but..." LeAnn began.

"Good." Jake opened the door to Ben's office.

"Jake! Jake you can't just ..."

Ben held up his hand to LeAnn. "It's ok, LeAnn."

"Sorry Dr. Thompson, I tried to tell him you weren't to be disturbed."

"No it's fine. Please shut the door." Ben smiled at her. She glared at Jake as she closed the door.

"Jake Weidner, this is an honor. What has you barging into my office today?" Ben said calmly.

"I need some answers about Olivia Curtis." Jake said, taking Ben's chair behind the desk. He refused to sit on the couch like a patient and Ben didn't deserve his respect.

"Jake you know perfectly well I can't divulge patient information to you and even if I could, I wouldn't." Ben said, shaking his head in irritation.

"Ben you asshole; this isn't about some historical beef you have with me. I know you don't think I'm right for Olivia but that's for *her* to decide. I care about her." Jake admitted.

"Sure you do. You don't care about anyone. Do you honestly expect me to believe Olivia Curtis is more than just another of your conquests? You're a player and you *always* have been! As Olivia's doctor, I think it would be best for you to stay out of her life. All you can do is hurt her more!" Ben said angrily.

"I get it. You don't trust me. That's fine. I don't expect you to trust me. But I'm not leaving her. I think she needs my help. Tell me how I can help her. Please Ben. I can't stand around and do nothing." He pleaded.

"You can't help her Jake! *You* can't! I don't think your involvement is healthy for her. You have no idea the scope of the issues she's dealing with, so bounding into her life like some lovesick puppy isn't going to help her. You are not what she needs right now!" Ben replied firmly.

Jake stood up looking angry and frustrated, turning away from Ben. "Then what do I do?" Jake asked, suddenly deflated.

"Alright, for arguments sake, why don't you tell me what happened? Why are you coming to me today?"

Ben knew he needed to give a little though it burned him. Jake sat back down. This time he sat on the opposite side of Ben's desk letting Ben take his own chair.

"We, she, she overslept and Dan Libby fired her from her job at the diner. She lost it, I mean, *really* lost it. She freaked out, started rocking and crying, panting and she told me it was a panic attack so I gave her something out of that drug store she calls a medicine cabinet and then she fell asleep. But it's more than that. She has no appetite and she has that scar on her wrist. It worries me. She worries me." Jake said sincerely, raking his hands through his hair, but he'd be damned, if he told Ben she tried to throw him out, or had called him 'Jackson' in her panic.

Ben pursed his lips. "First of all, *you* need to stay calm. You should have called me. You can't help Olivia at all if you go off half-cocked. *You* can't freak out."

"Is that a technical term Doctor?" Jake asked sarcastically.

Ben ignored him. "She needs the people in her life to be calming influences. If you can't do that then it would be better if you don't get involved. It *might* help if you can convince Dan to give her job back but it would be even better if she did that for herself. She needs to learn how to fight for herself. It would give her a sense of accomplishment but honestly I don't think she's ready for that."

"Ok that's what I'll do then. I'll go make Dan give her the job back." Jake was irritated.

"You aren't listening to me. Are you sure she wants it back?"

"You just said I should get it back for her so which is it?"

"The loss of her job represents loss of control. The panic attack was a reaction to *that*, not the job." Ben tried to explain.

"So she needs a way to feel in control?"

"Yes for the short term. For the long term she needs to discover for herself that she'll be alright even when things are *out* of her control."

"I still don't know how to help her" Jake said, sounding more frustrated than ever.

"You really can't help her, not the way you think. Olivia has faced a lot of tragedy. The fact she is able to have any semblance of life is a big step.

You need to give her time and you need to give her some space and that is all I'm going to say about *my* patient."

"Yeah, thanks for nothing," Jake slammed the door as he left. He went outside and jumped in his truck. He looked down at Olivia's keys. He was so frustrated. He felt helpless. He wished he didn't care so much but that felt too late. It could definitely be too late. He wanted to punch something or someone, namely Ben Thompson.

He drove back to Olivia's apartment and let himself in. Harper barked. "Good girl Harper. How's your mama?" Jake whispered. He walked into Olivia's bedroom. She was sitting up in her bed looking disoriented, but calm.

"Jake?" she said with a raspy voice.

"Yeah Darlin', I'm here. How are you feeling?"

"I don't know. I'm still here." She replied numbly. "Jake I don't want to be a burden and I know I am. Right now, I am."

"You aren't a burden to me." He sat on the bed beside her.

"Yes I am. I haven't been anything but a train wreck since you met me. I think you should go. You need to leave me alone. You can't fix me Jake. *I* have to fix me. You can't mend my broken heart. You need to go; you need to leave me. Please? Don't make me ask you again."

"Olivia no, I'm not leaving."

"Jake, take your coat. Take the boots, too. They should still be in the living room." She said clinically.

"Please don't do this Darlin'". He pleaded.

"It's for the best. I need to do this for myself. Now go." She ordered with finality.

Olivia looked off toward the window, unable to face him any longer. She wished he would disappear. She didn't want to hurt him but she hated the sound of her own voice. She hated the feel of her breath going in and out. She hated every beat of her heart. She hated there was life without her son; her angel.

Jake didn't understand. He couldn't understand. He didn't need to be here to witness her pain. She couldn't even tell him the worst of it. "How do you tell someone you know what's coming and you're powerless to change it?" Just like her family, he would think she was crazy. Maybe they were right, maybe she *is* crazy. "Crazy was the only way to describe what it felt like to see the future and have no one believe you."

"What was your son's name, Olivia? Tell me his name." Jake demanded, interrupting her thoughts.

The question shocked her back into the room. She jumped off the bed and ran past him into the kitchen. She grabbed a knife from the drawer and pointed it at him and suddenly moved it dangerously to her wrist.

"GO AWAY! GO AWAY! GO AWAY!" she screamed.

"No Olivia, I won't leave you! Tell me his name! Say it! SAY IT!" he yelled back at her.

"I CAN'T, I CAN'T! I DON'T WANT YOU! I WANT YOU TO GET OUT OF HERE!" She continued screaming at him. "I can't change what's going to happen but you can! You have to leave, Jake!"

"I'm not leaving. Tell me your son's name." Jake insisted. "Miles said he had a nephew who died. You are a mother. You are a mom, and you are being held hostage by this, this fear. Say it, Olivia. Say it. Start somewhere. Say his name. Be brave," he pleaded, more quietly this time.

He grabbed her by the wrist as she held the knife and she dropped it on the kitchen floor. She fought him, struggling against his overwhelming strength. He held her tightly and she was reminded of another struggle. She screamed a sound of agony unlike Jake had ever heard.

He quickly loosened his grip and taking her face in his hands whispered, "I'm sorry. I'm sorry. I'm sorry."

She stopped fighting him and leaned into him sobbing. "Dante', my beautiful angel, Dante'."

She didn't think she would ever cry this way again. She didn't want to feel this way. It was the same pain, just as excruciating.

Jake held her strong and firm. He held her not with violence or control but with sincerity and kindness. He didn't say anything. He just held her, held her as she cried tears of grief and sadness and admittedly, some relief. After a while, she looked up into his warm brown eyes.

"Dante was sixteen when he died, only sixteen. He was so smart and kind. He always seemed so grown up but he was a baby. He was *my* baby. He was sixteen; the same age I was when he was born," she whispered. "I named him Dante' because it means enduring."

"Olivia, don't try and send me away again." Jake whispered, stroking her hair. "I'm not leaving. I won't leave you."

She whispered again. "Yes you will."

"No, I won't."

She leaned her face into his shoulder.

"Why don't you move in with me?" he asked suddenly without even thinking about it.

"Jake, that's crazy. I thought *I* was the crazy one." She replied in shock.

"You aren't crazy and neither am I. It makes sense. I have a huge house and it would be great not making up excuses to see you."

"No, Jake. It's not a good idea. I need to be alone. I need to have my own place. What happened to 'taking it slowly'?"

"You could have your own room." He smiled, but then admitted, "Ok, ok, so maybe it's too soon."

"Jake" she said softly, took his hand and led him to her bed. He sat down before her with questions in his eyes.

"What is it?"

"As much as I would like to pretend none of this happened, I've had enough therapy to know that we need to talk about it." She sat next to him on her bed. "I just don't know where to start." She sighed.

"Ok well, let me help you. I'm sorry about your job and for falling asleep; truly I am. I'm not sorry for waking up next to you. I never regret spending time with you."

"I'm sorry you had to see me this way."

"I'm not" he said honestly.

"You know how everyone has baggage?" she asked, biting her lip nervously.

"Yeah, of course."

"I have a lot more than most people."

"It's ok, but I think you need to be honest with me about it. I don't want to hear who you are, or know what you're dealing with only when your brother lets something slip."

"I can't tell you everything, I just can't, but I promise to try, ok? I didn't want to care about you, but I, um, I do."

"So I'm not alone?"

"You're not." She blushed. "And about my job, it wasn't your fault. I'm not even that upset about it, now. I still can't believe Dan didn't insist on talking to me about it but whatever, it's done."

"I have a gut feeling you'll be hearing from him soon. He'll realize that he overreacted and he'll call you."

"I don't know if I even want my job back. I need to work, but maybe I'll find something better.

I need to stay busy. It's not good for me to have too much time to think, and dwell." She shrugged. "You know what they say about 'idle hands'?" She played an imaginary piano with her free hand.

"...they are the devil's playground but that doesn't sound so terrible to me." He smiled coyly.

"No, I need to figure out something to do." She paused, thinking of how to explain. "The panic attack wasn't really about my job, or you. It just happens sometimes. I didn't mean to scare you."

"That's what Ben said, too." Jake said and then wished he could press a rewind button. The look on Olivia's face flipped from serene to angry in less than a second.

"What the hell? Jake! You talked to Ben *about me?* When? What did you tell him? What did he say?" she demanded angrily.

"Nothing; he didn't tell me anything. He didn't tell me anything and you certainly won't tell me anything! I went there because I was scared for you. I didn't know what else to do, Olivia. I don't know what to do for you. I was sitting there watching you fall apart and it scared the shit out of me, ok? It scares me that you value yourself so little that you could ever consider *suicide*." Jake yelled.

She flinched at the word. It didn't seem like such a big deal until she heard Jake voice it out loud. She sat there in shock, looking at his face so sad and so angry.

"You can call it whatever you want but the outcome would still be the same. There's nothing pretty about it; not the word and certainly not the act. Suicide is selfish. Don't you see that? Do you think Dante' would be proud of you? Do you think he's up in heaven, looking down, just hoping you'll kill yourself so you can join him? Is that what you picture? Because trust me, he's not." Jake finished, knowing he'd gone too far.

Olivia stared at the floor, fresh tears slipping down her face and landing in her lap. As much as she hated to admit it; he was right. It wasn't even the first time she'd heard this. Isn't this exactly what Miles said to her in the hospital? They just didn't or couldn't fathom what it felt like for her to live without Dante'.

She had been a child when he came into her life. She and Dante' had grown up together. He was her one constant. He was the star she guided her life by. He was the reason she worked so hard to make something of herself. She always wanted him to be proud of her. Jake was right. Dante' wouldn't be proud of her now.

Olivia was quiet for a long time, staring at her hands in her lap. He watched her and waited. It was as if he could feel her processing his words. He wished she would say how she felt, say something. He hated the not knowing. He lifted his arm and put it in front of her face.

"What?" she asked, unsure of what he was doing?

"Dry your tears on my sleeve," he said and smiled warmly. So she did, and then smiled at him.

"I'm sorry Darlin'. I went too far and I shouldn't have talked to Ben about you." Jake admitted.

"It's ok, I know it's because you care about me." She understood, as she suddenly realized she cared for him in the same way.

"I do care about you; very much. I need you to hear that and really understand it just in case I ever act like an ass or go harass your therapist. Try and remember it's because I care about you." Jake chuckled.

"Just promise me you won't talk to Ben about me anymore" she insisted.

"I promise, but I want a promise in return." Promise me; no more knives and try and remember you can trust me. You can tell me anything and it won't change how I feel about you."

"I think that's actually two promises but I'll try." She said weakly.

"That's good enough for me." He smiled.

"You know we still don't really know each other all that well. I mean, I feel so close to you but there is still so much we don't know about each other. I don't know your middle name, your favorite color. I know how you take your coffee but I don't know your favorite food or what kind of music you like."

"I understand, but there's time." He looked at her face. She waited expectantly like a dog waits for its dinner.

Jake laughed, "My middle name is Knox. I am named after my Uncle Niccolo, my mother's brother. When Mom was a little girl she gave him the nickname and it stuck. The whole family calls him Knox. Sometimes I forget his real name."

"It's Italian right?" Olivia asked. "Is that why you have this olive skin tone?"

"I guess it explains the skin. My mother's side is Italian." He shrugged. "Mom would say I've had too much sun but she has lighter skin than I do. Francesca Giada Conti-Weidner likes to make sure I have my feet planted firmly on the ground.

Personally, I think she's just jealous." Jake laughed.

"That name's a mouthful," Olivia noted.

"Yeah, but everyone calls her Frankie."

"Really, that's adorable? No one would dare shorten *my* mother's name or give her a nickname at all. She would find it tacky." Olivia smiled.

"What is her name?"

"Antoinette" Olivia grimaced.

"What about you? What's *your* middle name?"

"Karen; I was also named after a relative; my grandmother. I never met her, though I'm told I resemble her."

"So, she was beautiful, too then?" Jake smiled and leaned in to kiss her. She closed her eyes briefly.

"Jake, I..." she began.

"This isn't where you're going to tell me to leave again, is it?"

"No you jerk, I was going to say, I'm hungry and I should probably feed Harper, as well. It's getting late." She said reasonably.

"Oh, I guess it is. What are you hungry for?"

"A cheeseburger but I don't feel like going to get one. I'm kind of tired."

"That's ok, I'll go pick up the food and you can feed the dog. Sound good?"

"Yes, perfect but where will you get a cheeseburger now?" she asked, afraid she already knew the answer.

"Maggie's; Tag makes the best burgers."

"I know and don't take this the wrong way but I don't want you in there giving Dan a hard time," she said cautiously.

"Whaaa? Meee?" he joked. "I won't. I'll just get the food and come right back."

"Alright, please, please don't do or say anything else. This is my problem, not yours. Besides, I think you and I could use some drama-free time, don't you think?" she asked, suddenly embarrassed for being the cause of all the drama.

"Darlin' you have my word." He said and kissed her before he left. A simple thing really, as natural as breathing and yet she couldn't get over the beauty of it. She decided she would take Harper for a quick walk so she left Jake a note on her door.

She didn't want him to have to wait out in the cold truck for her to return so she left the door unlocked. The note read:

Jake,
I took Harper for a walk to the park. Back soon, make yourself
comfortable.
Olivia, XOXO

Jake drove to the diner thinking heavily about everything. He was finally feeling like Olivia was letting him in, if only little bits at a time. It felt good, kissing her, being near her, holding her hand, hearing her speak; even the tears and anger felt right to him. Now the lady wanted a cheeseburger. "God bless that woman." He thought.

Olivia was doing some thinking of her own. A new glimpse of the future had lit up in her mind like a pinball machine. Just once she wished for some happy vision but that was never the case.

She was walking alone across built-up snow and ice. She kept her arms tightly wrapped, but she couldn't seem to get warm. The freezing wind and snow ripped at her face. She saw Dante' in front of her and she tried to run to him. She couldn't understand how it could be him. Her visions had never made sense but this was on a whole other level of crazy. Her boy had died. She had buried him. She had seen and touched his lifeless body and now she was having visions of him alive. How could this be?

CHAPTER THIRTEEN

Billy had been spending a lot of time on the corner near Olivia's house. He watched Jake Weidner come and go. It always burned him that guys like Jake seemed to have life handed to them on a silver platter and girls like Olivia were such suckers for it.

"That bitch didn't even give me the time of day." He thought. He stood in the shadows next to the abandoned house across the street. All that could be seen was the occasional light from his cigarette. He saw Olivia and her dog walk outside and head toward the park. Billy thought about following but watched as she placed the note on her door. Then suddenly a man he didn't recognize approached him.

"Hey man, do you have a light?"

"Sure" Billy answered, taken off guard.

"She's beautiful isn't she?"

"I don't know what you're talking about." Billy replied, handing the stranger his lighter.

"The woman who lives in that apartment across the street"

"Is she your girlfriend or something?"

"Or something…"

"Listen man, I don't want any trouble." Billy replied, getting an ominous vibe from this stranger.

"You won't get it from me. In fact, I think you should go over there and wait for her to come home. She would be into a man like you. She likes it rough and dirty."

"I, I don't know. You think so? How do you know?" Billy replied.

"I'm sure of it. Trust me. She wants it. Thanks for the light." The stranger walked away casually.

Billy thought about it. Maybe the weird dude was right. He took one long drink of his whiskey still wrapped in its paper sack then went to investigate the note left behind by Olivia. He read the note and was instantly angry. He was still left with an unsatisfied curiosity about the stranger. Billy turned the door handle and sneaked inside her apartment. Maybe that guy was right. Why else would she leave her door unlocked?

"Why should Jake get to be her welcoming party?" He thought.

"I'll give her a welcome she'll never forget." He said out loud. He crossed the room into her bedroom.

It smelled nice and clean but there was something else he noticed a whiff of, "That prick's cologne…" He yelled and shoved her lamp onto the floor.

Next door, when Mitch Jameson heard the sound of breaking glass, he dialed the police. He wasn't interested in any excuses from Olivia this time. He knew what real trouble sounded like.

Oblivious to anything but his own desire and fury, Billy walked through the broken glass and into the bathroom. He swung open the medicine cabinet and was astounded at the entire prescription bottle collection. He started opening them and popping pills indiscriminately. He figured something in there would give him a good high.

He wandered back into the kitchen to see if Olivia had any liquor. He had finished off the cheap whiskey he bought the day before. Just as he opened the cabinet, he heard the door open. "Olivia' he thought happily. He walked out of the kitchen and stood face to face with Jake Weidner.

Jake wasted no time. Grabbing Billy by his right arm he twisted it around his back. Jake was so enraged he thought he could snap Billy's arm off but thought better of it as "the little prick" yelped in obvious pain.

"Billy, what the fuck are you doing in this house?" Jake shouted. "Where's Olivia?"

Billy struggled. "Whoa Jake man, I mean come on. What's wrong man? I'm going to sue your ass off if you don't let me go. This chick has been beggin' for it since we met." Billy's words were slurred and his eyes were bloodshot.

"Good luck suing me from jail, Billy Boy." Jake shoved Billy's face up against the wall behind the door, still wrenching on his arm.

It wasn't long before police arrived. Right behind them was a terrified looking Olivia and Mitch Jameson. Harper was barking wildly, so Olivia picked her up in her arms.

"Jake?" she said with fear coloring her voice. "What happened? What's going on?"

Jake handed Billy over to the sheriff's deputy who began to question him.

"What's going on here, Jake? I got a call from Mr. Jameson. He heard glass breaking. He was concerned." Deputy Frazier said.

"Wait, what are ya askin' him for, Brad? slurred Billy. "I'm the one you wanna talk to.

I'm your brother, man. That bitch right there, she stole from me. I'm here to get my shit back."

"That weird guy told me she'd be all into me. He said she likes it rough and dirty" Billy slurred, and then laughed loudly as some of the drugs began to take effect.

"Alright Billy, what did she steal and what guy are you talking about?" Bradley asked.

"She stole my heart!" Billy laughed with a drunken grin at Olivia.

"I see, and what guy?" Brad repeated.

"I don't know; just some guy who asked me for a light."

"Right, ok." Brad rolled his eyes.

Jake went straight to Olivia, stood in front of her with his arms wrapped protectively around her. He suddenly reminded her of a bear; large, dark and dangerous. She wasn't afraid of him but she thought this Billy character should be.

"What happened?" she asked, trying to sound calmer than she felt.

"I came back from the diner to find Billy ransacking your house; you weren't here, thank God. Apparently Mitch called the cops and then you came home. I'm just relieved I got here before you did."

Deputy Frazier put his drunken brother in handcuffs and read him his rights. Billy was swaying back and forth in the middle of Olivia's living room, so the Deputy took him out to his squad car and then came back inside.

"What do you think, Brad?" Jake asked.

"I think she's going to have to press charges to keep him in jail for any length of time." Brad replied.

"Excuse me? Do you two know each other?"

"I'm sorry, Darlin'. It's a small town." Jake shrugged. "This is Deputy Bradley Frazier. He's a friend of mine and he's Billy's brother. We all went to school together." Jake smiled.

"Hello Ma'am, Brad said, politely tipping his hat.

"You should probably call me Olivia."

"Nice to meet you, though I'm sorry it's under these circumstances." the Deputy replied. "So Jake, Billy ransacked the place, then?"

"I think so. I didn't get a look around yet but there are open cupboards in the kitchen." Jake answered looking around the room.

"Ok, well I'll take a look around and file a report. Ma'am, I mean, Olivia, you will want to press charges, I assume?"

"No" she replied flatly.

"What? Yes you will." Jake insisted. "Olivia, Billy broke into your house. Who knows what he might have done if you had been here by yourself."

"I didn't lock the door, Jake. It was open. So my cupboards are opened? So what? There's nothing of real value here. He didn't hurt me. I just don't see the point." Olivia shrugged her shoulders.

Jake and Brad exchanged looks of concern and confusion.

"Ma'am, if he stole or destroyed any of your property, I advise you to press charges." Brad explained. "It doesn't matter that he's my brother. I've been down this road with him many times I'm sad to say."

Olivia sighed. She and Jake wouldn't be getting any breaks from the drama. Almost as if Jake could read her thoughts he said, "Darlin, I know this isn't what you hoped for tonight but I really think you should press charges. He needs to go to jail for this. You should take it seriously." Jake insisted.

"Fine, but then I would like to..." Olivia began.

Mitch interrupted. "Olivia, I hope it's alright I called the police. I heard breaking glass and got worried."

"Yes of course Mr. Jameson. I appreciate you looking out for me." Olivia said, feeling herself getting pushed around by all these men.

"I'm going to head back to my place if there is nothing more you need and you're sure you'll be alright." Mitch squeezed her shoulder.

"I'm fine, really. Thank you again."

"You're very welcome, dear." Mitch replied. He had seen Billy around town through the years but never heard of him getting in this kind of trouble. Usually the gossip around town was Billy was drunk and disorderly. "Poor Olivia", he thought.

Bradley, Jake and Olivia began looking through the house.

Jake went into Olivia's bedroom first. Glass covered the floor from the broken lamp. "Damn. Be careful Darlin', there's glass everywhere."

"It's ok. I'll go get a broom," she said sounding hollow.

"Let me take a few pictures before you start cleaning up." Bradley added as he stepped out to his vehicle to retrieve the camera.

Jake and Olivia followed Deputy Frazier around as he took pictures and then walked into Olivia's bathroom. Pill bottles were strewn about and most of them had been opened.

"Why would he do this? It just doesn't make sense.

I mean, my medicine cabinet, I guess I understand but why me at all? I don't..." Olivia began.

"Jake, I'm going to take statements from you and Miss Curtis and then I'll get out of your way." Deputy Frazier said, ignoring Olivia's comment. Better just to let Jake deal with the female emotions.

Jake squeezed her hand. "It'll be all right, Darlin'."

By the time the deputy left and they cleaned up the mess it was nearly midnight. They both looked like they'd been run over by a truck. It had been a mentally exhausting day.

"Jake would you stay here tonight?" she asked. She wanted to tell him everything. The words sat frozen on the tip of her tongue. She knew exactly who had spoken to Billy in the dark. She felt it in the same way one feels a winter chill in the air. There was only one person who had ever spoken of her that way. She stuffed the whisper of fear down deep inside and waited for Jake's answer.

He didn't have to say anything. He leaned down and kissed her neck in response. He was relieved she didn't want him to leave. He wondered if he would stop worrying about her alone in this place, ever again.

She let him use the bathroom first. She considered putting bedding on the couch for him but she really hoped he would want to be in her bed.

She felt so conflicted by her feelings for him. Her common sense and rationality battled it out with her physical desire for this man, on nearly a moment to moment basis. She wondered how Jake was able to tolerate her rollercoaster of emotions when she could barely stand it herself.

He walked out of the bathroom wearing only his jeans. "He looks like an ad from a magazine" Olivia thought. She could feel herself start to blush and her heart was pounding.

His face, freshly washed, his dark hair curling slightly around his ears; it was all so unreal. She didn't know how he could look so relaxed. "He looked so, so at ease all the time. It was as if nothing ever bothered him and if it did, he didn't show it." She was almost envious. Whereas, she felt like her life was in a constant state of upheaval. A fresh wave of desire washed over her as he leaned against the door frame looking at her.

"Darlin' you look like you're daydreaming. It's all yours." He said smiling and gestured toward the bathroom.

"What? Oh!" Olivia blushed again. "The bathroom; right, um, thank you."

"Where should I put my things?" Jake asked as she fidgeted in front of him.

"Uh, anywhere you like. I, I was just thinking some wine sounded good. Maybe you could pour us some and I'll be out in a minute?" She stammered.

"Sure" he smiled as she shut the bathroom door.

Olivia washed her face, brushed her teeth, combed out her hair and even thought about showering but didn't want to waste another minute away from Jake. She grabbed her oversized University of Oregon t-shirt and put on large fuzzy socks. She walked out and Jake was standing, waiting patiently holding a bottle of wine and two glasses.

"Where do you want this?"

Olivia took the bottle out of his hand. "In here." She backed up toward her bedroom.

"Are you sure about this? I mean we both agreed to take this slowly? This doesn't exactly qualify as slowly; not that I have a problem with it but I'm still trying to be a gentleman."

"I'm trying too" she smiled as she set the bottle of wine on the now empty bedside table. She reached over to the opposite side flipping on the only remaining lamp that hadn't been smashed to bits. Jake stood next to the bed waiting for more of an explanation.

"Here's the thing; I'm tired, you're tired. We've had a very long day. The bed is much more comfortable than the couch and for the sake of taking it slowly, I'm not offering sex. I'm offering a cozy bed, wine and some fairly innocent cuddling. What do you say?" She smiled, trying to make her insides stop quivering.

"How could I resist an offer like that?" he began pouring the wine. Olivia propped pillows for them in a sort of circular fashion that reminded Jake of a nest.

Jake had to admit it looked inviting and she looked downright irresistible.

He crawled onto her bed to lean back on the pillows. Slowly sipping his wine, he was able to really appreciate her natural beauty. She sat across from him and closed her eyes as if savoring every bit of flavor on her tongue. A smile lit her face as she opened her eyes and realized Jake was watching her.

"What?" She said, laughing a little.

"You're very beautiful, Darlin'." Jake said honestly.

"If you sweet talk me too much, we'll be doing a whole lot more than cuddling."

"Alright, alright; I said I was *trying* to be a gentleman. I can't say I'll succeed."

"We could just talk. I'd love to hear more stories about you and your family. You've led an interesting life, Jake."

"Oh no you don't, I'm pretty sure it's your turn to tell *me* some stories."

"I find it difficult to talk about myself. That's probably why therapy hasn't exactly been a shining success."

"Well tell me what it feels like when you play the piano. Tell me your favorite color, tell me your nicknames; something easy."

Olivia giggled. "That actually doesn't sound easy at all, but ok. The piano?"

He nodded.

"There is something about the piano that fits me or maybe I fit the piano. I took to it easily or so I've been told. It felt like I had to play; like I was *meant* to play."

"Truthfully, I was relieved to find something I was good at that wasn't the cello. And aside from a mind-blowing orgasm, playing the piano is the most cathartic thing I've ever done. Everything I feel comes out through my fingers. Sometimes it feels like lightning and passion and sometimes it feels like warm breath on chilled skin. It's hard to explain properly."

"On the contrary, I think you explain it perfectly. It makes me wish I played an instrument." Jake said, and then smiled. "A mind-blowing orgasm, huh?"

"Honesty is always best, don't you think?"

"And your favorite color?"

"Brown, since the first time I looked into your eyes." She wished she could keep her stupid, high school girl thoughts to herself.

"Now who's sweet talking?"

She set her wine down and crawled over on top of him. He set his wine down as well, refusing to let her take control.

She rubbed her hands over the strong muscles of his chest. She leaned in and kissed the skin of his bare shoulder. He reached up to feel the soft waves of her burnished hair. He gently kissed the delicate skin of her neck, just below her ear. She gasped lightly, desire flooding through her.

"Jake, do you remember what you said about wanting to get to know me? About not settling for less than everything?" she asked in a whisper.

"Yeah" he murmured into her throat.

"I want that, too. I want that with you." Olivia admitted.

He was surprised at how it felt to hear her say it. He couldn't name what he was feeling. He pulled her in closer and she leaned her head on his chest. He rubbed her back softly.

Olivia felt so peaceful listening to the beat of his heart, the breathing-slowly in and out. After a while, his hand stopped. He let his head fall back on the pillow, lightly. He slept. She pulled his arm around her like a blanket or a shield and she fell asleep, too. "Bliss"

CHAPTER FOURTEEN

The next morning Jake woke to find Olivia still snuggled on his chest. She had pulled a blanket over them and they remained surrounded by pillows. It was luxurious. He yawned and lowered his head to smell her hair. She smelled delicious and felt so warm on top of him.

The motion caused Olivia to stir and blink slowly awake. She lifted her head and looked at Jakes' half naked body. "Good morning" she said, still sounding sleepy. She smiled though she was beginning to feel the previous day pressing on her good mood.

"Good morning Darlin'; how about I go make some coffee? And then I have to hit the road. I have a conference call at eleven." He said casually but then added, "You could come with me out to the ranch?"

"Jake, I don't need a babysitter" she sat up, suddenly looking irritated.

"I didn't say you did. I just want to spend more time with you."

"I can't. I mean, I can't keep you from your work all the time and I have to figure out what I'm going to do with myself and *what* is wrong with you?" she demanded.

"I don't know what you mean?" He stared at her, puzzled.

"I mean here I am, a crazy rollercoaster of emotions, up, down, up, down, up, down. I'm a basket case. I have cried at least once every time we've been together; and it's not your fault, it's mine but you just keep coming back for more. It's like you have some desire to be jerked around by me. Haven't you had enough? I'm not trying to chase you away, I'm not. I just don't get how I haven't already. I am really attracted to you but how in God's name do you feel anything for me but pity? And to top things off, you genuinely seem to want me around. I can't wrap my brain around it, Jake! I can't! So, please tell me what is wrong with you because there has to be something!" She ranted and then looked at him expectantly.

Jake's face broke into a grin; that charming, devil-may-care half smile just like the first day they met. "Well..." he drawled.

"I'm serious Jake. Explain this to me. Tell me you're flawed."

"OK, I AM flawed! Let me correct you. You said I don't want you to go anywhere.
That's not true." Olivia looked like she'd been slapped.

"Darlin', I want you to go everywhere and anywhere you want to go. I just hope you'll let me come along." He smiled. "As for the rest of it; I'm nowhere near perfect. I have my own problems, God knows. I don't think I'm a glutton for punishment though either. I think when you find someone who makes you feel all the things I feel for you, you don't let go just because they happen to be dealing with something painful. In fact, that's when you hold tighter so they never feel alone. You aren't alone Olivia. You have me. You had me from the first look. You have me whether you like it or not." Jake squeezed her hand gently.

"Jake I'm tired. I'm tired of crying all the time. I'm tired of being weak. I'm tired of wondering if you pity me or if you somehow see beyond it; but mostly I'm tired of fighting the feelings I have for you."

"Good, then don't! Don't fight it."

"I'll try. But I do still have to find myself a life. I feel like, until I figure out who I am now, without my son, I have nothing of value to give you." She tried to explain but didn't think it was coming out right.

"Where does that leave us Darlin'? I don't think I can pretend you don't exist until you have everything figured out." Jake raked his hands through his hair in frustration. He sighed deeply and walked into the kitchen to make coffee. He leaned on the counter as it perked, thinking hard.

Olivia followed after a moment. He stood up to face her. She put her hands on his bare chest. His heart beat rapidly, steady and strong. "I won't ask you to leave me again."

He leaned down and kissed her passionately on her warm lips. The coffee pot gurgled its finish. Jake looked up at the clock.

"Damn, Darlin' I have to get a move on. Don't suppose you have a to-go cup for this do you?" He grabbed his shirt from the back of a chair slipping it on.

Olivia pouted a bit watching him dress. "No, but take whatever mug you like."

"Thanks, now are you sure you won't join me at the ranch today? You could have lunch with me, and dinner...and dessert?" he smiled and cocked a sideways plea.

"No Jake. No. You have work to do. Some of us still have jobs and you should do yours. I won't let you turn into a lazy dilettante because of me." She declared, only half joking.

"Ok, I'll go, but I'll call you later?" he asked, kissing her again.

There was an easy rhythm to moments between them that were undeniable. They could have been an old married couple. Olivia's thoughts shocked her as she watched him pull out of her driveway.

"Well Harper, what shall we do today?" Olivia asked her wiggly pup. "I know what I said. I wasn't going to let Jake in, he wouldn't get hurt that way; but I didn't expect it to be so hard to fight these feelings. I didn't know love felt like this." Olivia sat on her couch, "Love" she thought, "I do love him, I knew I would, and yet..." Still in her t-shirt and at a loss at what to do next, she sipped her coffee and reached for her phone.

Two hours later she was in her Jeep heading to Dr. Thompson's office. She hoped the timing would be perfect. Jake should be right in the middle of his conference call. She didn't want to have to explain why she couldn't talk and she didn't want to ignore his call and make him worry.

THERAPY SESSION II
Ben Thompson, M.D.

"Hello Olivia; have a seat. I was surprised when LeAnn told me you were coming in today. Is everything alright?" Ben asked.

"Yes, no...I don't know. There's a lot going on. My life has switched gears from very quiet to strangely noisy lately but in a good way, I think, or mostly in a good way. I've had a breakthrough Doc, or a mini breakthrough, I think." Olivia smiled, fully aware she sounded scattered.

"Well then, let's talk about it. I should tell you before you begin; Jake Weidner came to see me yesterday. He wanted to talk about you." Ben explained, hoping to shed some light on Jake for her.

"I know. He told me. We talked about it. I wasn't happy when he first told me, but he did apologize and promised never to do that again. I'm satisfied."

"So you believe him?" "You feel he is someone worthy of your trust?"

"Yes I do." Olivia replied honestly. It dawned on her she really did trust Jake. She hadn't thought about it in those terms until just now.

"How does that make you feel?" Ben asked feeling deflated. He couldn't seem to stay professional and detached from Olivia. It bothered him.

"I thought it would make me feel vulnerable and scared but even now, as I think about it, it feels good. I, I actually feel safe with him. I've never had anyone make me feel like this. He makes me feel protected but also, um, honored." She was finding it hard to look her doctor in the eyes. "I know Doc; I know you don't think I'm ready for a relationship. But isn't part of this whole process about trusting people?"

"Yes, it is. It is within family relationships and friends. There is a great difference between mending the relationship with your mother and romantic involvements with strange men."

Olivia had to laugh, unable to stop the scoff escaping her lips. If she didn't know any better, she would say Doctor Thompson sounded jealous. "Jake isn't a strange man and besides, mending my relationship with my mother is not on the menu."

"Jake is kind, patient, charming, and he's a gentleman. He seems to only want to protect me, care for me and be with me. I've never had that; not *ever*! I've been starving for so long and now I crave it. I want it. I know how it sounds but I just don't care."

"Is this your breakthrough, Olivia; misplaced trust?"

"Excuse me? Where do you get off calling it 'misplaced'?" She glared angrily; finally looking into his eyes.

"I will encourage any healthy relationship you may form. But, I don't think this falls into that category."

"You're wrong. We haven't even had sex. Doesn't that scream healthy? I wanted to. I wanted to but *Jake* insisted we take it slowly. Doesn't that say something about his character? What about coming here to speak to you? Didn't you find him genuine?" She accused more than asked.

"My personal feelings about Jake Weidner are irrelevant. Why don't you tell me about the panic attack?" Ben asked, switching gears as quickly as possible.

"It was an awful, wonderful, confusing, hugely emotional day yesterday but I got through it. I even spoke about D...I explained to Jake about Dante'." She declared, steadying her breath and keeping her eyes directly on the doctor. It was hard to believe she could say his name and it didn't kill her.

"That's good. I think it's important for you to talk about your son. It's one of the ways we honor those we've lost. We talk about them and keep their memory alive. I think that's very good. Will you, can you talk about him now with me?"

Olivia took a deep breath. She hadn't prepared herself for this part, but she was determined not to cry-not today.
"I know I need to try. That's part of what I'm finally realizing. For so long now, I haven't wanted to feel better. I haven't. I wallowed in my pain because I thought I didn't deserve better but now, today, I know I bring no honor to Dante' by

wallowing. Staying lost in my grief does him no good. It does *me* no good. So, yes, I'll try." Olivia bit down hard on her lip. Tears were hard to stop.

"I don't expect you to heal or move past your grief in one fell swoop and you shouldn't either. I'm glad you're willing to try. I think it's a very important first step.

Shifting gears, knowing he might be testing her resolve too much, Ben said, "Tell me if you would, about Dante's father."

"I don't know what else there is to say about Jackson."

"No, I don't mean Jackson Montgomery. I'm talking about Dante's biological father." Ben said seriously. "How old was your son when you married Jackson?"

Olivia took a sharp breath. "He was four, almost five, I guess." She said unsteadily. She knew she needed to say more, that he expected her to say more but she couldn't. There were parts of her past sitting in her throat like lumps and no matter how much she swallowed, they just wouldn't go down.

She knew Ben had all the information he needed in front of him, the police reports and hospital records. There were psychological evaluations and doctors recommendations and even some photographs. She sat motionless trying not to think about those things; all of the ugliness living in those files.

Ben waited patiently. He knew this wouldn't be easy for her. He had been a doctor for many years now and had never seen the kind of brutality Olivia had endured. She survived violence unlike he'd ever seen.

"Who was Dante's biological father?" He asked again, directly.

Olivia took a deep breath, willing herself not to cry. "Why should I cry?" she thought defiantly. "I didn't cry when I told Dante' and I won't cry now."

"His name is Patrick Hanson." She paused, looking down at the phoenix on her bracelet, rubbing it gently with her fingertips. She hated her scar but not in the way others hated it. To her it represented *her* failure, *her* lack of will and *her* inability to change her fate. She had known she wouldn't be able to kill herself. She had failed and knew she was going to. To others, her scar was a source of pity.

For some unexplained reason it was also beautiful to her. She hated it and she loved it. She remembered clearly the feeling of her blood pouring out of her body. Her first suicide attempt had been childish and half-hearted at best. Her second was different. Jake didn't know the scar was really two scars, one on top of the other. Both times a failure, just as Olivia had failed Dante'. If only she could have changed her fate and saved him.

"Olivia?" Ben asked gently.

"Huh? Oh sorry. I was just thinking." She said quietly.

"Patrick? Did you know him?"

"Yeah; he lived in our neighborhood. He went to the same school as my brother and I, though he was older, graduated." Olivia tried to sound casual.

"Tell me about the rape." Ben said solemnly.

Olivia held in a breath and then sighed. It seemed everything always came back to this. She began slowly. "I was home. Mother was at the club as usual. She was on the planning committee for some dinner or auction or something, I can't remember. My father was at work." She said, unwilling or unable to continue without a prompt.

"And your brother; where was he?"

"Miles was at a polo match. One of his best friends was on the team. I was supposed to go too, but I didn't. I don't remember why." Olivia lied and stared at the painting on the opposite wall. She could picture it all so clearly but wouldn't admit the reason she stayed home that day. Some things were hers and hers alone.

"It was a Tuesday. I went to school like normal but skipped the polo match in the afternoon. The doorbell rang, um, Patrick rang our doorbell. He didn't break in. He didn't have any weapons. He just rang the doorbell." She said slowly.

"Was anyone else in your household; a housekeeper, nanny, anybody employed by your parents?"

"Yes, we had a housekeeper named Amy, but she wasn't home either. She must have been out running errands for my mother. I answered the door. I recognized him. He was friendly and asked if he could use our phone.

I showed him into where it was but he didn't, he..." Olivia's breathing came rapidly. She tried to slow it down but couldn't. She could feel herself falling into that same dark abyss that always claimed her.

Ben's calm voice broke through the darkness. "Olivia, it's over. You are safe. This is all in the past." He soothed.

Olivia wrapped her arms around herself and inhaled deeply. "Can you go on?"

"Why should I? What's the point of telling this story again?" It was easier to be mad at this doctor than to face the gory details of her past.

"It's proof of your strength. You had the strength to survive a horrific attack and all that came after. *That* is what it will take to deal with the loss of your family. You need to see for yourself just how strong you are. You can overcome all of this."

"Patrick took the phone and ripped it out of the wall." She went on quickly, not giving herself time to think too much. "I remember laughing about it. I was a fifteen year old girl with the world at my fingertips. Everything was an amusement back then, even butting heads with my mother. Everything was easy for me, school, friends, parents; it was all so easy. I was laughing and asked Patrick just what he thought he was doing. He wasn't laughing; his face changed. He grabbed me and bound my wrists with the phone cord. I screamed at him to stop and kicked and tried to push him away, but he was stronger than me, stronger than he looked. He ripped at my clothes and I screamed and cried. He pulled out a knife; he cut at my clothes and slashed my skin. He didn't care how deeply the knife cut. It was like I was watching the whole thing from outside myself, from the stairs."

"I remember thinking just for a brief second, 'how could he ruin my new top', but then I also remember feeling embarrassed and there was so much pain where the knife had dug into me. I remember his eyes, he was going to kill me and then, I was naked, bloody and ashamed."

"I cried and tried to get away, but that was when he hit me. I remember that first hit most of all, right in the face like he hated me.

I'd never felt that kind of physical pain before and I couldn't understand why? That hit broke my jaw and I think about the broken bones sometimes. There were a lot. He bound my arms tightly behind my back and the force of him on top of me caused a separated shoulder and a break in my forearm. It seemed impossible. The whole thing seemed impossible. And all the while he kept talking to me." She paused for a second to catch her breath. It came out like a ragged sigh.

"He was sweaty, he crawled on top of me, his sweat dripped on my neck and chest, but, he didn't smell like sweat; he smelled like cheap cologne. Cologne? He put on cologne to rape me? It was like he had prepared himself to go on a date." She stopped again, feeling overwhelmed. The unshed tears felt like daggers behind her eyes.

"Take your time." Ben said reassuringly.

"He sat on me, held me down, ripped open his jeans and shoved his...he raped me, violently. He used his body to tear mine apart until he had nothing left. I couldn't breathe, I couldn't scream. I just closed my eyes and then he licked me, my face, my neck, my chest and stomach as though consuming my blood, sweat and tears gave him power. The sounds he made were horrible. I'll never forget those sounds, like an animal. He did the one thing to me I never thought would happen."

"When he was finished with me, he set fire to the kitchen. I don't remember much after that, except the look on his face and the sound of his voice in my ear, 'you were always mine'. Then he ran out. He went home as if nothing had happened. I lay bloody, exposed, and ruined on that kitchen floor wishing for death."

"I remember hearing a fireman say I was lucky we had an alarm system. He used the word 'lucky' that I didn't burn up in the fire. I was cut up, beaten, raped, knocked up and left to burn and someone had the nerve to call me lucky. I wasn't lucky, I was cursed. I am cursed." She said quickly, unable to look at Ben.'

"Patrick Hanson got me pregnant, but he wasn't a father, he isn't my baby's father!

I kept my baby. It was against the *adamant* advice of my parents, well my mother mostly and that's it." She said as if trying to push it back into the past where it belonged.

"But there is more, isn't there? Didn't you try to kill yourself before finding out you were pregnant?"

"Yes, I did. Miles found me and I was hospitalized again. I hadn't been out of the hospital for very long when I went right back in. I didn't know I was pregnant then. They told me. I don't know if they told me before that moment or not or if I just couldn't hear it or process it. The whole thing had me pretty messed up. It's all sort of blurry."

"When I found out about Dante'; I mean really started to wrap my head around having a baby, it changed something in me. I realized Patrick had turned us both into victims, Dante' and I, and *that* I couldn't stand. I wouldn't stand for it. I fought for us. I fought my family, the doctors. I fought in court and got Patrick Hanson locked up in prison. He only served two years of a six-year sentence. You said I was strong but it wasn't me. Dante' gave me strength and now he's gone and my strength with him." Olivia said sadly, a tear finally spilling over.

"How much did Patrick know? How much does he know? Did he ever know about your son?"

"Yes, somehow he found out about Dante'. I tried to hide the pregnancy in court, during his trial, but maybe he realized. I don't know. Sometimes, I think maybe it was his intention all along. I don't know how much he knows now. I don't care. There's nothing left for him to take or ruin and he *will* pay for what he's done. Dante' was never his. He was always mine. Miles always said Dante' looked just like me." Olivia said, and then paused, thinking. She hadn't meant to say it, 'always mine'. It was *the* phrase that haunted her.

"You know when you asked me about faith? There must be a God because Dante' was my miracle.
Everyone told me he would be a living reminder of what happened. He wasn't. He had the most pure heart. I didn't look at him and think about rape; I looked at him and saw beauty, and courage.

It was as if everything good in me was used to make him."

"My mother could never make sense of it. She was angry at me all the time and she just knew I was crazy. She told me so on several occasions. I can't mend my relationship with a woman who wanted me to kill the only good thing I ever had. Dante' *was* my gift for enduring."

"What do you mean 'he will pay for what he's done'? Are you talking about revenge or do you still think you can see the future?"

"Neither" she lied. "I just mean Karma's a bitch, that's all."

"Yes, well I agree, but I want you to be honest with me, especially if you *are* having recurrent delusions or visions."

"I told you I wasn't Doc, what more do you want from me?"

Ben decided to move on. "Do you think it's *possible* to mend your relationship with your mother?"

"No, I don't. She will *never* be satisfied with me. I'm not good enough for Antoinette Curtis. I never have been and I never will be. She wanted me to be a cellist, a socialite like her. She wanted me to pretend that everything was perfect and when I couldn't pretend, she was angry and embarrassed. Do you have any idea how hard it is to be told to stuff all your feelings down inside, to pretend they don't exist? I wasn't allowed to feel it, acknowledge it or talk about it. It's hard, no impossible, to move past something like that."

"Do you really think that's how she feels about you?"

"Yes. She may say a million different things to the contrary but don't be fooled.
She will only be happy if I finally do as she wishes."

"What does she wish for you?"

"Honestly anymore, I don't know. I don't speak to her. I imagine she still has some plan for me. Do you know that none of her friends know the real story of what happened? She's told everyone some bullshit version of my life that makes it pretty and acceptable."

"Are you sure that's the case?"

"I'm positive. The real story isn't pretty enough for country club luncheons."

"What are you most angry about where it concerns your mother?" Ben asked, hoping to get to the heart of it.

Olivia paused. It was hard to say but she knew she needed to. "I can't love someone who couldn't love Dante'." She finished simply.

Sometimes there was nothing but a patient's acknowledgement of their own truth. Ben knew he didn't need to comment. She merely had needed to say it.

"Are you afraid of Patrick Hanson now? Do you fear him?" Ben asked cautiously, switching gears.

"No. I have an unnatural fear of phone cords but I don't fear Patrick Hanson." She said sarcastically. "Like I said, there's nothing left for him to take from me. I haven't seen him since that day in court, so I tell myself he's moved on to new victims. There is part of me that thinks he should fear me though. I'm not a fifteen year old girl anymore and now, I have absolutely nothing to lose. What could he take from me? Dante' is gone." But, as she said it she saw Jake's face in her mind and fear trickled inside her again.

Ben worried about the ominous sound in her voice. "Was she planning something?" Feeling like she had nothing left to lose made her think she was invincible and yet, Ben knew there were fates worse than death and somewhere deep down, she knew it too.

He sat for a moment, watching Olivia. She had a natural grace about her. Even in the way she spoke, the way she moved through a room. It was in the way she looked at him now, elegant. Ben had to admit she was right about the breakthrough. He never expected to come so far in such a short time but he still was concerned about the reason behind the breakthrough; Jake Weidner.

"How are you feeling now? I have time if you care to continue or we can stop there for today. What would you prefer?"

"I'm tired but, it surprises me, I'm ok. For so long, I thought it would hurt *more* to talk about Dante' but it doesn't. It hurts the same as *not* talking about him." She smiled halfheartedly.

"Talking about the attack isn't easy though. That part's harder. I guess it makes sense. I could never be one of those people who wear it proudly like a badge of honor; counseling others as a way to heal myself. That just isn't me."

"It doesn't have to be. Everyone must find their own path. I thought perhaps you could tell me what brought you to marry Jackson? I only ask because there is value in understanding the choices you made and how you came to them."

"I thought we already went through this?" she said, oozing frustration.

It fascinated Ben that Olivia could have nearly the same level of anxiety and pain when talking about Jackson as she did when talking about Patrick Hanson. "We did discuss it some but I think there was more to the choice you made than you realize. It's time you think about 'why'. Why him? Why did you marry Jackson Montgomery?"

"I told you, I gave in. I caved and married someone socially acceptable, from a good family." She was irritated that she even had to speak about Jackson, again.

"So you want me to believe you went from being a fifteen year old girl who was so self-assured that you kept a baby 'everyone' said you should abort to a twenty year old who married a man you didn't love just because your family approved of him?" Ben said accusingly. "I'm sorry Olivia but I don't buy it. I wasn't born yesterday and neither were you."

"Go to hell!" Olivia snapped. Anger felt easier than sadness. In that moment she desired nothing more than to punch Ben in the face.

"Well before I go, let me tell you my theory. See, I think you married Jackson because he was the only kind of man you ever had any experience with. Did you date many men before marrying Jackson? No, and there's a reason for that. Your first experience with sex was violent and terrifying and you never had a chance to know tenderness or to experience real love from a man." Ben said, watching her carefully. He was dangerously close to the heart of her wound.

"Jackson didn't rape me! Jackson was an angry son of a bitch with a temper like hell fire but he didn't rape me!!

Your theory stinks, Doc!"

"Maybe he didn't rape you but he most certainly abused you. Didn't he? Didn't he yell at you? Didn't he call you names? Didn't he grab you and push you around? I read in your file how he hit you so hard you ended up in the hospital unconscious for two days. Was your mother ok with that?"

Olivia felt the heat of her shame. She *had* let men destroy her. She never stopped it. She was never going to be the battered wife and yet, she had allowed it to happen. A fresh tear threatened her cheek.

"I don't know. I didn't tell her. Jackson made me promise never to tell anyone." Olivia replied quietly, wringing her hands in her lap.

"Make no mistake Olivia, he may not have raped you but he certainly abused you." Ben explained sadly.

"I guess I didn't think I deserved better."

"You didn't *know* you deserved better." Ben corrected.

"Are you saying I married Jackson because I wanted Patrick Hanson?" She asked, beyond upset. "Is that what you're saying? Now, that's crazy!"

"It isn't crazy. *You* aren't crazy. I'm saying subconsciously, you were drawn to the only kind of relationship you'd ever known. Have you ever heard the term, Stockholm Syndrome?"

"Yes, but I wasn't held captive by Patrick Hanson either. I didn't have a bomb strapped to me."

"But you *were* held captive, by telephone cord and brute strength and whether you understand it or not, a bond was formed with your abuser. He put a child inside you. You knew nothing else. You still know nothing else. Patrick went to prison briefly but eventually you sought out his replacement." Ben explained.

"That's sick! That's fucking sick! I wouldn't do that!" She yelled but then cried in earnest this time. This was too much, too crazy. It didn't seem possible. "If that's true then my mother was right to have me committed."

"Olivia, let me assure you; you are **not** crazy. You were and are traumatized. They are not the same thing.

The reactions you are having and have had, are all normal for what you've been through. This is your mind's only way of coping or it *was,* and we are going to find better, healthier ways of coping...together. You married Jackson for other reasons, too. None of us are that single-minded."

"What would you say if I told you I married Jackson because he was the person I saw myself marrying?" she asked tentatively.

"I would remind you it was something you manifested because you couldn't deal with the reality of the rape. You admitted to your other doctors that you created this fantasy about psychic ability in order to have control over your future." Ben replied, unable to help his long exhale.

"Olivia, you chose Jackson in order to make your prediction come true, the same reason behind moving to Montana. You came here in order to make people believe you. That's not real psychic ability. I could tell you that tomorrow I'll have ham and eggs for breakfast. That isn't a prediction because I can make it happen simply by going to the store, buying ham and eggs and cooking them for breakfast tomorrow."

"I'm not delusional." She argued quietly.

"Good, because you have enough to deal with. So I'll ask you again, can you predict the future?"

"No" she lied. It was easier than trying to explain the truth and running the risk of being put in a mental hospital again. It could happen so easily. Though she had never seen herself being committed again it didn't mean it couldn't still happen. That was the worst of it. There were bad things she saw coming and bad things she didn't and not much in between.

"I think you should tell your family what Jackson did to you."

"No, that's not going to happen. He's dead and he can't hurt me anymore. There's no point." She replied seriously.

"At least think about it. It could really change things especially between you and your mother. You could have a fresh start. You're here. This is your chance." Ben said, encouragingly.

"I want to start fresh, but nothing will change my mother's heart." She admitted.

"Also it's hard to separate what I felt for Jackson from this strange feeling of relief that he isn't here. I feel guilty and I really can't separate my feelings about Jackson from my feelings about Dante'. In a perfect world I would have Dante' back and Jackson would still be gone." Olivia said, unwilling to say dead.

"Who says feelings come neatly categorized or that you should be the *one* person in the world who gets to put all your feelings in their own little box with labels. Life is messy. It wants to be messy. You can organize your closet but you can't organize your emotions." Ben explained. "Do you ever feel out of control? Not what other people would say about you but how you feel about yourself. Are you out of control?"

"Yes, all the time. I made a fool of myself in front of Jake, coming onto him. I couldn't even tell you why it happened the way it did. It isn't even the most recent incident either."

"What do you mean? What happened?"

She hesitated, and then said "some guy named Billy broke into my apartment last night and broke a lamp, stole some medicines and ranted about me breaking his heart. The strange part is that I wasn't mad. I was scared I guess, but not angry. I didn't even want to press charges. I wanted to shut down, crawl in bed, disappear but I knew from the look on their faces, the Deputy and Jake's, that I would seem crazy if I didn't."

"Did you go ahead and press charges?"

"Yes I did, but I felt completely out of control. Jake was in control. He was so sure of himself. He reacted the way I think normal people should react, but me, I just couldn't. Apparently stressful situations turn me into either a raging nymphomaniac or a zombie. Neither screams 'mental health', does it Doc?"

Ben had a number of reactions but needed to respond clinically and professionally. He ignored her question. "Are you having sex?"

"Do you mean with Jake or with anyone?" She asked sarcastically. She didn't like his tone when it came to Jake Weidner.

"I meant with anyone." He only half smiled.

"No, I told you, we are not having sex but not for lack of trying. I know what you said; I heard you. My mind knows the right things but sometimes I'm happier *out* of my mind."

"Also, and not to sound like a sappy teenager but I'm genuinely attracted to Jake. Talk about things that are hard to separate. Here I am going through all this stuff and yet, I'm having real feelings for a man. It's like there's some part of me that doesn't care about the grieving process, or the healing."

"Are you sure they're real feelings or is this a very small bandage on a very large wound?"

"God, you piss me off! Sometimes I think you don't want me to be happy at all. How does anyone know if what they're feeling is real or not? I guess I'm never going to be a good judge because I never had 'boyfriends'. Isn't that right?"

"I do want you to be happy. And I think you have the potential to make very good choices and decisions. I'm not even saying you haven't. I'm saying, slow down, think about it and don't jump into anything with too much haste."

Olivia complained. "I wish I could be normal, all the time lately. I wish I was divorced instead of widowed. I wish I'd been courted instead of raped so I could be the person Jake deserves." She couldn't help blushing lightly.

At that moment Olivia's cell phone began to ring. She smiled without thought and her blush deepened. It was Jake. Ben didn't need to guess who was calling.

She looked down at her phone and said, "Ben I'm sorry, do you mind if I take this? It will just be a minute."

"No I don't mind, I'll go get some coffee. Would you like some?" he asked politely, cringing on the inside.

"Yes, thank you; cream and sugar please?" Olivia said sweetly, "Hello?"

"Hello beautiful." Jake drawled in that sexy deep voice making her insides quiver.

"Hi" she said again, suddenly wishing she had gone to see him today.

"What are you up to Darlin'? I was really hoping you were going to change your mind about lunch."

Olivia looked at her watch. It was close to one o'clock. "I know. I'm sorry. I was going to but I got kind of busy." She said, unsure of how to explain.

"That's alright; my call ran long so it worked out. I just miss your face so, how about dinner? It'll be you, me, and some cheeseburgers we didn't get to last night? How does something like that sound to you?" He asked hopefully.

"That sounds wonderful. What time and where?" She asked dreamily.

"I'll come pick you up at six."

"Perfect." She smiled.

"I'm looking forward to it, Darlin'. You don't know how much." Charm colored his voice.

"Me too, bye."

"Bye." He said, longing for more. This reminded him of being a teenager and spending all his time on the phone with Sunny Roberts, his first real serious girlfriend. Jake would love nothing more than to bail on the rest of the work waiting for him and go pick up Olivia now.

Olivia hung up the phone and sat back down. She didn't realize she was still smiling until Ben came in with coffee.

"Something amusing?" he asked as he handed her the coffee.

"No, I mean, yes. Oh, I don't know, just ignore me. I'm being silly. I always feel better when I talk to Jake. It has to be real because the way I feel couldn't be a lie. I've tried to fight it, I did, but it was a ridiculous and futile effort. I don't know, like I said, just ignore me."

"It's my job *not* to ignore you but I do understand. I just hope you're cautious. It's a tall order to hope for a lasting, long term relationship at this point. I think you should keep your expectations in check and be careful."

"So I shouldn't expect to be happy with a man because I'm so screwed up by the two men from my past *and* by my mother? Great; that's just great, thanks, I feel like a defective piece of junk. Ugh! Tell me, is it because it's Jake?

I mean, I guess I shouldn't be so blunt but I get the impression if I had told you about some other man you would be offering different advice."

"I'll admit, Jake Weidner and I have a long and unfortunate history and it's possible it has clouded my judgment, but believe me when I tell you I would warn you to be cautious no matter who the man might be. I am telling you to take your time with anyone. I don't think a relationship is really what you need right now." He explained carefully.

"But I'm lonely. Don't you get that? I didn't know just how lonely I was until I met Jake and then my brother came to visit. I'm tired of having meaningful one-sided conversations with my dog. For a while I felt like I didn't deserve to create friendships and bonds with people. I was good at punishing myself. My solitude was part of that but now I have someone who wants to spend time with me. I'm starting to realize I had it all wrong. Jake is the reason for that. Don't you see?" She felt like she was pleading for his understanding.

"Yes I do, and I'm not without compassion, Olivia. I understand and I think it's good you aren't punishing yourself with solitude anymore. You just need to be careful about pinning all your hope of recovery and mental health on someone else. I hope you'll learn you can depend on yourself. I want you to recognize and rely on your *own* strength." He said emphatically.

"Yes, but isn't part of my healing about being strong enough to tell my story? Isn't it about realizing I can trust someone?" She said sounding almost hopeful.

"Yes it is. Let me ask you then; what have you told Jake? Does he know you tried to commit suicide and why? Does he know about the car accident and Jackson and Dante'? Did you tell him about being committed to a psychiatric hospital and being diagnosed with a delusional disorder?" Ben fired with both barrels sounding more like a jealous boyfriend than a shrink.

Olivia wasn't angry. Perhaps it was because she knew Ben was right; as much as she hated to admit it. She did owe Jake her story. It was that simple.

She would never know if what they had was real or not until he knew about all the baggage she still carried.

She refused to answer the question directly. Stubbornness was an outstanding trait. "So what do I do? Should I sit him down and tell him everything? I want us to have a real chance as a couple. And, if I do, what if I scare him away?"

"If your story does scare him away then he isn't the man you thought. If he would be willing, I would mediate a conversation in regard to your past. He could come with you to a session so I can help you navigate through it, but only if you want."

"I'll ask him today."

"There is no need to rush anything. You haven't known him for very long. If you feel you aren't ready, that's fine. My offer stands. I think you should keep things lighter for a while. That would be my advice."

"Things between us have been anything but light. No, I want to get it over with. I want to know where we really stand. I can't play pretend. I want to rip off the bandage and see if I've healed."

"Fine, but if you change your mind, just call me. I'm going to give you my cell number. If you need to talk about anything, I'll be available. I want you to think seriously about this before you proceed."

"I will. I'm sorry but I have to go. I'll see you next week. Thank you, Ben." She said and took the card he held out to her.

"You're welcome Olivia." He stood and watched her, even after she had shut his office door.

CHAPTER FIFTEEN

Olivia found it difficult to concentrate on any one thing. Her head was all over the place. There was a time when she would have played piano to focus her thoughts and energy but now she was back in her apartment doing yoga on the floor as Harper lay nearby sleeping. The phone rang and Olivia's meditation was abandoned.

"Hello?"

"Olivia, this is Sam. I was calling to see if you're in for girl's night?" Sam said happily. "I hadn't heard from you."

"Yes, I'm sorry I didn't call. I'm in. What should I wear? What time and where do I go?" Olivia hadn't decided for sure until the moment she heard Sam's voice but it suddenly sounded like a great idea. She liked the idea of having women friends, some girl talk and fruity girl drinks. It sounded perfect.

"Outstanding. I'm so stoked you'll be there. You'll have a great time. I'll text over details and honestly, wear whatever you'd like. So what are you up to?"

"I was just doing some yoga and wishing I knew a good massage therapist here in Troy."

"I didn't know yoga was so strenuous."

"It's not really the yoga. I've had a kink in my shoulder for the last couple days. I think it's just stress though."

"Yeah, well I can't exactly help you but I know someone who could." Sam said, her voice sounding sing-songy.

"Who?"

"Jake. I know how that sounds but he gives a great massage."

"Oh" Olivia replied, sounding more jealous than she meant.

"Olivia, you do know Jake and I are just friends don't you? He's like a brother to me. I'm an only child so Jake is as close as it gets." Sam said, feeling the need to explain. The last thing she needed was issues with Jake's new, um, whatever Olivia was to him.

"I appreciate it Sam but I have no claim on Jake. I don't know what we have going, to be honest."

"*I* think you have something special.
It's written all over his face every time he talks about you. I've never seen him this way." Sam admitted.

"You almost sound disappointed."

"No, I'm not at all.

I want Jake to be happy. I want him to fall in love, for real, to have the kind of love that takes his breath away and makes him feel like he could do anything. I just don't want him to get his heart broken."

"I would never intentionally hurt Jake. I promise you that. It's great he has a friend like you looking out for him."

"I try; it is a *monstrously* big job." Sam teased. "Oh crap, I have to get the office line. I'll see you Friday night and we will pick you up at your house. Six thirty, ok?"

"Ok sounds great, thank you Sam." Olivia replied smiling.

"You're welcome and have a good time tonight. Jake tells me you have a date."

"Oh, um, thanks." Olivia said, not sure how to feel.

The two women said goodbye. Olivia hung up the phone as she sat on her yoga mat. It seemed weird to be making friends with a woman who didn't want anything from her. It wasn't about status or who she was married to. It was just about fun and mutual interests. This was definitely new.

Olivia braved her spare bedroom. It was time to start facing some fears. That and she really wanted Jake to see her in something nicer than a polyester uniform. If she were truly going to change her life then she had to stop being so afraid all the time. She started digging through the boxes and although she didn't dig into Dante's things, she found a nice outfit to wear.

Olivia felt pretty; putting on a favorite creamy silk blouse, military jacket, black skinny jeans and high leather boots. She hoped Jake liked her look. There was no shortage of fabulous clothes to wear. The dark voice of fear spread once more in her mind. If she wore those clothes she had packed away, did it make her the same woman who married Jackson? She tried to push that nasty thought aside.

"He'll be here soon" she told Harper. Like clockwork, there was a knock at the door and Harper barked her announcement.

It was surprising how quickly things were changing for Olivia. She felt like she had been stuck in purgatory, burning forever; and then she met Jake.

"Hi" she said happily as she opened the door.

"Hi there Darlin'; you look incredible." Jake said, smiling broadly.

"You look pretty incredible yourself," her smile just as broad. He did, too. He wore a heather grey turtle neck sweater, jeans and his usual, boots. His jacket was black and looked to be down-filled.

Olivia liked it very much and smiled to herself wondering if she should have stolen this one, too.

Jake leaned in and kissed her. "Are you ready to go?"

"Yes, let me grab my coat and purse," she answered turning toward the side table near the door.

"Can I suggest you bring Harper too?"

"What? No. I'll just take the Jeep and that way you won't have to drive me all the way back into town after the movie."

"Or you could bring your dog and some other necessities in case it gets late and you would like to stay the night." He countered.

"Jake, I couldn't."

"You could and I'd very much like it if you did, but no pressure. You don't have to." He grinned, holding up both hands. "I'm just suggesting you give yourself the option. You've already stayed overnight at my house, so why not?"

Olivia thought for a moment. She took a deep breath and realized he was right. It would be nice to have the option and she could decide later, see how things went. It was time she started taking chances again, at least small ones. It was time to start living again, for her. It's what Dante' would have wanted. "Ok, let me grab some things. It will just take a minute."

"Take your time Darlin'," he sat down on her couch, pulling Harper into his lap happily.

"Can I ask you something?" She called from her bedroom.

"Anything" Jake replied, amused.

"Well sometimes I detect a bit of a Southern accent from you. Please tell me it's not my imagination?" She asked as she put her toothbrush and some other necessities in a backpack.

"No, it's not your imagination, not exactly 'southern', but I did go to the University of Texas in Austin. You spend enough time in Texas and you pick up the accent pretty easily. It sort of stuck, I guess. It drives my very Italian mother crazy. I used to lay it on really thick just to annoy her but anymore she ignores it." Jake laughed.

Olivia was looking at an open drawer of bras and panties and debating on what to bring. She finally decided to grab a silk teddy *and* her favorite oversized t-shirt. She smiled thinking of Jake teasing his mom with the accent. Finally ready, she gave herself one last look in the mirror.

"I like the accent. It's charming. It kind of goes with the house you live in." she said as she joined him in the living room. "

Sometimes everything about you and your life reminds me of 'Gone with the Wind'. Is that weird?"

"Perhaps that's Mom's master plan; to turn me into a modern day Rhett Butler only I hope not to be thrown in jail."

Olivia smiled but changed the subject. It was easy to see this 'modern day Rhett' was still looking for his Scarlett and the thought thrilled and terrified her. "Do you think I should bring food for Harper?"

"No Darlin, it's a ranch. There are a lot of dogs and a lot of food. I think we'll be able to find something for your fluff ball to eat."

"Ok then, I guess I'm ready." She said as she scooped up Harper who wiggled happily.

"So what are we watching tonight?" Olivia asked as Jake drove.

"It's a surprise." Jake said, keeping his eyes on the road. A few minutes later they pulled into the parking lot of Maggie's Diner.

"Jake, I, I'm not ready to go in there."

"You don't have to. I called Tag ahead of time, and our dinner order is ready. I'll run inside, it will only be a minute. And don't worry; I won't say anything about your job."

Olivia smiled. It seemed like every time she thought Jake was about to let her down or piss her off, he didn't. He just kept coming through for her. It was amazing and surprising. He couldn't know what little moments like that meant to her. But she worried about the rent that would eventually be due. She knew what this curse would cost her and she wasn't finished paying. She kept telling herself not to depend on him. She had to try to keep a bit of distance but that was only her brain talking. Her heart and sadly, her body betrayed every instinct her brain dictated. Even now as he approached the truck with their dinner, she felt overwhelming desire for him. This was all so new. She had never felt this way about Jackson and before him, well...

Jake hopped in and placed the food between them. "What did you do today?" he asked as he drove them toward the ranch.

"Uh" she paused, "actually I was going to talk to you about that but it can wait. I talked to Sam today though. I agreed to go with her for 'girl's night' on Friday."

"That's nice Darlin'. You'll have fun. Sam is a good friend."

"I like her very much. She is very straight forward."

"That's one way of putting it," Jake laughed.

They pulled up to the house and it seemed quieter than before, still grand and beautiful but more cozy and intimate somehow.

Perhaps it was because it was just the two of them this time. Jake grabbed the food and Olivia's bag and Olivia carried her purse and Harper.

"I should probably let her go potty before we go in. Is there someplace you'd prefer I take her?" Olivia asked politely.

"Here in the yard is fine. Better not let her wander too far in the evening like this."

Olivia set Harper down and asked, "Why?"

"A little dog, outside in the evening so close to the mountains? There are a lot of predators out there that think she would make a nice snack."

"Oh, right" Olivia replied in a breath. Sometimes she forgot just how different it was here in the wilds compared to the city.

"It's ok, you're safe here. I just wouldn't want you wandering too far away from the main buildings this time of night without a gun."

"Oh" she said, feeling uncertain. "Do you carry a gun with you all the time?" she asked.

"Generally, I do. There's usually something in my truck." He said as though it was the most natural thing in the world.

"Oh" was all she could say. "Well, I have no intention of wandering around. I was already warned about bears in the park. Have there really been bears in the park?"

"From time to time; who told you that?"

"My stalker friend, Billy" Olivia replied trying to sound amused and not frightened.

"He won't be bothering you anymore." Jake said seriously.

Olivia didn't reply. She just sighed and let her shoulders drop. There was no end to the trouble in her life. "Jake, um, today, I uh, I went to see Ben Thompson."

"Oh, well that's good, right?" He asked sitting down on the front steps.

"I don't know, but I have something to ask and suddenly I feel ridiculous."

"Spill it. You can ask me whatever you want."

"Ok, well, I wondered if maybe you would come with me to my therapy sometime. It's just, Ben suggested since you and I have um, wow, I don't what to say."

"What?"

"Now that we're seeing each other more often, he thought it would be helpful to me."

"Darlin' I'm not opposed to the idea but I am not sure why you would want me there." Jake said diplomatically.

"I want you to come so maybe you'll understand more about me. I don't know. I just, it's because I feel so close to you and Dr. Thompson thought I might have an easier time talking about my past with you if he were there to, uh, guide me, I guess?" Now, Olivia felt stupid. She shuffled her feet in the grass.

Jake stood and came closer to her. "We don't need him for that. I'm not saying no, it's just; is that what you want? If it's what you want, I'll do it."

"Jake", she sighed his name like a prayer. "There is so much about me you don't know and it's not things like what high school I attended. It's big, horrible things."

"Ok. I'll do it. Just don't let Ben, Dr. *Thompson* pressure you into it. I don't want you to feel pressured by him or anyone."

"He didn't pressure me." She said simply looking up at him. "Come on Harper." Her little dog ran over to her happily.

"You tell me when and I'll be there." Jake earnestly promised.

Olivia tried to change the subject again. "So where is Carmella tonight?" she asked as they stepped inside through the kitchen entrance.

"She's around somewhere I imagine. She's probably playing on my computer. Her latest passion is online poker. I keep telling her it's a good way to lose her money but she tells me she's pretty good. She said she's buying me a Christmas gift this year with her *winnings*." Jake laughed. "I guess I'll know how she's doing if she buys me a new car for Christmas, huh?"

Olivia laughed, too. First she discovered Carmella was on Facebook and now she learned she played online poker. She was truly an enigma.

"Let's eat before all this food gets cold." Jake suggested, and put their food on plates at the kitchen counter. "I didn't order drinks because I have lots here. What would you like?"

"May I look?" Olivia asked.

"Of course you may look, la mia casa 'e la tua casa", Jake replied in Italian.

Olivia opened the refrigerator and grabbed two wine coolers. "Where are we eating?"

"In the media room" Jake replied and tilted his head toward the hallway as he carried a tray and led the way.

Olivia and Harper followed. "You never showed me the media room," she said as they walked downstairs to a level of the house she had not seen.

"I couldn't show all my cards." Jake replied and set the food down. "Make yourself comfortable."

"This is so awesome." Olivia said and took her boots off to cozy up on a large overstuffed sectional.

Jake grabbed the remote and turned on the movie. Then he reached over and twisted the cap off of Olivia's wine cooler for her.

He did it almost mindlessly but that kind of chivalry was rare. It was a small thing but it spoke volumes. She smiled.

The movie began. Jake had chosen 'Sabrina' with Audrey Hepburn. Olivia laughed. "I love this movie; it's one of my favorites. Did you know that?"

"I did know that." He replied, smiling.

"How"?

"I called Miles. He said you were a sucker for Audrey Hepburn movies."

"That is really sweet, Jake." She had thought he might choose a film he liked. She was surprised and pleased.

They ate and snuggled up together to watch the movie; holding hands like teenagers. Olivia felt so at ease leaning into Jake and holding his hand. There were few things that brought her this feeling of comfort but Jake was definitely one of them.

It wasn't just comfort though; it was something else, too. There was electricity surrounding them when they were together. The feeling was so foreign to Olivia. Everything was new. She guessed this was what most teenagers felt. This was something she should have felt with her first puppy love or, again for her husband. In so many ways, Olivia was a virgin. The feel of Jake's warm body next to hers was powerful. She could have spent the whole night looking at him if she thought he wouldn't have noticed; but he noticed everything.

Jake did notice everything. He noticed the scent in the air that was somehow only Olivia. He noticed the feel of her body curled up next to him. He noticed the change taking place in her; how she seemed more at ease with him, more confident somehow. He noticed the soft skin of her delicate hands and her short, unpolished nails. He noticed the waves of auburn hair falling softly over his arm.

He noticed the same leather bracelet with the phoenix from his dream, staring at him. It willed him to understand her.

With a jolt, Jake noticed something else and the sudden thought scared the shit out of him. He was falling in love with Olivia Curtis. No, not falling; fell. It was too late. He was in love. Suddenly Jake couldn't sit still. It was as if someone had given him too much caffeine.

"Jake is everything alright?" Olivia asked feeling him squirm next to her.

"Yes, yes Darlin' everything's fine." He said as he hopped off the sofa. "I just need to go let Whitman out one more time. You just relax, I'll be right back. Enjoy the rest of the movie." He said, sounding tense and jumpy.

"Did you want me to come? I could take Harper out? Or we could wait just a little bit. The movie is almost over."

"No, no, you enjoy. I'll take Harper out with me. I'll be back before you know it." He said and scooped up Harper off the couch. He practically sprinted out of the room.

Olivia was blindsided. "What the hell just happened?" she thought. It had been so nice between them and now Jake was...she didn't know what he was now.

Olivia could feel the sting of rejection and tears burned at her eyes. "No, no tears." She told herself. She had opened a new chapter. There had been no deep subjects come up. There had been only fun, easy conversation and enjoyment and now suddenly, this.

It was as if Jake had been shoved into a light socket and not in a good way. Olivia tried not to overthink it. She attempted finishing the movie but Sabrina could no longer hold her attention.

"Why did I let my guard down?" she thought. Maybe he wasn't the man she had thought he was. Could Dr. Thompson be right? Maybe Jake was the man from her vision but it didn't mean he would ever love her back. She wished he hadn't taken Harper with him. She should have driven her own car and then she could just go home. "Why didn't I just drive my Jeep?" She thought angrily. She got up, grabbed her things and went in search of him.

Jake was standing out in the yard watching the dogs. His back was to the house. "Damn", he cursed. Whitman came to him as if he'd been called. "No boy, not you. Go do your thing." Jake waved him away. How could this happen?

He knew he liked Olivia Curtis. He really liked her but love? Love he had *not* planned for. Love didn't happen so quickly, did it? He felt so out of control and it was not a feeling he was used to. He wanted to get away, clear his head but how, without her? An indestructible cord had been attached to his heart and it led directly to hers. Maybe getting away *was* what he needed; even if it was only for a little while. He would go see Jess in New York. It was still more than two weeks before Thanksgiving. He had time. "I just need to slow down, that's all. I need to take my time." He said aloud.

"Who are you talking to?" Olivia asked from behind him sounding hurt and formal.

"Oh, uh, just the dogs, that's all." Jake said, surprised.

"I'm ready to go home now Jake. The movie is over." Olivia said, desperately trying to cover her disappointment.

"I'll go start the truck and be right back to help with your bag." He said and started for the driveway.

"No I can manage." She scooped up Harper and followed Jake to the front of the house where they had left his truck. Snow was falling steadily. Flakes stuck to her hair as she opened the passenger door. She refused to wait for him like some kind of helpless thing. She stepped up into the truck and only looked straight ahead as Jake silently cursed himself and went about removing the snow from the windshield.

He hopped in and started it up. "I'm sorry Olivia." Jake said quietly as he drove her home.

"Whatever for"? Olivia asked formally. When she was uncomfortable, she always resorted to cold formality, just like her mother. Jake didn't reply.

Olivia wanted to scream at him. She was so frustrated and confused. It was like a switch had been flipped in Jake but she'd be damned if she was going to wait around to see if it flipped again. Jake wouldn't get another shot. She couldn't let herself get hurt again. She couldn't. She would not fall in love.

Even if it felt as though he were deciding for her; Jake would be the one thing about her future she would change and then with any luck, everything would change. She had been right to want to put on the brakes and now he was making it easy for her. He would be safe and maybe she would finally stop seeing the future.

They pulled up to Olivia's place and she hopped out of the truck with dog and bag in hand before Jake could get around to her door.

She left him standing by the front of his truck.

"Goodnight Jake" she said from over her shoulder, not making eye contact.

Jake came around and shut the truck door she had left wide open and replied, "Goodnight Olivia". What else could he say? He was feeling overwhelmed and confused. He knew he had hurt her feelings but he had to figure out his own first.

CHAPTER SIXTEEN

The next morning Olivia woke feeling like she'd been run over by a train. She had not really slept much at all and the sleep she did get was riddled with nightmares. She was exhausted and irritable. There was no making sense of the change in Jake. Things had been so perfect and then suddenly, completely awful.

She sat at her kitchen table drinking her favorite coffee. But even coffee wasn't helping her mood this morning. She stared into her cup looking for answers and finding only more questions. "I need a job. I won't sit here without a life, waiting for him or anyone else to rescue me or figure this out for me." She said loudly.

Quickly she showered, dressed, and dug out a copy of her resume'. "Now, where to apply"? She thought. She picked up her phone, paused, took a deep breath and then dialed.

Sam picked up on the second ring. "Hello?"

"Hi Sam, its Olivia"

"Oh hi, what's up? Oh God, you aren't cancelling are you? I told all the girls you were coming."

"No I'm not cancelling. I'm actually calling to see if you had any suggestions for me."

"Suggestions?"

"Yeah, I need to find another job. I'm wondering if you know of anyone who is hiring. I know it's a small town but I'd really like to stay nearby."

"Well Jake knows everyone; he would probably be the person to ask."

"I, uh, no, I don't want to bother him with this."

"Ok, well I do know of one person who might be looking for some help but I don't know if you'd be interested. What happened at the diner, if I can ask?"

"Um," Olivia hesitated, then blurted out, "I overslept and got fired. I'm so embarrassed."

"Dan's such a dick. I bet he'd take you back if you spoke to him." Sam suggested.

"No, I don't think I'm ready to do that. It wasn't quite the right fit for me anyway."

"His loss." Sam wanted more detail, but Olivia didn't sound right. "So what's the job?

I'll do anything, but I need to stay busy." Olivia admitted.

"There's a little music and dance studio looking for a piano teacher. The place is called Tempo."

"I don't have teaching credentials."

"I doubt that would be a problem. It's privately owned by a really great lady named Denise. I'm pretty sure she doesn't care about credentials as long as you can play. Anyhow, it's worth a shot. You should go talk to her." Sam assured her.

"Ok. Ok, I will."

"I'll text you the phone number and address."

"Thank you Sam."

"You're welcome. Hey how was your date last night? I got the weirdest message from Jake this morning." Sam asked nosily.

"Well, it didn't go so well." Olivia replied sadly. She felt the burn of unshed tears and felt like someone had slugged her in the gut.

"Why, what happened?" Sam said, immediately on the defensive. It was obvious Olivia was upset.

"Honestly, I don't know. I thought we were having a great time and then suddenly it was...different. Jake was different. I don't know."

Sam was confused. "He left a message on my phone saying he was boarding the jet for New York. It was really early this morning. I wasn't up yet and he hasn't answered my calls since."

"He's gone?" Olivia asked, feeling sick to her stomach.

"Yeah, didn't he tell you? He said he was going to be gone about a week and he would check in about business when he landed. I'm supposed to call his cell phone or his sister's house if I need him." Sam explained, feeling like the bearer of bad news.

"No, he didn't tell me." Olivia said quietly. So Jake was gone. Jake was gone and she remained. Apparently, it was the story of her life; getting left. People left her for dead. People died. People left. It was a recurring theme.

"Olivia, are you ok? I'm sorry about this. I thought he would have told you. Did you have a fight?"

"No. Listen, I appreciate the help, more than you know. I have to go." Olivia said quickly.

"Ok, I'm really sorry. Call me if you want to talk." Sam offered.

"Bye."

Sam hung up the phone and immediately dialed another number.

"What the hell is going on, Jake?" She nearly shouted into the phone.

"Hello to you too, Sam" Jake replied sarcastically.

"Don't give me that shit. I just got off the phone with Olivia. She sounds like someone kicked her in the stomach with size eleven boots. Would those be your size elevens by chance? What did you do? What did you do?" she asked accusingly.

"You spoke to Olivia?" Jake's heart jumped into his throat.

"Yes I spoke to her. She didn't even know you were gone. What the hell happened? I thought things were going so well and you *know* normally I would be on your side, except she sounds truly wrecked." Sam was frustrated.

"What does it matter? I thought you warned me not to get involved with her?" Jake said defensively.

"Sure Jake, blame this one on me." Sam replied angrily.

"Sam it's none of your business, alright? I can't talk about it right now. Just call me at Jessica's if you have any *work* problems." Jake replied and hung up on her.

He couldn't face it. He couldn't face Sam and he definitely couldn't face what he was feeling...not yet. He couldn't be in Montana right now. He hoped Jessica could help him clear his head or at least distract him. She was always good at that.

He arrived at Jessica's apartment and her doorman, recognizing him, opened the complex door. Jess was working. Jake wasn't sure if he was glad to be alone or not. He sat near the window overlooking the city, not really seeing the view. Thoughts of Olivia filled his head. He missed her already. He wondered why she called Sam. He was tempted to call Sam back but instead paced a path in Jessica's living room carpet. He knew he should get his laptop out and get some work done but there was no point. He couldn't focus on work; not right now.

Jessica Brooke Weidner was a force to be reckoned with. There wasn't a person alive who intimidated her and she too was used to getting what she wanted. Her only major flaw was her addiction to bad boys. She knew Jake wanted to try and protect her from those situations but she couldn't help herself.

Jess was slender, like her mother with refined features; though she shared her brother's olive skin tone. Lately, she wore her hair in a short angled bob but it was always black. She was exotic and beautiful. She almost looked 'not of this world'.

She had been blessed with her father's crystal blue eyes; it gave her softness. She wasn't in a relationship right now and her work was going well so she wasn't sure why her brother found it necessary to come back to New York again so soon. She detested being checked up on like a child.

She walked into her apartment, looking stylish and suspicious. Jake was sitting on the sofa with his elbows on his knees. He looked like a pathetic version of The Thinker.

"Hey Jakey, to what do I owe the honor…again?"

Jake stood up to greet his sister with kisses on both cheeks. "I just thought I'd come visit. Is that a crime?"

"No but you look pretty well strung out and you were just here recently so I'm forced to ask; 'what's up'?"

"Nothing."

"Is it work?"

"No."

"I'm going to go change my clothes and we'll go have a drink at the most fabulous jazz bar you've ever seen. Then, you can tell me what's going on and cut the bullshit." She said as only she could.

Jake scowled at her but nodded.

When they arrived at the bar and were seated, Jess began again with the twenty questions. "What's really going on Jakey?"

"Maybe I should order a drink first."

They both ordered drinks and Jake took some big gulps of his beer.

"Ok spill it. You wouldn't come all the way here just to visit a month after you were *living here* for a month. Tell me before I'm forced to hire thugs to beat it out of you. Also, Thanksgiving is right around the corner and I'll be home, as instructed, for my obligatory visit so what gives? Talk to me," she commanded, rather unceremoniously.

He leaned forward over his beer and took in a huge breath. "I've met someone. Her name is Olivia," he said with near-reverence. "She moved to Troy while I was here with you."

"Oh, ok, so far this doesn't sound bad. Is she married? Is she an axe murderess?"

"No, nothing like that, thank God. She's wonderful. She's kind, funny, and sensitive. She's beautiful."

"So get to the part that has you looking like a drug addict. What happened?"

"Jess I..." he began with a sigh.

"You what? Jesus, Jakey you're killing me."

"I love her."

"Wow! Wow, really?" Jess giggled a little not really believing him.

"That's all you can say? Yes really? Why? You don't believe me?"

"No" she smirked. "Listen Jake, I love you. I have the best brother on the planet but you are not *that* guy. You don't fall in love. You date, you have sex, you go to great parties, you throw great parties, you wheel and deal and do business and handle things for your crazy family but you do **not** fall in love."

"Yeah, that's what I thought too, but I guess we were both wrong. It hit me like a ton of bricks. I swear to God, it was like lightning striking. She's the one, Jess. I was sitting there next to her and it hit me. And then I freaked out and left town. Holy shit, I'm an asshole!" He said as he rubbed his temples. "The woman I love is in Troy and I just took off to New York without a word. I suck. What is wrong with me?"

"You're not an asshole. You just don't do commitments. Look, you're used to having everything under control and love is something we *can't* control. Trust me, I know. It freaked you out. I get it, I do. You're a newbie, a novice. Freaking out the first time you realize you're in love is pretty normal for someone like you and let me just say, it's about damn time."

"Thanks, that's helpful." He still had an iron grip on both temples.

"What? Do you want me to tell you how wrong you were for leaving? Fine, you were wrong. That is not the bigger picture here. The bigger picture is that you, my commitment-phobic brother, are in love."

"I'm not commitment-phobic, but it is crazy. I must be out of my mind. I mean I knew I liked this girl right from the start but I thought we'd have a little fun and she'd end up hating me like most of the others, but it wasn't like that. This is different."

"Jess, I've always wanted what Mom and Dad have, that kind of spark, respect, you know the whole package. I just didn't think it would ever happen for me. I thought I'd be Jake Weidner, entrepreneur, businessman, terminal bachelor. But now I'm picturing a partnership, a family life. Can you believe that?"

"I'll admit I'm surprised. Over the years, how many of my friends have had the hots for you?

You would charm the pants off them (literally) and then leave them in your wake. Now you're telling me there is a 'someone'...a *one* someone that does it for you? It's hard to believe. Thank God I'm coming home for the holidays. I would hate to miss out on this drama!"

"Huh; yeah." Jake replied, taking another big drink of his beer.

"I have to tell you Jakey; I don't really get why you're here. I mean I heard you; you freaked out but you freaked out and left! If this girl is really that special, then what are you doing *here*?" She put a reassuring hand on his arm and stared directly into his eyes.

"I don't know. I couldn't think. I needed to clear my head." The excuses didn't sound reasonable even to him.

"How's that working for you?" she asked sarcastically.

"It's not. I can't stop thinking about her. I can't seem to clear my head; not even here."

"What are you going to do?"

"I don't know. I really messed things up. I didn't even tell her I was leaving." Jake sighed. "You know, when I first met her, she did not want to get to know me at all. She didn't want to open up and I pushed her. I made her break down some walls and now, when she finally does, what do I do? I leave. I even made her promise not to push me away anymore." Jake said, raking his hands through his hair. "I'm a chicken-shit."

"So are you really afraid to commit?"

"No, I mean; no. I don't know. Maybe I am. She has been through some awful stuff. What if she can't move past it?" Jake explained, rubbing his temples more.

"Jake, all I know is, if it was me, I think I could get through anything with the right guy. And yet here you are, three thousand miles away. Sorry, but you did fuck this up. Maybe I won't be meeting her after all." Jess teased. "I really doubt you're the only one feeling this way. Love isn't created in a vacuum, although sometimes it truly sucks."

"I think I'll just stay here a few days. I need to figure this out." Jake said, barely listening to his sister.

"Or, you could call her, apologize and then buy her some nice jewelry or a designer purse or maybe some great shoes. Shoes always say 'I'm sorry' so nicely. I know that would make *me* feel better." Jess laughed.

"I'm so glad my misery amuses you."

"Oh Jake come on; look on the bright side, you got to see your favorite sister again."

Jake stared into the last of his beer. "You know, I think I will buy her some jewelry but there is only one piece of jewelry that will do." Jake said seriously looking up in a sudden revelation.

Jess nearly fell off her chair. "You're shitting me? Are we talking engagement rings?" She was so enthralled; she didn't even notice the guy actively trying to flirt with her from a nearby table.

"That's precisely what I'm talking about. I won't propose right away. I need to plan this out. Are you up for some shopping tomorrow morning?" Jake smiled suddenly feeling like a weight had been lifted.

"Shopping is my middle name."

CHAPTER SEVENTEEN

Olivia worked up her nerve and called Denise. She found her to be friendly and very excited to meet her. They made an appointment to meet the following day at the music studio.

When she met Denise for the first time, she felt a strange sense of déjà vu. Denise was tall, elegant, and striking but still had warmth about her. She immediately smiled broadly when she saw Olivia. This put her at ease.

"Hello, I'm Olivia Curtis." She said and shook Denise's hand.

"I knew you had to be. Troy *is* a small town after all. I saw you at the diner a few times. I'm so pleased to meet you. I'm Denise Weidner," she said happily.

"Um, Weidner?" Olivia stammered.

"Yes?" she asked and laughed. "Oh, I gather you've met my nephew Jake." Denise smirked. "He's a bit of a rascal; I hope he made a good impression."

"Yes I've met Jake." Olivia replied flatly, unable to stop the sick feeling in her stomach.

"Why?" she thought. "Why couldn't I just have one day where I don't have to think about Jake?"

"Let's go into my office and we'll have a little informal interview, shall we?" Denise suggested.

Olivia nodded and looked around the studio as she followed Denise into her office. Above the piano in the corner of the large room was a poster of a phoenix. She knew it was her fate. This was where she was meant to be, though she couldn't see any darkness that usually colored her fate and had no visions of this place. She prayed it would stay that way.

After they sat down, Denise began to explain, "I hold numerous classes here at the studio including various dance and music lessons as well as voice lessons but I'm short a piano player. I would prefer someone willing to teach as well. My last pianist was also the organist from my church but she passed, poor thing."

"Oh I'm so sorry."

"Don't be, dear, she was as old as the hills. It was her time."

Olivia let a giggle escape and looked nervously at Denise who laughed out loud.

"I'm afraid I have no experience teaching but I play quite well." Olivia straightened in her seat.

"Would you be comfortable giving me a demonstration?" Denise asked and led Olivia to a piano at the edge of the rehearsal room.

"Yes of course; what would you like to hear? I can play quite a few songs without sheet music or I can grab some from my car. I apologize I didn't bring it in with me." Olivia blushed slightly. She could only imagine the kind of impression she was making on Denise *Weidner*. She couldn't help but see the family resemblance in Jake's aunt.

"That's just fine. You surprise me. I don't believe you would be here if you couldn't read sheet music."

Olivia had always excelled at auditions. Interviews were something altogether different but auditions were like breathing. She began playing Stravinsky's Patruschka for piano. It was one of the more complicated pieces she knew but she could still remember rehearsing it over and over as a teenager. Her piano teacher had been a cruel woman, strict and cold. She reminded Olivia of her mother. No surprise Ms. Ivanov was hand-picked by Olivia's mother.

Denise listened and watched as Olivia played. She could picture the dancers and was captivated by the sound coming from this old piano. She had never had a pianist of Olivia's caliber in her studio before. It was like finding a Monet at a yard sale. Olivia finished the piece and Denise said, "The job is yours if you want it. I would be an idiot not to hire you."

"Thank you; yes, I want it."

"I will have you play for most of the dance classes, especially as we approach performances and at some point I hope I might talk you into teaching piano. It would bring in a lot more business for the studio. People will want their children to learn from you, I can guarantee it."

"I'll consider it, but perhaps only for private lessons at first? I would prefer not to teach group classes yet. I'm honored by this opportunity."

"I'm the one who's honored. You're incredibly talented Olivia. I feel like our humble little studio in Troy just isn't good enough for a pianist of your skill level." Denise admitted.

"Please don't say that. I appreciate the praise, truly but I love Troy and I'm grateful to have a job again."

"Good, then it seems we have a deal. Let's go back into my office and we'll dot some i's and drink some tea." she chuckled.

"Wonderful. I should probably tell you, um, Jake and I sort of had a couple dates. I wouldn't mention it except I don't want you to get the wrong idea about me or make you think I was trying to hide anything; especially since he's your nephew. I can promise you I will conduct myself with professionalism. My private life will not interfere with my work."

Denise put her hand on Olivia's face and smiled. "You worry too much, missy. Has anyone ever told you that? I only had to take one look at you to know my nephew had probably been sniffing around. No offense. Anyhow, I'm not concerned about your professionalism in the least.

Jake is a charmer, he always has been. It wouldn't surprise me if he were outside drooling on the windows as we speak." Denise said lightly.

"I, uh, he and I, well, we aren't *together* or anything. I think he's moved on." Olivia felt the large painful knot roll in her stomach. She swallowed hard, as if it would help.

"He's moved on, huh? Well, I somehow doubt it, but then you are definitely Jake's type. Either way, it's none of my business." Denise clapped her hands together, "None of that matters to me. You are both grown up and you, my dear, play piano like an angel."

"Thank you." Olivia was relieved to have a job and a kindhearted boss but also she felt tense. She hated that Jake had dismissed her so easily. It shouldn't matter to her, either. She had no intention of "coupling up" again. No way. Maybe he would be safe if he stayed far away from her, regardless of how her heart broke over it.

But still, the feeling of rejection lingered like a bad smell in a small space. It just didn't seem possible; after all the emotion passing between them, he would just toss her away. Olivia couldn't make sense of it. There had been two separate visions involving Jake and meeting him was one, but the other one hadn't happened yet. Had *he* changed their fate by walking away? Could it be that simple? Somehow she doubted it.

Denise and Olivia spent the next half hour discussing business. She was relieved to take her mind off Jake and the future.

The next day was Thursday, her first day on her new job. Olivia enjoyed it so much she found herself smiling several times during the day. It was another new experience for her. She was especially happy when she was able to play for a toddler ballet class. They were sweet little round-faced cherubs in pink tutus.

This was a completely new feeling. Apparently Olivia had a biological clock and it was ticking. She subconsciously put her hand to her tummy. She leaned against the doorway and began to daydream about a dark haired little girl of her own taking dance class from Aunt Denise. Suddenly she felt the desire to slap herself. "Oh Olivia, you are losing it. You know that won't happen."

****

Jake and Jessica spent the day in all the best jewelry stores New York had to offer but he finally settled on Tiffany's. Olivia loved Audrey Hepburn movies after all. Jess was starting to lose patience with her usually very decisive brother. He had somehow let this whole thing turn him into a teenage girl in search of the perfect prom dress.

"Jake, seriously, I like both of those. I also liked the last five you had me look at. I've never known you to be such an indecisive nut bag. Pick the one *you* like the best; out of those two and then let's go. I want to go *shoe* shopping." Jess whined. "I'll even buy her some glass slippers to go with this fairy tale of yours, just move it. I'm bored."

"You're only bored because this isn't about you. Jess, this is serious. This is the ring I'm going to propose with. This is the ring my wife will wear forever. It has to be right. It has to be perfect. I'm pretty sure the shoes aren't going anywhere."

"Ha! Says you! You obviously haven't been shoe shopping in Manhattan then." Jess sighed. "Fine, but honestly I don't see you going through with this. You haven't even introduced her to Mom and Dad yet."

Jessica continued listing reasons why Jake wouldn't propose. "You haven't even met *her* parents; they could be crazy and then all bets are off. You do **not** want to end up with crazy in-laws. Besides, you left her and took off for New York without a word. What makes you think she isn't just going to tell you to pack sand?"

"I don't know. She could be really angry at me but I have to try. I didn't feel good about anything until I decided to propose. I know I haven't called her and I haven't fixed this mess with her but I will. Somehow, I will. I have to. I'm nervous about it but it feels right. Doesn't that prove it's different this time?" Jake asked holding up a two carat princess cut diamond ring.

"No, it only proves that you have horrible taste in jewelry. Princess cut? Really Jake?"

"I'm not talking about the ring; I'm talking about this feeling I have about her, about us." Jake said, wishing Sam was here instead of Jess, though they both had the same acerbic wit.

"Jakey, all I'm saying is you might want to patch things up first, *and then* buy the ring." Jess said, holding a pricey diamond necklace up to her throat. "You know I love you but you're a playboy. You always have been. The only difference is, instead of sticking around to see how much pain you caused by dumping some poor girl, you took off. That doesn't exactly scream, "Buy an engagement ring". But I'm not you and I haven't even met this girl; so maybe it is different." Jess admitted skeptically.

"Maybe you and I should just catch up later at the apartment." Jake suggested, wishing that killing ones' own sister wasn't a crime.

"No, no I'm sorry. You tell me this is the girl for you, I believe you. I want you to be happy Jakey, you deserve it. Maybe it would be easier picking out a ring if you told me something about her." Jessica suggested, hugging her brother around his neck.

Jake sighed. "The first time I saw her, it took my breath away. I mean literally, she took my breath away. I know how that sounds, believe me, but it really did. And it's not just the way she looks but the way she carries herself, the way she speaks. She reminds me of a bird in flight, graceful and elegant."

The young female clerk behind the counter leaned in to listen with a dreamy look on her face, her elbows on the glass case.

"Olivia is classic, like she was born in the wrong era. She's a bit stubborn but, she has a voice like melted butter and when she stands in the snow, I'm certain an angel fell from the sky. I go from wanting to kiss her to wanting to shake her in an instant. She has a smile that lights up the room and a temper too but it flames out as quickly as it appeared; and when I hold her, I feel like I found the missing part of me."

Jessica had goose bumps listening to her brother. He was right, this *was* different.

The girl behind the counter grabbed a tissue and dabbed her eyes. "That was just about the sweetest thing I've ever heard." She pulled a ring box out and opened it, and showed it to Jake. "There *is* this one, it's called Legacy. It has graduated side stones and its three point seven carats."

Jake could have kissed the girl. "Yes. That's the one. It's perfect. *That* is Olivia's ring. Thank you."

Jess put her hands to her suddenly flushed cheeks and laughed, "Jakey, you really *are* in love."

"I know; scary huh?" He smiled, holding the ring up in the light.

"No, I'm happy for you. Now, let's wrap it up so we can go buy my shoes. I'm thinking red Louboutin's for the holidays. Speaking of which, aren't you hosting the New Year's Eve Ball this year? I usually get my invite by now."

"Yes, I have your invitation. I wasn't going to send you one this year." Jake teased.

"Why ever not?" She asked, mock pouting.

"Because, every year I'm forced to wade through a ton of texts and emails with pictures of you in different gowns. I was hoping to avoid it this year. Don't you have girlfriends for that; or Mom?"

"I'll have you know I send those out to you *and* Mom *and* some of my girlfriends." She replied haughtily.

"Well how about this year you just surprise me, huh?"

"Fine, if you feel the need to go and mess with tradition." Jess said and smiled.

Jake chuckled. He couldn't help but be proud of his sister; she was resilient and hardworking and always the life of any party.

He purchased the ring and then indulged Jess with some retail therapy. When they arrived back at her apartment, Jake went into the guest bedroom and took the ring out of the box. He held it up and thought of Olivia. He could picture her wearing it, showing it off proudly.

He still hadn't called her. It was gnawing at him. It had been almost two days. "Grow some balls" he told himself aloud and began dialing Olivia's number. It rang and rang and then finally her voicemail message began.

"You've reached Olivia Curtis Montgomery. I'm unable to take your call at this time. If you would please leave a message; I'll return your call just as soon as I'm able."

Jake silently cursed. "Olivia, this is Jake. Please call me. I'm in New York staying at my sister's apartment. I'll be back to Troy soon but please, please call me. We need to talk." Jake said, not caring about the desperation that colored his voice.

He lay on the bed and stared at his cell phone; willing Olivia to call him. "Come on darlin', call me" he said to the silent phone.

After her first day of work Olivia felt better. Playing piano, meeting some wonderful people and seeing the children made her feel brighter, lifting her mood. She hadn't known it was possible but she'd found her place. Now, if only she could stop herself from thinking about Jake. But just like thinking about her son, some things were unavoidable. She had allowed herself to be vulnerable, to lean on Jake and tell him things. She let her guard down and now she was let down. Knowing he was gone left Olivia feeling empty. Tomorrow night she was supposed to go out with Jake's best friend and have a girl's night. She considered cancelling but she liked Sam and didn't want to hurt her feelings. And perhaps it was just what she needed to lift her spirits. She hoped it would.

Back at her apartment, she finally checked her phone. Listening to the message from Jake; she was hurt, angry, but also relieved. He sounded upset. She was glad to hear his voice but wanted to kick herself for feeling this way. She needed to let him go. He was gone, so why couldn't she let him be gone? She bit her lip and stared at the phone.

"I don't know what to do." She said aloud to Harper, who whined at her feet. She knelt and picked up her dog. She took a deep breath and dialed Jake's number.

Jake answered before the end of the first ring. "Hello? Olivia, is that you?"

"Yes, it's me. I saw you called." She said flatly.

"Oh God, Olivia," Jake sighed, nearly crying out, "I'm so sorry. I don't have an excuse for leaving like I did. I know I upset you."

"No, you didn't. I'm fine. I mean I get it now. At least now, I know how you really feel. I just wish you would have left me alone when I asked you. I gave you plenty of chances to leave. Either way, you left, so, it's done. You owe me nothing. Let's just call it what it is...a very brief acquaintance that has no future." She knew it to be a lie as soon as she said it especially if her vision was to be believed.

"Olivia no; that's not it at all. You've got it all wrong. I didn't leave because I don't care for you. I left because I do. Please give me a chance to explain this in person. I'll be home tomorrow."

"There's nothing to explain. You're off the hook. I wish you the best. Goodbye, Jake." Olivia hung up without waiting for him to reply.

"SHIT!! SHIT!! SHIT!!" Jake yelled loudly.

Jessica came running in. "What's wrong?"

"Nothing! Everything! Shit, maybe you were right. I've screwed this up too badly to repair it."

"I'm right about a lot of things but I seriously doubt I was right about that. Just go home tomorrow and make it right. Nothing ever gets fixed over the phone; you know that. If you want this girl, then make it happen. You're Jacob Weidner, golden boy of Troy, Montana. Go fix it. Take that big rock home and go get your girl." Jess encouraged.

"I wish it were that simple. This isn't a business deal I can negotiate, this is a person, the flesh and blood woman I love and I broke her heart. Damn it." Jake moaned sadly, his eyes filling with tears.

Olivia stood in her kitchen crying. She wanted so badly to call Jake back and tell him she'd lied. She wanted to go to him, kiss him and make him see he'd done nothing wrong. Who was she, to be angry about running away? How could she blame Jake for that when she had done it herself or tried to over and over again?

Harper began to whine, too. Olivia and Harper sounded like a pathetic duet of sadness. She slid down the cabinets to the floor sobbing.

She wasn't lying about letting Jake off the hook. That part she had really meant. She didn't feel worthy of him and there was still the question of whether she could protect him by letting him go. He did make her feel better and *that* she didn't deserve, no matter what anyone said.

Jake Weidner's life wasn't a mess like hers. He didn't carry around this huge burden of grief and tragedy. He came from a good family, not *just* a family with money. He had easiness, a kindness, and a generosity of spirit about him. She never had that and didn't feel worthy of it now.

Olivia felt sick, her stomach churned. Her head was deciding to let Jake go and it was physically making her sick. She could hardly believe how close she had come to knowing real love and now it was gone, or she'd turned it away. She knew deep down no matter how much therapy, no matter how great the man; she didn't deserve to feel better.

Slowly she pulled herself off the floor, shut off her phone, locked the door, set her alarm and went to bed. She crawled under the covers with her clothes on, needing the comfort of the fabric and the weight of the material. She slept, not caring that it was barely four in the afternoon on a Thursday. If not for her new job she would sleep forever.

"Livi, you have to stop this! You could not have known that Dante' would die in a car accident! You can't see the future!" Miles shouted angrily.

"Yes I can, Miles, only I can't stop it! I didn't know it was going to be in a car accident but I knew he was going to die and I couldn't do anything to stop it! I can't stop what's coming! Don't you see? Don't you believe me?" Olivia raved.

"No, I love you Liv but no, I don't believe you. The doctors all say it's your imagination, that it's part of the delusions. I think they're right, Liv. I'm sorry."

CHAPTER EIGHTEEN

The plane trip home had never taken so long. Jake hadn't enjoyed it and even though there was an engagement ring in his pocket, things were far from ideal. He was fairly certain Jessica was glad to be rid of him. He'd been a man on edge and he remained so. He called Olivia repeatedly, more times than he could count but her phone went instantly to voicemail. He was irritable, tense and wanted nothing more than to find her and make this right.

He couldn't just hop in his truck and go find her. He thought it might scare her off and *that* he didn't want; besides, Carmella would be waiting for him. He was certain Jess had probably sent out a press release about him by now so his whole family likely knew what was going on. Also, he needed to shower, shave and figure out the best way to approach Olivia now.

When he arrived at the ranch it was nearly lunch time. He dropped his bag in the foyer and went to find Carmella. He was surprised she wasn't waiting at the door for him. He heard a familiar voice in the kitchen along with Carmella's, both speaking Italian.

"Ciao Mama" Jake said, when he saw his mom in the kitchen.

"Ciao ragazzo dolce" Frankie replied. She had always called Jake her 'sweet boy'. He kissed his mom and greeted Carmella. These ladies had planned their attack, it was obvious. It was only a matter of time. "What are you doing here mama?" Jake asked "...as if I even need to ask. Did Jessica call you?"

"Of course she did and I can't believe I have to hear about my son's life from my daughter. We were heading this way for Thanksgiving so I told your papa we needed to come back earlier than planned. I'm surprised at you Jacob. Why don't you tell me these things? Have you lost my number?" Frankie asked.

"No, of course not. I'm just not ready to talk about it." Jake replied, feeling like a twelve year old answering to his mother.

"Can we at least see the ring, Jacob?" Carmella added.

"Sure, why not?" He pulled the ring box out of his coat pocket and placed it on the counter in front of the two women. He should have known this was coming but he was so distracted.

Frankie and Carmella opened the box with reverence. Sounds of approval found Jake's ears as he collapsed into a chair by the window.

It had snowed quite a bit while he'd been gone. He wondered how Olivia was getting around in it. He wondered if she was wearing his coat, if she was staying warm enough in her apartment. He stared out the window and daydreamed about her, picturing a snowball fight or making a snowman, maybe another horseback ride. He smiled. He could picture a smile on her face and them together coming in to cozy-up by the fire with warm drinks in their hands.

"Jacob!" Frankie yelled, interrupting his daydream. "Did you hear me?"

"No Mama, what?" He was irritated, frustrated and tired, propping his head up on his hands.

"Let's go into the study. We need to have a talk." Frankie said, grabbing her cappuccino and striding out of the kitchen, expecting Jake to follow. "Excuse us please, Carmella."

Jake was left with little choice. He gave Carmella a look of desperation but she just smiled at him and said, "She's worried about you. It's a mother's right to fuss over her children. Go talk with her."

Jake barely sat down in an overstuffed chair when Frankie began. "You can't marry this girl, Jacob. You can't. You haven't even met her family. We have not met her *or* her family. You don't know her well enough to marry her." She said with finality.

"Mama, I love you but I am thirty four years old. I'm fairly certain I'm old enough to decide who I want to marry. And I *do* know her. I know enough. I know I can't breathe without her. I know when I'm with her, everything is better, I'm better. I feel whole when I'm with her and when I'm not, I'm empty." He rested his head on the back of the chair and let out a long sigh.

Frankie waited as Jake continued, "She is kind, loving, beautiful and extraordinary. I screwed up with her by going to New York like I did and what's worse, I don't even know if she'll forgive me. I've messed up this entire deal, but I know you have to meet her. I know you and the family will love her. I wasn't going to propose right away. I want to meet her family and do all the right things, Mama. I want to ask for her father's permission. I do. Give me some credit." Jake said seriously, emotionally.

Frankie sat on the arm of his chair and put her hand on her son's cheek, smiled and said, "You are in love with Olivia aren't you mi dolce? It is Olivia isn't it?"

"Yes Mama, her name is Olivia Curtis. Why must you test me this way?" Jake asked.

"I have no idea what you mean. But you do have my blessing." She smiled, kissed her son's cheek and left the room. Jake smiled too. His mom always pushed him; it seemed to be her way of finding where his heart was.

He went to his room to clean up. After his shower he realized he had missed several calls. He scrolled through quickly hoping Olivia had called. She hadn't. Sam had called several times though so Jake called her back.

"Hello," Sam answered on the first ring.

"Hey Sam; listen, I'm sorry about before. I haven't been myself, I guess."

"It's ok Jake. I was rude. I know whatever happened between you and Olivia isn't my business. I felt so badly for her. She sounded really upset."

"Sam, you're my best friend, I can't expect you aren't going to wonder what's going on. Do you happen to know where she is now?"

"Yeah she's at work and then we're having girl's night tonight at Max's."

"Work? Did she get her old job back at the diner?"

"No she got a new job, with um..."

"With whom? Where?"

"She got a job with your Aunt Denise at Tempo. I sort of suggested it to her."

"That's wonderful. I can't believe I didn't think of it."

"Yeah, it's great. I spoke to her this morning and she said she really likes it."

"Maybe I should go see her there. I need to see her."

"You mean you want to go to her *new* job, with *your* aunt and patch up this fight you're having? Yeah, great idea, Jake! Seriously, get a grip. You can't just go busting in there like some knight on a white horse, trust me."

"I know but I have to make this right. I need to see her."

"You know I would **NEVER** suggest this to anyone else, but since it's you...maybe you should just *happen* to be at the bar tonight."

"Really?"

"Yes, just give her a chance to relax, let loose a little, have a few drinks and *then* talk to her. Be there about nine; just don't come any earlier than that. She needs to unwind first. I hope you have a nice fat apology planned because I'm telling you, she was really hurt, especially after she found out you left town."

"Yeah, well who told her I left town? Thanks a lot by the way."

"Hey, that is *so* not my fault. You're the jerk who flew off to New York without so much as a 'see you later baby'."

"I know; you're right. So I'll see you about nine, that way I can take a disco nap. I'm beat. I don't think I've slept in three days." Jake complained. "Did you know my parents are in town?"

"No, when did they get here?"

"Today I guess. Jess called them and they decided they needed to check up on me I think."

"What for"?

"Well...while I was in New York, I uh, I bought a ring."

"Whoa. What?"

"I'm going to ask Olivia to marry me?"

The phone was silent. Jake started to wonder if the news had killed her. "Sam?"

"Yeah, I'm still here; I think I just took an acid trip. Did I hear you say you're going to propose to Olivia?"

"Yes, I mean, not now...later."

"Uh, congratulations I guess."

"Don't congratulate me yet. First, I have to figure out how to get her to forgive me. I left her. I left the woman I love. I'm a dumb shit, now, I'm afraid she'll never trust me again."

"I think she will. Trust takes time. She'll forgive you because it's not like she's perfect either Jake."

"She's perfect for me."

"Ok lover boy, I get it. I'll see you tonight."

"See ya" He enjoyed making Sam uncomfortable with love talk. He knew it didn't really bother her.

Jake lay back on his bed in only a towel. He thought about Olivia in the studio playing piano. It made him happy. He considered calling Aunt Denise but thought better of it. He called the flower shop and had several arrangements sent to Olivia's house and then drifted off to sleep.

After work Olivia felt a little better though she was still tense and a bit distracted. She tried not to think about Jake but the more she tried, the harder it seemed. The family resemblance between Jake and his Aunt Denise made it especially difficult. When she arrived home there were flowers spilling over her front porch. The single card attached to a long stemmed red rose said, "Please forgive me". Olivia thought she should throw them in the dumpster but instead she brought them inside and filled her petite kitchen table with them. She smiled in spite of herself. They were the prettiest things in the apartment.

Later, after her shower, Olivia stood in front of her newly reorganized and now somewhat overstuffed closet. She had forced herself to unpack most of the clothes she'd left in boxes for far too long, but the closet in this tiny duplex was nothing compared to the huge walk-in at her prior home. She had beautiful clothes but she didn't have the first clue what to wear to a 'girl's night out' in small town Montana. She just didn't know.

There was a knock on her door. Harper barked and Olivia jumped. "Harper, hush." Olivia wrapped her robe tighter around herself and said a silent prayer that it wasn't Jake.

She looked through the peephole. She opened the door and said, "Either you're early, or I'm late."

Sam smiled. "I'm early. We have plenty of time. I thought we would get ready together. You don't mind, do you?"

"No, not at all. I'm relieved actually. Please come in."

"Great." Sam lugged a large duffel bag over her shoulder.

"Are you staying the night too?" Olivia teased.

"You never know, but actually this is supplies."

"Supplies?" Olivia repeated as Sam made herself at home and began digging through the bag.

"Supplies; clothes, shoes, make up, purses, liquor and even condoms. You never know." Sam laughed.

"You come prepared." Olivia giggled. "I was just trying to decide what to wear tonight. Maybe you could help me?"

"Sure. We've all decided to dress up a little. Sadly, it's not often we get a night on the town like this so point me to your closet. Let's see what we have to work with."

They stood in front of the open closet door. "Holy shit Liv. This is crazy. Look at all these designer clothes. You've been holding out on me, girlfriend."

Olivia shrugged as Sam rummaged through her closet.

"It's all so beautiful but do you have anything...sexy?"

"I doubt it. I don't know. Maybe I shouldn't go."

"You're going, if I have to sew an outfit for you, drug you and play puppeteer all night. You are going. I think it's exactly what you need. They have a DJ on Friday nights. We'll drink, we'll dance; we'll totally let our hair down."

"Ok, you're right." Olivia sighed. "So what do you think? Does anything have potential in there or is it a beautifully hopeless closet?"

"Well what's this?" Sam asked pulling a garment bag out of the back of the closet.

"I can't remember. Open it up."

Sam pulled out a layered ruffled mini dress in a pretty champagne color. It had a deep plunging, beaded neckline. "I just found your outfit." Sam gushed.

"Oh wow. I forgot I still had that. I bought it years ago to wear to an anniversary dinner with my husband but he didn't like it. He said it was 'inappropriate for a mother and wife of a prominent lawyer to wear.'"

"Well I say bullshit to that. This is gorgeous and sexy. Here try it on." Sam shoved it at Olivia and pushed her into the bathroom.

Olivia closed the door and Sam could hear her fretting about it. "What is it Liv?"

"This is so short and so low cut. I can't wear it. Maybe Jackson was right."

"No he wasn't. He was probably just scared everyone would start hitting on his wife. Most men are wickedly insecure. I'm holding out for a guy who is proud when other men look at me. Come out and let me see."

Olivia opened the door just a crack. "You should probably see the whole ensemble then. There are light grey boots that go with this dress." Olivia replied, smiling at Sam's bluntness.

"Man, Liv, you have a lot of shoes. I thought I had a lot, but this puts my collection to shame." Sam said, digging through the pile of boxes. "I can't find the ones you mean."

"They might be in the spare room closet. I just saw them when I was unpacking boxes. They have dark grey suede straps that wrap around the ankles."

Sam crossed the living room and rummaged in a few boxes. "Ok, found them. Whew, I know where I'm coming if I ever need to borrow an outfit."

Sam said and handed the boots to Olivia's waiting hand through the bathroom door.

"You're welcome to raid my wardrobe whenever you like. So what are *you* wearing?" Olivia asked, pulling on her boots and giving herself one last look in the mirror. "Please tell me you're wearing a dress, too."

"I am. Don't worry about me; just come out so I can see how *inappropriate* you look."

"Ok." Olivia took a deep breath and opened the door.

"Did I say 'inappropriate'? I meant to say,' HOT'. Olivia you look incredible. You have to wear that dress. It's amazing. You have to. Your husband was wrong sweetie. Now go finish your makeup and I'll get dressed."

Olivia smiled broadly, "Thank you Sam. That means a lot to me. I never allow myself to feel *sexy*."

"You're a woman; it's your God given right to feel sexy. It came with the creation of lipstick. Besides, if God didn't want women to feel sexy then he'd have given us udders instead of boobs."

Olivia burst into laughter, she was grateful she hadn't put on her mascara. When she did finally finish her makeup she came back out of the bathroom but didn't see Sam.

"Sam?"

"Yeah, I'm in the kitchen. I see Jake's been on the phone with the flower shop." Sam commented looking at the overflow on the table.

"I don't want to talk about it."

"That's ok, me either. I'm all ready and Ali and Cash should be here pretty soon. Let's have a little pre-party cocktail before they get here. I've got drinks ready."

"Sam, you look gorgeous, that is a beautiful dress." She was wearing a midnight blue one-shoulder sparkler with matching leather stiletto booties.

"Thank you. I've always liked this." Sam smiled and held out a drink.

"What are we drinking?"

"Sea Breeze, I hope you like them. I probably should have asked."

"I do like them. Thank you."

The evening with the girls was much more fun and relaxing than Olivia had anticipated. Dinner was filled with laughter and talk of men, mostly.

All the girls wanted details about Jake but Olivia changed the subject quickly. She felt the sting of regret at the mention of his name. Sam helped her out by suggesting another round of drinks.

Olivia was beginning to relax again and really enjoy herself. The multitude of cocktails helped tremendously. The food and the company were both excellent. She had friends back in Oregon but they were always so caught up in gossip and keeping up with each other's latest purchases that they never really knew how to be 'friends'. This was different. These women really cared for each other. They weren't competing for men, or money, or prestige; they were just friends. Olivia made the group five.

Alison, everyone called her Ali, was bubbly, fun and a mother of two, though Olivia couldn't tell to look at her. She was married to Cash since college and they were still madly in love, so it seemed.

Kate was very pretty, petite, single, and loving it. She taught first grade but cussed like a sailor. Olivia liked her right away. She and Sam had been friends since grade school.

Gwen, who was very quiet and reserved, was a beauty in her own right but not in an obvious way. She worked as the librarian in town. Olivia thought if she wore glasses, it would complete the picture.

Cash drove the girls to Max's Bar at around eight thirty. Olivia was already buzzed from the drinks with dinner. This was nice; she wasn't drunk, just chilled ever so slightly. It felt good to 'let her hair down' as Sam had said. Olivia hadn't expected so many people to be at the bar. She felt a twinge of nervousness but followed the rest of her group to a booth. Everyone seemed to watch them enter, as if they were celebrities or something. Olivia found it amusing. "Should I go order drinks?"

"No" they all said in unison. Sam explained. "Someone will buy us a round. Trust me."

"So we're waiting for men to buy us drinks?" Olivia asked trying not to sound prudish.

"Liv, don't look so shocked. It's a small town and most of these boys are happy to have a little eye candy on a Friday night." Kate answered.

"Yeah, but it's not like we can't buy ourselves a drink." Olivia countered.

"We can, but it's like...um, chivalry. They *want* to." Ali explained.

Gwen added, "They want to because they think they're going to get in our pants. Let's be honest."

Olivia laughed along with the rest of the girls.

"Let's dance!" Sam suggested, "We can get our drink on later."

Olivia followed as the girls all made their way to the dance floor. It was so much fun. She was having a blast. The music was loud and pulsing and it was easy to get lost in the moment. They came back to the booth, giggling and excited and a little breathless when Ben Thompson approached their table. A slow song was playing now and the mood in the bar changed.

"Hello, Olivia. Would you like to dance?"

"Oh, um, hi, sure" Olivia felt instantly uncomfortable. This was her therapist but then she reminded herself that this was also a 'small town' and at least he wasn't a stranger.

"Have fun Liv" Sam said and watched as Jake came through the front door. He stood near the doorway his eyes like lasers on Olivia.

"Oh shit; I hope you girls are ready to see some action." Sam said as Jake walked up to Ben and tapped him on the shoulder.

"What are you talking about?" Ali asked, turning in her seat to where Sam was looking.

"Jake is here and Olivia is dancing with Ben." Sam explained to the others.

"Excuse me, may I cut in?" Jake asked politely.

Jake was seething on the inside to see Olivia in the arms of Ben Thompson. It was one thing to hear Olivia saw Ben in a professional setting; it was a whole other feeling to see her dancing with him. It was too intimate.

"Sorry Jake, but you'll have to find someone else to dance with tonight." Ben replied and twirled Olivia around and away.

At the sound of Jake's voice Olivia's insides felt like jelly. She was awash with different emotions; relief, anger, irritation, joy, regret, and pain like a knife stabbing into her gut. It all jumbled inside her and all she could do was look up at him with big eyes. No words came.

Jake ignored Ben's snarky reply. "Olivia, will you honor me with the next slow dance?"

For less than a breath Olivia considered saying, 'no' but she'd seen that same look in Jake's eyes the night Billy was in her apartment and she had no interest in watching him tear Ben apart.

"Sure." She said as Ben scowled and Jake headed off to the bar.

"You two *really* don't like each other much, do you?" Olivia observed.

"I don't want to talk about Jake Weidner. I don't want to *talk* at all." Ben said and kissed her roughly on the mouth.

Olivia was taken by surprise but then leaned back and pushed Ben away by the shoulders. "Ben, this isn't right. This isn't going to work." She could smell the liquor on his breath.

"Of course it is." Ben disagreed. "We would be great together, Olivia. I could be everything you need. I know I'm crossing a line here but I know we have something. I know you've felt it, too." He had completely lost his professional manner.

"Ben, you've been drinking. This isn't the time. Let's put this behind us and move on. Thank you for the dance." Olivia said and began to walk away but Ben grabbed her by the wrist.

Jake had seen enough. He tried not to watch but he couldn't help himself. He moved quickly grabbing Ben by the scruff of the neck. "I believe your dance is over. Let the lady go, Ben." Jake said roughly.

Ben released Olivia's wrist. She rushed back to the booth and sat down.

Sam went over to Ben and Jake to deal with the idiocy. "Jake, let's go order another round of drinks? Ben, if you ever grab one of my friends again, I'll make sure you're walking with a limp! Do we understand each other?"

"Oh that's nice Jake; having a woman fighting your battles for you." Ben goaded.

Jake pulled back to take a swing at Ben but Sam pulled him away toward the bar.

"Shit Jake, why don't you just write him a check. He'd love nothing more than for you to hit him so he can sue your dumb ass for assault. Come on, use your head. Jeez!" Sam scolded.

"I know, I know but he pushes my buttons. He **kissed** Olivia and grabbed her like some piece of meat. You saw it, for God's sake! I won't stand for that, even if *she* will." Jake replied angrily leaning his elbows on the bar.

"Nor should you when she is your wife or hell, even your girlfriend but as it stands, she is neither, and you come off looking like a jealous asshole. All she knows right now is you took off on her. Perhaps instead of fighting with her therapist, you should buy us some drinks and then dance with the girl. Just try and remember to be a gentleman. She's a little fragile right now. Look at her; she'd probably be in tears if it wasn't for all these drinks. She is *supposed* to be having fun tonight. Let her have some fun, ok?"

"Ok, ok, you're right; you're right. What are you girls drinking? It's my treat. I'll take care of the bar tab tonight." Jake offered. "Hey Matt, put all the girls drinks on my tab tonight, ok?"

"Sure thing, Jake" The bartender replied.

"Thank you Jake." Sam smiled and patted his cheek. She walked back to the table and sat next to Olivia. "Are you ok, Liv?"

"I don't know. I could have handled Ben; I just don't want them to fight." Olivia remarked looking toward Jake still standing at the bar.

"Hell, those two have been fighting since they were kids; this is nothing new. Jake feels badly for overstepping his bounds, just give him a chance. He wasn't trying to upset you." Sam defended her best friend, whom she knew was in love.

"Sam, Jake and I aren't going to work out." Olivia said quietly. "I'm not mad at him but he'll be better off without me. He deserves better. It turns out I'm not the right girl for Jake Weidner."

"Good luck convincing *him* of that." Sam smiled as Jake approached the booth with a tray of drinks.

"Thanks Jake, you'll make somebody a good husband someday," Ali teased and winked at Olivia.

Olivia looked like she might throw up but attempted a smile anyhow. She glanced up at Jake.

He looked better than she remembered. She wished she could just tell him to piss off and forget about him but she couldn't. There was tension in him, like a bowstring being pulled back for a shot. The muscles in his arms flexed through his shirt. Olivia yearned to touch him.

"Olivia, would you care for that dance now?" Jake asked sweetly, holding out his hand. Another slow song was playing.

"Ok", Olivia replied without thinking. She reached for his hand and again she felt their electricity. It was physical, palpable.

They moved out to the dance floor and she was close enough Jake could taste her. For him, they were the only two people in the world.

Olivia looked up at him and sighed, biting her lower lip nervously. They swayed to the music and he held her close, securely. No matter what else was said or done, in that moment she never wanted to be apart from him again.

Jake had practiced and planned what he would say when he saw her but now he had no words. She was stunning. She was as beautiful as he had ever seen her. Her dress showed off every curve and had him imagining intimacies between them.

Her hair was curled and fell in soft waves down her back. He loved the feel of it brushing lightly over his arms.

"Olivia", he said finally. "What can I do to make this right? Please, tell me what I can do. I'm in misery."

"I don't want to talk about this. Not here, not now."

"Then when?" He said, rather petulantly.

"I don't know. I shouldn't have agreed to a dance. It's over Jake, it has to be. I will only cause you pain." Olivia couldn't believe the words coming out of her mouth. She held back a sob, pushing away from him, running to the door and out into the freezing winter night. She stood in the parking lot trying to catch her breath and stop the tears from falling.

"Damn. Damn. **DAMN!**" She yelled, not caring who heard her. She stomped her feet like a child throwing a tantrum.

Jake grabbed his coat and followed her out into the parking lot. Olivia stood with her back to the front door, her face in her hands. He could tell she was crying. He gently laid his coat on her shoulders and started to reach around to hold her but she cried louder and spun around. She backed away from him, the coat landing on the ground between them.

"Don't Jake! You don't get it! You have to be sensible. You have to see! You aren't safe with me!" Olivia said, backing away and pointing at him like the accused in a trial.

"Darlin' I don't understand. I know you're mad at me for leaving. I would be mad too, but I made a mistake. I was just so surprised at how I was feeling, shocked really and I panicked. But my feelings for you haven't changed. What is it you think I don't see?"

"You-you-you," she cried, "you have to..."

"What Darlin'? What is it?"

She continued to point at him as if she was frozen that way. He reached out slowly for her hand.

"No. No. Don't touch me! I can't think when you touch me. Don't touch me!" She said, finally lowering her hand and crossing her arms around her body for warmth.

"Alright, alright" Jake said soothingly as if trying to tame a wild animal.

She wasn't far from it. She was beautiful, wild, and scared. He didn't think she had any idea the power she held over men, over him. She couldn't know how powerful she was in this moment.

Jake asked softly, "Please, talk to me Darlin'. Tell me what you're feeling. What don't I get? What do you mean I'm not safe with you?"

Olivia shivered, both from the tension and the cold. She didn't want to say it. She thought if she said it, it became truer; somehow more real. She needed to tell him the truth and set him free. She needed him to believe her but he wouldn't. She needed to protect him but she couldn't let him go.

"Don't call me 'darling'. I'm not good enough for you. You deserve better. You have to believe me. Please believe me." It was all she could think to say.

"I *don't* believe that. I didn't believe it when I left and I don't believe it now. Why don't you let me be the judge? Olivia, I love you. Don't you see that?" He reached for her, his arms aching to hold her.

She blinked, shook her head and pushed him back. "You can't Jake. You can do better. Bad things are going to happen to you, if you're with me." Her voice was strained and raspy. "You can't love me."

"But I do. There is no one better for me than you. I love you. You, Olivia Curtis are the love of my life. You can't,,,won't change my heart."

"I'm trying to change your fate." She argued quietly. Olivia couldn't look him in the eyes. She continued to shiver and look at the ground. She was afraid of possibly seeing doubt in his eyes.

This time Jake came closer but didn't try to hold her. "Olivia, look at me, please."

"No." she sniffed, tears still falling heavily. "I can't trust it, Jake. I'm afraid to want it. I'm afraid of wanting you. I can't watch you get hurt."

"I know Darlin' but you won't hurt me."

"No you don't, you don't know."

"Then tell me," he tilted her chin up so she was forced to look at him. Her eyes still filled with tears.

"I'm afraid of...loving you. You'll be hurt."

That was all it took. They kissed passionately in the still cold air, and new snow began to fall. The kiss felt like medicine for all the wounds between them. Jake wrapped his arms around her, trying to keep her as warm as possible but he was all the warmth she wanted. She couldn't believe she had worked so hard to pass up this feeling.

She couldn't believe she had tried to throw it all away again, when she knew there was no way to change what would happen to him. "I must truly be a masochist." She Thought.

They didn't' care about the time, or the people passing by, or the falling snow. They kissed like it was the first time. He felt so good to her. She didn't want this moment to end but her body betrayed her and she shivered again.

"Darlin' we need to get you inside where it's warm." He took her hand and she leaned into him as they walked. Jake picked up his coat off the ground.

"Jake?" she stopped, just before the door.

"Yes Darlin?"

"I do love you."

"I love you, too." Jake felt relief and joy. He'd really been in misery being away from her. This was better. This new hopeful feeling replaced the sickness he'd felt in New York. He hated knowing he had hurt her. He vowed to himself never to do it again.

They walked inside and Sam eagerly approached. "Is everything ok with you two?" she asked.

They looked at each other and nodded.

"That's good. So, Liv are you staying or are you two taking off?"

"Oh well, um," she looked at Jake unsure of how to answer. She wanted to stay but she wanted to be with him, too.

"Darlin' I'm all yours. If you want to stay, then we'll stay." Jake said and kissed her on the forehead.

"Maybe for a bit?" She asked, hoping not to make him angry. She was so accustomed to Jackson's reactions to everything; but then Jackson wouldn't have let her go out on girl's night in the first place.

"That sounds great. I've always wanted to see what girl's night is all about." Jake teased and leaned down to kiss her in earnest on the mouth. Suddenly drinking and dancing was holding far less appeal but Jake set her down, smacked her on the ass and said, "Go have some fun."

Olivia giggled as Sam grabbed her hand. They went back out to the dance floor while Jake made his way to their empty booth. He sat back and watched as Olivia danced and laughed with her new friends. As much as he desired to take her home, he knew she needed to have some fun with other women. He was lost in thought when Ben nearly stumbled into the table.

"You always get whatever the fuck you want, don'tcha Jake? Wait until that girl gets a front row seat to *your* bullshit. She's going to get dragged through the mud and then she'll see. You won't be able to buy your way outta this one, you piece of shit." Ben slurred his words. He was obviously drunk. He slammed his fist down on the table.

"Why Ben Thompson, if I didn't know any better, I'd say you were jealous. How about you go home and sleep it off?" Jake replied sarcastically.

"And leave you alone with all these fine women? I don't think so. Olivia deserves to know what a lowdown piece of shit you are." Ben spit on the floor.

"Olivia is a smart lady. I don't think you give her enough credit. Besides Ben, you've had plenty of opportunity to enlighten her about my character, or lack thereof, and you haven't. What's holding you back, man? Is it that you have no earthly reason for hating me the way you do or that you know she'll choose me anyway? Can't handle the competition can you, Ben? What's new? You never could!" Jake stood up as he raised his voice. His fists ached to make contact with Ben's face.

"What's going on here?" Olivia asked as she stepped in front of Jake facing Ben. Jake put his hand on her arm protectively. The two men were practically nose to nose. Olivia felt like the middle of a very angry sandwich. She pushed hard on Ben's chest and he stumbled backward. He looked at her in confusion.

"Olivia, there is so much you don't know about him. I'm trying to help you." Ben wailed.

"Ben, I know you think that's true but this is not the time or the place. You can't help anyone tonight."

Olivia tried to appease him and she stepped forward, laying her hand, gently this time, on his chest. Ben put his hand over the top of hers.

"Please, couldn't we go and talk about this, just you and I?" Ben lifted her hand to his lips and she pulled away.

"No, Ben. We will talk, but not tonight. I'm not trying to hurt you but I think the conversation we need to have should take place when we're both clear-headed. You know this." Olivia said, feeling very little of the happy buzz she'd had earlier.

"Fine maybe you're right." Ben replied but pulled Olivia toward him and kissed her on the mouth again.

"Stop it." Olivia said, and stepped back into Jake's arms.

"Ben, you've crossed the line." Jake said angrily, grateful he had his wits about him tonight.

"You don't even know her and she certainly doesn't know you! Go to hell, Jake!"

"After you, Ben" Jake growled.

Ben scowled at him but finally made his way to the door. Olivia turned in Jake's arms and looked up at him. "You **will** tell me what this is about," she demanded.

"Yes Darlin', but not tonight." Jake kissed her sweetly on the cheek.

"I think I've had enough 'fun' for one night. Would you mind just taking me home?"

"I'm sorry. I never wanted to ruin this for you," he said sincerely.

"You didn't ruin it. I mean, it definitely could have been better but I am happy you're here." She stretched up to kiss him.

She liked how tall he was. There was comfort in it and it made her feel so feminine. She loved kissing him. This was right where she was meant to be; when she stopped fighting her feelings. She curved her body around him, desiring nothing more than to be as close as possible to this man she loved. She would figure out how to keep him safe later. She had to.

Jake's response was instant and primal. He would no longer deny the feelings he had for her. He wouldn't refuse. His hands explored her back and tangled in her hair. Again, they were lost in their desire for each other.

"Hey guys, I like a good porno as much as the next girl but you might want to tone it down a bit since we're in public." Sam said teasingly.

They barely relaxed their hold on each other. Jake smiled and Olivia blushed.

"Sorry" Jake said. "I think I'll be taking this lady home now." Olivia nodded in agreement, and leaned her head against his strong chest. The small intimacy renewed Jake's passion but he thought better of making love to Olivia in the middle of Max's.

"Thank you for tonight, Sam. It was so nice to meet everyone." Olivia turned to hug Sam.

"It was my pleasure. You *are* coming next time, too." Sam replied. "I think we should do it more often."

They said their goodbyes to the rest of the girls and walked out to Jake's truck.

"Where would you like to go Darlin'?" He asked as they sat in the truck waiting for it to warm up. Olivia was seated as close as possible to Jake. It seemed so cliché to her, but being far away from him again was out of the question.

"Your place," she said quietly and maneuvered herself onto his lap. She kissed his neck and earlobe and ran her fingers through his hair. He gently pulled her face back to his to kiss her mouth. His teeth finding her lower lip and biting it, pulling and sucking on it. She moaned slightly.

The windows were fogged up and the defroster had difficulty keeping up. Jake's hands moved down and he could feel the delicate lace of her panties. He wanted her so badly and apparently, the feeling was mutual.

"Jake" Olivia said breathlessly, "We should probably take this someplace more private."

"Yes we probably should" he said raggedly and kissed her neck again before she could scoot off his lap.

She remained close, eager to wrap herself up in him, in every sense of the word. She was intoxicated by the feel of him, that warm, earthy scent of him, the sound of his deep voice, and the escape from reality she knew was coming.

She realized she had lied. It wasn't just that she couldn't think when he touched her; it was that she couldn't think when he was around at all. His voice, calling her 'darlin'; it made her tingly all over just to think of it. She loved this man, in a way she had never known.

"Darlin', Jake said, interrupting her fantasy. "Maybe we should just go to your apartment."

"I thought you hated my apartment."

"I don't hate anything of yours. Uh, see, my parents are in town and I'm not sure if they're at the ranch or not."

"Oh, oh I thought you said they stayed at your Grandpa's house when they were in town."

"Usually, but they aren't exactly predictable. I didn't even know they were here in town until this afternoon."

"You don't want me to meet them?" Olivia asked, feeling fresh butterflies in her stomach.

"I *do* want you to meet them, very much. I just want some alone time with you. And, it's the middle of the night."

"That's a good point and I have been drinking and you came close to a fight."

"Close only counts in horseshoes and hand grenades Darlin'" Jake replied, teasingly. "So, you're place then?"

"Yes, my place." She agreed. She realized there was a part of her that worried about going back to the ranch anyway.

They pulled into her driveway parking behind her Jeep. They hadn't been very far away and Olivia was grateful for the short drive. He took her house keys to gallantly open the apartment door, but twisting the knob, realized she had left again without locking it.

Harper barked until she realized it was Olivia and Jake, and then put herself back to bed.

"For the sake of your safety and my sanity will you please start locking your door when you leave?" He asked and didn't wait for a reply. He pulled her through the doorway, pushed it shut with his foot and began kissing her again.

He knelt down and her hands moved naturally to his shoulders. She needed to steady herself. He kissed her bare legs as he unzipped her boots and pulled them off. She shivered slightly from excitement and nervousness though she didn't want him to stop. He continued kissing through her dress and reached to pull down her panties. A blissful, helpless sound escaped her lips. Her hands were in his hair, on his face, his shoulders. She felt as though she wasn't in her own body at all. She had lost control and she didn't care.

He worked his way back up, holding her waist, kissing her everywhere, over the top of the dress, her hands, her arms, her shoulders. He reached around to unzip the beautiful slip of a dress and slid it down. It fell in a silky heap at her feet. Her bra was all that remained. He unhooked the clasp and kissed the exposed taut flesh of her breasts, one at a time, slowly, passionately. He kicked his boots off while still covering her with kisses.

She pulled the shirt over his head and tossed it aside. With only his jeans left between them, he stood to his full height and picked her up effortlessly. She wrapped her legs around his body.

They continued to kiss as he walked them to her closed bedroom door. Jake shoved the door open with a foot and laid Olivia down gently on the bed. He turned on the bedside lamp and removed his jeans and underwear. Olivia reached for him, not wanting any distance between them. She sighed as he rolled on top of her. He kissed the thrilled skin of her body and she did the same, covering him in kisses and nibbles.

He was unreal, exotic and sexy. His body was so perfectly chiseled; it was hard to believe this was happening.

His long, powerful muscles tensed and flexed as he moved over her. The anticipation was excruciating. Olivia's body responded in kind. There was nothing between them but sweat slicked skin and the intensity of the passion they felt for each other. Her hot breathy words in his ear drove him closer to the edge. He needed to be inside her, to fill her with himself. The need was so great he thought it might burn them both.

"I love you, Darlin'" and he pushed the full length of his manhood inside her. She gasped and cried out in blissful oblivion. He moved in perfect rhythm with her body. She gripped the strong muscles of his back.

Further and further, they pushed each other closer and closer to the edge. The flames of passion licked at their skin, every cell was burning with intensity. There was nothing between them but this beautiful love. There was no one else.

Olivia screamed his name as the passion overtook her again and again. Strangely, a tear slid down her face as he released himself inside her. "I love you, Jake" she gasped breathlessly.

They lay tangled together for some time as their hearts slowed, and their breathing returned to normal. Jake stroked the soft skin of her thigh. There was such peace between them now.

Olivia felt like rejoicing, or crying or both. Sex had never felt like this before. She'd finally experienced what it was to be truly loved, to be filled and she vowed she would never settle for less; not ever again.

They slept. They slept like two people who'd been searching for each other forever. All of her bad dreams were kept at bay.

Saturday morning Olivia woke with her head resting heavily on Jake's chest. She lifted it and he stirred, pulling her back to him almost out of reflex.

He yawned, "what's your hurry Darlin'?" He asked and stretched.

She sat up slightly and smiled. "Eleven o'clock isn't exactly hurrying." She looked at her clock on the bedside table.

Jake chuckled. "No, I guess it isn't."

"Now what?" she sat up fully and suddenly was feeling self-conscious. She pulled a blanket up around her.

"You don't have to be shy around me Darlin'" Jake said smiling.

Olivia ignored him, unsure of even how to respond. She waited for him to say something.   "Alright, alright, I vote we stay in bed all day. I have no wish or need to go anywhere.

It's Saturday." He reached to pull her back down on top of him. She gave in but still propped herself up so she could look at him.

"We really have a lot to talk about." She said insistently, though her determination was waning as he kissed the inside of her forearm.

"Mmm hmm" he moaned.

That was all it took. Her resolve was gone. She had planned to tell him how different everything felt. She wanted to explain the shock she felt at her own desires and that finally she was no longer a virgin. She was going to be wordy and tell him how much had changed so quickly but instead her body wanted him; it was all consuming.

They made love again with the same intensity as before but with less urgency. They took their time, relaxing into each other, exploring each other more completely. Finding they had an easy physical chemistry was like a gift.

Their bodies moved as if only one heart beat between them.

Later, much later, they cooked some eggs and ate them in Olivia's bed. They laughed and talked and neither brought up anything serious.

But then Jake remembered, "Darlin', my family always gets together at Thanksgiving. It's quite a big deal. Have you thought about your plans for the holiday?"

"Not really, no. I wasn't planning on celebrating the holidays at all." She squirmed uncomfortably.

"Well, I thought since my parents are here and my sister will be here, you might join us. I would like you to be part of my family's tradition." He said hopefully.

"Jake, I don't think it's a good idea. I mean, a lot has changed in a very short time but it doesn't seem right for me to take part with your family, when I don't even do that with *mine*."

This was just what Jake had hoped she'd say, "Then by all means, let's invite your family, too."

Olivia had been railroaded. She immediately tried to backpedal. "I doubt they'd even come. I mean Miles might but my parents, I don't know." She thought of her mother. "This would be coming from so far out in left field. I don't, I don't, I haven't spoken to them in so long." Olivia sighed deeply.

"All the more reason they'll be glad to hear from you." Jake assured her.

"You just don't get it." She said, shaking her head and rubbing her temples.

"What Olivia? What don't I get now?" Jake asked, beginning to sound irritated.

"I'm sorry, I shouldn't have said that. My mother and I have a very difficult relationship. I'm afraid it would ruin a perfectly lovely Thanksgiving dinner. I'm already nervous about meeting your family. I don't think we need to have any added stress, do you?"

"Darlin', I come from a very close knit family and I promise you they would love nothing more than to have you all join us. It might be good for your parents to see how well you're doing. They should see how happy you are."

"Jake, I am happy but it's a lot of pressure."

"Don't think of it as pressure. It's a holiday, a family holiday. It's supposed to be fun. You asked me last night if I was embarrassed to introduce you to my parents. Obviously I'm not. In fact, maybe we should go see them now, today. That way when you come on Thanksgiving, it won't be awkward for you. Then, all that's left is for you to invite your family."

"You're determined to have your own way, aren't you?" She didn't know how to take in all these changes so suddenly.

"Yes and you'll find I usually get what I want." He answered and smiled that same irresistibly charming smile.

"Oh what must that be like?" She noted, sarcastically.

"It's pretty great actually."

She took a deep breath. He lifted her hand to his lips and kissed each finger individually. She wanted to be irritated with him but found it nearly impossible. "Fine" She sighed heavily. "But I can't meet your parents looking like this."

"Then go get that sexy body of yours in the shower." He said playfully.

"No" she said, "Not unless you're joining me."

"You don't have to tell me twice." He laughed.

CHAPTER NINETEEN

Later in the afternoon, they finally got on their way to Jake's parents' house. Jake had made some calls to find out where they would be and asked his mom to make sure Dad would stay put.

Every time Dacey Weidner came to Troy, he was hard to track down. He would check out the local businesses, check up on how Jake was running things and he spent a lot of his time on the ranch with the hands who worked for the Weidner family.

Olivia commented on the way to the historical Weidner family home. "So your dad's name is Dacey? That's an unusual name. I like it, I've just never heard it before."

"Yeah, Dacey is a Gaelic name. I'm Italian, *and* Irish. Sort of strange combination I guess."

"Jake, I'm nervous." Olivia admitted resting her hand on his thigh.

"I know, but I promise you, they won't bite. They are going to love you. I love you. Trust me?" He asked and squeezed her hand gently.

She nodded, "I love you too. It's the only reason I'm doing this." She forced a smile.

"Does it make you feel better that I'll be just as nervous about meeting your parents?"

"No, it doesn't. I doubt you'll be nervous at all. I wouldn't even mind if you didn't meet them. In fact, I prefer you didn't. My mother is crazy, you know." Olivia continued, only half-joking. "I think she might have some dead bodies in the trunk of her Mercedes. It might be safer if you didn't meet them."

Jake just laughed. "Darlin' I get it. I do. I understand this is not something you're looking forward to but it's important to me. You are important to me. I feel like the most important people in my life should meet each other."

Olivia let out a deep breath but said nothing. She knew she was being ridiculous but this was all so overwhelming. Yesterday morning she was nursing a broken heart and today she was meeting her lover's parents. So much for taking it slowly; it seemed her life, the future, everything was now on fast forward. Though she sat next to Jake in the truck, she continued staring out the side window. There was still so much they didn't know about each other but it didn't seem to matter. They would figure it out together.

They pulled up to the house and to her it looked like a Christmas card. Fresh snow covered the roof and yard. She could imagine standing in front of it for a picture on a holiday greeting.

"What are you thinking about?" Jake asked, looking over at her.

"Nothing" she replied, but he made a face. "I'll tell you later, ok?" she said as they walked up to the door.

"Ok" he smiled and knocked on the heavy oak door.

The sound felt like nails being hammered into her coffin but she tried to look calm. Jake squeezed her hand again as Frankie opened the door.

"Ciao, ragazzo dolce, come in, come in. It's freezing outside. Your Papa is in the kitchen probably taste-testing all the food I made."

"Ciao, Mama. Allow me to introduce Olivia Curtis. Olivia, this is my mother, Francesca Weidner."

They stepped through the doorway and Frankie kissed Olivia on both cheeks.

"Ciao, Olivia, our Carmella was right, you are *very* beautiful. My boy has good taste, ah?" Frankie said and patted Jake on the cheek.

Olivia smiled, "Thank you, that's very kind of you. It's a pleasure to meet you, Mrs. Weidner."

"Please call me Frankie, everybody does."

"Ok" Olivia said feeling awkward.

"Let's go in the den and save the food from my husband." Frankie yelled down the hallway, "Dacey, get out of that artichoke dip and come meet Olivia."

Dacey Weidner walked out of the kitchen to greet them all in the den. Olivia was astounded at the resemblance between Jake and his father. The only noticeable differences were the streaks of silver highlighting his dad's hair and the fact that Jake had darker skin. She stood next to Jake.

"Olivia, I'm Dacey Weidner, Jake's dad. It is Olivia, isn't it?" he asked, looking at Jake.

"Yes, this is Olivia Curtis." Jake said proudly.

"Well Olivia, it's an honor to meet you. I must say this is a happy surprise. Jake never introduces us to anyone. I think he must be ashamed of us." Dacey teased.

"Papa, that isn't true, you know it's not." Jake made a face at his father who just grinned.

"Let's sit down and get to know each other better.

Frankie made some incredible artichoke dip." Dacey smiled as Frankie lightly smacked him on the shoulder.

"Might there be any left, mi amore'?" Frankie teased.

"Oh there's a bit. Do you want me to go get it, luce mia?" Dacey said lovingly.

"Yes would you?"

"I'll help you, Papa." Jake offered.

The two women were left alone to face each other in the den. Olivia was more nervous than ever as she looked to Frankie.

"Olivia, tell me about yourself. My Jacob didn't really tell us much but then we haven't been in town for quite some time."

"Well, I'm, uh, I'm from Oregon originally. I moved here about a month and a half ago and I uh..." Olivia didn't really know what else to say.

Frankie leaned forward and put her hand on Olivia's knee. "Bella ragazza, you have nothing to fear. Jacob loves you."

Something about the way she said it made Olivia want to cry. Here was her mother's polar opposite, trying to put her at ease. "Thank you. I love him, too. I can imagine what you must be thinking though. This is all so new and we know so little about each other." Olivia admitted.

Frankie nodded and gave her a knowing smile. "Sometimes what you feel is a lot more important than what you know. The knowing comes in time."

Jake and Dacey returned from the kitchen at that moment carrying trays of food and drinks. Jake looked questioningly at Olivia. She smiled but said nothing as he sat down next to her.

"So Dad was telling me you've been in Victoria, British Columbia? What on earth for?" Jake asked his mother.

"It's beautiful for one. We've been there for a while; didn't you get my emails? I sent you pictures. In October we went on an amazing whale watching tour. The photos I took were unbelievable. There is some interest from a local shop in purchasing some of them." Frankie said proudly.

"Wow, I guess I should check my emails more often."

"Victoria is quite a place. I'm looking into some real estate there." Dacey added.

"For private use or is this a business deal?" Jake asked.

Olivia watched Jake's eyes light up. He was obviously dedicated to his family's business.

"Both, if everything goes as planned. There are several small businesses I'm looking into and I think it would be a nice place to have a vacation home. It could prove to be very lucrative. I've been running the numbers with Tom and I called Paige about a home there. She has a few appointments lined up for us after the holidays. You'll need to be there too, Jake."

"How about P&L's and tax returns, do we have any of that yet? Any tours of the businesses set up?" Jake prompted.

"Do Olivia and I need to be here for this, or shall we come back later when you too are done discussing business?" Frankie scolded her two men.

"Sorry, Mama. Olivia, my apologies." Jake offered.

"Yes Olivia, I'm sorry, Frankie is right, this isn't the time for business." Dacey patted his wife's knee. "So what brings you to Troy?"

Jake rolled his eyes. "Dad!"

"What? What did I say?" Dacey looked at his son.

"It's fine." Olivia interjected. "I moved here from Lake Oswego, Oregon. I needed a change though it was chance that brought me to Troy. I had an appointment in Spokane and afterward, I went for a long drive. I sort of ended up here. I really feel lucky; Troy is a great place to live." Olivia said sincerely.

This was news to Jake. He realized then just how little he really knew about her.

"Well, we're glad you're here. I spoke to my sister-in-law Denise. She said you are working at Tempo." Frankie said.

"Yes I am. I play piano for some of the classes. She's encouraging me to start teaching piano, but I'm hesitant."

"Why is that?" Frankie asked.

"I've never taught before. I've been playing since childhood and I went to school for music but I don't have teaching credentials." Olivia explained.

"I think you'd be a wonderful teacher." Jake said enthusiastically.

"I always wanted Jacob and Jessica to play an instrument but neither of them showed much interest." Frankie admitted.

"If I thought I could play as well as Olivia then I might have. She's amazing, Mama." Jake smiled at Olivia.

"Will you play for us at Thanksgiving? You are coming aren't you?" Dacey asked quickly.

"Oh, well, I, uh, I'm not sure yet. I hope to." Olivia suddenly felt very uncomfortable. Not only was she expected at a large family Thanksgiving dinner but now she was expected to be the entertainment as well. It was bad enough Jake wanted her to invite her family. This was shaping up to be a disaster of epic proportion. She could only smile.

"Dacey, her family might be expecting her in Oregon." Frankie said, sensing Olivia's tension.

"No they aren't." Olivia said honestly.

"I suggested to Olivia she invite her family to join *us*." Jake interjected.

"That would be wonderful though you haven't given them much time to think about it Jacob." Frankie said.

"You should offer them the use of the jet." Dacey added.

"That's a great idea." Jake smiled.

Olivia was taken aback. She turned to Jake. "You have a jet?" She couldn't even smile. Jake and his parents had sufficiently railroaded her. What excuse could she use now to not invite her family? She thought if Jake could have waited, then she might have had a chance to do things in the right order. She sat frozen by her thoughts.

Dacey grinned, "Yeah, our family takes a lot of trips. Several years ago we realized we needed a faster means of travel."

"Won't your sister need it?" Olivia asked, thinking desperately how to get out of this mess. The current situation was making her nauseous. She wished she could just have Jake all to herself and not have to share him with *either* of their families. She knew it was selfish but family had become an overwhelming concept since Dante' had died. But then if she were honest, her family had always been overwhelming.

"No, Jess will be here much sooner. What? Monday Mama?" Jake asked.

"Yes, Jessica will be coming on Monday. She wants to stay with you at the ranch of course, Jacob. I don't need to guess why." Frankie replied.

"Why?" Dacey asked, in between more bites.

"Because, vita mia, Jessica is excited to meet Olivia. You know how she is." Frankie explained.

"That's true," Dacey admitted. "Olivia dear, you look like you don't feel well. Are you alright?"

Jake looked at her. She was white as a sheet. "Darlin' what's wrong?" Jake asked looking concerned now.

Olivia leaned into him. She was feeling overwhelmed and should probably eat something but refused to give in to yet another weakness. She straightened up. Jake held her firmly.

"I'm fine really." She protested.

Jake smiled at her. "Ok Darlin', if you're sure."

"I am." Olivia reassured him and placed her hand on his knee. Jake covered it with his.

Frankie and Dacey watched the exchange approvingly. Francesca had always wanted her son to be in love; real love. She felt the rightness of this match. Her son was so loving, so attentive to Olivia. He reminded her of Dacey.

Out of the blue, Dacey asked, "How did you two meet?"

Jake chuckled, "Olivia was working at Maggie's when I got back from New York. I went in for some breakfast and there she was, like an angel. Like an angel who couldn't stand me." He grinned at Olivia.

Olivia blushed, "That is not true. I liked you fine, though you seemed to take pleasure in teasing me."

"I still do." Jake said, laughing again.

The conversation went well into the evening. Dacey and Frankie invited them to stay for dinner but they declined. Jake felt as though Olivia had more than held up her end of the bargain to meet his parents and he looked forward to having her all to himself again.

"Darlin' thank you." Jake said as they stepped up into his truck.

"You don't have to thank me Jake. You have great parents. You are the spitting image of your dad."

"I think I've heard that a couple times." He chuckled. "So what were you thinking about before? You said you were going to tell me later?"

"It's really nothing. I just think this house would make a perfect Christmas card."

He tilted her face up by the chin and kissed her.

"Where are we headed?" Jake asked as they sat in the truck waiting for it to warm up.

"My place, I have to go check on Harper since I don't have a team of people working for me, like some people I know."

"Darlin' I haven't been at home much. Why don't you just come with me out to the ranch? You can stay, bring your dog, bring whatever you want."

"We should just call it a night. I'm pretty tired. Just drop me off at home and I'll come see you tomorrow." Olivia said firmly.

"What's going on?" Jake glanced at her, sounding disappointed.

"Nothing; a lot has happened and I need some down time. You've been away and probably need to get caught up on things as well."

"I won't be able to get any rest or anything accomplished without you." He said as they pulled up to her apartment.

"You won't be able to get anything done with me there, either. It's really ok. It's one night apart."

"We've only had one night together."

"That's not true."

"Why do I feel like there's something else going on here?"

"I have no idea. Maybe it's jetlag." Olivia said bitterly but wished she could take it back.

"That's it, isn't it? You're punishing me for leaving? Olivia please don't pull this passive-aggressive crap on me. Talk to me for real. I'm not leaving until you do."

"I'm not trying to be passive-aggressive but fine, if you must know, I don't want to be at your house right now."

"Why?"

"Because the last time I was there was great, perfect in fact, right up to the point where it all went to shit. I'm sorry but I can't deal with that again, not tonight! I want to be with you, I truly do, and I'm not trying to hurt you but I *can't* be there right now, not feeling the way I do. I need to slow down. I need for *us* to slow down. I hope you can respect that." She opened the pickup door, hopped out not waiting for him and walked up to her front porch.

Jake followed behind her. At her front door he wrapped his arms gently around her and laid his head on top of hers.

"I'm sorry Darlin'. I never meant to hurt you. It's killing me that I did, please give me another chance. It's just a place, just a house. Please come with me. I want to wake up with you tomorrow morning. Nothing feels right without you."

"Oh Jake, I feel the same but there's still so much we haven't talked about. Aren't we doing the **one thing** we said we weren't going to do? Aren't we rushing this? I didn't even tell you about my job. You probably had to hear about it from your aunt. You didn't tell me anything about your trip to New York."

"Actually I heard about your job from Sam."

"Come on!" Olivia said in frustration.

"I hear what you're saying but how can we talk about any of that when we're apart? Come with me. Be with me."

Olivia leaned into him. She let out a deep breath. "Ok, just don't leave me tomorrow! I don't think I can take it."

"Darlin' from now on, I'm not going anywhere unless you're comin' with me." Jake kissed the top of her head.

Inside he helped her pack up a few things, put Harper between them and drove out to the ranch. Olivia told Jake all about her new job on the way then asked, "Will Denise be at the Thanksgiving dinner, too?"

"Yes and my cousin Cameron, her son."

"Oh, I didn't know she had a son."

"That surprises me. Denise likes to talk about three things: music, dance and Cameron."

"Well you can't blame her, can you? I'm sure your mom brags about you all the time, too. She's very proud of you. Both your parents are."

"I hope so. Thank you for coming to meet them. I hope it wasn't too unbearable for you?"

"No but..."

"What?"

"You shouldn't expect a similar experience when you meet *my* mother. I don't know why you had me pack a swimsuit." Olivia said, desperate to change the subject. "I'm not a strong swimmer."

"Then I'll have to make sure you keep to the shallow end." Jake smiled. "Or you can relax in the hot tub."

"Of course there's a hot tub."

"What?"

"I don't think you have any concept of the kind of life you lead Jake; private jets, huge homes, multiple businesses, it's all sort of unreal to me."

"Your father's an investment banker and your mother's a musician. I kind of thought you'd be used to this kind of lifestyle."

"It was completely different than all this. What surprises me is how you act about it. Even with all this *stuff* you still drive a pickup truck. You eat at a diner. You ride horses with western tack on trails through wild mountains; hunt, fish. It, it just doesn't add up."

"Sure it does. It's always been important to my family to keep a level head regardless of how successful we might be."

"Well it's refreshing, that's for sure."

They pulled up to the ranch and Olivia had another strong sense of déjà vu. Harper must have felt Olivia's anxiety because she began to whine softly.

"Does she need to be out for a while?" Jake asked.

"Yeah probably, I'll watch her though."

"Darlin' it's freezing out here, why don't you let me do it?"

"Jake I'm fine. I have a coat on and she'll move along faster for me anyhow."

"Ok. I'll take your things inside."

"Thank you" she said and set the wiggling little dog down on the ground.

"You're welcome. I'd do anything for you." Jake said as he grabbed her case and walked toward the house.

Olivia just needed a minute to get her head together. She had to remind herself the only reason he left was because of his feelings for her. He plainly said as much. Now, she just needed to believe him and trust him.

Dante' would have liked Jake. She knew it. She knew he would have wanted her to open up to someone like Jake and to have a real life. On the other hand, Jackson would have been pissed about Jake. Whether dead or alive, Jackson never wanted Olivia to be happy.

"Come on Harper, go potty baby." She said softly. Jake was right, it was really cold out tonight. Olivia looked around. She could still make out the landscape in the fading light. The mountains were incredible and so was the ranch. It all seemed as though it had sprung from the ground, fated to be here. The outbuilding, the fencing, all of it was so perfect here and in the center of it all, the main house, big and majestic. It gave off an unreal quality like a mirage and although she loved it, she knew it wouldn't last. It couldn't last. Nothing good in *her* life ever did.

Suddenly a vision took over and Olivia could see a woman she didn't know with Ben and Jake. All three were angry and tension filled an unfamiliar room. Jake yelled, "Can we just cut through the bullshit?" Olivia saw herself waiting for something. They were going to tell her something. The news would tear them apart. Jake had a child! Suddenly, Olivia couldn't catch her breath. Who was this woman and why didn't Jake know about his own child? The image faded. She sighed heavily, "Come on, Harper; let's go."

Carmella greeted her in the entry. "Bella ragazza, it's so good to see you again. Jacob has put your things in his room," Carmella said coyly. "And he is in his office. You should make yourself at home. Are you hungry?"

Olivia blushed. "It's good to see you too, Carmella. I'm not hungry, but thank you. I would be perfectly happy sleeping in a different room. I, I don't think Jake meant..."

"The two of you are grown-ups, well, you are at least." Carmella smiled.

Olivia laughed. "Thank you Carmella. Should I leave Jake alone then? I don't want to interrupt his work." Olivia asked, unsure of what to do.

"Darlin' you do whatever you like." Jake said as he wrapped his arms around her.

Olivia gasped and whirled around to smack him on the shoulder. "You scared me."

"It took you long enough out there. I was starting to think you ran away with one of the hands."

"Jacob, stop teasing the poor girl and help her get settled. One would think you've been raised by wolves the way you act. I've left Chicken Kiev in the oven if you're hungry." Carmella said and left Jake and Olivia alone.

Jake was still holding on to her. He rested his chin on the top of her head as he held her. "I'm so glad you're here. I already feel better. What do you want to do?" he asked.

"Honestly, something quiet and relaxing." She confessed.

"I think I can handle that. Would you like to sit in the sauna for a while?"

Olivia shivered, thinking how cold it had been outside and how cozy and warm the sauna sounded. "You have a sauna? What don't you have around here?"

"Someone to share it with" Jake turned her in his arms, kissed each of her cheeks softly and then her mouth savoring it all, the taste of her lips, the feel of her breath. She was heaven to him.

"The sauna then?" he asked before he got carried away.

"That would be perfect." Olivia whispered, still just inches away from his lips and feeling breathless from his kisses.

As they sat in the comforting heat of the sauna, Jake could feel a new mood invading the space, like grey clouds rolling in and threatening rain.

"Jake, I was thinking, after what happened with Ben at the bar, we can't very well have a therapy session with him. I mean, that just wouldn't work." Olivia sighed deeply.

Jake was tempted to laugh. Subtlety was not Olivia's strong suit. He knew he needed to approach this subject with caution. "No, it probably wouldn't be a good idea for you and me to go in there together. I'd still like to hear anything you have to tell me, though."

Olivia sighed again. She wasn't sure if she was relieved or nervous. She wanted to be open with him and really put her cards on the table but to do it,
especially without some help was a daunting prospect.

"Jake, I have so much to say but..."

"You can tell me anything, I promise you that. I love you."

"I love you too..."

"But?" he asked feeling the apprehension and the tension looming.

"But it's hard to know where to start. Will you tell me what happened between you and Ben?"

"Quid pro quo, then?" Jake smiled.

"Yes, I suppose so. I would rather you go first."

"Of course Darlin' let's go shower and change and then we'll talk over dinner. Does that sound fair?"

"Fair." She replied, knowing she would have no appetite until this talk was over. They needed to talk, that's why she had pushed for it but she was terrified of how it might change things between them. And here she was *again* with no car of her own, no means of escape. "You really need to start driving your own car Olivia," she thought.

The dining room, the setting of their first dinner together was dimly lit. Candles flickered on the sideboard. Jake looked terrific. He wore a blue dress shirt and casual jeans. He had given her privacy in the guest bath after the sauna. When she finally was ready he was waiting patiently for her.

Jake stood as she entered and pulled out a chair for her kissing her lightly on the cheek as she was seated. "You look stunning." He whispered in her ear.

"So do you," she smiled at him.

Jake poured them both a glass of white wine and sat down casually, leaning back in his chair watching her over the top of his glass. It looked more like a seduction scene than two people about to have a difficult discussion.

"Why do I feel like this is going to be the Spanish Inquisition?" He smiled.

"I have no idea. You don't have to talk about it." Olivia replied seriously.

"No, I told you I would tell you why Ben and I have a great desire to tear each other's heads off and I'm a man of my word. Though what happened is not something I'm proud of." He took another drink of his wine.

Carmella came in carrying two plates. She had fantastic intuition and knew Jake and Olivia needed their privacy. She set the dinner in front of them and disappeared before they could even say 'thank you'.

Olivia tried to eat. Something needed to help the sick feeling she had in the pit of her stomach. She really wasn't too worried about what Jake was going to say, but was curious to know more. Mostly, she was terrified to tell him her own story. She knew it could destroy any hope of starting a new life.

Jake could see she was waiting for him to talk. "Ben Thompson grew up in Troy, just like Tag and I. The three of us were best friends, inseparable." Jake let out a breath filled with frustration. He wasn't one to regret any of his choices but there wasn't another word for how he felt about what had happened so long ago.

He continued while holding his fork. "We did everything together, all through grade school, junior high and most of high school. I think my mom felt like she had three sons sometimes." Jake smiled but there was little happiness behind it.

"During our junior year of high school a new girl moved to town. Her name was Sarea Scott. Ben fell hard for her right from the start. It's safe to say Sarea was the death-nail in our friendship. They started dating and that's when Ben stopped telling me everything. I couldn't understand it at the time. He became closer with Tag then and I found out it was because Sarea had a crush on me. Actually I guess it was more than a crush."

"Did you have feelings for her?" Olivia asked.

Jake flinched at the question. "I guess I did but no more for her than any other girl back then. Ben would say I pursued her; that I stole her but it really wasn't like that. She, they came to a party and I was there. It was a bonfire outside of town after a big football game. We won. I was the quarterback..." "Of course you were." Olivia teased.

"What does that mean?"

"I just mean you have this hometown hero, star of the football team thing about you, so I guess I'm not surprised."

"Oh, well, I'm no hero. That night I'd been drinking and was feeling *pretty* good. I was still amped about our win and I felt...invincible."

"I can picture it." Olivia said, thinking about what Jake must have been like, so handsome and so cool. It was easy enough to picture, she thought not much had changed.

"There was a crowd of people there and the next thing I knew Sarea was all over me. I didn't stop her. I should have, I knew it but I didn't. We..."

"You had sex." Olivia finished his sentence.

"Yes but it wasn't...ugh." He raked his hand through his hair. "Olivia, this is hard to explain. I guess you could say I was a, a playboy. I was young and stupid and thought I had it all, right up to the moment when Sarea told me she was pregnant."

Olivia sat perfectly still. She didn't look surprised, rather the opposite. She forced her face to move into what might pass as surprise. She didn't trust herself to say anything. Why in her vision did he seem surprised? So far, it didn't make sense.

Jake looked at her. He thought her feelings of disappointment were written on her face. He continued, "I think it was the news of the pregnancy that hurt Ben the most. He might have forgiven me the sex, but a baby, he couldn't."

Olivia needed to tell him but how could she when she knew he wouldn't believe her. "You have a child." She blurted.

"No I don't. That's not the whole story. See, Sarea took it upon herself to have an abortion. She didn't tell me about it until after." Jake replied shamefully.

"I'm sorry Jake. I shouldn't have..." It was useless. He would learn the truth in time and she would be there to watch it tear them apart. And if she'd learned anything from her visions, it would be soon.

"It's ok. I was preparing myself to be a dad. I never asked her about an abortion. I figured I had to pay the piper but she didn't see it that way, I guess. It all happened a really long time ago. Sarea moved away and I'm pretty sure Ben blames me for that, too."

"Do you stay in touch with her?"

"What would be the point? We didn't exactly part on good terms.

The last thing she said to me was 'I ruined her life'. I figured I needed to leave her alone."

"Does she have family here?"

"No, her family moved away together. Her dad worked for my dad. He up and quit and they took off."

"Oh." Olivia replied, trying to process it all. Jake suddenly didn't have much of an appetite either and pushed his plate away.

"You know, there are worse things than unprotected teenage sex, Jake." Olivia said, thinking of her own tragic life.

"Maybe but I do regret what happened. I ruined a great friendship over it."

"I think Ben will forgive you." Olivia said suddenly.

"He won't. He hasn't forgiven me in over sixteen years."

"Well, one thing I know for sure is you can't change your fate, even when you really wish you could."

"What would you change, Darlin'?" he asked before he thought of Dante'.

Olivia shook her head. "So many things."

"I'm sorry. I shouldn't have asked you that. Forgive me?" Jake reached over to hold her hand.

"There's nothing to forgive."

"I love you Olivia."

"I love you, too."

Jake stood up and came around to her other side. He bent down to kiss her and leaned back against the table. "Your turn, Darlin'."

"I still don't know how to start."

"Let's go cozy up together in front of the fire in the library and we'll see where it takes us. No pressure." Jake suggested. He felt relieved knowing her reaction to his past. There was nothing she could say that could bother him now. After all, he already knew about the death of her husband and son. What more could there be?

"That sounds good." She replied trying to keep the apprehension out of her voice.

They carried their wine glasses down the hall.

"You know, I think the library might be my favorite room in your house." Olivia commented.

"Really? That surprises me a little."

"Why are you surprised?"

"I just figured you would say the ballroom or maybe the white room."

"They're both beautiful but the library is perfection. I love the tall ceilings, the books, the smell, the huge fireplace. It's like something out of a storybook, you know, magical. I like the warmth of it and it's more like you than the rest of the house. I mean, um, it's all so pretty, it's just..."

Jake chuckled as she sat down and he started to light a fire. "Just another similarity between my dad and me. Mom designed this room specifically with him in mind."

"Don't they miss it? All the work and passion they put into designing a home the way they wanted it then they just leave to travel around; I don't get it."

"Honestly, I don't think they do miss it. For one thing, they're here a lot more than you realize and two, they never seem to care where they are as long as they're together. There isn't a board, a brick or a painting on the wall that means more to them than each other."

Olivia smiled but said nothing. It was hard to imagine a love like that. She began to feel like maybe, just maybe, it was possible but was so scared of trusting it especially now before he knew just how badly she'd been burned.

He sat down beside her. She kicked off her shoes and curled her legs underneath her. Jake held her hand and looked into her eyes. They glowed like emeralds in the firelight. If he thought she would let him he would forget about all the things unsaid and make love to her right now but her face held the fear and the anticipation of a dark secret, unshared.

She began, "When I was very young, I was placed in lots of classes. There was an army of people to shape me into exactly what my mother wanted me to be."

"Which was?" Jake asked.

"A prodigy. I took dance, art, music of all kinds. You name it; I was forced to do it. I was also enrolled in equestrian classes. They were my favorite, even though it was all about competition, I loved being with my horse. His name was Maestro. It was always the best part of my week but at the same time, I was taking piano and of course, cello, like my mother. I began to refuse. I didn't like the expectation of playing the cello." Olivia explained thoughtfully.

"I stayed with the piano though and it became my mother's leverage. One day out of the blue she pulled me out of equestrian lessons and sold Maestro. She told her friends it was because of my particular skill at the piano.

She told them she was afraid I would hurt my fingers but never explained a thing to me. What she did say was 'it was not my decision to make and I would do as I was told or I would never see my horse again'. She'd planned all along I would never see him again and I didn't. Everything changed after that."

Jake could picture a young piano virtuoso heartbroken over losing her horse. It made him sad and angry. He wondered what kind of a mother could do that to her child. It was still evident how much she cared for her horse.

"Anyway, one day," she continued. "I was supposed to go to a polo match with Miles after school but being the rebellious and angry teenager I was, I couldn't go and watch other people with their horses."

Jake could understand that. It was hard to watch other people getting what you wanted.

Olivia looked up as if she was hoping to find solace somewhere in the room or stop the shimmer of tears that suddenly glinted in her eyes. "I was home alone when the doorbell rang." Olivia took a breath. "It was a guy from my neighborhood and he asked to use our phone." Olivia looked at Jake expectantly, willing him to fill in the blanks but knowing he couldn't.

"You know, back when most phones still had cords?"

Jake could suddenly feel where this story was going either by the sound in Olivia's voice or his basic intuition.

"...he, uh, he took, he took, um," she took another deep breath. "He took the phone and ripped it out of the wall." She bit her lip and braved a look at Jake. He was obviously beside himself. It was the same look of horror everyone had when they heard her story. She wished it ended there.

He squeezed her hand and tried to pull her closer but she stopped him.

"Jake I can't. Just let me tell you and then if you still want to hold me..."

"Ok, ok." Jake said feeling helpless and violent toward a nameless faceless man. He was overcome with anger but sat very still holding her hand gently.

"He tied me up. He beat me and cut me with a knife and he, he, um, he..." Olivia willed herself not to cry. Jake had seen too many of her tears already.

"He tied me up with the telephone cord. Right there in my own house." She let out a deep agonizing breath and then cleared her throat.

"And then...he raped me." She whispered unable to say it any louder.

Jake's eyes welled up with tears, anger and shared pain spilling over. Olivia had to look away.

"Jake, I'm sorry." She reached up and put a hand to his cheek.

"Oh my God, Olivia don't, please. Stop telling me you're sorry for shit you didn't do. I'm angry for you! I'm hurt for you! You have nothing to apologize for." Jake sniffed. "I'm so sorry that happened to you, Baby."

"There's more." She said, feeling spent but knowing she couldn't stop there. "He set the kitchen on fire around me and left me for dead, broken and bleeding and I um, I got pregnant. He was Dante's biological father."

Jake was stunned. He could barely breathe let alone process this whole incomprehensible story. "Darlin' I don't know what to say." His raspy voice was barely audible.

"Most people don't understand it, couldn't understand it. I just felt like all of my choices had been taken away with that one violent act and I couldn't let *us* be victims to it. Given the choice, I would have chosen not to be raped but then I never would've had my Dante'."

"I am not judging you for your choice, Olivia. I mean I don't know what to say because this is all so horrible for you."

Olivia took a deep breath and watched him carefully. She debated on whether or not to tell him about the visions and all the rest of it. There was so much more and none of it was pretty.

"Come here" he said.

She moved closer to him and let him hold her. The rest would wait.

"You are an incredible woman. I don't think you have any idea."

"I guess I don't." Olivia smiled relieved she had gotten through yet another retelling of her horror but it wasn't the whole story.

Jake lifted her up off the couch and carried her up the stairs to his bedroom. It was a large, elegant room with windows stretching across one wall. The windows were covered in heavy, dark brown draperies over cream colored sheer panels.

The furniture was just as masculine; a four poster bed of dark mahogany and luxurious bedding, the color of champagne with touches of chocolate brown trim.

It looked like Jake had picked it directly out of a catalog and said, "This one."

Olivia was tempted to tease him about living in a 'Better Homes and Gardens' catalog but this wasn't the time. The truth was it was gorgeous.

He laid her on the bed and began undressing her slowly, savoring each moment. He noticed the way she smiled, the happy sigh, the feel of her skin as he unbuttoned her blouse. He held himself over her naked body and kissed her exposed breasts. Jake thought if there was ever an angel on earth it was her. She was beautiful, powerful and intoxicating and he marveled at the thought that she didn't realize her beauty or her power. Jake wanted to breathe her in and feel her in every cell in his body. A tragic thought struggled to life in the back of his mind. "Someone tried to ruin her."

Olivia reached up to remove his shirt, not wasting time with all the buttons but instead pulling it over his head. Jake chuckled, "Slow down Darlin' we have all the time in the world."

But she didn't want to take her time. She wanted to drown in his kisses, suffocate in his passion and forget all the horrible things of her past. She needed him to take away her pain. She ignored his teasing and pulled his face closer to hers and kissed his mouth, licking and kissing. He responded matching her passion. The need was too great, the fire, too intense. She reached down and unbuttoned his jeans. She pushed desperately at his clothes. She held him firmly in her hand and stroked with ease. He gasped. He found it impossible to slow down. They were on fire and it threatened to consume them both. Jake moved closer to the end of the bed and lifted up her foot. He kissed her instep, her calf, and worked his way up careful not to miss a thing. She shivered with delight and anticipation.

He kissed her body like a man dying of thirst and she was his water. She moaned and writhed beneath him. His body was perfect on hers, like puzzle pieces. She would wait no longer. She wrapped her legs around him and pulled him inside her.

He wouldn't resist. His need was as great as hers. He brought her to climax again and again. She felt as though she might explode into tiny pieces and float around the room like feathers on a breeze. She knew this was what lovemaking should feel like. This is what burning should be.

Afterward, she lay cradled in his arms watching him sleep so soundly.

She was very cozy but her brain wouldn't shut off. She knew he would ask again about inviting her family for Thanksgiving. It weighed heavily on her mind. Even with Jake by her side and her dad and brother here for extra support, she wasn't sure she was ready to face her mother. Antoinette was nothing like Frankie. She would come here and suck all the oxygen out of the room. Olivia was sure her mother would like Jake but it would be because he had money and power. She wished her mother didn't need to be told about the Weidner jet. To her it would be icing on a very affluent cake and she would give Olivia no peace. She guessed her mother wanted her to marry into high society so she could once again be respectable. At least Antoinette could stop lying to people at the country club if her daughter married a very rich man. Olivia could picture her mother bragging about it at the latest luncheon. "Gag" is all she could think. "Why couldn't she have an adorable, kind hearted mother like Jake's?" she thought with a bit of jealousy.

She sat up, looking back at his peaceful, handsome face. Quietly, she slipped out of bed and put on her swimsuit. She kept looking back nervously at him hoping he wouldn't wake. Reaching for a robe she stepped lightly out of the room and made her way to the hot tub. The house was mostly dark save for the hallway lights marking her way. She considered turning on the tub jets but was worried it might make too much noise, so instead she slipped carefully into the calm, warm water. It was heavenly.

Both Jake and Carmella had told her to make herself at home and it was too easy to get lost in anxious thoughts about her family and her life while lying in bed but here in the warm water, everything was better. She laid her head back closed her eyes and tried not to think about anything, except for perhaps, Jake's handsome face and sexy body. She sighed.

Jake's internal alarm clock woke him around six on Sunday morning. Something was amiss. He felt it right away. "Olivia?" He called out and got up, slipping on his jeans from the previous night. "Olivia?" he called questioningly. The door to the master bath was open but she was nowhere in sight. He didn't think it was part of Carmella's job to hunt down his girlfriend so he walked down to the kitchen and was greeted by two hungry dogs. Harper and Whitman had become fast friends. It seemed they had slept snuggled up together on Whitman's big, round dog bed.

"At least someone got to snuggle." He thought.

"Hey guys, come on, let's go outside." Jake threw on boots and a coat and walked the dogs outside. It was still dark and cloudy. The sky looked heavy with unshed snow. "Olivia has barely had a taste of the kind of winter that's in store." Jake thought.

In the quiet dark he thought about everything she had told him, the pain, anger and brutality of this near-death experience. How could she have survived it all and then, the loss, the anguish? The thought crossed his mind; "God, had I hurt her myself?" Physically, she seemed to want him as much.

It occurred to him she never said the name of her attacker almost as though she had omitted it on purpose. Jake needed to know his name. He was compelled to know though he couldn't really explain why. He thought better of asking Olivia. She hadn't said if the man was in prison or out, dead or alive. Jake hoped he was dead. For the horror that Olivia endured, he hoped the man was not only dead but that he had been castrated in prison and died slowly. It would have been deserved.

It bothered him he didn't have more information. He felt like he couldn't protect her without knowing who he had to protect her from. Was this why she told him he wasn't safe with her? Was this man still a threat? "And why would she worry about me and not herself?" He thought. He doubted she would be happy to know he felt this way but his love blinded him.

Olivia didn't know it but Jake had made it difficult for Billy Frazier to make bail. There were benefits to being a big fish in a small pond like Troy. He placed a couple calls to some longtime friends and created a few legal road blocks for him. Jake and Brad had been keeping pretty close tabs on Billy since he was released from jail but between Billy, Ben and the dirtbag who raped her, Jake really wished she would reconsider moving out to the ranch. That apartment in town where she never remembered to lock her doors just wasn't safe. Not even with Mitch Jameson as her neighbor.

Jake thought about the ring in his desk drawer. If he thought she would say yes, he would ask her today but he knew she wasn't ready, not yet. Besides, his Mama was right, he needed to meet her parents. He needed to be at least somewhat traditional and ask for her father's permission. However, getting Olivia to invite her family here was proving difficult. He could understand now, at least in part, why she had run.

Olivia woke up in the library. She wanted to go back and crawl in bed with Jake but it had been one of the many nights where restlessness and bad dreams prevailed. Talking about her attack twice in two weeks had brought back the nightmares about Patrick Hanson.

Patrick had come for Dante' and Olivia couldn't seem to hold onto him. She tried so hard to hold him but he just slipped away and Patrick laughed. It was that same horrible laugh she heard when he finished with her and left her for dead on her kitchen floor. The dream was so real she could smell the smoke in the air.

The fire had gone out in the library so she had wrapped herself in a blanket from an obliging chair but she was still so cold. She got up stiffly and walked to the window. There, out in the snow-covered yard stood Jake. There was light beginning to peek around the tops of the mountains in the places where the clouds parted. She watched as Jake talked to their dogs and she felt so grateful. Here was this man who was so loving, so kind, and somehow, against all odds, he loved her. She didn't know how to feel worthy even after they had shared their own personal stories. She had seen his tears and anger and had felt his tenderness in their lovemaking.

The story about his past seemed so inconsequential compared to hers and yet it wouldn't be. Olivia knew it would shape Jake's future and in turn, hers. It didn't change how she felt about him though. Dante' would have said, "Mom, go for it." And he'd be right, too. It would be a lot easier if she could stop having bad dreams and start having a real life, a life without fear.

As if Jake could feel her presence, he turned toward the house and saw her in the library window. He blew her a kiss.

"Come on kids, let's go in." he said to the happy dogs. He quickly fed them in the mudroom off the kitchen and went to Olivia. She was still standing in the window, wrapped in a blanket.

He came up behind her and put his arms around her. "Good morning Darlin' I missed you last night."

"I couldn't sleep and I didn't want to disturb you."

"You can always disturb me anytime you want, I'm yours." Olivia rested her head back on his chest and he kissed her hair.

"Did you go swimming?" Jake asked, feeling dampness in her hair and realizing she was wearing her bikini.

"Not exactly; I did go in your hot tub for a while though. I hope you don't mind."

"Not at all. I want you to feel at home here. How would you like a swim with me before breakfast?"

"Jake, I told you I'm not a strong swimmer."

"Then you can sit on the edge while I do laps and when I'm finished, I'll tow you around the pool like a barge." He teased.

"What a horrible thing to say." She squeezed his arm as if to punish him. "Ok, I'll let you show off your *skills* to me."

"Good, I want you to be really impressed so maybe you could say 'ooh' and 'ahh' a lot. Deal?"

Olivia giggled and nodded. Jake went to change into his suit and Olivia sat next to the pool, her feet dangling in the water.

"It's warmer than I thought it'd be but I still don't know if I want to get in."

Jake dove into the water and swam up to her legs. His face and hair glistened. He was so good looking it was almost shocking. He kissed her knee and then swam away to begin his laps. There was a beautiful rhythm to his strokes.

He had long lean muscles that pulled him through the water as if he was a child of Poseidon, born to glide and move with the water. Olivia envied his graceful movements. Swimming was a hobby she never took part in. She'd made it a priority for Dante' because of his interest in sailing but for her, land was where she was meant to stay.

After a while, he swam up to her. "Ok Darlin', let's give it a whirl shall we?"

"Jake" Olivia shook her head in protest but it was too late. He picked her up and carried her through the water. She felt surprisingly safe though she wondered when he would stop surprising her. He placed her hands around his neck and he stretched out in the water. Olivia relished the feel of him beneath her. Later he swam them both to the side.

She kissed his wet mouth. "Thank you. That was so...it was perfect." She was again at a loss for words.

"You're perfect," Jake kissed her neck.

"No, I'm not."

"Well, you're perfect for me Darlin'. Let's go shower and change and have some breakfast. I'm starving."

Jake didn't wait for an answer. He grabbed her hand and walked her up the stairs out of the water.

Olivia wished she had a photo of this moment. "Jake, I was thinking I'd really like to have a picture of you." She said as they dried themselves off.

"Sure Darlin' or we could get a picture of the two of us together." Jake answered. She looked surprised he said it but then *he* was thinking about an engagement photo.

Later on, they were in his office. He sat at his desk looking over paperwork while she sat in an overstuffed couch by a warm fire. Harper and Whitman sat together as close to the heat as they could get. Olivia thought it was amusing. She had her head resting on the back of the couch, watching Jake, lost in thought.

"Sorry Darlin', you're probably bored out of your mind. Normally I'm not so consumed with work on a Sunday but this is just one of those times it won't wait."

"It's ok really. I was just daydreaming anyway. You know, you're going to have to take me home sometime tonight?"

"Are you sure you won't just stay? I love having you here."

"No, I really can't. I have work tomorrow, remember?"

"Why don't you call your family about Thanksgiving? There's a phone on the side table there." Jake suggested.

Olivia sighed but knew he would just keep pushing until she did it. She caught her breath and could only hope they wouldn't be able to come. She was tempted to just pretend and make up an excuse but she didn't feel good about lying to Jake. She wanted their relationship to be better than that and didn't want there to be games or lies between them. She picked up the phone and gave Jake a look of despair.

"Shall I sit with you and hold your hand or would you prefer privacy?"

"Neither, just stay where you are and pretend to be working."

Jake laughed. Olivia had a wit about her he found completely charming.

She dialed the phone and held her breath.

"Hello?" Antoinette answered. "Curtis residence."

"Hello Mother" Olivia said flatly.

"Olivia? Where are you? What's going on? I don't recognize this number." Antoinette asked nervously.

"I'm calling from Montana, Mother; of course you don't recognize the number."

"Well, what's happened now?

You know your father is beside himself over your leaving? If I had known you were going to keep driving and then shut us out completely, I would have..."

"It couldn't be helped." Olivia cut her off. "I'm sorry. I just couldn't stay there and pretend for you."

"I've never once asked you to pretend, Olivia. Don't be melodramatic. I do expect you to, at the very least; let us know where you are. For all we knew you could have been dead in a ditch somewhere. Miles said you looked thin. Are you eating? Are you staying on your medications? What about therapy? Are you still in therapy?" Antoinette bit harshly.

"You knew where I was, Mother, I don't want to get into this right now. The reason I called was to invite you, Dad and Miles here to Troy for Thanksgiving, unless of course you have other plans." Olivia crossed her fingers.

"As a matter of fact we do, but I think your father would feel better if he could see you so I'll cancel *my* plans. You'll need to make hotel and flight arrangements for us. I wouldn't know where to begin, traveling to a place like Montana. And call your brother and make sure he has all the details."

"Mother," Olivia sighed, "I'm going to send a jet for you. You won't have to arrange anything. I'll set everything up here and I'll call Miles. I'll text you an itinerary as soon as I have one."

"A jet? Who's jet? Not yours? Please tell me you didn't buy a plane Olivia."

"No Mother, I did not buy a plane. Listen, I should probably call Miles before it gets too late. I will be in touch."

"Olivia..." Antoinette began to protest.

"Goodbye Mother."

"Goodbye Olivia." She replied sounding put off.

Olivia hung up the phone and stared at the fire. She must really love Jake to be willing to put up with her mother for a holiday. "Jake, I can hear you thinking over there. Just say whatever's on your mind."

"I was just thinking that can't have been easy and I'm really proud of you."

She turned to look at him over her shoulder. He sat at his desk looking at her. "Humph" Olivia pouted. "I feel like throwing something at your head, just so you know."

"I'd prefer you didn't. Did your mother actually think you bought a plane?" Jake asked, smiling broadly.

"Yes, thanks for that, by the way. They are coming." She replied grumpily.

"Do you want to talk about something else?" Jake asked, smiling at her.

"Yes please, anything else." Olivia was relieved.

"Can I ask you something then?"

"Sure."

"What do you miss most about Dante'?"

Olivia hadn't been expecting that and choked back a sudden sob. She was so used to keeping all things concerning Dante' inside it was difficult to switch gears.

"I miss the little things most of all." She said quietly, pausing. "Dante' had decided he liked coffee, just like his mom, so he would get up early to come down and drink a cup with me in the mornings before school. I think he put more cream in than coffee." She smiled. Jake smiled, too.

"He would sit in his robe with his hair all funky from sleep and we would talk. We talked about everything. I miss those moments the most."

"That does sound nice. He sounds like a good kid."

"He was an amazing kid. I was so blessed by him." Olivia wiped away a tear. "His life, the kind of person he was; it was all proof I made the right decision no matter what it feels like now, without him." She paused and groaned at herself. "Ugh, sorry."

"Don't apologize to me. You love your son. You miss him. There's nothing to apologize for." Jake came over to sit next to her on the couch. He pulled her in for a hug.   Olivia sniffed and then laughed, "I sure do cry a lot, don't I?"

"I hadn't noticed." He teased.

"Jake, as much as I'm enjoying this, I really do need to get home. It's already late in the afternoon and I have a few chores to get caught up on. Not all of us have a sweet Carmella."

"Alright Darlin' but I don't really want to let you go." He emphasized by squeezing her tightly and kissing the top of her head.

"I don't want to leave you either but..."

"I know, I know, you have things to do. I still have some more work to do anyway. Our family's lawyer, Tom Braxton sent over some information about Dad's Victoria deal.

In fact, would you mind if I let Dent take you home?"

"Dent? What is a dent?" Olivia looked skeptical.

"Denton Taymore is our ranch foreman. I promise you you've never met a more decent fellow, except me, of course. He will get you home safely, I promise."

"Alright I guess I'll go gather up my things. Come on Harper" she kissed Jake and at the sound of Harper's name, both dogs were up. "Jake, is this the brush off?"

"Oh God, no, it absolutely is not. Don't think that, please. When you're ready, just buzz down and I'll come get your bag."

"It's one bag Jake, I'm pretty sure I can manage."

Olivia sat with her dog on her lap in Jake's pickup being driven home by a very quiet man named Denton Taymore. Dent, as he was called, was a tall, skinny cowboy with a black hat. It looked like it was a permanent fixture on his head and you could see the sweat stains from many hard days' work in the sun.

He had bright blue eyes, weathered skin and a scruffy salt and pepper beard, so there was no way for her to tell his age. He seemed friendly enough but Olivia had no idea how to start a conversation with him, so instead she sat and stared out the window.

As promised, Jake was true to his word and didn't fly off to New York, at least, not that she knew of but he didn't put up much of a fight to have her stay longer either. That surprised her a little, though she could have just told him she wanted to stay. She hadn't minded entertaining herself while he worked. She had perused the books in the library, made them both a snack in the kitchen and took the dogs for a walk around the grounds.

The ranch was much bigger than she realized. She had considered walking through the stables but wasn't interested in explaining who she was to any of Jake's employees.

"Oh well," she thought. "I really do need to get home and do some laundry and go get some groceries." The cupboards were incredibly empty; it was pathetic.

When they arrived at her apartment, all Dent said was, "Afternoon, ma'am." Olivia smiled and hopped out of the truck. "Thank you" she replied.

Jake sat back at his desk. He had promised to call Olivia tonight before he went to bed but in the meantime, there were some other calls he needed to make.

He didn't want to run the risk of having Olivia in the house when he made them. He dialed the phone.

"Hello?"

"Hello Tom, its Jake."

"Hi Jake; do you have any questions about the Victoria deal? I faxed over everything I have so far." Tom Braxton explained.

"No, no that all looks good. I'm still reviewing it. No, the reason I called is I need some advice."

"You aren't in jail are you Jake? I thought that sheriff liked you?" Tom joked.

"I'm not in jail. No, I actually need to hire a private investigator. I need someone reputable and discreet." Jake explained.

"I can give you a name. He's not local though. Do you mind telling me why?"

"I'd rather not."

"Are you in some kind of trouble?"

"No, it's not about me or the family."

"Ok, well, let me see what I can do. I'll send you a text with a name and phone number. Does that work for you?"

"Yes Tom, thank you."

"You're welcome but you know you can trust me. I've been your family's lawyer for twenty years. Are you sure you don't want to talk about this?"

"I know I can trust you, I just want to play this one close to the vest for now, ok?"

"Ok. Let me know if there is anything more I can do."

"Thanks." Jake hung up the phone. He hoped he was doing the right thing. "Time will tell" he said aloud.

Just then Carmella walked in. "Jacob, did you take Miss Olivia home already?"

"I had Dent take her. She needed to get home and I had some work to do."

"That isn't right Jacob. Are you sure you didn't hurt her feelings? You should have taken her yourself." Carmella scolded.

"Yes ma'am. You're right. I'll call her and apologize."

"Good boy. Oh, the reason I came in here; your parents called and are on their way over for dinner."

Jake rubbed his forehead and sighed, "Ok."

"I think they were hoping to see Olivia again." Carmella continued, looking at Jake expectantly.

"Thank you Carmella." Jake said dismissively.

"Humph" Carmella snorted and walked out.

Jake picked up the phone again and dialed Sam. She answered almost instantly. "Hello."

"Hey Sam, what's happening?" Jake asked casually.

"Nothing, I was just doing a little housekeeping.

Jake could picture it, too. Sam always cranked up the music to do chores. He was surprised she could even hear the phone ring.

"What about you?"

"My dad has his sights set on Victoria, British Columbia; so I was just going over some paperwork."

"Victoria, huh? I hear it's beautiful. So does that mean the Weidner family will be international business owners then?"

"We already are, but this would be a first in Canada. That is, if everything pans out. He has Tom working on it, too."

"Uh huh" Sam said quietly. "Jake; what is that I feel?"

"What do you mean?"

"Oh, I know...its tension. Why do you sound tense? Did you fuck up things with Olivia again?"

"No, for your information, I did not. We had a really good weekend together and I even took her to meet my folks. I think it went well."

"So why is there a big, fat elephant in the room with you then?"

"Olivia and I did have a pretty major talk and I told her, um, I told her about what happened with Sarea."

"Oh, that's good, isn't it? At least now she'll understand why Ben's not your number one fan. Did she tell *you* anything?"

"Yes, she did and that's all I'm going to say about it. That's not why I called."

"Oh so you did call for a reason and here I thought you just missed my witty banter."

"...and your foul mouth? No, not exactly. Actually, I was wondering if you could track down a horse for me?"

"Don't you have cowboys to do that sort of thing?" Sam teased.

"It's about a horse I want to buy, smartass. Listen, please. When Olivia was a little girl in Oregon she had a horse named Maestro. And considering she came from a country club background, I'm willing to bet he was registered and likely came from a good bloodline which means there would be a paper trail..."

"Likely yes, but Jake, if this horse was say a three year old when she had him, well, odds are he's either dead or really, really old. I'm sorry to burst your bubble."

"I know that, but I just want to find out if he was a gelding or a stallion and if he sired any foals."

"And you couldn't just ask Olivia because...?" Sam asked, and then it clicked. "You want me to track down this horse as a gift?"

"Possibly, I don't know. That depends on what you find out. I'm merely asking you to gather some information for me."

"Based on what Jake, the horse's *name*? That isn't much to go on!" Sam complained. "Maybe she just liked the name. It may not have been his registered name if he was registered at all. What breed of horse was he? Who was the owner of record? Where did she ride? What type of riding? And, did she compete? Jake seriously, you've given me very little to work with here."

"Are you saying you can't do it?" He knew Sam couldn't resist a challenge.

"What if I just ask Miles about it? It would make this a ton easier." Sam said, taking the bait.

"If you must, just make sure he doesn't say anything to Olivia about it because if I find out that Maestro has any progeny for sale, I'm going to find a way to make it happen."

"Isn't that rock of an engagement ring a nice enough gift? I mean, hell what is it, two carats?"

"It's a little over three actually. Maybe the horse will be her engagement present." Jake liked the sound of that.

"Ok lover boy I'll see what I can do."

"Thank you Sam you're the best. Do you know that?"

"Yeah, well I have to be, to put up with you." She teased.

"Is that so?" Jake laughed.

"Yes, yes it is. Hey before I forget, Mr. Tanner got his moose this weekend. So you have one very pleased client at the lodge. You told me to keep you posted about that and he flies out tomorrow morning."

"That's great news. I'll give him a call later. Why don't you send over a nice bottle of whiskey, too?

"It's already done. His favorite brand and commemorative glasses were waiting for him when he returned from the hunt."

"Damn you're good. Ok, let me know when you have anything on that horse, ok?"

"I know. What can I say? It's a gift. Yep. I'll keep you posted about the horse."

****

Olivia had suffered through yet another restless night and wasn't feeling so great at work on Monday morning.

Denise approached her at the piano with a handsome man in tow. "Olivia, I want to introduce you to my son Cameron Peterson. Cameron, this is Olivia Curtis."

"Olivia, it's a great pleasure to meet you. My mom says you are an incredible asset here at Tempo." Cameron shook Olivia's hand.

It was official Jake's family was filled to the brim with beautiful people. Olivia would say that perhaps they got more than their fair share of the pretty. Cameron stood approximately six foot two, had dark hair, and a very refined face. He wasn't as rugged as Jake but still terribly handsome; like he'd walked right off the cover of GQ. He had ice blue eyes and wore a blue and white pinstriped shirt that complemented them perfectly. Olivia found his good looks to be a little intimidating. She blushed. "Thank you, I'm happy to be working here and it's very nice to meet you, too."

Denise beamed. She was definitely proud of her son and obviously trying to set them up. Olivia thought perhaps she should have filled Denise in on the details of her weekend.

"Olivia, we won't keep you, I know there's another class coming up but since Cameron stopped by, I thought I should introduce you." Denise said proudly.

"I'm glad you did."

She realized in that instant it would be completely too easy to flirt with this good looking man standing before her. Internally she sighed.

"I hope to see you again soon, Olivia." Cameron grinned.

"Oh we will, at least I think so as Jake has invited me to the ranch for Thanksgiving." Olivia said, using the opening to mention Jake. The last thing she wanted was to cause any problems between the cousins.

"That's great. Yes, we'll be there. We'll see you then." Cameron replied recovering quickly.

"Great," Olivia said and smiled at both of them, then returned to the piano.

~ 236 ~

As she sat down, Olivia's cell phone rang in her pocket. "Hello."

"Hey beautiful, sorry to bother you at work. I just called to tell you I talked to your brother and everything is arranged for your family's visit."

"Everything? What about a hotel? My parents can't stay with me Jake. Hell, my parents *wouldn't* stay with me." Olivia replied feeling nauseated suddenly.

"I told Miles that everyone could stay here at the ranch..." Jake paused, waiting for Olivia to react.

"What?! Jake! I don't want my parents staying at your house. I don't think it's a good idea at all. I'll call Miles; we're going to have to figure something else out, oh my God." Olivia's nausea went from a three to about a seven. The next dance class began filing into the room.

Jake burst out laughing. "Darlin' I was just teasing you. I made arrangements for your family to stay at the Lodge."

"Jacob Weidner, how could you? I was so freaked out. I thought I was going to have a heart attack. Don't ever do that to me again! I'm nervous enough as it is about seeing my mother."

"I'm sorry Darlin', I couldn't resist. Seriously though, it's all going to be fine. I'll be right beside you." Jake said sincerely.

"Jake where is this lodge? Do you think my mother will find it acceptable?" Olivia fretted.

"I think so, but you should go see what you think. Tonight after work just run up to the Outfitters and Sam can give you a tour."

"It's at the Outfitters? How could I have missed that?"

"It's just up the road from the office, in the trees. I think you'll be pleased but go check it out and call me later."

A new vision emerged. Olivia would never get used to the way she saw the future. The visions weren't peaceful moments like daydreaming on a sunny day. They were intense flashes of anger, violence or fear. She saw blood and words from Patrick's mouth blended like poison and razor blades. She didn't feel any compassion for him. She didn't feel human toward him at all. For so long he held power over her and now, Olivia knew there would be an end, a bloody and terrifying end.

"Why do you hate me?"

"I don't hate you Olivia, you're mine, always mine."

"I'm not yours. I belong to no one."

"You belong to me. You are my bird and you will sing for me."

"I am a bird! I am the phoenix. I will burn and be reborn. Your blood will be my fire and I will rise."

It was her vision. Olivia knew what was to come with more clarity now, but would it change her fate? Would her visions die with Patrick Hanson and how would it affect Jake?

"Darlin', did you hear me?" Jake asked over the phone.

"Yes, I heard you. Um, you want me to call you after I visit the Lodge." She replied numbly.

"Yes, are you alright? You sound strange?"

"I'm fine, I just, I um..." Olivia didn't know what to say.

"Did something happen?"

"No, I just have a class coming in so I have to go." Olivia whispered and hung up the phone. Jake called her right back but she let it go to voicemail. She couldn't explain right now.

CHAPTER TWENTY

Later as promised, Olivia called Jake.

He answered quickly as if he were waiting for her. "Darlin' what happened? I tried to call you earlier and it went to voicemail. What's going on?"

"Well, thankfully you aren't my keeper. I had to go and I am calling you now, just like I said I would." Olivia was suddenly feeling suffocated and defensive. A new feeling when it came to Jake. She refused to let this relationship resemble anything she had endured with Jackson.

"No wait; I'm not your keeper. I was just worried about you. What I meant to say was 'how was your day'?" Jake drawled.

"It's disgusting to know just how charming you can be." Olivia giggled in spite of herself. "My day was ok. Oh, and the Lodge is perfect. It's beautiful and slightly rustic but still classy. I think my mother will like it. I'm sorry for doubting you."

"No problem. I would have suggested you check it out either way. I'm glad you like it. It's where we put up clients from the Outfitters."

"Well, I think it *is* perfect. Hey, I met your cousin, Cameron today?" She smiled as she said it.

Jake bristled on instinct alone. The way she said it sounded less than casual. "You did huh? Well, I told you my aunt would probably be keen on introducing you to him."

"Jake, if I didn't know any better I'd say you were jealous. I mean, I can understand it. He looks like a GQ model. Is that what he does for a living? Does he model? I meant to ask him but I couldn't seem to form a thought around him."

"He, uh, he, I, well, you..." Jake didn't know what to say in the wake of such obvious attraction. He was jealous. He was so jealous in fact, that the idea of beating the crap out of his cousin came to mind.

"I'm teasing you back. But maybe next time *you'll* think better of pressing my buttons." Olivia laughed.

Jake was surprised and relieved and laughed, too. "Darlin' I can't tell you how much I enjoy pressing your buttons, though."

"You do huh?" Olivia purred.

"Yes I do. I wish you were here now. Speaking of which, part of the reason I didn't offer my house to your parents was I'm hoping *you'll* stay here during the holiday. When is your last day at work?"

"Tomorrow," she answered. But Jake isn't your sister staying with you and what about your other family? Besides, I don't want to have to explain it to my parents or yours for that matter."

"Jessica is the only family I have staying with me. And what would you explain; the birds and the bees? If you would be more comfortable, you could have your own room. There are seven of them, you know."

"I don't know." Olivia bit her lip. "Let me think about it, ok?"

"Of course. You know you don't ever need to wait for an invitation, not ever. You are always welcome in my home."

"Thank you, Jake. The same goes for you, not that you'd want to come to my little apartment."

"Darlin' I can be there in about fifteen."

Olivia giggled. "Ok."

Around midnight they laid facing each other in the dark. Olivia could just barely make out his outline but could feel his warmth and closeness like a favorite blanket. Jake rubbed her arm, slowly, methodically.

Olivia asked quietly, "Are you nervous about Thanksgiving? I know you said you would be nervous about meeting my parents, but I still don't believe you."

"The truth? The truth is I'm excited. I'm happy. You have no reason to believe me after my crazy trip to New York but it's true. I'm happy here with you. I love you Olivia Curtis. Family and being together is what Thanksgiving is all about. Besides, what's the worst that could happen?"

"What is the worst thing that could happen? Hmmm, let's see, my mother could make a scene. She could monopolize every conversation, she could treat you or your family like second class citizens and she could basically embarrass the hell out of me."

Jake chuckled. "Well if she does, then she does and we'll deal with it. She can't be that bad. Does she really bother you that much?"

Olivia thought about it for a moment. "I don't know if *bother* is the right word, but yes, she does. See, she was the one who had," Olivia sighed deeply. "She had me, um, Jake, she had me committed." She waited with her eyes shut, terrified.

"Committed?" Jake asked quietly touching her cheek in the dark.

"I know I should have told you this part, I just, I just didn't know how to say it. I mean, how can I explain something like that?"

"What happened?"

"My mother did what she thought was right, I guess. I don't know. I was such a mess after the accident and things went a little wonky for me-- a lot wonky. The doctors diagnosed me with what they call Mixed Delusional Disorder. They said it was brought on by what happened to me when I was a teenager and made worse by the accident and death of.... I tried to kill myself, Jake, once after the rape and once after Dante' well..." Olivia cringed, and was grateful for the darkness. She hated how those words tasted in her mouth.

Jake slid his hand down to her wrist and rubbed his thumb over the bracelet that he now realized, she never removed. "I know Darlin', I know. I didn't know you were committed but I've noticed this bracelet. I should have told *you* before, but I moved it aside, when I was tucking you in that first night you stayed with me. I sort of guessed what the scar was from. But, oh my Lord, Olivia, I'm just so thankful you weren't successful and that you're ok, now."

Olivia buried her face in his arms. "I don't know if I am."

"But, you will be. Just look at how much has changed already. You moved to Montana on your own, you've got a job where they love you, you met a handsome, eligible bachelor who makes you laugh..."

Olivia did laugh. "Stop it, you turd, this is serious. What was that eligible bachelor's name again? I keep forgetting."

"Ok, that's it." Jake started tickling her wildly.

They shared early morning coffee together before Jake headed back to the ranch. Olivia almost told him she had decided to stay with him for the weekend but stopped herself. He would like the surprise.

"I love you Darlin'. Have a great day at work today."

"You too"

"Call me later?" Jake asked in between kisses.

He left and Olivia hurried to get ready for her day. After, she went over and knocked on Mr. Jameson's door.

"Hello Olivia, how are you?"

"Hi Mr. Jameson, I'm good thank you and yourself?"

"I'm terrific. Would you like to come in?" he asked politely.

"No thank you, I don't have time. I just wanted to let you know I won't be around this weekend. I didn't want you to worry. I'll be at the Weidner Ranch for the holiday."

"Oh that's nice Olivia. I'm glad you won't be alone."

"What about you Mr. Jameson, do you have plans for Thanksgiving?"

"Yeah, don't worry about me. I'm a social butterfly, didn't you know?"

"Well, if your schedule opens up, we would be happy to have you join us at the ranch. Jake and I would love to have you."

"Thank you dear, I appreciate the offer. Have a happy Thanksgiving." He hugged her.

"To you as well."

All day at work, Denise had been asking Olivia what she thought of Cameron. Apparently Olivia hadn't been obvious enough. Finally, she said, "Denise, I'm sort of dating Jake. That's why I'm having Thanksgiving at the ranch. I don't mean to hurt your feelings but I didn't know how to tell you."

"Oh, oh I see. Olivia, I didn't mean to be so pushy about Cameron. I just want him to meet a nice girl and settle down. You have my sincere apologies, truly."

"Don't apologize. Cameron seems like a great guy and I didn't want to mislead you or him. I enjoyed meeting him. I hope it won't make things awkward."

"It won't at all. My son *and* my nephew are both grown men. I shouldn't be meddling. I told you before you are definitely Jake's type. I'm happy for you."

"You weren't meddling; you were being a good mom." Olivia smiled. Denise had such a big, kind heart.

"Thanks for that. I do try. So, I'll see you Thursday then."

"Yes Thursday."

Olivia went home hoping Jake was too busy to call her. She knew if he did, he would ask her about staying out at the ranch again. She really wanted to surprise him. She rushed to get everything ready and loaded in her Jeep.

Harper seemed more hyper than usual. She knew something was up, or maybe she just sensed Olivia's excitement. As quickly as she could Olivia went through some boxes until she found what she was after. She stopped for a moment, looking at the keepsake in her hand. She knew Jake would understand but sometimes moving forward was very, very hard.

On the drive out to the ranch she started to second guess this impulse. She hadn't really considered what Jake's sister would say when Olivia showed up on the doorstep. She took a deep breath and Harper barked. "I'll take that as encouragement.

The rest of Jake's family has been great. It'll be fine, right?" Harper wagged her stubby tail.

It was beautiful out. Everywhere she looked was like a postcard. Snow covered the trees and ground and ice formed on everything. Olivia was reminded again how grateful she was for her new car. She knew Miles had paid for it but it had seemed important to him she not know, so she kept her mouth shut about it. Someday she would have to thank him, for many things.

Olivia pulled up the driveway toward the house. She didn't see Jake's truck anywhere. She hoped Carmella would answer the door. It wasn't that she was unwilling to meet Jessica; she just thought it would be better to be introduced differently.

She left Harper and her bags in the Jeep and went to ring the doorbell. "Please God; don't let it be Jessica who answers this door." She prayed silently.

The door opened as she glanced back at her Jeep. She turned back and .... "Hi! Are you Olivia? You must be. Come in, come in. I'm Jessica Weidner, Jake's sister."

"Hi, yes, I'm Olivia Curtis." She silently cursed her unanswered prayers but smiled warmly at Jessica.

"Well get in here, it's freezing out there."

The two women shook hands but Olivia didn't enter. She was suddenly frazzled. She hadn't thought of what she would say. "I came out here to...Jake invited me to stay for the holiday weekend and well I, I never gave him an answer. I thought I would surprise him."

Jess smiled in understanding. "That's a great idea. You have perfect timing, too. Jake isn't here. He and my dad are out with some of the hands for the afternoon feed."

"Oh good," Olivia said, feeling suddenly shy.

"Pull your car around and I'll open the garage for you."

It wasn't a question. Jessica shut the door quickly in excitement and Olivia was left standing on the front porch. She did as she was told and Jessica was waiting near the garage door. Olivia thought she was stunning. She was chic and stylish, but still had the same laid back casualness the rest of the Weidner family possessed. It amazed Olivia. They all were incredibly good looking but incredibly down to earth. They made it seem effortless. It was all vastly different from the tweezed, primed, botoxed, lipo'd people from the country club her mother seemed to favor. Olivia pulled Harper and her bags from the car.

"Do you need any help?" Jessica asked excitedly.

"No thanks, I think I've got it. So, you think Jake will be happy about this?" Olivia asked, attempting to make conversation.

"Are you kidding? He'll be over the moon. Who's this?" Jess asked, gesturing to her dog under her arm.

"This is Harper. I hope it's ok I brought her. I don't have anyone to watch her."

"Of course it's ok." Jessica replied as they climbed the stairs and turned toward Jake's bedroom.

"Um, I should probably stay in a guest bedroom."

"Why? That's silly. Unless you and he aren't well, you know...Anyhow, are you sure?" Jessica asked, smiling brightly.

"It's just that with your parents here and everyone." Olivia was blushing wildly.

"Let's ask Mom, then." Jessica replied, and pushed the intercom button on the wall next to Jake's bed. Olivia was shaking her head and had a panicked look on her face, but it went unnoticed.

"Mama, would you come up to Jake's room?"

Olivia didn't hear a reply, she was suddenly cast underwater. She was silently kicking herself for not thinking this through more thoroughly.

After a few moments Frankie Weidner walked in. "What is it Jessica?" she asked but then glanced over at Olivia. "Olivia, this is a nice surprise! Are you here to stay?" reaching out to hug her.

"Yes, I am. I just..." Olivia began but Jessica interrupted.

"Mama, Olivia is here to surprise Jake. Isn't that great? Except she thinks she should sleep in a guest bedroom and I think she should sleep in here. What do you think? She's worried what you and Papa will think of her."

Olivia's blush only deepened, she was sure her face was purple.

"Olivia dear, you stay wherever you are most comfortable. I know my son well enough to know he will want you in here with him but it's completely up to you. Though I should warn you, if you don't choose to stay in his room with him, he'll likely end up sneaking down the hall in the middle of the night like a teenager, believe me." Frankie said teasingly.

Olivia smiled sheepishly. "But my family is coming as well."

"Yes, I know but they're staying at the Lodge, aren't they?"

"Yes they are." Olivia replied.

"Then relax. You don't owe anyone an explanation, not even me." Frankie said.

"Yeah, lighten up. Jakey is going to be so excited you're here. Make yourself at home." Jessica said. "Oh and it's really nice to meet you Olivia. Come down to the kitchen when you get settled in. The guys won't be back for a while. You can help us if you'd like. We're making desserts."

"Thank you, both of you. I'll be down in a bit." Olivia said and hugged them both. They were so warm and friendly.

She had always dreamt of this kind of family. She thanked God for Miles. He was the one piece of her family puzzle that seemed to fit. She let Harper down who wiggled and barked. "You'd better be on your best behavior; there are a lot of people coming." She told her sweet little dog.

She unpacked a few items from her suitcase to hang in Jake's closet but most of it she left in the bag, unsure of where to put anything. It wasn't like she was in a hotel, this was Jake's home. She opened up the top drawer of his dresser just out of pure curiosity. Everything was neatly folded. She had a feeling it was Carmella's doing.

She took Harper outside for a short walk and then came back to face the jury of women though she was feeling much more relaxed. There were yummy smells wafting from the kitchen.

Carmella was the first to greet her as she entered. "Ciao. Come in. We're making some of the desserts for Thanksgiving, join us. I was so happy when Jessica said you were here."

"Ciao Carmella, it's good to see you again."

"Jessica tells me you are here to surprise Jacob."

"Yes, he had invited me to stay and so..."

"We need to come up with a plan; something sneaky." Jess added.

"What do you mean?" Olivia asked turning toward her.

"I mean, I think we should let him wonder where you are for a bit, build the suspense a little."

Frankie interjected. "Jessica, that isn't nice; your poor brother. He will worry about Olivia."

"We won't let him suffer very long, Mama. It's good for him and there is nothing poor about *my* brother. He'll live. We should hide Olivia somewhere in the house and let him find her. I need to think of a reason to send him to his room so he can find you there. Hmm" Jessica said thinking out loud.

Olivia reached into her back jeans pocket and held out her cell phone to Jessica. "If I'm really going to do this I guess I should turn this off, then. I don't know if I feel right about it. Your mother is right, he'll worry."

Jessica took it and smiled wickedly. "He'll be fine. I promise it will only be a few minutes. You should wait in his room. I'll tell him he needs to change his shirt after being out with the cows and there you'll be. Voila'."

"I like it." Carmella added. "I think Jessica is right. It will be fun."

Frankie rolled her eyes at the conspirators, but agreed. She called Dacey on her cell and asked how soon they would be heading back to the house.

Olivia overheard Jake in the background asking if anyone had talked to her and then the house phone rang.

"Hello" Jessica answered innocently.

"Jess, do you know if Olivia has called? I can't seem to get a hold of her." Jake asked.

"I can ask Carmella. 'Carmella, did Olivia *call* today?'" Jessica asked loudly.

"No, Miss Olivia hasn't *called*" Carmella replied, happy that she didn't have to lie.

"Shit, I wonder where she could be. Her phone just keeps going to voicemail." Jake hung up on Jessica.

"Rude!" Jess said into the phone. She looked over at Olivia who looked miserable.

"Seriously, you look like you murdered someone. It's only a little joke."

"Yeah, but what if he heads to town to look for me?"

"He won't. He doesn't drive anything but his own truck unless he absolutely has to."

"Ok, I hope you're right. Should I go to his room now?" Olivia questioned.

"Yes, it shouldn't be too long now and don't forget Harper, she'd be a dead giveaway." Jessica smiled.

"Ok" Olivia said, uneasily trying to come up with a little simpler plan. "I could help here in the kitchen. He would still be surprised."

Frankie looked sympathetically at Olivia but Jessica insisted and nearly pushed her down the hallway. "It will be fine, trust me. He'll be here soon."

Not five minutes after Olivia shut the door to Jake's room, he burst in through the kitchen door looking dirty and disheveled and supremely anxious. Dacey followed casually, amused by his son's behavior.

"Still no word from Olivia?" Jake asked anxiously.

"No, sorry" Jessica replied. "Maybe her phone just died. I'm sure she's fine."

"Yeah" Jake said dismissively, not sounding sure at all. "I'm going to her apartment and make sure she's ok." Jake headed back toward the door.

"Jacob wait," Frankie intervened. She didn't want Jessica's little joke to get out of hand and suspected he would tear apart the town of Troy looking for his girlfriend. "Before you go, change your shirt. That one's filthy. She won't want to hug someone covered in cow shit." It was more of a motherly order than a request. She looked down and continued cutting pie crust into strips as though she knew he would obey.

Jake began to protest, not concerned about his shirt but then looked at himself and realized she was right. "Ok" he said and began taking his shirt off before he was even out of the kitchen. He took the stairs two at a time and swung open his bedroom door. There, sitting next to the window was Olivia. She rushed to him and threw her arms around his naked torso.

Jake was instantly relieved. Olivia didn't let go, she just held him tightly. He kissed the top of her head.

"You're here." Jake sighed. "I was just about to go looking for you. I thought something had happened because I couldn't reach you. I'm so glad you're here."

"Me too" she said softly. "I'm sorry if I worried you. I wanted you to be surprised."

"I am surprised. But this, oh this has my sister written all over it. I should have known."

"I shouldn't have agreed. I'm sorry."

"Don't be sorry. I know those women really well. You're here and you're safe. Does this mean you're staying?" Jake asked hopefully.

"Yes, I'm staying." She kissed his chest and then, happily, his lips. He kicked the door behind him with one foot.

She giggled. "Jake, your family, they're all in the kitchen; they'll… We can't." she giggled again.

"Oh yes we can." He replied sexily.

Later on Olivia sat up in Jake's bed, covered with only a sheet shaking her head at him. He stood by the door. He had already taken a shower and was dressed in clean clothes.

"Darlin' we have nothing to be ashamed of. Please get dressed and join me." He said, holding his hand out for her.

She hadn't been thinking about how embarrassed she would be and wished she'd thought ahead to how this would feel but she couldn't resist making love with him.

"Jake I..." Olivia blushed.

"Darlin', no one will say anything. I promise you."

Olivia sighed. She knew she couldn't hide out in Jake's room all weekend. "Alright FINE!" she said and put her clothes on and ran a brush through her hair.

"How do I look? Do I look, um, ruffled?"

"You look gorgeous," Jake said, grinning.

"You look like the cat that swallowed the canary. And thank you but do I look, ruffled?" She asked again, smoothing her hair.

Jake laughed. "Ruffled? Is that what we're calling it? No Darlin' you don't look ruffled."

Olivia took his hand and leaned into him. "Ok, let's go face the firing squad."

"There won't be one." Jake assured her. He was right; everyone was kind and courteous and greeted them happily. The only thing they teased Jake about was hiding Olivia away from all of them.

He squeezed his sister's shoulder. "You always have to give me a hard time don't you Jess?"

"What are sister's for?"

Just then, Olivia's cell phone rang in her pocket. "Excuse me" she said to Jake's family and walked out into the foyer to answer it. "Hello."

"Olivia, this is Ben Thompson."

"Hello, Dr. Thompson. How are you?" Olivia asked formally.

"I'm fine. I'm calling to apologize to you. I was out of line the other night and I'm sorry. How are you doing?"

"Very well, thank you."

"I'd like you to consider coming in for an appointment."

"No, that isn't a good idea. A line has been crossed and I'm not sure I'm comfortable seeing you."

"That's why I'm recommending an appointment, in office, a professional setting."

"I don't know." She began to waver. She looked around at the beauty surrounding her. She smelled the comforting scents coming from the kitchen. She felt at home here. Suddenly, she wanted to cry. She hadn't felt at home in so long she nearly forgot the phone in her hand.

"Olivia?"

"Yes?"

"Will you come? I have time tomorrow morning."

"Alright what time?" she said, still filled with uncertainty.

"Nine a.m."

"Fine, see you then." She hung up and turned to rejoin the rest. Jake was leaning against the door jamb with a look of concern on his face.

"You startled me." She jumped slightly.

"I didn't mean to. What's going on?"

"I have an appointment tomorrow morning."

"With Ben?" Jake asked.

"Yes Jake, I have an appointment with Ben. I hope you'll understand."

"No I don't really understand. Are you sure it's a good idea after what happened? It's obvious he's attracted to you." Jake ranted like a jealous boyfriend. If it wasn't for the look on his face she would be tempted to tease him about it.

"He apologized for his behavior and to be perfectly honest, I'm not sure it's a good idea either but what am I supposed to do?" she asked.

She needed to explain more and she knew it. "I'd like to get things back on track for myself. On my release from the hospital, it was impressed on me how important it is to continue outpatient therapy for my, let's say, issues. Ben Thompson is still my therapist and he's the only one in town."

"I won't tell you what to do. It isn't my place so if you're going to go, then at least let me take you."

"That's not necessary. What would you do while I'm there; sit in the waiting area and torment LeAnn? Besides, I need you to greet my family."

"Olivia, your family won't be here until tomorrow afternoon."

She looked seriously at him. He looked genuinely worried. "If you really want to take me, then you may." She acquiesced.

"Good; it's settled then, I'll take you." He hugged her tightly, not waiting for her response.

Olivia woke feeling tense and tired. She had a terrible nightmare and woke up screaming sometime during the night. Jake tried to get her to talk about it but she just couldn't. It was too awful and too real.

She was in her home in Oregon that she had shared with Jackson and Dante' but instead of beautiful and warm, it was dark and plain and somehow she was locked inside like a prisoner. She tried all the windows and doors but nothing would budge. She couldn't understand the powerful need to get out. She beat her fists on the glass and suddenly it shattered. She was covered in shards of hot broken glass that burned her skin like fire. She looked down at her wrist and instead of the scar she'd had for so long, there was a jagged piece of glass sticking out. She pulled it out and her wrist gushed blood like a memory. She watched in helpless horror as her blood poured out onto the floor around her. Slowly she grew weaker and slumped down unable to hold herself up anymore.

In her weakness, she heard his voice, low and terrifying and sadly familiar. Patrick Hanson was kneeling in the blood with such a look of satisfaction on his face. He came very close to her and whispered in her ear. "It should have been you. I should have killed you. It should have been you. I should have killed you. It should have been you. I should have killed you..." He covered her mouth with his bloody hand as he kept repeating it over and over again. She cried, too weak to cover her ears. She finally released her terror in screams.

Unable to catch her breath, part of her still stuck in the nightmare, she was crying and sweating profusely even though the air in the room was cool. "Leave me alone!!" she screamed.

"Darlin' it's ok, it's me. I'm here. It's me, Jake. It was just a dream. It isn't real," he tried to soothe her, holding her arms tightly and pulling her close into his chest.

At some point, Olivia was able to calm herself and go back to sleep. Jake watched her sleeping; worrying about this fragile bird beside him, so fearful, so tormented.

In the morning they prepared to leave for her therapy appointment. Jake noticed Olivia was especially quiet.

"Darlin' don't get angry but maybe it's best to postpone this appointment until after the holidays."

"No!" she snapped. "I want to get this over with."

"Ok" he replied knowing it was a losing battle today. He could clearly see she was irritable and tense but more than that, she looked worn out.

"I'm sorry; I don't mean to bite your head off. I'm just tired."

"It's going to be ok. We'll get through this, all of this, even your nightmares."

"Thank you my love," she kissed his mouth warmly trying to calm herself.

"Mmm, I like the sound of that. Let's get going, shall we?"

They pulled up to Ben's office and Jake opened Olivia's door.

"What are you going to do?" she asked.

"I'll think of something don't worry about me. I won't be far away in case you need me. Just call when you're ready. Darlin' are you sure about this?" He asked and kissed both her hands.

She reached up and kissed him again. "I love you." She said simply, becoming more comfortable every day with her feelings. He was her rock, more than that he was her mountain.

Olivia sat on the couch once again watching as Ben flipped through paperwork. She felt like he was stalling.

"Ok, sorry about that. I planned on being more prepared." Ben said.

"It's fine." She replied stiffly.

"First off Olivia allow me to apologize again for my behavior the other night. It was completely unprofessional and out of line and I'm so very sorry. I guess it's one of the risks of practicing in a small town."

"I accept your apology, though I'm still not sure I should continue therapy."

"Olivia, I can understand why you feel that way but please, let me assure you, it will *never* happen again. Besides, you are making really great progress."

"I think you're right. I have made progress. Things have been progressing nicely with Jake too, against your advice." She said willfully.

"Are you baiting me?"

"No, I'm not. I, Jake told me all about what happened between you."

"What did he tell you?"

"He told me why the two of you aren't friends anymore."

"Did he mention Sarea Scott?"

"Yes, yes he told me about the three of you in high school."

"Did he tell you she was bought out of Jake's life by his family and they paid her to have the abortion? Did he give you that little detail?" Ben asked angrily.

"I don't believe you. The Weidner's wouldn't do that!" Olivia yelled. In her heart, she knew she shouldn't be involved. Her love for Jake and the vision she'd had were clouding her judgment.

"Olivia, calm down." Ben said, choking on his own temper.

"No, I won't calm down! Jake didn't lie to me, he wouldn't!" She bit her lip furiously.

"Well then I guess you have a problem because I'm not lying to you either."

"It was a mistake to come here. Jake was right." She jumped to her feet to leave.

"Olivia please, please sit down." He gestured to the couch.

"There's nothing more to say."

"There *is* more.

This work isn't about Jake or me; this has to be about you. Now, let's focus on your life, your needs. Do I need to remind you that you are required to continue outpatient therapy?"

"No, you don't need to remind me but this won't work. I'm in love with Jake. How am I supposed to talk about my life when he is such a huge part of it now? I can't share that with you. How can I tell you anything?"

"I can keep my personal feelings out of this I assure you." Ben said sincerely.

"I very much doubt that. I think you and Jake should have remained friends regardless of what happened but I don't think I can come to you for therapy knowing what I know. I know what will be in the back of your mind and worse than that, I know the truth of what really happened."

"What does that mean?"

"I just mean I believe Jake."

"I'm sorry you feel that way. I'll be in touch with Dr. Cline's office in order to find you an appropriate referral. His office will be in touch with you. Good day to you, Miss Curtis." Ben stood and offered his hand.

Olivia refused his hand. She stepped back feeling shell-shocked. Ben ushered her into the waiting room and closed his office door.

Inside, Ben sat back at his desk frustrated and angry. Jake Weidner had won again and he didn't even know what he'd won. "Asshole" Ben thought.

Olivia walked out to the parking lot and stood in the cold. It dawned on her she'd been summarily dismissed. She wanted to scream at Ben Thompson until her lungs gave out. "No one dismisses Olivia Curtis-Montgomery" she said to herself but the anger gave way to tears. "Damn it."

She knew she should compose herself first but she longed to hear Jake's deep, soothing voice. With shaking hands she dialed his number.

"Hey Darlin', that was fast. Are you done already?"

"J-J-J-Jake, would you c-c-come get me?" She asked and the phone went dead. She wasn't sure if she disconnected the call or if Jake had hung up on her. It didn't matter. She was frustrated and hurt.

Jake had been visiting with Tag over at the diner when Olivia called. As soon as he heard her shaky voice he was on his way; reaching her in a matter of minutes.

Olivia stood outside in the cold with her face in her hands.

She brushed away the tears when she realized Jake was there. He quickly jumped from his truck. "Darlin', what happened?" Where's Ben?"

"Jake please, will you take me home." She asked as she hugged him tightly.

"You wait in the truck. I think Ben and I need to have a word." Jake said angrily.

"No, please." She begged and clutched at him. "Let's just go."

"I'll only be a minute. It'll be alright."

Olivia took a deep breath and tried to push the anger and sadness down inside. "Then, I'm going with you."

"I think its best you wait here." He tried to sound calm and controlled.

"No, we either talk to Ben together or not at all," she countered.

He didn't reply, he just held her hand and they walked into the office together. Jake ignored LeAnn and opened Ben's office door.

Ben sat at his desk and looked up from his reading, "Have a seat. I didn't realize we were conducting couples therapy today." He said sarcastically.

Olivia could feel the unleashed anger washing over Jake like waves about to crash. She decided she'd better start this conversation. "Ben, I was hurt by the way you *dismissed* me. You seemed determined to take out this vendetta you have against Jake, on me." Olivia sat down but Jake remained standing.

Ben replied in the best clinical voice he could muster. "I'm sorry you feel that way. It became clear to me that you wish to remain blind to a great many things in the past. As a psychologist, it is sometimes my unfortunate duty to recognize a hopeless case."

Olivia inhaled sharply as if she'd been slapped.

Jake seethed. "Ben, I think the lady is right. I think you're so pissed at me you couldn't help someone out of a paper bag. Talk about being blind. I told Olivia about Sarea. I told her what happened between us."

This time Ben stood up and slammed his fists on his desk. "You didn't tell her anything! You told her some pretty, make-believe version of what happened but you didn't tell her that your family *paid* Sarea to get out of your life and she was forced to have an abortion! You just happened to omit that ugly little detail!"

Olivia looked back and forth between the two men. They both looked like bombs about to explode.

"Is that what you think happened?" Jake was suddenly more confused than angry.

"Ben, I planned on marrying Sarea! She took off without so as much as a word to me! She chose to have an abortion! I found out later from her dad. She wasn't paid by anybody. She never even talked to me about it. Maybe you need to get your facts straight!"

"I have the facts, Jake! Sarea told me exactly what your family did. She wrote me a letter explaining how you refused to see her and how she was all alone.
She said your family's lawyer offered her a lot of money to terminate the pregnancy and she was required never to contact you AGAIN."

"Ben, I swear to God that is NOT how it happened. And if it did, it was without my knowledge. I did try to reach her, to see her."

Out of the blue, both men looked less sure of themselves. Olivia felt the urge to laugh but could tell neither man would appreciate her dark humor. The silence was overly long and Olivia began to feel uncomfortable. Both men stood with the desk between them. Neither could find words, nor barely able to look at each other.

Olivia couldn't stand it any longer, "I guess the only way to know what really happened is to ask Sarea Scott in person. In the meantime, maybe you two gentlemen should shake hands and call a truce. It is the day before Thanksgiving after all." Olivia offered.

After gulping, Jake offered his hand; Ben shook it. There would be no apologies today, only quiet understanding. To Olivia, Ben said, "I'm sorry to drag you into the middle of all this. If you can forgive me and only if you are interested I would like to continue with your sessions, but if you can't, I understand. It's your decision."

"Thank you Ben. I'll be in touch. Oh, and I hope you have a nice Thanksgiving."

Once outside, Jake stopped her spun her around and kissed her. It had started to snow again and the flakes fell lightly on their heads. "Who are you?" he asked.

"I'm just the girl who loves you."

CHAPTER TWENTY-ONE

Jake was rather quiet on their way back to the ranch. He had a lot to think over.

Olivia broke the silence. "Do you think your family could have done what Ben said?" she asked quietly.

"No, they wouldn't. I think she probably made up that story to get some sympathy out of him."

"Are you ok about all this?" she asked, still worried for the quietness lying over him like a blanket.

"Yeah, I'm ok." He said. "You know, your family will be arriving soon."

"I'm excited to see Miles again. Is he driving them from the airport? Oh, how will they get to the Lodge?" She asked, suddenly remembering.

"Everything is arranged; there's a car waiting to pick them up, that way they can get settled in before we visit. I thought it would be best."

"Yes, I suppose I should see them before tomorrow. Oh God, Jake. I cannot be trapped in their room with them. My mother makes me claustrophobic; she sucks all the air out of a room."

Jake turned to see her pale suddenly. "Darlin' relax. Miles is going to call when they are ready and we'll join them in the lounge for a drink. Apparently you're going to need one."

"One isn't going to be enough." Olivia sighed heavily. "So, what should we do in the meantime?" She asked nervously.

"Do you have your keys?"

"Yes why?"

"Why don't we go to your apartment to freshen up?"

"Oh no, I look horrible don't I?"

"You look beautiful but I can tell you've been crying and if I can tell then..."

"Then my mother will be able to tell from fifty miles away. Ok, my place, so I can try and work a miracle on my face without makeup. Shit everything is at the ranch."

"We'll stop at the store and you can pick up what you need, or I can take you out to the house, you decide."

"Store and then my place it'll be quicker." Olivia pulled down the visor mirror to repair some of the damage. She looked like a very sad raccoon. After a whirlwind trip through the store, Jake drove them to her apartment. She ran up to the door not waiting for him. He followed stopping briefly to talk to Mitch who was shoveling the walk.

"Hey Mitch, how are you?"

"I'm good Jake and yourself?"

"Terrific. I meant to tell you we'd love to have you join us for dinner at the ranch tomorrow if you're interested, about four o' clock?"

"Thanks Jake but I'm bound for Libby. The in-laws are there. You know how it is."

"No I don't, but I hope to." Jake smiled. "Have a safe trip Mitch and happy Thanksgiving."

"Will do, you too." Mitch returned to his snow shovel. He always liked Jake and the whole Weidner family for that matter. He was glad Olivia had Jake now and from the looks of Jake, she definitely *had* him.

"Olivia?" Jake called as he walked in.

"Yeah, I'm in the bathroom. Is Miles going to call you or me?" she asked.

Jake noticed the frantic sound to her voice. "Me I think. Did you change your clothes too?"

"Yes I did. Why?"

"I thought you looked beautiful already."

"Jake I was wearing jeans. I don't wear jeans around my mother. Jeans are not acceptable attire."

He smiled to himself. He was beginning to think his future mother-in-law was a serious bitch on toast. He looked down at himself. "Darlin', I'm wearing jeans, is your mother going to have a hissy?"

"No, I don't want you to change anything about yourself. Besides, my mother is much more forgiving of men. Don't be surprised if she tells you how quaint or charming your lifestyle is here in the country." Olivia said, mocking her mother's attitudes.

"So it's just you she's tough on, then?"

"Yes, but then I'm the only girl. Miles can do no wrong and Dad, well; he does what he's told. Lucky me I guess, I get to be the only daughter of Antoinette Curtis – I must adhere to **very** high expectations."

Jake didn't comment. It took a lot to injure him but he feared for the kind of damage a mother like Antoinette Curtis could and would inflict on a daughter like Olivia.

"What?" She was still trying to perfect her fresh makeup when she saw him watching her in the bathroom mirror.

"Nothing, so what *are* you wearing then?

"This" she said as she pulled open the bathroom door.

She looked ravishing as usual but more proper this time. Jake had never seen Olivia like this. It was strange. Her hair was pulled back into a smooth up-do. Her makeup was elegant, sophisticated. She wore a pearl necklace, white button up blouse and grey wool trousers. The whole look screamed Park Avenue chic and although she wore it perfectly, it seemed like a cloak to shield her from her mother's attacks.

"You look great Darlin'."

"Are you sure? I can't believe how nervous I am to see my own mother. The last time she saw me I was..."

"What?"

"Nothing, never mind."

"You are beautiful. So does your dad make you nervous, too?"

"No my dad is different."

"How so?" He reached for her hand pulling her down next to him on the sofa.

"Well for one thing, he calls me 'Slugger'." Olivia smiled. "He's very kind and quiet. Reserved, I guess."

"Slugger? Are you close?"

"As close as we can be but somewhere along the line, he let my mother take control when it concerns me. I think my dad feels sorry for me." Olivia said, making a face.

"...and you hate that, don't you?"

"I hate it more than anything. I don't want pity, especially from my family."

"What do you want from your dad?"

Before Olivia could answer, her phone rang. "Hello" she said, happy to change the subject.

"Hello Liv." Miles' voice sounded cheery.

"Hi Miles, how was your trip? Are you all settled in?"

"The trip was great; Mom took a sedative while Dad and I played cards. Yep, we're all settled in. Mom is really anxious to see you. You and Jake are coming for drinks aren't you?"

Olivia sighed. She could picture just how 'anxious' her mother was. She could only hope the sedative hadn't worn off. Her mother had never been fond of flying, apparently not even on a private jet. Olivia could never understand it, she loved to fly.

"Yes we are on our way. Miles, I..." Olivia paused.

"I know Livi, it feels like you're about to be executed but don't worry, Jake and I will both be there. It'll be alright."

The tension rose off of Olivia like heat waves off a road on a hot summer day. Jake squeezed her hand and leaned over to kiss her cheek.

"I'm fine. They're here. I'll grab my coat."

"Ok Darlin', I'll go start the truck." Jake smiled as he hopped off the couch.

Olivia didn't say two words on the way up to the Lodge. She was stuck somewhere in her own head. They pulled up in front and Jake stepped around to open Olivia's door. He stopped her briefly as she stepped down.

"Just remember they love you, it'll make this easier. If that doesn't help, then remember *I* love you." Jake said and kissed her gently.

Olivia's family was seated at a low table in the lobby near windows facing the mountains, trees and the slow-moving river below. Her father and brother rose to greet them. Olivia's mother remained seated and watched them from behind her martini.

Miles picked up Olivia in a hug and she giggled. "Livi, it's so good to see you again. You look good. Hey Jake, how are you?" Miles asked and reached to shake his hand.

"I'm good Miles, thank you. I'm glad you made it."

Miles turned slightly as Olivia's dad was giving her a hug. Her dad's eyes glistened with unshed tears. "Hey, Slugger," he whispered, "I've missed you so."

"Hi Dad, I've missed you, too." Olivia said and sniffed, holding back her own tears. She needed to steel herself for what came next.

"Jake, allow me to introduce you to my dad, Jonathan Curtis." Miles said.
The two shook hands. "Mr. Curtis, it's an honor to meet you, Sir. How was your flight?" Jake asked.

"The honor is mine. Thank you for setting all this up. It means the world to me to see my girl again. And the flight was great."
Jonathan's eyes crinkled when he smiled. Olivia's dad had a kind face, an easy smile but still held intensity about him, a sharpness.

It was hard to imagine he would let his wife run the show. At that moment, Olivia's mother set down her drink and stood to join them. She laid her hand on her husband's arm somewhat deliberately.

It was easy for Jake to see where Olivia got her good looks but while Olivia was warm and full of passion and heart, her mother was cold and unapproachable. Jake was well studied in people like Antoinette Curtis. He came across them in business all the time.

"Hello Olivia," Mrs. Curtis said formally and air kissed her daughter's hair. Already Jake felt himself bristle. He already knew Olivia hated this kind of pretentious bullshit and he agreed with her. He noticed Miles rolling his eyes.

"Hello Mother. You look well. I'm very happy you could come to share Thanksgiving with us." Olivia said stiffly; rather unconvincingly.

"Don't lie to me Olivia, it's unbecoming. You look tired. Are you still not sleeping?" she accused more than asked.

Olivia ignored the comment and pasted a smile on her face. "Mother, this is Jake Weidner, our host for the weekend. Jake, this is my mother, Antoinette Curtis."

Mrs. Curtis' demeanor suddenly changed and her smile warmed ever so slightly. "Hello, Jake. May I call you Jake or is it Jacob? We are so pleased to be here. It was incredibly gracious of you to include us." She was oozing with charm.

"It's a pleasure to meet you, Ma'am. Please call me Jake." He replied somewhat amused. Out of the corner of his eye, he could see the look of irritation on Olivia's face. "Let's order some more drinks, shall we?" Jake suggested.

"Yes, that would be lovely. We have a table just over here." Antoinette replied.

As they were all seated, Jake made sure to be next to Olivia. She looked to need his support. He reached over to hold her hand but she had them clasped tightly together in her lap. She sat bolt upright, looking rigid and tense but inclined her head toward him at the gesture.

A waitress came over to take orders but Olivia hesitated. She dreaded her mother's judgments and realized instantly there was no safe choice. If she ordered something with alcohol then she was an alcoholic and if she didn't then her mother would wonder if she were pregnant or some such nonsense. There was no winning.

"What would you like, Darlin'?" Jake asked.

"Just water for me thank you," Olivia replied. As suspected, her mother eyed her suspiciously.

"Are you sure you wouldn't like a cocktail?" Jake asked politely.

"Perhaps a glass of white wine," she said quietly.

"May I suggest the rose'?" the waitress added, "it's really quite good."

"Yes, that would be fine, thank you." Olivia answered quietly.

"Just bring the bottle Kimberly and a glass for me, as well." Jake told the waitress. She nodded and took the rest of the orders.

As soon as the waitress was out of earshot Antoinette said, "Jake, you know this waitress here?"

"Troy is a small town so, yes, I pretty much know everyone."

"Oh, how quaint," Antoinette sniffed.

"My family owns this Lodge, Mrs. Curtis." Jake replied, hoping to dissuade her from thinking he was some kind of playboy, small town or not. Olivia looked at him in surprise.

"Oh that's wonderful and have you always lived in Montana?" Antoinette continued, enunciating 'Montana' like the name of some wretched disease.

Jake ignored the tone. "Yes I have, mostly. I lived in New York for a while and Texas for college, but Troy is my home."

"The lodge is lovely. Is this how you make your living, then?" Antoinette asked snottily.

Olivia's eyes widened in horror but Jake merely chuckled. "No Ma'am, I have a few other irons in the fire." He smiled slightly.

"Mother, are you touring with an orchestra?" Olivia asked, desperate for a change of subject.

"You would know the answer to *that* if you would ever call." Her mother replied. "But to answer your question, I do have plans to tour starting in the spring. I have too many obligations at the club during the holiday season. You know that."

"Of course, I'm sorry, I should have called. I've been very busy." Olivia said, kicking herself for opening that can of worms.

Her mother laughed slightly, but there was no humor in it. "I'm sure you have been. What was it you told me she was doing, Miles, waitressing?" Antoinette asked glaring as if she just learned her daughter was a prostitute.

Miles nodded and looked at Olivia for forgiveness.

Olivia slouched slightly at the blow but then took a deep breath and pushed her shoulders back almost defiantly. Miles cringed. He had seen this battle waged many times.

Jonathan intervened before Jake could. "Troy is sure beautiful. I would love to see it in the spring. Do you have a golf course here, Jake?"

"Yes Sir, we sure do. I play a bit of golf myself. Perhaps you could come back and we'll play a round or two." Jake suggested sincerely.

"I'd like that very much."

"Hey, I want in on that." Miles added jovially.

"Of course Miles, I would love to have you both come."

Olivia was grateful for the reprieve but knew it wouldn't last. Her mother would continue taking bites out of her. It was simply how things were. "Excuse me for a moment," she said and escaped to the restroom. She needed a minute or twenty to regroup. She prayed her mother wouldn't follow her. Odds were good she wouldn't. Her mother had always enjoyed the attentions of men. She would take this opportunity to have the spotlight.

Olivia stood in the restroom looking in the mirror. "Keep it together Olivia" she told herself. She tried to steady her breathing. "How can I let one comment from my mother throw me into a tail spin?" she thought.

The door opened. Olivia quickly turned on the water in the sink. She didn't need an audience for this little breakdown.

"You're not planning your escape are you Darlin'?" Jake drawled as he put his arms around her waist. "Not that I would blame you."

She smiled, turned in his arms and leaned her head on his chest. "Jake, you're in the ladies room." Her voice was slightly muffled with her face in his shirt.

"I am? Shit. It's kind of nice in here. Women always get the better bathrooms. Why is that?" Jake teased.

"We spend more time in here." She smiled. "You know what I want to do right now?"

"I know what I want to do but I think the bathroom echoes too much."

She ignored his innuendo. "I want to crawl into your bed, pull the covers over my head and maybe never come out."

"That isn't exactly what I had in mind, unless I get to join you." He chuckled.

"Jake, be serious. I'm freaking out here. My mother makes me crazy and not just a little crazy but like, loony-bin crazy! And I can say that because I've been there before." It was her half-attempt at humor.

"Olivia, your mother isn't quite the monster you portrayed, but she's damn close, I'll admit. Listen, your family is here, for better or worse and we may as well enjoy it for what it is. I like your dad, he seems cool."

"Yeah, Dad's great. Ok go, you have to go now. I'll be out in a minute and no, I'm not going to escape. I promise. I love you too much to leave you alone with my *mother*."

Jake laughed and kissed her before leaving the bathroom.

When Olivia returned to her seat, her mother looked irritated. She was sitting across from Jake listening to the men discuss ranch life.

When there was a lull in the conversation, Antoinette asked, "What kept you Olivia?"

A thousand smart-ass replies crossed her mind but instead she said quietly, "I'm sorry. I didn't mean to be rude."

"Yes well, I do worry about your affinity for bathrooms." Antoinette announced.

The entire room could hear a pin drop. Jake wanted to take back what he said about Antoinette Curtis. It was quite possible this beautiful, cold woman sitting across from him was the devil. Maybe she *was* the monster Olivia had described. Jake squeezed Olivia's hand.

She couldn't look at her mother. Instead, she looked at her dad whose face was filled with shock and pain. He remained quiet. It shouldn't surprise her. Her dad rarely spoke up on her behalf.

"Mother, why don't you...?" Miles began, but Jake interrupted.

"I don't know any woman who doesn't spend a lot of time in the bathroom. I've been told by my mom *and* my sister countless times that looking beautiful doesn't happen by magic. But, I will spend every last breath trying to convince the women I love they don't need all that stuff to be beautiful." Jake's declaration was pointed toward Olivia's mother.

Olivia didn't realize she'd been holding her breath. She let it out slowly.

"Is that so?" Antoinette asked. "So, you don't appreciate the adornments of women? You want a natural, scrubbed-face girl who wears flannel and stinks of sweat?"

"On the contrary" Jake said seriously. He looked Antoinette directly in the eyes. "I love Olivia for exactly who she is, makeup or not. So, if she chooses to adorn herself, as you say, or scrub her face and get sweaty, I still think she's beautiful."

Olivia, Jonathan and Miles all looked at Jake in shock. Miles jaw dropped slightly.

Before Antoinette could reply, Miles said. "I think that deserves a toast." He held up his glass and they all joined him. Antoinette didn't smile.

"Here's to my sister Olivia and also to you Jake and to spending time with family." Miles lifted his glass proudly. He knew how to defuse his mother at least temporarily.

"Thank you Miles and thank you Mr. and Mrs. Curtis. I am honored to have you here." Jake lifted his glass toward Olivia's parents.

Olivia leaned over to whisper to Jake, "You make everything better. I love you."

"I love you too Darlin', so much." He whispered back to her and kissed below her earlobe quickly.

This intimacy was not lost on Antoinette. "Olivia, perhaps we could take a little walk and let these men get to know each other better." Her mother quickly rose to her feet.

Olivia immediately looked like a deer in the headlights but wouldn't refuse her mother. "Yes of course" she replied nervously.

Jake stopped her long enough to kiss her briefly. "There's a nice sunroom next to the pool," he suggested, pointing across the lobby to the hallway. She smiled slightly but said nothing.

Olivia was quiet as she and her mother strolled toward the pool. She knew it wouldn't take long for her mother to say something. The only question was how badly it would hurt.

"Olivia I find this whole situation unacceptable. I don't hear from you for over a month and then suddenly we are called to show up at a stranger's house for Thanksgiving dinner as if nothing has happened. Jake seems nice enough but that does not change the fact you don't belong here."

"I don't belong anywhere Mother." Olivia replied sadly.

"What is that supposed to mean?" Antoinette asked, not waiting for an answer.

"Perhaps though, if you marry Jake, I won't have to worry quite so much about whether or not you are dead in some bathroom somewhere. I don't think you should be alone. Do you think he'll propose? Would he move the two of you out of Montana?" 'Montana' came out once again like she was describing a disease. Olivia sank heavily into blue and white striped pool chair.

"Did you hear me Olivia?" Antoinette demanded.

"Yes, Mother I heard you. You think I should marry Jake and move out of Montana so I'm no longer a burden to you and your poor overwrought nerves."

"You have **no** right to speak to me in that manner. I have only ever wanted what's best for you. Jake obviously has enough money to provide the kind of lifestyle you deserve, so once you're married you won't have to be a *waitress*. Though, I personally feel there is never a need for *you* to be a waitress. Miles told me Jackson provided you with more than enough money. You should quit that job. No decent man wants to marry a *waitress* from a diner."

"Actually I was fired." Olivia replied rebelliously, knowing the reaction she would get.

"They fired you? What did *you* do?" Mrs. Curtis asked angrily.

"It doesn't matter Mother, I'm working in a dance studio now. I play piano for dance classes and have been asked to do some teaching."

"A piano teacher! Really? With your talent you should be back at Carnegie Hall but instead you have decided to throw it all away on a music studio in backwoods Montana.
I'll never understand you Olivia. This may sound harsh but after you left the hospital, I thought you would have a fresh start. I thought you would finally have the career you were meant to have before you had *that boy*."

Olivia stood up in her mother's face, her anger finally released. "You do NOT speak to me about Dante'! You will not ever call him 'that boy'! I do not and I will not regret having him! He was *not* a mistake! Do you understand me?"

Her mother wasn't even fazed by Olivia's sudden outburst of anger. "Of course he was a mistake Olivia! Granted, it wasn't his fault but you never should have been a mother!"

"Neither should you!" Olivia shouted matching Antoinette's tone. "And, as for a fresh start, this is it!

I love it here in Montana and I love Jake Weidner, not for his money or his standing in the community or even his good looks but for his heart, his kindness. He is one hundred times the man Jackson ever was!"

So much venom, regret and emotion were built up inside Olivia and her mother needed to hear it, even if it changed nothing. She continued, "And, if by some miracle Jake Weidner wants to marry me I will consider it but not because you say so. I am meant to be here in Montana! Believe me, I am staying!"

"You've always been too stubborn for your own good. I think you enjoy screwing up your life just to spite me. A man like Jake isn't going to wait around while you have another meltdown. So I'd suggest you find a way to pull yourself together before you lose what may be your *last* opportunity to change your life for the better. He won't want a delusional, suicidal wife!" Antoinette replied, knowing just how to injure her only daughter.

Olivia physically felt this last kick in the stomach. Suddenly, she pictured Dante' standing behind his grandmother flipping her off! Olivia took strength from her son's memory. "I'm not suicidal Mother and I'm not delusional. It's not like being an alcoholic."

"Does he know about your past?"

"Yes, and he loves me anyway!" Olivia replied defiantly.

"Well just try and keep it that way. I'd hate for you to lose another man."

Olivia shook her head. It was almost comical her mother would say 'lose' as if she had merely misplaced Jackson.

"Have you played the piano for Jake or his family?" Antoinette asked, changing tack as if they hadn't argued at all.

It was apparent her mother was taking a break in her assault. Olivia replied quietly. "I played for Jake once. It was a while ago. He has a lovely piano in the ballroom of his home."

"A ballroom? Well, I think tomorrow we should play something for them. I brought my cello." Antoinette suggested with pride.

"Mother I don't want to be a spectacle and besides, we have nothing prepared."

"I brought some sheet music. We'll play Dustin O'Halloran's Prelude Two." Antoinette said, as though she'd planned it ahead of time.

"Mother, I haven't practiced. I won't play and be the cause of your embarrassment."

"Then you'll go back tonight and practice. I'm sure Jake won't mind if you practice at his house and he can set everything up. You said there's a ballroom?"

"Yes, but, they may have other plans, Mother. We are their guests. I think it would be better if you were to play without me."

"Olivia, stop this childishness. I want these good country folks to see what real talent looks and sounds like. They should see what they'll be getting if Jake marries you." Antoinette said sarcastically.

"Why do you have to do that?"

"Do what?" she asked, falsely innocent.

"Insult everything you think is beneath you and then make it sound like you're selling me off like some prized cow at a county fair. You should know Jake and his family are very cultured and very well-traveled. He speaks four languages."

"How special for him. *I* speak four languages. I would hate for you to be wasting your time and your talent here for nothing. I really think you should speak to him about relocating with you. You simply cannot stay here."

"I'm not moving back to Oregon."

"I didn't say Oregon but he said he had lived in New York once. Oh Olivia, the two of you could move to New York and you could have an amazing career."

"That is *your* dream Mother, not mine! I don't want what you want."

"How can you know what you want when you've never had it? I don't want to see another man holding you back."

"Which is it? Is Jake too good for me or am I too good for Jake? I wish you'd make up your mind."

"Olivia, I only mean it's because of men you didn't have a better life. As far as Jake is concerned, that remains to be seen. I hardly know him after all." Antoinette replied bitingly.

"Mother, you hardly know me." Olivia looked around for an escape, any escape.

"If it weren't for this little crush you're having, would you consider relocating? All the best therapists are in New York anyway."

"I'm not moving."

Antoinette ignored her. "I'll get the sheet music you'll need. Please, do practice tonight."

"Fine, I'll meet you back in the lounge." Olivia turned away facing the closest wall.

Her mother walked away completely unaffected by anything said between them. Olivia never understood how her mother could be so impervious and yet *she* was left feeling she had just spent the last thirty minutes being used for target practice. She sighed heavily and willed herself not to cry. She stood up, feeling heavier than before, weighted down by her mother's expectations again. There were lead weights in her pretty grey pumps.

Jake saw Olivia first, before her dad and brother. He rose and walked to her purposefully to create a little distance between her and her family.

"Are you ok?" he asked sincerely.

"Yeah."

"You said you wouldn't lie to me Darlin'." Jake kissed her forehead. "More wine?" he asked as he led her back to the table.

"Where's your mother, Slugger? Did you drown her in the pool?" Jonathan asked with a smile.

Olivia smiled. "No, she's run up to your room to gather some sheet music for me."

Jake looked at her quizzically.

"Apparently we are putting on a little performance for everyone tomorrow after dinner." Olivia said stiffly.

"You don't have to do that." Jake looked at her in sympathy.

"Jake's right Liv; if you don't want to play, don't play." Miles added. Her father shook his head in agreement.

"It's fine. It's what Mother wants."

Just then Antoinette returned. She placed the sheet music on the table in front of Olivia. "Call me if you have any questions Olivia."

"I'm sure I can figure it out Mother."

Antoinette looked at Jake ignoring her daughter's discontent once again. "Jake, Olivia was telling me you have a ballroom with a piano. She and I would like to play for you and your family tomorrow as a thank you for including us and making us feel so welcome."

Jake couldn't believe how easily Mrs. Curtis turned on the charm. "Of course Mrs. Curtis, we would be honored."

Mrs. Curtis smiled up at him and said, "You may call me Antoinette, of course."

Olivia took the opportunity to escape. "We should probably be going Jake, don't you think?" She asked attempting to keep her voice even and in control.

"Yes, I suppose so. We'll see you all tomorrow afternoon then at the house? Miles, there's a car here at your disposal; we've left the keys at the front desk. You remember the way, don't you?"

"Well, thank you Jake, but Sam is coming to pick us up, so we're good." Miles said politely.

Olivia felt completely in the dark. "Sam is coming with you?" She asked Miles.

"Yeah, why?" Miles asked.

"No reason, I just didn't realize. Ok well goodnight, we'll see you tomorrow." She hugged her brother. Then she hugged her father with emotion coloring her voice,

"I love you, Dad."

"I love you too, Slugger." He replied, getting misty again. It was such a relief to Jonathan Curtis to see his daughter looking so well. He didn't know if it was because of the passing of time and distance from her tragedies, a new start or being with this new young man, but to him, she looked and sounded happier and more self-assured than he'd seen her in a very long time. That made his heart glad. Though, when he looked at Olivia he was struck with the emptiness of Dante's absence. He would forever miss his grandson.

Olivia gave her mother an obligatory hug and air kiss. Jake shook their hands and he escorted Olivia out into the cold winter air. She carried the sheet music. She wished somehow it would spontaneously combust in her hands. She felt like *she* might spontaneously combust right along with the music. She was angry, hurt and once again had been railroaded by her mother. Turning to ash and soot seemed like the only logical thing to happen next and yet, she stood in the cold air next to Jake who couldn't know how badly she'd just been burned.

She didn't know what to say about her family, or about what just happened. Forming words around the moment seemed impossible. She should probably apologize to Jake, or thank him, or maybe both. He just walked quietly beside her holding her hand warmly. He helped her into the pickup. She looked at him helplessly and he simply kissed her hand. When he closed the door on the driver's side, he laid his head on the steering wheel. Olivia's insides began to turn to jelly. She figured she knew what was coming. She began to say, "I'm sorry" when Jake burst into laughter.

"What?" She was completely in the dark. Nothing was funny. "Jake, what is it?"

He looked up at her and smiled brightly at her still chuckling. "Your mother is a Royal BITCH!" He said and then burst out laughing again.

No one had ever said that out loud about Antoinette Curtis, at least not to Olivia. She couldn't help it and let out a wheezy laugh, partly from shock and partly because it helped relieve the pressure inside. Her mother took everything so seriously. It actually helped to laugh.

Finally getting his laughter under control Jake apologized, "I'm sorry Darlin', I shouldn't have said that. It wasn't nice of me."

"Don't apologize for the truth Jake. I'm just sorry she acts this way. It's not about you. She's angry with me."

"Oh, God, Olivia, don't apologize for *her*. You're not the reason she's so hateful."

"Maybe not but I've been her excuse for so long, I guess I'm just used to it."

"That isn't something any child should have to get 'used to'. What I want to know is how on earth you and Miles turned out to be such good people with a mother like her?"

Olivia didn't know how to respond. She didn't think she had 'turned out' all that well; she was sad, angry, moody, stubborn...all horrible qualities.

Jake's phone rang. Olivia listened as he answered.

"Hello - Uh-huh - Ok, yeah we're on our way home now. - When did he call? Alright, is Mama at the house also? - Ok, thanks, Dad. - Bye"

Olivia loved the sound of Jake's voice as he spoke to his father. There was so much love, respect and almost reverence when they talked.

"That was my dad."

"I heard" Olivia smiled.

"I'm sorry Darlin' but I have some business to discuss with Dad when we get back to the ranch.

"That's ok, I need to monopolize the piano for a while if that's alright?"

"Of course; it's all yours."

Olivia sighed deeply and leaned on Jake's shoulder.

"Tomorrow morning we'll sleep in, have a late breakfast, and relax, no pressure, ok?"

"That sounds good. I think I'm overtired."

"Why not just practice in the morning then?"

"If I know my mother at all, she has chosen a difficult piece and I'll probably need to practice in the morning as well. I don't want her to be disappointed."

They pulled up to the house and went inside. Harper and Whitman greeted them at the back door like old friends.

"Hi kids." Jake smiled roughing Whitman's ears."

Olivia couldn't help but smile. "Jake I'm going to change and then get busy." She kissed him softly on the mouth. "Thank you for today. I wouldn't have gotten through it without you."

"Yes you would have, you're tougher than you think." Jake replied. "I'll be in my office if you need anything Darlin'. Are you hungry for some dinner before you get started?"

"No, my mother killed my appetite. Thank you though."

"Ok" Jake smiled. "I love you." He swatted her butt as she headed up the stairs. She laughed.

He headed for his office and found his dad already there sitting at his desk. "Hey Dad" Jake said kindly as he shut the door locking it behind him.

"Exactly what's going on, Son?" Dacey asked looking seriously at him over the rims of his reading glasses.

"What do you mean?" Jake asked.

"I mean, why have you hired a private detective?"

Jake sighed, "I really can't talk about that right now, Dad."

"Well you have me worried, Bud. Is there anything I can do? What is it regarding, can you tell me that much?"

"It's not about business. It's about Olivia."

"Olivia? Is she in some kind of trouble?"

"I don't know yet. There's someone from her past who's potentially very dangerous and I just want to make sure he stays there in her past. I'll feel better knowing he isn't anywhere near her again."

"Do you think it's a possibility?" Dacey asked concerned pulling his glasses off, leaning forward on the desk.

"Unfortunately yes, I do. I'm handling it Dad, but thank you for your concern. Olivia has had a hard enough life. I won't let anyone hurt her again."

"Well, just know I'm here if you need me. Your Mama tells me you're going to propose to Olivia. So what is her family like? You met them today, right?"

"Eventually I'll propose. And yes, we just came from the Lodge. We had drinks with her parents and her brother, Miles.

Her brother is great and so is her dad. Her mother, well, her mother is not the nicest person I've ever met, let's just put it that way."

"That surprises me because Olivia seems so kindhearted."

"She is, but she didn't get it from her mother, that's for sure." Jake said thoughtfully.

"Where is she? I thought she was staying here?"

"She's going into the ballroom to practice a new piece of music on the piano. Her mother is a cellist and has decided they should play for everyone tomorrow. Oh, that reminds me, I need to set up some chairs in there."

"That sounds nice. Why don't you let me do that? It will give me a chance to get to know Olivia a little better, unless you think I would disturb her."

"I don't think she'd mind at all. Thanks, Dad."

You're welcome. I think she's a lovely girl Jacob, not that you care about my two cents but there it is." Dacey smiled as he closed the office door behind him.

Olivia heard a knock at one of the doors to the ballroom. "Come in" she called out.

"Am I interrupting?" Dacey asked, peeking around the door.

"No, of course not Mr. Weidner, this is your home."

"You call me Dacey. And, well, technically this is Jake's home. Frankie and I haven't lived in this house since the kids were in school. When Jake graduated from college, we signed it over to him as a gift of sorts."

"This is quite an amazing gift. My parents gave me some Luis Vuitton luggage for graduation. It was ironic because my son was little and I wasn't doing much in the way of traveling."

"You have a son, Olivia?"

"Uh, well, I had a son but he passed away last June."
Dacey came to her and squeezed her hand. "I'm so sorry for your loss, dear." Dacey said simply and honestly.

"So much like Jake," she thought. "Thank you." Her words were catching in her throat and she swallowed down the pain yet again.

Dacey could plainly see this subject was upsetting her, so he cleared his throat. "The reason I came in, uh, would I be bothering you if I set up some chairs for tomorrow? I know you are practicing, so I could come back later."

"No, no not at all" was all she could manage.

CHAPTER TWENTY-TWO

The private detective Jake hired picked up on the first ring. "Hello?"

"Hello, this is Jake Weidner. I'm returning your call. You have some information for me?"

"Yes I do. I did as you asked and ran a background check on the woman Olivia Curtis. Formerly, she went by Mrs. Olivia Karen Curtis-Montgomery. She was married to one Jackson Kyle Montgomery, deceased. Mr. Montgomery died in a car accident last June along with Mrs. Montgomery-Curtis' biological son. The son's name was Dante' River Curtis-Montgomery. It's a mouthful isn't it? Anyhow..."

Jake listened intently, but felt tightness in his chest. He would never have wanted to feel the loss of a child and though it was just a name on the paper to the investigator, he was a very important person to Olivia.

"The boy's biological father is one Patrick Hanson, uh, excuse me, Patrick Michael Hanson. The strange thing is that Mr. Hanson is related to the deceased Mr. Montgomery."

"Wait, what?" Jake asked in disbelief.

"Yeah, it seems Patrick Hanson and Jackson Montgomery are second cousins."

Jake gulped. "Is it possible Miss Curtis didn't know that?"

"Sure, that's possible. A lot of people don't even know their second cousins. So, yeah, I'd say it's possible."

"Patrick Hanson was charged and convicted of raping Miss Curtis and when he went to trial, Jackson Montgomery wasn't in the picture from what I could gather."

The investigator continued. "Patrick Hanson served two years of a six-year sentence for the rape. There were also attempted murder charges filed but the judge threw them out. The court documents showed the fire was ruled as accidental. Sir, I think someone paid off the fire marshal but that's just speculation."

"What makes you say that?" Jake asked, not believing what he was hearing.

"Mr. Weidner, I've been doing this a long time and the only answer I have is my gut tells me something was fishy about that whole deal.

I would bet my life Patrick Hanson set fire to the kitchen to cover up the assault and any evidence he might have left behind and yet the judge throws it out? It doesn't add up."

"Ok, go on." Jake was barely breathing.

"After two years, Patrick Hanson was paroled but then later convicted of assault in a separate incident. That victim was also a woman. He spent another, almost two years in a maximum security prison and then paroled again. Eighteen months ago he was released from parole and has kept his nose clean as far as I can tell. He is currently living in Sandpoint, Idaho, unmarried and working as a..."

Jake cut him off. "He lives in Sandpoint?"

"Yes sir, he works nights stocking shelves in a supermarket. He rents an apartment, has no girlfriend and no children. He doesn't have much of a life, though he spends a great deal of time on the internet. He has a top of the line home computer system. He's a registered sex offender and though he visits a lot of porn-sites on the internet, he seems to be flying under the radar these days. That's pretty much where the trail ends on him. As for Mrs. Curtis-Montgomery, well, she..."

"What?" Jake asked, his blood running cold.

"I just feel bad for the lady, Mr. Weidner. I don't usually take a personal interest in my cases but she's been dealt a pretty bad hand."

He continued the report. "At fourteen she performed at Carnegie Hall and had some other big performances on her schedule but then she was raped at sixteen. She attempted suicide and was hospitalized briefly. Obviously she carried the child to term and her son, Dante' was born on May 10th. She finished high school, went to college and graduated with honors from the University of Oregon School of Music and Dance. She married Jackson Montgomery and became a country club wife. I think we can both safely assume she doesn't know she married her rapist's second cousin. She chaired a few fundraisers but didn't perform much after marriage. Last year, shortly following the car accident that took the lives of her husband and son, she attempted suicide again and was committed involuntarily to Oregon State Hospital for psychiatric evaluation and care for almost three months. Shortly after she was released, she moved to Troy, Montana."

"Ok, that's plenty." Jake said. "I'd like you to fax me this report and any other details you have including photos. Do not email me, is that clear?"

"Yes sir. Are you sure you want to see these photos? They're brutal. I mean really bad."

"Yes" Jake replied simply though his head was spinning and his heart was breaking for Olivia. If a rough and tough P.I. says they're brutal, then it must be really bad.

"May I ask what you plan to do with this information, Mr. Weidner?"

"That's none of your business." Jake snapped.

"I know, Sir, but then usually I'm investigating cheaters and dirt bags. This case is completely different."

"I intend to keep Miss Curtis safe."

"That's good to know, thank you."

Jake hung up the phone and sat at his desk. This was a helluva lot to take in. On several occasions he'd thought of Olivia much like a frightened bird, this was just confirmation of those thoughts and of his dream. Though it was pointless, he wondered what a different person she would have been if she hadn't had to survive such a tragic life. Now, the cause of all of her pain was living less than a hundred miles away. It didn't take a genius to figure out why or the reason behind his internet obsession. People were easy enough to find and keep tabs on thanks to the internet revolution. He wondered how Olivia would feel, knowing her attacker lived nearby. The investigator was probably right; Olivia likely didn't know Jackson was related to Patrick Hanson. Jake hoped she never had to find out.

There was a note from Carmella on his desk saying he was to call Sam, but he would see her tomorrow. Right now he wanted to be with Olivia.

He didn't feel like thinking about her past anymore tonight. Instead, he wanted to think about their future together. He could hear music coming down the hall from the ballroom as he approached but it wasn't what he had expected. His dad was singing.

Jake smiled to himself as he leaned on the doorjamb to watch the two of them. Olivia was playing an Irish song by ear and Dacey was singing loudly, sitting next to her on the piano bench. It was a surprising and heartwarming sight. All the chairs were arranged and Olivia was smiling brightly as she played for his dad.

She noticed him first and stopped playing, blushing slightly. "Excuse me, Dacey" she said and got up to rush into Jake's arms. She reached up and kissed him quickly on the lips. "Jake, your dad is teaching me some of the Irish songs he grew up with."

"You two will be going on tour soon, I think." Jake teased.

"You never know." Dacey smiled. "Olivia is the one with the talent. This girl can play."

"Thank you, Mr. Weidner."

"No, no we talked about that; you call me Dacey."

"Ok, thank you for taking my mind off of things Dacey. I appreciate it. It was fun."

Dacey rose from the piano bench and kissed Olivia's cheek. "It was my pleasure, dear. We'll see the two of you tomorrow. Your mama and I are going home now but we'll be back in the morning. She wants to be here for all the preparations, you know."

Dacey left and Olivia sat again at the piano.

Jake followed to sit beside her. "I was in my office but I couldn't stop thinking about you. Are you about done here?" he asked hopefully.

She kissed him again, this time slower, softer. His lips felt so warm and perfect on hers. She didn't want to stop, not ever but her obligation won out. "Yeah I just need to go over this song one more time. Do you mind? You can be my audience?"

"Of course Darlin' but won't I make you nervous?"

"No, I'm happy to play for you. It's my mother who makes me nervous."

"Ok" he said and kissed her on the forehead. He took a seat in one of the chairs his father had set up, right in the front row.

He watched and listened closely as she played. So much passion came through her fingers, her body. He remembered how she described it. He could see clearly how it would feel that way. The music was sad and haunting and Jake's mind wandered. Against his will he thought about her attack, how violated she was, how it broke her, how it burned her. His fists clenched in reaction to his thoughts.

"Jake, what's wrong?" she stopped playing.

"Nothing Darlin', I'm just tired is all."

"Oh, I'm sorry, I can be done. It's not going to matter how much I practice, my mother will crucify me tomorrow regardless."

"I thought you played beautifully." Jake replied as he turned off the lights to the ballroom.

"You're biased."

"Perhaps I am" he said teasingly, and scooped her up and carried her up to his bedroom. They made love in the dark.

Olivia felt a heaviness coming from Jake that hadn't been there before. She wondered what was on his mind. Was he carrying around some sort of burden? She struggled over asking him about it but instead buried herself in his caress and the tenderness of his kisses. She didn't want to face anything; she simply wanted to escape into his love.

Thanksgiving morning Jake awoke alone. He and Olivia had another magical night together and now she was gone, as if she were an apparition. He sat up looking around the dimly lit room.

Olivia sat on the floor in front of the cold fireplace. She was completely naked. She hugged her knees like a child, still as stone. Jake couldn't see her eyes but instinctively knew something was wrong.

"Olivia?" He touched her shoulder; her skin was cool to his touch. Still, she didn't move. Again he said her name louder this time. She gasped as if waking from a nightmare.

"It's just me." He picked her up off the floor and laid her back in bed pulling the covers over her. He held her tightly.

"I couldn't sleep."

"I think you *were* sleeping. Are you alright? You're freezing." She shook her head but said nothing more.

Jake held her, rubbing her back and shoulders, warming her up. If he didn't know any better he'd swear she'd been outside in the snow. She shivered as if her body was just registering the cold and her teeth began to chatter.

Jake turned on the gas fireplace to warm up the room. "What happened?" he asked.

"Bad dream" she whispered.

"Do you want to talk about it?"

She turned to face him. He could tell she'd been crying either in her sleep or awake, he didn't know.

"I dreamt about an argument I had with Dante'. He was about twelve and he was so angry with me. He'd overheard Jackson and me fighting again. He told me we should leave Jackson. He said I was a coward if I didn't. I refused and tried to reason with him. I tried to explain but didn't have a good excuse. He saw right through me and accused me of only staying for the money and the comfort and he swore he would never be that kind of person. Maybe I *was* a coward. Dante' didn't know Jackson had threatened our lives if we left.

He screamed at me 'when he was grown he wouldn't live his life being afraid of everything'. He couldn't understand and I couldn't explain. I let him down so horribly."

"Did he know about his father?" Jake asked softly.

"That was the day I explained it to him. I told him about the man who raped me. I didn't cry. Somehow, I didn't cry. I told my twelve-year old son about my being raped; his conception and I didn't cry. I kept telling him how blessed I was to have such an incredible child. How special he was, how loved he was. He was so angry. He said it was just one more reason not to stay with Jackson. That night he ran away but I knew he would come back to me and he did in the morning. He said he didn't ever want to talk about it again. So we didn't."

Olivia wiped away the tears. "Jake, I can't face my mother today. I can't." She pulled the covers up over her head. With a muffled voice she said, "Can't I just hide under here today? You could sneak me some turkey."

Jake was so surprised she said it, he laughed and kissed at the covers over her face. "It won't be so bad, Baby. Miles and your dad will be disappointed if you don't visit them but if you're going to have Thanksgiving dinner in bed, then so am I."

"Perfect. Maybe Carmella will bring plates to both of us? Dad can come in here and say hello."

"Come on gorgeous, let's go face the music." Jake chuckled.

Olivia sighed deeply and pouted, "Dante' was right; I am a coward."

"No you aren't. You are brave and strong and have nothing to fear except maybe your mother." Jake said, hoping to lighten her mood.

"She hates me."

"Olivia, I realize I have only spent one afternoon with her but I don't think she hates you. She might hate *me* for tempting you to stay in 'Montana' but she definitely doesn't hate you."

"Yes she does. You wouldn't believe me if I told you what she said to me yesterday."

"What?"

"It's not worth repeating. She's still deciding whether or not I'm too good for you or if you're too good for me. I'm fairly certain after some deliberation, she'll vote in your favor."

"Don't let it get to you. Just let her be who she is and you, you be a duck."

"What?" Olivia giggled.

"Let whatever she says to you just roll right off you, like water off a duck's back. Be a duck."

"I may have *that* tattooed on my ass." Olivia replied.

"Don't you dare. I like your ass just the way it is."

"Ok, I guess it's unavoidable. I'm going to shower."

"Ok Darlin'," Jake replied. He waited for the door to close and took out his cell phone.

"Hey Jake, what's wrong? Did you forget something for Thanksgiving?" Sam asked.

"No, I was returning your call."

"Jake, I'm coming to your house in like four hours."

"I know but I thought there might be something you needed to tell me in private."

"Oh yeah, well, I found that horse. It took some digging but Maestro did have championship bloodlines. That made it easier. The best prospect I can find for you so far is the sire of Maestro and Wayward Lass. It's a horse called Caithness Mochaccino; a bay gelding, sixteen hands, born in 2010. The owners aren't offering him for sale though. He's a beauty. Apparently her horse was a Swedish Warmblood. How they managed to get him from breeders in New Zealand is beyond me. They have another gelding and a mare for sale but neither are the caliber I know you're looking for. I've got some contact info for you. I also sent you an email with some pictures. I think you'll be pleased. The rest is up to you though. They're going to want to play hardball on the price and I can't negotiate that for you. I have no idea how much you want to spend on a horse that isn't even for sale or that Olivia may not even want."

"She will, I'm sure of it. If I'm wrong, I'll sell him for a profit. Thank you. What time are you picking up the Curtis family?"

"At two o'clock, why? Are they awful? Miles told me his mother can be sorta harsh."

"Then, she is exactly as Miles described, though she might like you more than she likes me."

"Wow, I can't wait." Sam said sarcastically.

"I have to get in the shower. I'll see you later Sam."

"Ok, see you Jake."

Olivia came out of the bathroom as Jake was setting down his phone. "Working on Thanksgiving?" she asked, looking fresh and cozy in a big, white bathrobe.

"No, it was just Sam." He said. "How was the shower?" changing the subject.

"It was delectable but I missed you in there." She wrapped her arms around him.

"Hmm, you did, huh?"

"Yes sir I did."

"We'll make up for it tonight after everyone has gone."

"Tonight? Jake, I want to make love to you now," faking a pout.

"How could I refuse an offer like that?"

They made love again and Olivia felt renewed. Later on, they were both finally dressed and ready. They walked into the kitchen together to see if they could help Frankie and Carmella.

Frankie told her son, "Jacob, go find something to do. Go turn on the football game or see what your papa is up to while we entertain Olivia."

"I'm happy to help with the preparations, Mrs. Weidner." Olivia replied as Jake smiled and left the kitchen happily.

"Now I told you, call me Frankie and, of course you can help."

Olivia felt so at home here with Jake's mom and Carmella. It was the kind of moment she always secretly wished for with her own mother but Thanksgiving had never been celebrated like this in her family. On the rare occasion the Curtis family was all together for the holidays, the meals were catered, never home-cooked. The phrase 'home-cooked meal' wasn't in Antoinette Curtis' vocabulary.

In this moment though, Olivia felt all the things she wanted as a child and all the things she wanted for Dante' if she hadn't married a man like Jackson. The kitchen was filled with delicious and tempting smells. The turkey was roasting and food filled every countertop. It all looked incredible. It suddenly occurred to Olivia she was starving. She hadn't eaten dinner last night or breakfast this morning and now she was ravenous. Olivia snagged a carrot from the relish tray but Carmella caught her.

"Bella ragazza, manga. Eat if you're hungry. You need to eat. Keep your strength up." Carmella said.

Olivia was shocked Carmella would say that, especially in front of Frankie. She thought she better clear things up.

"Carmella, uh, I'm not pregnant."

"I know you aren't, not yet at least." Carmella grinned as she stirred something.

Olivia gasped and blushed deeply. "Carmella!"

"Oh Carmella stop teasing the poor girl, you'll give her a heart attack before I have a chance at *really* having grandchildren. You know Jessica isn't getting it done. My Jacob is my only hope." Frankie laughed.

Olivia knew it was all in good fun but she couldn't help panicking a little. She and Jake had only been together a very short time.

"Where is Jessica?" Olivia asked, changing the subject.

Frankie and Carmella exchanged knowing looks. "Whenever she visits the ranch she spends a lot of time in the stables or down at the bunkhouse. She's a sucker for strong, handsome, young cowboys." Frankie explained.

"That is a horrible lie, Mama." Jess said as she breezed in through the back door. "I was simply being hospitable to the poor men forced to work on Thanksgiving by my slave driving brother." She smiled. "Hi, Olivia!"

"They only had to do some feeding. Your brother doesn't have anyone doing anything extra today. Don't be naughty. The only people here today are having dinner with us and you know it. You're going to give Olivia the wrong idea about Jacob." Frankie scolded.

"Hi, Jessica. How many people are coming?" Olivia asked turning to Frankie.

"We're expecting about twenty." Carmella replied.

"Well my mother should be pleased." Olivia said, sighing.

"Why's that?" asked Jessica pulling off her boots in the doorway of the mudroom.

Olivia sat down on a stool next to Jessica. "Mother loves an audience."

"Oh right, Papa told me you two are going to play for us. What does your mom play?"

"She plays the cello."

"Wait, Curtis, right?" Jess asked.

"Yes."

"What's her first name?" suddenly very interested.

"Antoinette" Olivia replied, her shoulders slumping a bit.

"Oh my God, your mother is Antoinette Curtis? Holy shit!"

"Jessica, please don't talk like that, especially on Thanksgiving." Frankie scolded.

"Mama, Olivia's mother is famous. I saw her perform at Lincoln Center. Do you remember when I dated that Icelandic painter named Varick"?

"No I don't but go on, tesoro mia." Frankie replied.

"He took me on a date to Lincoln Center. He said there was a cellist performing he *had* to see. The cellist was Antoinette Curtis. Olivia, your mother is incredible. I can't believe I didn't make the connection sooner."

Olivia suddenly felt nauseous. This had been the way of things her entire life. Her mother was always the center of attention. It wasn't that she didn't want to be proud of her; she was *expected* to be proud of her. And worse, was the expectation Olivia would be just like her.

The expectation was overwhelming. The look on Jessica's face was the same one everyone had when they 'made the connection'. It was a look that said, "Wow, how lucky you must feel to have such an amazing, talented, beautiful woman as your mom. How come you don't measure up?"

Maybe it wasn't what they thought but that's what she felt. Olivia never regretted choosing piano over cello. It would have been too much to bear.

"Olivia, are you alright? You look a little peaked. Carmella's right, you should eat something." Frankie suggested.

"I'm ok, thank you but if no one would mind, I'll just go lay down for a bit before my family arrives."

"You go right ahead." Frankie said.

"Olivia, did I upset you?" Jessica asked.

"No, you didn't, I just didn't sleep very well."

Carmella handed her a little plate of hors de 'oeuvres. "Here, you need to eat something too," she said. "That will help. Would you like a cup of tea?"

"Thank you, no."

She returned to Jake's room and set the plate on his bedside table. She was too tired and too stressed out to worry about her hair and makeup. She kicked off her shoes and crawled onto Jake's bed. She buried her face in his pillow. It smelled like his shampoo and the undefinable scent that was authentically Jake. It was so comforting.

The only thing missing from this day of Thanksgiving was Dante'. If he were here, he would probably be watching football downstairs with the guys. He would have loved the normalcy of this place and of Jake's family. He would have laughed at her neurotic behavior and somehow him being a part of this, would have made everything easier. She fell asleep thinking of her son's smile.

Jake had fallen asleep in front of the TV but awoke to the sound of the doorbell. He hadn't realized how late it was and wondered where Olivia had disappeared to.

Frankie greeted Miles, Sam and Mr. and Mrs. Curtis at the door. Mr. Curtis held a large case that was quite obviously Mrs. Curtis' cello.

"Ciao, come in. Ciao Samantha, happy Thanksgiving. I'm Frankie Weidner and you must be Olivia's family." She said warmly inviting them into the foyer.

"Yes, I'm Jonathan Curtis. This is my wife Antoinette and our son Miles."

"I'm just so pleased to meet all of you. Welcome to our home. Let me take your coats. Samantha, would you show everyone into the dining room please?" she asked.

"Of course" Sam replied.

Jake walked in just then and smiled. "Hi, I'm glad you made it. I'll help with the coats and we'll be right in and join you. Miles, do you and Sam want to open a bottle of wine?"

"Sure Jake, where's Liv?" Miles asked. "Did she take herself a walk?"

"No, she's uh, she'll be right down. Make yourselves comfortable."

Jake followed Frankie into the kitchen. "Mama, have you seen Olivia?"

"She went to lie down a while ago. If you see your papa, tell him we're going to eat without him if he doesn't get in here."

Jake rolled his eyes and smiled. He went up to his room to find Olivia curled around his pillow like a kitten and sleeping soundly. There was a plate of untouched food next to the bed.

"Darlin'?" he said gently. He hated to wake her. He had witnessed just how difficult sleeping was for her.

Olivia rubbed her eyes with the back of her hand and yawned. "Hmm?"

"Your family is here. It's time to wake up."

She sat up quickly. "Oh no, are you kidding me?"

"No, I'm afraid not. It's alright though not everyone is here yet. You have time."

Olivia rubbed her face. Jake bent down and picked up her shoes and placed them on her feet. Then he leaned over and kissed her.

"How bad do I look? Tell me the truth."

"You look fine."

Olivia squealed like a frightened teenager and flew off the bed and into the bathroom. Jake heard her squeal again from inside. Five minutes later, she came out looking gorgeous.

"You look beautiful. No one would ever guess you'd been napping."

"Thank you, this is as good as it's going to get I think. I can't believe I slept and like the dead, too. I can't believe I let myself."

"You needed rest. I took a little nap too."

"Who's here?" Olivia asked, kissing Jake on the lips.

"Who cares?" Jake said, holding her close to him.

"Jake!" she protested.

"Probably everyone now, let's get to the table before Carmella or my mom come looking for us."

"Yeah, or worse, my mother."

Jake laughed.

The dinner wasn't the catastrophe Olivia thought it would be. There were enough people around the table to keep her mother occupied and to run interference for her. She was grateful for all the outgoing personalities and loud voices, for the funny stories and shared family jokes.

All of the introductions had gone smoothly with the exception of Jake introducing Miles to Jessica. Olivia noticed Sam bristle slightly. Her brother had always been a flirt and she desperately hoped he had no plans to break either girl's heart. Apparently her brother was a hot ticket and was enjoying all this female attention.

The fabulous dinner was beginning to wind down but the drinks were still flowing freely when Olivia's mother leaned over to speak to Jessica. Strategically, they had been seated next to one another.

Jessica stood up and tapped her wine glass lightly. "Ahem, excuse me everyone, if I could please have your attention?"

The group quieted. Olivia put her hands in her lap and took a deep breath.

Jess continued, "Tonight we have the distinct honor to enjoy a private performance by a musical legend, Mrs. Antoinette Curtis and she will be accompanied on the piano by her equally talented daughter, Olivia Curtis. We'll give them a moment to set up and then join them in the ballroom."

Olivia smiled and looked to Jake. "I guess that's my cue."

"Don't worry Darlin', you're among friends." Jake whispered in her ear.

"Yeah, but I have to play with a dragon-lady." Olivia replied quietly forcing a grin. She joined her mother in the ballroom. "Mother, I asked that this not be a spectacle."

"It's not a spectacle but someone had to tell them we're going to play. I like Jessica Weidner very much. She works in an extremely well known art gallery in New York City. Did you know that?"

"Yes I did." Olivia replied dryly and thought, "Jessica would make a superb daughter for her mother."

"Did you practice today?" Antoinette asked as Olivia sat at the piano, feeling suddenly cold and exposed.

"Yes, well, not today but last night I did." Olivia replied, feeling like a twelve year old.

"Olivia, I wish you would be more disciplined and learn to take things seriously."

"I wish *you* would..." but Olivia didn't finish, as people were entering to take their seats.

Jake, Sam and Miles came in first and everyone else followed rather casually with their glasses in hand. It gave Olivia some peace hearing the conversations and laughter from Jake's family and friends. At least *they* weren't taking this too seriously.

Jake couldn't take his eyes off Olivia. She looked radiant and as she began playing, the moment was compelling. Her mother joined in and it was as if their dueling personalities somehow lent to a perfectly balanced duet.

Olivia had a look of contentment and satisfaction. Jake would almost call it a smirk. He glanced around at the crowd of people and everyone was mesmerized.

After their third song everyone cheered. Olivia and Antoinette smiled politely and bowed their heads but as Olivia rose, Antoinette said, "Olivia will now play one more piece for you."

"No, Mother I..." she began but Antoinette gave her a look that burned through her.

"Of course" Olivia replied quietly sitting back down. Situating herself and taking a deep breath she began to play Rachmaninoff's Piano Concerto Number Two Opus Eighteen as passionately and as loudly as she could muster. She'd been pushed as far as she would be pushed by her mother. Without a misstep or forethought she bridged into 'Grandma Got Ran Over By a Reindeer'.

She didn't dare look away from the piano but she knew with certainty that her mother was seething. The audience began to chuckle and Jake laughed loudly. As she finished, everyone cheered and she stood without looking over to her mother and presented a grand bow. "Thank you everyone." Olivia said over the sounds of their laughter. The audience cheered again and quieted.

Olivia winked stealthily at Miles, she couldn't help her smirk. He decided to rescue her from immediate punishment. "Mom, would you mind playing a little Bach for us?"

"Of course I will Miles." Antoinette replied trying desperately to keep her composure.

Olivia sat down next to Jake who whispered, "Darlin' you were incredible and that was so funny. I never expected it."

"Thank you; neither did my mother. I'm sure I'll hear about it." She said gritting her teeth.

Antoinette played one last piece and Olivia listened carefully. As much as she wanted to hate her mother, there was magic in her playing that made it impossible. She couldn't really hate anyone who could create music so passionately. Her mother looked beautiful and regal and she began to feel a twinge of regret about her "outburst." She watched as Antoinette Curtis took the whole room on a musical journey. She always pictured pretty English gardens and grey skies like something out of a classic novel when her mother played Bach.

As the song ended and everyone applauded, Antoinette gave Olivia a meaningful look. "Jake, I think I'm being summoned. Would you mind showing my dad around the ranch before dark?"

"It would be my pleasure. Are you going to be ok with your mother?"

"Yes, or you might be attending my funeral...I'm not sure which." Olivia tried to joke.

"Don't let her get to you, remember," he whispered, "be a duck." He kissed her gently, but briefly on the lips.

Dacey and much of the group headed to the media room for dessert, football and more drinks and Jake sought out Olivia's father. Jake had hoped for just this opportunity.

"Mr. Curtis, would you be interested in a tour of the ranch or would you rather watch the football game?"

"A tour sounds great Jake. I don't really follow football." Jonathan admitted.

"I'll just grab our coats and we can go take a look at the stables."

"Great, a walk sounds terrific after such a fantastic meal. Carmella is an excellent chef."

"Yes she is. She and Mom have been cooking Thanksgiving dinner together for as long as I can remember."

"It was wonderful. Your family has been so welcoming and gracious. It means a lot to me."

They stepped outside into the cold air. Snow fell lightly. "Olivia means a lot to *me*, Sir."

"I can see that Jake. You know I've spent most of Olivia's life worrying about her. She probably doesn't even realize how much. My wife, well, my wife has always tried to "handle" Olivia but I think she does better when people aren't trying to "handle" her. Don't you Jake?" Jonathan said as though he were hinting at something.

"Yes sir, that sounds about right." Jake replied, smiling. They walked into the stables and out of the weather. They stopped in front of one of the stalls and a horse approached the gate hoping for a treat.

"This is quite a place you have here." Mr. Curtis said admiringly.

"Thank you; my family has worked very hard for this. I just hope to continue their legacy and make them proud."

"I'm sure you do make them proud." Mr. Curtis said and clapped Jake on the shoulder kindly.

"Thank you. You certainly have a very talented family, Mr. Curtis. Mrs. Curtis and Olivia have made today very special."

"Yes, they are both exceptional musicians, I just wish my wife would take it easy on Olivia."

Jake nodded, but said nothing.

"Oh come on Jake, you're no dummy. My wife can be "confrontational" let's say and her favorite subject? Our daughter."

"I don't know what to say Mr. Curtis. This is your family we're talking about."

"You don't have to say anything but I don't think we should pretend otherwise. Do you?"

"No Sir. I've never been good at pretending."

"I want you to understand something. I don't know how much Olivia has shared with you, but she has had it really rough, not just because of Antoinette but for many reasons and if you really care for her then you won't make it any harder on her. My wife is determined that Olivia leave Montana and from what I've seen, *I* think she should stay. She seems happier here.

She seems happy with you. Just try and keep it that way, ok Jake?"

"Yes Sir. I'll do my best." Jake replied. "Mr. Curtis, uh, I need to say something too."

"Spit it out Son."

Jake smiled, took a breath and continued. "I love your daughter, Sir. I was serious about that. *I am* serious about her. I know it probably seems like we don't know each other very well but I can tell you honestly, she is the best thing that ever happened to me. All I want is to see her happy. She's my whole world and I love her truly, so I'm asking your permission to marry Olivia."

Jonathan Curtis stood with his arms crossed over his chest and watched as this good man expressed his love for his only daughter. It was a new experience for him. Jackson had never been so thoughtful or traditional. Jonathan had a good feeling about Jake. He was honest, sincere and obviously passionate about Olivia. Jake was all heart where Jackson had been merely appearance.

Jake waited nervously as Mr. Curtis seemed to be thinking it over.

Jonathan spoke slowly, "I haven't really talked to Olivia much lately. How does *she* feel about getting married again? You do know she was married before, don't you?"

"Yes, I know about her husband and her son. As for marrying again..." Jake half-smiled, "I don't know exactly. I haven't asked her yet. I'm afraid to push things too quickly. I won't pressure Olivia. I don't want to scare her off."

"So are you asking my opinion or my permission?"

"Both" Jake replied, hoping he hadn't blown it.

"Jake you have my permission." He paused. "As for my opinion, I think you should wait, at least for a while. Olivia does seem better, a lot better than she was a few months ago but I also feel like some of that is," he paused again, "just an act. She wants everyone, including and probably especially you, to think she has it all together."

Jake listened and nodded, but his face betrayed him.

"Don't get me wrong Jake, I can tell she's getting better but grief isn't something you can shut like a door. My grandson was her whole world; she lived and breathed that boy. I would say it bordered on obsession. Can you imagine the one thing that makes your world turn being taken away from you? That's what happened to Olivia. Dante' used to complain to me about his mom's overprotective nature but I know as much as he complained, he loved *her* just as much."

Jonathan's eyes glistened as he spoke about his grandson. "Dante' would golf with me on Saturday's. Did Olivia tell you that?"

"No sir, she didn't."

"Mrs. Curtis could never fully accept Dante'. The circumstances surrounding his birth were, well, she just couldn't get over it. To her, he represented all the things that went wrong in Olivia's life, but to me..." he choked, "to me he was the one good thing *in* her life. I don't know if that makes any sense to you. I honestly don't know how much she's told you. I guess I should keep my mouth shut."

"No, you're fine. Olivia told me about, um, well, how her son came to be. She didn't want us to have any secrets." Jake explained, trying to be as delicate as possible. He refused to use the word rape with Olivia's father, especially now that he could see how much the man loved and missed his grandson.

Mr. Curtis nodded his head and sniffed. "I'll never forgive myself for what happened to her and for everything after." He looked at Jake seriously.

"There's nothing you could have done."

"There's plenty I could have done and should have done. I should have protected her better. Did you know that maggot is still a free man, after everything, he is still walking the streets?"

"Yes, I do know that. I respect you Mr. Curtis and so I hope you won't judge me too harshly but I did some investigating.
I wanted to find out if *that maggot* was still a threat to Olivia."

"...and?"

"He lives less than a hundred miles from here and I'm willing to bet it isn't by chance."

"Oh, my, maybe Olivia *should* move back to Oregon with us." Mr. Curtis said, rethinking his position.

"With all due respect, I think he would only follow her there. I'm almost certain he followed her here." Jake said seriously.

"He had good lawyers. When Olivia had to testify at his trial, they shredded her. She probably never told you that. There was no chance he would get the maximum sentence because he went on that stand, so innocent, so believable."

"They never even talked about the fire he set. There was even speculation in the papers that she had set the fire herself because she was depressed and wanted to die. He nearly killed her. Somehow my daughter endured it all, the humiliation of the trial, the rumors that plagued her, the dirty looks, somehow she survived it all."

"I'm so sorry Mr. Curtis, truly."

"I have to do something! I can't let him get to her a second time!" Jonathan said angrily pounding his fist into his own hand.

"I spoke to my attorney and he informed me no legal action can be taken as long as the scumbag hasn't broken any laws. I've hired an investigator to keep tabs on him and I intend to squash him like the bug he is just as soon as he sneezes in the wrong direction. I won't let him get anywhere near Olivia, Sir. I promise you that. I honestly think she's safer here than anywhere. It's a small and close knit town. People look out for one another. If someone like him came to town, I would hear about it before he could even order breakfast."

"I appreciate it Jake but I think I would feel better if she just came back to Oregon. She should be with her family. I'm sorry."

"If that's what she wants, I won't stop her."

Jonathan chuckled, "You and I both know she won't come home. There are too many bad memories there.
I can't say I blame her but I can't just sit back and watch her get hurt again, either."

"I would give my life for Olivia. I **won't** let her get hurt!" Jake vowed seriously.

"I'll tell you what, if Olivia decides to stay here, then I'm going to put my trust in you to keep her safe but I'm still going to suggest she move home to live with her mother and me. Whatever she decides I'll support but if she stays here, I want you to keep me informed. Is that clear, Son?"

"Crystal" Jake said. They shook hands in agreement.

"So, you're going to marry my Slugger?" Jonathan said, lightening the mood a bit.

"If she'll have me. I'd appreciate it if we could keep this between you and me, at least for the time being. I don't want her to find out before I've had a chance to ask her properly."

"My lips are sealed."

"Thank you, Sir, for your trust, well, for everything" Jake said sincerely.

"You should probably call me Jonathan." He smiled, placing a hand on Jake's shoulder. He had a feeling he was really going to like his future son-in-law despite what Antoinette did or thought.

They walked back to the house after dark.

Through the windows they could see the family eating pie, drinking coffee, laughing, talking. But Jake didn't see Olivia or her mother. They came through the kitchen door and Carmella set a plate of pie in Mr. Curtis' hand. She could always be depended upon to feed people. Jake waved off the dessert and headed for the ballroom. Jonathan stayed behind talking with Carmella and savoring the most delicious pumpkin pie he had ever eaten.

The doors to the ballroom were closed. Frankie and Jessica were standing in the hallway outside as Jake approached quietly.

"What's going on?" he asked.

"Shh" they said in unison.

"Are you two eavesdropping?" He whispered.

"No, yes, no, well..." Frankie mumbled quietly. "Mrs. Curtis said she needed to have a word with Olivia, alone."

"Oh great, my sister *and* mother are listening in on a private conversation?" Jake shook his head and rolled his eyes.

"I'm sorry, but I asked Mama to stay because I overhead Mrs. Curtis speaking very meanly to Olivia and I felt bad. I thought we should wait and make sure she was ok. It's my fault." Jessica explained.

"What did she say?" Jake asked, still whispering.

"Just trust me, it was awful. I don't think she liked the way Olivia played piano but I thought she played beautifully; everyone did."

As Jessica said that, they could hear Mrs. Curtis raising her voice. "I don't know what I've ever done to deserve this kind of treatment from my own daughter. I've only ever wanted you to be successful but think of how this reflects on me. What if it were recorded? Did you think of how you could damage my career? Do you even care?"

Then they heard Olivia raise her voice as well. "Mother I do care and I would never try to damage your career. All I've ever wanted was for you to accept me as I am, not the vision you have of me, but really who I am, inside. When have you ever been on my side? You weren't supportive with Dante' and now again I feel your disappointment in me. Why am I never good enough for you?!"

"How long have they been in there?" Jake asked quietly, his temper flaring.

"Since you and Mr. Curtis went outside I guess. It's been awhile." Frankie shook her head, feeling sorry for Olivia.

"Ok, I'll take care of this. You two amateur spies go on and I'll deal with it." Jake told them.

"Ok Jacob, we'll leave you to it." Frankie said, and ushered her daughter down the hall.

Jake opened the door quickly as if he had no idea what was going on. Olivia was seated at the piano facing her mother who was standing over her. They both looked over when he walked in. Olivia's face was filled with relief and Antoinette's face was filled with barely restrained anger.

"There you are Darlin'. You're missing out on dessert. Carmella is serving pie if you are interested Mrs. Curtis."

Olivia looked at him with wide eyes and then down to her lap with obvious embarrassment.

"We'll be there in a moment. Olivia and I just need to finish our talk and then we'll join you." Antoinette said smoothly with a pasted-on smile.

Jake walked over to Olivia and took her hand, "Come on Darlin', you don't want to miss Carmella's pumpkin pie, trust me."

Olivia stood up and Antoinette grabbed her by the wrist. "Jake, I said we needed another minute alone." Mrs. Curtis said firmly as if she were scolding a child.

"I heard you Ma'am but there's plenty of time for that later. I don't want you to miss out on all this great food and conversation." Jake insisted.

Olivia felt like the rope in a game of tug of war. Her mother's nails dug into her skin, delivering a very clear message, Olivia would stay or face more of her mother's wrath later. Internally, she sighed.

"Let's go be social Mother. We'll finish our talk later, ok?" Olivia unwound her mother's hand from her wrist.

"Fine, of course you're right. Now isn't the time. You have my apologies, Jake." Antoinette, pursing her lips let out a long breath to control her frustration at being maneuvered.

"There's nothing to apologize for. Let's have some fun, shall we?" Jake smiled politely but Olivia could see the anger and intensity behind it.

Olivia hugged Jake. She felt like a prisoner who'd finally been released. The moment made Mrs. Curtis retreat from them. Olivia watched as she strode down the long hallway.

When they were alone, Jake said, "What the hell was that about?"

Tears began to form at the corners of her eyes. But she was determined not to let them spill over. Jake wanted to run after 'The Dragon Lady' and tell her how he really felt but he knew he couldn't.

"I'm just a disappointment, that's all. I shouldn't have played that silly song. I lost my temper."

Jake held her tightly by the shoulders and looked her right in the eyes. "Well if that's what it looks like when you lose your temper, I guess I've got nothing to worry about." He laughed. "And, you are **not** a disappointment. Do you hear me? Your mother is wrong. Are you alright?"

One tear did escape onto Olivia's cheek and Jake touched it gently with his finger.

"I am now." She leaned into his strong chest.

He wrapped his arms around her and held her close. "I love you Darlin', keep that in mind.

After some time, the party began to wind down and the only ones to remain were Jake's family. Olivia sat in the kitchen on a barstool. She had kicked her shoes off and held a glass of wine. Jake had gone off to the media room to spend some quality time in front of the television with his dad while Frankie and Carmella were now surveying the cleaned kitchen.

"Olivia, what are you thankful for? I usually require everyone at my Thanksgiving dinner to tell me what they're thankful for but this year, I completely forgot. So, you're it." Frankie mused, swirling her little glass of sweet wine.

Olivia smiled sadly, trying to push thoughts of Dante' from her mind. "I'm thankful for Jake. He saved my life."

Frankie came to her and put her hand on her face. "Dacey told me about your son. I hope you won't be upset with him."

"No, I don't mind; I never planned on him being a secret."

Carmella looked at Frankie questioningly.

Olivia saw the look and explained, "See Carmella, I had a son who passed away this last year. I feel like Jake has helped me get through some really tough moments."

"Oh my, oh dear, I'm so sorry." Carmella leaned forward to cover Olivia's hand. "I had no idea."

"Thank you but I'm doing ok. So Carmella, what are you thankful for?" Olivia asked.

"Good wine and good friends" she said, "but not necessarily in that order."

Olivia and Frankie laughed and toasted each other.

"I'm thankful for my family, tipping her glass to include Carmella, "and now, for you Olivia." Frankie said tipping her glass toward Olivia.

"Me? Why?" Olivia smiled.

"You saved my Jacob too." She said sincerely. "He has never been this way before, so loving or so attentive. I hate to tell you this but women have only ever been a dalliance for him. He's always loved his family fiercely and worked so very hard and he's passionate about the outdoors, but never has he been truly passionate about a woman. He's needed you, Olivia. You're the one for him and whatever circumstances brought you into his life and ours, I'm grateful."

Olivia hugged Frankie. "Thank you. No one's ever said that to me before; not ever." She couldn't help the tears welling.

"No, thank *you*. I mean it. You are exactly what I've always hoped, for Jacob."

"Alright you two, that's enough sappiness." Jessica said as she joined them in the kitchen. "Tomorrow is Black Friday, let's talk shopping."

"Where have *you* been hiding?" Frankie asked, pouring Jess a glass of wine.

"I was just socializing. I met the new guy Matthew. He is so cute and he's just so eager to please Jake in this new job. I guess Jakey has him working with the horses at the Outfitters." Jessica replied happily. "And Olivia, he's from Oregon too, from around Portland I think he said. Did you know Jake had a cowboy from Portland working here?"

"No, I didn't realize that. I guess I should have done more socializing tonight."

"No biggy, your mother did sort of monopolize you for quite some time." Jessica said bluntly.

"I'm sorry about that. She and I haven't seen each other in so long, we needed to catch up."

"It sounded like more than "catching up"." Jess said, pushing the subject.

"Jessica!" Frankie scolded.

"It's ok. It *was* more than that. It's not like it's a secret anyway. She wants me to move back to Oregon and as I expected, she was very angry about my little added performance. She also felt like I bailed on her when I went to sit with Jake. Let's see, what else? Oh yeah, she hated my clothes and was embarrassed I didn't get my nails done." Olivia sighed, inspecting her hand. "She was right about my nails."

Actually glad for a chance to unload, she looked up at the women who all shared a look of confusion, shock and sadly, pity. "Please don't look at me that way. It's ok, really, I'm used to it. My mother has *never* been satisfied with me. It's nothing new." Olivia shrugged, taking a gulp from her wineglass. "Is Jake still in the media room?"

Jess, glad for a change of subjects said, "No I think he and Dad went into Jake's office."

The door to Jake's office was open but Olivia's heels clacked on the hardwood floor as she approached so the men quieted when they heard her. She stopped in the doorway and knocked on the doorframe.

"Come on in" Jake said lightly, though he still looked serious. Dacey smiled at her warmly.

"Are you sure; I didn't mean to interrupt?"

"You aren't interrupting anything. Jake and I have plenty of time to talk business, don't we, Son?" Dacey rose to take his leave.

"Yes Sir, we do." Jake answered.

"Why are you waaaay over there, Darlin'?" Jake drawled.

"Jake, um..." she began.

"Uh oh, what's wrong? Is it about your mother? I'm sorry she cornered you."

"No, it's not that. It was bound to happen after what I pulled. She needed to vent, so I let her."

"What is it then?"

"My parents want me to move back to Oregon. It's one of the things my mother brought up during our 'talk'. I should say she is *insisting* I move back." Olivia sighed deeply.

"Oh" Jake said, noncommittally.

"That's all you have to say?"

"Olivia listen, I don't want you to go. Do you need to hear me say it? Don't go. Of course I don't want you to go but I also don't want to stand in the way of what you want either."

"I want you. I want you Jake! I want Montana and Troy and this small town life. I want the opposite of everything I left behind. I can't go back there! I won't."

Jake felt like he'd been holding his breath. "Good, because I don't think I'd like living there and I'm not letting you go without me."

"What *aren't* you telling me?" she asked, feeling there was something beneath it.

"Your dad already told me he was going to ask you to come home as well, and I told him I really hoped you wouldn't, but that I wouldn't stand in your way. I also promised him I'd look out for you here, if you decided to stay."

"I don't need a babysitter. I'm a grown woman." She said petulantly.

"Well how do you feel about a boyfriend?" he smirked.

"A boyfriend, I can handle."

"Good, now will you come sit with me?" he asked, closing the laptop on his desk.

The motion didn't go unnoticed by Olivia but she decided not to overthink it. He looked completely inviting and completely charming in his leather chair. She sat on his lap and kissed him gently at first but working up to the same crazy intensity that thrived between them. The flames of passion lapped at their skin and enticed every nerve ending.

Jake stopped for a moment, catching his breath as if he were coming up for air after swimming deep in the ocean. "We should probably say goodnight to my family before I get lost in you again." He whispered nuzzling her hair.

"Ok, I suppose we should." She was feeling just as breathless. She stood up straightening her slacks and touched her hair.

The gesture was reminiscent of their first night together. "You look beautiful. Did I tell you that?" he asked as he linked his arm with hers.

"I'm pretty sure you did." She smiled naughtily.

After saying goodnight to Jake's family they went upstairs together. It was so quiet in the house and Olivia was feeling the exhaustion begin to sink in. She kicked off her shoes and opened her overnight bag.

She took something out and put it behind her back. "I didn't wrap this but it's something I want you to have." She held out a small framed picture.

He took it and turned it over in his hands. Here was a wonderful picture of Olivia and a young man. They were standing on a beach both with their shoes off and their jeans rolled up. Dante' was taller than his mother by a couple inches. It was the first time Jake had seen her son but it was obviously him. She looked so happy.

"Darlin' I love it. Are you sure you want me to have it?"

"I'm positive. I love you both."

CHAPTER TWENTY-THREE

The next few days were busy and Olivia couldn't wait for her mother to go back to Oregon. She was never so grateful for Sunday to arrive. She'd barely seen Miles since dinner on Thursday and could only guess he and Sam were keeping each other entertained. That left Olivia to act as the perfect hostess to her parents. Mrs. Weidner was helpful in that department and made an excellent buffer between Olivia and her mother.

On Saturday, Olivia arranged to have lunch with her parents at the restaurant in the Lodge. She needed to have a very frank discussion with them, without any members of the Weidner family present. "I'm not going to move back to Oregon." She began rather bluntly, leaving her salad untouched.

"Of course you are Olivia, don't be ridiculous. Your father and I have discussed it and it's what we think is best." Antoinette pronounced sipping her wine as she faced Olivia across the table.

"Dad, is that really how you feel too?" Olivia asked, hoping just once her father might have her back.

"I think it would be best. You need your family, Olivia." He looked at his plate, rather than at her.

Her heart sank yet again. "I'm not moving back." She protested trying to draw him in.

"Olivia, have you even considered it? We worry about you, so far away." Jonathan said finally looking at her and laying his hand on her arm.

"I know you worry Dad and I'm sorry but I won't; I can't move back there."

"It's because of Jake isn't it?" Antoinette asked.

Olivia stumbled a bit. "Partly, but it's not just about him, it's about me. It's about what I want."

"Jake would relocate to Oregon for you. You seem to have him wrapped around your little finger, though for the life of me, I really don't know what you see in *him*. I think you can do better Olivia."

"Of course you do Mother."

Jonathan still with his hand on Olivia's arm, looked at his wife, "Now Antoinette, I think Jake is a very good man who loves her and seems to make her happy, but Olivia, I think your mother has a point,

Jake would likely move to Oregon for you."

"No please, both of you. Listen to me, for once! I am **not** moving back to Oregon! I'm not moving in with the two of you and I'm not leaving Montana. *This* is my home."

"No, it's not. Your home is in Lake Oswego. Your home is with us!" Antoinette ordered fiercely.

"I don't belong there Mother! I will not live in that fucking house!" Olivia said darkly.

Antoinette grabbed Olivia's hand and squeezed. "Do not speak to me that way, you selfish child."

"I'm not selfish and I'm **not** a child! If you expect me to live in that house where I was raped, you're out of your mind, Mother!!!" Olivia grimaced through her teeth. She could only see red. That place haunted her dreams and life. It would never be her home again.

"Both of you stop this, right now." Jonathan intervened. "Antoinette, we cannot force our grown daughter to do something she doesn't want to do. She's right, she's not a child. She has to make her own decisions to be able to heal and move on with *her* life. Olivia, I expect you will at least consider this offer and understand that we want to help you, to even live in your own apartment or condo. I don't think it's too much to ask to consider it. Now, that's about enough, both of you. Let's discuss something else; anything else." He was ashamed of the words he let come out of his mouth. The guilt he'd carried for so long like a tumor grew in size again and threatened to overtake him. Why didn't he fight for her? Why had he never fought for her?

The rest of the lunch was like a slow march through hell but somehow, Olivia endured.

Later they met with Frankie at the Weidner home for tea. Frankie had suggested it as a way to get to know Olivia and her mother better. Olivia had dropped her dad off at the ranch to meet Jake and then drove back into town. Her mother was quiet on the drive, simply staring out the window. Olivia was grateful.

As Frankie was serving the chai tea, Antoinette said, "Frankie, we've suggested to Olivia she move back to Oregon."

"Oh dear, Olivia, I hope you aren't considering leaving us. You know, you are very welcome here." Frankie said still holding out the cup and saucer to Olivia, then sitting in her chair a little stunned.

Olivia could have killed her mother and then died her own humiliating death. "No, I'm not moving back, I'm quite happy here Frankie, thanks to you and all your family."

"I would think you would understand not wanting to be so far away from your children." Antoinette said pointedly to Frankie.

Frankie chuckled, "Sure, when they were little, but my children are grown and it seems, so are yours. We can't hold onto them forever. I always tell my kids to remember they have roots and wings. They have the love of a family and a place to call home, but also the ability to choose as they please. I don't let the distance bother me. It simply makes the time I *do* spend with them all the more precious. Besides, it's a good excuse to go to New York once in a while."

"Yes, but then Troy isn't exactly New York, now is it?" Antoinette commented harshly.

Olivia noticed her mother's claws were especially sharp today.

"So you would be happy if Olivia chose not to come home to Oregon but moved to New York City?" Frankie observed.

"It would be more fitting for someone with her talent." Antoinette seemed to forget Olivia was in the room.

"Perhaps, but what would make *her* happier?" Frankie asked, particularly sharp herself.

Olivia interjected, trying desperately to change the subject. "Um, anyway, so this is really good tea Frankie. It was so nice of you to invite us."

"*You* are welcome anytime." Frankie replied, leaving Antoinette out on purpose.

Olivia's mother had always been a frustrating and confusing woman. She wanted Olivia to have a career and forget about ever having a family but when Dante' was born, suddenly she was shoving a husband down her throat for appearance sake. Now she seemed to want the Weidner's to like Olivia but recognize how unworthy of her they were. In the end, it was always Olivia who felt unworthy. The Weidner's were sweet, kind people and Olivia had nothing to offer but her terrifying mother. She knew what she wanted; she just couldn't convince herself she deserved it. And no matter what her heart desired, she knew fate would win out.

On Sunday morning, Olivia and Jake stood on the tarmac finally saying goodbye to her family.

"Will we see you at Christmas Olivia?" Antoinette asked pointedly.

"I don't know yet Mother." she replied. "I'm glad you all came."

"Yes, well I had to see you were alright. I hope you change your mind about moving."

"I won't."

Antoinette made a 'humph' sound and turned to Jake. "Thank you Jake for your hospitality. You'll tell your parents thank you as well, won't you?"

"Of course I will, Mrs. Curtis. Thank you for coming and have a safe trip."

Antoinette pulled on Jake's sleeve and walked them away from everyone else. "I realize now how much influence you have on her, Jake. I want you to convince her to move home. If you love her, you will do what's best for her and this, is what's best. You can see her as often as you'd like. You have a plane; you could fly to see her, when she isn't performing, of course."

Jake clenched his fists. Never had he felt such a desire to hit a woman in his whole life. "Ma'am, I'm going to say this in the most respectful way I know how. You don't have the first clue what's best for your daughter. If you did, you'd realize it isn't living in the same house where she nearly died or living in the same town where her son is buried. You would know she has so much strength and determination that if she really wanted that precious career you keep pushing; she would reach for it herself. Now, I'm going to smile and pretend we never had this conversation and you Ma'am, are going to go home and think about all the ways you can work on being a better mother."

Antoinette stood there her mouth gaped open. Olivia watched from afar unsure of what had just transpired.

Jake smiled and rejoined the others. "It looks like the pilot is ready for you." he said happily.

Miles hugged Olivia until her eyes started to water. "I love you Liv. You'll see me again soon."

"I'm glad, Miles. I love you too." Olivia swallowed hard.

Then Jonathan shook Jake's hand and hugged his daughter tightly. "I'm sorry, Slugger. I know we don't make it easy on you. I never meant to let you down."

"I'll live." Olivia said, a tear slipping down her cheek.

"If you need me I won't be far away. I promise. You can call me anytime ok? I love you." Jonathan's voice cracked.

"I love you too, Daddy. I'm going to be ok."

"I know you are. You're strong, you're beautiful and your smart and I'm very, very proud of you."

Her family boarded the plane and Olivia felt a mix of relief and regret. She hated to admit it but seeing her dad made her feel a little homesick. Though she knew very much more time spent with her mother and that feeling would pass.

Jake turned to Olivia as they watched her family board the plane. "Slugger, huh?"

"Yeah, you know when I was in kindergarten I hit a boy in the eye because he teased me about my red hair. My dad thought it was pretty funny and called me Slugger. I guess it stuck."

"I like it. Your mother sure doesn't like me." Jake said looking toward the plane.

"Why do you say that?" Olivia asked turning to him. "What did you talk to her about?"

"You, Darlin', we talked about you. She wants me to encourage you to move back home."

"Jake, I *am* home." She squeezed his hand and held on.

As she said it, she couldn't help flashing back to her vision of Jake falling, maybe dying. She didn't know if he would survive and the unknown was like a knife in the dark. She thought, "You never know when you'll run into it." She couldn't make herself leave him and she couldn't think of another way to save him. Her mind filled with terror and blackness gripped her heart. The dark and horrible voice of her curse slithered in her mind like a snake preparing to bite. "You cannot save him. Your destiny is carved in stone from an ancient curse and you shall never escape it. Fall for him and watch him fall. It's already too late. Your fate is sealed."

"There must be a way." She thought desperately.

"Are you alright, Darlin'?" Jake asked warmly.

Olivia shook her head to try and clear the vision. "Yeah, I'm just worn out. My mother has that effect on me."

They watched as the plane flew away.

"Are you sure that's all?" he asked, his arm around her shoulder.

"Yeah" she said, feeling irritation at holding onto this horrible secret. "I just need to be home. It's been a really long, really exhausting weekend. I need to be alone. I'm sorry."

"I'm not going to be able to sleep tonight you know."

"Jake, I don't need a guilt trip. I just need a break."

"Is this because I asked you to move in with me? Is that where this sudden mood swing is coming from?"

"We already discussed this. I can't move in with you."

"I don't understand why. Give me one good reason." Jake said seriously.

"It's not because I'm old fashioned it's, well, maybe it's partly that but..."

"Don't tell me why it's not, tell me why it is."

She blurted out quickly, "I pay for my apartment. I have a lease on it. It would be ridiculous to waste the money in order to get out of my lease early."

"I'll pay the fine. How long is your lease?"

"No Jake, I'm sorry but no. It's getting cold, we should get going. I've got all my things and Harper's already in my Jeep so I'm sorry but I'm going back, to *my* apartment. I said goodbye and thank you to your family so now all you have to do is say goodbye to me." Olivia said, wishing he would accept her decision.

She'd already been through the ringer with her parents about moving and now Jake wanted her to move out to his ranch. He brought it up the previous night while they lay in bed and Olivia tried to laugh it off but then he mentioned it again this morning. She felt badly about lying to him about the apartment. She hadn't been required to sign a lease but she just couldn't think of a reason he would accept.

"Darlin' I don't *want* to say goodbye to you, not ever. That's the point. Will you at least let me see you home safely?"

"Why?" Olivia asked, sounding more irritated than she planned. "I mean, that's not necessary." She soothed.

He didn't answer. He just stood there looking at her but it was a look she didn't understand. He couldn't stop himself from thinking about the possible danger. He knew he should tell her about Patrick Hanson living so close but even her own father wasn't inclined to tell her. Jake figured they were both thinking the same thing; she'd already been through enough. He was afraid it would make her run back to Oregon or worse, someplace new she might not tell him about. There was no point in her running all over the country when he could better protect her here, in Troy.

"Fine" Olivia sighed audibly. "You can follow me home.

I just don't think I should stay another night and I don't think I should move in with you. I love you Jake and I love spending time with you but it's too much, too soon."

"I understand. I do. Let's go. It *is* really cold. It's supposed to snow another six inches in the next couple days. Be careful when you're driving." He warned, feeling a difference in Olivia. He got in his truck and watched as she started up her Jeep. He followed her to her apartment thinking of ways he might stop that scum, Patrick Hanson.

CHAPTER TWENTY-FOUR

"Thank you for everything. I loved meeting and being with your family." Olivia said as she was unlocking her apartment door.

"You're welcome, of course." Jake replied, opening it for her.

Harper bounded in ahead of them.

Olivia laughed at her happy dog and then gasped as she looked up at the wall of her living room. In red dripping paint, someone had sprayed, "**Always Mine**."

"Jake, I was wrong!" Olivia gasped frantically.

"What are you talking about? I'm calling the police." He replied when he saw the wall.

"No, don't. There's nothing I can do." she cried out. "I wanted to save Dante' and look what happened. I want to save you too but I can't. It doesn't work that way. Everything that's meant to happen *will* happen, no matter what I do. That's why you have to leave! I can't protect you, only you can." Olivia begged, and pushed on his chest.

"Darlin' you're talking crazy. It's ok. You'll be ok. We'll figure this out." Jake quickly dialed his phone.

Olivia felt helpless and sick. Jake didn't believe her, wasn't even listening to her. No matter what, she knew she wouldn't leave Troy, not until fate played its final, painful note.

Jake had instinctively pulled Olivia behind him. Her head was spinning. Her hands clutched his jacket. Harper growled at her feet. Olivia couldn't focus on anything Jake was saying on the phone. She knew she should be doing something but she didn't know what. Her mind was scattered and her hands were cold and numb.

Jake reached around with his free hand and placed it protectively on her back.

She followed him as he slowly walked through the icy cold apartment. When they stepped into Olivia's bedroom, he realized why. The window was open and the wind was blowing snow into the room.

Jake turned to face her. "Darlin' I want you to take Harper now, go over to Mitch's apartment and stay there. Ok?"

Olivia could barely find her voice and when she did, it was shaky. "I want to stay with you."

"I'll be right behind you. I'm going to wait here for Brad to arrive."

"Jake, I don't think I can." She gulped, her hands shaking in fear. For some reason she couldn't seem to calm herself. She had the urge to jump in her Jeep and drive away, whether Jake came with her or not.

"Ok, I'll call Mitch." Jake said dialing his phone.

"You have his n-n-number?" she asked quivering.

"Yeah, I've known Mitch a very long time Darlin'."
Mitch answered, "Hello."

"Hey Mitch, this is Jake, Olivia and I are here in her apartment and she's had a break- in. Could you come over right now?

"Sure Jake, are you guys ok? I just got back myself. I ended up staying at the in-laws for longer than I'd planned. I'll be right over."

"We're ok, thanks" Jake replied, and hung up.

When Mitch knocked on the door, Olivia jumped.

Jake almost said, "Criminals don't knock" but then remembered what had happened to her before. In her case, they did. Instead he put his warm hand on hers, "it's just Mitch. Come on in." He called out.

Mitch opened the door and came right to Olivia. "Olivia, I'm so sorry. If I'd been here..."

"This isn't your fault. I j-j-just have bad luck, I guess."

"I'm going to wait here for the police. I thought maybe you could take Olivia over to your place." Jake said meaningfully to Mitch.

"Of course, just come with me Olivia and I'll fix you some hot tea. We'll wait together." Mitch replied, placing a warm hand on her arm.

"You won't be long?" she turned to Jake, picking up Harper, whose hair was standing on end from the tension in the room.

"Nope, not long at all." He said kissing her gently on the cheek.

He waited and was relieved when his friend Bradley Frazier showed up to handle this.

"Hey Jake, more trouble in paradise?" the deputy joked.

"Yeah, or something like that."

"Tell me what you know."

"We weren't here. Olivia stayed at the ranch this last week. She came to my house on Tuesday night I think it was, and we just came back here tonight. Oh, and we were here on Wednesday too but nothing was out of place then, but now there is, well, this." Jake explained, pointing to the obvious red graffiti on the wall.

"Where is Miss Curtis, I need to take her statement, too?"

"I sent her next door with Mitch Jameson. This has her pretty rattled and to be honest, it does me, too. First she has a run-in with your brother and now this. I think I have an idea who it might have been."

"Well Jake, it's probably just teenage kids messing around 'cause I've been keeping tabs on Billy, and I don't think it was him." the deputy replied, feeling the cold in the room.

"I don't think it was Billy either but why would teenagers put 'Always Mine' on Olivia's wall inside her house? No, I think this is someone from Olivia's past. A long time ago she was attacked by a man named Patrick Hanson. I found out he currently lives in Sandpoint and I don't know for sure, but I think it's worth looking into, don't you?"

"Do you have any other reasons to suspect this Hanson character?"

"No, not really, just gut instinct."

"Alright Jake, I'll do a little digging but if I turn up anything, I'll have to inform her."

"I understand, but in the meantime, don't say anything about Hanson unless you find out something, ok?"

Mitch made tea but Olivia just sat very still, holding the cup. She stared off into space feeling the comforting warmth in her hands. She really didn't like tea all that much and had pretended for the sake of Jake's mom but it didn't matter, nothing sounded good right now. Harper perched herself protectively on Olivia's feet.

Jake rushed in and kneeled down in front of Olivia. Harper put her paws up on Jake's knees. "How you holding up Darlin'?" Jake asked, rubbing Harper's head absently.

"I don't know." Olivia replied quietly.

"Deputy Frazier is going to come over in a minute to take your statement."

Olivia nodded.

Jake sat down next to her and spoke with Mitch.

They could have been talking about architecture or the state of the union for all Olivia heard. She couldn't focus on anything but those red drippy letters.

Deputy Frazier came into Mitch's apartment and politely stood in front of Olivia. "Hello Miss Curtis, I'm sorry we have to meet again under these circumstances."

Olivia stared up at him.

"Is there anything you can tell me about what happened? Have you had any problems with anyone recently? Any suspicious phone calls? Is there anyone who would want to hurt you?"

Olivia looked up as he spoke and simply shook her head.

"I told you, she's been with me. She hasn't received any threats." Jake said, getting slightly irritated.

Olivia looked at Jake. She couldn't understand his reaction. This had him more upset than it should. He was different this time. He hadn't acted so upset and nervous when he found Billy in her apartment.

She needed to pull herself together. She set her cup down and stood up face to face with the deputy. Harper let out a single bark as if to punctuate Olivia's thoughts.

"Are you going on the assumption this vandalism has something to do with your brother, Deputy? He is the only person I've had any kind of confrontation with." She asked clinically, chasing her mind away from the words on her wall.

"It's a possibility of course, but I wouldn't be doing my job if I went on assumptions. Not to speak out of turn Ma'am but there's a rumor around town you and Jake had a bit of a scuffle with Ben Thompson last week. Is there any truth to that?"

Jake stood up looking angrier than before. "Damn it Brad, you know that wasn't about Olivia. Ben and I have our own issues going back a long time, but I don't think he would do something like this."

"Easy Jake, I'm just asking. I have to cover all the bases here."

"Jake is right, it couldn't be Ben." Olivia agreed.

"Ok, well I have some work to do next door but if you think of anything, anything at all that might help, just let me know." The deputy replied.

"Sorry Brad, I know you're just doing your job." Jake apologized.

"I'll be in the apartment for a few more minutes and then I'll be taking off. I'll let you know if I find out anything."

"Thanks" Jake said.

Jake paced the floor as Olivia sat back down, nearly motionless, across from Mitch.

"Have a seat, son." Mitch suggested. "Would you like a drink?"

Jake raked his hand through his hair and looked at Olivia, realizing instantly he should probably sit down.

"Sure, that would be great, maybe just some ice water if you don't mind." He sat on the couch next to Olivia.

She watched Mitch disappear into the kitchen and she turned to Jake. He looked so worried. He reached for her hand and squeezed it gently.

"Jake, I need to say something to you." Olivia said quietly.

Jake steeled himself. He didn't like how she sounded, detached and unemotional. This could have easily been her cold-hearted mother sitting next to him instead of Olivia.

"Darlin' I told you, you can tell me anything."

"I know. The thing is, bad things happen to me and I'm getting better at dealing with them. I'm almost used to it but it doesn't mean anyone else should be. And, I know I told you I wouldn't try to chase you away anymore but there is no reason for you to be involved in all of this. Look at the stress you're under, all because of me. I don't want that. I never wanted that."

"Olivia, do you love me?"

"Yes, I love you, that's why..."

He cut her off. "...and I love you, so can you really imagine I see any of this as a burden to me? Really? All this is, is a shitty situation. I intend for us to deal with it *together*. There is no more you or I and yours or mine, there is only us and *we* are in it together. That's how I see it, but if you don't, then you need to tell me right now."

Olivia opened her mouth to protest but then closed it again. She needed to think about it. She couldn't respond instantly, she needed to process it first. Could that really be how he saw things, already? Could that really be how he saw the two of them? This was an epiphany. Jake constantly surprised her and in nearly a lifetime of no surprises, she wasn't sure how to deal with it. She had foreseen that Patrick Hanson would come back into her life and in doing so, Jake would be hurt. How could she love this man beside her, so honest and true and not try to protect him? There had to be a way to keep him safe. If she could keep Jake from harm, then perhaps the curse that plagued her life would finally take its' leave.

"I've never had that, not ever. I have never been part of a 'we' or an 'us' except with Dante'."

"Well, you're a 'we' now, so figure it out, please, for me, ok? Because you love me.." Jake said and kissed her. "..and because I love you."

Her lips knowingly submitted to the kisses they desired. It was intoxicating. Olivia could have forgotten everything and everyone but then Mitch returned with Jake's drink.

"Sorry to interrupt." Mitch said smiling and handed a glass to Jake.

Jake only moved back an inch or so from Olivia's face and looked her in the eyes as he replied. "Thanks Mitch" and smiled at her. Finally he turned away and took the glass.

"So Olivia, what are you going to do?" Mitch asked, sitting in his easy chair.

Olivia knew Mr. Jameson was probably only asking about the vandalism on the wall, but she began thinking about the bigger picture. It was time to change her life. It was time to push back at her accursed fate. Her life up to now had been like a building being torn down and bulldozed over and over. Now it was time to rebuild, starting with a solid foundation. She would no longer run, she would make a stand, stay and face this curse head on.

She had to find her courage. "Well Mr. Jameson, I'm going to move in with Jake." She said smiling at him and turning to see Jake's face. "That is if your offer still stands."

Olivia couldn't think of any more reasons why she shouldn't. The best she had felt, the most normal, the happiest times had all been with Jacob Weidner. Why deny herself of this happiness anymore? Fear still sat perched like a parrot on her shoulder squawking in her ear. Everything she predicted had come true. There had to be *something* she could change and in changing one thing, she would change it all and save her beloved.

Jake was completely surprised. "Of course, of course my offer still stands." He stammered happily.

This time, an audience or not, she leaned in and kissed him. He was on cloud nine. One minute he feared she was about to leave town and the next she was agreeing to move in with him. His thoughts suddenly jumped to the ring box in his desk drawer. He hoped the time to propose would come soon. But there couldn't be a sociopath spray-painting her world with threats. He couldn't wait to make Olivia his wife, but the timing had to be exactly right and he had to protect her.

Deputy Frazier knocked on the door once more. When Mitch let him in, Olivia straightened her shoulders. There was no escaping the current nightmare or the sick feeling in her stomach. Although she knew who painted her walls as a reminder of his presence, she wouldn't tell anyone. She knew as soon as she saw it; only one person would have chosen those words and though she had not predicted the act, she knew he would be coming for her.

She felt his presence like the icy wind that had blown through her apartment, like the chills running up her spine now. He was, after all, the one who had cursed her, and theirs was a connection of pain like a long sticky thread between them.

Doctor Thompson was right about that, she *had* bonded with her attacker, but not in the way he had explained it.

"*Always mine,*" Patrick had said to her as he violated her and planted the life that would be Dante' inside her young womb. That was the first day she began to foresee her future and know she would never be believed.

"Well Miss Curtis, I'm done at your apartment for now. I've made sure it's secure and locked the windows for you. The heat was running, so it should warm up shortly. You'll be safe there as long as you keep your doors and windows locked." Bradley said hoping to scare her enough that she would do as he asked.

"I'm moving out of the apartment Deputy, but I thank you for your diligence."

"I'm just doing my job and you are most welcome. Do you have another contact number, then?"

"Just my cell phone, but I believe you already have that." Olivia replied, feeling like she was acting out a scene in a movie. She reached for Jake's water and took a long drink.

"Brad, she's moving in with me, so you can call out to the ranch, too." Jake told him, unable to keep the pride out of his voice.

"Ok, I'll let you know if I get any leads. I'm going to go, it is Sunday after all. I'll be at the station for a while writing out my report, so if you need anything else, call."

"Thank you, Deputy." Olivia said politely.

"You're welcome."

Mitch had been very quiet as he showed Brad to the door.

Jake stood up next to Olivia and said, "Hey Mitch, I want to thank you for everything."

"There's no need. Olivia, I'm going to miss you as my neighbor."

"I was a horrible neighbor." Olivia smiled sheepishly. "I'm just sorry there's been so much trouble since I arrived."

"You're not to blame for any of this and remember, if you ever need anything, I'll be right here."

Olivia hugged him. "Thank you, so much." she said sincerely. Mitch Jameson was such a kind man. She was grateful for his friendship.

"Darlin' if we're going to get you moved out of your apartment, we'd better get started."

As they walked back with Harper in tow, Olivia asked, "Jake, are you sure?"

"Sure about what?"

"Are you sure you want me to move in with you? I'm a horrible sleeper. I have awful nightmares when I *do* sleep and it's quite possible I snore. You are essentially agreeing to have a crazy person move in with you."

"Well, when you put it that way..." he joked. "Darlin', I want to be near you more than anything. I want you just as you are."

"Well, don't say I didn't warn you."

As they walked inside together, Olivia was struck once again by the horror on the wall. She held Jake's hand but walked up to the wall to touch it almost mesmerized by it.

"Billy Frazier didn't do this," she uttered, going back on what she had promised herself. She realized she'd slipped, but she couldn't let Billy get in trouble for something he hadn't done. She knew this was not Billy Frazier's handiwork.

"What makes you think that?"

She didn't answer right away. All the memories of her life began to jumble together and she desperately wished she could forget. "I just know," she admitted.

"No matter who did this, I don't want you to worry about it, we'll let the police handle it. Whoever did it isn't going to be bothering you again." Jake said confidently.

Olivia nodded unconvinced. "So, where should we get started?" she asked, turning her back on the wall, hands on her hips and trying to sound lighthearted.

"I would leave word with your landlord. You may not be able to get a hold of him today though. Also, after we get out to the ranch and get you settled, you'll need to compose a letter formally withdrawing from your lease. For now, let's just pack the absolute essentials and fit what we can in my truck. You have a lot of boxes already packed up in the spare bedroom, right?"

"Yeah, how did you know that?" she asked.

"Miles showed me. He wanted me to see the extent of your OCD, I think."

"That's not funny." Olivia said, but smiled anyway.

"That room won't be much work then. Let's start with clothing, whatever you need from the bathroom, things like that. Did you keep any of your empty boxes?"

Olivia noticed he was very good at organizing and telling people what to do. She had to admit it was kind of funny to see Jake in his 'work mode'. They spent the remainder of the day, packing and loading and ignoring the message left on the wall.

Mitch came over to pitch in and help load boxes into the truck and her Jeep. Harper followed each of them in turn out to the vehicles acting as supervisor. Jake called his house to prepare Carmella for this change, but he already knew she would be thrilled and lay out the welcome mat.

They continued working until evening and were very nearly finished. Olivia was grateful she didn't have much in the way of furniture. Jake offered to come back for what little she did have. They worked very well together, not saying much just getting it done.

Olivia was beginning to feel the exhaustion set in when they piled in their loaded vehicles. Harper had no room to sit in the Jeep so she rode on Olivia's lap.

Olivia drove with one hand and softly stroked Harper's furry coat with the other. "I sure hope we're doing the right thing, girl. You like it at the ranch, right? And Jake is such a good man. I just don't know. I hope I can be the kind of woman who deserves a good man."

Harper slept. "But, it was always easier spilling your guts to a dog; sleeping or not." Olivia thought, and she bit her lip as she pulled into the big garage next to Jake. It was snowing again and this time big, heavy flakes. She parked and took a deep breath as Jake came over and opened her door. Harper lifted her head.

Jake picked up Harper setting her down on the garage floor. He leaned in and kissed Olivia on the lips first, then the cheeks, then the earlobes and then he spread little kisses all over her face and neck. Olivia giggled.

"Are you ok Darlin'?"

"Sure, of course. I'm wonderful. Today was *awesome*. In the morning I got to deal with my mother one more time and say goodbye to my brother and Dad. Then, later I received such a very nice message left at my apartment from a crazy person and now both of our vehicles are filled to the brim with my stuff that I have no clue what to do with. Really, why can't everyday be like this?" she said sarcastically.

"That's it!" Jake growled playfully. He pulled her out of the car and threw her over his shoulder running out the open garage door into the snow.

Olivia laughed loudly, completely surprised, snowflakes falling heavily. Jake had never heard her laugh like this; it was incredible, so natural and happy. He spun her around, eventually letting her down in the snowy yard. She staggered dizzily. He stepped back and planted a snowball on the front of her coat.

She laughed again, balling snow in her bare hands to make her own. "Two can play at that game." She shouted and nailed him on the side as he tried to move away.

They pelted each other in a full-on snowball fight until both were freezing and covered with snow.

"Shall we call a truce?" Jake held up his hands as a plea.

"Yes, we probably should" she laughed, but when Jake moved in for a hug, she put her ice cold hand up the back of his jacket.

He made an uncomfortable groaning sound. "That's just wrong. You're going to pay for that." He faked a growl but kissed her lovingly.

"What? Are my hands cold?" She asked with mock innocence.

"Just a little."

They walked hand in hand into the lights of the garage. Olivia stopped, looking at her Jeep. "Jake what am I going to do?"

"About what?"

"It's late, we're tired and we both have to work tomorrow and we haven't unloaded a single thing yet." Olivia said, sighing deeply.

Jake gently put a hand to her face and smiled. "Long day huh? Ok, let's just unload your Jeep tonight and I'll worry about the rest tomorrow."

"Don't you have to work, too? You'll need your truck."

"This is a ranch, remember? You can't throw a rock without hitting a truck and besides, my office is here at home. Trust me; let me take care of things for you. Let's just unload your Jeep and then have some dinner and call it a night."

"Are you sure?"

"Yes" he said as he kissed her cheek.

Carmella came into the garage from the kitchen doorway and saw them leaning against the Jeep. "How do you two expect to get anything done when you're out here fooling around?" she scolded.

Olivia backed up, blushing. Jake just remained where he was; a lazy, satisfied grin on his overly handsome face.

"Jacob, there is much to be done. I have organized your room and made space for your things, Olivia. Also, there is a casserole in the oven in case you two are hungry."

"Thank you Carmella, you're right. Olivia and I were just discussing how much we should try and get done tonight." Jake replied grinning.

"Sure you were; now stop *discussing* and get busy." Carmella ordered.

"Carmella, you should have been a drill sergeant. You really missed your calling." Jake teased.

They worked until late and finally Jake called a halt to it. "Come on Darlin'. I'm pretty sure the rest can wait. We made a good dent."

"I suppose you're right and I *am* very tired and hungry."

"We'll heat up some of Carmella's casserole then."

"Did she go to bed?"

"Yes, but she said she would help more tomorrow."

Olivia asked sincerely, "Please don't let her. I've already inconvenienced you both enough as it is."

"There is nothing about you or this situation that inconveniences me. To be perfectly honest, the only thing inconvenient would be to have worried about you alone in that apartment tonight. This, having you here? This is perfect."

"Thank you Jake." She hugged him tightly. "I love you so much."

"I love you too Darlin'."

The next morning, Olivia woke at five thirty knowing she had a laundry list of things to do. She had slept like the dead and was grateful for it. She wanted to tell Jake how nice it was to sleep so soundly and maybe thank him properly for how gracious he'd been but he wasn't in his bed, or *their* bed. "Oh hell" she thought, "I have no idea what to call it."

She'd hoped to get a few more boxes out of Jake's truck before she left for work but she knew she'd also have to leave earlier to compensate for the longer drive. She peeked out through the curtains to see what kind of a day it was going to be. The world was white and cold and she longed to crawl back into bed. Normally she loved the way snow made everything so pretty but today she was looking at a treacherous drive and a long day at work when all she really wanted was a few more hours of sleep.

She could see lights on out at the barn.

"I guess cowboys really do get up at the butt crack of dawn" she said aloud.

"Well we have to; there are animals to take care of." Jake chuckled from behind her.

"Jake!" she said happily and rushed to kiss him.

They were quite a contrast, him in boots, coat and hat and she in a little slip of a nightgown.

"I slept so good last night and I want to tell you thank you for everything."

"You're welcome of course. I'd do anything for you, Darlin'." He kissed her again.

"Is Harper ok? I haven't seen her this morning," Olivia asked.

"Yes, she and Whitman are on clean-up duty in the kitchen, in case Carmella drops anything. I fed them both, but you wouldn't know it, the way they're begging."

"What time did you get up this morning?"

"Four-thirty. I tried to be quiet. I didn't want to wake you."

"I didn't hear a thing. I'm going to shower and bring in some more boxes. I feel bad we left stuff in your truck."

"Don't worry about it. Just get yourself ready for your day and then come and have some breakfast with me, please? Leave the rest of the unloading to me."

"I couldn't do that." She said feeling a little guilty.

"Of course you can. I'll see you downstairs." He kissed her again before she could protest further.

The next few days were filled with unpacking, work and more unpacking. Olivia couldn't believe how easily her things found homes here at the ranch. There was plenty of room and Jake and Carmella made sure she felt welcome.

Olivia liked having a purpose and staying busy with Jake. She even talked him into waking her early so she could help him with the morning chores. She discovered right away that feeding the horses was her favorite part and although Jake had a crew of people to do it, Olivia could understand why he was always a part of it, when he could be.

She would linger longer than necessary at each stall talking to and petting each horse. Jake left her to it while he would go on ahead and do whatever he did. Olivia still didn't really know but was content to have her own moment in the stables every morning.

Jake's horse at the ranch was Olivia's favorite. His name was Guiness. Jake said he named the horse for the dark, rich color of the beer he loved.

One morning Olivia was feeding Guiness when Jake walked up behind her. "Darlin' we need to talk," he announced.

"That sounds serious. Are you kicking me out already?" she teased.

"No, of course not," he said and hugged her around the waist.

"I know I've still got boxes to go through but..."

"No, it's not about the boxes. They could rot there for all I care."

"What is it then?" she turned to face him finally.

"You haven't so much as mentioned the incident at your apartment. I think we should talk about it. It's been over a week, the police have no leads, and..."

"There's nothing to say," she interrupted. "Are you afraid I have some unresolved issues about this, because I don't." she said irritated.

Jake didn't know how to reply. He wondered if he should bring up Patrick Hanson finally and just lay his cards on the table.

"I'm sorry Jake. It's just that there's really nothing to say. Someone came in my house and spray painted my living room wall. It was probably teenage kids or something like that. It doesn't matter, really. I'm here with you and I'm safe. You make me feel safe so let's just forget about it, please?"

"Ok, you're right. I just want you to know you can talk to me about anything."

"I do know that, but, I just want to move forward. I want normal."

Jake hugged her still but he couldn't help worrying that she might be shutting down when she should be opening up. He wouldn't mind some 'normal' too but he didn't want it to be an act. She hadn't mentioned her therapy and he certainly wasn't going to bring it up. He wanted to believe she was really ok, but the question nagged him.

"Darlin' what do you think about having some friends over for dinner on Friday night?"

"I thought you had poker night on Friday?"

"I could reschedule it."

"No, that's silly. Why would you rearrange something already scheduled for something completely out of the blue? Besides, who would we invite?"

"I was thinking maybe Ben Thompson and a few other people."

"I'm not an idiot Jake. Please tell me you're kidding."

"I think it's high time I really mend that fence, don't you?" Jake suggested.

"Yes I do, but you should just invite him to the game, then."

"That's not a bad idea. Would you play? Sam will be here?"

"No, I don't play poker. It's not my thing."

"What would you do? I don't want you to be left out."

"I can keep myself occupied for one evening. Honestly Jake, I'm a big girl. I can deal with one Friday night all alone you know." She said, pouting a bit.

"I know Darlin'."

CHAPTER TWENTY-FIVE'

When Friday rolled around Olivia was relieved. The snow had been piling up and getting to and from work seemed to take longer every day, or maybe she was just overly cautious. Jake always had one of the ranch hands plow the lane and the county maintained the roads leading up to it but it was still sketchy.

When she arrived home that evening Carmella was busy in the kitchen making an array of snacks for "Jake's" guests. Olivia decided she wasn't going anywhere near his card game tonight. "Hello, Carmella!"

"Ciao, bella ragazza. How was your day?"

"It was good, I'm glad this week's over though because I'm ready for some downtime. Have you seen Jake?"

It amazed Olivia how quickly she and Jake had settled into a routine of daily life together. In only one week, Olivia would come home from work and Jake would greet her practically at the door. Today though, there was no Jake and his truck wasn't in the garage; not that it meant anything. Jake loaned his truck out all the time to employees at the ranch or to friends.

"He should be back soon. He said he was heading to the Outfitters but he'd be back well before the guests arrive. You can always call him. He loves it when you call him." Carmella teased.

"How do you know that?"

"He said so. Jacob is a pool of mushy goo around you. Haven't you noticed?"

"Oh, I don't know. I suppose so, but then I have nothing to compare it to." Olivia smiled.

"Call the boy. Make him smile."

"No, he'll be back soon I'm sure. I think I'll just go shower and change." After her shower, she dressed and went back down to the kitchen to offer Carmella some help, but she had already finished.

"Did Jake come back?" Olivia asked, surprised she hadn't heard from him yet.

"Yes, haven't you seen him?"

"No, but that's ok." Olivia replied, looking a bit upset.

"Don't fret; I'm sure he just has his mind on work."

"Yeah, I'm sure. I'm going out to the stables."

"Would you take the dogs please, I think it's been some time since they've been out."

"Of course" she replied. "Come Harper. Come Whitman."

The two dogs rushed to the kitchen door and waited impatiently while Olivia put on the coat she had stolen from Jake and pulled on her riding boots. She opened the door and the dogs raced past her. She stepped outside into the same winter wonderland they'd been living in for a while now, but this evening, it felt different somehow.

No one had said anything but the house was showing all the signs of holiday cheer. It suddenly dawned on her it was only a few weeks until Christmas. Carmella had worked her magic and Olivia instantly felt horrible for not noticing sooner.

Sometimes, she still had to pinch herself. Being with Jake didn't seem possible. She likened it to traveling a very long, very hard road and feeling there would never be an end to her difficult journey but then suddenly, there was. "Out of the blue a tall, handsome stranger invites you to stop and rest." She thought. With Jake, she could rest. With Jake, she could let go. With Jake, the death grip of fear loosened a little. She didn't trust that this peace could last. Lately, even Jake seemed like he was about to tell her to get back on her road of pain. Mostly she knew Jake wanted her to talk, to keep talking about her past and her pain. "She just didn't want to, after all, why would she risk jinxing this new life?' She wouldn't risk it.

Whitman found a snow-covered ball and dropped it at Olivia's feet. It sunk heavily in the snow. She picked it up and threw it for the happy dogs. Harper was much slower and the deep snow made it worse but she jumped and chased along behind Whitman happily, her cottony fluff disappearing often.

Olivia and the dogs made their way to the stables. She smiled when she entered and was greeted by sounds of horses stomping in the stalls and nickering their 'hellos'.

Olivia loved this ranch more than she had a right to really. At least she loved what she had seen of it. Jake told her she hadn't even been on half of their land yet. Of all the things she had seen, she loved the stables the most. The building with its indoor arena was just what she thought all stables should be. It gave her such a feeling of nostalgia every time she set foot through its wide doors, and yet, a bit of regret. Even now she wondered how her mother could have torn her away from something she loved so dearly. She missed Maestro.

She opened Guiness' stall and hand fed him some grain. Almost out of habit, she put her arm around him and leaned into his large, powerful neck.

"You remind me of Jake, you know that?" she told him.

"And here I thought you liked me more than that, Darlin'." Jake drawled. He loved teasing her.

"Jake!" Olivia's head snapped up and she turned to face him. "Must you scare me like that?"

"I guess I must. Of course it's not intentional." He smiled and propped his boot on the railing.

"Humph" Olivia said and reached for a brush, successfully turning her back on him.

Jake opened the stall-gate, grabbed her hand and pulled her into an embrace. She refused to look up at him. He reached up to tilt her chin to meet his gaze.

"What particular type of bee is in your bonnet today?"

"Whatever do you mean?" She lied in her best 'Scarlett' voice.

"You know exactly, have I done something to upset you?"

She ignored his question. "Is *your company* here?" she asked.

"What is it?" Jake asked impatiently now.

"It's just that I haven't seen you all day, and now you have guests coming to the house and I guess I'm just, just..." she heard the childish sound in her voice and internally scolded herself for it.

"Petulant? Jealous? Moody?" Jake teased, unable to keep from smiling.

"I am not petulant!" she yelled.

"Darlin', I have the perfect solution to this little, um, *problem.* Join us tonight. You don't have to play cards; just be there, relax, have fun, have a drink and socialize. It's not some super-secret meeting. Its friends and fun and it is *our* house. Besides, I tried to suggest a dinner party and you didn't like that idea, remember?"

"It's not *our* house and I do remember. Alright, so maybe I'm being a little petulant. I just don't want to sit there like some kind of third, fifth, or seventh wheel. I'd rather have something of my own to do. I'd rather have something that makes me feel like I have a life."

"You do have a life." He soothed.

"Right, and what am I doing with it? Nothing! You know when I was walking out here tonight I realized it will be Christmas soon. I mean, seriously, when did that happen? I feel so disconnected, like I'm living on cold medicine that makes me fuzzy.

I'm going through the motions Jake, it's not normal to only be passionate about one thing..."

"One thing?" Jake asked, not understanding at first.

"You Jake, you! I'm only really alive when *you* are with me. It's not enough. I have to figure out what I'm going to do with the rest of my life." She sighed and leaned heavily on his chest.

"Well, you don't have to have it all figured out tonight, right?"

"No, I guess not.

"Good, then let's go in, have some fun and greet our guests, shall we?"

"I really don't feel like it. Do you mind if I don't join you? I was going to groom Guiness and then ride for a while. I need to clear my head."

"You aren't going outside are you?" he asked a little concerned.

"No *Dad*, I was just going to stay in the indoor arena." She replied sarcastically.

"Just be careful. That's all I ask. I worry about you out here by yourself."

"I've got the animal kingdom here keeping me company. I'll be fine."

"I'm sure one of them can call 911 if you happen to take a fall then?"

"No, but I could probably get Whitman to go find you." She smiled.

"Great, I won't worry then."

Jake kissed her on the mouth and she felt the warmth spread through her body like an electric current. He felt it too and could have easily forgotten about anything else.

He couldn't wait for her to meet Mochaccino. Jake had moved heaven and earth to get that horse here before the holidays and now he just had to keep her away from the Outfitters until then. The horse was perfect for Olivia, well-bred and well trained. He was elegant like her. They would be good together, he could feel it. It had always been a talent of his, matching people to horses. Jake decided his guests would be fine for a bit longer without him, so he saddled up Guiness for her and gave her a leg up. He admired how she looked, so diminutive on such a big horse, but still relaxed and in control. Olivia couldn't see it but she had already found more than one passion.

Jake nodded before leaving the stables. The cars in the driveway told him he was late for his own game, and he saw the one car he hoped would be there. Ben had shown up after all.

When Jake had called him, Ben had been suspicious but Jake hoped to explain everything tonight. Jake would put his pride away for Olivia. She needed someone to talk to and Ben was the only one who had gotten through. She talked to Jake but it wasn't the same. He loved her too much to be objective and he knew it. It burned him every day that Patrick Hanson was walking the streets a free man and he may be stalking her. If Jake had his way, that beast would be a dead man. Olivia needed someone with objectivity and Jake definitely wasn't. He hoped Ben could be objective, Jake was counting on it.

He walked back to the house and chuckled to himself that the dogs stayed with Olivia. Wherever she went, they went. They both sat at the edge of the arena like sentries watching quietly as she rode.

Ben was just coming up the walk and Jake knew it might be his only chance to talk to him. "Hey Ben, I'm glad you came." Jake said truthfully.

"You are, huh?" Ben replied dryly.

"Yeah, I am. I need to talk to you for a minute."

"Damn it Jake, so this isn't an olive branch is it?" Ben growled and started walking back to his car.

"No, it is. Wait, please. After all these years, I'm more than ready to bury the hatchet." Jake said.

"What? You need a hug?" Ben replied sarcastically.

Jake laughed. "Maybe later; no what I need is for you to talk to Olivia. She needs you. I hate to admit it, but she does. She needs someone she can talk to. We talk but it isn't the same. She needs someone objective and well..." he raked his fingers through his hair. "...that's not me."

"That can't have been easy for you to admit. Have you told her?" Ben asked.

Jake looked guiltily at him but only shook his head.

"Have you told her you feel she should continue therapy?"

"No, I haven't" Jake admitted.

"You should tell her, you know?" Ben encouraged.

"Will you talk to her or not?" Jake asked, already feeling stupid. A feeling he hated worse than anything.

"Does she have any idea what a pussy you are?" Ben joked.

Jake ignored his digs and waited as Ben considered it.

"Alright, I'll call her on Monday and we'll see how it goes." Ben replied at last.

"She's here. She lives here now, with me. I thought maybe you could talk to her tonight."

"I'm glad to see she's taking it slowly like I advised." Ben rolled his eyes.

"She was going to but then someone broke into her apartment. Didn't you hear about it?" Jake asked.

"Yeah, I did know about the break-in because the police questioned me about it. Thanks for that, by the way. I didn't know she'd moved in with you, though."

"*I* didn't give the police your name and neither did she. Brad heard about our little scuffle at the bar."

"It doesn't matter. You and I both know I didn't have anything to do with what happened."

"I do know that and so does Olivia. I'm sorry."

"Listen, I'm willing to continue therapy with Olivia and I already have apologized and told her just that, but she has to want it. I can't just ambush her and expect she'll open up. It doesn't work that way."

"Fine, it doesn't work that way. I'm just asking you to talk to her. Say to her whatever you would have said on the phone."

"I guess I won't be playing cards tonight will I?" Ben asked.

"You might. I did invite you to play poker." Jake replied with a wry smile.

"Don't lie to me Jake."

"You want the truth? The truth is I'm sick and tired of being your enemy, Ben, especially over a girl who probably hasn't given either of us a second thought in years." Jake reached out.

Ben stood silently and contemplated alternatives then decided to meet him halfway and shook his hand. Jake hoped this was the first step to finally burying the hatchet, for good.

"Where is she? I may as well go talk to her now. Though, I think you should know the prospect of having her bite my head off doesn't sound so good."

"You aren't scared of Olivia are you, Doc?"

"Scared? No, I'm not scared, but I'm smart enough to be cautious. If you had the sense God gave you, you would know that under that calm, serene exterior is a whole lot of fear, anger, grief and resentment. Those things aren't exactly pretty when they finally make their way out."

"She's out in the arena riding. You might want to wait until she's finished." Jake said.

"No, as much as it would please me to sit in on the first round and take some of your hard earned money, I think it will be good to get this over with." Ben replied and headed to the stables.

Jake went inside hoping this plan would work when he nearly ran into Tag and Samantha who had obviously been watching from the window.

"What's going on Jake?" Tag asked.

"Nothing. Are you ready to lose some money?" Jake asked, needing to redirect their attention.

"What Tag meant to say was, why in the hell is Ben here? Last time I checked, the two of you hated each other's guts with a passion. I had no idea you and Ben were suddenly chummy." Sam remarked, her hands on her hips.

"I wouldn't say we're chummy, but I did invite him to join us tonight. Cam is out of town and I thought maybe it was time to bury the hatchet."

"I'd suggest you bury it in his skull." Sam said angrily.

"Wow Sam, and here I thought I was the one that he screwed over. Something you want to tell me?" Jake asked.

"Excuse me for giving a shit about my friends." Sam retorted.

"I appreciate it, but listen; I don't want to fight with Ben anymore. It just makes things more difficult for Olivia and..."

Sam interrupted "...and you are officially whipped. I mean, it's cute, seeing you wrap yourself around her little finger like this. I like her Jake but come on, Ben has been shitty to you for more years than I can count and now you're suddenly going to let it all go?"

"Yes, I am. Hating Ben Thompson hasn't gotten me anywhere. Sam, I love you. You *are* one of my best friends and I'm lucky to have you, but I have to let this go. Now, let's play some poker."

"Ok Jake. We understand. I for one think it's great." Tag added. He'd been very quiet. He patted Sam on the shoulder sympathetically.

"Fine, Jake" Sam replied. "But if he turns on you like a rabid dog, don't say I didn't warn you."

"Just try and be civil to him. Can you do that please?" Jake asked.

"Sure, why not. Is he playing cards then or is he too busy flirting with *your* girlfriend?"

Jake rolled his eyes. "He'll be in soon, probably our second hand."

Ben watched Olivia for only a moment before the dogs alerted her to his arrival. He petted them both and then waved to her. She rode over to him, looking incredibly surreal.

She dismounted the tall horse athletically and stood holding the reins with her arms crossed over her chest. She said nothing. She only stood glaring at him.

"Hello Olivia. How are you?" Ben asked.

She ignored the question. "The card game is in the house, not the barn."

"Did you know I was coming?" he asked.

"Yes, Jake tells me everything." Olivia replied, lifting her chin defiantly. "If you'll excuse me, I need to get this horse cooled down."

As she said it, she led Guiness away and began walking him around the arena, her black riding boots kicking through the sawdust.

Ben followed after her. "I thought perhaps we could talk."

"Ben, I want you and Jake to get along, I do. I even suggested he invite you to play poker with him, but as I said, the game is in the house. You and I have nothing to discuss."

"I understand. I think you have everything you want here."

"What do you mean by that?" she demanded, taking the bait.

"You have a nice house, away from everything, a family, too far away to confront you, a man who's terrified of what you'll do if *he* confronts you. There's nothing and no one to tear down these walls you've built around yourself. You're safe. You're safe from everyone but yourself." Ben explained.

She dropped the reins and kept walking but Guiness kept following her. She turned to face Ben, a tear falling down her cheek. "I want you to leave, now."

"I was invited to play poker. I think I'll go join the game now." Ben said provokingly.

Olivia slapped him hard across the face. "Go home, Doc."

Ben touched his cheek and shook his head at her. He turned and walked out of the stables straight up to the house. He wanted to make sure Olivia realized she couldn't chase him away. He knocked on the door and Carmella answered with a big smile. Ben was always one of Carmella's favorites of Jake's friends. She prayed eventually they would work out their differences.

"Hello Benjamin. It's so good to see you at our door again. When Jacob told me you were coming, well, it made me very happy. You're late though. The game has started already."

"I'm happy to see you too Carmella" he replied and gave her a big hug. "I was out um, talking to Olivia."

Carmella gave him a stern look. Ben put his hands up. "Jake asked me to."

"Oh" she said. "That's different then isn't it? Everyone is in the parlor. Do you remember the way?"

"Yes ma'am, thank you." Ben smiled.

When Jake saw Ben at the doorway, he waved him over to the table. "Ben you're just in time we're about to start a new hand."

Ben smiled and sat down at the card table.

"Would you like a drink? Tag is playing bartender tonight which means your liver may never recover." Jake teased.

"Jake, you've always been such a lightweight. You don't even drink your coffee black." Tag replied jokingly.

"So how did it go out there?" Jake asked nervously.

"We can discuss it later." Ben replied.

"Are you missing any appendages?" Jake asked.

"Luckily, no" Ben replied.

CHAPTER TWENTY-SIX

Olivia groomed Guiness methodically. She took her time enjoying the solitude of the stables. More than ever she wanted to be by herself but it was dark outside, she was starving and rather disgusted. She wasn't stupid; she knew Jake had sent Ben to 'talk' with her. She had mixed feelings about that. She wanted to be angry with Jake but also, she worried what it meant to him. Did he really think she was still so screwed up that she needed more therapy from a man he couldn't even stand?

Maybe she *did* still need to talk to someone. She had been very irritable with everyone and maybe even more so with Jake. And, there was still so much she hadn't said, but would her saying it really make it better? She had her doubts, especially when she was certain she couldn't say it all.

She had moved in with Jake and her curse moved in with her. This was just geography. She'd been shut down ever since. She bristled, hating to admit to herself that Ben might be right. Maybe she was hiding out. Hiding was so much easier than talking. She hadn't felt like crying in some time now, and yet Ben walks into the arena and immediately, tears. It was truly annoying.

Olivia decided to sneak into the kitchen and avoid the human contact all together. Perhaps she would eat in Jake's bed and be sure to drop crumbs on his side. It would serve him right for sending Ben out to talk to her.

The kitchen was dimly lit. Carmella had obviously turned in for the night. Olivia opened the door and the dogs rushed in past her ready to find some warmth. She sat and removed her boots and hung up her coat. There was a special charm to the little mud room off the kitchen. She sat for a minute on the bench and sighed heavily.

"Is there something on your mind?" Sam asked peeking around the corner.

Olivia gasped, thinking she had been alone. "Oh my God, you scared me. You must have learned that little trick from Jake."

"Sorry, I needed to get out of that room. There's too much testosterone and bullshit. I love men, God knows I do, but sometimes they annoy the crap out of me. I wish you would have joined us. You could have kept me company."

"Sam, from what I hear, you handle yourself just fine with all those guys. You don't need me."

"You'd be surprised at what I need."

Olivia put her head in her hands.

"What's going on, Liv?"

"I'm being railroaded, that's what's going on."

"You mean by Ben?"

"By Ben, by Jake; they obviously want me to spill my guts but I've been dealing with some of this stuff for so long, sometimes it's better *not* talking about it. My mental health has been the subject of discussion and study for far too long if you ask me. It's getting old."

"Let me ask you this...do you feel like you *need* therapy?

Olivia stared up at Sam in the dimly lit room.

"Honestly, I feel like I'm getting pretty damn good at trying to put it behind me and pretending it never happened until someone comes along who thinks they know better."

"So stuffing it down is better?" Samantha asked honestly.

"Yeah, sometimes it is."

"Huh! I guess that's one way of doing it. It seems kind of gutless if you ask me."

"Excuse me? I thought you were my friend." Olivia replied giving her a sideways glance.

"I am, and any friend of mine will get to hear exactly what I think. Olivia, just because you hide a dead body in your basement doesn't mean it won't still stink up your house. Jake wants you to deal with this for *your* sake, not his. Don't you get that?"

"Yeah, and you're both probably right, but it doesn't make it easy. I see how close I am to having a different life. I'm close, really, really close to changing my destiny but it feels like the price of admission is more than I can afford. My ticket will cost me having to truly confront my past, and I don't want to pay."

"Nobody really wants to pay, Liv, but we do."

"I guess I know what you think I should do then?"

"Yeah, you should deal with this, head on, so there's nothing left to stuff down inside. Bury the body, once and for all. Then, maybe you'll feel like you finally deserve a new life."

"Maybe *you* should be my therapist." Olivia smiled.

"Thanks, but I already have a job, and I'd rather just be your friend."

"I guess I should apologize to Ben and get back on the mental health train then, huh?"

"I wouldn't go that far. Let Ben suffer a little." Sam replied, "He needs it."

"I slapped him. I owe him an apology." Olivia admitted.

"Oh really? I'm pretty sure he's fine." Sam said, rolling her eyes.

After Sam had left the card table, the game sort of fizzled out. Apparently no one was really 'feeling' it tonight, least of all their host. Jake wondered just how much trouble he was in with Olivia. As much as he hated to admit it, he had set her up, and he had forced Ben to play a part in it.

Tag headed home mentioning something about a big storm coming. Jake and Ben remained at the bar in the parlor. Both silently staring down their drinks, finally Jake couldn't take it anymore. Though, he wasn't sure if he knew how to hold a casual conversation with this man who had once been one of his best friends.

"Next time, we'll be more organized." Jake said, floundering a bit.

"Oh, so I'm getting invited back for cards, then?" Ben asked.

"Sure, I told you the offer was sincere. And listen, I really appreciate you talking with Olivia."

"She's really angry Jake. She slapped me and told me to go home." Ben admitted, absently putting his hand to his cheekbone.

"She did?"

"Yeah, I'm not sure I did any good. Time will tell, I guess. You know, you can't force her to talk. Right now she seems determined to hide out here and pretend nothing happened."

"It was never my intention to give her a hideout."

"I know." Ben admitted.

"You do? Hell Ben, I thought you were determined to think the worst of me."

"I wanted to, but that grudge wasn't helping either one of us and it never helped Sarea one bit. I never could help her. It's time I come to terms with that. As far as Olivia is concerned, she would have found a way to hide, no matter where she lived. You should know that Jake."

Jake didn't know how to respond. He took his glass and tipped it to Ben's. It seemed to Jake that a girl had torn their friendship apart and now incredibly, a woman was helping them to mend it.

"So, on a scale of one to ten, how pissed off is my darlin' Olivia?"

"Do you mean at me, or at you?"

"Both."

"I'd say a ten, at least."

Just then, Sam's voice came over the intercom. "Sorry to break up the party but Jake, I need you and *Dr. Thompso*n to join us in the library. Oh, and bring a bottle of wine."

The two guys looked at each other skeptically. Jake pressed the button and replied. "Ok".

"I guess we've been summoned by the queen." Jake laughed.

When they walked into the library holding the wine and four glasses, Olivia and Sam were seated next to each other on the sofa. Jake suddenly felt like the fly who had accidentally wandered into the spider's web. He looked cautiously at Olivia who smiled at him, with sort of false warmth. He knew it, he was definitely in trouble.

"Come in gentlemen. Have a seat." Sam gestured toward the chairs that had been arranged facing the women. "Thank you for bringing the wine. Olivia and I thought it sounded nice."

Jake poured the wine. "What's going on?" he asked as he handed a glass to Olivia. She said nothing. She only nodded to Jake and took the glass from him softly. Jake leaned down and kissed her forehead.

"I love you, Darlin'" he whispered in her ear.

"Ok lover boy, sit down. We need to talk." Sam interrupted.

Jake winked at Olivia but sat down compliantly. Sam looked at Olivia expectantly. Ben began to speak but Sam shushed him.

"Sam and I were talking and it seems you men have been scheming." Olivia began and Jake tried to speak up but was quickly hushed by Sam. "Let her finish, Jake."

"I have decided that having other people discuss my life and make decisions for me is unacceptable. Everyone here in this room pretty much knows about my unfortunate past, however all of us, in different rooms at different times talking about it, or whispering about it, just isn't working for me."

"First of all, Jake, I love you, too. She smiled at him and he started to get up but she held up her hand. "But if you love me, really love me you have to be honest with me. You can't send Ben out to *deal* with me. It's not right. I'll admit, I've been shutting down and..." Looking at Ben said, "...building walls. I'm sorry about that but I'll talk when I'm damn well good and ready."

She continued, "I needed a break. I needed time. I needed some space and time without drama. I wanted to know what it felt like to be 'normal'; you know, to have a simple life.

I wanted to just be a girl in love who had a normal family and no exceptional talents or expectations. I needed to lie to myself for a little bit. But I get it, I can't keep doing that. I'm not normal. I don't get to be that girl, not yet, at least. The things that are coming won't wait forever and I know it."

Olivia sighed but went on. "Ben, I'm willing to continue therapy, but there needs to be some boundaries. There needs to be rules that we don't break. You and I, we can't be friends, not yet. Not now. If this is going to work for me and you, then it has to be a strictly professional relationship. If you and Jake are friends, then I'm happy for it, but keep me out of it. If you guys go do whatever guy friends do together, don't bring up my name. You two don't get to discuss me, without me. Maybe someday you and I will be friends, but right now, I need a doctor, not a friend."

Olivia picked up her wine with an unsteady hand and took a sip. She waited.

Ben spoke up. "I can agree to that; so I'll see you in my office on Monday, then?"

Olivia straightened in her seat, "Yes that would be fine."

Jake laughed but Olivia gave him a sharp look. "I guess that means I'm not out of the hot seat?" He asked.

"We'll talk later, privately."

Jake nodded, but had a feeling that may be a difficult conversation.

Sam merely sipped her wine but patted Olivia's hand warmly.

Jake and Olivia stood in the front hall and said goodnight to Ben and Samantha, then he followed as she walked back into the library. He added more wood to the fire and sunk into a cozy chair. It was late and he was tired but he could see she still wanted to talk. He motioned for her to sit on his lap but she remained standing staring into the glowing fire.

"Darlin', it's late, let's go to bed." He suggested. "We can share a bowl of ice cream and see where it leads. Doesn't that sound good?"

"Yes, actually it does, but I need to say something to you."

"Ok shoot, um, well, don't shoot." Jake teased and put his hands in the air.

"Jake, that's not funny"

"It's a little funny."

"I just want you to understand that I wish you would have said something to me, instead of sending Ben out to ambush me in the stables.

You could have said, 'Olivia, I think you need to get back into therapy'."

"I couldn't have said that to you. I don't want to hurt you, don't you see that?"

"It hurts me more that you would go behind my back."

"I'm sorry, Darlin', I am; I couldn't watch you close yourself off like that."

"I'm sorry I haven't been more open, truly, I am. I just can't tell you everything Jake. I want to be the kind of woman you deserve but you don't deserve me dumping all my baggage at your feet."

"I told you before, I love you and if that means baggage, then so be it. You matter to me, that's all there is to it."

There was something about the way Jake loved her that touched her so deeply. She suddenly couldn't stop the waterworks.

Jake came to her quickly and wrapped his arms around her.

"I want this to work, Jake. You are the only good thing in my life." She admitted.

"It will work. I love you come hell or high water, do you get that? I just hope someday you'll trust it."

"I'm trying. I love you, too. I just don't think I deserve you."

Jake wanted to spill his guts right then and there, confessing his fears and just how much he knew about Patrick Hanson, but now was not the time. He would walk through fire to protect his future wife and he would just have to trust Ben to help Olivia work through and settle her past.

The rest of the weekend was fun and relaxing and Olivia felt better getting some things off her chest, but there was always the one thing she wouldn't say, not to anyone, not ever again.

They made plans to spend the following weekend in Spokane to do their Christmas shopping.

She was still reluctant to talk about the graffiti in her apartment but made a promise to herself that she would discuss it in therapy.

Monday afternoon came too quickly for Olivia's taste. She wasn't sure she could go through with this. She spent the day feeling nervous, sick to her stomach and generally, out of sorts. She wondered if she could admit to Ben that she was still having visions and maybe, just maybe, he would believe her. She had been short-tempered with Jake that morning and she knew it had been uncalled for. As usual he'd been patient with her and much kinder than she deserved.

She thought about it as she drove to Ben's office. "That man loves you Olivia Karen Curtis, don't screw it up." She scolded herself as she pulled up to the office. She looked around, hoping no one saw her talking to herself. She didn't see anyone but suddenly got the chills as though someone *were* watching her. Quickly, she hopped out, locked up her car and nearly ran inside.

"Hi Olivia, is everything alright?" LeAnn asked.

"Yes, I'm fine, just letting my imagination run away with me." She replied as she looked back through the glass door behind her. She sat down and began thumbing through a magazine, not really seeing what was on the pages.

Ben's voice came over the intercom. "LeAnn, go ahead and send in my next patient."

As she entered his office Ben looked up, "Hello Olivia, come on in. I hope you didn't have to wait, I got stuck on the phone."

"Its fine, I didn't wait." She smiled politely before sitting down on the couch.

"Good, that's good. Can I get you something to drink?"

"No thank you."

"I thought we would begin by talking about your goals."

"Really?" she asked, sounding amused.

"Yes, it's important to clarify what you want to achieve in therapy." Ben replied patiently.

"That's simple; sanity, normalcy."

"There is nothing simple about that, and let me share a little secret with you, there's no such thing as normal."

"No I suppose there isn't. But Doc, the thing is," she sighed. "The thing is, I can't seem to convince myself that I deserve to be happy."

"Do you feel you've done something that warrants punishment? What's your crime?"

"It's not that I've done something bad. It's all the bad that's been done to me."

"So, because bad things have happened to you, you feel you aren't worthy of anything good happening?"

"Yeah, though it sounds stupid when you say it that way" she curled her lip.

"That's because it is stupid."

"Great, now I'm stupid."

"No, you aren't. You're punishing yourself for things that are out of your control. Choosing to do that; is stupid. The upshot is you can make a different choice."

"I'm like food left out of the fridge too long, I've been spoiled."

"What about your marriage to Jackson? What about the birth of your son?"

Olivia thought for a moment. "They were different."

"Explain that."

"Marrying Jackson never felt like something good had happened to me." Olivia admitted.

"So because you were 'spoiled' (your word) Jackson was your punishment?"

Olivia nodded.

"What about Dante'?" Ben asked, watching carefully as he spoke her son's name. He noticed she flinched a little but her reaction was getting less intense.

"Dante' was like, like a reprieve. He was my angel. Since he died, I have spent so much time wondering if I *ever* deserved him. I tried to change what happened to him but I couldn't. Maybe I was wrong from the very beginning."

"Wrong about what?" Ben asked.

"Um, everything. Maybe I should have tried harder to spare him from a miserable life with an asshole stepfather."

"Do you truly think Dante' was miserable?"

"He always seemed happy, not around Jackson but with me. But it can't have been easy knowing he was the product of, the product of..."

"Of rape" Ben finished for her.

"Yes" Olivia wanted to say it. She wanted to be stronger than her pain, but she just didn't' have it in her; not today.

"If you're right, then there wasn't a decision you could have made that would have satisfied you completely." Ben surmised.

Olivia thought about that. Could it be true, that she would have been just as unhappy regardless of what she chose?

Ben could see her wheels turning. "Olivia, every day we are given the opportunity to make choices and we never can say with complete assuredness how our choices will affect our future or the future of others. You don't have a crystal ball. That is the beauty and sometimes the tragedy of life. You love Dante'. Choosing to bring him into this world wasn't wrong, it was just a choice. How could it be wrong when you said yourself he was your angel? Do you understand?"

"Yes, you are telling me to stop torturing myself for the past."

"Yes, I am, but also stop second-guessing every choice you ever made. You can't go back in time and change things so why waste even one second on regret?"

"That's the thing...I feel like that's all therapy is sometimes. I'm supposed to rehash my whole life and beat that dead horse until I'm..." she waved her hand in the air. "Fixed? Is that how it works? And yet I'm not supposed to have regret when I knew what was coming and I couldn't stop it."

"I know it feels that way but the goal isn't to beat a dead horse, it's to give you some perspective, and hopefully change your perspective to something more positive. It's to help you grieve so you *can* stop beating that dead horse. You aren't broken, you don't need fixing, and you couldn't have known what was going to happen to your son."

She wanted to blurt out, "Lord, why can't you believe me?" But, he, like all the others doesn't believe me either, she simply answered, "I feel broken and the sad thing is I can barely remember a time when I didn't feel broken."

"I understand, I truly do but that is why you're going to need some perspective. I'll show you what I mean. On a scale of one to ten, one being as broken as you've ever felt in your whole life and ten being as happy as you can imagine yourself being, what number were you when you were committed to that hospital?"

"Zero" she replied quietly, simply.

"What number were you when you looked upon your child's face the first time?"

"I can't answer that."

"Why can't you answer that? Are you afraid to say you were happy? How about this? What number are you now?"

"Four or five, maybe" she admitted.

"What brought you from a zero to a four? Just list a few things. Here, take this notebook, and write them down.

I want you to write in the heading, 'Going from Zero to Ten'" Ben held out a leather-bound notebook and a pen. "This journal is for you to keep. It isn't meant for me or anyone to see, it's for you, and you alone."

"Time has helped. I know it sounds cliché but time has helped."

"Good, write that down. What else?"

"Drugs; it's embarrassing to admit but at first, the drug therapy helped me."

"Are you taking anything currently?"

"No, I stopped taking all the meds. I saw Jake's face when he opened my medicine cabinet one day. I didn't want to be that person. I wanted to get better for real and I can't do that when I'm on drugs. Not anymore. Does that make sense?"

"Yes it does, though I would've preferred you discuss it with me first. Some of those meds can have serious side effects when you stop them cold turkey. The fact you want to be clearheaded is a good thing though. What else?"

"Moving away from Oregon helped me feel better. I know you think I should mend my relationship with my mother but the truth is, I love not being close to her, under her immense shadow and I love not being judged by her. Having her here for Thanksgiving just proved to me she and I can't ever be close. I'm better without my mother."

"Well, perhaps in time, even that can improve. What else?" he prodded.

"Jake" Olivia said simply, though there was nothing simple about her feelings for Jake.

"Tell me about that."

"I didn't want another man in my life, not ever. I had intended on being as alone as a person could possibly be. But that is nearly impossible, as I've discovered. I got that job at the diner and I was forced to interact. That's what it felt like. I didn't isolate myself as much as I thought I would and then, one day, Jake walked into the diner and somehow, right into my heart, even though I told myself I wouldn't let it happen."

"I'm going to admit something because I think it can only benefit you to hear it. I think Jake *has* been good for you. Not to devalue anything else that has helped but I really see the affect he's had on you. If you had succeeded in isolating yourself like you planned, I don't think you would be so far along in this process of healing and forgiveness.

Now, I want you to add to that list whenever you think of things that make you happy, that make you feel better, even if it's simple things or little things."

"Ok, then I should add coffee. I love coffee. I love the warm cup in my hands and the sweet aroma. It does help."

Ben smiled, "That's good."

Shifting gears more directly Ben said, "So, let's talk about the graffiti in your apartment. Have there been any new developments? Do they know who did it?"

Olivia bit her lip. "Jake hasn't told me anything about it."

"Why would he know and you wouldn't?"

"He asked me if he could deal with the whole mess for me. I told him he could. Honestly, I don't even care, except..." she hesitated.

"Except what?"

"Except that since it happened I keep feeling, I don't know, kinda, on edge, I guess. I even felt like I was being watched on my way in today. I guess I'm more rattled by it than I'd like to admit."

"That's understandable. Have you mentioned these feelings to anyone, to Jake?"

"Oh right, 'I'm sorry Jake but your crazy girlfriend has one more thing to pile on your plate.' I don't think so Doc."

"Olivia, you aren't crazy and Jake loves you. You need to tell him. If it's your imagination, then it will get better in time. If it's not, then it's worth checking out. Sometimes just saying it out loud helps."

"Perfect, since I just told you, I should be all better and stop getting the chills all the time."

"You should inform the police and your boyfriend, better safe than sorry."

"I hate that expression but I'll think about it." She agreed.

"Now I want you to start a new page and list your redeeming qualities. It can be anything but it has to be about you. It can't be about someone else."

Olivia rubbed her head. "This is silly."

"No, you need to start seeing yourself differently. You need to change how you feel about you."

"And what if I can't think of anything?"

"I'll help you." Ben replied. "You're polite."

"No I'm not; I slapped you across the face. That isn't exactly polite. I'm sorry about that, by the way."

"An impolite person wouldn't apologize for that. And you're forgiven.

I shouldn't have spoken to you the way I did. Trust me, you are polite. Write it down. Now you; it's your turn."

"Fine, I play piano well."

"What else?"

"I am good with horses."

"Good, that's good. What else?"

"I don't know. There isn't anything else."

"If someone else were to describe you, what would you hope they would say?" Ben pushed.

"I would hope they would say I was smart, kind, and witty; that sort of thing."

"Ok, that's great. Write those down. Now, how about physically, do you like the way you look?"

"The way I look shouldn't matter."

"Maybe it shouldn't but it does and you and I both know it. People respond first to physical appearance. Do you consider yourself beautiful?"

"I, I guess other people would say I was, but I don't really think so."

"Can you name one moment in your whole life when you felt beautiful; your wedding day perhaps?"

"God no, my mother picked out the dress and I, um, no; I don't see how this matters. I am not beautiful. It's ridiculous and if someone else thinks I am, who cares?"

"Jake thinks you're beautiful. Doesn't that matter to you? Why so defensive about this?"

"How do you know Jake thinks I'm beautiful? And no, it doesn't matter. It doesn't make me *feel* better. It doesn't, I don't understand the point."

"The point is to start focusing on the good. The good about who you are. You are a good and beautiful person, inside and out, and you've never been able to see yourself that way."

"How I look has only ever brought trouble."

"Tell me about that."

"I don't want to."

"Say it, Olivia, say it out loud. He picked you to rape because you're beautiful. Say it!" Ben demanded.

"Go to hell." She said, though not angrily.

"Isn't that where you live, already in hell? Aren't you tired of being a prisoner to that feeling? What if he picked you because he was too lazy to leave the neighborhood? What if he picked you because he liked the color of your house?

What if it doesn't matter why he picked you? For every bad thing that has ever happened to you, you look to blame things that are out of your control. Do you understand what I'm saying?"

"Yes" she sat with shoulders slumped and a look of misery on her exquisite face. She had no idea just how powerful her beauty was or perhaps, Ben thought, she did know and feared it.

"I need to say something, but I'm afraid." She looked up seriously.

"This is where you are safe to say whatever you need to say."

He sounded too clinical, too much like every other doctor she knew.

Olivia changed her mind in that moment. He wouldn't believe her. It was simply how the curse worked. She would be burdened by the knowledge of what was coming and no one would ever believe her. She felt as though there was a heavy stone in her heart; everything she foresaw would come to pass. Invisible bricks rested squarely on her shoulders.

Instead she said, "I wish I could shake this fear."

"You will, and the best way to do that is to be open with those who care about you. Let's move on. Tell me about the visit with your family."

"My mother was the same as always. It was nice to see my dad though, and my brother." She was reluctant to say more. Talking about her mother always felt like a hot button.

"Did you fight with your mother?"

"I wouldn't call what we do, fighting. She tells me all the things wrong with me, my life, my choices, my mistakes and I eat shit politely with a knife and fork."

"Have you ever stood up to her?"

"Yes, in my own way. It doesn't matter though, she still pushes me. She still punishes me. That is the nature of our relationship. She expects that if she pushes me enough, eventually I will be perfect even if it kills me."

"Do you think your mother won't love you if you aren't perfect?"

"Haven't you been listening? My mother *doesn't* love me. I know you think you know better, but I can guarantee you, she does **not** love me. She wouldn't love me, even if I *was* perfect."

"The woman I spoke with on the phone is profoundly worried about her daughter. She wouldn't worry like that if she didn't love you." Ben replied earnestly.

"Then you are now the proud owner of ocean front property in Arizona. I've never been more than a performing monkey to that woman.

~ 339 ~

If the monkey behaves badly, she scolds it, shames it and pushes it harder. If the monkey performs well, then it could probably do more so she pushes it harder."

Ben was astounded at the venom she spewed toward her mother. He had no idea the depths of Olivia's resentment and maybe even hatred.

"Do *you* love *her*? Ben asked.

Olivia put her fingers to her temples. "I have to get going."

"Don't run away from this. Answer the question."

"Do I love my mother? Yes, in spite of everything, yes I do. Which I'm pretty sure makes me a masochist."

"If she was as evil as you say then I guess you would be a masochist, but I'm unconvinced your mother doesn't love you. She may be hard on you. She may not be a warm person, but in her own way, I think she loves you."

"People have told me that...my whole life and *I'm* unconvinced. I don't know a lot, but I know loving a child doesn't feel like this. It isn't supposed to feel like, like being the daughter of a stone cold bitch." She already had said more than she wanted to. She was so angry. "I'm sorry Dr. Thompson but you don't know what it's like."

"Then tell me."

"I'm afraid anything I say will sound petty."

"Try me."

"She sold my horse! I had a horse I loved and she sold it. She never even asked me. She said it was for my own good. She said my time was better spent practicing the piano. And then, she, she wouldn't let us move out of the neighborhood after I was raped. She told my father that if he tried to take me somewhere, she would divorce him and take everything including custody of me and my brother. During my pregnancy, she remodeled the kitchen and threw a party when it was completed, so the rumors about us would be put to rest. She hired a nanny and I was told not to mention my baby, at all, no matter what anyone said. My mother made me dress up and smile and lie to fifty of her closest friends about what happened. I still remember what she told me to say. 'I don't know how vicious rumors like that get started. The kitchen was in need of a remodel. Me? I'm fine. No I was not attacked; what a horrible thing to say. Awful reporters made up that story. They're being sued.' Of course that last part was only to be said if someone asked me directly."

"She gave me a valium that night to relax me so I wouldn't have any "social anxiety". That's what she called it. She said, 'Here Olivia, take this.

That way you won't have any social anxiety. I don't want you to say something inappropriate to my friends.' I mean, really, why would I have any social anxiety? I was only brutally raped and beaten, left for dead and then very nearly burned by a man from my neighborhood. It seems strange I would be anxious at all, don't you think? Then, I found out later that she had begged my doctor to give me an abortion without my knowledge. When he wouldn't do it, she tried to pay him for it. Miles told me he heard her talking to the doctor outside my room. I had to fight and fight hard to keep my precious baby."

Olivia fought back her angry tears and continued, "I think it was part of her reasoning for having me committed later on. I think she was angry she didn't get *her* way. She told me during the visit last week that Dante' was a mistake and now that my son and husband are dead I should get a fresh start and begin performing again. She wanted, wants me to have the career I never really had. She wants Jake to marry me and move us to New York so I can be all she's dreamed of for me. She wants to finally be proud of me. But perhaps I'm being too hard on her. Perhaps you're right and she really does love me. That is how a mother loves a child, right?"

Ben had been shocked before but this was more than he'd expected. He understood better now why Olivia had such venom for her mother.

"I owe you an apology Olivia."

"Does that mean you believe me?"

"I believe your mother has not handled things well, but I still think there is a way to have a better relationship with her. I think it's possible. I'm not saying she'll change but it doesn't have to be like this."

"I guess *I* have to do the changing then."

"Unfortunately, that is usually the case. Do you have much communication with her?"

"No, she calls me but I usually don't answer. If there is an emergency or if there is something she really needs to discuss then she calls my brother and then Miles calls me."

"That's probably best for now. You've heard of toxic friends? I think what you have is a toxic parent and right now it's better if you limit your contact with her."

"That would be great but she wants us to get together for Christmas. I'm hoping to avoid it. Jake's family is so kind and welcoming and with them I don't feel like I'm under attack."

"You're an adult, it's your choice. What do you want to do?"

"I want to do anything except spend Christmas with my mother."

"That's ok. You should surround yourself with people who build you up, not tear you down."

"This is the first time I've ever had that option, except with Dante'. I'm sorry, but can we be done for today?"

"Of course; I'll see you next week. Just take that journal with you and work on it. Reread what you wrote. There is good progress there. Try and add to it if you can."

"Ok, I'll try."

Olivia headed for the exit as quickly as possible. She decided she needed a ride tonight, to clear her head.

CHAPTER TWENTY-SEVEN

Jake had been on edge all day. He didn't mind that Olivia had been grumpy with him this morning. He was more concerned with the reasons behind the bad mood.

It was obvious entering into therapy again was weighing heavily on her and he still felt like an ass for pushing her into it. He had promised himself he wouldn't push her and yet he had done it anyway. He sincerely hoped it had gone well.

He couldn't even remember what he had done all day. His mind was overtaken by thoughts of Olivia. He called her during her lunch but she was quiet and didn't have much to say. She would be home soon and Jake would feel better. 'Home', it made him happy this was Olivia's home. She belonged here, with him. *That* he was sure about. He opened his desk drawer and looked at the ring again. Even with everything else going on, he was looking forward to finally proposing to her. He felt like he'd been in limbo since buying the ring; like money burning a hole in the pocket of a child.

He wondered if the proposal he planned would be too much for her. He didn't want to overwhelm her. He needed some sound advice so he picked up the phone but then stared at it for a moment. Who to call? The only person who might be remotely helpful was his mom. He dialed.

"Hello Jacob, did you need to speak to your Papa?"

"No Mama, actually I called to speak to you."

"Tesoro mia, is everything ok?" Frankie could hear the distress in his voice.

"Everything is fine, it's just, well, I bought Olivia a horse and I planned on proposing to her when I show it to her but now I'm second-guessing the plan."

"Oh dear, you don't do anything half way, do you?"

"No, I guess I don't. I've got the horse hidden up at the Outfitter's and the ring is in my desk drawer and I just want everything to be perfect."

"It *will* be perfect. It will be perfect because you love Olivia. As for overwhelming her, I think you worry too much."

"Yes, but she's been through so much Mama." Jake twirled the ring around his little finger as he talked.

"She has been through so many *bad* things, dolce' mia, it's not the same when it's something good. Either way, trust your heart, you'll know what to do."

"Thank you, Mama. Can I ask you something else?"

"Of course, ask me anything."

"Was Sarea bought out of my life?" Jake asked bluntly, unable to sugar coat it. He wasn't even sure he wanted the answer.

"Sarea? What? Why would you ask me that Jacob after all these years?"

"Ben and I are finally talking again and that's the story he was told. I'm not blaming you or Papa for anything, I'm just asking."

"What did I tell you when you came to me with the news that Sarea was pregnant?"

"You said I'd better be ready to be a grown up. You said I was foolish and stupid and my childhood was officially over and you told me to prepare myself for a lifetime of parenting and all the responsibilities that go with it."

"That's right, now why would I give you that lecture if I had been planning to bail you out? God had other plans for you Son, and for her I think."

"She didn't have a miscarriage Mama." Jake repeated what he now believed.

"Yes, yes she did. Jacob, she had a miscarriage. Her father told us, your papa and me, right there in the library and *she* was to tell *you* before they moved away. How is it you don't know this?"

Jake sighed in frustration. "Because she told everyone different stories, I guess. She told Ben she had been forced to have an abortion under a threat from our family; she told me she chose to have an abortion, and she told her father she had a miscarriage. I think the only person who knows the truth is Sarea Scott."

"Then my question for you is; why are you calling me and not Sarea Scott?" Frankie asked reasonably.

"I don't know. I guess I'm afraid of what she might say. I'm sorry, Mama, I shouldn't have asked you about this. I knew better than to think my family would pay someone off."

"Jacob, I love you, we love you, I'm certain Olivia loves you. Now, try and relax. Everything will work out, have a little faith dolce' raggazzo. How *is* Olivia?"

"She's good, I think. She went back to therapy today thanks to me and I feel awful about the way I manipulated her into it.

I don't think I've been very helpful to her."

"Oh Jacob, sometimes you men just don't get it, do you? It's not your job to fix every problem she faces. You love Olivia, all she needs is for you to listen to her, support her and let her feel what she needs to feel. Let her vent if she needs to vent and cry if she needs to cry and don't look at her like she's a problem that needs your fixing. If you can do that, then you'll be a much faster learner than your papa."

"So you're saying I should back off, then?"

"I'm saying, don't be Mr. Fixit every time she wants to tell you about a bad day. It's annoying."

"Thank you, Mama, I love you. I'd better go; Olivia should be getting home soon. Ti' amo"

"Ti' amo, Ciao"

Olivia was distracted while driving out to the ranch. She didn't even remember to put her Jeep in four wheel drive and she wasn't paying attention to the snowy road. She just kept replaying her conversation with Ben over and over in her mind. She had finally spilled her guts about her mother, but wasn't that supposed to make her feel better?

The hard wind was making the snow blow sideways across her windshield. It drifted over the road making it hard to see where the sides of the road actually were. Without warning the Jeep pulled to the right and she was instantly in a ditch.

She cursed herself for her distraction. She hadn't been driving very fast so she was frustrated and confused how it happened. She wasn't hurt but her ego was bruised.

"This is so ridiculous" she said aloud as she put the Jeep in four wheel drive and tried to back herself out onto the road. The tires spun but the Jeep didn't move. Underneath the snow was a sheet of ice. "Damn" she cursed. "Damn, damn, damn."

She reached for her cell phone. "No power, really?" Olivia sighed. How could she really be stuck in a ditch in Montana with a dead cell phone, no charger and to really add insult to injury, it was already getting dark.

"Ugh" she groaned. "This can't be happening. What a shitty day." She wasn't sure therapy had really gone very well and now this.

She looked over at the notebook Ben gave her. "You won't do me any good. Stupid book! Stupid Ben Thompson! Stupid Montana!" she yelled and slammed her fist on the steering wheel.

She tried once more to slowly back the Jeep out of the ditch, but again the tires spun on the ice. She bit her lip. "Now what? I have my heavy coat on, I have boots on. Do I walk or do I wait? It can't be that far." She thought.

Thinking it could be awhile before someone would drive by; she decided to try to walk to the ranch. She put on her gloves and grabbed her purse and keys. The wind blew the cold through her like a screen door. She had never seen weather like this, let alone been out in it. This was such bone chilling cold.

She wrapped her scarf around her ears and neck and crossed her arms over her chest. She wondered just how long it would take before Jake came looking for her.

"Please God don't let me see a bear, especially a hungry one." She prayed as she tromped through the deep snow. The icy wind took bites at her face.

"Doesn't anyone ever drive on this road?" She wondered. She forged ahead trying to focus only on walking. Already her fingers were cold so she shoved her hands in the pockets of her coat.

Jake stood in the kitchen staring out the window. The phone was in his hand. He didn't know or care how many times he called Olivia's cell phone. All that mattered was she didn't answer. Every attempt went directly to her voicemail. Jake let out a deep breath and jumped at the sound of Carmella's voice.

"Call Benjamin and ask when Olivia left his office." She suggested.

"That's a good idea." Jake replied, wondering why he hadn't thought of it already and dialed Ben's number.

"Hello?" Ben answered.

"Ben, this is Jake. Is Olivia still there in your office?"

"No, she left about an hour ago. Why?"

"She isn't home yet. I gotta go." Jake replied and hung up the phone.

"I'm going to look for her. Call me if you hear anything." He said to Carmella as he practically sprinted to the garage. His mind was racing and his heart was pounding. He wasn't the only one.

Olivia's mind was racing, too. She couldn't understand why she hadn't seen the Weidner Ranch sign yet. Fear kept her moving quickly, but she turned to look behind her. Her tracks were swept away by the wind and the snow and nothing around her looked familiar. Nothing looked right.

She told herself it was just the storm making everything look different, turned around maybe? "If only I'd been born with a better sense of direction." She thought. She was beginning to sweat and then shiver. Her body began to move more sluggishly, even though she told herself to keep going.

"You idiot, you should have stayed in the Jeep. You're an idiot and you don't belong in Montana; the home of bears, wolves and rugged men like Jake. Your mother was right. You should go back to the city. If you get out of this mess that is exactly what you should do. You should go to the city, get your nails done and hope Jake likes long distance relationships." She thought darkly.

She was too mad and afraid to cry. The fear and the cold were overwhelming but the fatigue scared her even more. The snowflakes were sticking to her eyelashes and she rubbed at her nose and could barely feel it with her numb fingers.

She stopped and looked around again searching for something familiar. "Why don't I recognize anything?" she mumbled to herself, sniffling and trying to hold back tears.

Then she saw him, just ahead of her in the trees. "Dante'", she cried out. "Come back baby. Please Dante', come here to Mommy." He just kept walking away and she was so confused. Tears fell, but turned to ice on her cheeks.

After what seemed like an eternity, Olivia saw headlights approaching and Dante' was gone, as if the wind had swept him away. She tried to wave her arms and yell but her limbs felt heavy and her voice came out like a whisper. "Stop, please stop."

When Jake saw her, he let out the breath he'd been holding. He stopped his truck next to her and jumped out. She collapsed into his arms. He picked her up, adrenaline and fear propelling him.

"Oh my God, are you ok? Are you hurt? Oh Olivia, you scared me." He shouted in the wind as he carried her through the deep snow. He placed her in the warm truck and closed the door.

"You have to find Dante'. The wind took him." She said so quietly, Jake barely understood her.

"He's not here Darlin'. Let's get you warmed up."

He noticed she shivered violently. He turned up the heater as high as it would go and reached for her hands. He pulled off her soaking wet gloves and held her ice cold fingers up toward the heat vent. It was obvious she was in the early stages of hypothermia.

His heart pounded as he reached down to take off her boots and socks. Both were soaked through.

It was difficult to undress her in the confines of the truck but he knew she needed to get out of the wet clothing as quickly as possible. She tried to help but was shivering and still somewhat delirious. He pulled off her jacket and sweater wrapping a warm blanket around her and then drove as fast as he could go.

"Don't touch me," she said angrily and her head lolled back onto the seat. To her, this was wrong, it all felt wrong. She was tired, angry and she couldn't understand why Jake had undressed her. Was he crazy? Why didn't he go back for Dante'? How could he leave her boy out in this cold? What was wrong with him? She pushed at him, trying to get him to stop the car. "Please stop. He needs me. You can't leave him. He'll die."

"You're going to be ok Darlin'." Jake kept repeating, he didn't know what else to say. He picked up his cell phone and called Carmella.

"I found her. She's hypothermic." Jake shouted. Carmella didn't stay on the phone.

When he got them safely home, Jake carried her up the stairs. Carmella had prepared heat packs for the bed, turning up the fireplace so the room was toasty warm. Jake laid her in bed and placed the heat packs around her feet, hips and under her arms.

Olivia was unaware of what was going on. She felt so tired, especially as her body warmed. The shivers began to subside. Even though she wanted to talk to Jake, the words wouldn't come and sleep took over.

Jake sat in a chair next to the bed and watched her. He could tell she tried to say something but drifted off instead. He took her pulse and her temperature. She barely moved. She was a rag doll again.

"Did you call the doctor?" he asked Carmella quietly.

"Yes, he said to warm her slowly, monitor her vitals then call him and take her to the hospital if she gets worse. He said it's likely early to moderate hypothermia. He's going to make a house call tomorrow. Don't worry Jacob, you found her, she's alive and she's safe. She'll be alright." Carmella soothed.

"I was really scared." Jake admitted. He checked her feet and legs again adjusting the heat packs.

"I know. I'm going to make some coffee. You should lie down. I will watch her for you. You need sleep too Jacob."

"No Ma'am, I would take some coffee though."

"Alright" Carmella replied.

Jake spent the night watching over Olivia. The next morning he called his Aunt Denise to let her know what had happened. Carmella had gone to bed at some point realizing Jake wouldn't leave Olivia; he refused to sleep. He wouldn't even allow himself to crawl in next to her. He feared he wouldn't be able to stay awake.

After the phone call, Carmella came in and saw Jake rubbing his eyes. It reminded her of when he had been a little boy. "My turn" Carmella said quietly.

"What?" Jake asked, barely conscious.

"It's my turn. You lie down in that bed and let me keep watch for a while, over *both* of you. Her temperature is better; her breathing is normal, let me take over." Carmella insisted.

"No, it's ok." He whispered.

"Jacob Knox, I'm not asking, I'm telling you. I'll be right here."

"I guess I could sleep for a bit."

"You could sleep for a week by the looks of you."

Jake smiled and crawled on the bed next to Olivia. He draped his arm over the top of her protectively. "She *is* looking better." He said, the sleep took him instantly.

Olivia opened her eyes. She felt groggy, like she'd had another bad dream. Jake's arm lay heavily over her. She smiled and turned to look at him. He lay on top of the covers in his jeans and a t-shirt. Olivia had no idea what time or even what day it was. Why hadn't he undressed? She only knew she was incredibly thirsty and really hungry and something smelled delicious.

Gently, she lifted Jake's arm from her. He didn't even stir. Olivia kissed him on the cheek and slipped quietly out of bed. She realized she only had underwear on, so she grabbed a bathrobe and pulled it tightly around her. Her legs were shaky and there was a chair sitting next to the bed. She rubbed her eyes and felt the sensation of standing on wobbly legs.

She remembered most of what happened and was totally embarrassed. She had driven into a snowdrift and started her walk toward the ranch but it must have been farther than she realized. She remembered seeing the headlights and Jake lifting her into the truck. It was like trying to recall details from a nightmare.

She looked into the bathroom mirror and was shocked to see her reflection.

Her color was closer to grey than pink and her eyes were bloodshot with dark circles under them. If she hadn't been so famished, she would have showered first.

Carmella was in the kitchen humming to herself.

"Hello Carmella" Olivia's voice cracked.

"You shouldn't be out of bed, yet. We were so worried about you. Here, sit down before you fall over. What can I get for you?"

"Water please. I'm so thirsty."

"Of course, I want you to drink this tea though. Your body still needs the warmth. This isn't the first time we've dealt with hypothermia around here." Carmella replied, setting the tea mug down in front of her.

Olivia obeyed even though she didn't enjoy tea and took a slow sip at first but it was so good, she began to drink it faster.

"Here is some oatmeal, too. Nice and warm with cinnamon sugar. Are you ok for a minute? I'm going to wake up Jacob."

"Please don't wake him, he is so tired."

"I promised I would wake him if there were any changes. He needs to see that you're ok." Carmella replied as she left the kitchen.

Olivia wanted to protest further but didn't. She ate as much of the oatmeal as she could but then felt slightly nauseous and sleepy again. She rested her head on the counter for just a moment.

"Jacob, Olivia is awake" Carmella touched him on the shoulder gently.

"Ok, thanks, where is she?" Jake asked, jumping out of bed.

"In the kitchen, she was hungry. She's alright." Carmella assured him.

"Thank you" Jake replied and rushed downstairs in his bare feet.

"Darlin'" Jake said, and then realized Olivia was asleep again; fast asleep with her head resting next to her bowl of oatmeal. He leaned down and kissed her cheek.

"Hi" she said drowsily.

"I'm going to take you back to bed Darlin'."

"I can walk."

He ignored her and lifted her easily into his arms and carried her upstairs. Gently he placed her on the bed. It was pride and stubbornness that kept her from admitting she probably wouldn't have made it upstairs without his help.

"Thank you" she said lying on the fluffed up pillows.

He pulled the comforter around her as he sat on the bed next to her. He pulled out his phone.

"What are you doing?"

"I'm calling the doctor, love. He's coming out today to check on you and I need to know what time. The storm has passed, so he can make it."

"Please don't. Just tell him I'm fine. I don't need a doctor's visit."

"It's only a precaution. It would make me feel better. You just rest." Jake said as he dialed.

"Jake, I don't want..." she began to protest.

"Please don't fight me on this. Hypothermia is no joke. People have died from it."

Olivia nodded guiltily. There was no fighting the look in his eyes. It was a combination of fear and anger. She hated that she had caused it.

"It seems I have more to make up for." She whispered.

"Hi, this is Jake Weidner. Dr. Harris was planning on making a house call today. I just wanted to find out what time he would be out here." Jake waited. "Ok fine, thank you."

Jake hung up the phone. "You have nothing to make up for. I should have shown you what to do in this sort of situation. I'm not mad at you, I was worried about you. And you don't seem to be bouncing back as quickly as I thought you would." He explained, trying to remove the sound of tension from his voice.

Later that afternoon, when Dr. Harris arrived, Olivia was more alert and Jake was beginning to wonder if she had been right about not needing to see a doctor.

Olivia had washed her face and brushed her teeth and hair. She sat up in bed in an oversized light grey sweatshirt and yoga pants. The sweatshirt said DIVA in rhinestones on it and hung off one shoulder, a fleece throw covering her feet. She had a smile on her face when Jake escorted Dr. Harris in the room.

"Olivia, this is Dr. Shane Harris." Jake said politely.

"Hello, Dr. Harris; I tried to tell Jake this was unnecessary but he insisted." She gave Jake a mischievous look.

"Hello Olivia. Jake did the right thing, it's always better to err on the side of caution."

Olivia liked Dr. Harris right off. He had a warm smile and he reminded her of her own grandpa.

"Jake, how about you give Olivia and me a few minutes alone. You should go and eat something, Boy. Carmella tells me you haven't eaten anything since this lovely lady went missing."

"No, I..." Jake began.

"We'll be fine here Jake, now get." He told him firmly, and Jake begrudgingly left the room.

Olivia giggled. "Dr. Harris, I wasn't lost. It was just a longer walk than I realized."

"My dear girl, they tell me Jake found you several miles from the ranch road. You are very lucky he found you when he did."

"I wasn't even on the right road?" she asked, confused. "I didn't know that."

"The confusion and delirium you felt was due to the hypothermia."

"I don't think I was delirious."

"No matter, I think you're probably fine now, though you seem to be a bit dehydrated. Do you drink much water?"

"I'm not very good about drinking water." Olivia admitted.

"Ok, well I'm going to start an I.V. and get you properly hydrated."

"Is that really necessary?"

"I think it'll help. Have you been ill recently? Have you had any vomiting, diarrhea, anything like that?"

"I've been nauseous, but I haven't had any other problems, why?"

"Is there a possibility you are pregnant Olivia?"

"No, I..."

The doctor waited. He had seen that same look of shock many times before.

"When was your last period, dear? Perhaps we should do a pregnancy test, just to be sure."

"No, I'm not pregnant; I just haven't been drinking enough water. I'm sure that's it."

"Alright, if you decide you want to find out for sure, you can make an appointment in my office anytime."

Jake walked back in with a very large, half-eaten sandwich. "An appointment for what?"

"Olivia needs to make a follow up appointment so I can see how she's doing, let's say, this Friday?" Dr. Harris replied winking at Olivia.

"That sounds fine. I'll make sure she's there." Jake mumbled through a bite of his sandwich.

Olivia suddenly felt like she was drowning. "Dr. Harris wants to start an I.V. on me Jake. Will you hold my hand? I hate needles."

"Of course I'll hold your hand." Jake said and reached for her hand kissing it gently.

Dr. Harris left the room to get the supplies he needed to start the I.V.

"I'm so sorry, Jake. I had no idea I was lost. I thought I was on the right road. I've caused you so much trouble and so much worry."

"Don't be sorry, but from now on, don't leave your vehicle. I found your Jeep long before I found you."

Olivia sighed. She felt like a ridiculous city slicker. More bits and pieces of what happened came back like embarrassing flashes.

"I thought I saw Dante'." She said, and her eyes welled with tears.

"I know Darlin'. That's how hypothermia works, it can really mess with your head."

"Thank you for finding me." She said simply.

"I never would have stopped looking for you, not ever." Jake kissed her softly on the mouth, but then with more urgency, more intensity.

Dr. Harris cleared his throat from the doorway.

"Dr. Harris, can Jake stay for this part? I really don't like needles."

"That's fine with me." He replied, and then took her hand and turned her arm over, looking for a vein. He inadvertently moved her bracelet aside and couldn't help but notice the scar on her wrist.

"That's some scar you have there."

Olivia blushed miserably. "Yeah" was all she could say.

Jake held her other hand and watched her face as Dr. Harris started the I.V. Olivia thought how strange all this was, and strangely familiar. It was the part she detested the most.

Dr. Harris left instructions for Jake and Carmella and Jake walked him to his car. "Jake, I've been your family doctor for many years now, I didn't need an escort." He teased.

"I wanted to talk to you but not in front of Olivia. I was going to surprise her with a trip next weekend. Is she alright to fly?"

"I think it'd be fine. See if you can get her to drink more water, I'm a little concerned about dehydration and it isn't due to hypothermia."

"What could it be?"

"Oh, it could be any number of things. Just make sure she comes to see me on Friday for that follow-up before you leave." Doctor Harris said vaguely.

"I will. Thanks Doc."

"It's my pleasure, Jake. Say hello to your folks for me."

"Will do."

When Jake came back up to the bedroom, Olivia was standing in a robe next to the I.V. pole.

"Darlin', what are you doing out of bed?" he asked. "Crawl in love, you need rest."

Olivia had her little pouty face on. It was a look Jake was beginning to know well. She was biting her lip and her brow was furrowed.

"Is it Tuesday?"

"Yes."

"Have I lost another job?"

"No, of course you haven't. I called Aunt Denise and everything is fine." Jake held her, but she was tense.

"Maybe I could just take a shower or a bath." She began to cry. She hadn't meant to, of course, she never did mean to, but tears flowed against her will. "I don't even know why I'm crying."

"It's probably just exhaustion. You've been through a lot, Darlin'." He helped her back into bed. "As soon as the I.V. is finished, we can take it out and then I'll draw a bath. I think we could both use one." He just smiled.

Over the next couple days, Olivia found herself in awe of Jake. It was the first time she really was able to watch what he did every day. It was impressive how much he could accomplish. He and one of the hands hauled her Jeep out of the ditch and brought it back to the ranch, he bought her a car phone charger and stocked the Jeep with some sort of emergency kit he promised to show her later. He fielded numerous phone calls and easily dealt with all the Weidner businesses including greeting new clients at the Outfitting Company.

He arranged for Olivia to have plenty of company including Sam, his parents, Carmella of course, and even Tag. He took time out of his day to play board games with her and brought dinner to her every night, insisting she stay in bed. He rented her movies and watched many of them with her. He oversaw all of the crew at the ranch and did a lot of "cow business" as Olivia had begun to call it

But as nice as it was, by Friday, she'd had her fill of bed rest, so she got up early to get ready for work.

"Denise isn't expecting you back until Monday, Darlin', and you have an appointment with Dr. Harris this afternoon."

"I know, and I'll be there. I'll go to work and then to Dr. Harris' office. When I get home, I'll pack for our trip. We are still going aren't we? I love Spokane and I'm excited to get away for the weekend."

"Yes, we're still taking a trip, but you don't have to work today."

"I can't stay in bed any longer, Jake, I'm getting cabin fever. I'm not ill, I'm fine. In fact, I'm better than fine, I'm well rested, but now I have to go do my job."

"I'm not trying to hold you prisoner, I just don't want you to overdo it."

"I'm sorry, my love, I know I sound like an ungrateful bitch. I appreciate how you've taken care of me, truly. It's just, now, I'm all the way better, I promise and so it feels like I'm skipping school or something. I want to go."

Jake growled playfully and picked her up in a bear hug. He bit softly at her ear. She squealed and laughed.

"Ok, just come home safely to me." He said seductively.

"I will." She replied softly.

She kissed him on the mouth and then the nose. He continued to hold her off the ground. Jake loved how she fit so perfectly in his arms.

"I don't want to let you go, Darlin'."

"I know, I feel the same way, but it's temporary. Just think, this weekend, you and I will have nothing but time to..." she paused. "Shop" She teased him.

"Actually, shopping was the last thing on my mind." He whispered in her ear.

It caused a delightful chill to cover her whole body.

"I have a hotel room reserved and dinner reservations and I thought we might have a little champagne."

"Are we celebrating something?"

"Yes, we're celebrating us."

"That sounds amazing, but we really do have to get some Christmas shopping done."

"We will; Portland has some great shopping I hear."

"I thought we were driving to Spokane?"

"No, we're flying to Portland."

Olivia sighed. It would mean visiting her family. It was obligatory; the weekend wouldn't be so relaxing after all.

"Ok" she said begrudgingly, but tried to sound accommodating. "Is there anything in particular I should bring?"

"Just you" Jake said happily.

Olivia drove herself to work and as promised, she called Jake when she arrived. She didn't want to worry him again. It seemed to throw him into overprotective mode.

It was good to be back at work. She was glad not to be a patient any longer, even though she still had the follow up with Dr. Harris.

Olivia thought a lot about Jake as she played piano. He was probably at his desk making phone calls or up at the Outfitter's pestering Sam, or perhaps he was out and about at the ranch. Jake's career seemed to be about managing and delegating more than anything else and yet she knew just how hard he worked every day.

At three in the afternoon, she cut out early at the studio and went to see Dr. Harris. She was kind of surprised that a doctor would even hold office hours on a Friday afternoon. But, then, this was small town America. Dr. Harris was sweet and charming and still reminded her of her grandpa.

"Well Olivia, what about that pregnancy test now?"

"I took one already. It was negative." She lied.

"It wouldn't be the first time I've been mistaken. How are you feeling then? Anything going on that I should know about?"

"Nope, not a thing, I'm feeling good."

"Are you still feeling nauseated?"

"No, that went away. I'm fine, seriously."

After she left the doctor's office, she realized she'd missed several phone calls. At first she was irritated, but then she realized Jake had only called her once. The rest of the calls were from a number she didn't recognize. She decided to call Jake back first.

"Hello Darlin'," Jake answered.

"Hi." Olivia loved the sound of his deep voice.

"How was your day?"

"It was good. Dr. Harris gave me the all clear, so now I'm on my way home."

"That sounds great, call me if you need me."

"Hey, I missed some phone calls today, did you happen to call me from a different phone?"

"No, you don't recognize the number?" Jake asked suspiciously.

"No, oh well, it was probably just a solicitor. I love you. I'll see you soon."

By the time Olivia arrived at the house, she had completely forgotten about the missed calls.

"Jake, I thought we weren't leaving until tomorrow?" Olivia said as she folded a sweater and placed it in her suitcase.

"We're leaving just as soon as you're ready." Jake replied. He stood behind her with his hands on her hips.

"Jake, nothing's changed."

"What do you mean?"

"I mean I still can't think when you're around. Isn't there something you can do while I pack? Go boss someone around. Go make sure Carmella doesn't mind looking after Harper for me, something?"

"Oh alright but really, everything is taken care of. Dent is waiting to take us to the airport, Carmella runs this house better than I ever could and I've already finished up business for the weekend. Maybe I could help you. Should I pick out some lingerie for you?" he teased.

Olivia groaned jokingly, but turned and kissed him.

About an hour later, they were sitting quietly on the jet. Jake held her hand and gently rubbed with his thumb absently. It was one of those quiet moments between them where Olivia could picture forever with this man. He didn't represent stress or anger or drama, just love. Loving Jake felt like that first deep breath of air after being under water for a long time, or that first blissful stretch when you wake up in the morning. It was indescribably good.

"I'm a little nervous about going to Portland, you know. What if I see someone I know?" she asked, feeling silly, but needing some reassurance.

"You might, but who cares. You don't owe anyone an explanation."

"Do my parents know we're coming?" she asked dreading his answer.

"Yes, and I promised them we would join them for dinner tonight but after that it's just you and I."

"Dinner? Where? Who did my mother invite?"

"I think it will just be your family and the two of us, at their country club."

"I don't want to go. You have to cancel."

"Why?"

Olivia stood up and paced as much as she could, though there wasn't much room for it on the jet. "Because, Jake, Mother is an evil woman who would love nothing more than to see me suffer and we'll be in *her* territory. I told her I won't ever come back to Oregon."

"You make her sound like a predatory animal Darlin'. When you put it that way, I guess I better cancel."

"No, no don't, we'll just deal with it. It's one dinner, right?" Olivia said, changing her mind remembering what she had discussed with Ben.

"Right" he replied, looking at her skeptically.

Olivia spent the remainder of the flight perfecting her hair and makeup and silently praying her mother didn't have anything up her sleeve; though, she had a sneaking suspicion she did. Her mother's 'surprises' were never good.

When they arrived at the country club, Olivia was a beautiful bundle of nervous energy. She had far too many memories of this place and most of them were not good.

Though many of those memories included Dante', and that just put a knot in her stomach. Here she was walking down memory lane, only this time, stripped of everything she used to be.

"Jake, Olivia, it's good to see you again." Miles said and hugged his sister.

"Hello Miles. Good evening, Mr. Curtis, Mrs. Curtis; I'm happy we could get together." Jake replied courteously.

Jonathan stood to hug his daughter and shake Jake's hand. Antoinette stood also.

Another person joined their table and waited patiently. Olivia turned and nearly gasped.

"Olivia, you remember Layne don't you?" said Antoinette a sly half-smile on her face.

Jake could feel Olivia stiffen next to him.

"Of course Mother; he *was* my brother-in-law, how could I forget?" she replied without smiling.

"I'd like to think we're still family, Olivia." Layne leaned over to kiss her cheek.

"Of course, how are you Layne?" Olivia asked tensely.

"I'm terrific, I was so glad when I bumped into your mother and she invited me to join you for dinner. It's been too long. I think the last time I saw you..."

"You were fighting me over the inheritance from my husband." Olivia cut him off.

"Right, well, that worked out nicely for you, now didn't it? Who's your new fella?"

Olivia felt the sudden urge to beat the shit out of Layne Montgomery; partly for the poor excuse for a human being he was and partly for how much he resembled Jackson.

"This is Jake Weidner. Jake, this is Layne Montgomery, Jackson's brother."

Jake shook his hand but refused to be friendlier to someone Olivia obviously didn't like.

"Why would you come here?" she asked Layne as everyone was seated at the table.

"Mother, how could you invite him?" Olivia asked angrily.

"Olivia!" Antoinette snapped. "That is uncalled for. I expect you to be civil."

"Let's all have a drink, shall we." Jonathan suggested raising his arm for their waiter.

Layne smiled and nodded, but it was obvious to Olivia it was an act. The only reason he came was to try to get under her skin. She decided not to give him the satisfaction.

"Miles, what are your plans for Christmas?" she turned to her brother.

"Well I'll be spending a little time in Montana actually. Didn't Sam tell you?" he asked and smiled mischievously.

"You're welcome to stay at the ranch if you would like Miles. We would love to have you." Jake offered.

"Thank you, Jake, that's very kind of you."

"Are you married then Jake? Is our Olivia just your girl on the side, or are you shacking up with someone already Liv?" Layne said sarcastically.

"Layne you low down piece of shit, son of a bitch! How dare you come here pretending to play nice with me! You and I both know what you really think of me and what you've always thought of my family. Why don't you cut the crap for once?" Olivia growled.

"Olivia! Layne asked a simple question." Antoinette defended him.

"Thank you Mrs. Curtis. I didn't mean to offend you, Olivia. I didn't realize you were so sensitive about your new life in Montana. It is Montana, isn't it?"

Jake didn't give Olivia a chance to respond, taking her hand under the table. "No, I'm not married and none of that is any of your business. I think perhaps you should leave, as you *are* offensive." Jake said, as calmly as he could.

Layne put on his best boxer's face, ready for a challenge. "I'm a member here at this club; so perhaps *you* should leave and let Olivia's family take care of her."

"Layne, you can go straight to hell, and Mother," Olivia stood. "If you knew what kind of person Jackson really was, you would be dancing on his grave, not inviting his asshole brother here to take bites out of me. I'll never forgive you for this. Layne, the one good thing your brother ever did, was making sure you never got a penny of his money. Jackson may have been an abusive terrorist, but at least he took care of that part. Now, if you'll excuse us, Miles, Dad, Jake and I have other plans. I love you Daddy, I'm sorry, I'll call you later, Miles." Olivia choked back an angry sob and strode out of the dining room. Jake followed looking like the cat that swallowed the canary.

She waited in the foyer on some weird high. It was like an adrenaline rush to stand up to Layne like that, and to her mother, in front of all those people. She felt like celebrating or hitting something, she wasn't sure which.

If Olivia would have been a man, Jake would have slapped her on the shoulder or given her a high five. He was so impressed. She was badass, and he was proud.

He picked her up and spun her around. She laughed out loud.

"Darlin' you were awesome in there. Who was that badass chick who put that piece of shit in his place?" Jake laughed.

"I don't know!" She said with a look of shock on her face. "I can't believe I stood up to them like that! I don't even know where it came from. I never swear like that. I was angry and I just, I just...oh my God, I did it!"

"You did it! You were amazing! " He said and kissed her passionately.

People were passing by them staring and some even made noises suggesting they should stop making out in the foyer but they didn't care. She didn't miss this stuffy atmosphere of the country club. As far as she was concerned, she'd never belonged here in the first place.

"Let's go, Darlin'. I have a surprise for you."

CHAPTER TWENTY-EIGHT

When they arrived at the hotel, Olivia was still buzzing. She told Jake all about Layne and also explained a lot about her relationship with Jackson. Both Layne and Jackson had been emotional and physical terrorists and thrived on making Olivia jump and fetch. For whatever reason, she had. It was yet another point of shame.

She also explained the main reason for Layne's current disposition...money. For all his faults, Jackson left a will providing very well for his wife and her son. It had surprised her when she first found out and it still surprised her. She never could understand how he could treat her so poorly and yet left everything to her. Because of him, Olivia's financial situation was enviable. She had her own money and plenty of it, but the irony was she had no need of it.

She could only reason Jackson knew that if he left it all to Olivia, Layne would fight her for it. Perhaps it brought him some sort of sick satisfaction to know his brother would pick up where he left off. The joke was on him though, because the will had been written too well. He was a lawyer and prided himself on doing his job perfectly-it was iron clad. Layne didn't have a leg to stand on. Or maybe Jackson had a soul after all.

They settled into their suite at the hotel and decided an intimate dinner for two trumped anything they left behind at the country club.

Olivia changed into a deep burgundy silk dress. It hugged her minimal curves seductively. She looked ravishing, but then Jake had yet to see her and not think that.

"You are beautiful Darlin'." He said as they were seated at a table for two overlooking the twinkling lights of the city on both sides of the river.

"Thank you, you look pretty good yourself." She gave him her dazzling smile.

"I should apologize and tell you I've learned my lesson about your mother."

"It's not your fault. I thought she might invite some of my old friends or worse, her friends, but I had no idea she would invite Layne. She has sunk to a new low; not that I should be surprised."

Their waiter approached with a bottle of champagne.

"Did you call ahead?" she asked Jake, smiling.

"I might have." He said, reaching for her hand across the table. "Olivia, I need to tell you something."

"Oh God, what? Jake I can't handle any more bad news. I can't. I've met my quota, seriously. Is it bad?"

"Darlin', you need to let me speak." He said quietly, smiling.

"Sorry," she sighed. "Go ahead."

"You might find this hard to believe but I've never felt like I had a purpose, or even a direction. That is, until I met you and then everything changed. Suddenly, I know my purpose, I've found my direction and it guides me to you, always." He paused, trying to collect his thoughts. "I love you. I love you Olivia Karen Curtis like I've never known was possible. I don't ever want to lose this feeling. I don't ever want to lose you, so..." he knelt down in front of her, still holding her hand.

Olivia's brain went into overdrive. Could this be happening? Something broke inside her but not in a way she'd ever felt before. She couldn't process all the thoughts and feelings she was having. Her eyes searched his face and she couldn't help the tears sliding down her face.

"I would be so honored if you would be my wife. I want to spend forever with you. Will you marry me, Darlin'?" He pulled a small Tiffany box from his jacket pocket and opened it. Through her tears Olivia saw the most perfect ring she had ever laid eyes on. It had been made just for her; Jake had been made just for her.

Olivia couldn't catch her breath. In her head she was saying yes, but nothing audible escaped her lips, she simply nodded as the tears fell. She looked into his eyes. There was so much love there, so much patience.

He held her hand gently and waited. "Darlin', is that a yes?"

An alarm sounded in her head. "Say something Olivia. The man of your dreams just asked you to marry him. SAY SOMETHING!!" Her brain was on fire. "Yes" she said and continued to nod like a bobblehead doll.

Jake smiled broadly and placed the ring on her shaky finger. He reached for a napkin and dabbed at her tears.

"I love you so much Jacob Weidner."

"Oh Lord, Darlin' I was hoping you'd say that." He pulled her to her feet and they kissed. The entire restaurant exploded with clapping and cheers.

Olivia's feet weren't touching the floor, or maybe, just maybe they were.

They sat back down at the table but Jake didn't let go of her left hand. This was just what he had been hoping for, the ring on Olivia's finger, that look in her eyes. Somehow, Olivia looked different to him, happier and unencumbered by trauma, anger or pain.

As they walked hand in hand through the myriad of well-wishers, Olivia was still walking on air. She'd never felt like this with Jackson or with anyone before Jake; so everything seemed new, and shiny.

There still remained a glimmer of sadness as she only wished Dante' could be here to share in her happiness. It was what he'd always wanted. She knew that wish would never go away but the pain of missing her son was changing, too. It was ever present, but less intense. Jake had done that for her.

"Jake?" she murmured softly in his ear.

They were wrapped around each other like two branches from the same exotic tree. They had spent the night making love until the early hours of the morning. Olivia was still blissfully and incandescently happy and so was Jake.

"Are you still awake?"

"Mmmhmm" he replied sleepily, but content.

"Jaaaake?" she teased and nipped at his ear.

"Yes Darlin'," he said with a bit more conviction.

"I can't sleep," she said, as if that explained everything.

"Ok, ok, I'm awake." He said through a yawn.

"How long have you known?"

"I don't know what we're talking about?"

"How long have you known you wanted to marry me?"

"Oh, well," he paused. "I bought the ring in New York."

"You bought an engagement ring for me when I was barely speaking to you? I don't know what to say."

"I tried to tell you how miserable I was, being away from you. I've been trying to wait for the right time, and I know we haven't known each other long, but I couldn't wait any longer. I saw that ring and I knew it was meant for you."

"Mmm, that's good."

"What about you, Darlin'? Were you surprised? Are you happy?"

"I am *so* happy Jake, I've never been this happy. I wish Dante' could see me this happy."

"He does see you." Jake replied, kissing her fingers one at a time.

A tear slid over the bridge of her nose and landed on Jake's strong chest. "I really am happy," she smiled through the tears.

"I understand. I wish I could have known him. Speaking of family, shouldn't we announce the good news to *your* family while we're still in the city?"

"What about Christmas shopping? We have a lot to do, besides, I don't think I can face my mother today, not after what happened at the club."

"It won't take long and then after a short visit, we'll go get the shopping done. Besides, I think Miles and your dad need to hear from you in person about our engagement."

Olivia could picture her mother's reaction and a cold chill ran up her spine. "Either one of two things is going to happen. One, she'll throw a hissy fit and tell me all the reasons why I shouldn't marry you; or two, she'll turn this whole thing into 'her' party and it will be the social event of the season. Either way, the spotlight will shine brightly on my mother, just like it always does." As an afterthought, she said, "we don't have to tell them. She will hire a wedding coordinator, probably the same one she hired for my last wedding and she'll want us to get married here in Oregon. Promise me something." Olivia said seriously.

"Anything" he replied sweetly.

"You must promise me we'll get married in Montana, no matter how many different ways my mother tries to take this away from us."

"That's easy enough. I promise you, Montana it is."

"Thank you, Jake."

"You know, it doesn't really matter to me where we get married. So, I guess we're agreed then?"

"About the wedding?"

"Yes, and that we need to pay your family a visit?"

Olivia sighed, "Yes, we're agreed. This is going to take some serious coffee and perhaps some liquor."

"Ok, I'll get the coffee and you get in the shower." Jake said and patted her butt.

"I don't get liquor?" she asked jokingly.

"Uh, it's probably not a good idea to tell them when you're three sheets to the wind, Love."

"You're probably right. Would you call Miles and have him arrange to meet us at my parent's house? I'm going to go throw up and try to build up my courage in the shower!" she announced.

There was a new ease to Olivia he hadn't seen there before. His fiancé was happy. It seemed like the kind of happy that even her mother couldn't destroy.

"Sure Darlin'" he reached for his phone as he watched her cross the room.

The neighborhood where Olivia had grown up and the home where her parents still lived was just as Jake had pictured. It was upper class lakeside suburbia at its finest. People there put all their wealth on display; they were trying to "keep up with the Jones's. The 'Jones's' in this neighborhood were the Curtis family.

These homes were large and elaborate with expensive cars parked out front along expansive driveways. Jake thought it almost comical. He didn't know or care how much money these people had but *they* obviously cared a great deal. He decided not to share these observations with Olivia. He already knew her feelings about pretentious behavior. It was one of the things he loved about her. She seemed to prefer the horses, the gravel roads and the sweet simplicity of Troy; though he also could admit his own home was somewhat 'over-the-top'.

She was quiet as the driver pulled up to her former home.

Jake held her hand, as he always would. "It's very beautiful." he said hoping she was calmer than she seemed.

"It's cold." Olivia replied, not referring to the weather.

They walked up to the front door and Olivia was visibly tense. The vibe here was most definitely formal and completely different from the day she met Jake's parents. He was beginning to rethink insisting she come here, but he decided he could be her buffer.

He had wondered for some time now why her family had not moved out of this house after she was attacked. He couldn't understand it. It seemed strange to want to live in a house full of nightmares and bad memories. Why would anyone want to stay?

If it had happened at the ranch, Jake would have burned it to the ground for her. To him, it was the only logical way of thinking about such things.

Kay, the Curtis's newest housekeeper, opened the door. She was warm and kind. Olivia didn't guess she would last much longer in this job.

"Olivia! What a wonderful surprise," she gushed.

"Hello Kay, it's good to see you. Are my parents around?"

"Yes, your mother is in her practice room and your father is in his office. Come in and I'll let them know you're here."

"Kay, this is Jake Weidner." Olivia said before she could slip away.

"Hello Mr. Weidner. Welcome." Kay replied formally.

"It's a pleasure to meet you." Jake nodded.

Olivia led Jake into the living room. "This is all so surreal." She whispered.

Jake smiled and kissed her hand. "I'm here Darlin'."

Antoinette entered the room with a flourish. Her face was taut with unleashed anger. Always reserved, Jake could see she was livid with her daughter.

"Hello Olivia, Jake. Come in, your brother isn't here yet. He called to say he was coming over. I can only assume you would like us all to be here so you can apologize for your behavior last night?"

"No, I'm not here to apologize." Olivia replied quietly keeping her eyes on her mother.

Jake was overcome with the urge to strangle Antoinette with his bare hands. She seemed to take pleasure in ruining everything for Olivia.

"Why am I not surprised? Go fetch your father, will you? I would like a moment alone with your *boyfriend.*" Antoinette said stiffly.

"I don't think that's a good idea, Mother." Olivia countered.

Jake interrupted, "its fine Darlin', go visit with your dad for a bit. Give your mother and me a chance to get to know each other better."

Olivia looked at Jake with a pained expression on her face; he just returned the look with a wink. Slowly, she stood up and walked out of the room.

"I gather you have something you'd like to say, Ma'am." Jake began.

"Yes, I do. You're wrong about Olivia. She isn't going to play house with you in the mountains forever. She won't like it; she'll get antsy just like she always does. I had to fight tooth and nail to get her to stay in her marriage to Jackson Montgomery, and *he* was a prominent attorney. So, do you really think she'll stay with you, a rancher; especially without my blessing and insistence? Don't misunderstand Jake, you seem like a fine man, salt of the earth and all that, but Olivia needs a stronger hand than yours. She always has."

"Is that what you're calling it, a strong hand? From what I understand he was an overbearing son of a bitch who used that strong hand to beat the hell out of her. I can't for the life of me, understand why *that* is what you would want for your daughter."

"You don't know anything about it! Jackson took care of Olivia and **that boy**, when no one else wanted them. He made sure they had everything they could ever want."

"And it came at a very high price. Were they happy? Did she love him? Or does love even factor in for you? You may think you're trying to help me; hell, you may even think you're trying to help Olivia, but let me tell you something about me. Yes, I'm from the country. Yes, I get dirt and cow shit on my clothes on a fairly regular basis. I even drive a truck, but that strong hand you speak of so fondly, all that is? Another name for abuse! I don't want to control Olivia. I don't want to *force* her to do anything. I want her to be happy, safe and know without a shadow of a doubt she has my love, forever. Love, that's that word you don't get. Maybe you should look it up!"

Antoinette gritted her teeth, "Don't say I didn't warn you when she starts looking for the exit, because she will!"

Jake stood as Jonathan and Olivia came in. "Hello Mr. Curtis." Jake said as smoothly as he could.

"Jake, Olivia tells me you two wanted to speak to us?"

"Yes sir, we do." Olivia crossed the room to him and placed her hand on his arm. She could feel his muscles flexing under her hand, so she looked up at him with trepidation.

"Well go ahead Son, let's hear it." Jonathan smiled.

"Mr. Curtis, Mrs. Curtis; I've asked Olivia to marry me and by some miracle, she's agreed."

Olivia smiled and reached up to kiss his cheek.

"That's wonderful news." Jonathan beamed at his daughter.

Jake smiled, relieved that at least one of Olivia's parents wasn't a raving lunatic.

Olivia watched as Jake took the ring out of his pocket. She had asked him to hold onto it for her. He placed it back on her finger where it belonged.

"Congratulations." Antoinette said stiffly.

"Thank you, Mother" Olivia said. She was curious why her mother looked like she'd been slapped in the face.

Just then Miles cleared his throat from the doorway. "What'd I miss?"

Jonathan turned still smiling, "Well Son, if you had been here a bit earlier, you would know that your sister is engaged to be married."

"To who, do I know the guy?" Miles teased crossing to his sister.

"Miles, you are so going to get it." Olivia replied and hugged her brother and her dad.

"Congratulations you two, that's really great news." Miles said sincerely and offered his hand to Jake.

Olivia looked at her mother who sat on the sofa as still as stone. Even though Olivia was happy, the look on her mother's face threatened to steal it away. She began to feel panic rising up inside her. Her throat was burning.

"Mother, wouldn't you like to see the ring?"

"I see it. It's lovely. Perhaps you'll make time for a manicure while you're here." Antoinette replied coldly.

Jake turned to hug Olivia but she ducked under his arm. "Excuse me; I need to, um..."

Olivia rushed out of the room and down the hall to the guest bathroom, willing herself not to cry. She'd only been in there for a second when the door opened behind her. One look at Jake and the tears flowed like a river.

"Why does she hate me?" Olivia asked sadly.

There was nothing he could say. He just held her as she cried. Olivia sniffed and grabbed a tissue. She took a deep breath. "I'm so sorry. I don't know what she said to you, but knowing her, it wasn't good."

"It doesn't matter Darlin'. This, all of this, it isn't about her remember, it's about you and me. She can't tear this apart. I won't let her, I promise you that." He affirmed, wiping her face with the hand towel.

Olivia sighed, "You're right. Do we have to invite her to the wedding?"

"It's your wedding to plan; invite whomever the hell you want." Jake said and lifted her chin up. "I love you, Olivia. You're going to make an exceptional Weidner."

Olivia laughed. "You think?"

"Definitely."

"Let's go. I don't want to be here anymore. Let's go buy the ice queen a snow globe for Christmas."

Jake looked at her, not sure he'd heard her correctly, but then seeing the look on her face, he laughed out loud. She hugged him tightly before letting him leave the bathroom. "You make everything better."

"That's funny, that's how I feel about you, too."

Nothing more was said between Olivia and her mother. They stayed just long enough to let Mr. Curtis pour some champagne and toast the happy couple. Olivia only took a small sip. All the drama had given her an upset stomach, again.

Suddenly, she couldn't wait to get back to their home in Montana. "Jake, I'm sorry, my mother *is* Satan. What did she say to you?" Olivia asked as they drove away.

"Don't apologize for her, Darlin', she's not your responsibility."

"So, what did she say?"

"She said I better take good care of you, or she will chop me into little pieces and scatter me around the rose garden at the country club."

"You're a horrible liar."

"It doesn't matter what she said."

"Jake, I want to know." Olivia replied, her stomach churning. "Did it make you wish you could back out? You can, you know."

"Back out of what, of marrying you? Are you out of your mind? I love you, Olivia. I love everything about you, from the top of your head to the tip of your toes. I love the way you apologize too much. I even love your bitch of a mother, because if it weren't for her, there would be no you. I love every part of you. You aren't getting rid of me, not ever. Unless you don't want to be with me, but sure as hell I want to be with you."

"I do want to marry you. I'm just scared I come with way too much baggage."

"Bring it on. I'm strong and I'm steady. I can handle anything if we're together."

She let out a deep breath like she'd been holding it forever.

Late on Saturday night, they sat together on the Weidner jet. They decided they didn't want to stay in Portland another night. Olivia had never been able to sleep on airplanes, but then the accommodations were never so luxurious either and after everything they had just gone through, she could have slept anywhere.

Jake was engrossed in 'cow business' on his laptop. Olivia was so exhausted he could have been watching porn for all she knew.

The jet was stuffed with packages from their shopping excursion. Jake was even more excited than usual for Christmas this year. He would be with his fiancée, the beautiful goddess sleeping heavily on his shoulder.

Out of the blue, Jake remembered Olivia mentioning all the phone calls from a number she hadn't recognized. He couldn't help but wonder who it could be. There weren't any leads on who vandalized her apartment either and Jake couldn't shake the feeling it was Patrick Hanson. Would he contact her? And why did he live in such close proximity to her? It couldn't be coincidence.

Olivia let her phone battery die so Jake had no way of seeing the number. He would have to ask her. He would have to tell her what he knew. That wouldn't be an easy discussion. He hated having to say anything now when she was so happy and things were going so well.

When they landed at the airstrip, Olivia was still sleeping. Jake woke her as gently as possible. She was yawning when she pulled herself into Jake's pickup.

"Thank you for this weekend. It was all so incredible." She said admiring her engagement ring.

"You're welcome Darlin'; hey, did you ever figure out who the missed calls were from?" Jake asked, trying to sound casual.

"What are you talking about?" she asked absently.

"Before we left, you know, you said you'd missed some calls."

"Oh I'm sure it was just a solicitor."

"I guess you're probably right. Maybe you should change your number though, as a precaution." Jake paused.

"There's no point Jake. I missed some phone calls; it's not a big deal." She sighed heavily.

"Yeah, it's probably nothing."

Olivia was gritting her teeth and feeling irritated and apprehensive. She felt like she wasn't allowed to have a moment of peace and even though none of this was Jake's fault, she could feel in her gut; the moment she had been dreading was quickly approaching.

"You obviously have something on your mind. Why don't you tell me what it is?" she demanded.

Jake looked at the road ahead. He was regretting not being completely honest with her from the beginning. "After your apartment was vandalized, I hired a private detective."

Olivia felt sick. "You've been investigating my life?

Jake, I told you everything ...everything!" she said angrily, though she knew it was a lie as it came from her mouth.

"You told me everything you *know*. I wanted to find out everything you didn't, so I could protect you."

"So what don't I know Jake?" Olivia asked, feeling like she'd been sucker-punched.

"Patrick Hanson lives in Idaho. I'm concerned he might have been in your apartment." Jake said seriously, trying to look at Olivia without her notice.

Olivia felt terror and betrayal mix up inside her like a poisonous cocktail. "Jake, please pull over, I'm sick."

He pulled the truck over to the side of the road and she jumped out. She barely got the door closed before she vomited in the fresh, white Montana snow. Jake quickly came around to comfort her but she put her hand up and waved him away.

"Jake, don't." she choked and sobbed.

"I should have told you sooner." He said, the alarm sounding in his voice.

"Can we talk when I'm..." She wretched again, "... finished puking my guts out, please?"

He said no more, just waited on the other side of the truck, frustration and fury like knives in his heart. Brad was right; he should have told her what he knew.

She was finally able to get herself under control, but she didn't get back in, not at first. She stood leaning on the pickup door looking off toward the mountains, willing herself to drift off into the sky like smoke.

Finally, she got back in and slammed the door. Jake got in, shifting the running truck back onto the road. Neither of them said anything. Jake knew from the look on her face just to keep his mouth shut.

He pulled into the garage at the ranch and turned off the engine. He started to get out but Olivia quickly grabbed his arm. "I don't want to talk about this now, but tomorrow maybe? Would that be ok?" she asked quietly.

Jake nodded and pulled away. He began unloading the truck. He was ominously quiet. She couldn't imagine what *he* had to be angry about.

After a quick chat with Carmella, Jake and Olivia went up to bed. Olivia wanted to scream.

The silent treatment from Jake was the last thing she needed now. Jackson had played those kinds of games with her. Though, as she looked closer at his face, he didn't seem angry as much as introspective and quiet.

"I've changed my mind." She said quietly turning on the bedside lamp.

Jake looked up in shock. All he could think was she had changed her mind about marrying him.

"We need to talk about this now. I can't stand you not speaking to me."

Jake sighed in relief and then almost chuckled. "This isn't the silent treatment Darlin', I'm just frustrated with myself for not handling this whole thing better."

Olivia wrapped her arms around his waist and laid her head on his chest. "I didn't handle it well either. I'm sorry."

"No, *I'm* sorry."

"You know what? I think all the psychopaths from my life can wait until tomorrow. Let's just go to bed, make love, and not talk about them anymore tonight."

"Are you sure?"

"Positive."

He began to undress her slowly, methodically. She couldn't help the moan escaping her lips. Why not lose herself in Jake's caresses for one more night? What if it were their last? Hadn't she already seen how brutally short life could be?

Sunday the house was especially quiet. Carmella had gone to church. Jake woke early as usual to feed and water the cattle with his crew while Olivia was left to sleep in. When he came back, she was still in pajamas and slippers. Jake had to laugh at how cozy she looked sitting at the island in the kitchen a cup of coffee in her hand.

Jake poured himself a cup too, kissed his fiancée on the mouth warmly and then sat next to her.

"Where do I start, Darlin'?" he asked, refusing to let himself off the hook any longer.

She knew she could no longer put this off. "I guess tell me what the detective told you."

He held his coffee mug with both hands. "Patrick Hanson lives in Sandpoint, Idaho, it's not very far away. I can't prove he's been here or even that he had anything to do with vandalizing your apartment, but something tells me he did.

Call it a gut feeling, or intuition, but it just smells fishy to me."

Olivia felt a fresh wave of terror sweep over her. She knew she needed to come clean too. "It *was* him."

"What? How do you know? Are you sure? Did you see him?"

Olivia took a deep breath. "No, I haven't seen him, but what was written on the wall, it was...it was exactly what he said to me when, um, before."

"Why didn't you tell the police?"

Olivia's hands began to shake. She tried in vain to stop herself and draw warmth and comfort from her coffee but even that wasn't helping today. The nausea plaguing her lately reappeared. She reached over and grabbed her cell phone.

"I didn't tell you or the police because I didn't want to be right."

She scrolled through her missed calls and redialed the unknown number and put the phone on speaker. She couldn't look at Jake. The phone rang once, twice, and then,

"Hello Olivia" a man's voice answered.

Olivia pressed 'End' as her bravery gave out. She looked seriously at Jake, "That was him". She stood up abruptly. "I'm going to change and go for a ride."

"Olivia, I won't let him hurt you."

"Can we talk about this later, please?"

"No" he said and grabbed her arm, more forcefully than he intended.

She looked at him warily but saw the look of worry on his face.

He didn't fear the man who answered the phone. No, what he was worried about was something much more fearful. Jake feared she would run almost as her mother had predicted.

Her tears escaped once again. She leaned into him and as if she had read his mind she said, "I'm not going to run, Jake. I've made up my mind."

"If you did, I'd find you." Jake said and hugged her more.

"I know. I am scared, though." She looked up into his warm brown eyes. So much love lived there; how could she ever run from that? "I'm really, really scared."

"I won't ever let him hurt you again. If I have to hire a bodyguard; if I have to *be* your bodyguard, nobody is going to hurt you like that ever again. Do you hear me? Do you believe me?" Jake said seriously.

"Yes, I believe you." Again he reminded her of the mountains he loved so much; so big and strong and immoveable.

Her phone rang on the counter next to them. They both jumped and stared at the number, the same mystery number.

Jake picked it up. "Hello" Jake said gruffly. The phone went dead.

"What do I do Jake? I knew this would happen. I knew it."

"What do you mean, you knew?"

"Nothing, I just, nothing..."

"I'll tell you what we're going to do; we're going together to the police station. You're going to give them the phone number, all the details you can, and then we're going to change your cell number. Also, tomorrow when you have to go to work, I'll drive you, just to be safe."

Olivia stared blankly and nodded. Finally she said, "Ok" but there was no conviction in it, no comfort.

"Is it better I told you?" He asked.

"Huh?" Olivia's mind had been wandering, racing. She kept picturing Patrick Hanson in Troy. She hadn't wanted to face it before but now there was no avoiding it. He was back, or near. Either way, it sent chills up her spine. She wasn't safe, not anywhere and neither was Jake. How soon before she lost everything, again?

The rest of the day, she followed Jake around like a puppy. She knew it seemed silly but near him was the only place she could relax and even then, it was only a little. She asked him to come out to the stables with her but the tension she was feeling made Guiness skittish. Jake suggested instead they go inside and watch movies. She knew she wouldn't be able to keep her mind occupied, but she agreed.

Her thoughts began to drift into darkness, the place in which her visions lived. She stared at the TV screen but all she saw was Patrick in front of her.

"Olivia, you are *always mine*. How come I have to keep reminding you of that? Are you stupid? You are *always mine*. You weren't supposed to be with Jackson for long and you don't belong with the cowboy either. Do you have any idea how hard it was to get Jackson out of your life? That was no easy trick, I can tell you that. Come with me now, or the cowboy will die, too." Patrick's distinct voice echoed in her head; or maybe from the television.

"No, I won't!" she said aloud unaware of Jake sitting beside her.

"Darlin', are you ok?" He inched closer and took her hand.

"I think Patrick Hanson killed my son."

CHAPTER TWENTY-NINE

Patrick wasn't the sex offender he had been accused of being. He had no interest in other women. He was a nice guy, a decent guy; he was simply a guy who knew what he wanted. Or rather, *who* he wanted. Olivia Curtis was his, always. He knew she was what he deserved. He deserved to finally have her back in his life, the way she should have been all along. She was meant to be with him and she was the *only* woman for him. That didn't make him a sex offender. "That makes me a romantic." He thought.

Though he had tried to find her replacement a few times but the hair was always wrong, it wasn't dark enough or thick enough. The eyes were always wrong, they weren't green or they weren't shaped the same. Often it was the voice that was wrong, but then Patrick was grateful for duct tape. He hated the sound of their voices, begging him. It was pathetic. There was only one voice he wished to hear begging him.

Patrick was getting aroused just thinking of Olivia and her thick, dark red hair, her piercing green eyes and her soft voice.

"Olivia, you will be with me." He spoke softly to his favorite picture of her. He had collected many photographs but the one he loved best was at their son's funeral. He loved the look of the tears falling down her face, the anguish and the pain. He loved seeing her filled with darkness.

Patrick spoke to the picture as if Olivia were there in the room. "I know you miss our son, but if you're a good girl, we'll make another one. Don't worry, our next child will call me Daddy and we will be a perfect family. Oh Olivia, the things I'm going to do to you."

He masturbated to the photograph as he'd done so many times before. Patrick couldn't contain his excitement. It would be soon, and he couldn't wait.

"That dumb hick from Montana isn't good enough for you. I'm going to prove it to you, when I put a bullet in his skull."

Olivia must be shown the error of her ways. She would have to be shown her mistakes. She would be punished for her mistakes. She would see.

****

"Listen, Brad, I think Olivia is in real danger. I know it's him, Patrick Hanson. He wrote on her wall, he called her, and she thinks he's responsible for killing her family. And I think she's right."

"Jake, do you have any proof to back that up? These are serious accusations based on no solid evidence. I can look into it, but I can't promise anything."

"If that man is capable of raping someone isn't it possible he's capable of murder?"

"Jake, I'm not saying you're wrong; I'm saying we need proof. I'll see what I can find out, but if I can't prove harassment at the very least, then legally, we don't have a leg to stand on. There weren't any leads with the vandalism case; no fingerprints, no witnesses and nobody has even seen any strangers in town."

"That doesn't mean he wasn't here!" Jake exclaimed.

"I'll run a trace on that number and see if anything comes of it. In the meantime, just cool your jets!"

"Brad, don't tell me to cool my jets. I'm telling you this guy is trouble!"

"Off the record, you've got a concealed weapons permit, I'd say make sure you're packing."

"I am, but I don't know how Olivia would feel about that if she knew."

"Tell her, trust me."

On Monday morning Jake had dropped off Olivia at the studio, both looking around carefully, but not saying anything. He waited until she was inside and then drove off to the police station. Olivia planned on going with him, but had backed out. Jake decided not to force the issue.

Later, he drove back toward the studio. The streets were quiet and as he pulled into the parking lot he could see Olivia through the large windows on the front of the building. She was smiling and talking with his Aunt Denise. A tiny little girl in a pink tutu with ribbons in her hair had crawled up on the piano bench next to Olivia. Jake's heart felt full.

He was sure Olivia had been an amazing mother to Dante' and he hoped they would someday get the chance to be parents together to a child of their own. It was one of the many subjects they hadn't discussed. Now that he had settled happily into the thought of being a husband, he knew he definitely wanted to be a father.

When he walked in the studio, the little girl was giving Olivia a great big hug with her tiny arms. Olivia looked up at Jake and smiled.

"It seems you have an admirer, Darlin'."

"So it would seem." She smiled.

The little girl looked up at Jake and beamed. "Miss Olivia plays pretty music for me."

"She does? Well, that's because pretty little girls deserve pretty music."

The little girl blushed. Apparently, Olivia wasn't the only one affected by Jake's charm.

"Hello Jacob, how's my favorite nephew? Sydney, your mommy is here." Denise said from the doorway with a smile.

The little girl squealed happily and ran to her mom.

"I'm doing well. I apologize for the interruption." Jake replied to his aunt.

"You aren't interrupting, we're about to go have some lunch. Would you care to join us?" Denise asked.

"I would love to, in fact, it's my treat." Jake answered.

Olivia was quiet, and it didn't go without Jake's notice. He drove them to the diner in his truck and Olivia's eyes widened. "Don't worry Darlin', no one's going to bite you."

Denise couldn't help but comment. "Are you worried about Dan? If he's rude, just kick him in the shin." She laughed.

"It's silly I guess, but I haven't been here since I was fired." Olivia replied quietly from the back seat.

Jake held Olivia's hand and sat beside her in a booth across from Denise. Dan waved and then approached them.

"Hi Jake, Denise, Olivia, how is everyone today?" He smiled sociably.

Olivia didn't know what to say so she just smiled but gave no reply.

"We're good Dan, how about you?" Jake asked.

"To tell you the truth Jake, I'm not good, not good at all. I'm filled with shame and regret. I've been to church and confessed my sins but I still feel terrible...because I never should have fired the best waitress I ever had." Dan said, looking falsely pitiful and batting his eyes at Olivia.

They started laughing and Jake said, "Serves you right."

"Olivia, can you forgive me and just put me out of my misery?" Dan asked.

"Of course I can forgive you, Dan; I think it all worked out for the best."

"Oh I see, well, I deserve that I guess." Dan said and then took their orders personally.

Olivia reached for her drink and the engagement ring caught the light and Denise's attention. "When did that happen?" Denise gushed pointing at the sparkler.

"I didn't have it on this morning." Olivia replied, blushing and looking at Jake for help.

"Oh yeah, Aunt Denise, Olivia and I are engaged." Jake said happily.

"So I gather. Congratulations to you both; this is wonderful news!" Denise replied reaching across the table for both their hands. "Did you tell your dad yet?"

"Not exactly; we told Olivia's parents and Mom knew it was a possibility but we haven't officially told them. We've been gone all weekend. I thought we'd tell them tonight." Jake grinned.

Olivia looked at Jake in shock. She hadn't heard this plan and was feeling a bit overwhelmed.

"Olivia, is everything alright? You're engaged and you aren't shouting it from the rooftop. What's going on?" Denise asked pointedly.

"I'm, I'm very happy. We're *both* very happy." She said plainly.

"And yet I don't believe you." Denise replied frankly.

Olivia knew she should be happy. She should be just as happy now as the moment Jake proposed. This time in her life should be amazing and blissful but somehow, her past kept grabbing at her, holding her down with powerful, evil hands.

"It was a long weekend and dealing with my family is um, stressful." Olivia explained. Although she spoke the truth, she knew it wasn't her family getting her down.

After lunch, Jake drove the two ladies back to the studio. Denise thanked her nephew for the meal and went on inside.

"I'll be back to pick you up after work, ok Darlin'?" Jake said between kisses.

"Jake I have an appointment this evening after work, remember? Maybe I should just cancel."

"No, don't cancel, I'll drive you to your appointment and wait for you at the diner until it's over."

"That's ridiculous; I'll just walk to Ben's office and I'll meet you at the diner."

"I don't want you walking by yourself in the dark. I won't let this affect your life."

"It already has, but it's a short walk to the diner and then we can have dinner together. Patrick Hanson has ruined so much. I won't let him ruin everything for us." She decided firmly.

"Ok" he replied, throwing his hands up in mock defeat. But don't worry, I spoke to Brad today and he's going to find out for sure who's been calling you. Here's your phone. I'll see you later. Now, can I have just one more kiss from my sexy fiancée?" Jake purred.

"Of course you can." Olivia relished in the feelings his kisses gave her. She melted into him and secretly wished she could leave with him now and lock out the world for a while.

Later, as she walked to her therapy appointment she reminded herself not to freak out. Maybe there was no one out to get her, but the niggling thought of the voice on the phone and the words on her apartment wall was anything but comforting. Maybe Patrick Hanson wasn't in town now but he had been. There was no denying it. "I HATE HIM" echoed with every step.

Memories of her vision of Jake flooded in to view. She hoped to see details that might help her figure out when and where it would happen. She knew she would see Patrick Hanson again soon. She knew the confrontation with him was coming and like a moth to a flame, it felt unavoidable. She wanted to change this next part, but she couldn't see how. Her mind raced trying to think of ways to keep Jake out of it and safe.

She had seen blood all over Jake. She had seen glass breaking and could hear her voice screaming. She still couldn't see if he would live. Trying to recall more from the vision than had been revealed was like looking into an empty room. There was nothing left but memories. She saw his eyes close and nothing more. Jake would fall and she couldn't stop it. Jake would fall. Her breath caught and then she sighed deeply as she opened the door to Dr. Thompson's office.

THERAPY SESSION V

"How are things Olivia?" Ben asked.

"Crazy, and good, and terrifying" She said with honesty.

"Ok, let's start with the terrifying."

"The man who attacked me so many years ago now lives in Sandpoint and he's been calling my cell phone. Then, recently I had a dream that he was responsible for killing my, Dante'."

Olivia made sure to call it a dream though if she were truly honest; it had been a vision just like all the rest, except this one had happened in the past so the whole thing confused her.

"...and Jackson?" Ben added, wondering why she would omit her husband.

"Yeah, that's what I meant."

"And yet you didn't say his name."

"They were in the car together. I guess I didn't think I had to be so specific." Olivia replied, becoming irritated.

"Or maybe your dream was just that and it wasn't about Jackson at all."

"I don't know."

"Ok, that's ok; I'm trying to get you to be clear."

"Does it really matter? What if he did? What if Patrick killed my son?"

"...and your husband; again you omit Jackson as if you have forgotten he was in the car, too."

"It's not that."

"Then what is it?"

"I omit Jackson because I don't care that he's dead." She said ominously.

"Aha, that's progress." Ben smiled.

"How is that progress? It makes me sound awful."

"It's progress because no matter how many times or ways you wished Jackson dead, you didn't make it happen. You are beginning to separate your feelings about Jackson from your feelings about Dante'. I'd say it's good to admit it, get it off your chest. You had a really bad marriage and you aren't all that upset Jackson is gone from your life. That's ok. You're not guilty. You still didn't kill him. I want to know why you think Patrick Hanson did though."

"He told me so. The voice on the phone, it was him, also, the graffiti on my wall at the apartment, it was him, I'm sure of it. The words 'always mine' were spray-painted in red.

'Always mine' is just what Patrick said to me the day he raped me and he mouthed those same words to me in court. I tried to tell my lawyer but he told me I was mistaken. Patrick is back."

"Did he say those words? On the phone or ever, did he confess to killing your son?"

"No, but I feel it." Olivia replied, nervously.

"Have you contacted the police? Have you told them what you told me?"

"I told Jake and he talked to the sheriff's deputy but I just couldn't go. I couldn't. I'm stuck and I'm scared. Jake even talked about getting me a bodyguard. I seriously hope he doesn't."

"I wouldn't put it past him."

"But, I just want to be 'normal'. I want to be average. I don't want to be the girl who was raped or the grieving widow or the heartbroken mother anymore...I just want to be **NORMAL**!"

"I know you do, but you can't go back, you can only move forward. How you do that is completely up to you. When you're scared, or stuck, or fixated on the pain of your past, then you give your power away. You have to take your power back and live your life in a way that makes *you* happy. There is no normal, but there can be better. You can have it, but no one can give it to you, you have to take it."

"Jake and I are engaged." Olivia said out of the blue.

"When did that happen?" Ben asked feeling suddenly a little sick.

"Just this weekend, and now I want to move on more than ever."

"I'm sure you do and you can but you also have to be patient with the process of healing."

"How can I heal when I am being tortured by the thought of Patrick Hanson breaking into my apartment, calling my cell phone and haunting my life? He won't stop!"

"You let the authorities handle him and we figure out how to help you move on. In no way would I ever suggest that you deal with Patrick Hanson on your own. He's obviously a dangerous person."

"Right, because what could I do to someone like him? I'm a woman. I couldn't fight him before, why would I be able to fight him now?"

"If it came down to it, you'd fight back. You aren't a child who's been taken by surprise. Don't underestimate yourself."

She sat quietly. It was as though he could see the wheels turning and then a light was turned on. "You said I should take my power back."

"Metaphorically speaking, yes"

"You're right."

"I strongly urge you not to do anything rash."

"I wouldn't, Doc. This isn't the time for rash decisions." She lied, putting up that practiced façade. "Doc, would you mind if we stopped here for today. With everything that's been going on, I'm really tired. I think I need an early night."

"Olivia, this is the second session you've cut short and we've only barely begun."

"I know, I apologize but you did say I have the control."

"Yes, but not to the detriment of your therapy.

"Are you saying I can't go home yet?"

"No, of course I'm not saying that. Do you have a ride home?"

"I'm meeting Jake at the diner." She said, sounding distracted.

"Ok, I'll see you next time, but, Olivia?" Ben looked at her feeling unsure about what was really going on.

"Yeah? She looked over her shoulder.

"Remember, nothing rash!"

CHAPTER THIRTY

The wind blew bits of ice harshly against her cheeks as she tromped toward the diner. There was a soft glow from behind the mountain. It was a 'light of hope'. She hoped. Olivia kept flashing back to earlier that afternoon; she and Jake kissing like a couple of high school kids. When she was with him, she could escape from everything bad and she knew the only way to have that feeling all the time was to shed her past like a poisonous skin. That meant confronting Patrick Hanson and getting him out of her life for good.

Could it be that simple? Did she only need to tell him "stop" in order to meet her fate head on? That was it. She would call Patrick Hanson and pray that somehow there would be an end to this curse and that it didn't result in more loss.

Olivia's fingers shook from fear and cold as she scrolled through her recent calls. She took a frozen breath and hit, 'Send'.

Patrick knew better than to stay in Troy for very long. Instead of going right back to Sandpoint immediately though, he needed to stay just long enough to get some missing information. Small towns were all the same and it was better if he kept a low profile. He had done what he came to do but he had miscalculated Olivia's reaction to his message. It was only meant to keep her fresh and tense. He should have known the cowboy would move her in with him.

It was next to impossible to get close to her out on that ranch, there were always people coming and going and out in the country people noticed unfamiliar cars. It wasn't like when she was in the city and he could watch her for hours, uninterrupted. He wished she would go back to the city.

He decided that when they were together again they would move to a city. They would live somewhere people didn't ask too many questions. He liked anonymity and being anonymous meant there would be fewer people to misunderstand him. Olivia understood him. She longed for him as he longed for her.

Patrick hated being misunderstood. Even his parents had turned their backs on him. They were so worried about what other people might think. They cared more about public perception than their own son. "You and I have that in common don't we, Olivia?" he asked her photograph.

Patrick sat in the dark, dreaming of the time when Olivia would be his again. Having her would mean having her money, too; his rich, dead cousin's money, which made it all the more sweet. He relished the thought of getting back everything she had taken from him. He would punish her for the years he spent in prison. He would punish her for the way his parent's abandoned him. He would make her grovel, beg and plead. He would bring her to the edge of darkness and then, when the time was right, when he'd finally had his fill, he would release her from her pain.

"Perhaps I will end your suffering though I will have my fill of you first. I like the idea of keeping you around until you've lost your shine, Olivia. Right now you are so shiny."

"You are still sexy, but I will fuck the shine off you. Yes, I will..." Patrick couldn't finish the thought, he was too excited. His mind was racing along with his pulse. Soon he would go to Troy again and claim his prize. Soon she would be alone. The thoughts aroused him even more.

****

This had to be the one thing she would do right and pry herself from the grasp of this wretched curse.

"Hello Olivia." Patrick answered smoothly as if he'd been expecting her call.

It threw her off. "Hello" she replied, as forcefully as she could.

"I was just thinking about you." He growled huskily.

"Don't speak to me like that, in fact, don't ever speak to me again. I called to tell you to **leave me alone**! I'm done."

"I don't know what you mean, Olivia. I am being courteous to you. I have not seen you in so many years and now I feel I'm being accused of something. Perhaps we should iron out our differences in person. Wouldn't that be nice?"

"No! Absolutely not!"

"I want you to know that I've changed. I'm not the same as I was in our youth. Please give me a chance to prove it to you?"

Jake had been hovering near the door of the diner holding a forgotten cup of coffee when he saw her. He set the cup on a nearby table and rushed out the door to meet her.

"Darlin', are you coming in? I'm starving and Tag's shutting off the grill soon."

Olivia's heart raced. Jake had such a beautiful strong voice. There was no way Patrick hadn't heard him.

"I have nothing more to say to you and I don't care what more you have to say to me." Olivia replied into the phone quietly.

"Intimate dinner for two at Maggie's tonight?" Patrick asked.

Jake took Olivia's hand and they crossed the street back to the diner. As Jake opened the door, Olivia's stomach rumbled but she wasn't hungry. The smell of comfort food filled her senses but it was not enough to calm her. She wondered if Jake would notice her hands trembling. They sat in their usual booth and Olivia faced the door, unable to stop her eyes or thoughts from drifting to the inevitable. She hadn't stopped her vision.

"May I ask how it went?" Jake asked taking her hand.

"What?" alarm coloring Olivia's reply.

"Your appointment?"

"Oh, it was fine. We should order, I could use some coffee and I thought you were 'starving'."

"I am starving. Can't you tell?" Jake chuckled, and caught Tag's eye.

Tag came up to their booth. "Hey guys. What do you think of my waitressing skills?"

"Where's Ella tonight?" Olivia asked politely.

"It's hard to say. I don't know why Dan keeps her around. Seriously Olivia, he fired the wrong waitress." Tag smiled broadly.

"Of course he did. He's an idiot. Unless he's listening in the back and then I didn't mean it." Jake replied loudly.

"Nope, it's just me tonight." Tag said. "So, what'll ya have?"

"Darlin'?" Jake asked, looking over at her.

"Oh, uh, um just whatever you're having." She said slowly.

"Then we'll have two steak dinners but she likes hers medium well and I'll take mine rare and bleeding on my plate."

Olivia's breath caught in her throat. "Jake, that's not funny."

"It's just an expression." He said kindly.

"How about drinks?" Tag asked.

"I'll just have coffee." Olivia ordered absently.

"And Jake, how 'bout you?"

"Just water for me, thanks buddy."

Tag headed back to start their steaks and Jake reached across the table and squeezed her hand. "Who were you talking to earlier?"

"Sam called. Girl talk." Olivia said no more. She was trying to remind herself that less is more when telling lies.

Patrick's mind was filled with desire. He could barely contain his excitement as he drove toward Troy. Today was the day. He could picture tears falling down her face just as before. He'd spent so much time imagining scenarios between them and he was about to make his dreams come true. Every word, every nuance would be as he'd pictured so many times in his head. This short drive from Libby to Troy would be the last time the scenes would only be imagined and he allowed himself one last daydream. He could vividly see Olivia's quivering frame in the seat beside him. She would cry. He would make sure he heard that sweet sound. "Ah the sentimentality, it's so beautiful." He knew he would hold his anger until they were alone. "You cry because you know I'm right. You need me. This time I won't hit your face, it's hard to fuck something so ugly and swollen. I do regret that," he would tell her.

She will fight and whine like a child. "You can't have me! You won't have me! I will see you dead before you ever touch me again!"

"I do have you. You are *always mine*, my love. I want your body, your money, your blood, your fear, your soul, you are **mine**..."

He stopped the car and the bright image that had been burning in his head was now right in front of him. There she was. The light from Maggie's diner shone brightly onto the snowy street. "I was right" he clapped and laughed aloud.

Jake had pulled Olivia out of her own worried mind, if only briefly. Over the now empty dinner plates she looked at him and longed for a different sort of crystal ball, not the dark visions of loss and pain but a glimpse at possibility.

If only God could tell her it would all be ok. How dare she hope, even now, and yet, she did. Jake's smile reached his eyes as he told a story about the new orphan calf at the ranch and Dent's unsuccessful attempts at bottle feeding. The bell on the diner door chimed suddenly.

Olivia looked up to see the face of her nightmare only this time she wouldn't wake up. He had that same cold death in his eyes.

It was the one thing about Patrick she wished she had known all along. The unleashed fear and anger rumbled inside her like a volcano. Ben was right. She *was* different now. This time, she *would* fight back.

"Hello lover" Patrick said as he slid into the booth beside her.

Jake met his eyes with fierce conviction and the anger shone through like fire. He squeezed Olivia's hand again more forcefully this time to reassure her. He wanted to break Patrick's nose but he caught the quick flash of the gun shoved into Olivia's ribs.

The fear threatened to overtake Olivia, but she pushed it down siding with anger instead. She forced herself to feel only the fire of rage.

"Don't ever call me that, you sick fuck." She spoke angrily through her teeth.

"Olivia, dear Olivia, so naive, I've come to you because you called me. We've been apart far too long. You know we're meant to be together."

"You don't belong here!" Jake growled.

"No, **YOU** don't belong here! The only extra person at this little reunion is you cowboy, now shut the fuck up!" Patrick returned his attention to Olivia who felt sweat roll down and stop where the gun pushed into her ribs.

"Your marriage to my cousin didn't work out so well, but our son was special now, wasn't he?"

"Your cousin?" Olivia's mouth gaped in realization.

"Oh, oh you didn't know, did you?" He replied happily.

"Oh my God" she shuddered. She had married her rapists' cousin. Nausea threatened to overwhelm her but she fought it back. "*You* didn't have a son!" She said forcefully.

Patrick placed his other hand heavily on her shoulder and whispered, "Of course **we** did. You and Jack kept him from me, that wasn't nice. It is a shame what happened, and you looked so upset at the funeral. Convincing Jack to marry you wasn't so easy. He didn't like having my leftovers at first, but I explained how important it was to keep you close. He came around to my plan soon enough."

Olivia stared into Jake's eyes. She silently pleaded with him not to react. He seethed. Unleashed fury rose off his skin in pulsing waves.

"You..." she began, turning to Patrick.

"I was there at the funeral, of course. Our son died so tragically and Jack needed to give me back what was rightfully mine.

Jack wasn't exactly a big loss, but then you didn't think so either did you sweet thing? You can thank me later."

"What do mean?" she asked, feeling lightheaded.

"It doesn't matter, all that matters is that we're together now. You are with me and we don't have to worry about anyone getting in the way; except this fucking cowboy. He is just asking for trouble, isn't he?"

"Jake hasn't done anything to you. Let him go and I'll do as you say."

"The hell you will" Jake exploded! He was raging, darting his eyes between them and watching the gun, looking for the smallest opening.

"Please Jake, I'm begging you, don't." Olivia pleaded.

Patrick's face burned red with anger. "You don't beg him! You beg **ME**! You will be punished for this disloyalty Olivia."

The way he spoke, as though he were teaching a kindergarten class sent chills up her spine. Those words rang in her ears.

"I've done nothing except endure your torments and attack, and then Jackson, I...."

"Tsk, tsk, Olivia, I did not attack you. I was only claiming my property. You tried to ruin my life, Olivia. You sent me to prison for my love."

"Love? How dare you!" Olivia replied in a venomous whisper.

"I loved you then, and I love you now. I told that snake cousin of mine to give you back, but he refused. He's your example of what happens to people when they refuse me. He bragged to me you made a nice trophy wife, even through your stupidity. I told him he would pay for his disloyalty but he didn't listen to me. So you see, you deserve everything I'm going to give you."

"You beat me nearly to death and raped me. How did I ever deserve that?" Olivia said, feeling the threat of tears. Her eyes were burning, her throat, her brain was burning.

Patrick was outwardly angry, now. He would no longer control himself for their sake. **"You are mine, you dumb bitch! You've always been mine! You are my bird and you will sing for me! You will pay for your blindness!"** He yelled wildly.

Olivia could feel him shoving the gun deeper into her side in his rant. A tear escaped and slid down her cheek, born of all the pain living inside, but all she could feel was fury. She wanted to beat him with her bare hands until blood spewed from his mouth and nose, until her fist could no longer be the instrument.

She wished to hear his last gurgling breath spit from his mouth in blood and fear so he could know just what he took from her and just what she would never let him take again. She wanted to scream her rage at his remains, so loud and so long that even God would weep and the Earth would rumble. She said nothing, just stared at Jake.

Everything happened in slow motion for Olivia as Jake explosively lunged across the table for the gun, desperate and blind to the danger. In that same moment, Patrick easily pointed it toward him, pulling the trigger as though swatting a fly.

The sound of the gun was the same as a nail in a coffin. It rang in her ears. She watched as Jake's body was thrown back against the vinyl. He convulsed for a split second and slumped in the seat.

She screamed in horror. "Oh my God! Jake, no, no, no, Jake you're bleeding! Oh my God, oh God, no, God! Tag! Tag! Call for help!"

"Olivia..." Jake said strangely as he slid lower into the booth.

Patrick's cold fingers grabbed at her shoulder. She was not destined to live happily in the mountains. She was destined for pain and grief that comes from losing everything good; the misery of her curse. Here was another moment she hadn't changed at all.

"When are you going to learn? It didn't have to be this way, Olivia. This is *your* fault! Look at this mess you've made! I have tried and tried to teach you, but now look what you've made me do! Look at your cowboy there. His blood is on your hands, now!" Patrick smiled oddly and tapped on Olivia's temple with the barrel of the shiny pistol; then he pulled on her arm roughly. "Come on now, we have to go. No time to waste." He said calmly.

Tag had heard the stranger's voice screaming at Olivia and looked out the pass-through getting a glimpse of the pistol, hearing the shot, and seeing his friend slump down in the seat. He listened to Olivia's horrific screams as he crawled quietly through the kitchen door and behind the front-counter still able to see Olivia and the shooter. Reaching for the phone on the nearby wall, he dialed quickly. His heart drove him to act but his mind stayed calm. He knew this was the only way to help his friends.

Before Patrick could pull her completely to her feet, Olivia's hand instinctively curled around a forgotten steak knife on the table. She shoved the blade up and into Patrick's throat as hard as she could, propelling them both to the floor.

It felt different than she had imagined. Strangely she felt she had been waiting for this moment and somehow she had wished it into reality. She pulled the knife back and stabbed him again, and then again and again. She didn't know or care what she hit, just that she couldn't stop herself. She heard the guttural sound of her cries but didn't really recognize them as her own.

She stabbed at him until there was no life in his eyes. She screamed and cried and stood up staring at the blood-soaked rapist slumped to the floor in front of her. There was a strange satisfaction from it. He had cursed her, and in his blood she would wash herself clean of it once and for all. She had done to him what he had done to her. She had raped the life from his body with the sharp blade in her hand. She wiped at her tears, but only streaked his blood on her face. She looked down at her hands and dropped the knife to the floor.

■ ■

CHAPTER THIRTY-ONE

Jake's blood was pouring from his shoulder. The blue shirt he'd been wearing was covered, his eyes struggling to stay open. Tears fell down Olivia's face like rivers of anguish. Everything seemed to move in slow motion.

"It's ok, Olivia. It's going to be ok. Jake, buddy, you're going to be ok." Tag yelled nervously rushing to the booth.

Olivia stumbled forward over Patrick's lifeless body. Tag carefully moved Jake toward the floor and ripped off his apron stuffing it into Jake's bleeding shoulder. He looked to Olivia for reassurance. Her face read nothing but uncertainty. She placed her hand over Tag's and helped to apply pressure blankly staring at Tag. "I'm so sorry. I didn't want this. I tried to stop it," she cried.

Jake moaned in pain just as the bell on the door chimed again.

"Jesus! Jake! Tag! What happened?" Brad blurted out as he knelt beside Jake. Still holding the bloody apron in Jake's shoulder, Tag moved aside to let the deputy come in closer.

"Jake, man, you ok? What the hell?" Brad looked to Olivia for answers.

Her body was numb, her eyes vacant. She couldn't answer. What could she say? There was no easy answer.

Cool air rushed in as the door kept opening and closing. It hadn't taken long before people in uniforms and voices and a swarm of activity filled the diner around her. She had been placed at a table on the opposite end of the room. She could see Jake's boots. She loved those boots. She remembered hearing a story of a mom who had walked her son to the bus one morning and a short time later, she heard sirens nearby. Being curious the mom turned back to the bus stop only to see her son's shoe beside the road. Jake's boots were his symbol of vitality and life. Would his boots be her final token from an unlived life?

She watched as they covered Patrick's body with a sheet. It wasn't big enough to cover all the blood. There was nothing about the body on the floor that broke through to her heart. She was consumed by fear for Jake and all the questions that remained unanswered, but for the dead rapist, she would not mourn or cry or feel any remorse. But, she also felt no difference.

Even in his death, Olivia was still cursed. She was going to lose Jake.

"Miss Curtis? Olivia? Can you hear me?" Deputy Frazier asked worriedly. "Miss Curtis I need you to talk to me." Brad said patiently.

"Is, is Jake alive?" she asked quietly.

"Yes Ma'am he is" he replied. "He was shot in the shoulder and it looks like the bullet went straight through. We're going to get him to the hospital. Miss Curtis, can you tell me what happened? Did Jake shoot that man? Did you know him?"

"That was Patrick Hanson" she replied numbly. Her eyes were trained on the commotion surrounding Jake as they loaded him onto a stretcher. If only he would wake up. If only he would say her name. If only. He was so pale and lifeless and Olivia felt her heart shatter. Patrick was right, she had done this.

Tag held her hand and helped Olivia to her feet.

"Can I go with him? With Jake?" she spoke softly to the deputy.

Brad battled between his friendships and his duty. "Yeah, but at some point, we'll need to take your statement. Likely it will be a State Police detective."

The lights on the ambulance were like a beacon as Tag drove Olivia to St. John's hospital in Libby. It felt like an eternity to wait. She was grateful for the dark and Tag's kindness. She listened as he made phone calls to Jake's parents and then another to Sam. A heavy stone sat on her chest as he spoke solemnly.

When she and Tag arrived at the hospital, they were told to wait. Jake's family and quite possibly the whole town of Troy were in route and Jake had been rushed into surgery. She and Tag tried to be patient as they'd been told little else.

Olivia sank into a light blue chair with wooden arms. The well-worn finish on the arms made the surface rough. People stared blatantly at the dried blood covering her face and chest. She hadn't even washed it from her hands. Olivia looked down to see it flaking off in pieces and falling to the floor like bloody snow.

"He is all I have." Olivia said quietly, tears streaming down her face once again. Tag gave her a half hug from the chair beside her.

"Why don't you go wash up a bit?" he offered.

Olivia nodded her response and walked shakily to a restroom.

"Excuse me sir, I'm looking for Olivia Curtis." A tall, serious, uniformed officer stood in front of Tag.

"Uh, yeah, she's in the restroom, but I'm Tag Porter. I work at the diner."

"I'm detective Brandon with the state police. Were you working tonight, Mr. Porter?"

"Yes, I was. Did you want to talk to me first? Olivia will be out shortly."

"That would be fine; there's a private waiting room just over here. Follow me please."

Tag followed the detective to a very small, very bland room like something out of the movies.

"Miss Curtis wouldn't leave, would she?" the detective asked skeptically, glancing toward the hallway.

"No, absolutely not. Jake's here-she's here." Tag replied earnestly.

"Why don't you just tell me what happened tonight?" the detective began, pulling out a notepad and pen.

"Well, where do I start?"

"Who came in the diner tonight? Was anyone else working?" The detective had been through this many times.

"No, it was just me and it was dead quiet until my buddy Jake came in. He told me he was waiting for Olivia, um Miss Curtis, while she was at an appointment. Since there weren't any other customers, Jake and I were just hanging out, shooting the breeze. When Olivia came, I took their dinner order and got back to cooking."

"What about the other man? When did he show up?" the detective prompted.

"You mean the dead one?" Tag asked sounding more sarcastic than he'd meant to.

The detective frowned. "Yeah, that one."

"Uh, yeah, he came in sometime after I brought their steaks out. I was in back cleaning up and shutting down the grill. I saw the guy through the pass-through when I heard the door. It looked like he said something to them and then sat down next to Olivia. I couldn't hear because of the dishwasher and the grill fan."

"Did you recognize him?"

"Nope, but I figured Olivia and Jake did because of the way he just sat down."

"Then what happened?" the detective continued.

"I got back to my cleaning. I started out to tell him I'd already shut down the grill but that I could still take his order. I heard him shout something and that's when he pulled a gun on Jake and shot him!"

"What was Miss Curtis doing and where were you standing at the time?"

"She was screaming. She screamed at me to call the cops. I ducked down and was just about to the front counter when she grabbed a knife from the table and stabbed the guy. That's when I grabbed the phone. I don't know what happened to the gun."

"Were you able to see anything else from where you were?"

"I saw Olivia trying to protect Jake."

"What do you mean by that?"

"I mean my best friend was just shot by this guy and Olivia did what she had to do to get him to stop!" Tag replied angrily. He felt his face flush.

"Calm down Mr. Porter. I'm only trying to find out what happened."

Olivia walked past the open doorway and saw Tag talking to an officer. Her face and hands had been scrubbed clean, but her hair and shirt told a different tale. Olivia looked at the officer with wary eyes.

"Olivia, this is detective, uh, Brandon? Is that right? He's with the state police."

"Miss Curtis, why don't you have a seat. Thank you for your time Mr. Porter. I'm going to ask you step back across the hall and wait." Reluctantly Tag left the room as Olivia took the seat on the old brown sofa he'd just vacated.

The next few hours were a blur to Olivia. She had told the detective everything she could think to tell. The only thing she left out, as usual, was her vision. If there were any part of her story that would make this all seem premeditated, it would be that.

When he had finished with his questions and seemed satisfied, at least temporarily, the detective left her alone. She wondered if Jake's family had arrived but couldn't bring herself to go find out. She needed a minute without questions or looks or company at all.

Olivia let out the breath she'd been holding. Would a jury believe this to be justified? Would anyone really understand she hadn't intended to kill anyone? I only wanted to protect Jake. Did it even matter? Olivia thought deeply as she sat alone in the room. A heavy sigh escaped her lips. So much had happened and she would have to live with the label of murderer, even if only in her heart. She took Patrick's life from him.

She wondered when her next vision would come, and how would it be colored now that he was gone.

The visions had started with him, would they end with him also? There were too many unanswered questions. Olivia laid her head in her hands as the held-back tears escaped.

She needed to pull herself together. The Weidner's would be here already and Miles would arrive soon. She paced in the small room then forced herself to face them. There were familiar faces in every available chair. Deputy Frazier was standing nearby and noticed Olivia first.

"Where are Jake's parents?" she asked him.

"I think they're in the chapel. How'd it go with the detective?" he asked, but she didn't answer.

Olivia felt heavy. She had no tears now, just the overwhelming burden of pain and grief. How long had Jake been in surgery? Again, too many questions and not nearly enough answers. She found an empty seat, pulled her knees up to her chest and wrapped her arms tightly around them. The smell of Patrick's death filled her senses. She rocked back and forth wishing none of this had happened. She was lost somewhere in her own head longing for Jake to hold her hand.

"Olivia?" a familiar voice said. Frankie walked into the waiting room followed by Dacey and Sam.

Olivia couldn't stop the tears. The flood gates were opened. "I'm so sorry Frankie. Have you heard anything? No one has told me how Jake is doing."

"We haven't heard anything." Frankie bent down to Olivia and held her like a small child. They cried together. Dacey stood and smoothed his wife's hair. After some time, Olivia spoke, "I feel so awful. This is all my fault." She admitted.

"This is **not** your fault. You did not hurt Jacob and we're just glad you're ok." Dacey replied.

Everything had gone so terribly wrong. She should be wrapping gifts with Jake at home on the ranch not sitting in a hospital hoping doctors could save his life.

"Did you kill the man that shot Jacob?" Frankie asked bluntly.

"Yes" Olivia cried. "I k..k..killed him."

"Good, good girl! If you hadn't then I would have!" Frankie replied fiercely.

"God, I can't wait any longer!" Olivia cried and got up to pace, not waiting for Frankie and Dacey to follow her. She walked to the nearby desk hoping someone could tell her something about Jake.

"Can you tell me anything about Jacob Weidner? Please? He's been in surgery for a long time and his parents are here and we still haven't heard anything!"

"Yes ma'am, I believe the doctor will be out in just a few moments to speak to his family."

"Thank you" she said politely. It just dawned on her, "I'm not his family." She watched as Frankie and Dacey sat down again. She wondered why she had never taken up smoking. People in movies always seemed so comforted by it. She could use a cigarette right now.

She watched as Frankie started to cry anew. Fresh terror swept swiftly through her. She scolded herself for her cowardice and went to sit with Jake's mother once again. She loved these people and needed to be brave for them.

"He's going to be ok. He has to be." Olivia said, not knowing exactly what to say, but desperately hoping it was the truth.

Olivia thought about the ring that held a quiet vigil in her purse. She wanted to put it on but she and Jake hadn't officially announced their engagement to his parents and family.

"Does Jessica know?" Olivia asked suddenly.

"Yes we called everyone we could think of. Jessica is on a plane as we speak. Oh Lord, Olivia, we didn't call your parents. I'm so sorry we should have thought to do that for you."

"It's ok, I called Miles and he's on his way. I'm sure Miles told them."

"Are they coming as well?"

"I don't know."

Olivia watched as a doctor in a surgical gown walked through the far doors toward them. She felt her heart stop. She watched him approach Jake's dad. "Are you with Jacob Weidner?"

"Yes, he's my son." Dacey replied with a gulp.

"He's going to be ok." The surgeon smiled. "He's lost a lot of blood, but the bullet exited his shoulder without too much damage. I'd say he's lucky, considering. He's in recovery so it will be a while before you can visit with him."

"Thank you, doctor. Thank you so much. When can his mother see him?" Dacey asked.

Olivia let out the breath she'd been holding and cried in earnest. She wanted to say, 'when can *I* see him?' but didn't want to be selfish. He wasn't hers.

The ring in her purse wasn't really enough to insure Jake belonged to her. He didn't belong to her, he never really had. This whole tragedy and the fact Jake was hurt so badly was just further evidence to prove she was cursed to be alone. Look at everything he had endured because of the evil that plagued her life. This was proof and she knew she didn't deserve Jake.

The surgeon said, "Give it about twenty minutes and you may go sit with him Mrs. Weidner and just keep the visitors to family, one person at a time for now. The nurse will take you to him when he's ready."

"Excuse me" Olivia said and rushed out of the room. She needed to be alone. She followed the signs to the hospital chapel. She sat down on a pew in the back of the quiet little room. There were flowers placed on the altar and she noticed the fragrance in the air. It reminded her of the first time Jake was at her door. He had mistaken Miles for her boyfriend so he had tried to downplay the flowers. Olivia had never met a man like Jake before. He was always so comfortable in his own skin. He gave her that bouquet as if it was the most natural thing in the world; except for Olivia, it was so touching.

She prayed.

****

Frankie held her son's hand softly. "Tesoro mia, you have to get better. I know you don't like to be told what to do, but you allow yourself to heal and get better. Is that clear?" she said firmly.

"Yes ma'am" Jake croaked. "Where's Olivia? Is she alright?"

"She's fine; she's waiting to see you."

Frankie kissed her son's cheeks warmly and then went to get Dacey. "You can go in now, vita mia." She said to Dacey, tears still streaming down her face.

Frankie walked into the chapel and watched Olivia for a moment. "Jacob is awake and he asked for you."

"Ok, I'm sorry. I just thought I should say a prayer, you know?"

"Yes, I know, I've said many today. Now come with me. God knows your pain. We are going to get you changed, something to eat and then you're going to go see Jacob."

"Could I? Um, see him now?"

"His papa is there with him. He's going to be ok. Did you hear the doctor?"

"Yes, but I'm not..."

"No buts; you are going to eat and you are going to be strong for Jacob. Starving yourself isn't going to help him and by the looks of you, a strong wind could blow you over right now." Frankie said and grabbed Olivia by the hand.

It seemed to Olivia that she hadn't heard Jake's voice in days or weeks. It was hard to believe it had only been hours. Olivia sat in the cafeteria across from Frankie, strong, willful, Italian mama that she was.

"Olivia, you're wearing your guilt like a coat made of stone and bricks. You need to stop this. This isn't your fault. I know you think it is but you didn't know that man had a gun. How could you know? If it weren't for what you did, he might have tried to shoot Jacob again, or you, you just don't know."

Olivia took bites of a muffin that had no flavor. Nothing had any flavor. After they ate, Frankie walked her to Jake's room and very nearly shoved her inside. She looked childlike in the oversized scrubs Frankie had borrowed for her to wear. She wasn't sure why she was afraid but she was.

His eyes were closed. Olivia reached for his hand. She could barely stand to look at the bandages covering his shoulder. The sound of the monitor in the room was strangely comforting. She laid her head next to his thigh.

She cried quietly. Slowly, against her will, her eyes closed as well. She didn't deserve sleep any more than she deserved food, but it took her just the same.

"Mama?" the child said, "why is daddy still sleeping?"
Olivia looked down at her son with big brown eyes, his daddy's eyes, and smiled.
"He's very tired, my love. He had a big day." She whispered sweetly to the beautiful child in her dream.
"Will he wake up? Wake up daddy? Wake up."
Wake up Olivia! Wake up...

Olivia jolted awake, unsure of her surroundings. She couldn't remember what day it was or where... She rubbed her eyes and looked up at Jake. He moved his hand.

"Where have you been?" he croaked.

"I've been here" she cried.

"I asked Dad to find you and then I guess I fell asleep, are you alright Darlin'?"

"How can you ask me that when you're the one in a hospital bed? This is my fault Jake. I'm so sorry." She shook her head and cried.

He held up her hand and she stopped. "Where is your ring?" he asked, beginning to sound a bit more like his old self.

"It's in my purse, Jake. We haven't told your parents yet and I just..."

"Put it on" Jake demanded, though he didn't look angry, just frustrated and he was. He didn't like being stuck in a hospital bed when all he really wanted to do was hold Olivia and kiss her and make her feel better and make that look of guilt and shame on her face go away.

Olivia reached into her purse and put the ring back on her finger.

"Good, now go get my parents."

"You're only allowed one visitor at a time." Olivia protested.

"I don't care; just have them come in with you. No one will say anything. I'm ok." Jake insisted.

Olivia did as instructed and when Frankie came in the room she kissed her son on the cheeks again and spoke to him in Italian.

"Mama, Papa; Olivia and I are engaged to be married." Jake said and reached for Olivia's hand.

Olivia looked sheepishly at Frankie and Dacey but both of them hugged her and smiled and congratulated them. Suddenly Olivia knew what it was supposed to feel like when a family embraces you.

Jake smiled and reached for Olivia's hand. He wouldn't let go again.

CHAPTER THIRTY-TWO

Over the next few days half the town of Troy came to see Jake in the hospital and Olivia's parents came, as well. She had never seen her mother quite so beside herself. All she wanted to talk about was Olivia's new "legal issues" as she had begun to call them. For some reason, Antoinette Curtis didn't seem to be relieved that her daughter's rapist was now dead. More than anything, she seemed embarrassed that people might say her daughter was a murderer. They only stayed one night and when Antoinette could not convince Olivia to move back to Oregon with them, she became angry and flew back home with Mr. Curtis in tow. Olivia wasn't sure if she'd hear from them again anytime soon. Miles stayed awhile longer but by Friday, even he said his goodbyes too, on the promise that Olivia would keep him posted on everything.

Jake kept telling Olivia not to worry about her mother and as long as she listened to their lawyer, all this would work out just fine and they would handle it all together.

Jake had to push his doctor a bit. "Christmas day is on Monday. I want to go home. I am ready to go and spend Christmas with my fiancée and my family. I won't overdo it, I promise. I'll just sit there; maybe open a present or two, that's it. Come on doc. Let me go home please?"

Olivia sat on the edge of Jake's bed listening. It seemed he was in fighting form. Jake was back. He still needed to rest and recover but the wit, the sense of humor, told her he *was* back.

The doctor finally agreed and Jake was allowed to go home as long as he didn't try to drive himself. Jake slept while Tag drove them both to the ranch.

Even though Carmella had visited at the hospital several times, she had managed to do everything under the sun to prepare for his arrival home, including cook his favorite meal. She had also finished decorating the house.

There wasn't a square inch that wasn't festive. It was beautiful. There were white twinkle lights on everything that would stand still, all the trees and fences. There was a huge white lighted star over the barn. It was all magical, but having Jake come home was the best magic of all.

Dacey and Frankie had followed in their car and when they pulled up to the front, everyone rushed to help Jake. Olivia, Frankie and Carmella all hovered like frantic helicopters as Tag and Dacey helped Jake inside and up to his room. Carmella arranged the pillows. Frankie poured Jake a glass of water and Olivia pulled back the covers. They were all talking at the same time.

Jake was trying not to lose his temper but he detested this sort of fluttering treatment. His frustration was building. He was, admittedly, not a good patient.

Dacey could tell his son was about to lose it so he intervened before the well intentioned women got their feelings hurt. "Ladies, why don't you let me get Jake settled in here."

Tag agreed. "Yeah, I'm taking off, too. Jake, if you need anything, just call me, ok buddy?"

"Thanks for everything" Jake said as Tag left the room.

All the women stopped talking and gave Dacey a look that could have melted the skin off his skull.

"Mama, Carmella, please. I want to talk to Dad alone, for a few minutes." Jake pleaded nicely.

Olivia tried not to get her feelings hurt. She told herself she was being childish. "That man loves you. He took a bullet for you. Give him some time." She thought.

"Darlin'" Jake said, interrupting her thoughts. "I need a couple minutes, ok?"

"Of course; I'll be in the um, I'll be in the ballroom if you need me."

She walked out of the room and heard Frankie say, "No business talk. I mean it." And then she and Carmella followed behind Olivia.

Olivia wanted to scream. "Don't take it personally, Olivia." Frankie said seeing the look on Olivia's face. "Jake has been like this since he was a child. He never takes sick days, even when he should, so being forced to stay in bed, well, it makes him grouchy. He only tolerates his papa at times like this because Dacey doesn't baby him like we women."

Olivia nodded and smiled but said nothing. She went to the ballroom and sat angrily at the piano and began to play. Her thoughts were dark and heavy. She felt like she wanted to run. She was furious. She kept picturing Patrick's dead eyes, as she nearly pounded on the keys.

There was a jumble of relief and sadness, fury and fear about what she had done and about what had been done to Jake. Patrick was dead and yet she still felt damaged. How could that be? How could she still be so broken? Patrick had admitted he killed Dante' and Olivia wondered, did she kill Patrick for revenge, or did she kill him to save Jake? Or, could it be that after everything, did she do it for herself? She tried to let it all go in the music. She wanted to lose herself in the melancholy sound.

As soon as they were alone Jake asked, "Papa, I need your help. Sam brought that new horse over for Olivia and he's out in the barn. Can you keep her out of there until Christmas morning?"

"Yes, of course, but we need to talk about some other things." Dacey added.

"What?" Jake asked with a look of concern.

"I'm so grateful to God that you *and* Olivia are both ok, but I still don't understand what happened there, Jacob, and I really don't understand the attitude you have toward your mother, Carmella or Olivia. They are your family. Those women were terrified and now they only want to take care of you. I suggest you figure out a way to control yourself and get your feet on the ground. Have you even talked this whole thing out with Olivia?"

"What's there to say? The monster that attacked her shot me and she..."

"She killed him. You both could have been killed. It might be time to say your prayers, boy." Dacey scolded.

"I'm not upset with Olivia, Dad, I'm scared for her. How's she going to handle it? I should have protected *her*, not the other way around. What am I supposed to say?"

"Why not the other way around? She's your fiancée. I think you better figure out what to say to her, and soon. I know you're frustrated about what happened, and this whole thing has you rattled, but I also know if you don't let those women in, you'll be dealing with much worse than a gunshot wound."

Jake rubbed his forehead and smiled. "You're right."

"I'm right?" Dacey teased.

"Yes, Papa, you're right. Could you ask Olivia to come up here?"

Olivia walked down the hallway with Harper wiggling at her feet. She didn't know if she should just walk in, or knock. She hated the tension she was feeling between her and Jake.

~ 403 ~

Things were definitely different and she didn't know how to get them back to the way they were. What if Jake didn't want her anymore? Would he change his mind about getting married? She looked at the beautiful ring on her finger and felt suddenly sick to her stomach. She felt like she was stuck on the outside, looking in at the life she had always dreamed of, but knew she didn't deserve and couldn't have.

She stood in front of the big French doors to her bedroom, her husband, her life. Her future was through those doors, but would she be allowed to have it. Perhaps her dream life would be only that. She couldn't walk in and hear him tell her it was over. She couldn't handle those words coming out of his mouth.

She bent down and picked up Harper. She rushed back down the hall and into the kitchen, the gathering place of the family she wanted. She grabbed her purse and spoke to Frankie who was having tea with Dacey and Carmella. "Tell Jake I'm sorry." she said through tears.

"Olivia, wait!" Frankie called after her, but it was too late.

She rushed out the door to her Jeep and drove away.

Harper was whining on the passenger's seat. "Shut up, Harper" she yelled.

She didn't really know where she was going, just that she needed to go. She drove carefully but wished she could be reckless, just once. She screamed her frustration as the tears continued to fall. She drove up toward the lodge and stopped at a pretty little cabin-house on the corner just a mile from the Outfitter's.

The snow fell heavily up here amongst the trees. Olivia felt a huge wave of relief that a light was on. She picked up Harper and tromped through the snow up the walkway. Sam opened the door before Olivia could even knock.

"Come in before you catch your death out there." Sam said, holding the door open with a serious look.

Olivia sobbed out the words, "I didn't know where else to go." She put Harper on the floor in Sam's living room. There was a crackling fire in the stone fireplace.

Sam looked at her with arms crossed. "What's going on?"

"Where's your bathroom?" Olivia asked looking wrecked.

"The first door on the right, are you ok?"

Olivia couldn't speak. She sprinted to the bathroom and lost her lunch or whatever meal she'd eaten last. She couldn't remember.

Sam followed grabbing a washcloth for her. Olivia continued to cry and puke, hovering over the toilet like a skilled party girl.

After a while, she finally felt a bit better and straightened up. She took the cool wash cloth from Sam and wiped her face.

"I'm so sorry." She said, still sniffling.

"Do you want some water?" Sam asked.

"Yes please" Olivia replied as they came back to sit together in the kitchen.

"What's going on?"

"I don't know where to start." Olivia replied, rubbing her face and taking sips of water.

"Why don't you start with; why you aren't home?"

"I should be. I know I should be, but I think, um, I think Jake's going to break up with me. He's been so short with me and I just don't think he wants me there."

"Did he tell you he doesn't want you there?"

"I didn't give him the chance."

"Liv, he's a horrible patient, trust me. But he needs you, now more than ever. He was shot just three days ago. I don't care how he's acting, he needs you. What happened?"

"Well, I..." she began.

"Hold that thought. I'm going to make some coffee and then we'll talk."

"Ok" Olivia replied sadly. Her phone rang. It was Jake.

"That's him, I'll bet. Answer the damn phone Liv!" Sam growled over her shoulder.

"Hello?" Olivia answered, trying not to sound like she'd been crying.

"Where did you go? I was worried sick. Are you ok?" Jake asked.

"I can explain."

"Great, that's great; I can't wait to hear why you've taken off again." Jake replied grouchily.

"I just couldn't, I didn't, I just..."

Sam grabbed the phone out of her hand. She'd had enough of this crap. "Jake, it's Sam." She said not-so-sweetly. Olivia tried to take the phone back but Sam wouldn't let her.

"Olivia is at your house?" he asked, feeling relieved and confused.

"Yes, she's having a rough time but we're going to have a talk and then she'll be home safe and sound. You just rest and don't worry your handsome little head about this. You need plenty of rest if you're going to get better quickly." She said as though she were speaking to a child.

"Tell her I love her. Tell her to come home to me, please? And tell her I'm sorry I've been so, such an ass."

"Your words, not mine. Alright, I got this lover boy." Sam said and hung up looking at Olivia. She looked pitiful. "Drama, drama, drama" Sam muttered.

"If I didn't like you so much and think you and Jake have the potential to make excellent grown-ups someday, I would smack the crap out of you both right now." Sam paused, waiting for Olivia's reaction but she just sat back down, stared at her engagement ring and burst into tears again.

"...but I happen to think that once the two of you get past all this crap and pull your heads out of your asses, you'll be a spectacular couple." She placed a cup of coffee in front of Olivia.

"Thank you" Olivia snuffled.

"For the coffee or the ass chewing?"

"Both, I guess."

"So lay it on me; what's going on with you and don't leave anything out."

Olivia relayed the whole sad, screwed up story to Sam. It felt like she had retold it a thousand times already, but this time she talked about killing Patrick and the fear that she would face charges. Sometimes, it felt like there was nothing more to her than a very long, very sad story.

"I have always wished him dead." She admitted in one breath. "It was like I made that moment happen and now I don't know if Jake can see past it. Am I a murderer?" she sobbed again.

"What? You're not a murderer Olivia. You killed the man who raped you, who shot your fiancée and planned to do horrible things to you, who may have even killed you. And it sounds like he killed your husband who just happened to be his cousin? And let's not forget that means he also killed your son! I know they haven't been able to prove that, but come on...if there was ever a case of self-defense honey, I'd say this is it!

"I couldn't walk into Jake's room and face him. I was afraid."

"Oh, you mean, of Jake? You mean the man who was just shot and desperately wants you to come *home* to him? You mean the guy who said to say, 'he loves you', that Jake? I'd say you're worried over nothing." Sam smiled.

"You've been through so much more than any one person should have, and I definitely understand you wanting to get that crazy dirt bag son of a bitch out of your life for good! What I don't understand is why you don't seem to realize how much Jake loves you? He doesn't just *love* you, Liv, he needs you? Jake is a different guy since he met you. Why aren't you fighting for it?"

Olivia took a deep breath, "It's simple really; I don't deserve somebody like Jake. Everything I've been through makes me undeserving and unworthy." Olivia paused. "Girls like me don't get to be with guys like him."

"Now I might just have to slap you. What a bunch of bullshit, Liv. You think because horrible things were done to you that makes you a horrible person?"

"Yeah, I guess that's how I feel." Olivia admitted.

"What would you have said to your son if someone had violated him? That it makes him unclean, unworthy of love? Is that what you would have said?"

"No, of course not" Olivia yelled!

"Then why do you say that to yourself?" Sam yelled back!

"I'm..."

"What?"

"I'm scared. What if this falls apart, too? What if it doesn't last? What if Jake leaves me or worse, what if he dies? It will kill me!"

"So you'll walk away before love has a chance to hurt you? I didn't know you were such a coward!"

The kitchen was dead quiet. Sam sat staring at Olivia with her piercing blue eyes. Olivia looked down, fresh tears coming into her own.

"I'm not a coward." She whispered.

"Prove it." Sam replied loudly.

Olivia pushed herself out of the chair and walked around the table and hugged Sam fiercely. "Where were you through all my years of therapy? You're the best Sam."

"So I've been told." She smiled, tears in her eyes now, too.

Olivia grabbed her purse and scooped up Harper.

"What are you doing?" Sam asked, not surprised.

"I'm going home."

Sam smiled.

The kitchen was dark when Olivia arrived back at the ranch. She was relieved.

She didn't think she could handle a confrontation with Jake's family.

Olivia took off her shoes and hung up her coat. She tiptoed up the stairs to his bedroom. The bedside lamp was on. It was obvious Jake had tried to wait up for her, but being on pain medication, he couldn't. He slept propped up, his head lying back heavily on pillows. Olivia sat next to him on the bed and gently kissed his lips.

Jake opened his eyes and pulled her in closer kissing her passionately. "Don't leave me again, Darlin'. I can't take it." Jake whispered seriously.

"I know. It's just, well, after what I did, I wasn't sure if you still wanted me."

"Of course I still want you. I always want you, Darlin' I need you."

"I, I *needed* to go but I promise I'm done, no more running. Come hell or high water, you're stuck with me."

"I want to trust you and I want you to trust me, but that means really trusting you won't run away every time things get tough or something freaks you out. I couldn't come after you. I'm stuck here in this damn bed! Do you know how frustrating that is?" he groaned.

"I'm sorry, really, I'm so sorry. I shouldn't have left. How are you feeling, my love?" Olivia asked, smiling coyly.

"Olivia, I mean it. I'm serious. You are grounded young lady." Jake said, returning her smile.

"Oh I'm grounded huh?" Olivia laughed. "You're the one who's grounded. You need to rest so you are well enough to dance with me at the New Year's Eve Ball."

"Is that so? You want to dance with me?"

"Yes, I do, but first you need sleep."

She wanted to ravage him in that moment but instead, she kissed his forehead and helped him get more comfortable, fluffing the pillows around him.

"Are you leaving?" he asked.

"I'm just going to get something to eat from the kitchen, do you want anything?"

"Just you" he said through a yawn.

"I'll be back. Now sleep and I'll be here when you wake, ok?" She said and kissed him again. He began to snore before she could leave the room.

She went down to the kitchen feeling much better and very hungry. She felt like she hadn't eaten in days.

"I gather you're staying then." Frankie asked from the dimly lit kitchen.

"Oh, you startled me."

"I'm sorry, Olivia."

"That's ok; I'm the one looking for a snack in the dark. I probably startled you." Olivia replied and grabbed a yogurt from the fridge.

"Sit down, we need to talk." Frankie said seriously.

Olivia sat at the island, wondering just how many 'talks' she would end up having before this night was over.

"Is this some sort of a game to you?"

"What? No!"

"I'm going to sound like an overprotective mother, and maybe I am but I won't let you hurt Jacob. I want to know what your intentions are here."

"Mrs. Weidner, um, Frankie, I know Jake has been through the ringer because of me, but I promise you and I promised Jake, too; I'm done with all of that. I'm finally starting to feel like I can move forward and I want to move forward with your son. I love him more than anything. I can't even explain it. There are no words for what he means to me and what he's done for me and I'm sorrier than you can know for what happened to him. Jake is my whole life." Olivia said sincerely.

Frankie looked at her. "Jacob will heal from his physical injuries. It is not your fault he was shot, but I worry for his heart. I worry you'll leave and not come back. You can't do that to him. I've seen his face when he looks at you. Don't break his heart. I think you are a good person Olivia and I care for you, but don't hurt my boy and, well, that's all I'm going to say about it."

"I'm so sorry Mrs. Weidner, I truly am; I've made a lot of mistakes."

"I know you're sorry, and Jacob isn't perfect either, God knows. I heard how he ran off to New York without so much as a word to you. I'm not blind, I'm just overprotective."

"You are a good mother. I was always very overprotective of my son Dante'. I think I must have driven him crazy with it sometimes."

"I'm sure I drive Jacob crazy, too. You would think I would be used to seeing him hurt." Frankie smiled.

"What do you mean?"

"Oh Jacob played football and was injured. He played lacrosse and was injured. He was involved with rodeo for a while and seemed to look like one giant bruise. Training horses for the ranch and for the Outfitter's, he was always getting hurt. He was kicked in the hand when Guiness was a yearling. You name it, he has done it."

"I had no idea." Olivia sighed. Sometimes it was glaringly obvious how little she and Jake knew about each other.

"None of that could compare to being shot, but a freight train wouldn't have stopped him from trying to save you. You know that, right?"

"I do know. I just wish none of this would have happened. I never should have called Patrick. It was obviously the thing that brought him to the diner. Jake would have handled this better if only I would have been honest with him. I have lived with fear for so long that I thought maybe I could..." Olivia shook her head "free myself from it."

"Did you?" Frankie asked sincerely.

"In a way, yes, I think I did. It just doesn't feel like I thought it would. I mean, I killed someone and I don't know how to be ok with that."

"You protected yourself and the people you love. Are you sure you aren't Italian?" Frankie smiled.

"Maybe I am." Olivia looked at Frankie with a new perspective. Her mother never would have made this better and somehow all in the stretch of one short conversation, Olivia did feel better. She felt forgiven and more than that, she felt loved.

"If not yet, you will be. You're my honorary Italian daughter. Jacob loves you and he wants to marry you, that makes you family."

"You don't know what this means to me." She replied looking down at the lovely ring on her finger.

"Did Jacob tell you about this ring? Did he tell you what happened in New York?" Frankie asked.

"Just bits and pieces really. I still can't believe he bought it for me when we weren't even officially together."

"Well Jessica told me he was a wreck that week. She said he wasn't himself at all. He was tense, grouchy, and bossier than usual; and that *is* saying something. She said all he did was mope around until they went shopping. She said he was in Tiffany's and started talking about you and suddenly, he was calm, peaceful almost and happy."

"I guess even the clerk was listening to him and started crying at his description of you and then she handed him *that* ring. She said Jake knew instantly and called it 'your ring', 'Olivia's ring'. You're future husband is very much in love with you."

"I love him too, so much."

Later, Olivia crawled into bed next to a sleeping Jake. Her love, her mountain was resting. She could kick herself for causing him so much worry and pain. She thought about Christmas. It was only two days away. She hoped Jake would like his gift. She seriously hoped he hadn't gone overboard on something for her.

Thoughts of Christmas at the ranch filled her head, but finally, after days of unrest and tension, she was able to sleep soundly, listening to Jake's quiet breathing beside her. She held his hand under the covers and there were no dreams.

Jake woke the next morning feeling sore but definitely a bit better. Olivia slept heavily next to him and was holding his hand. To Jake he was always the one holding on and Olivia was the one letting go. And now, she held his hand. Something had changed.

He wanted to be angry with her. There was a part of him that wanted to lash out and stomp around like a caveman about everything that had happened since the day he met her. There was the really angry and frustrated part of him, but when he looked at her, all of it just melted away. He couldn't be angry with her, not really. Most everything that had happened was not her fault and he really didn't blame her for her reactions. It was purely self-preservation and grief. He understood her more clearly now.

Jake smiled. She wore that same U of O t-shirt she'd had on the first night they spent cuddling on her bed with pillows all around them like a nest.

So many times, Olivia was like a frightened animal, maybe a timid deer; but now that he studied her, she *was* a bird. She belonged to no one. She liked the coziness of a nest, she still frightened easily, she barely ate anything and she carried herself with elegance on those long limbs. She was a bird born of fire, just like in his dream.

"Darlin'" he said sweetly.

"Hmm?" she refused to open her eyes.

"Hey sleepyhead, I hate to wake you but the doctor is coming out to check on me this morning. I thought you might want to get up."

"Oh, oh yes, I do." She sat up, rubbed her eyes and yawned.

"Good morning Darlin'." Jake said and started to lean over to kiss her, but then winced. "You might have to come to me."

"Oh baby, I'm so sorry." Olivia obliged him and kissed him gently.

"I had a long talk with Sam *and* with your mom last night." She said as she got up and put on a robe.

"Oh yeah, how did that go?"

"Well. I've never had much of a mother, as you've seen, and I've never had such a friend like Sam. It helped to talk to both of them. If I'd had those two around to talk to, maybe I wouldn't have needed so many therapists or meds, who knows?"

"So no more running off in the middle of the night?"

"I promise you, I won't do that to you again."

"Good, because what you need to understand is, when you're not here everything is wrong." He said sincerely.

"I know; it's that way for me, too."

"Really?" he asked, not sure he heard her correctly.

"Yes, Jake, really, it's just so hard to process everything. What I did? I was so scared it would change how you felt about me. I was so afraid of losing you that I wanted to leave before you left me. I kept thinking, 'what if you died', 'what if because of, um, what I did to Patrick, what if you left'? I couldn't take the thought of it."

"And how do you feel now?" he asked his hand stroking her shoulder.

"And now, I know I have to be brave because I need you. I need you alive and well and by my side for always. When you were shot I didn't know if you would survive; I've never been so scared."

"I wouldn't change a thing." Jake smiled.

"Baby, how can you say that? You could have died." Olivia felt nauseous thinking about it.

"Because that monster had every intention of taking you with him and if you hadn't stopped him, there would've been no one to stop him. I couldn't, Tag couldn't. You saved me, you saved us! And you will not spend a day in jail over this, do you hear me?" Jake had needed to reassure her. He felt guilty for not saying it sooner, but he had no intention of her ever being punished for this. It was Jake's turn to feel queasy. He hated thinking of Olivia being touched again by Patrick Hanson. Jake was glad he was dead.

"I hear you. I only wish the whole thing was over. I wish none of this would have happened."

"I know, but it did and look at me, I'm fine. Aside from going out of my mind because I'm not supposed to work, I'm perfectly fine."

"Work? Jake are you crazy? You were shot, I'm pretty sure you shouldn't be out riding horses or feeding cows."

"There are other things I could do. There's no reason I couldn't be at my desk or you could get my laptop up here for me."

"Jake, the surgeon said you needed rest and that is exactly what you'll do!"

"When did you get so bossy?" he smiled.

"When I realized that I'm engaged to a stubborn man who thinks he's a super hero."

Jake laughed. He'd never seen this side of Olivia. It would have been a turn-on if he wasn't trying so hard to hide his pain from her.

"What time is Dr. Harris coming?" she asked, looking sadly at the robe she wore and the cluttered mess their bedroom had become.

"About an hour I think."

"Are you hungry? Do you want me to fix you something to eat?" Olivia asked.

"I thought you didn't cook."

"I can cook. I can't cook like Carmella, but I can cook." She retorted.

"Sorry, but how about you let Carmella make us both some breakfast and we'll eat in bed together." He suggested.

"I'm going to shower and put some real clothes on. Eat whatever you want." She said and shut the door to the bathroom.

If he was feeling better he would have thrown her over his shoulder for that little tantrum but instead, he reached for the intercom button next to the bed. "Carmella?"

"Yes Jacob, how are you feeling? Are you ready for breakfast?"

"Yes please and for Olivia, too. Have you seen Mama this morning?"

"I'm here too Jacob. You aren't overdoing it are you?"

"No, Ma'am, I'm not."

"Good. You had better be decent Jacob. I'm coming up there right now." Frankie replied.

"I'm in pajama pants. That's as decent as it's going to get this morning."

Less than a breath later, Frankie walked in the room, barely knocking. "You sound exhausted, have you taken any pain medicine this morning? I think you need more sleep. Where is Olivia?"

"She's in the shower and no I haven't taken anything this morning."

"Carmella will be up with breakfast for you both in just a bit and I spoke to Shane, he's on his way." Frankie said and began picking up the clutter in the room. She opened the curtains and hung up clothes.

"Mama, Dr. Harris isn't coming to see if my room is clean."

"I know but there's no reason for him to see a mess."

Olivia opened the bathroom door looking clean and refreshed. She wore black and green yoga pants and a matching top. Jake thought about saying something about a 'downward facing dog', but then realized she was wearing her pouty face.

"Oh Frankie, I'm so sorry. I was going to clean up in here before Dr. Harris arrived, really." She said, blushing as she noticed her bra lying on the side of the bed. She grabbed it quickly and stuffed it in a drawer.

Jake chuckled, but both women gave him unkind looks. Apparently he was the only one in a good mood this morning, though as he took a deep breath, he winced in pain and moaned slightly. He had been trying so hard not to make anything of it, but both his mother and Olivia rushed to him.

"You need a pain pill, dolce'." Frankie said reaching for the meds on the dresser.

"Yeah, I haven't had anything since last night." He admitted.

"Oh Jake, you should have said something." Olivia added.

"I didn't want you to worry Darlin'. It's just a little pain, it'll pass."

Carmella came in with breakfast on a tray. Jake ate enough to take his meds. Olivia ate like a hungry coyote. She was famished for the first time in a long time. Jake watched in amusement as his eyes became heavy. Olivia helped him ease into the pillows.

"You were hungry weren't you, Darlin'?" Jake asked sleepily.

"Well, I haven't had much of an appetite since my fiancée was shot."

Her reply was mostly lost on Jake as he fell asleep again. Olivia took their plates to the kitchen and greeted the doctor.

"Hi Dr. Harris, come in. It's nice to see you, though I wish it were under different circumstances." She said politely.

"Hello Olivia, dear. Yes, I agree but Jake is a tough kid, uh, 'man'. I guess he'll always be a kid to me."

"That's understandable."

"Is he upstairs then?" Dr. Harris asked.

"Yes, he's up in his room. He just fell asleep though."

"That's good; the rest will do him wonders. I'm not in a hurry. Perhaps you'll join me for a cup of coffee, then?"

"Yes of course. Here, just make yourself comfortable and I'll get it."

"Where are the mother hens?" Dr. Shane asked.

"They're probably watching Jake sleep, or knitting him a sweater or curing cancer. You know, it's hard to say about Frankie and Carmella!"

Dr. Shane laughed. "So Olivia, how have you been feeling? Have you had any problems since I saw you last?"

"Just some indigestion, but I think it's because of all the stress. With Jake being in the hospital, and I'm sure the whole town knows what I did, so..." Olivia didn't know how to finish that sentence. She felt like she was going through a never-ending therapy session. The one person she hadn't talked to was her therapist, but not for lack of trying. Olivia hadn't been home long enough to get in touch, or go to see Ben at his office.

"What kind of indigestion?"

"Oh, I'm sure it's nothing."

"Have you had any nausea, vomiting, or heartburn?"

"I guess a bit, but Jake was shot! He was shot, so really I'm fine. Seriously Dr. Harris, I'm not the patient here." Olivia replied more gruffly than she meant.

"I don't mean to be pushy but just make sure you're taking care of yourself. You won't be any good to Jake if you're sick. Promise me you'll let me know if the symptoms get worse or if anything changes health wise, ok?"

"Sure." Olivia replied dismissively.

"By the way, did you hear that Jake and I are engaged? She asked showing Dr. Harris her ring.

"I did hear that, from Dacey. Congratulations! You won't be leaving Troy will you?"

"No, definitely not, Montana is our home. Jake and I both love it here."

"Do you have family in Montana?"

"No, my family is in Oregon."

"They're going to miss you." Shane replied as he finished his coffee.

Olivia just smiled and nodded.

"Shall we go wake the patient?"

"I guess so; he was in a lot of pain this morning. I should've made him take his meds sooner. He tried to hide it from me." She said as they rose from their chairs.

"That sounds like Jake." Shane smiled.

"I just hope he heals and starts to feel better soon."

Dr. Harris knew she meant well. Jake wasn't a very *patient* patient. "Did you know Jake cut off his own cast when he was thirteen?"

"No, really?" Olivia replied looking at him sideways as they ascended the stairs.

"Yep, he decided it'd been on there long enough, so he and Ben Thompson took a hack saw or something to it out there in the barn. I don't think I've ever seen Dacey so mad. The funny thing was, Jake was right; the x-ray showed he was healed. If I remember correctly, Dacey still grounded him for it." Shane smiled.

Olivia quietly opened the bedroom door. She was surprised to find Jake alone. She was sure his mom or Carmella would have been in here.

"Jake? Jaaaake? Dr. Harris is here." Olivia said sweetly.

Jake's eyes opened slowly, heavily.

Although she knew how necessary they were, she hated the medications he had to take. She knew it was driving him crazy, too.

"Olivia, would you give me some time alone with Jake, just so I can examine him?" said Dr. Harris, opening his black bag.

"Yes, of course. I'm sorry." She said turning toward the door.

Without looking up, Shane said, "Not at all. Would you mind letting Dacey know I'm here?"

"Sure" she replied as she closed the door behind her. It was puzzling, but Olivia decided she wouldn't overthink it like she had been doing with everything lately.

She went to look for Dacey and maybe spend some time in the barn. The sun was shining brightly on the snow and Olivia wished she'd thought to put jeans on instead of workout clothes, and then maybe she could sneak Guiness out for a ride. She stood in the kitchen looking at the mountains as Dacey came in from outside.

"Hello" he said. "How's the patient this morning?"

"I think he's ok, in some pain, but ok. Dr. Harris is upstairs with him now. He wanted to make sure I told you he was here."

"Thank you, so how are you holding up Olivia?"

"I don't think I'm much help around here. I don't like not having a chore or something to keep me busy. The house is already decorated and I can't seem to help Jake at all. I already wrapped the presents we bought in Oregon. I don't send out Christmas cards. The studio is closed for the holidays and I feel useless.

"I think I'm just going to go out to the stables and groom the horses or something. I just need something to do." She looked at him with a half-smile on her face.

"Oh, you can't go out to the stables. With some of the storms we've had this winter, there's some structural damage that's getting repaired. It's not safe out there. Sorry."

"Great, that's just great." Olivia complained. She hated feeling trapped and this long Montana winter on top of everything that happened was making her feel suffocated.

"I have a project for you if you're interested?"

"Yes please, whatever it is, I'll do it."

"I have a whole stack of gifts to wrap and deliver. Frankie usually helps me but well, with Jake laid up in bed, she's told me I'm on my own. Anyhow, would you mind helping me with that?" Dacey asked with a grin on his face. It was Jake's grin.

"I would be happy to help you."

"That's great Olivia, thank you."

"Where are all the gifts and how will I know who gets what?" she asked.

"I'll show you. Everything is at the house in town."

"What about Jake?"

"Just tell him you're helping me and you'll be back around dinner time."

"Ok" she said grateful to feel useful.

"You can leave Jake in his mama's capable hands for today. He'll be fine." Dacey reassured her.

"Alright, I'll be right back down." She went upstairs to change and talk to Jake.

Olivia knocked lightly and leaned into the doorway. "May I come in?"

"Come in Darlin'." Jake looked up, smiling.

"I'm sorry to interrupt but I didn't want you worrying about me. I'm going to your parent's house to wrap gifts for your dad."

Jake chuckled, grinning mischievously, "So, you're this year's sucker then? And you aren't interrupting.

The Doc and I were just arguing about how long I have to stay in this dang bed."

Olivia smiled and sat next to him on the bed. "Jake" she purred "you had better do as the doctor says or I will personally chain you to this bed if I have to and I'm **not** a sucker. I'm happy to help your dad."

"You'll chain me to the bed, huh?" he said teasingly and kissed her on the lips.

Jackson had never wanted to kiss or even hug in public so this was all new to Olivia; a man who didn't care who was watching. She didn't quite know what to make of it.

She blushed as Dr. Harris cleared his throat. "Jake, let's try and keep your blood pressure down, shall we?"

"Come on, Doc. How am I supposed to keep my blood pressure in check when I'm engaged to an angel like this?" he said and kissed Olivia again, this time on the forehead and then the nose.

"Sorry Dr. Harris. Jake will behave I promise you. So how is he?" she asked.

"Well he has a serious case of stubbornitis but other than that, his recovery is coming along remarkably well. The pain and the exhaustion are normal, the stitches look good, and he has no sign of infection. Jake and I were just discussing his work when you came in."

"Doc here thinks I should let Dad take over for a month."

"Take over?" Olivia asked.

"Yes the businesses, the ranch, everything. But I didn't work my whole life to hand the reins back to Dad in his retirement just because I have an injury. I'm not calling in sick for a month Doc, hell no."

"Like I said; stubbornitis" Shane replied.

"Jake you need to listen to what Dr. Harris has to say. I want you to get better and healing takes time."

"I'll be fine Darlin', don't fret." He said as if he was speaking to a child.

It pissed her off. "Don't patronize me Jake. If you don't give yourself enough time to heal properly then you're going to end up feeling worse. But you know what, do what you want. You will anyway. Dr. Harris is right. You are stubborn, a stubborn ass." She threw her hands in the air, hopped off the bed, grabbed some different clothes and hurried into the bathroom. She didn't exactly slam the door, but her point was made.

She wasn't going to sit there and argue with her fiancée while he acted like a dumb jock.

Olivia walked out of the bathroom all changed and glared at Jake who grinned happily at her.

Dr. Harris just rubbed his temples. She walked up to Jake and kissed his cheek. "Not that you ever *need* anyone but if you happen to need me, I'll be at your parent's house. I love you." She turned sharply and headed out.

"Darlin' wait." Jake said, unable to stop his laughter from escaping.

"Do you *need* something?" she asked haughtily, flipping her hair over her shoulder.

"Yeah, would you ask Carmella to make me a grilled cheese sandwich before you go?" he smiled, oozing charm.

"Ugh!" she yelled in frustration as she slammed the bedroom door. He was the most infuriating, obstinate, charming pain in the...

"Ugh!" she yelled again from the hallway. She could hear Jake's laughter as she made her way downstairs. She shot one more look of disgust toward the ceiling and ran right into Dacey.

"Is Jake alright? What's wrong?" he asked, concerned.

"Yes, he's fine. I'm fine. Sorry."

"Ok, well here's the key to the house, just make yourself at home there. All the gifts, tags and names are in the study and there is a list of who gets what. If you have any questions, just give me a call."

"Ok" she replied. "It sounds easy enough."

"Thank you again for doing this." Dacey said politely.

Olivia smiled but said nothing more. She considered mentioning the grilled cheese sandwich to Carmella but decided Jake could press the button on the intercom just as easily as she could deliver the message. Besides, Olivia needed to get outside for a while. She realized in that moment Jake felt the same way, but there was nothing she could do about that, not now.

"As she pulled her Jeep out of the garage, she saw a truck coming. Olivia stopped and rolled down the window.

"Where are you off to?" Sam asked her.

"I'm going to Jake's parent's house to wrap gifts for Mr. Weidner."

"So you're the sucker this year, huh?" Sam laughed.

"I am *not* a sucker! What is the big deal?" Olivia said for the second time this morning.

"Nothing, there's just a lot of gifts. Trust me; I've done that job before. It's sweet of you to help out, though. In fact, when I'm done here, I'll stop by and help too, if you want?" Sam offered.

"That would be great. I would love the company. I need to thank you too, for what you said last night. I needed someone to set me straight. Jake and I are better, or at least we would be if he would listen to Dr. Harris's orders."

Sam smiled. She knew Jake too well. If he were forced to be stuck in bed too long, he would start tearing the room apart or worse, Olivia. "He's never taken doctor's orders in his life, why would he start now? But don't worry, if he's dishing crap to Doc then he's probably starting to feel better."

"I guess you're right, it's just so frustrating. He's such a pain in the ass."

"Yep, and you love him." Sam teased.

"Yes I do." Olivia sighed and smiled. "I'd better go."

"Ok, I'll be there in a bit."

Sam went in the house after a brief knock on the kitchen door. There was no answer, and even stranger than that, there was no Carmella.

"Hellooo," she called out happily. Samantha had always loved Christmas especially at the Weidner home, and this year was no exception. She noticed the dogs even had on shiny, red and green Christmas collars. Sam patted their heads and went to find her surrogate family.

She passed by the library and saw Frankie. "Hello, Frankie."

"Hi Sam."

"Where is everyone today?" Sam asked.

"Dacey and Dr. Harris are in the office. Carmella ran to the store for a few odds and ends and Jake is pretending he isn't working on his phone, but he doesn't fool me. And I haven't got a clue where Olivia is hiding out."

Sam laughed, "I just saw Olivia. She's on her way to your house. She's Dacey's elf this year."

"That man! I tell him every year just to pay someone to do all that wrapping or start earlier so he could do a little at a time, but does he listen? No. He always waits until the last minute. I told him this year I was not doing it."

"That's ok, I think Olivia needed a distraction and I told her I'd help her.

~ 420 ~

When we're done wrapping, I can help her deliver too, if you want?" Sam offered.

"Would you? That would be so helpful. I'm sure Dacey didn't really show her what needed to be done."

"I don't mind. I'm just going to visit with Jake for a little while and then I'll go over there."

"Thank you, Samantha."

"You're welcome."

The door to Jake's room was open, so Sam didn't bother knocking. Jake was engrossed in his laptop computer he had obviously snuck in somehow.

"Aren't you supposed to be resting?"

"I find this very restful." He replied, not looking up.

"How are you today, lover boy?" Sam teased.

"You know how I am. I hate this. I'm stuck here in this **damn** bed. Olivia's pissed off at me. I'm not supposed to be doing anything. I'm bored. There's nothing on TV. I'm going stir crazy already! We've got clients coming to the Outfitter's right after Christmas that will expect to meet me." He complained. "We're supposed to be starting part of the herd on that new supplement and I can't even supervise. I have a meeting scheduled in Victoria just after New Year's and Doc wants me to take a month off. This sucks and I'm grumpy. That's how I am!" he ranted.

Sam smiled and shrugged her shoulders. "Ce la vie."

Jake laughed. "Sorry, I guess I needed to vent."

"No biggie, but isn't this a very similar predicament to what Liv went through not very long ago? Being stuck in bed?"

"Yeah, and she didn't even make it a week before she went back to work. No one stopped *her*." He countered.

"I bet you gave it your best shot though, didn't you?"

"Yeah, but she's just as stubborn as I am."

"Speaking of which, I can't keep putting bandages on your relationship, Mr. Weidner. You're going to have to pull your head outta your ass."

"I know, I know, I should have talked to her before but I was having a hard time with everything that happened. It was intense. We talked a lot of things out though. We're ok now. I just hate being stuck in bed. I feel like I can't do anything." Jake explained, and then smirked at what he'd said.

"Oh my God, you're such a perv. Just out of curiosity though, how long before you can, you know?"

"Have sex? Doc says a month, and I say he's crazy. It probably won't bother Olivia as much as it bothers me."

"Then you're the crazy one. Have you not noticed how she looks at you? That's probably part of the reason she's been grumpy lately, too."

"Yeah maybe, but she's a woman and women don't think about sex the same way men do."

"Well you're a man and men are idiots. Just because we don't have a physical barometer for our sexual excitement doesn't mean we don't feel it."

"What?" Jake asked, only half listening.

"A dick, Jake! Just because we don't have a dick that gets hard every time the wind picks up, doesn't mean we don't have desires."

Jake laughed. He appreciated Sam for many reasons, but most of all he appreciated her no bullshit way of putting things. She laughed, too. If he didn't have a hole in his shoulder, she would happily smack him.

"So, what are you working on the day before Christmas eve?" she said, changing the subject.

"I'm just returning some emails about this Victoria deal. Also, payroll didn't get done at The Boot Barn because Pamela is out of town for the holidays. I need to get everyone their paychecks."

"Here, let me do that. I'm better at it anyway." Sam said and took his computer. She walked it over to the bench near the window and began clicking the keys. "So how did you manage to get your hands on your laptop?" she asked casually.

"I snuck downstairs to my office in the middle of the night and hid it under the bed. There's nothing wrong with my legs, ya know?" Jake grumbled.

"I know. You're a machine. Hush while I finish this up." Sam smirked.

So again, Jake was left with nothing to do. He sighed deeply and a sharp thread of pain ran through his shoulder into his neck. Even though the doctor said it was normal, Jake detested feeling less than one hundred percent. Samantha tapped away on his computer so Jake decided to call Olivia. He wished he would have asked her to stay.

He felt like they hadn't spent any time together and when they did, it seemed as though they didn't talk as much as pick at each other like two kids on a playground, or maybe he was the one doing the picking. He felt another sharp pain and although he hated the thought, it was time for another pain pill. He took one then dialed up Olivia from the house phone.

"Hello?" she answered.

"Hello Darlin'. I was just calling to tell you I miss you."

"You do huh? I find that hard to believe." She said sharply.

"Of course, I miss you and I love you. You know I was just teasing about the whole grilled cheese thing, don't you?"

I know and I love you, too. I just need to feel useful right now. I can't help you and I hate that there is nothing I can do for you." She sighed.

"Just having you around helps me. Why don't you tell Dad you can't do it, and come home to me."

"Jake, I can't do that to your dad, besides, I'm making some good progress. This shouldn't take too long and I will come home to you just as soon as I can. Hey, if Sam is still there, will you ask her to bring more tape? I'm running out."

"Sure" he said sadly.

"Jake, if that's Liv, tell her we're going to do some deliveries after we're done wrapping." Sam interrupted.

"Sam says the two of you are delivering the gifts, too. What about me?" Jake asked, and Sam rolled her eyes.

"I guess you'll have to make do without me." Olivia whispered, "Sorry Sweetheart."

"This blows." Jake complained.

"You're such a baby," Olivia teased. "But I promise you tomorrow, you and me, all day."

"I'm going to hold you to that. I love you so much Olivia."

"Jake, relax now, I love you, too." She replied and hung up. Olivia had been in a strange, undefinable mood since she spoke to Dr. Harris. She looked around at the piles of gifts, many wrapped now, but many more still unwrapped and decided not to think about what was bothering her...not now, or at least, not yet.

The Weidner's home was completely quiet. Would she and Jake someday move into this house too and leave the ranch to their own child? Would there be a child? Olivia balked at the direction of her thoughts. Guilt overwhelmed her.

There was so much to feel guilty about. And it seemed she was good at it.

She wanted to talk to someone about this but there really wasn't anyone who wouldn't judge her, except...

She dialed the phone as she continued wrapping gifts, it rang in her ear.

"Hello."

"Ben, its Olivia. I'm sorry to call like this on your cell, but I need to talk to someone."

"I'm actually in my office, did you want to drop by?"

"You're there now?"

"Yes, did you want to come in for a session? I called, spoke to Jake and suggested we have another session. Didn't he tell you?"

"No, he probably forgot."

"I'm sure. Are you working or free to come over and we'll talk?" Olivia didn't want to lie to Jake and she didn't want to let Dacey down either, but she was really feeling stressed and could use some perspective and hopefully some objectivity.

"Ok, I'm in town now, but I can't stay long."

"That works for me, too. I have family in town for Christmas."

"I'll see you in a few minutes."

THERAPY SESSION VI

"Have a seat." Ben met her to unlock his office door.

"Thank you."

"I can fix some coffee? What would you like to talk about?"

Olivia shook her head but felt like she could burst into tears. "I, um, I've been thinking about children a lot. My fiancée was shot just over a week ago and already I'm thinking about kids. There must be something wrong with that. Isn't there?"

"Not necessarily. Perhaps it's because of what happened to Jake that you *are* thinking about children. Have you and Jake talked about having kids?"

"No. But, I'm around a lot of kids at Tempo and I miss Dante' so much. Maybe you're right. Maybe it's because Jake was shot, but there is something else."

"What do you mean?"

"I don't know." She just looked confused.

"Ok, we'll leave that for now. How are you feeling about what happened in the diner?"

"I still f--feel guilty. I worried that Jake wouldn't want to be with me, you know, after, after what I did. And then, he and I finally talked about it and he's been really supportive. I just don't want it to be something that keeps coming back to haunt us. Do you know what I mean?"

"I think so. If you could say something about it, what would you say? What haven't you said out loud?"

"Oh, God. That I'm a murderer?"

"Is that how you see what happened?"

The tears started to come. "Maybe?" she replied quietly.

"Murder is not the same as self-defense, Olivia."

"Except I wasn't defending myself, I was blinded by rage and fury and fear. Patrick Hanson wouldn't have killed me, he..."

"He what?"

"He loved me in some sick, twisted way. I think he loved me."

"He tried to kill you once before, Olivia. What makes you think he wouldn't have hurt you again? Did he hurt you? Did he hurt Jake?"

"Yes, but he would have let me live, made me suffer."

"The answer is still the same. You would never have done what you did if you hadn't watched him shoot Jake. Were you planning on finding Patrick Hanson and hunting him down like a dog?"

"No, but I still killed a man and that's so awful..." She panted and gasped for air.

"I've seen the police reports Olivia and I don't think what happened was your fault."

"I didn't stop after he was dead. I didn't, I couldn't stop."

"You broke, but you can also mend."

"I don't feel mended."

"In time you will. Remember what I told you before about healing? You and Jake *both* have to heal and be patient with the healing process. It won't happen overnight, you know. I understand he's been his usual handful."

"Who told you that?"

"It's a small town Olivia and Carmella loves me." Ben smiled.

"I shudder to think what this town says about me, especially now." She half smiled.

"I wouldn't worry too much about it. A person can drive themselves crazy worrying too much about what other people think."

"Yes I suppose you're right." She was beginning to numb herself to the "crazy" word, having heard it so many times before.

She replied, thinking hard about what she was about to say. "Patrick Hanson was Jackson's cousin. He told me so. Did you know that?"

"No, but I honestly don't think it changes anything. Regardless of their family connection and even regardless of whether or not they somehow plotted against you together, none of that changes the facts. Honestly, I think it explains a lot about why Jackson was the person you described." Ben explained.

"I feel like I should have known. I've known so much ahead of time and I know you think that was all about my delusions but Doc, it can't be. I promise you I knew Dante' would be killed. I promise you I saw myself coming to Troy and even predicted that Jake would be hurt. I didn't tell you before because I was so scared you would think me crazy." There was that word again.

Her pulse raced. "Every time I tell someone about my visions, they blame drugs or a delusional disorder, or some other nonsense." She explained keeping her voice level.

"Olivia, how long have you been feeling this way?"

"What do you mean?"

"Did you lie to your doctors in order to get out of the state hospital?"

"No" she lied again.

"You were diagnosed with mixed delusional disorder. That can seem exceptionally real.

It may be you need to continue some sort of drug regimen. And I think it's important we contact your family as well."

"I'm not going back! You don't believe what I saw was real either or that I predicted bad things happening, fine! But I'm not going back to that fucking hospital! Jake would never let that happen."

"I'm not suggesting that; but Olivia I need you to separate delusions from reality."

"You couldn't humor me, even for a second?" she asked sadly, feeling suddenly very close to a breakdown.

"Fine, let's pretend for arguments sake, you 'predicted' Jake being hurt. Why didn't you push him out of the way? Why didn't you know Patrick would be carrying a gun? Why didn't you know he'd show up at the diner?"

"The visions aren't that detailed. I didn't know what town he would be in! I didn't see a weapon! All I saw was Jake, covered in blood and he fell! It's not like watching a movie!"

"I don't think this is productive. You need to remember that delusions are not predictions."

"So you don't believe me?" she asked, not really surprised. It was always the final kick in the gut of the curse; after seeing the horror that would come, to **never** be believed.

"No I don't. I'm sorry. I think because of this recent traumatic event, you have slipped into old habits. That's why I think we should consider drug therapy again and continued regular outpatient therapy."

"I can't take the drugs."

"What do you mean?" he asked. "Are you concerned about side effects?"

Olivia sat looking at her engagement ring.

She should just admit to Ben, the one person who was bound not to say anything, the main reason she came today. "Jake and I aren't married yet."

"I didn't think you were. What is it? What are we talking about here?" Ben pushed, looking perplexed.

"I think I might be pregnant." She said heavily.

Ben didn't know exactly what to say. There was still some disappointment even though his chances with Olivia had gone away the moment she met Jake Weidner. He took a deep breath and continued. "How do you know? Have you taken a pregnancy test?"

"No, but stupid Dr. Harris keeps asking me how I'm feeling and then when I'm forced to think about it, I realize I've had some nausea lately and I've been even more emotional than usual and I'm late, you know? I don't know what to do."

"Well, for arguments sake, what if you are? What do you see happening?"

"I think Jake would be happy. I think I would feel guilty and scared and maybe like I somehow dishonored Dante's memory. I think I would be really disappointed in myself for not doing all this in the proper order. I mean, aren't I supposed to fall in love, get married, and *then* have a baby?"

"Sure, in some magical fairyland that's exactly how it happens. But life rarely follows our plans. We all have that same plan in our head, Olivia, but nobody lives a life that goes according to plan."

"Mine certainly hasn't." she agreed.

"So maybe it's time to throw the plan in the trash and start accepting your current reality; beginning with finding out whether or not there is a baby. You can't decide anything without all the information."

"Yeah, you're right." Olivia replied, biting her lip.

"You said Jake would be happy and you would feel guilty. Isn't it possible you would feel happy, too?" he prodded.

"I don't know. What if I had another boy? What if something happened to him, too? I don't think I could handle that."

"I understand, but that's a whole lot of 'what ifs'. Just remember the circumstances surrounding having a child now are completely different than what you experienced before, therefore *everything* will be different, including how you handle things. Your choices are different."

"Shouldn't I feel guilty about giving this hypothetical child a better life than what I could give Dante'?"

"You've answered your own question."

"What do you mean?"

"I mean, you said 'what I *could* give Dante'. You gave Dante' the best you could at the time. So no, you shouldn't feel guilty. Just like you shouldn't feel guilty for surviving. I believe your son loved you and would want you to live your life to the fullest. You dishonor him only when you *aren't* doing that. You see, guilt is of no use."

Olivia looked up as silent tears started to flow. He was right. Again she was being reminded of her son's beautiful spirit by people who didn't even know him. She needed to honor her son by truly living.

"I'm sorry. I lied to you. I really thought I was doing the right thing. But now you see why I can't go on drugs again. I can't. If there is a baby, I can't do that to him, or um, her."

"You're forgiven; now stop beating yourself up for every little thought." Ben smiled.

"Jake said that too. Oh gosh," she looked at her watch. "I have to go. I'm sorry. Merry Christmas, Ben." She said, standing up to leave, then changed her mind and hugged him. Ben was taken off guard by it but hugged her back.

"Merry Christmas, Olivia. I want to see you back here after the holidays. And I want to know the results so we can get you started on some new meds if we can. Don't hesitate to call if you need me before then."

"Thank you." she replied. "Can I tell you one more thing?"

"Of course you can." He smiled.

"I think you need to call Sarea Scott."

"Olivia, I don't..."

She interrupted, "I know I probably shouldn't say this, but you have unfinished business, too. I can feel it." Olivia said, placing her hand on his arm.

"Let's focus on you, ok?"

"Just think about it."

As she left, Ben watched her walk out into the cold, mountain air. He wished things had been different. He wished he had spent more time at Maggie's and been the one to meet Olivia first. He wished he could say Olivia was wrong about him and Sarea. But she wasn't. He ached. Olivia had never been his and sadly, neither had Sarea Scott. He decided right then, it *was* time to find her and mend old wounds, once and for all.

CHAPTER THIRTY-THREE

Olivia returned to the Weidner's home just as Sam was pulling in the driveway behind her.

"Where did you go?" Sam asked jumping out of her truck.

"I, uh, just um, I needed to go get something to eat."

"Oh, what did you get?"

"Energy bar, but I ate it already."

"Oh, well thanks for getting me one." Sam teased.

"Sorry."

"It's ok, I was just teasing. So how are the elf duties going?"

"Good, I'm almost done. He had a lot of gift bags so there wasn't much more wrapping involved. I'm glad you brought more tape," she said seeing the package in Sam's hand.

"That's great, because we need to try and deliver as many as we can tonight. I already called ahead to most of them to see who was available."

"Oh, that's a good idea." Olivia answered, still trying to recover as she opened the door and switched on the lights in the den. "How is Jake?"

"He's grumpy, bored and pouting because you and I both left him alone with his mom." Sam laughed.

Olivia laughed, too. "I do feel a little guilty about that, it's just, there's nothing I can do for him."

"You don't have to tell me! I offered to play some cards with him and he wasn't having it, then I suggested he take a nap and he nearly bit my head off. So, I finished the Boot Barn payroll for him made what phone calls I could and then left."

"Great, so now I know what I have to look forward to tomorrow. I told him we would spend the day together."

"He'll probably be fine. He just hates being stuck in bed, but if you're in bed with him..." Sam teased.

"I was thinking I might play piano for him."

"I'm sure he would love that. He loves everything you do."

Olivia snorted. "No, he doesn't."

"Ok, maybe not everything but he is sort of a mush-ball around you. When I told him I was coming over here, he looked like the kid who got picked last on the playground.

He wanted to come but Frankie wouldn't let him." Sam smiled.

"I just hope he heals quickly or he is going to drive everyone nuts."

"Is something wrong Liv? You look like, like the holiday blues."

"Just anxiety I think, and I'm still just freaked out and sad. I should be happy right? I'm going to marry the man of my dreams but everything else still sucks. I hate that my son can't be here. I hate every breath without him and on top of everything; I think I might be..." she stopped, wishing she could reel the words back into her mouth. Her hand flew up to her mouth as if she could stop what she had just said.

"Are you pregnant? I mean, are you? That's what you were going to say, isn't it?" Sam's eyes grew wide.

Olivia nodded with her hand still over her mouth. She took a moment, and then finally replied. "Please don't say anything. I'm so freaked out! Nothing is going like I thought it would. Oh God, I don't even know if I am, so please, please don't say anything."

"Don't you want to find out? I could be back here in five minutes with a pregnancy test." Sam said, smiling.

Olivia didn't think there was anything to smile about. What she needed was for life to slow down, not speed up. What she needed was boring, not this potential new drama.

"No, no, I don't, I just don't want to think about this, now. I'm dealing with one thing after another and I'm seriously at the end of my rope. I just cannot deal with this right now, I can't." Olivia sounded completely frantic.

"Liv, calm down. How can you spend any time alone with Jake and not tell him something like this?" Sam asked, as if it were obvious.

"Because there is nothing to tell. I don't know. I honestly don't know. It's probably too early."

"Olivia, just pee on a stick and get it over with. At least then you'll know one way or another." Sam said seriously.

Olivia sighed again deeply. Lately she felt like she just couldn't catch her breath. She didn't want to know, not yet.

The thought of facing something new made her feel very, very tired. Right now she had the urge to crawl in bed with Jake and sleep for a month. Then maybe she would be ready to face this; if there was a 'this' to face. But these things never waited, just like the rest of her life. Life wouldn't wait.

"Fine, go get a damn test before I change my mind."

Sam practically sprinted out the door. She worried Olivia had the potential to bolt and leave Jake and somehow a baby might be the one thing that would make her stay for good. She wouldn't admit it but after Olivia showed up at her house the way she did, well, it made her more concerned than ever for Jake's heart.

Olivia was left alone again with her thoughts and worse, her fears, but not for long. Sam came back in the door just as jazzed as when she left and this time she was holding a paper bag.

Olivia wondered if soon *she* would be left holding the bag. "I changed my mind." She looked up at Sam, clearly panicked.

"Olivia Curtis, you **will** grow some balls and take this test! Mrs. Milton at the store has probably called fifty of her closest friends by now to inform them that *I* am the one who is pregnant. If I can subject my nearly spotless reputation to that kind of gossip, then you can damn well pee on a stick and see if it's to be champagne or apple cider for you!" Sam yelled.

"Oh my God," Olivia complained. "You are such a bitch! Fine, give me the test." She said and held out her hand like she was ready to accept her punishment.

Sam handed her the bag and stood with her arms crossed, looking stern. "Yes, I'm a bitch, shocking." Sam said sarcastically.

Olivia couldn't help it and started to giggle. She wasn't sure if it was honest humor or just nervous energy.

"What's so funny?" Sam asked.

"You told me to grow some balls." She said laughing harder.

"Ok so grow some metaphorical balls, then." Sam laughed, too.

"It's better to know, right?" Olivia asked at last.

"It's *definitely* better to know." Sam replied.

The next few minutes felt like an eternity to Sam and Olivia felt as she was awaiting her execution. Her heart pounded. This wasn't what she had planned; she hadn't planned any of this. She kept reminding herself what Ben had said, 'guilt was of no use'.

Olivia whispered a prayer. "Dear Lord, I know I don't deserve your mercy, but I figure this is as good a time as any to tell you, I'm not sure I can handle this. Maybe it sounds strange coming from me because somehow I've handled everything else. Well, I haven't handled as much as survived, but somehow I'm still here. Lord, please don't give me anything else to survive. I'm spent, I'm exhausted and I don't know if I can take much more. I am here in spite of being raped, in spite of my crazy mother.

I survived being a single mom, marrying an asshole, losing my angel-son, and nearly losing Jake. I have survived taking someone's life and I still don't know how to wrap my head around that. I have survived this wretched curse and I can't deal with anything else. I want to be Jake's wife and then, maybe, someday, decide to get pregnant. I don't think I'm as strong as you think I am. Amen."

"Liv? Well?" Sam asked through the bathroom door.

"I don't think I can look."

"Oh for crying out loud!" Sam yelled.

Without looking at the results, Olivia stuffed the test back in its wrapper and put the whole thing in her pocket. She would look, just not yet. She washed her hands, looked at her haggard face in the mirror then came out of the bathroom with the paper carton in hand. No way was Mr. or Mrs. Weidner going to find a pregnancy test in their trashcan.

"Did you look?" Sam asked.

"No, not yet; I will, just not yet, ok?"

"Samantha felt like tackling her and stealing the test. She detested waiting for anything. "Ok, but when are you going to look?" she asked, not able to understand Olivia right now. Who wouldn't want to know?

"I don't know, maybe after Christmas." Olivia replied, biting her lip again.

"If you're pregnant though, wouldn't you want to tell Jake on Christmas?" Sam asked, trying a new approach.

"He isn't supposed to do anything to raise his blood pressure. Come on; let's finish wrapping and get all this done." Olivia replied as calmly as she could manage.

"The suspense is killing me. Just so you know. How is it *not* killing you?" Sam asked.

"It is, but I don't know what I want the answer to be. Can we just work, please?"

"Sure" she said sounding angry "we can work. Jake was right, you are **really** stubborn! You two ought to get along swell!"

Olivia ignored the comment and went to work. She didn't feel like talking about this anymore. She and Sam didn't speak at all. Olivia felt like she should apologize but wondered if Sam would understand. The only apology Sam was looking for would be hearing Olivia read the results of the test.

As they finished the wrapping, Sam began to load the gifts in her truck. Olivia tried to help but Sam stopped her.

"I'll get this. You should go on home."

"Sam, I..."

"Don't, ok? Just don't. Because here's the thing, whether you know it or not or whether you appreciate it or not, you are living the dream. All the bad stuff that happened to you before, all of it; it's over. Now, you have a chance at a new beginning, the kind of life that most women only dream of, and you're standing there staring at it like you aren't sure what to do with it." Sam set her jaw and her eyes drilled into Olivia's face. "You might be pregnant by a man who has literally taken a bullet for you and happens to think sunshine shoots right out of your ass, and for some unfathomable reason, you're too afraid to read the damn test. I don't get it. I don't fucking get it. Do you have any idea what it would mean to me to be in love and have a baby? By being this gutless, you piss on every woman who has never had what you have and wishes with every fiber inside her that she did!" Sam yelled.

"Fine! You're always so sure of yourself, right? You and Jake, my mother, Jackson, Miles, all the damn doctors including Ben; you're all so sure you know what it feels like to be me. You all seem to think you know what's best and how I should live my life, fine! Here!" Olivia yelled back at Sam and threw the test at her. "Here, Miss I'm-right-all-the-time-about-everything! You look!"

Sam grabbed the test before it hit the floor and yelled back at Olivia. "Fine, I will!" Sam didn't want to admit just how jealous she was. She and Miles had chemistry, but Olivia's brother didn't seem interested in anything more than a little casual fun. Miles didn't look at her the way Jake looked at Olivia.

Jake was her best friend in the whole world and he was truly and deeply in love. If Olivia was pregnant, he would love that baby fiercely. He would be a great dad and she could only hope that Olivia could appreciate him.

Sam looked at the test. She wasn't a mushy girl. She wasn't someone who cried at the drop of a hat. She had spent all her time around cowboys and horses and had very little need for tears. She left the emotional sappy junk to women like Olivia, but now as she looked down at the result of Olivia's pregnancy test, big crocodile tears ran down her cheeks. "Liv, you're pregnant." She whispered through a tear-soaked smile.

She moved closer and hugged Olivia. "I'm sorry for yelling at you." Sam said sincerely.

"I deserved it."

"Yes you did. Are you ok?" she asked and squeezed Olivia's hand.

"Can I have the test?" Olivia asked, ignoring the question.

"Of course you can, here. I'm really sorry. I shouldn't have blown up at you that way. I guess I was just..."

"Jealous?"

"Yeah, I was, I am, but not because of Jake, I mean, Liv, I really don't have a thing for him I promise you. It's just what you and Jake have together. I hope you recognize how special it is." Sam admitted. "When are you going to tell him?"

"I know how special it is. Olivia crossed her arms. She had decided this subject was closed. Her mind shut the door on it. "Let's get moving ok? Are you going to let me help you?"

The day had turned to evening as the two women delivered Christmas gifts around town. Neither of them said anything more about babies. Olivia was relieved. She truly wanted *not* to think about it for a while, even if it was only for a couple hours.

Olivia got to see firsthand just how much of Troy was influenced by the Weidner family and by the generosity of Dacey and Frankie Weidner.

She was sure by the time she and Sam finished deliveries, she'd met almost everyone who lived here. Sam kept introducing her to people as Jake's fiancée. Most were warm and friendly, though a couple women in town gave Olivia the cold shoulder. She wondered if Jake's whole romantic past lived right her in Troy. She certainly hoped not.

"Do you think Jake will be happy?" Olivia finally asked Sam.

"Do you mean about the baby?" Sam paused, trying to be sensitive to Olivia. "Yes, without a doubt. He will be delirious."

"Sam thanks; I'm sorry about our fight. I'm just not very brave, I guess."

"Don't be silly Liv, you *are* brave and that was not a fight. Can I tell you something?"

"Of course."

"I wasn't too sure about you, not at first. I kept seeing Jake walk around with that dopey look on his face and I felt like smacking it off him; but now I am, and not just because of a baby. I want you to know that."

Sam looked straight ahead and kept driving. "Jake and I, we're more than friends; he's the brother I never had. His family is my family and I've never seen him like this. He's a better man because of you. He's focused, driven, and passionate and he's always been that way about his family and his work, but now he's that way about you, too. It's kind of a big deal. I just thought you should know." She parked the truck back in the Weidner's driveway.

"Don't make me cry." Olivia said, but it was too late. "Thank you for everything. We will see you on Christmas?" Olivia asked, wiping the tears away.

"No, I'm heading to Kalispell. My parents live there but I'll be back on Wednesday; the Outfitter's has some new clients and I need to be here for that."

"Have a Merry Christmas and drive carefully, then."

"You have a Merry Christmas, too and Liv, don't worry, it's not good for the baby! Just tell my best friend he's going to be a daddy and if for some reason he doesn't respond like I think he will, I'll knock some sense into him when I get back."

"Ok." Olivia smiled and squeezed Sam's arm and whispered, "Sam, thank you." She shut the door of the truck and watched as she drove away.

It was way after dark and she was kind of surprised she hadn't heard from Jake again. Maybe he was angry with her. She really hoped not. She already felt the pangs of nausea and couldn't tell if it was from the baby or her own anxiety.

"The baby" she said out loud, feeling the words in her mouth, gently laying a hand on her tummy. "You are going to be quite the Christmas surprise, aren't you?"

The drive home to the ranch seemed especially short this time. For a moment she wished for a summer road with the top down and a long drive in front of her. She needed time to clear her head and tackle this fear but instead she pulled onto the driveway at the ranch and hoped that somehow she could keep it together. Jake deserved that and so much more.

She had promised Jake and his mother things would be better. She had said no games, and no running. This feeling in her stomach made her want to run more than ever but that thought made her sick, too. There were still no easy answers, not yet. She'd planned on parking in the garage but the opener wasn't working, so she parked out front instead and looked at the time on her phone.

"Ten thirty; maybe Jake would be sleeping." She thought hopefully. That thought gave her a guilty twinge, but she just wasn't ready to talk about this again yet, not with Jake.

Sam was right about a lot of things today, but not about Olivia being brave. She never could get a grip on things. Maybe Ben was right. Maybe if she wrote this all down, maybe if she could stop the guilt; but, he didn't believe her either. She was either falling backward into things or grasping too tightly to things that seemed to slip away no matter what she did. She wanted control. "God, something in my life, could I just get something under my control, but nothing…." A tear slid down her cheek as she walked into the house. She quickly wiped it away and was greeted by Harper.

"Hi girl" she whispered, picking her up. "Is everyone sleeping?" She set her back down on the floor and watched as she returned to her spot next to Whitman on his bed. Whitman had only lifted his head with recognition and little interest in anything other than sleep.

Upstairs she opened the bedroom door and saw the bedside lamp was still on. Jake was lying down with his back to the door so she couldn't tell if he was sleeping or not. She began to undress. With Jake's family all ascending tomorrow, she knew better than to sleep naked next to him, just in case someone decided to barge in tomorrow morning.

She washed her face and brushed her teeth. She considered showering too, but changed her mind. Sleep was calling her; at least she hoped it was. She could do without another sleepless night or worse, a night filled with bad dreams. She crawled into bed and Jake's eyes opened halfway.

"Hey Darlin' how did it go?" he yawned, clearly tired and likely drugged.

"Fine; Sam and I got it all done. Some people were out of town already, but we got most of the deliveries made. Sam's a jewel, you know?" Olivia answered quietly.

It felt strange to have small talk with Jake right now. She leaned in closer to kiss him. She needed to give her mouth something else to do.

Jake smiled. "Uh huh, I'm so glad you're home. I love you. "I love you, too." In that moment she considered just telling him everything but then his eyes fluttered closed again. She kissed him lightly on his injured shoulder as she reached to shut off the lamp. It would all wait.

CHAPTER THIRTY-FOUR

Olivia opened her eyes to the bright morning. Gratefully she'd had a heavy and dreamless sleep. She felt good, strong and rested but as she stretched, the morning sickness overtook her and she rushed into the bathroom. She hadn't noticed the door was closed but as she opened it, there stood Jake.

She couldn't even say hello. Her hand was clamped over her mouth and though she wished she could kick him out and wait until he was gone, her body would not allow it. She rushed past him and vomited in the toilet while he brushed his teeth. There was a look of concern and disbelief on his face.

"Olivia, are you alright?"

She couldn't talk as she heaved again. She finally replied, "Yes, I'm alright", wiping her face and flushing the toilet.

"Merry Christmas, I'm pregnant." She blurted out. She walked back into the bedroom and crawled onto the bed, pulling the covers up over her face.

Jake's limbs wouldn't move. His entire world was spinning without him, or he was spinning and the world had stopped. He couldn't be sure. He rinsed his toothbrush and walked slowly into the bedroom and sat carefully on the bed. He was irritated by how slowly he had to do everything, or "maybe I'm just numb"? He wondered. The covers over Olivia shook with her sobs. He pulled them back to see big tears on her flushed face. She couldn't look at him so she covered her eyes with both hands.

"Pregnant?" he asked, making sure he'd heard.

"Uh huh" she moaned. She clapped her hand over her mouth immediately and flew again for the bathroom. She ran water over her face and rinsed her mouth. She slowly came back across the room, all the color washed from her face.

Then it hit him, rather like a ton of bricks. "I'm going to be a daddy." Olivia was pregnant with his child. "Darlin' that's amazing, that's wonderful. I can't even tell you...I am just so...I," he didn't know quite what to say, so instead he kissed her hands that still covered her face.

"So you're happy then?" she asked nervously peeking through her hands.

"Darlin', I'm more than happy. Whatever the word is for a hundred times beyond happy, that's what I am." Jake replied excitedly.

"Jake," she whined his name.

"You aren't happy!" he said it as a statement.

"I haven't gotten to happy, yet. I'm still stuck at the corner of nervous and freaked out." She burst into loud, dramatic sobs. Jake wanted to laugh but he thought it might make it worse.

"So, is this hormone tears?" He asked unsure.

If he hadn't already been injured she would like to pummel him with her fists. Instead she just continued to cry.

"Darlin' this is a good thing. You are going to be such an amazing mom to our child. We're going to be married and we're a family. It's a good thing."

She sat up and leaned on his uninjured shoulder. "I, but the timing isn't really great, is it? I wanted to get married, and *then* have a baby. This time, I just wanted to do it right. I wanted to be um, traditional." She sniffled.

Jake turned to kiss her forehead. "I know Darlin', really I do, but it's still going to be incredible. We'll wait until the baby is born and then we'll have the wedding."

"No, no I don't want that." She said seriously, almost inspired. Jake could see her wheels turning.

"What do you want, Darlin'? You can have this however you like. I just want you to be happy."

"I know and I'm grateful. I sound like such a spoiled brat."

"I don't think you've been spoiled enough really. So how do you want to do this?"

She looked into his warm brown eyes and could see herself reflected back. She should, at the very least, get on board the happy train with him, but all she felt was tension. "What do you mean?"

Jake leaned back on the pillows and pulled her with him. It wasn't without some serious effort but he was tired of resting. He wanted to properly hold his obviously distraught fiancée.

"I mean we're engaged and we have a baby on the way. When do we tell everyone about the baby and shouldn't we set a date for the wedding?" he asked, unable to keep the smile from his face.

Olivia felt dueling urges; one to smack him and the other to make love to him. Jake was just too charming for *her* own good. She kissed his bare chest gently and lightly ran her fingers over the bandaged shoulder.

"I don't want to tell anybody about the baby, yet. I haven't even seen a doctor. As for setting the date, what if we just had a surprise wedding on New Year's Eve, at the ball? Everyone will already be here." Olivia suggested.

"Darlin', we don't have that kind of time. New Year's Eve is only a week away." Jake said reasonably.

"Of course we do. What do you need to get married? The house is already decorated. People will already be here. I'll already be in a gown. We would need a, a license and a pastor. That's it! Unless..."

"Unless what?"

"Unless you don't want to marry me," she turned her eyes up to him for reassurance.

"What? Darlin' I'd marry you right now if that's what you want."

"You would?"

"Yes definitely. Let's do it. But we're going to need some help and I know just the people to recruit for this." Jake said, reaching for his phone.

"Wait" Olivia said and grabbed his hand.

"What?" he asked.

"Wedding yes, baby no."

"I know, I know, I won't tell anyone about the baby." Jake smiled. He was beginning to like that word in his vocabulary. "I thought I would call Jess and Sam."

"Just call your sister for now. Sam went to Kalispell and we can fill her in when she gets back. Is it a deal?"

"Deal," Jake dialed his sister's number.

Jessica answered on the second ring. "Jake, I'm coming for Christmas in five hours, what do you need?" Jessica asked a little frustrated.

"Hello to you, too; I just needed to catch you before you get on the plane."

"Why? What's wrong? Is it your shoulder?"

"No, I'm ok. I'm great actually. Olivia and I are going to get married."

"I know dummy, I already received that little piece of 'intel'."

"I mean we are getting married on New Year's Eve, at the ball. It's going to be a surprise and we could seriously use your help."

"Jakey, that's awesome! What can I do?" Jessica asked suddenly excited.

"Olivia needs a wedding dress." Jake smiled.

Olivia overheard and protested, "Jake, no I don't. I told you, I already have a ball gown. I don't need two dresses."

Jessica nearly choked the words out, "Oh wow, ok, well that's a tall order in five hours, less actually, but I'll see what I can do. Tell Olivia to go to your office, lock the door and call me back. She's going to need your computer for a while but since you aren't supposed to be working, I guess it won't be a problem." Jess instructed.

"Ok got it, what else?" he asked.

"Call the pilot and tell him I need a later flight out, but not too late or everyone will know something is up."

"Ok and Jess, thank you." He replied.

"You're my big brother; I'd do anything for you. Besides, someday I might need your help hiding a body." Jess laughed.

"I love you Jess." He hung up the phone and kissed Olivia's pouty face.

"Didn't you hear me? I don't need a wedding dress." She protested.

"Yes, you do. So, go to my office, lock the door and call my sister back. She's waiting for your call."

Surprisingly Olivia didn't protest any further. He wondered if perhaps it was because she really *did* want a wedding dress. Jake smiled.

Olivia dressed and locked herself in Jake's office to gown shop with Jessica via the internet and phone. Jess was surprised at how quickly Olivia picked the gown she liked. The only tricky part would be getting it to Montana in less than a week since alterations would be needed.

Thankfully, Olivia already had her ball gown, and when they announced the surprise, she would change into the wedding dress. That way, no one would get an early preview, especially Jake.

Around midday, Olivia finally emerged from her virtual shopping trip. Hopefully Jake had come up with some excuse to his parent's for her hiding out all morning. She walked into their bedroom and Jake too quickly hung up his phone.

"Hey, who was that?" She smiled.

"That was none of your business. It's a surprise." He replied teasingly.

"Jake, no more surprises, promise me."

"I can't promise that." He grinned again.

"Where is your nursing staff?"

Jake laughed, "My mom is, um, you know what, I don't know. She and Carmella were in here earlier but I told them I needed to rest and you were very busy and shouldn't be disturbed."

"Oh," Olivia sat on the edge of the bed looking at her shoes. Jake could tell she was still a little pouty.

"What is it?"

"Maybe you were right; maybe there isn't time to pull a wedding together in a week."

"I was wrong. We can do this. Let's make a list of things we need to do to prepare. Grab a pen and paper and we'll get organized."

Olivia looked at him, tempted to roll her eyes but he looked so sincere. "A 'to-do' list?"

"Yes, the way I figure it we need your dress, a license, a pastor, and a cake, family, witnesses..." he smiled, waiting for her reaction, but she was lost in thoughts of her own.

"We need rings, at least you do."

"Darlin', I've got that covered."

"You do?"

"Yes, now is there any other family or friends you want to invite?" Jake asked. He sounded overly cheerful and Olivia was finding it hugely annoying.

She shook her head. She thought about the 'friends' she had left behind in Oregon. She couldn't think of one person she considered a friend. She could think of plenty who liked her for her family name, or the money, or the prestige, but no one genuine.

Olivia wished she had at least one friend to offer up as proof that she was just a normal girl, with normal friends, but alas, no one came to mind.

There was nothing normal about what she'd been through. There was nothing normal about a violent rape or being a teen mom or suffering so much loss and grief. There was nothing normal about an undeserved fresh start with a handsome, kind, hardworking mountain of a man like Jake.

Olivia sighed deeply. "My brother and my parents are coming, that's good enough." She replied at last, hoping to sound more upbeat than she felt.

"What about aunts, uncles or cousins?"

"No" she replied.

"You don't have any cousins?"

"Jake, please, can we talk about something else? I'm not close with my cousins."

"Darlin', I need to say something to you and I want you to hear me out before you jump my shit."

Olivia smirked.

"We don't have to do this, and this isn't me saying I don't want to, this is me saying if you aren't happy, then I'm not happy. What do you really, truly want?"

"I want this. I do." She said sincerely. "I'll admit I did not plan on this baby. Hell, I didn't plan on a lot of things, but I know this is right, it's just..."

"Just what?" he asked trying desperately to understand her apprehensions.

"Scary, it's scary, overwhelming and very fast." She spoke softly. "You aren't even healed all the way, now Christmas, a baby, a wedding and what if.... What if there's, there's charges against me? It's all, well, so much all at once."

She took his hand. She needed him to know she meant what she was about to say. "But, no matter how scary this is, it doesn't change how right it is. Just bear with me, ok?" she said and looked in his eyes. She could see herself reflected there.

Darlin', first things first. We will handle EVERYTHING together, ok? I already told you, there will NOT be any charges; our lawyer is handling all that. You did nothing wrong. Now, we will handle ALL the rest!" He kissed her mouth and pulled her bottom lip through his teeth gently. She moaned. It had been forever since she'd lost herself in his touch. The internal alarm clanged in her head.

"Jake, we can't make love." she said and pushed gently on his healthy shoulder.

"I can't make love to my fiancée, I know! I know, but this sucks! Ugh!" he said in sincere frustration. He raked his hand through his hair. "I will make love to you on our wedding night. I don't give a shit what the doctor says. I miss you Darlin'."

"I miss you, too." She shifted gears quickly, looking back to his list. "Ok, so what else has to be done today?"

"Honestly, nothing! We have Christmas waiting for us. If we hole-up in this room much longer my parents are going to get suspicious."

"You're right; let's go down and be social then, shall we?" Olivia said, trying to keep his mind off his sexual frustration.

"Yeah, let's go. I love you Darlin' and I love our baby, too. I'm as happy as a man can be. Do you know that?" he said sweetly and touched Olivia on the tummy.

"Jake! That is a dead giveaway. You cannot do that! Can NOT!" she replied, only half teasing.

"I know. I'm just excited." He said hugging her and kissing her neck.

The Christmas tree was grand and elegant. Olivia began to think Carmella and Frankie had missed their calling. They both would have made amazing interior designers. Olivia only wished she'd had half that kind of talent. She recognized beauty when she saw it, but couldn't seem to create it. Her house in Oregon had been beautiful, but it was someone else's creation. And her apartment had merely been a shrine to her sadness.

Olivia sat down on the sofa next to Jake. She saw Dacey pouring wine for himself, Frankie and Carmella and felt a sudden twinge of nervousness.

"Where have the two of you been all morning?" Frankie asked kindly.

"Would you like some wine?" Dacey asked in their direction.

Jake replied first, for which Olivia was grateful. "We were just resting, enjoying the time together, and no thank you Papa, no wine for us."

"Dacey, our son can't have wine with the medicines he's on. Jacob, I thought Jessica would be here by now. Have you heard from her?" Frankie asked.

"She had some last minute errands to run in the city, so she arranged for a little later flight. She'll be along shortly. Dent will pick her up." Jake said casually.

"Oh, that's good. Olivia, is everything alright, you seem very quiet?" Frankie asked.

Olivia cleared her throat. "I'm fine, thank you. I think I just need some caffeine. Is there any coffee?" she asked trying to shift attention away.

Carmella nodded and stood up to get it for her.

"Carmella, I'll get it. Sit down, please." Olivia said and went off for the coffee herself.

"Uh, Darlin', are you sure you want coffee with all that caffeine in it? I thought you said you wanted some chamomile tea."

The look on Olivia's face was priceless but not in a good way. "I could strangle that man with my bare hands and raise this baby without a father!" She thought, only half joking.

"Oh, that's right, tea does sound wonderful." Sounding clipped.

"Let me make you some tea, then." Carmella said, ignoring Olivia's comment.

Olivia sat down. "That would be lovely, thank you."

The rest of the afternoon and evening was very relaxed and even Olivia who had been uptight since finding out she was pregnant was finally beginning to relax and enjoy herself.

The Weidner family had a tradition of serving lobster and king crab on Christmas Eve. Olivia walked into the cloud of heavy aromas wafting from the dining room and then, pulling away from Jake's side, turned and quickly walked out. She ran down the hall to the guest bathroom. A feeling of déjà vu swept over her; here she was being sick in the guest bathroom, again. Someone knocked on the door. "Just a minute please."

"Darlin' it's me. I'm coming in." Jake whispered loudly.

"Jake, no, I don't want you to see me like this again." She begged but he ignored her and opened the door.

He took a washcloth and wet it under the faucet. Gently, he stroked her hair back from her face and held the cool cloth to her forehead.

"We'll tell them it's the flu." He soothed.

"Can I just go lay down for a while?"

"Of course you can. I'll get you tucked in upstairs, then join the family for dinner and I'll check on you later."

"I should be taking care of you, not the other way around."

"You do take care of me and I'm right as rain. I'm not even taking as much pain medicine today." He told her as they walked together up the stairs.

Olivia took off her shoes and crawled on their bed. Jake covered her with a blanket and she fell asleep almost instantly.

He joined his family and was hit with a barrage of questions. He held his hand up to them, including his sister Jessica who had just arrived.

"Olivia has a touch of stomach flu but she made me promise to wake her when we open presents later. She will be just fine." Jake said with a self-satisfied grin.

"I put all my 'things' in the blue room. Is that alright Jakey?" Jess asked pointedly.

"Of course, wherever you want is fine."

Dacey said their grace and they dug into their traditional lavish dinner but, never being one to mince words, he said, "You kids are all acting weird today. What's going on?"

"I don't know what you're talking about Papa." Jessica lied.

"I'm talking about you showing up here on Christmas Eve at dinner time. You, asking Jake if you can sleep in the blue room, Olivia has some flu bug and Jake, in spite of everything, you have a big fat smile on your face." Dacey explained. "I want to know what's up with my family."

"Dad, I'm just happy to be alive. You know, being shot gave me a new perspective and I'm feeling good. I'm healing and I'm engaged to an incredible woman. So things are good. I can't let the little things get to me. My perspective has changed. That's the difference you see in me." Jake said truthfully.

"You know what Son, you're right. That deserves a toast." Dacey raised his glass and his family followed his lead.

"Here is to counting our blessings. May neighbors respect you, troubles neglect you, the angels protect you and heaven accept you."

After dinner, Jake went to wake Olivia as promised, but she wasn't in bed. He found her standing in front of the bathroom mirror fixing her makeup. "How was dinner?" she asked, sounding disappointed.

"It was horrible without you. I brought you some of Carmella's homemade bread."

"If I wasn't so hungry, I'd kiss you." She said walking past him to the table where Jake had left the plate. She devoured the bread, unsure if she chewed any of it.

"This is so good." She said in between bites. "I was really hungry."

"I guess you were. I don't think I've ever seen you eat like this before." Jake said smiling.

Olivia stopped mid-bite and spoke with her mouth full. "Jake, I have to fit into a ball gown and my wedding gown in a week. I can't be eating all these carbs, oh my God."

Jake smiled and kissed her forehead. "Yes you can. It's a good thing. You need to eat."

"What if I'm showing by then?" She gestured like she was holding a ball on her stomach.

"Olivia, take a breath, relax and stop worrying so much. I don't think your body is going to change that much in a week. My family always gives one gift on Christmas Eve so come with me now."

He said happily. "I want you to open yours."

She sighed. Jake was right. Stressing out about everything wasn't going to change anything and it wouldn't be good for the baby. "The baby" she thought, somewhat dreamily. She was slowly beginning to embrace this new joy but for her it took time. "Thank God Jake is so understanding" she thought. "Ok" she said and took his hand.

He led her downstairs to the kitchen. "Put your boots and coat on. It's snowing again and very cold tonight." Jake said, helping her with her coat.

"Why are we going outside?" she asked, hoping he hadn't bought her a car. The engraved watch she had bought him would pale in comparison to a car.

"I can't tell you why. It's a surprise."

"Where is your family? Should I get their gifts now? What about your gift? Jake, I'm freaking out. Do you realize how bad I am with surprises?"

Standing on the path in the snow he turned her around to face him. "I love you. I have never loved anyone the way I love you and I know you love me, too. That's why I feel confident in telling you..." he paused, trying not to grin like an idiot.

"What? What is it?" she asked, feeling upset all of a sudden.

"You need to chill out. No more questions." He started laughing. She smacked his good shoulder.

"Jake, how can I marry such an infuriating man?" she said but her eyes lit up and she kissed his mouth. "I do love you. That must be it."

"Good, now let's go. It's freezing out here." He took her hand.

As they approached the barn, Olivia noticed a big red bow on the door. "The barn is fixed?" she asked.

"The barn is fine." He said as he opened the door.

"Surprise!" everyone yelled as Olivia walked inside.

Frankie, Dacey, Jessica and Carmella were all there, standing in front of a stall.

"Hi" she said questioningly to all the smiling faces. "I don't understand."

"Darlin' my family is standing in *front* of your gift. Go look." Jake said, and urged her forward.

Olivia's face froze as she approached the gate. A beautiful gelding stepped forward from the back of the stall, a bay, tall and perfect. He nickered at her. She smiled and turned back to Jake with a look of childlike wonder in her eyes.

"You bought me a horse for Christmas?" She looked at all their happy faces. "You, he bought me a horse?"

"Yes, but not just any horse, this is Mochaccino, sired by a horse named Maestro. Your Maestro, Darlin'." He said softly.

"Really?" she cried happily. "Jake, I don't believe this. How did you...?"

She never thought she would have him back and now she did and Jake had made it happen for her. She couldn't stop the flow of happy tears. "Thank you, I love him" she said sincerely.

"Merry Christmas" Jake said happily.

After some time socializing and talking pedigrees in front of Mochaccino's stall, the family retreated to the house leaving Jake and Olivia alone, leaning on the stall gate.

"So did I do alright on your gift?" Jake asked, resting his arm over her shoulder.

"Are you kidding? He's the best present I've ever, ever received. I'm so happy Jake. Maestro meant the world to me and you remembered that. What you did for me is incredible, truly."

"You know you can't ride him though right?"

"Why, isn't he trained?"

"He's perfectly trained. This horse will do just about anything you ask of him, including shovel the driveway I think." Jake smiled.

"Then what is it? I don't understand."

"You're pregnant Darlin'. You can't ride." He said, feeling strangely like he was stating the obvious.

"The hell I can't."

"Olivia it's not safe."

"We're not going to discuss this right now. I refuse to let you ruin such an amazing moment." She said stubbornly.

Jake followed as Olivia walked toward the door. He was trying hard not to laugh out loud. He reached for her hand but she pulled away.

"Don't be mad." He chuckled.

She turned halfway back to the house and stopped in front of him. "Nine months!! Do you get that? Do you understand that I will be walking around getting bigger and bigger by the day and that **whole** time I'm supposed to be caffeine free, alcohol free, drug free and apparently horse free...for nine **DAMN** months!!! So Jake please, if you love me at all, then let the doctor tell me what I can and cannot do so I can be pissed off at him instead of you. Please?"

"You're right; we'll let Dr. Harris be the bad guy." Jake said sincerely, stifling a smile.

"That's all I'm saying." She said, satisfied she'd made her point.

The rest of Christmas Eve and all of Christmas Day was a happy blur. Jake loved the watch and especially the inscription. It read: "With Love from Your Darlin' Olivia". She wanted him to know regardless of what happened, she would love him forever. Her heart belonged to Jake for better or worse. She had adored the whole day in the lap of Jake's family with their fun, comforting traditions, the laughter and being a part of it all.

The day after Christmas the house was terribly quiet. Jake had convinced Dr. Harris to let him do some light work. He just had to promise to leave the heavy, physical stuff to the employees. His first stop was to the Outfitter's to make an appearance with the new clients as promised and take over Sam's office.

Jessica had told Olivia the dress was being personally flown to Montana by a friend of hers and would arrive the following day.

Dacey and Frankie were back at the house in town and Carmella was busy shopping for the New Year's Eve Ball. Sam and Jess were hatching some wedding plans Olivia wasn't allowed to know about so Olivia was all alone in that great big house. It was *her* great big house. That was fast becoming a strange new reality.

She never really realized how quiet it was here. Maybe it was the ranch, maybe it was Troy, maybe it was Montana, but it was awfully quiet. Olivia wasn't quite sure what to do with herself. The house was always perfectly maintained and work at Tempo wouldn't resume until after New Year's.

She went to the kitchen and was tempted by the coffee, but summoned the willpower to drink juice instead. She figured Jake would be pleased, not that a little sip of coffee would hurt anything.

She liked being here with no one to tell her what to do. Jake had told all of the employees at the ranch about their engagement so as Jake put it, Olivia was the new 'lady of the house'. She laughed at that, but it seemed to make him happy.

Even though she knew Jake was against it, she decided a short ride on Moccachino was just what she needed. After all, it seemed a terrible waste not to ride such a beautiful horse.

She called out to the stable to have him saddled for her and went to change into her jeans and boots.

She was completely excited to ride her new horse; she just wished Jake could be there with her for this first ride. She started to rethink it, but the rebellion, or perhaps it was stubbornness won out.

She didn't want to blatantly defy his wishes but she couldn't stand being a prisoner to her own body so early in the pregnancy. Even though she was being plagued by the occasional bout of nausea and moodiness, she felt fine otherwise.

It was a beautiful morning. The sun was shining brightly on the snow. Olivia felt great and was glad to have something exciting to do.

As she walked into the stable, Kyle, a young man who worked the stables as a groom was sitting on a stool next to Mochaccino's stall. Olivia had gotten to know Kyle pretty well because of all the time she'd spent riding Guiness in the arena.

"Hi Kyle, how are you?"

Kyle stood up quickly. I'm fine Miss Olivia. How was your Christmas?" he asked politely.

"It was so wonderful. How about you?"

"Real good thanks. Miss Olivia, I didn't saddle up Mocha for you because, um, well...before Mr. Weidner left this morning he gave me instructions that I shouldn't." he said guiltily.

"Oh really; what exactly did he say?" Olivia fumed.

"He said I'd be fired if I let you get on a horse. I'm sorry Miss Olivia but I need this job. I'm saving up for college."

"Ugh!!!" she yelled her frustration at him. "Of course you are. Kyle you should go to college. How much does Mr. Weidner pay you? I will double it, whatever it is just to saddle up the horse and keep your mouth shut."

"He said you might say that." Kyle looked at the ground, dusting the toe of his boot in the sawdust.

"Oh, he did, did he?" Olivia stomped angrily out of the barn and into the sunlight. "You have got to be kidding me! That man thinks he can boss me around like I'm one of his employees!"

She took a deep breath and went back inside the barn.

Kyle was now mucking out another stall.

"Kyle!"

"Yes Ma'am" he said, looking more nervous than before.

"Did Mr. Weidner say anything else?" she asked, trying to keep her cool.

"Just what I told you; I'm not to let you on a horse or accept any money from you."

"Did he say I couldn't do any groundwork?"

"No, Miss Olivia" Kyle smiled. "I'd say you can do all the groundwork you want. I'll get you a lead rope."

"Thank you Kyle" she said sweetly.

She spent the rest of the morning getting to know Mochaccino in the arena. He had a sweet disposition and Olivia discovered quickly he *could* do just about anything, just like Jake had said, short of making coffee. "So, is that why they called you Mochaccino?" she asked him, rubbing his strong jawline.

She had no interest in going back to the house, instead she helped groom all the horses, helped with feeding, and even mucked out a few stalls, much to Kyle's dismay.

"I just need something to keep me busy" she said grumpily, when Kyle protested.

"Mr. Weidner is going to fire me for this."

"He will not, I promise you."

She was placing fresh bedding in a stall when Jake's arms wrapped around her waist. "You and I are not friends right now. I don't think you want to hug me." She said stiffly.

"Of course I do Darlin'. I missed you today." He said happily. "You know, Kyle is pretty good at cleaning out stalls."

Olivia could tell he was in an especially good mood. He had been to work today. It made her want to scream at him.

"Is this about riding? Is that why you have your pouty face on?" Jake asked, turning her around to face him.

"It's about you thinking you can tell me what to do! I'm not one of your employees Jake! You told Kyle you would fire him if he let me get on a horse!"

"Apparently it was necessary." He said chuckling.

"That's not funny."

"It's a little funny." He replied and kissed her on her pouty mouth.

"I thought you were going to let Doctor Harris be the bad guy? You are supposed to be on my side."

"I am on your side, believe me."

"Then act like it, please? It wouldn't have been the end of the world if I had taken just a little ride."

"I'm trying to keep you and the baby safe."

Olivia decided there was no point in arguing. She knew she was being petulant and if she could put her stubbornness aside for a moment, she would admit he was probably right.

CHAPTER THIRTY-FIVE

The rest of Christmas week flew by. Olivia felt like her head was spinning again. It was so strange and surreal and sometimes she had to question if she was really in the moment.

Planning a surprise wedding in a week was a huge undertaking and she was relieved to have Samantha and Jessica secretly helping them. Her wedding dress arrived in high style and just in time on Wednesday thanks to Jessica's friend Charles. And by some miracle, no alterations were needed. Olivia took it as a good sign and she was especially happy her baby bump wasn't yet showing. She and Jake drove to the county courthouse on Thursday and applied for their marriage license. She was a little nervous about it, but it all went smoothly.

Olivia's family arrived on Saturday and she built up her courage to make her obligatory visit to the Lodge to spend some time with them. Jake said he had some loose ends to tie up and couldn't make it. She was not happy to be facing them alone and worried Jake might have more surprises up his sleeve. She could only guess what he was cooking up.

Mostly, she was afraid to face her mother and prayed she wouldn't guess about the wedding or the baby. Antoinette Curtis was a professional when it came to seeing right through her daughter. It came from years at picking at her flaws.

She walked into the lounge wishing Jake would have come. She needed him.

Olivia's dad greeted her first. "Hey Slugger, how's my girl?" he asked sweetly, giving her a big hug.

"I'm good Dad. I'm glad you're here." She said and moved to hug Miles.

"Olivia, where is your fiancée?" Antoinette asked pointedly. She barely looked at her daughter.

Miles caught the sourness of his mother's comment and said, "Livi, you look great. So where *is* Jake?"

"He's so busy preparing for the annual ball. He sends his apologies and says to tell you he is looking forward to seeing you all there."

"Of course, we understand." Jonathan replied happily.

"Mother, how was the flight? Did you find a gown?" Olivia asked trying to deflect.

"The flight was perfectly fine, and of course I found a gown. Why are you acting so strangely?"

"I think I'm just nervous." Olivia replied, biting her lip.

"What on earth do you have to be nervous about? Honestly, you need to calm yourself. Last I checked this is still only a dance in a small town. Will it be in the barn?"

Olivia tried desperately not to rise to that little dig. "No, it will be in the ballroom. You remember."

"Sit down. Let's have a drink." Antoinette snapped.

"Yes, let's" Olivia replied, screaming at herself on the inside.

"After they ordered and the drinks arrived, Antoinette started up again like an archer with an endless quiver of arrows and always the same target.

"Since Jake isn't here, I think we should have a little family discussion about how you treated Layne Montgomery. That poor man hasn't stopped calling me about it."

"Mother, I've said all I'm going to say in regard to Layne. I know you don't understand, and perhaps you never will, but my life has changed and I want to move on. Layne is not my family and he was never my friend. I hope you'll accept my judgment."

"I will not. He *is* your family. His brother is dead and you seem to have no sympathy for the Montgomery's at all."

"You think I should be sympathetic? They, their favorite sport was coming up with new ways to torture me and yet you can sit there with a straight face and say that? My fiancée was shot and nearly died. I don't give a shit about Layne Montgomery!" Olivia finished angrily.

"That *is* enough, Antoinette." Jonathan said sternly. "We are here to enjoy a holiday with our daughter, that's all."

"No Jonathan, I raised these children to remember their manners in all situations. What Olivia did in the country club was beyond an embarrassment. Layne was very put off by the whole thing, and I truly don't blame him."

"Layne can go to hell!" Olivia said angrily.

Antoinette was not going to back down. "Your father may have given his blessing on this little train wreck you call an engagement but I certainly have not. I'm starting to think Jacob Weidner is a bad influence and **not** the caliber of man you should be marrying."

She continued her venomous rant, "First of all, he lives here in this joke some would call a one-horse town, not the kind of place *you* should be living.

Jake is completely unrefined. I think he is intent on you being a small town piano teacher and *that* is not the life I planned for you at all. If only Jackson were still here, then none of this would be happening," she bemoaned, "I wouldn't be flying out to the middle of nowhere trying to talk some sense into my daughter." Antoinette sniffed. It was the same fake cry her mother had been pulling for as long as Olivia could remember.

Jonathan, Miles and Olivia all stared at Antoinette in sheer astonishment. She was certainly on one today.

"Dad, why don't you and Miles go tour the Outfitter's? Miles, you remember the way, don't you?" Olivia asked, through a practiced smile.

"Are you sure?" Miles asked, nearly gaping at his sister.

"Yes I'm sure. Mother and I need to continue this discussion in private."

The men left the table. Antoinette sipped her martini and glared at Olivia. "You didn't have to send them away. I'm not ashamed of what I've said because it's the truth. You don't belong here. I don't know how many different ways I can say this, Olivia. Just give up this foolishness and come back to Oregon. We'll arrange some concert dates for you; and later you may want to move to a larger city. I know an amazing young conductor living in New York and he's single. He knows all about you. When we get you settled back in Oregon, he is expecting your call."

"Mother! I'm engaged to Jake!"

"Engagements are broken all the time. Jake tried, I'll give him that, but he is not right for you. He's a cowboy." She said as if the taste of the word was bitter on her tongue.

"I love him." Olivia replied, frustrated at the tone in her own voice. She knew she sounded like a whining child.

"No you don't, you love to rebel. You love to defy me just like you did when you were twelve and fifteen and you still do. Nothing has changed."

"Everything has changed Mother. Don't you see? I've changed. Look at me please? For once can't you see who I really am? Marrying Jake is the first thing I'll ever do that is really and truly and authentically my choice. Me, Mother, Jake is for *me*! He is *my* choice!" Olivia cried.

"Stop this childishness. My God, but you're emotional. Believe it or not Olivia, I really do want what is best for you.

So tell me then *why* is he your choice? What makes you choose a cowboy over success and the potential to have the kind of man you truly deserve? Tell me that?" Antoinette asked trying to understand.

"Jake is *exactly* the kind of man I deserve. It just took me a *really* long time to realize it. Not that it matters anymore, but Jackson was not for me. I never loved him and I should never have married him. I only married him because I wanted *you* to be proud of me finally, for something, for anything."

"And so I was." Antoinette admitted coldly.

"No you weren't. You were just happy because to you, you were winning, but it's not really winning when the other team forfeits. That's what I did. I forfeited for you and still you weren't proud of me. Jackson made me feel worthless; nothing I ever did was good enough, just like you make me feel."

"Oh Olivia, you..."

"Mother, did you know that Jackson was Patrick Hanson's cousin? Did you know?" Olivia had not planned on telling her mother.

"What? He was not!" Antoinette replied astonished.

"Yes, he was. In fact, that makes him Layne's cousin, also! And, I'm sure Layne knows it, too! Doesn't that change your mind? What do you think of your precious Jackson now?"

"You don't know that it's true. I think you would say anything to smear that man's good name.
You should be ashamed of yourself, Olivia."

"No, let me tell you something, it's too late. You won't change my mind. Jake makes me feel powerful, strong and sexy. He trusts me and he makes me feel like I can do anything and if you love me at all, if you've *ever* loved me, then you'll want me to have him. And if that is asking too much, then at the very least, try and keep your mouth shut."

Olivia stood up, turned and walked to the door, leaving her mother in her wake. She tried not to let the whole floodgate of tears open until she was inside her Jeep. She sat in the driver's seat with the engine running. She dialed up Jake on her phone. She needed his voice, so strong and steady.

"Hello Darlin'" he said answering happily.

"Hi" she said through sniffles.

He knew immediately, without needing to ask, who was making Olivia cry the day before her wedding. "Oh shit, I knew I shouldn't have let you go without me. I'm so sorry." He said softly.

"I'm ok; I just needed to hear your voice, that's all." She took a deep breath. "I think I'm going to be fine."

"Do you want me to come get you?"

"No, where are you?

"I'm home."

"Then I'm coming home, too."

Jake was in his office when Olivia arrived. The remains of tears had dried sadly on her face. She sat in his lap and held him tightly as if she feared he would disappear.

"Do you want to talk about it?"

Olivia shook her head. "You are my family Jake. You and this baby are my family. You're all I need." She said into his good shoulder.

"Rough day, huh?"

"You have no idea." She said and laughed in spite of herself. She sighed deeply as she let all of it go. She kissed her fiancée on the mouth, but then she stood up and took a seat on the chair opposite the desk.

"You don't have to get up."

"Actually I do, there is something I need to say to you and I don't think you're going to like it."

"What is it?"

"I want our wedding to be a bit more traditional, so I was thinking we would sleep apart tonight."

"No." he complained. "Why don't you just borrow something blue and call it good? I don't want to sleep apart from you."

"Jessica, Sam and I are having a little girl's night tonight. Jess made up some story to Carmella and they have everything all set up. I'll still be in the house, but I just think it will be nice to keep this one tradition." Olivia explained nervously.

"Fine, but tomorrow night you're all mine. I want to spend every night for the rest of my life with my wife." Jake said with mock anger.

"I understand" she replied, sounding falsely submissive.

"Will I see you at all tomorrow?"

"I'll be at the ball."

Jake stood up and came around the desk. He pulled her up to him and kissed her neck. "You're going to hide in our own house from me all day?" he said playfully as he tickled her.

"Yes" she squealed with laughter.

Olivia marveled at moments like these.

She had just been dragged so far down into the abyss with her mother and now here with Jake, she was floating on air. "You're feeling a lot better aren't you?" she asked, realizing how strong he felt to her.

"Darlin' I'm pretty sure I could fly." He said and kissed her as he held her.

He had a way of making her feel diminutive and it was delicious. "Well?" she was still waiting for his answer.

"I can't tell you no, Darlin'." He replied, smiling.

"Yes you can, you tell me no all the time." She teased.

"I wouldn't say no to this unless you are planning on bungee jumping or skydiving."

"We thought about it." Olivia replied dryly.

"Maybe I'll get the guys together tonight then too and play some cards."

"That's a good idea. Then, please invite Miles?"

"Of course, he's your brother."

"And Ben?" Olivia added.

"You are bound and determined that we kiss and make up, aren't you?" Jake asked.

"I'd prefer you don't kiss him, but yes. I think you both should just get over this whole Sarea thing. If she cared about either of you she would clear this up herself." Olivia replied cautiously, feeling the edges of a vision.

"You're probably right." He replied. "I'll invite Ben."

"Good" she smiled. "I love you Jake."

I love you too Darlin'. So, is this the part where you leave me?"

"I'm afraid so." She sighed and kissed him again for good measure.

"Alright then, go before I change my mind."

Olivia didn't want to let go any more than Jake did. She held onto his hand as she began to walk to the door. He sat on the edge of his desk, his arm extending until they could no longer touch. She shut the door slowly behind her.

Jake suddenly felt antsy and frustrated. He wanted her so powerfully and that feeling seemed to be getting more intense with each day, each breath together. He raked his hand through his hair, picked up the phone and called his friends, and Ben.

Later, while the girls were engrossed in manicures, hair and lots of girl-talk, Jake was in his office in the middle of a private discussion with Ben Thompson. Jake figured some things were better discussed face to face.

Though he was surprised Ben had agreed to come over so quickly.

"I'm bringing a date to the ball tomorrow." Ben said nervously.

"That's great, is it anyone I know?" Jake asked feeling relieved at this piece of news.

"Yeah, actually it is Jake, um…it's Sarea."

Jake didn't know what to say, so he waited.

"I took Olivia's suggestion and I tracked her down. We've been talking on the phone the last few days and well, I invited her."

"No, absolutely not. Why can't you just let it go Ben? There are plenty of women out there, why can't you just let Sarea Scott go?"

"Well that's a relief, and here I thought you might overreact." Ben responded sarcastically.

"Right, this is my fault, just like it's always been."

"I'm not blaming you. Sarea's doing well and she wants to talk to you and explain everything. She apologized to me Jake. She wants to make it right."

"She wants to talk to me?" Jake asked surprised.

It wasn't the reaction Ben had expected. For some reason Jake sounded worried. "Yes, just give her a chance."

"This isn't fair to Olivia." Jake replied. "She didn't want me telling anyone but, I have to tell you now so you'll understand; we are getting married tomorrow."

"Wow, you guys don't waste any time, huh? Are you sure about this, Jake?"

"Yes, absolutely. I won't let Sarea ruin our wedding day." Jake said seriously.

"She won't. I'll talk to Olivia about it. It's the least I can do since I'm the one who brought Sarea back to Troy."

"Ok, but you better think of a way to make this right. I don't want Sarea causing any trouble."

Jake told Ben about Olivia's little girl party and sent him on upstairs, hoping the women wouldn't turn into a lynch mob once they heard what he had to say.

"I think someone just knocked on the door." Olivia said from underneath a cucumber mask.

"It's probably Jake. He has no willpower. How can you be marrying such a pushover Olivia?" Jessica asked, laughing.

"Oh, you mean your brother the pushover?" she replied happily. "I happen to love him and he's only a pushover for me."

"I'll get the door." Sam said. "The groom can definitely not see the bride in her cucumber mask before the wedding."

Sam opened the door while she was talking. "Jake, you're so predictable...oh um, Ben, what are you doing here?"

"May I speak to Olivia for just a minute?"

"It's not really a good time."

"It's important." Ben replied with a serious look.

Olivia sat up when she heard the exchange. She was torn between irritation and concern.

"Just come in," Jessica demanded loudly.

Ben remembered this room very well from his childhood. It was the room where the friends had always held sleepovers. They called it the bunk room. The walls were lined on two sides with full size, built in bunk beds that were made to look like part of the architecture, all finished in a dark mahogany wood.

Ben noticed the bedding was different than he remembered but the room still had a magical feel to it, like stepping back into childhood. It was a bittersweet memory.

The three women all washed the green gunk from their faces and the first to emerge from the bathroom looking happy and fresh-faced was Olivia.

He decided just to get to the point. "Olivia, I'm bringing a date to the ball tomorrow." He said quickly.

"That's great Ben really, and I'm sure you'll have a lovely time together..." Olivia began.

"Who is it Ben?" Sam asked suspiciously, interrupting.

"Oh my God, it's not that bitch that works for Jake at the Boot Barn is it?" Jess interrupted nosily.

"She does not like me." Olivia said frankly.

"She's a gold digging skank, *nobody* likes her." Sam said. "You should have seen the stink eye she was giving Olivia the other night."

"Sarea Scott" Ben blurted out before one more woman in the room cut him off. "I'm bringing Sarea Scott to the ball."

The silence was deafening. A look of anger and sadness flashed quickly across Olivia's face.

Ben continued. "Listen, I still really care for her and she wants to clear up the past, make amends. She asked me to speak to Jake and she wants to talk to him in person about what happened." Ben explained.

"Ben, you're an incredible douche bag if you think she doesn't have ulterior motives." Sam said, rolling her eyes.

Ben ignored the comment. "Jake asked me to talk to you, to tell you about this and he told me about the wedding. He wants to wait until later to have any serious conversations with Sarea. I thought that was reasonable."

"She had Jake's baby." Olivia said, feeling that slick, dark thread of terror knot in her stomach.

"No one knows exactly what happened. She doesn't want to tell me about any of it until she can discuss it with Jake. She feels she owes him that much."

"She had a baby." Olivia said again, but they all ignored her tone.

"Yeah, seventeen years ago, she owed him an explanation." Jess said bitterly. "My family went through a hell of a lot of turmoil because of her."

"I realize that Jessica, I do, but she regrets how she handled things back then. She wants to make it right. I think she deserves a chance to do that." Ben replied in his best therapist's voice.

Olivia's stomach was doing somersaults. The emotions were running through her like lights changing at an intersection. She didn't know what to say, but tears ran down her face. She knew this moment was coming, but as usual, the harshness of it shocked her. No one ever believed her.

"Tell Jake to come up here please." Olivia said quietly turning away.

Ben said no more, just did as he was asked and returned after a few moments with Jake.

"Can we have some privacy?" Olivia asked them all, holding on to the doorknob.

Everyone left them alone, standing face to face in the bunk room. "There is something you need to know and it can't wait until after we're married." Olivia admitted.

"What do you mean?" Jake asked.

"I mean you need to sit down with Sarea Scott tomorrow and have a conversation that has been delayed far too long. I won't marry you with this still unresolved. You need to hear the truth about your past before you can have a future with me. I'm sorry."

"Are you sure that's what you want?" Jake asked, worry, confusion and frustration coloring his voice.

"No, but it's what has to be. I won't pretend, Jake and I don't think you should either." Olivia replied earnestly.

"Are you still going to marry me?" he asked, a worried furrow appearing between his brows.

"I'll be the one in white." She said somewhat sadly.

She turned without kissing him and walked into the bathroom locking the door behind her. She sat on the floor pulling her knees up to her chest and cried silently. She had known this moment was coming, but it felt worse than the vision she had of it. There was a knock at the door. "Please go away." Olivia cried.

"Olivia, it's me, Ben."

She stood up and unlocked the door to face Ben. She didn't let him speak. "Tell Sarea Scott she and Jake are having brunch tomorrow. This has waited for seventeen years, it shouldn't wait any longer."

"I'm truly sorry, Olivia."

"Are you?" she asked angrily.

"Yes, I never wanted to upset you like this." Ben admitted.

"I know I encouraged you to reach out but I never thought you would do it now, not like this. Please leave. I need to be alone." Olivia said, sniffling.

Ben turned and walked into the hallway. Jake was standing with his arms crossed, looking down at the floor.

"Olivia wants me to set up a brunch for you and Sarea tomorrow." Ben explained.

"I heard and you're coming, too. I refuse for there to be any more miscommunications about this train wreck and besides, I have no interest in being alone in any room with Sarea Scott on my wedding day. My fiancée can barely look at me. You're coming."

"Jake, I'm sorry. I'll bring her here tomorrow at ten in the morning. Is that alright?"

"Fine" Jake replied through clenched teeth.

Jake walked back downstairs to join his unattended guests but everyone had already left, except Miles who was sitting in a lounge chair sipping whiskey.

"I'm sorry about that, Miles. I had some things to take care of. It looks like everyone left, huh?" Jake said, trying to sound casual to Olivia's only brother.

"What's going on Jake? It doesn't take a genius to sense the tension in the air around here."

"I guess the long and short of it is Olivia's not the only one with a past."

Just then a text came through on Jake's phone from Sam. "She's fine. Stop stressing. She is out in the barn. She said she needed to think. Leave her alone, I mean it."

Sam always knew how to get to the point.

"Everyone has a past Jake, Olivia of all people understands that." Miles pointed out.

Just then it occurred to Jake that Olivia didn't need him just then, she needed her brother, the one person who had always been there for her.

"I'm going to bed; it's a big day tomorrow and I'm wiped. Feel free to stay here tonight if you'd like Miles. Olivia is out in the barn. I think she may want to talk to you." Jake suggested.

"Ok, um, thanks Jake." Miles said, more confused than ever. He watched as Jake left the parlor, shoulders slumping.

When Miles opened the door to the stables, he saw his little sister right away. She was sitting on an up-turned bucket. She wore riding boots over leggings and a very large men's coat he could only assume belonged to Jake. Her hair was pulled into a ponytail down her back just like when she was a kid.

Very little about Olivia had changed and yet everything had changed. She was no longer the tag-a-long from his childhood, nor was she the rebellious teen oozing with potential and big dreams that had all of his friends drooling like hungry wolves. She wasn't the grieving mother wanting to end it all anymore, either. No, this was a new incarnation of Olivia. Even in the way she sat on a bucket and murmured to the horse in the stall next to her; even that was different. There was a new calmness to her, a peace that hadn't been there before. Her unending sadness had changed into something new, something undefinable.

Looking at her now from the doorway, Miles knew all of this change was because of Jake Weidner. Somehow miraculously, Jake had plunged headlong into the dark abyss to find her and bring her out. She had clung so tightly to her grief for so long and yet, Miles knew Jake had led her to release her grip. A task not easily done, that was for sure. A man had broken her and a man was helping her to mend. Miles only had a touch of regret that he wasn't the one who had done that. He was after all, her big brother, her protector.

"Hey Livi, whatcha doing out here?" he asked at last.

She stood abruptly and wiped tears away.

"Hi I'm just, um, visiting my new horse. This is Mochaccino. Jake bought him for me for Christmas. He was sired by Maestro. Do you remember Maestro?" she asked.

"Yeah, I do. This is a beautiful horse."

"Yes, he is."

"What's going on Liv?"

"What do you mean?"

"I mean, what is going on? Jake seemed to think you needed someone to talk to and it isn't him, so what happened?"

"I don't know where to start." Olivia said candidly.

"Start anywhere you want."

"Jake has a child."

"What? Where? With whom? He would have said something."

"It doesn't matter."

"Liv, tell me what you mean. I don't understand."

Olivia retold the story of Jake's past with Sarea Scott and how Ben Thompson played into it. Miles was very quiet, listening intently, but when Olivia had finished, Miles said, "You don't know for sure Jake has a child, you just think he does."

"Sure, if you would rather I put it that way, then yes, I think Jake has a child out there somewhere that he has never met."

"Would it really change anything?" Miles asked thoughtfully.

"Miles, it will change everything. The man I intend to marry never even wondered, never looked, and never questioned this. I can't understand that."

"You can't understand wanting to pretend everything is fine? Really?" Miles asked skeptically.

"Fine, I suppose I'm the last person to sit in judgment but the fact remains, he might be a dad."

"And wouldn't you love him just the same?"

"Of course I would still love him. I am forcing him to meet with her tomorrow so he can hear the truth. He wanted to wait but I..."

"But you wanted a reason to run." Miles filled in the blank.

"No, I mean, I don't know, maybe. This is all so much harder to deal with than I thought it would be. Why am I so afraid to be happy?"

"You don't trust it." He said knowingly.

"Is it happiness I don't trust or is it everything?"

"I don't know Liv, but I don't think you're being fair to Jake. You know I have your back, but when he told me to come out and talk to you? I could see he is really worried. You have him scared that if the news isn't to your liking you'll up and pack your bags. And I can't assure him otherwise because I've witnessed your vanishing act before." Olivia was quiet, so Miles continued, "What's the worst that can happen? So maybe he has a kid out there or maybe this chick lied to him, or both? So your fiancée has a past? So do you. He needs your support Liv and there is nothing supportive about always having one foot out the door."

Olivia was taken aback, her big brother had always been on her side, but this was different. He had her pegged. She realized she needed to hear it though, and at least the men in her family liked and respected the man she was about to marry, even if her mother didn't.

"You're right" she admitted.

"Wait, can you repeat that? I'm not sure I heard you correctly."

"I said, you are a huge jackass, but you're also right. Jake is a good man and he needs to know I support him. I've been so selfish."

"Well, you are a Curtis; we tend to be that way sometimes." He joked.

"Let's go in." Olivia suggested.

"Yeah, any chance there's some coffee?"

"I can make some for you, but I'm sticking to tea."

"What gives, you love coffee? You probably love coffee more than you love Jake." He took her by the shoulders, looking into her face. "Oh my God, I can't believe I'm just now putting this all together, Liv are you..."

"Miles" Olivia grabbed her brother sharply by the sleeve. "Here's the thing, Jake and I are getting married tomorrow. It was supposed to be a surprise, only I can't seem to keep my mouth shut."

"Is this a shotgun wedding we're having?" Miles grinned.

"Fine, I'm pregnant, but no, I didn't know I was pregnant when he proposed, so this isn't technically a shotgun wedding. I don't know, it doesn't matter, and you just have to keep this quiet, please? I, his parents do not know and I certainly don't want ours to find out, yet."

"A wedding and a baby, you guys don't waste time do you?"

Olivia sighed. "No, this whole change feels like a tornado. You know, I really wanted to be traditional."

"Don't worry Liv, I won't tell anyone, but you better call me the instant I'm allowed to say anything.

I'm going to be an uncle again!"

"I will." Olivia replied, finally smiling. She and Miles walked to the house in search of coffee and tea.

"Miles, what am I going to do about Jake?" Olivia asked as she poured their hot drinks in the kitchen.

"Marry him, have his baby, I guess." Miles teased.

"I'm serious. I forced him to deal with this and now he's probably miserable because of it."

"He went up to bed, just go talk to him." Miles suggested.

"I can't."

"Why not?"

"I'm trying to hold with the tradition of him not seeing the bride before the wedding."

"How's that working for you?"

"It's not working so well, to tell you the truth. I already spoke to him once. Just please go speak to him for me?" Olivia begged in her best little sister voice.

"What do you want me to say to him, Liv? I mean, I like the guy don't get me wrong but it's going to be a little strange to go knocking on the bedroom door of my 'soon to be brother in law', don't you think?"

"Just make sure he's ok and ask him if he thinks I should be there tomorrow when he speaks to Sarea."

"Fine, but you owe me for this one, little sister." Miles grumbled.

"You are the best brother in the world."

Miles went upstairs at Olivia's urging and knocked on the door as quietly as he could, secretly hoping Jake might not hear him.

Jake opened the door. "Miles, what's going on?" Jake asked, tying on a bathrobe.

"Olivia wanted me to talk to you."

"Oh, ok, yeah, hey, I'll meet you in the parlor ok?"

"Sure," Miles replied, nervously, not really knowing how to approach this touchy situation. He hated awkward conversations and it felt like he was about to have one.

Jake walked into the parlor after a few minutes dressed in jeans and a t-shirt which made Miles relax a bit. He wasn't sure he could take him seriously in a Hugh Heffner style robe.

"Is Olivia ok?" Jake asked, mixing them both a nightcap.

"Yeah, she's ok. I heard about the wedding, and well, I guessed about the baby."

"That's good, I hate keeping secrets, especially from family."

"We aren't family yet."

"Soon though, I'm just hoping Olivia goes through with it, considering everything that's going on, I'm worried."

"She's worried, too." Miles admitted.

"She is?"

"Yeah Jake, she's worried about you. She thinks she has painted you into a corner with this whole Sarea situation. She wants to know if she should be there with you tomorrow."

"See, she's trying to hold with the whole tradition about the wedding I know, but there is a part of me that really doesn't want to deal with this at all, let alone without Olivia. I need your advice Miles, what should I do?"

"Well, my advice would be to get it over with, without Olivia. She's convinced you have a teenager out there somewhere that you don't know about; but I think she's just letting her nerves get the best of her. I love my sister dearly but, in case you haven't guessed, she can be very emotional and I don't think you want to take emotion into that room with you tomorrow. Meet with the lady, find out what really happened and then tell Olivia in your own way." Miles said reasonably.

"Won't she feel excluded, not being there when I talk to Sarea?"

"Honestly, I think she's hoping you *don't* want her there. With Olivia and this other woman in the room together, one of two things is bound to happen; either Liv gets angry or she gets intimidated. Neither really sounds too appealing on your wedding day. I would just leave Livi out of it as much as possible."

"I hope you're right."

"I guess we'll find out."

Jake walked Miles to the door and watched through the window as he drove away and then decided since it wasn't midnight yet, he wasn't technically breaking with tradition.

Olivia heard footsteps in the hallway and opened the door, expecting her brother. "Jake!" She practically threw herself into his arms. "I'm so sorry baby, I've been so stupid and selfish and bitchy." She kissed him all over his face.

"You're not any of those things. Let's sit down for a minute, Darlin'. I want to talk to you."

"Ok" she said, barely letting go of him.

He kissed her forehead and put his hand gently on her belly.

He kneeled down and laid his head where his hand had just been. He was tired and worse than that, he was stressed and a little pain was lingering in his shoulder.

The gesture brought tears to Olivia's eyes. She had done this. All of it was her doing, and though she had known it was coming, it was her fate, like a train on a track. She sighed deeply, "Jake I..."

"Let me say something to you." He said, holding her hand as he moved to sit next to her on the bench at the end of the bed.

"Ok" she replied nervously.

"I think you were right about all of this. I need to find out what really happened. I need to meet with Sarea without you. It's the right thing to do. I know you want to be there for me and I love you for offering, but I think it best to speak with Sarea, and then you and I will talk. It's my past and I need to know for sure."

"Ok" she said a bit too quickly.

"Talk to me, don't just placate me, say something."

"Fine, do you want to know what I keep thinking? Do you want to know what keeps plaguing me? You have a child, Jake. You have a teenager that you've never met and suddenly after all this time, Sarea's ready to spill her guts about everything. Inconveniently, it's our wedding day. She's going to tell you about your son tomorrow and it will change everything and you've still got your head buried in the sand about it."

"You say that like you already know I have a son. You can't know that. Did you speak to her?"

"No, I wouldn't know her from Eve, but I just know. Your life is about to change and where does that leave *our* baby?"

"It won't change how I feel about you or our baby. Trust me. Please, trust me?"

"Things change when you find out you're a parent."

"You don't know that she had a child. You don't. You're wrong about this Olivia. I doubt she was ever pregnant in the first place."

"She was. I know it." Olivia pulled her hand away and looked at her engagement ring.

The only word that seemed to fit now was numb.

"Are you really going to marry me tomorrow? Jake asked quietly. "I know if we're together we can handle anything."

"Please don't, Jake." Olivia said sadly, she didn't like the defeated sound of his voice, or the sad slump of his shoulders.

She especially hated knowing what tomorrow would bring and having no way to stop it.

"Don't what? Don't love you? Don't worry about you? Don't wonder if you're going to run away? I'm sorry, but I can't help it. I'm exhausted." He was falling apart in front of her.

Olivia touched his cheek. "I'll be there. I want to be your wife. I just wish we could skip this part. I wish we could skip the stress, the drama and the tragedy. I want our child to have the kind of life *you* had growing up. I just want him to have some peace."

"Him?"

"Or her, you know." Olivia smiled.

"Darlin' I'll do everything in my power to bring peace to our family. I promise you."

"I know you will. You're a good person with a big heart. Why do you think I'm marrying you?"

"And here I thought it was my body you were after." He teased.

"It is. It's your body and your money, that's it." She laughed.

"Sleep with me tonight?" he asked hoping one last time, she'd change her mind.

"No" she smiled, and pushed his hand off her thigh.

"You drive me crazy." He smiled and groaned.

"I love you." She kissed him once more before kicking him out of her room. She was glad she had moved into the white room, leaving Jessica and Samantha to sleep in the bunk room.

CHAPTER THIRTY-SIX

Jake hadn't slept well. His conversation with Olivia kept playing over in his mind. She seemed so convinced he had a child already but he couldn't believe that. It seemed impossible. He hoped she was wrong.

There was a knock on the door, it was Sam. "I'm here so you can vent. I've known you for a long time now and I have a feeling you need to get some shit off your chest, so let's hear it." Sam said, sounding more matter of fact than usual.

"Ok, yeah." Jake appreciated Sam's honesty more every day. "What if Olivia's right? What if I have a seventeen year old somewhere out there? What if I have a kid I never bothered to find out about? Sarea's dad told my parents she miscarried. She told Ben that my family had Tom Braxton pay her to have an abortion. Why didn't I ever find out for sure? Am I that much of an asshole? And why does Olivia seem so sure about this?"

"You aren't an asshole. Honestly? I think you were just scared, and I think Olivia's scared, too. So, in her own head she is trying to come to terms with this, in case she's right, but I don't think she is. I think that if there had really been a baby, you would know about it."

"Yeah, I just hope you're right. What's Olivia doing now?"

"She's having breakfast and then we're getting beautiful all day."

"I'm grateful you're here for both of us. It means a lot to me." Jake said and hugged his best friend.

At ten, Jake went down to the sitting room. Carmella had already shown Ben and Sarea in and both were seated. Sarea was just as Jake had remembered, blonde, skinny, with that same upturned nose, except a few matured lines now shown around blue eyes. He suddenly realized the blindness of his youth. This was not his type of woman at all.

"Have you been waiting long?" he asked as he entered the room.

"No, not at all, we just arrived actually." Ben said and smiled.

"How are you Sarea?" Jake asked, lightly kissing her cheek.

"I'm very well Jake, how are you?" she said awkwardly.

"I'm great, thank you." He said, equally as awkward. "Are you hungry? I think Carmella fixed us some food in the dining room."

"Sure Jake, thank you." Ben said. Sarea just smiled and followed the men into the dining room.

They each dished up a plate of food in silence and found seats; Jake on one side, Sarea and Ben on the other.

Sarea seemed very out of place but then he couldn't blame her. He often forgot how people could be overwhelmed by the grandeur of this place. And this situation was not comfortable for any of them.

"Thank you for allowing me to come to the ball tonight. I've always wanted to attend, ever since I was a..." Sarea began.

"You're welcome." Jake said, wondering how to get this conversation started.

Sarea began it for them, "I've been living in Denver. I was very surprised when I got a call out of the blue from Ben but then I thought, what the hell, why not take a chance and come to my hometown for a visit."

Jake finally asked, "Can we just cut through the bullshit?"

"Excuse me?" Sarea asked.

"Jake, I don't think that's helpful." Ben interjected.

"Forgive me if I'm not exactly in the mood for small talk today." Jake replied honestly.

"You're right; I just don't know how to talk about this." Sarea admitted.

"Were you really pregnant?" Jake blurted out.

"Jake, I think maybe you should..." Ben began.

"Ben, I want to know. Don't you? That *is* why we're here, right?"

"Ben, Jake's right, that's why we're here. Yes, I was really pregnant, but I had a miscarriage. I'm so very sorry for all the lies I told. I just felt so isolated and I was scared."

"Did my family's lawyer try and pay you to have an abortion?"

"No" she cried, though Jake doubted the sincerity in it. "I'm so sorry you guys. I'm just so sorry. We were, I, was so young and dumb."

Ben looked shocked and Jake just felt relief. He had never wanted Olivia to be more wrong about anything.

"It's ok, Sarea. I wasn't there for you back then, not really and I'm sorry for that." Jake admitted.

"Ben, can you ever forgive me?" Sarea asked pathetically.

"I do forgive you, but I just was so sure that you had told *me* the truth." Ben replied.

"I know." She looked down in her lap.

Jake was so happy when they left. He went to find his beautiful fiancée, but then remembered he wasn't allowed to see her today.

He grabbed the phone and called her. Silly to call her with them both in the same house but he had to tell her the news.

"Darlin', I love you." He said happily.

"Oh God, I was right, wasn't I?" she said, breathlessly.

"No, she had a miscarriage. There *is* no child."

Everything seemed to grind to a screeching halt. Olivia had never been wrong about what was coming, not ever. Since the day after she had been attacked by Patrick she had visions and they were always accurate...always. She had known she would lose Dante' and be unable to prevent it. She had known she would meet Jake. She had known he would be hurt. She had even seen Troy, Montana as the backdrop to her life. In all she had seen, no one ever believed her. She had stopped telling people.

Just like Ben had accused her of doing, she began to lie. That was how she convinced her doctors to release her from the hospital. That was how she coped with this curse. She played it close to the chest, never revealing what was to come, no longer trying to change anyone's minds, even if and especially when it was painful.

She had been sure there was a teenage boy that had Jake's smile and charming mannerisms. Who could that have been? How could she be wrong? Everything else had been right. Everything had been so horrifyingly accurate.

Was it possible that this boy in her vision was, was their own son? A new feeling washed over Olivia like standing in a rainstorm; she was unable to see what was coming next. She could physically feel the curse lifting, leaving her body like the very last drop of poison. She sunk to her knees and cried tears of joy and relief. She didn't know what had broken the curse, but she knew with certainty that it was broken. Everything had changed, absolutely everything.

"Olivia? Are you alright, Darlin'?" Jake was asking.

She refocused on his voice. "For the first time in so long, yes I am." Olivia cried.

It was a perfect day for a wedding. The sun was shining on the snow and everything glistened and sparkled. Olivia was glowing too and she felt light as air, if a little nervous. Tonight she would marry the man of her dreams and she didn't know what was to come. This was a new sensation, a new chapter. This was a new life.

CHAPTER THIRTY-SEVEN

Oregon State Hospital
Discharge Evaluation
September 15, 2010

Patients Name: Olivia Karen Curtis-Montgomery
Attending Physician: Alex M. Woodley, M.D., PsyD.

Upon my initial assessment of the patient, I concluded she suffers from severe mixed delusional disorder. The patient was convinced quite violently so, that she could see (predict) the future and her life had been cursed. The patient mentioned Greek mythology and a princess of Troy.

She called it the Cassandra Curse. The patient spent several nights screaming the name Cassandra from her room. According to the patient, the curse of Cassandra entails psychic vision and the inability to change her fate. She claims this curse was placed on her by Patrick Hanson, the man who brutally raped and attacked her when she was a teenager. She described in detail her own future and chronicled her "new life" in a small Montana town named Troy (not coincidentally) where she would meet a man she would fall in love with. The patient went on to say this man would learn of a child he fathered when he was a teenager. She also stated quite sincerely she would see the same man (she refers to him as the one) get hurt, though she is unclear exactly how that will happen. She states only that she will see him fall.

The most worrisome of her delusions has been her commitment to the idea of killing the man who raped her. She describes in terrifying detail the manner in which she kills Patrick Hanson, going so far as to describe the type of knife and the amount of blood.

As part of her therapy, we have discussed the driving force behind these delusions, namely the recent trauma she faced in losing her son and husband in a car accident. It has been only three months since their passing and Olivia has created a scenario for herself in which she escapes; namely, the previously mentioned delusions.

We have also tried to impress on the patient some simple facts, like her extensive knowledge of Greek mythology and how it impacts her delusional state.

Recently, her status has improved greatly due to intense psychotherapy and the use of medication. The patient has at long last given up these delusions and has admitted she cannot see the future; hers or anyone's, nor has she ever been able to. The patient is currently trying to establish a family connection and has become especially close with her older brother, Miles Curtis. She continues to struggle in her relationship with her mother, Antoinette Curtis.

It is my belief the patient is now stable enough to be released from inpatient care and continue with her treatment on an outpatient basis.

I will be referring her to Dr. Cline for further treatment and consult with him in regard to medications.

Ben Thompson read this report in disbelief. He couldn't understand why he hadn't seen it before. He looked through Olivia's file again in astonishment. He thought he had reviewed everything. He *had* reviewed everything. It was as if this paper appeared out of nowhere. It wasn't making any sense.

He smiled. Olivia was right. She had been right all along about everything, except about Jake's child. He found it all puzzling. It had been one year since Jake and Olivia's wedding. They were an amazing couple and happily, his closest friends. He was going to propose to Sarea tonight at the stroke of midnight. He thought maybe it would be too cliché but Olivia encouraged him to go for it.

He couldn't put down the report in his hand. How could she have known all those things? Had she made them happen?

Olivia had been cleared of any charges concerning Patrick Hanson, but Ben knew this medical report could be construed as premeditated murder. He couldn't let that happen to the person who had become one of his best friends. He wouldn't let that happen. He had let Olivia down with his behavior, with his disbelief, but no more.

He picked up the phone and dialed the hospital where Olivia had been committed.

"Hello, my name is Dr. Ben Thompson. I'm calling to speak to Dr. Alex Woodley. We have a mutual patient. Yes, I'll hold."

Ben waited nervously. He hoped this man could be reasoned with, just in case there were ever any follow up.

"Hello" a woman's voice answered.

"I'm sorry; I must have been connected with the wrong person. I'm holding for Dr. Alex Woodley."

"Speaking, my name is Alexandra Woodley. Don't worry, it happens all the time." Dr. Woodley replied.

"My apologies, Doctor. I'm calling to discuss a mutual patient. Her name is Olivia Curtis."

"Yes, of course, Dr. Thompson, let me pull up her file."

Ben waited again, still not sure what he should or could say to convince this person to keep her mouth shut.

"That's odd" Dr. Woodley returned to the phone. "I find no record of a patient by that name. Is there another name I can try?"

"Try Montgomery or Curtis-Montgomery" Ben added. Again he waited.

"No, I'm sorry. I don't show her ever being a patient at Oregon State Hospital. Are you sure she was a patient here?"

"Yes, I believe so. Is there another place where past records are kept?" He asked completely puzzled.

"No, they're all integrated into the statewide computer system. Do you have a date that I could cross reference?"

Ben gave her the date of the report in front of him then waited as he heard tapping on a computer in the background.

"No, I don't find any patients with that name during that time. I wish I could be more help." Dr. Woodley replied sincerely.

"Thank you, Doctor. Actually you've been a great help. I must've gotten it wrong. Thank you for your time." Ben smiled at the phone as he hung up.

Ben read the paper on his desk once more. He laughed heartily as he placed each page in the shredder next to his desk.

Maybe someday he would tell her. Maybe…

EPILOGUE

Olivia woke to the morning sun peeking through the windows. She felt rested and stretched lazily, savoring the moment, but suddenly she realized it was too quiet. She sat up.

Jake wasn't there, but there was nothing unusual about that. She didn't hear her baby. That was the unusual part. She slipped out of bed and threw on a robe. She rushed down to the kitchen.

"Good morning bella ragazza." Carmella said happily.

"Hello Carmella, have you seen my boys?" she asked, now only slightly concerned.

"Yes, Jacob wanted to let you sleep in so he took the baby out to the stables to see the horses."

"Oh good, thank you." Olivia replied relieved.

She slipped on some boots and a coat and rushed outside not taking time to put on real clothes. She opened the door to the stables and saw Jake. She snuck up behind him quietly and put her arms around him. Her hand gently brushed her son's soft cheek.

"Good morning Darlin'. How's Mommy today?" Jake turned and Olivia easily cozied up under his arm.

"I'm good. I was worried about our little man since I didn't hear him on the monitor this morning." She leaned to kiss her baby on the nose.

"I told him his mama needed some rest on her wedding anniversary."

"Happy Anniversary" she said, smiling up at Jake.

"Happy Anniversary Darlin', I'm surprised you didn't sleep in longer."

"I couldn't; I kept dreaming about the performance in New York. I haven't been on stage in so long. I usually never get nervous but this time, I'm nervous. Lincoln Center is no joke. What could my mother have been thinking starting me out with such a huge venue? I'm scared I'm not really ready and this little angel is still so new. I don't know if I can leave him yet. He's so little."

Olivia took their son and held him close. Jake knew she always felt more at ease when she was holding him. River Curtis Weidner seemed to bring peace to everyone, except perhaps when people were arguing over who got to hold him next.

Even Olivia's mother seemed to soften a bit when she'd held her grandson for the first time.

Antoinette's only complaint had been his name, but Jake and Olivia didn't care.

After the surprise wedding, she and Jake left on a honeymoon to Italy and visited some of Jake's extended family. Jake had planned it as a special surprise for Olivia. She had put on the bulk of the baby weight in homemade Italian food. She was beginning to regret it now with her first concert looming on the horizon.

"He'll be in good hands and my parents are really excited about watching him for us. We're only going to be gone for two nights and you Darlin', are going to be wonderful."

"I'm going to miss him so much Jake." She replied, a tear filling her eye.

"I know, I will too, but we agreed it would be good to have some alone time. Maybe we'll get pregnant again?" Jake replied grinning broadly.

"Oh no, no way" She laughed. "I still haven't lost all the weight."

"I love every curve." Jake growled sexily.

Olivia smiled at River, humming and rocking him in her arms. Everything had changed. She had fallen in love and lifted the curse. It was strange not knowing if more tragedy would occur, but she reminded herself that God never intended us to know our own fate, not usually. ;)

"You are my mountain. I sit in the safety of your shadow and know that you protect me from the approaching storm. Apollo has cursed me but beside you the curse shall be no more and fate will finally smile upon me, a princess of Troy."

Cassandra

THE END

J.D. Greenfield was raised in Eastern Oregon. She's currently living in Western Washington with her husband of 21 years and their 11 year old son. She describes herself as a bit of a weirdo; very open-minded, outspoken, loves sarcasm, laughter and enjoys drinking wine and cussing like a trucker.

This is J.D.'s debut novel.